Archie

MODERN

CLASSICS

• VOLUME ONE •

Publisher / Co-CEO: Jon Goldwater

Co-President / Editor-In-Chief: Victor Gorelick

Co-President: Mike Pellerito

Co-President: Alex Segura

Chief Creative Officer: Roberto Aguirre-Sacasa

Chief Operating Officer: William Mooar

Chief Financial Officer: Robert Wintle

Director of Book Sales & Operations: Jonathan Betancourt

Production Manager: Stephen Oswald

Lead Designer: Kari McLachlan

Associate Editor: Carlos Antunes

Editor: Jamie Lee Rotante

Co-CEO: Nancy Silberkleit

Published by Archie Comic Publications, Inc. 629 Fifth Avenue, Suite 100, Pelham, NY 10803-1242

ISBN: 978-1-68255-831-7

STORIES

DAN PARENT, ALEX SIMMONS, ANGELO DeCESARE,
RON ROBBINS, BILL GOLLIHER & FRANCIS BONNET

ART

JEFF SHULTZ, BILL GOLLIHER, BILL GALVAN,
PAT KENNEDY, TIM KENNEDY, DAN PARENT,
JIM AMASH, BOB SMITH, RICH KOSLOWSKI,
GLENN WHITMORE & JACK MORELLI

CONTENTS

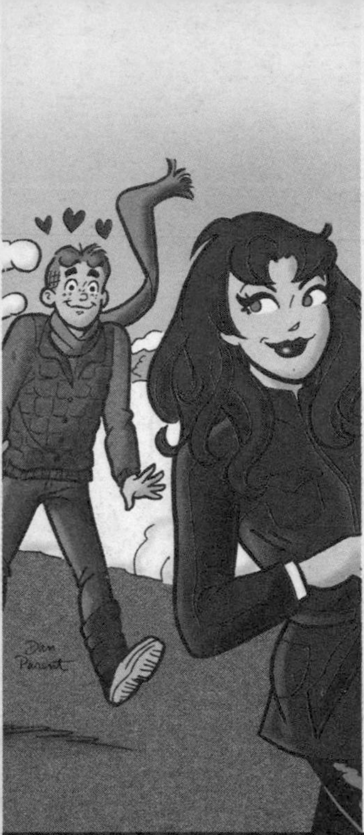
Dan Parent

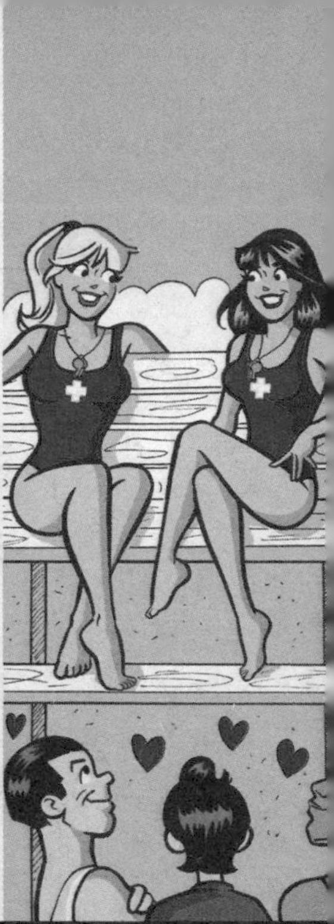

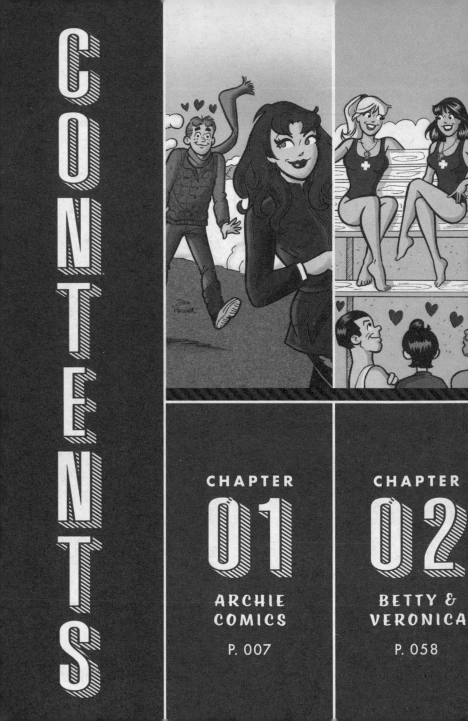

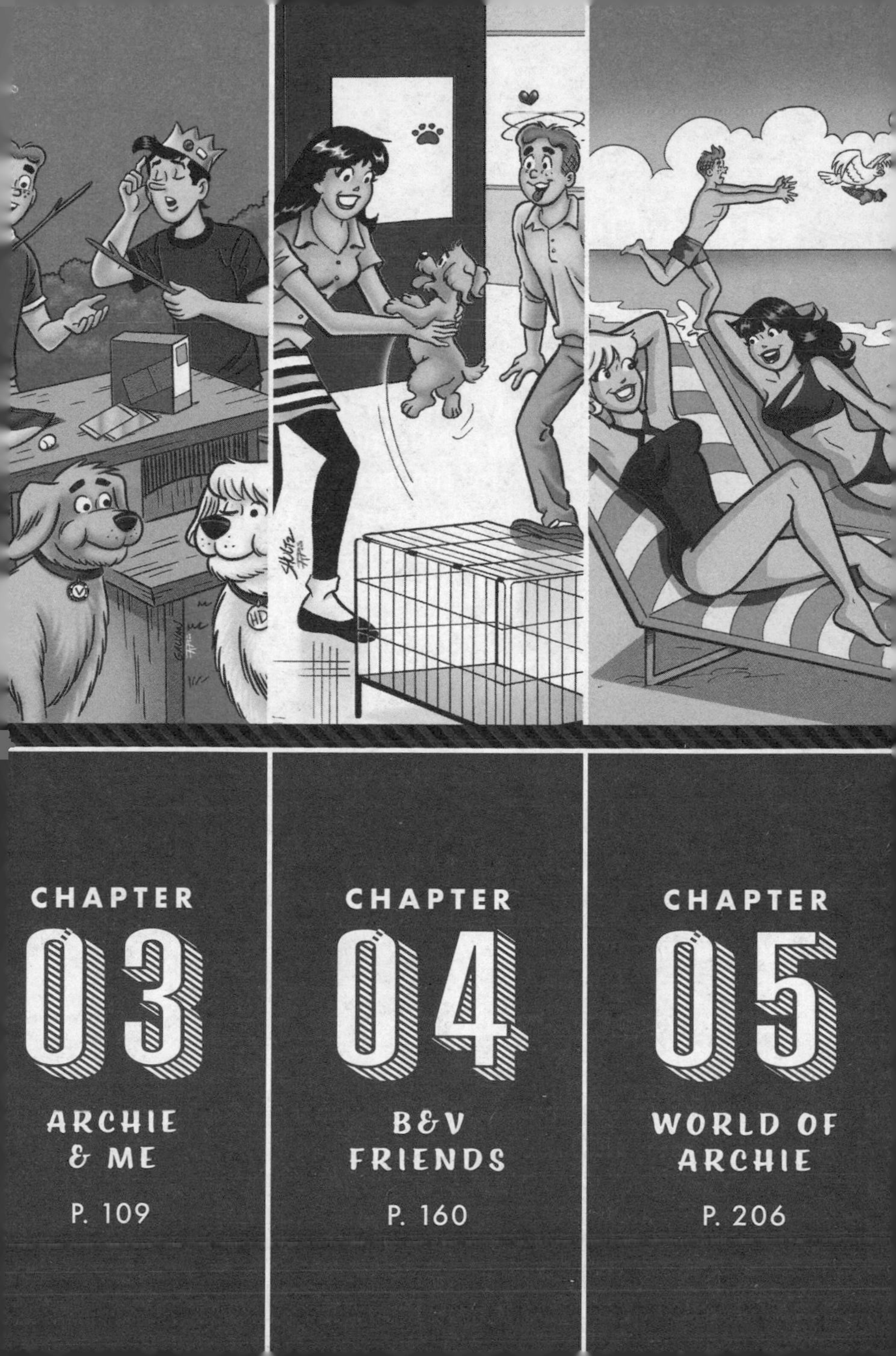

Wow! The last few years of Archie Comics have been jam-packed with fun and surprises!

Between the CW *Riverdale* TV series continuing to grow in popularity, the brand-new *Chilling Adventures of Sabrina* Netflix series joining *Riverdale* in success and having everyone talking, the launch of the widely popular Betty & Veronica fashion line, PLUS a number of new, well-received comic launches that further push the limits of what our characters can do, these past few years have been landmark ones for Archie Comics.

And it hasn't just been good for TV, fashion and new releases—our classic-style stories were more loved than ever! From new comic series *Betty & Veronica: Friends Forever* to our ever-popular brand new digest stories, Archie fans new and old were looking to reconnect with their favorite teens in meaningful ways!

Here's your chance to take a look at some of the most memorable recent Archie stories!

01

ARCHIE COMICS

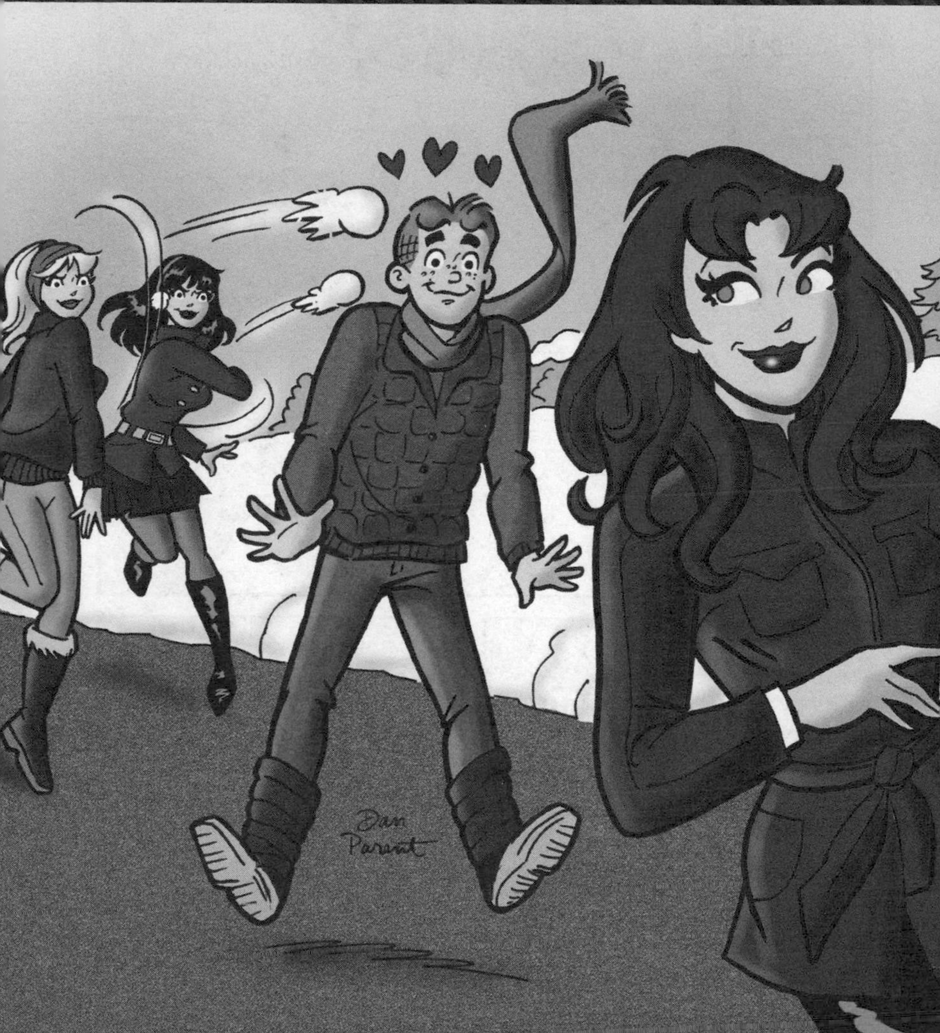
Dan Parent

Archie in READY, SET, GO!

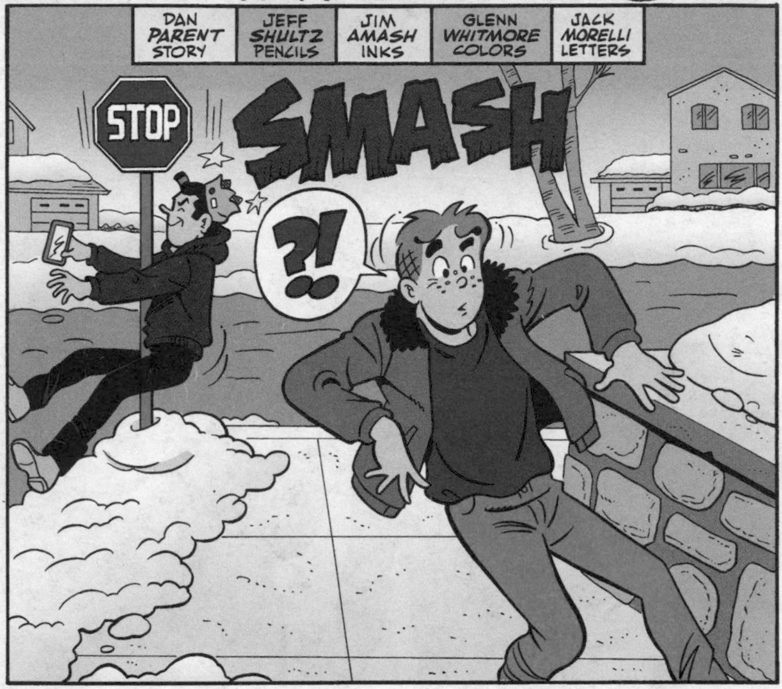
DAN PARENT STORY
JEFF SHULTZ PENCILS
JIM AMASH INKS
GLENN WHITMORE COLORS
JACK MORELLI LETTERS
STOP
SMASH
?!

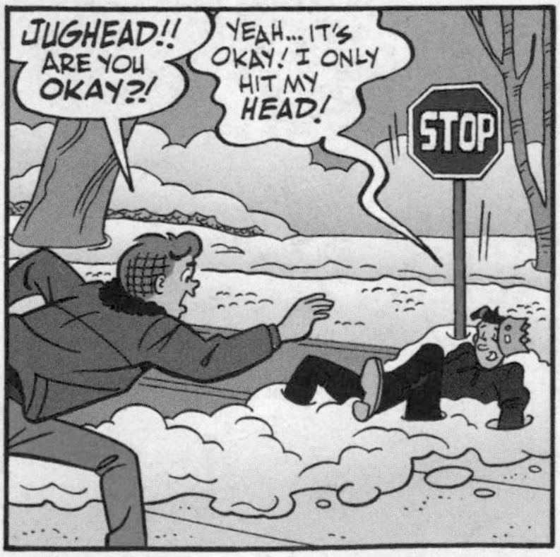
JUGHEAD!! ARE YOU OKAY?!
YEAH... IT'S OKAY! I ONLY HIT MY HEAD!
STOP

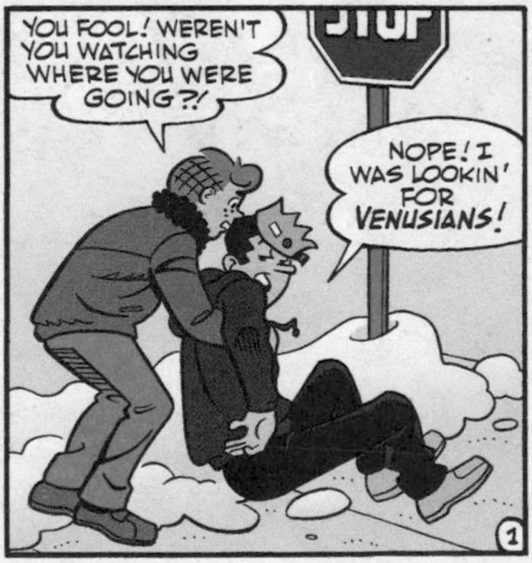
YOU FOOL! WEREN'T YOU WATCHING WHERE YOU WERE GOING?!
NOPE! I WAS LOOKIN' FOR VENUSIANS!
1

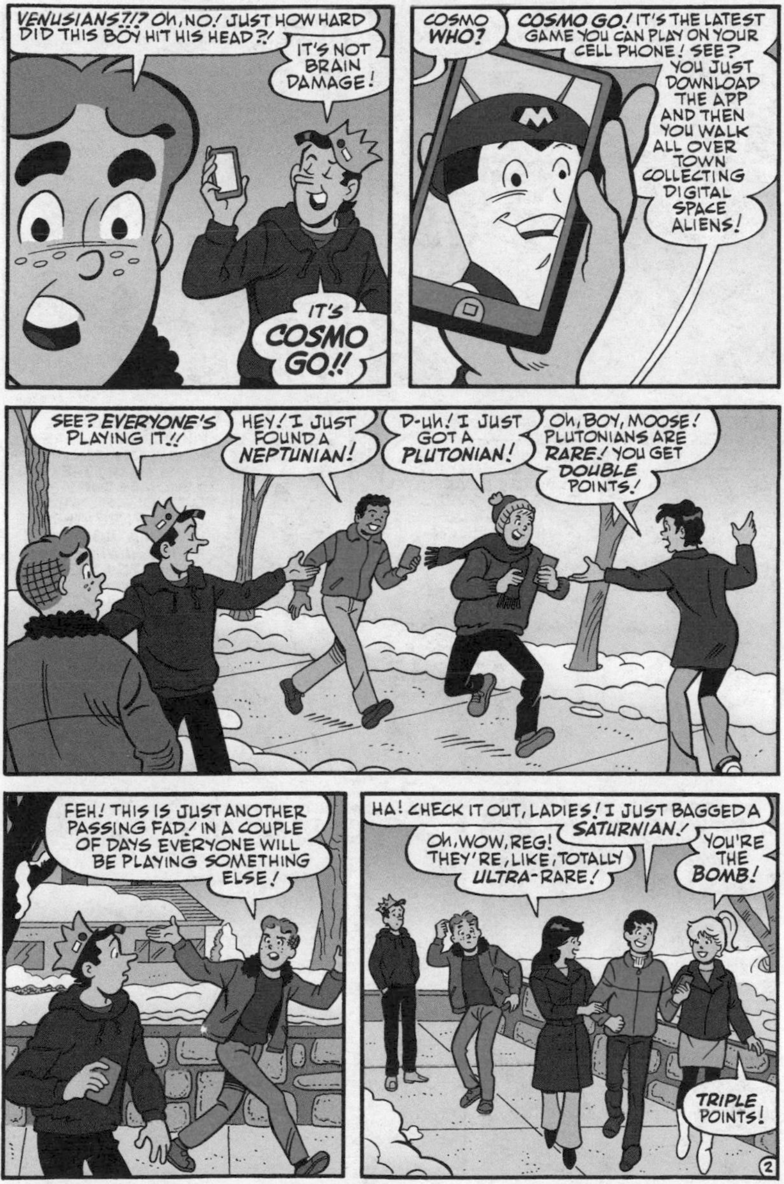
VENUSIANS?!? Oh, NO! JUST HOW HARD DID THIS BOY HIT HIS HEAD?!
IT'S NOT BRAIN DAMAGE!
IT'S COSMO GO!!
COSMO WHO?
COSMO GO! IT'S THE LATEST GAME YOU CAN PLAY ON YOUR CELL PHONE! SEE? YOU JUST DOWNLOAD THE APP AND THEN YOU WALK ALL OVER TOWN COLLECTING DIGITAL SPACE ALIENS!
SEE? EVERYONE'S PLAYING IT!!
HEY! I JUST FOUND A NEPTUNIAN!
D-uh! I JUST GOT A PLUTONIAN!
Oh, BOY, MOOSE! PLUTONIANS ARE RARE! YOU GET DOUBLE POINTS!
FEH! THIS IS JUST ANOTHER PASSING FAD! IN A COUPLE OF DAYS EVERYONE WILL BE PLAYING SOMETHING ELSE!
HA! CHECK IT OUT, LADIES! I JUST BAGGED A SATURNIAN!
Oh, WOW, REG! THEY'RE, LIKE, TOTALLY ULTRA-RARE!
YOU'RE THE BOMB!
TRIPLE POINTS!
2

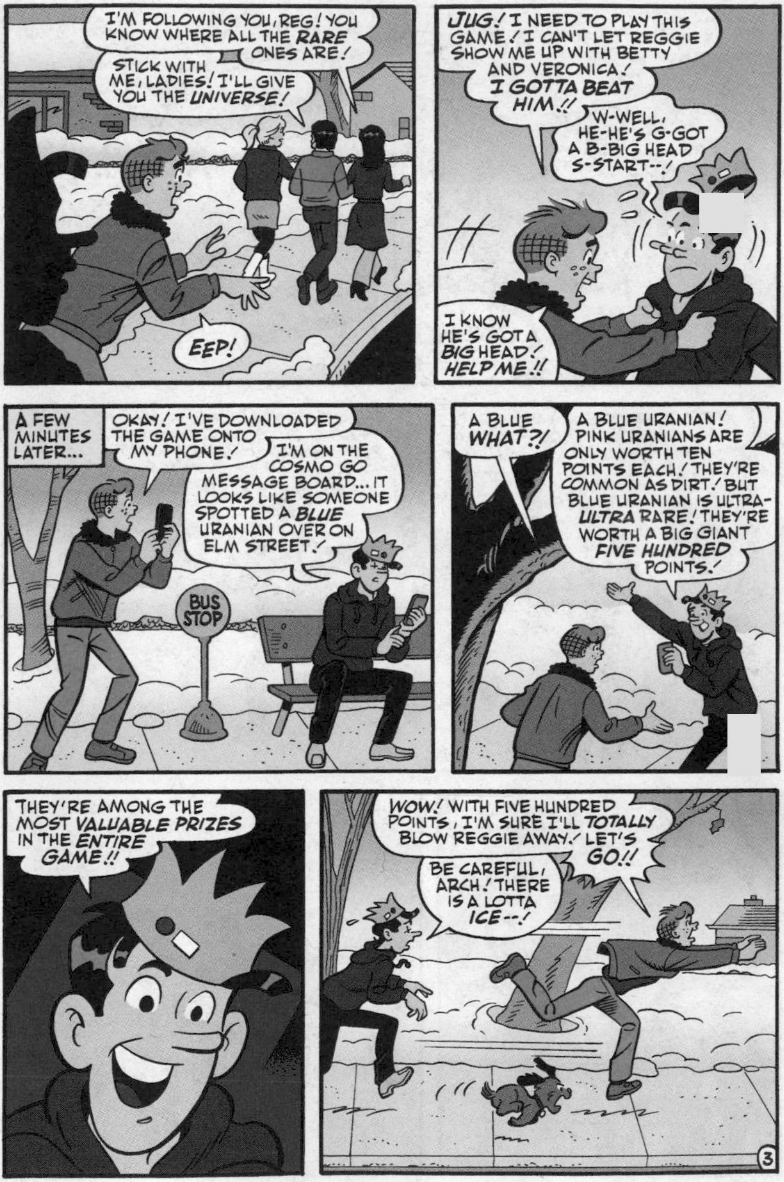
I'M FOLLOWING YOU, REG! YOU KNOW WHERE ALL THE RARE ONES ARE!
STICK WITH ME, LADIES! I'LL GIVE YOU THE UNIVERSE!
EEP!
JUG! I NEED TO PLAY THIS GAME! I CAN'T LET REGGIE SHOW ME UP WITH BETTY AND VERONICA! I GOTTA BEAT HIM!!
W-WELL, HE-HE'S G-GOT A B-BIG HEAD S-START--!
I KNOW HE'S GOT A BIG HEAD! HELP ME!!
A FEW MINUTES LATER...
OKAY! I'VE DOWNLOADED THE GAME ONTO MY PHONE!
I'M ON THE COSMO GO MESSAGE BOARD... IT LOOKS LIKE SOMEONE SPOTTED A BLUE URANIAN OVER ON ELM STREET!
BUS STOP
A BLUE WHAT?!
A BLUE URANIAN! PINK URANIANS ARE ONLY WORTH TEN POINTS EACH! THEY'RE COMMON AS DIRT! BUT BLUE URANIAN IS ULTRA-ULTRA RARE! THEY'RE WORTH A BIG GIANT FIVE HUNDRED POINTS!
THEY'RE AMONG THE MOST VALUABLE PRIZES IN THE ENTIRE GAME!!
WOW! WITH FIVE HUNDRED POINTS, I'M SURE I'LL TOTALLY BLOW REGGIE AWAY! LET'S GO!!
BE CAREFUL, ARCH! THERE IS A LOTTA ICE--!
3

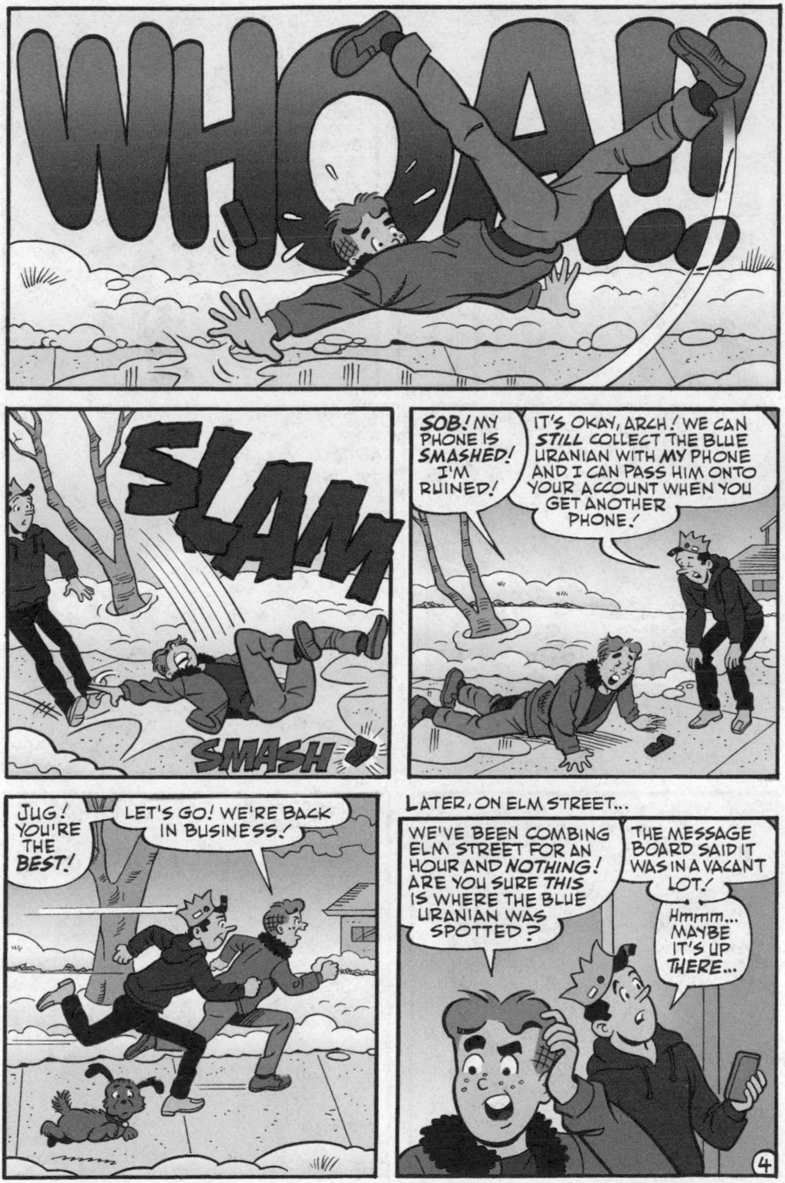
WHOAH...
SLAM
SMASH
SOB! MY PHONE IS SMASHED! I'M RUINED!
IT'S OKAY, ARCH! WE CAN STILL COLLECT THE BLUE URANIAN WITH MY PHONE AND I CAN PASS HIM ONTO YOUR ACCOUNT WHEN YOU GET ANOTHER PHONE!
JUG! YOU'RE THE BEST!
LET'S GO! WE'RE BACK IN BUSINESS!
LATER, ON ELM STREET...
WE'VE BEEN COMBING ELM STREET FOR AN HOUR AND NOTHING! ARE YOU SURE THIS IS WHERE THE BLUE URANIAN WAS SPOTTED?
THE MESSAGE BOARD SAID IT WAS IN A VACANT LOT!
Hmmm... MAYBE IT'S UP THERE...
4

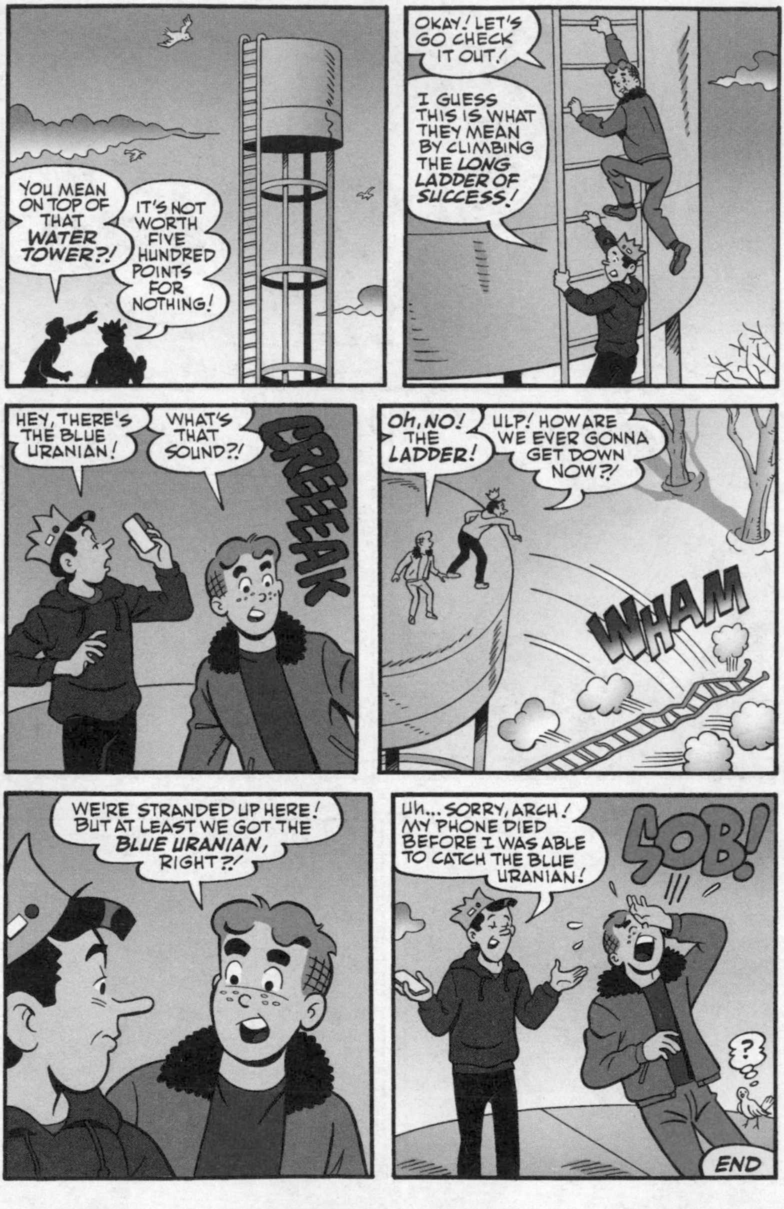
YOU MEAN ON TOP OF THAT WATER TOWER?!
IT'S NOT WORTH FIVE HUNDRED POINTS FOR NOTHING!
OKAY! LET'S GO CHECK IT OUT!
I GUESS THIS IS WHAT THEY MEAN BY CLIMBING THE LONG LADDER OF SUCCESS!
HEY, THERE'S THE BLUE URANIAN!
WHAT'S THAT SOUND?!
CREEEAK
Oh, NO! THE LADDER!
ULP! HOW ARE WE EVER GONNA GET DOWN NOW?!
WHAM
WE'RE STRANDED UP HERE! BUT AT LEAST WE GOT THE BLUE URANIAN, RIGHT?!
UH... SORRY, ARCH! MY PHONE DIED BEFORE I WAS ABLE TO CATCH THE BLUE URANIAN!
SOB!
?
END

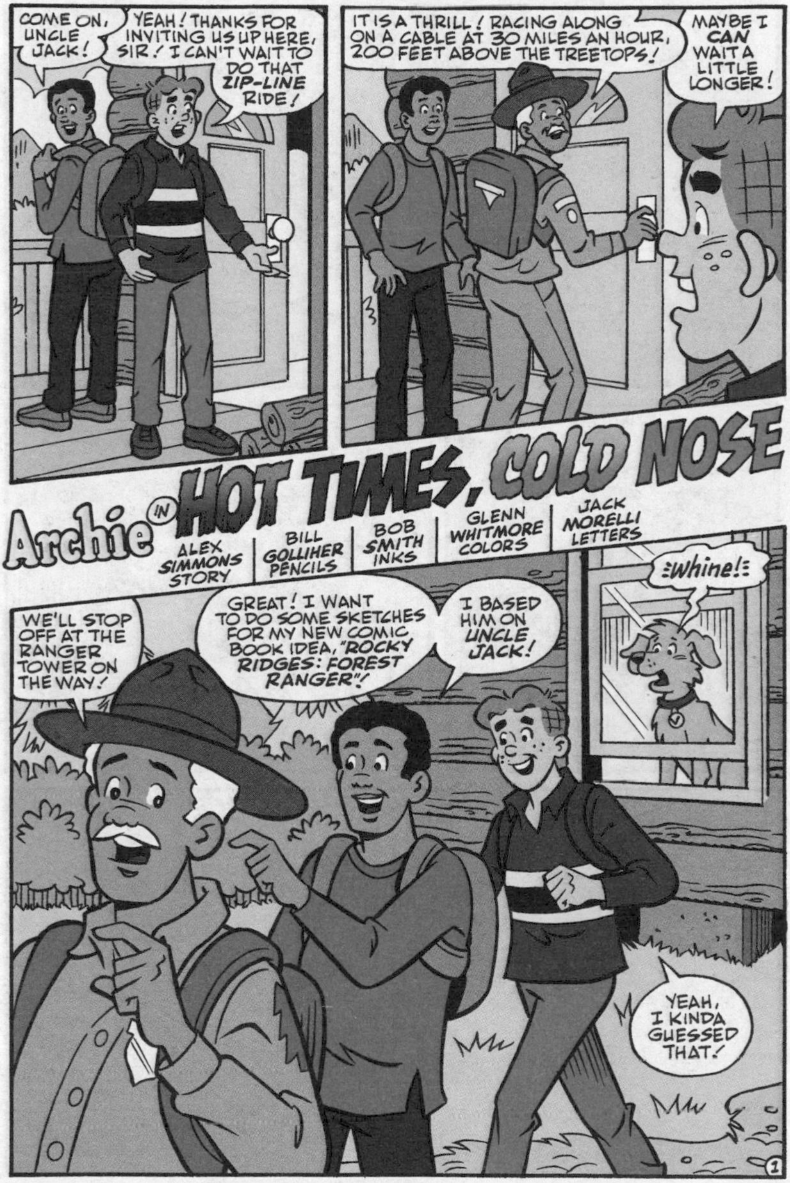
COME ON, UNCLE JACK!
YEAH! THANKS FOR INVITING US UP HERE, SIR! I CAN'T WAIT TO DO THAT ZIP-LINE RIDE!
IT IS A THRILL! RACING ALONG ON A CABLE AT 30 MILES AN HOUR, 200 FEET ABOVE THE TREETOPS!
MAYBE I CAN WAIT A LITTLE LONGER!
Archie IN HOT TIMES, COLD NOSE
ALEX SIMMONS STORY
BILL GOLLIHER PENCILS
BOB SMITH INKS
GLENN WHITMORE COLORS
JACK MORELLI LETTERS
WE'LL STOP OFF AT THE RANGER TOWER ON THE WAY!
GREAT! I WANT TO DO SOME SKETCHES FOR MY NEW COMIC BOOK IDEA, "ROCKY RIDGES: FOREST RANGER"!
I BASED HIM ON UNCLE JACK!
:Whine!:
YEAH, I KINDA GUESSED THAT!
1

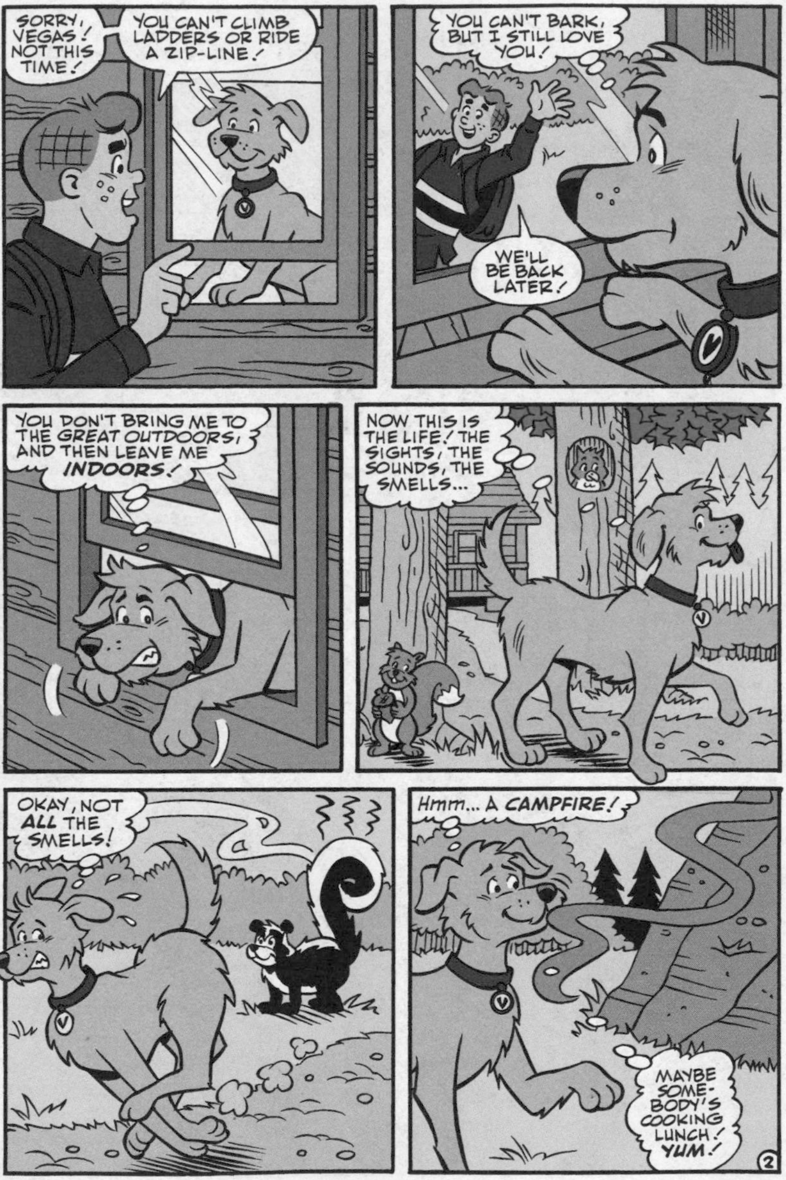
SORRY, VEGAS! NOT THIS TIME!
YOU CAN'T CLIMB LADDERS OR RIDE A ZIP-LINE!
YOU CAN'T BARK, BUT I STILL LOVE YOU!
WE'LL BE BACK LATER!
YOU DON'T BRING ME TO THE GREAT OUTDOORS, AND THEN LEAVE ME INDOORS!
NOW THIS IS THE LIFE! THE SIGHTS, THE SOUNDS, THE SMELLS...
OKAY, NOT ALL THE SMELLS!
Hmm... A CAMPFIRE!
MAYBE SOMEBODY'S COOKING LUNCH! YUM!
2

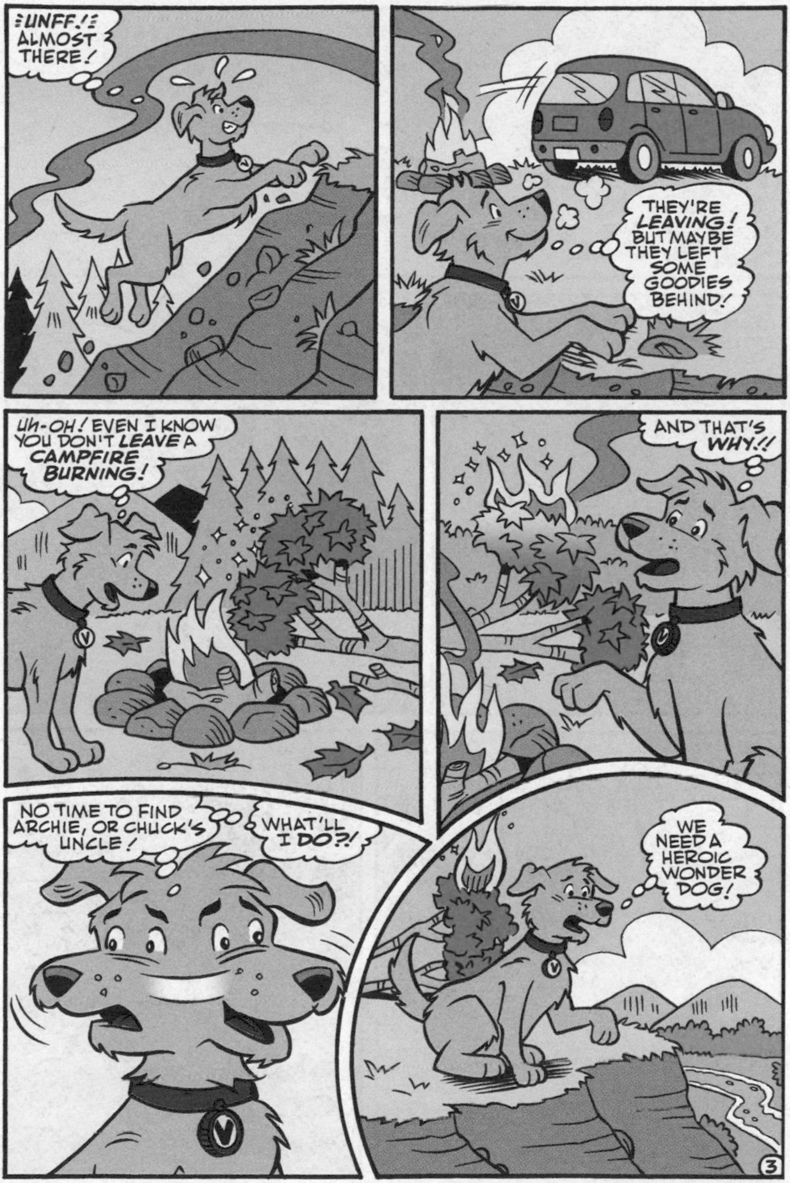
UNFF.! ALMOST THERE!
THEY'RE LEAVING! BUT MAYBE THEY LEFT SOME GOODIES BEHIND!
UH-OH! EVEN I KNOW YOU DON'T LEAVE A CAMPFIRE BURNING!
AND THAT'S WHY!!!
NO TIME TO FIND ARCHIE, OR CHUCK'S UNCLE!
WHAT'LL I DO?!
WE NEED A HEROIC WONDER DOG!
3

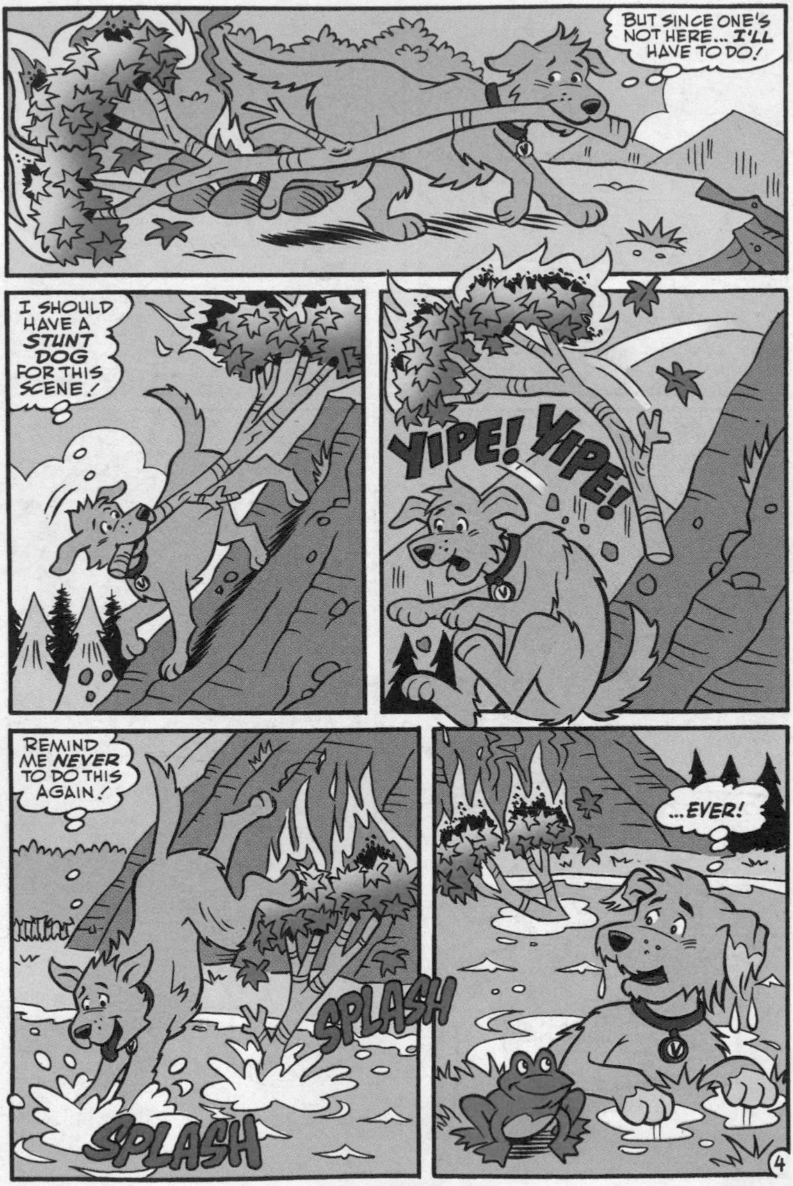
BUT SINCE ONE'S NOT HERE... I'LL HAVE TO DO!
I SHOULD HAVE A STUNT DOG FOR THIS SCENE!
YIPE! YIPE!
REMIND ME NEVER TO DO THIS AGAIN!
SPLASH
SPLASH
...EVER!
4

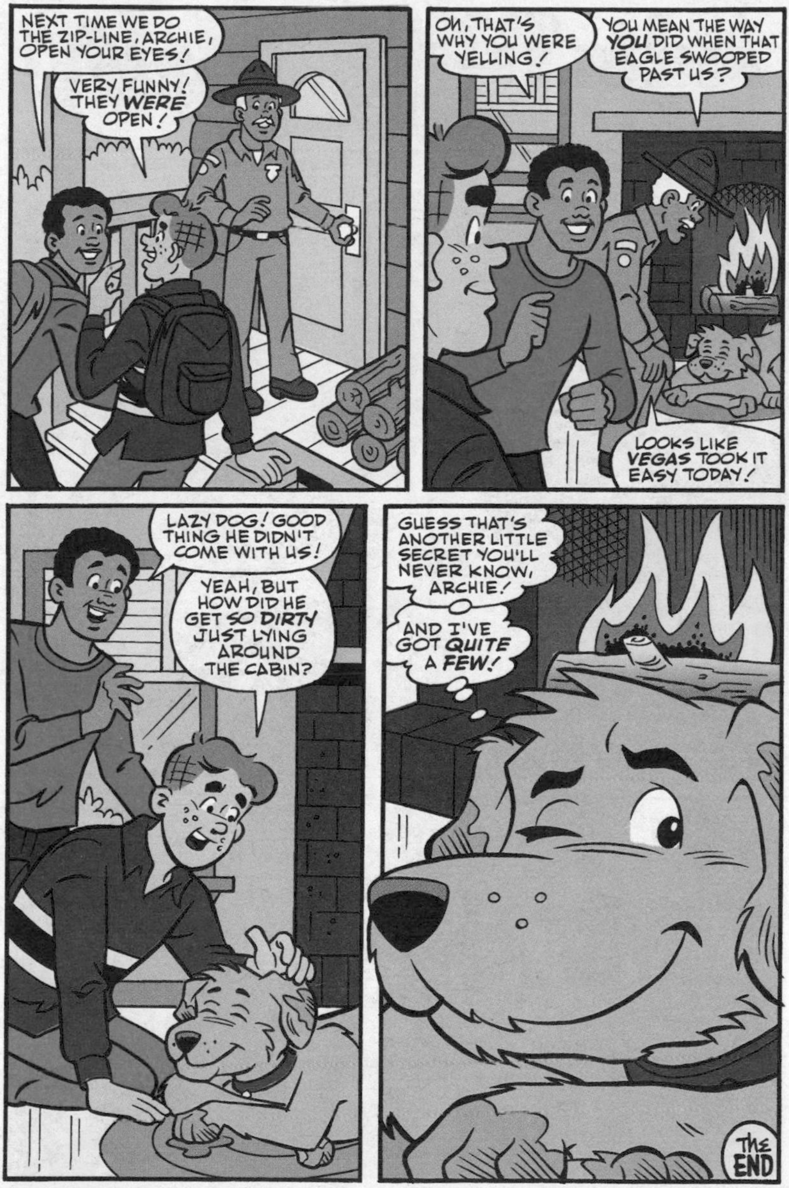
NEXT TIME WE DO THE ZIP-LINE, ARCHIE, OPEN YOUR EYES!
VERY FUNNY! THEY WERE OPEN!
OH, THAT'S WHY YOU WERE YELLING!
YOU MEAN THE WAY YOU DID WHEN THAT EAGLE SWOOPED PAST US?
LOOKS LIKE VEGAS TOOK IT EASY TODAY!
LAZY DOG! GOOD THING HE DIDN'T COME WITH US!
YEAH, BUT HOW DID HE GET SO DIRTY JUST LYING AROUND THE CABIN?
GUESS THAT'S ANOTHER LITTLE SECRET YOU'LL NEVER KNOW, ARCHIE!
AND I'VE GOT QUITE A FEW!
THE END

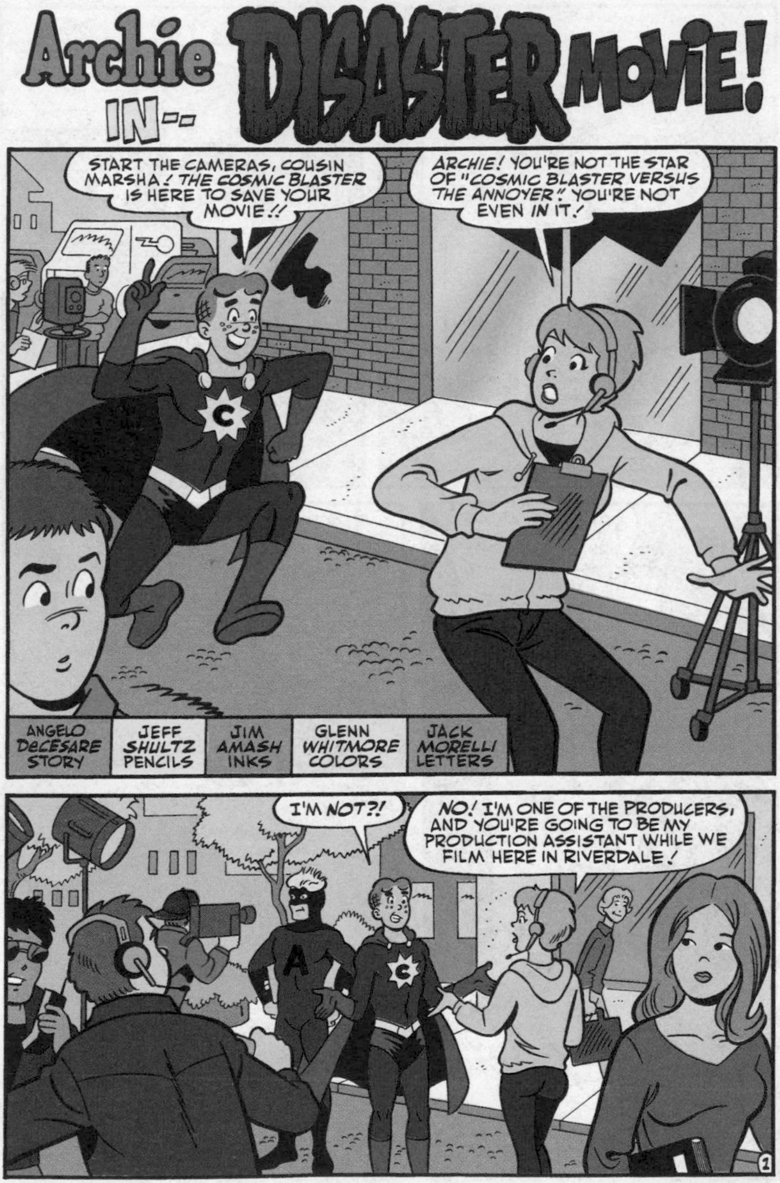
Archie IN-- DISASTER MOVIE!
START THE CAMERAS, COUSIN MARSHA! THE COSMIC BLASTER IS HERE TO SAVE YOUR MOVIE!!
ARCHIE! YOU'RE NOT THE STAR OF "COSMIC BLASTER VERSUS THE ANNOYER"! YOU'RE NOT EVEN IN IT!
ANGELO DeCESARE STORY
JEFF SHULTZ PENCILS
JIM AMASH INKS
GLENN WHITMORE COLORS
JACK MORELLI LETTERS
I'M NOT?!
NO! I'M ONE OF THE PRODUCERS, AND YOU'RE GOING TO BE MY PRODUCTION ASSISTANT WHILE WE FILM HERE IN RIVERDALE!
1

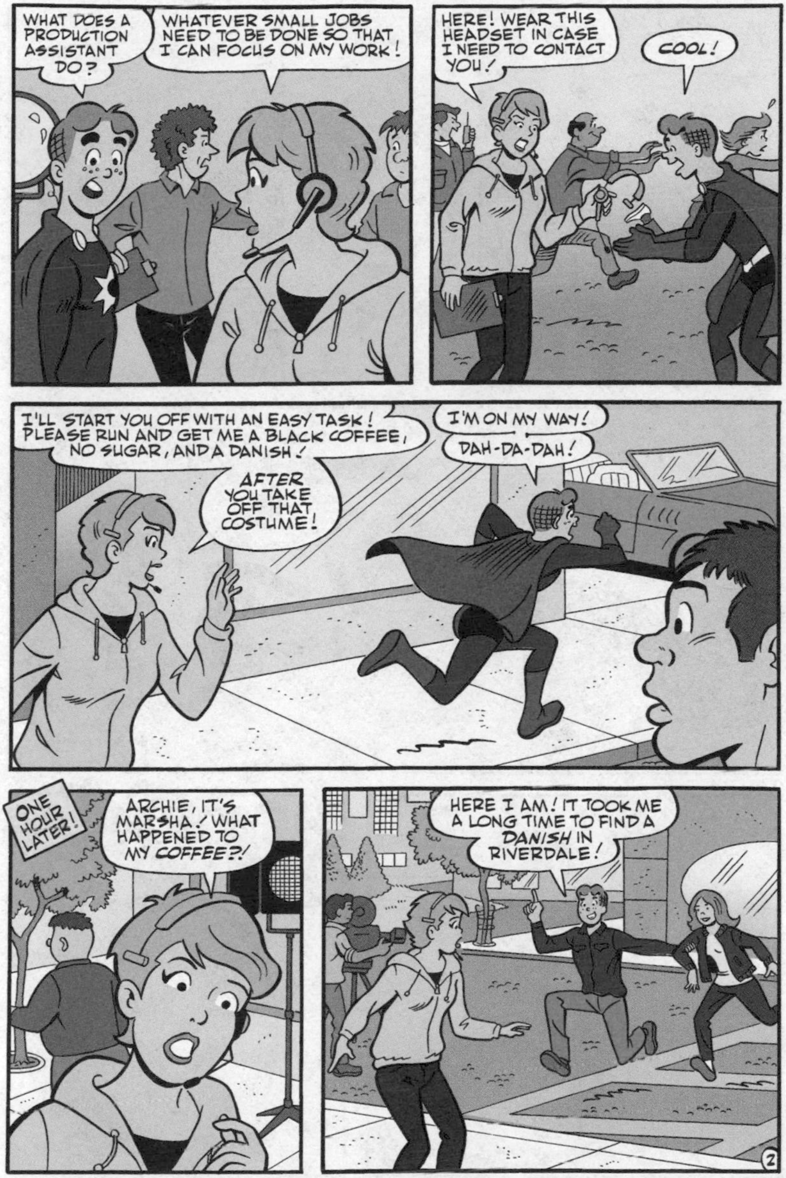
WHAT DOES A PRODUCTION ASSISTANT DO?
WHATEVER SMALL JOBS NEED TO BE DONE SO THAT I CAN FOCUS ON MY WORK!
HERE! WEAR THIS HEADSET IN CASE I NEED TO CONTACT YOU!
COOL!
I'LL START YOU OFF WITH AN EASY TASK! PLEASE RUN AND GET ME A BLACK COFFEE, NO SUGAR, AND A DANISH!
AFTER YOU TAKE OFF THAT COSTUME!
I'M ON MY WAY!
DAH-DA-DAH!
ONE HOUR LATER!
ARCHIE, IT'S MARSHA! WHAT HAPPENED TO MY COFFEE?!
HERE I AM! IT TOOK ME A LONG TIME TO FIND A DANISH IN RIVERDALE!

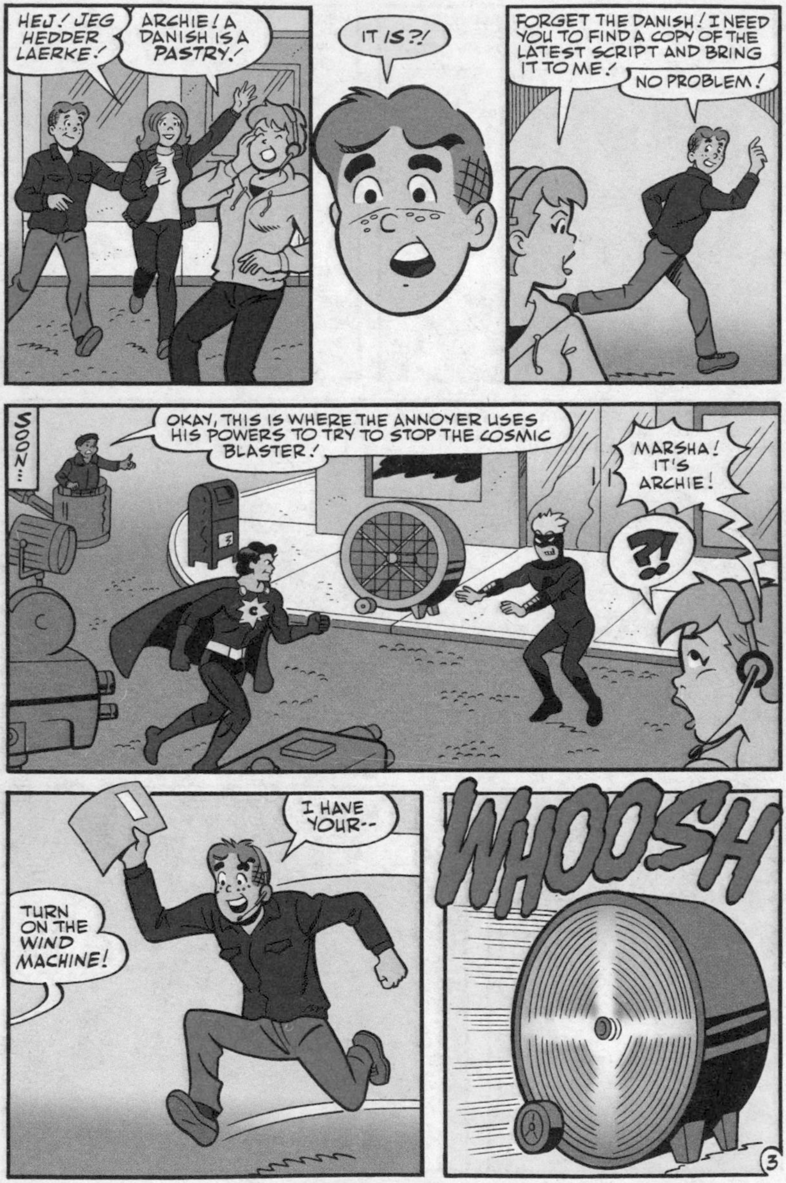
HEJ! JEG HEDDER LAERKE!
ARCHIE! A DANISH IS A PASTRY!
IT IS?!
FORGET THE DANISH! I NEED YOU TO FIND A COPY OF THE LATEST SCRIPT AND BRING IT TO ME!
NO PROBLEM!
SOON...
OKAY, THIS IS WHERE THE ANNOYER USES HIS POWERS TO TRY TO STOP THE COSMIC BLASTER!
MARSHA! IT'S ARCHIE!
?!
I HAVE YOUR--
TURN ON THE WIND MACHINE!
WHOOSH
3

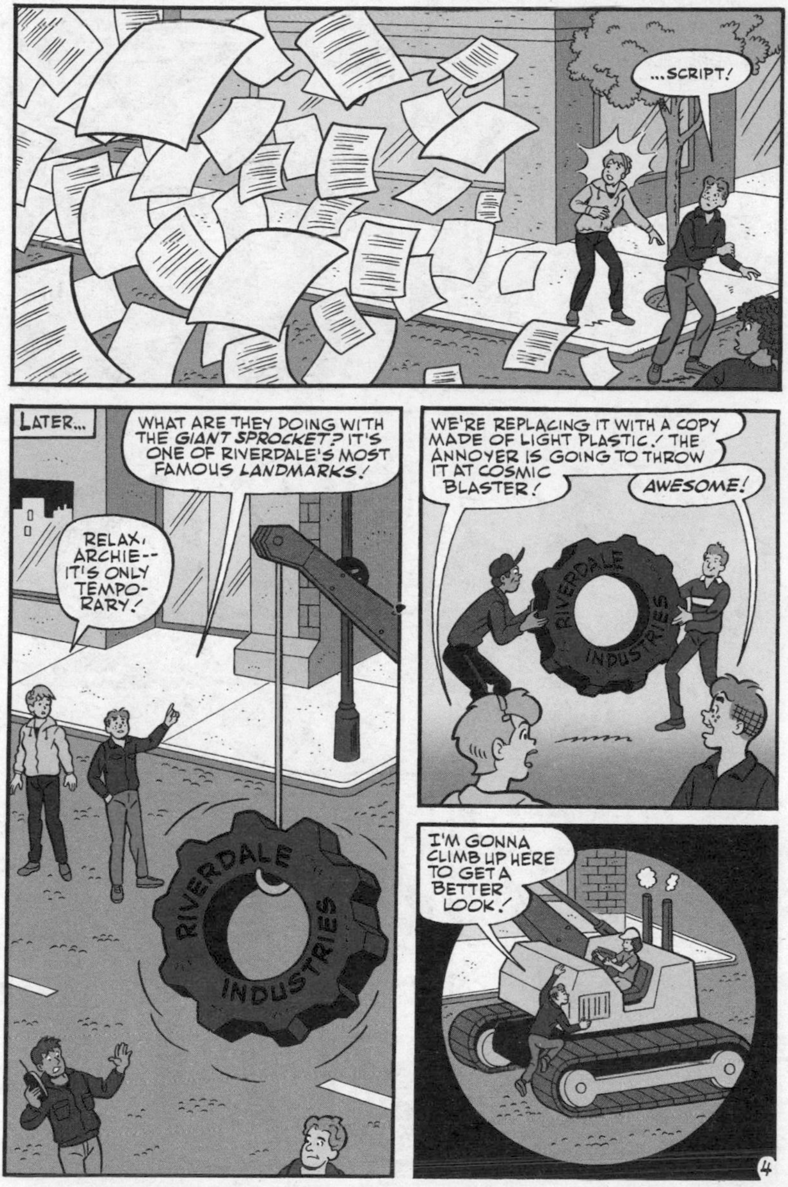
...SCRIPT!
LATER...
WHAT ARE THEY DOING WITH THE GIANT SPROCKET? IT'S ONE OF RIVERDALE'S MOST FAMOUS LANDMARKS!
RELAX, ARCHIE-- IT'S ONLY TEMPORARY!
RIVERDALE INDUSTRIES
WE'RE REPLACING IT WITH A COPY MADE OF LIGHT PLASTIC! THE ANNOYER IS GOING TO THROW IT AT COSMIC BLASTER!
AWESOME!
RIVERDALE INDUSTRIES
I'M GONNA CLIMB UP HERE TO GET A BETTER LOOK!
4

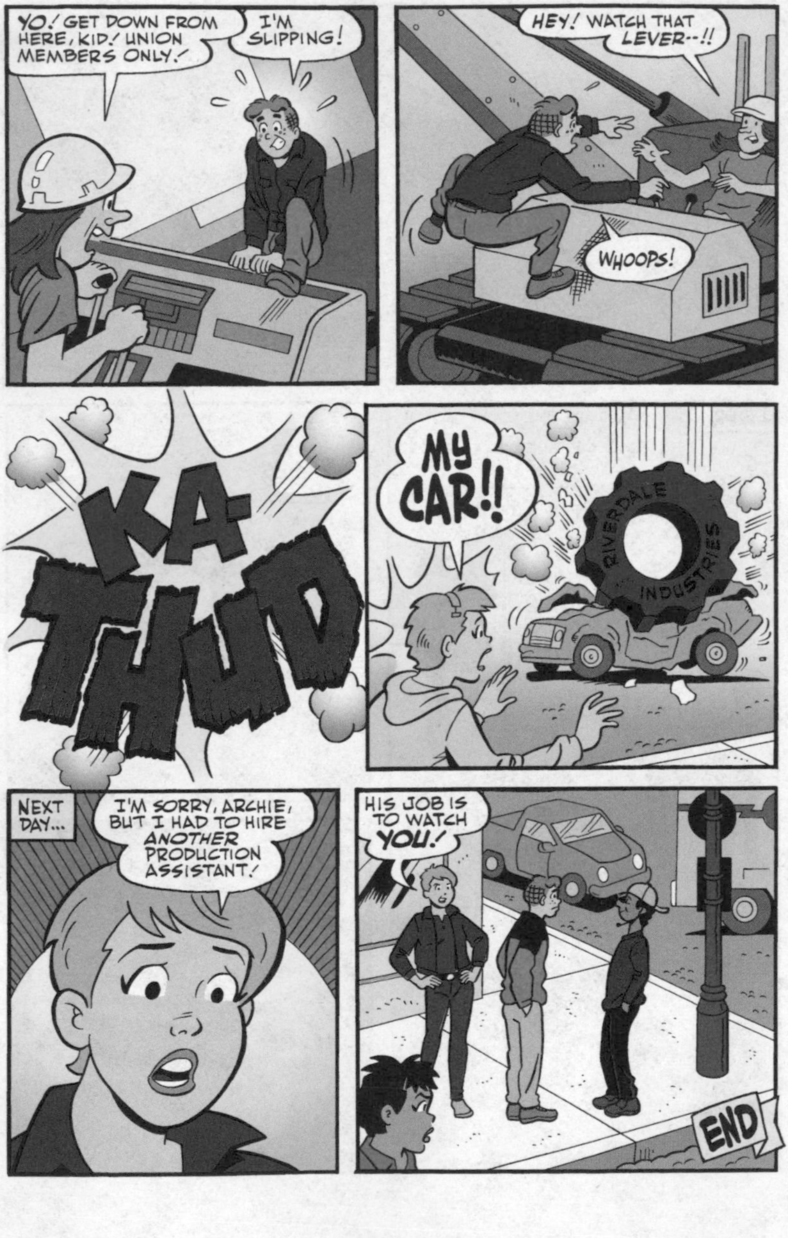
YO! GET DOWN FROM HERE, KID! UNION MEMBERS ONLY!
I'M SLIPPING!
HEY! WATCH THAT LEVER--!!
WHOOPS!
KA-THUD
MY CAR!!
RIVERDALE INDUSTRIES
NEXT DAY...
I'M SORRY, ARCHIE, BUT I HAD TO HIRE ANOTHER PRODUCTION ASSISTANT!
HIS JOB IS TO WATCH YOU!
END

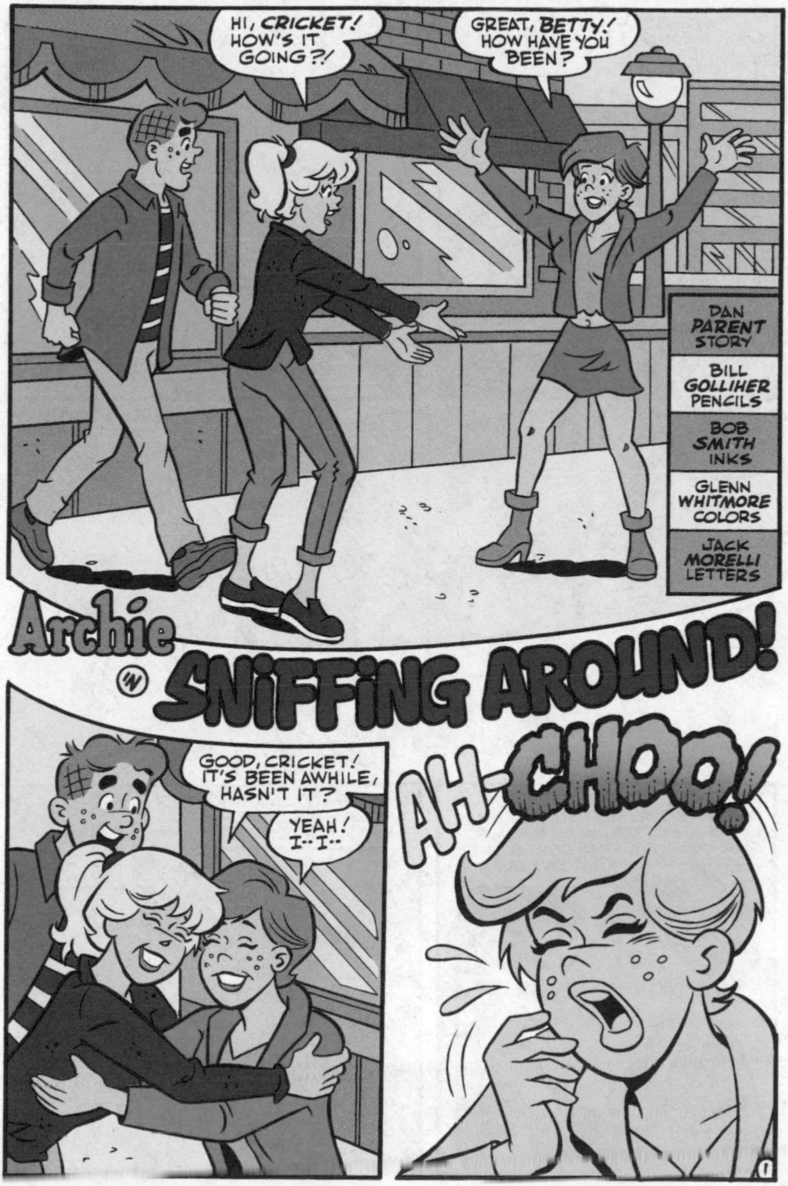
HI, CRICKET! HOW'S IT GOING?!
GREAT, BETTY! HOW HAVE YOU BEEN?
DAN PARENT STORY
BILL GOLLIHER PENCILS
BOB SMITH INKS
GLENN WHITMORE COLORS
JACK MORELLI LETTERS
Archie 'N SNIFFING AROUND!
GOOD, CRICKET! IT'S BEEN AWHILE, HASN'T IT?
YEAH! I-- I--
AH-CHOO!
1

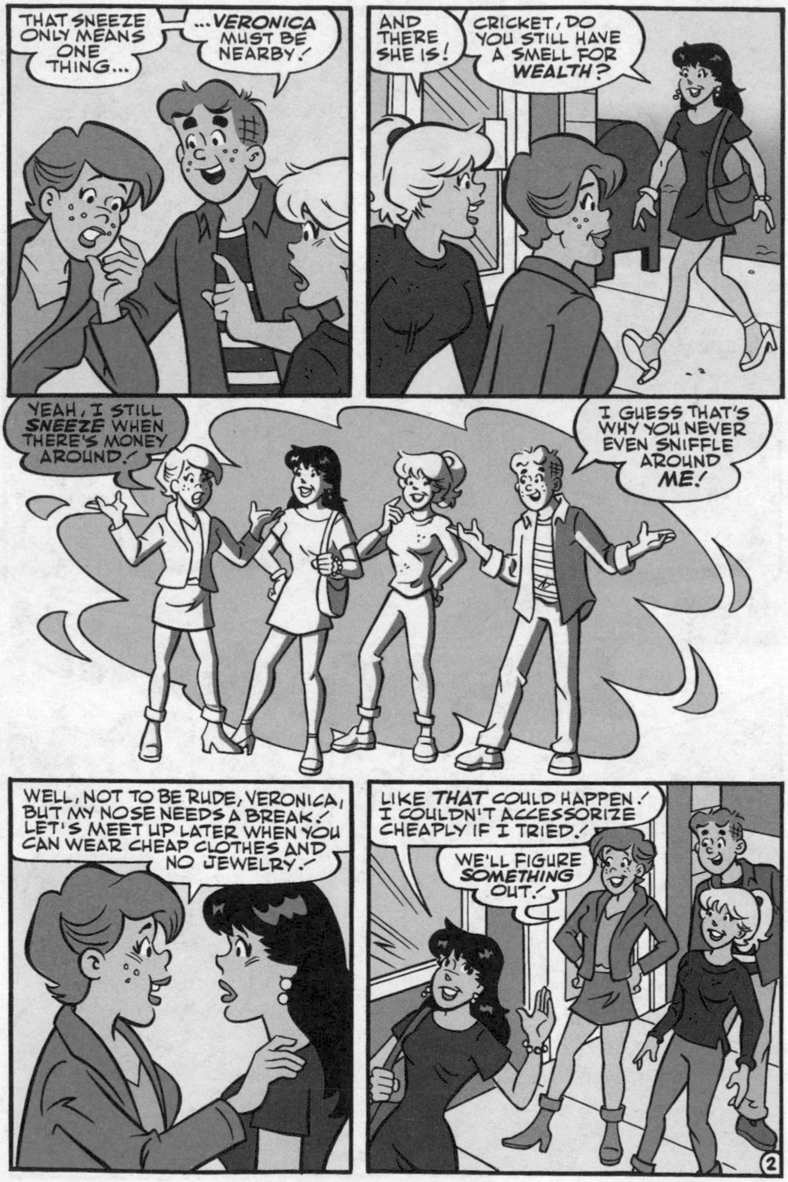
THAT SNEEZE ONLY MEANS ONE THING...
...VERONICA MUST BE NEARBY!
AND THERE SHE IS!
CRICKET, DO YOU STILL HAVE A SMELL FOR WEALTH?
YEAH, I STILL SNEEZE WHEN THERE'S MONEY AROUND!
I GUESS THAT'S WHY YOU NEVER EVEN SNIFFLE AROUND ME!
WELL, NOT TO BE RUDE, VERONICA, BUT MY NOSE NEEDS A BREAK! LET'S MEET UP LATER WHEN YOU CAN WEAR CHEAP CLOTHES AND NO JEWELRY!
LIKE THAT COULD HAPPEN! I COULDN'T ACCESSORIZE CHEAPLY IF I TRIED!
WE'LL FIGURE SOMETHING OUT!
2

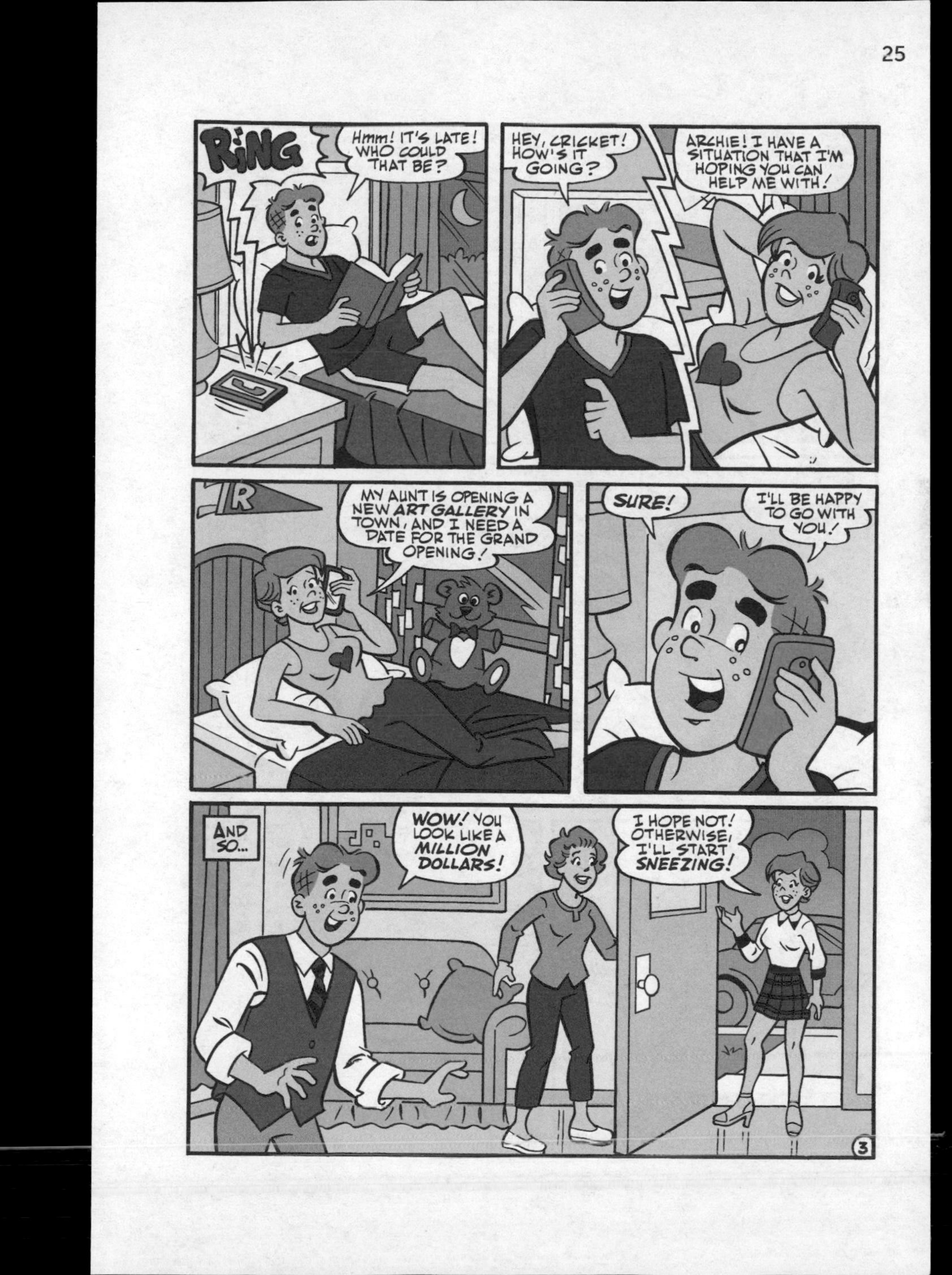
RING
Hmm! IT'S LATE! WHO COULD THAT BE?
HEY, CRICKET! HOW'S IT GOING?
ARCHIE! I HAVE A SITUATION THAT I'M HOPING YOU CAN HELP ME WITH!
MY AUNT IS OPENING A NEW ART GALLERY IN TOWN, AND I NEED A DATE FOR THE GRAND OPENING!
SURE!
I'LL BE HAPPY TO GO WITH YOU!
AND SO...
WOW! YOU LOOK LIKE A MILLION DOLLARS!
I HOPE NOT! OTHERWISE, I'LL START SNEEZING!
3

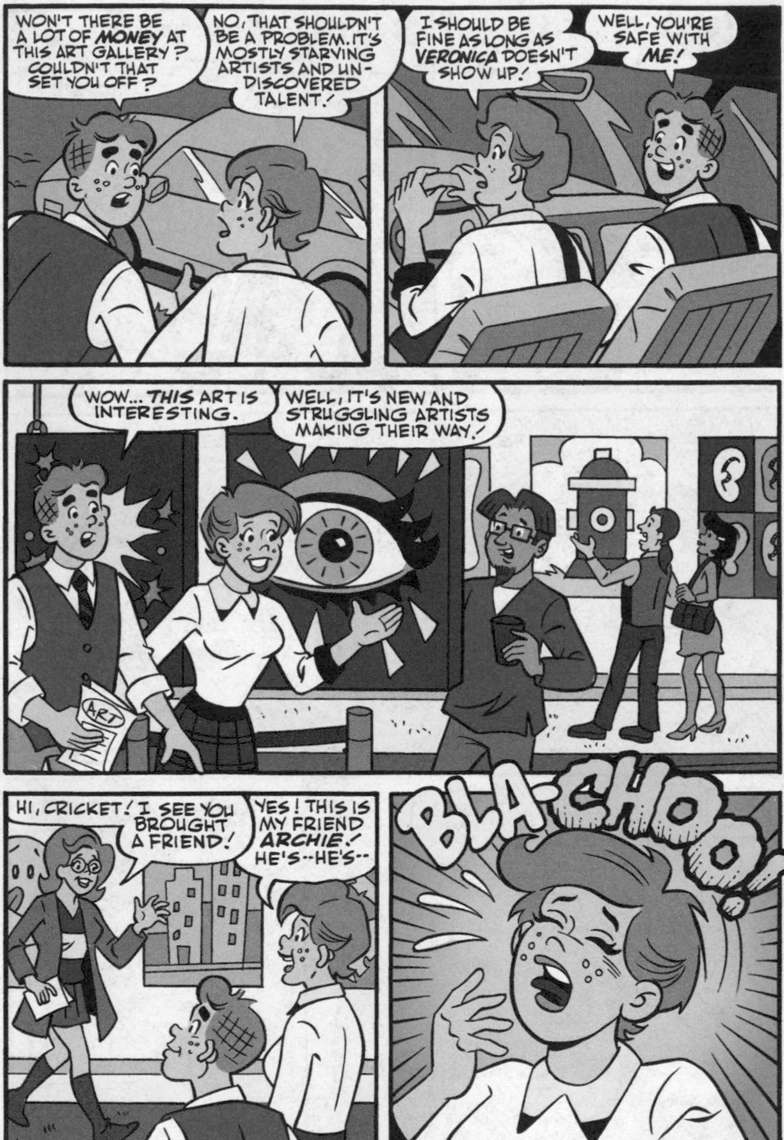
WON'T THERE BE A LOT OF MONEY AT THIS ART GALLERY? COULDN'T THAT SET YOU OFF?
NO, THAT SHOULDN'T BE A PROBLEM. IT'S MOSTLY STARVING ARTISTS AND UN-DISCOVERED TALENT!
I SHOULD BE FINE AS LONG AS VERONICA DOESN'T SHOW UP!
WELL, YOU'RE SAFE WITH ME!
WOW... THIS ART IS INTERESTING.
WELL, IT'S NEW AND STRUGGLING ARTISTS MAKING THEIR WAY!
ART
HI, CRICKET! I SEE YOU BROUGHT A FRIEND!
YES! THIS IS MY FRIEND ARCHIE! HE'S--HE'S--
BLA-CHOO!
4

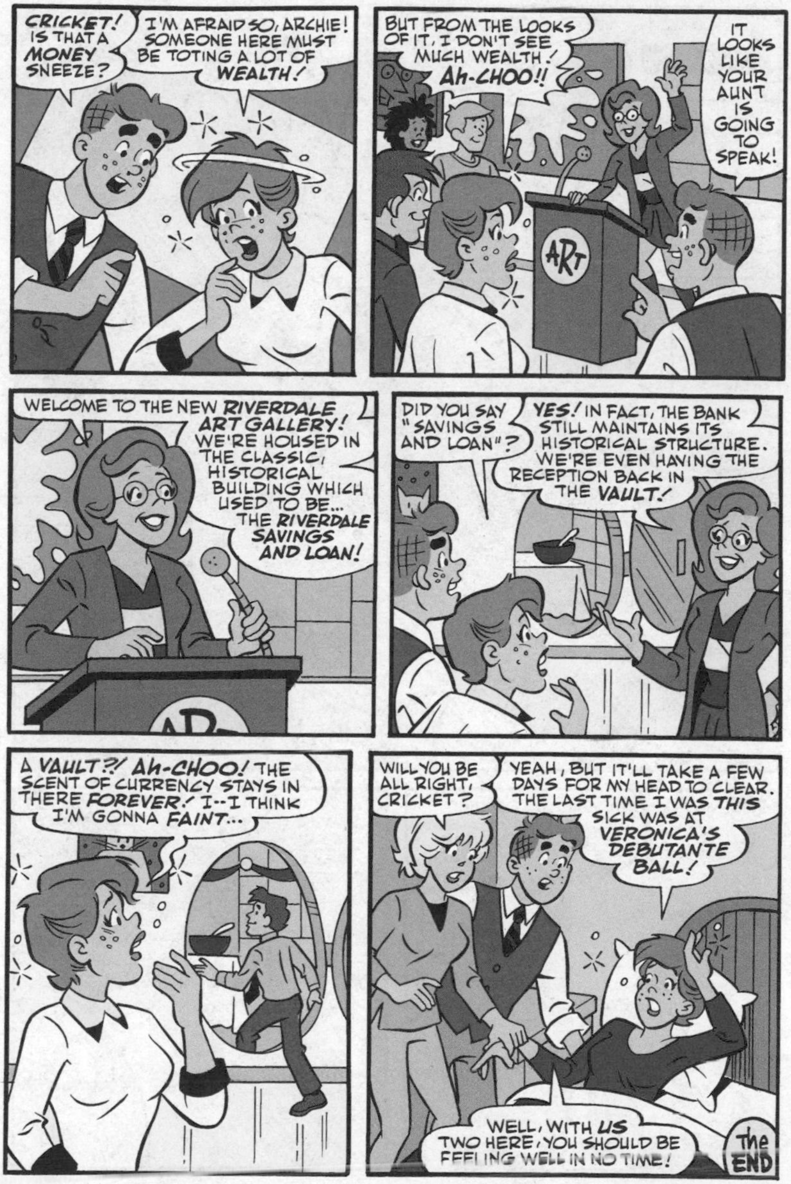
CRICKET! IS THAT A MONEY SNEEZE?
I'M AFRAID SO, ARCHIE! SOMEONE HERE MUST BE TOTING A LOT OF WEALTH!
BUT FROM THE LOOKS OF IT, I DON'T SEE MUCH WEALTH! Ah-CHOO!!
IT LOOKS LIKE YOUR AUNT IS GOING TO SPEAK!
ART
WELCOME TO THE NEW RIVERDALE ART GALLERY! WE'RE HOUSED IN THE CLASSIC, HISTORICAL BUILDING WHICH USED TO BE... THE RIVERDALE SAVINGS AND LOAN!
DID YOU SAY "SAVINGS AND LOAN"?
YES! IN FACT, THE BANK STILL MAINTAINS ITS HISTORICAL STRUCTURE. WE'RE EVEN HAVING THE RECEPTION BACK IN THE VAULT!
A VAULT?! Ah-CHOO! THE SCENT OF CURRENCY STAYS IN THERE FOREVER! I--I THINK I'M GONNA FAINT...
WILL YOU BE ALL RIGHT, CRICKET?
YEAH, BUT IT'LL TAKE A FEW DAYS FOR MY HEAD TO CLEAR. THE LAST TIME I WAS THIS SICK WAS AT VERONICA'S DEBUTANTE BALL!
WELL, WITH US TWO HERE, YOU SHOULD BE FEELING WELL IN NO TIME!
The END

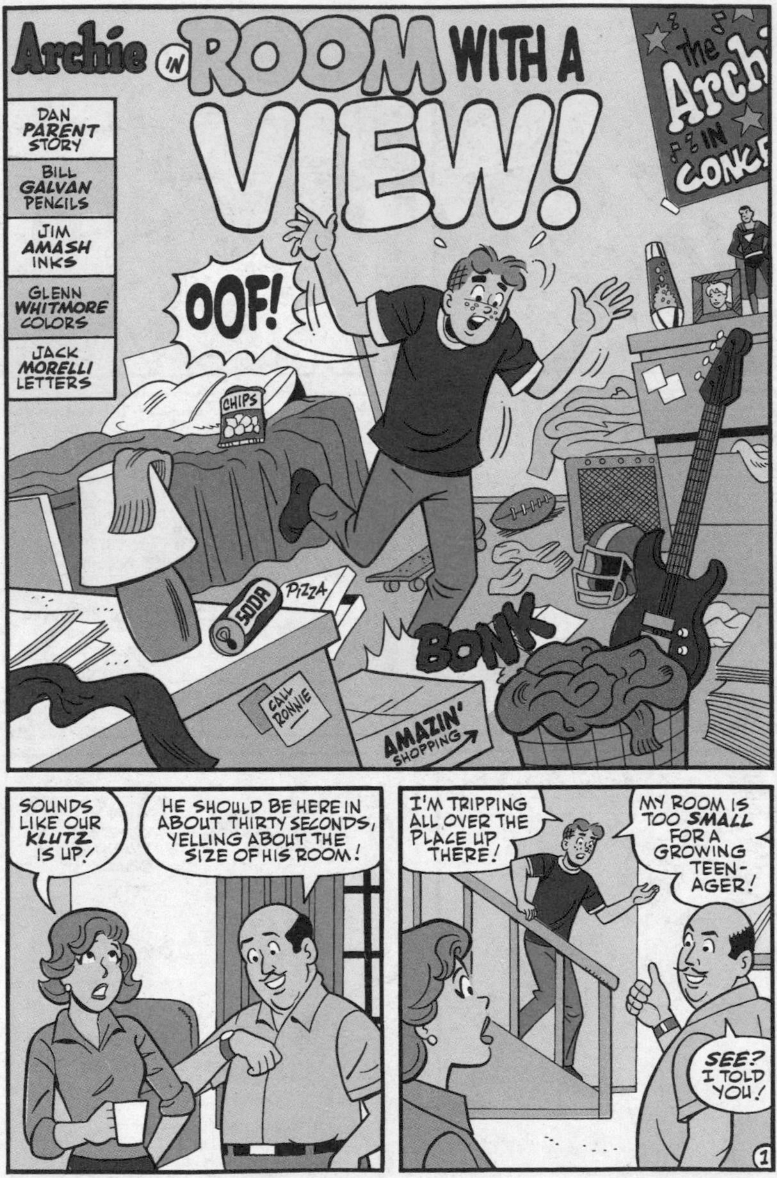
Archie in ROOM WITH A VIEW!
DAN PARENT STORY
BILL GALVAN PENCILS
JIM AMASH INKS
GLENN WHITMORE COLORS
JACK MORELLI LETTERS
OOF!
CHIPS
SODA
PIZZA
BONK
CALL RONNIE
AMAZIN' SHOPPING
SOUNDS LIKE OUR KLUTZ IS UP!
HE SHOULD BE HERE IN ABOUT THIRTY SECONDS, YELLING ABOUT THE SIZE OF HIS ROOM!
I'M TRIPPING ALL OVER THE PLACE UP THERE!
MY ROOM IS TOO SMALL FOR A GROWING TEEN-AGER!
SEE? I TOLD YOU!
1

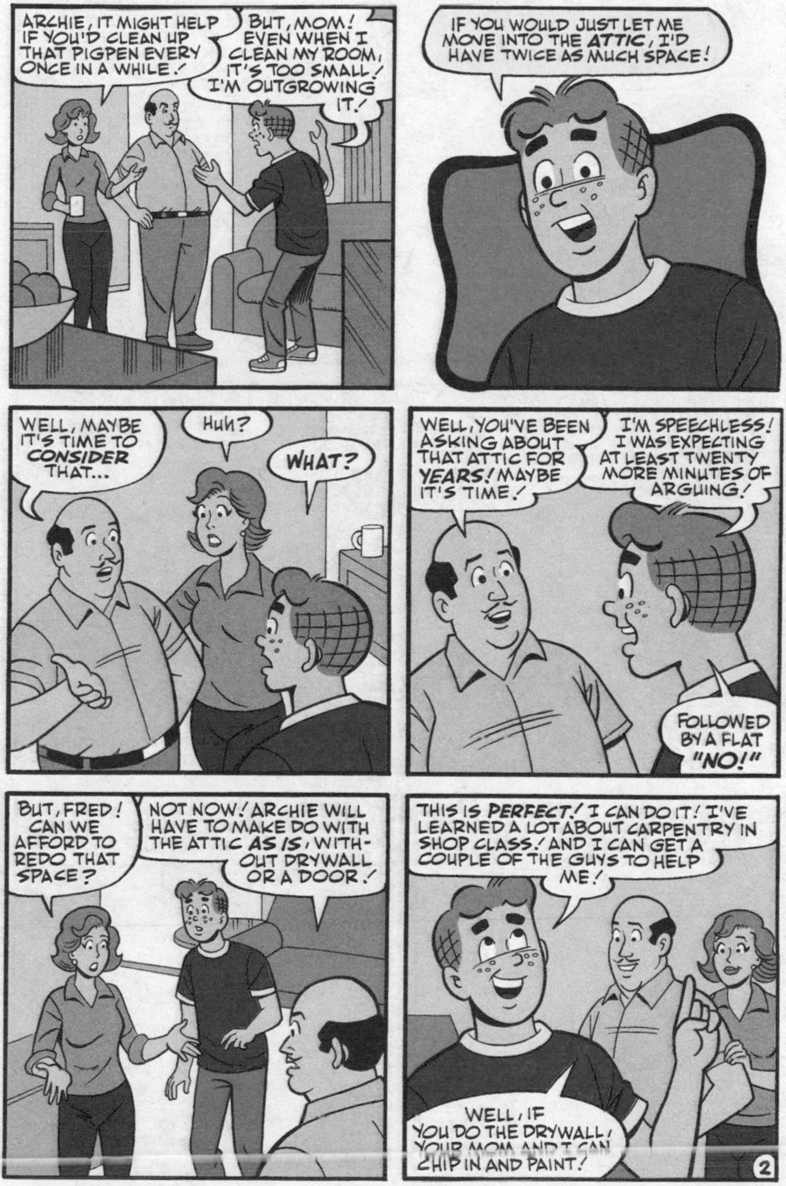
ARCHIE, IT MIGHT HELP IF YOU'D CLEAN UP THAT PIGPEN EVERY ONCE IN A WHILE!
BUT, MOM! EVEN WHEN I CLEAN MY ROOM, IT'S TOO SMALL! I'M OUTGROWING IT!
IF YOU WOULD JUST LET ME MOVE INTO THE ATTIC, I'D HAVE TWICE AS MUCH SPACE!
WELL, MAYBE IT'S TIME TO CONSIDER THAT...
Huh?
WHAT?
WELL, YOU'VE BEEN ASKING ABOUT THAT ATTIC FOR YEARS! MAYBE IT'S TIME!
I'M SPEECHLESS! I WAS EXPECTING AT LEAST TWENTY MORE MINUTES OF ARGUING!
FOLLOWED BY A FLAT "NO!"
BUT, FRED! CAN WE AFFORD TO REDO THAT SPACE?
NOT NOW! ARCHIE WILL HAVE TO MAKE DO WITH THE ATTIC AS IS, WITHOUT DRYWALL OR A DOOR!
THIS IS PERFECT! I CAN DO IT! I'VE LEARNED A LOT ABOUT CARPENTRY IN SHOP CLASS! AND I CAN GET A COUPLE OF THE GUYS TO HELP ME!
WELL, IF YOU DO THE DRYWALL, YOUR MOM AND I CAN CHIP IN AND PAINT!
2

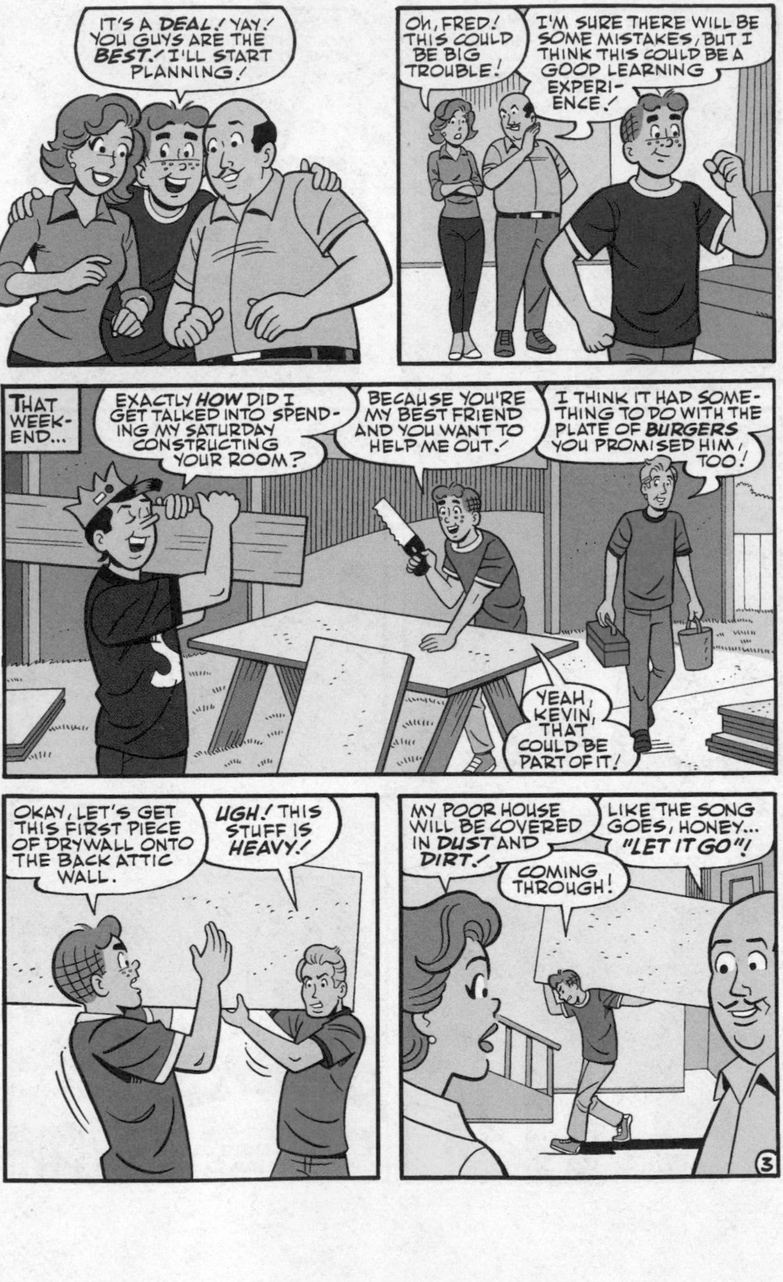
IT'S A DEAL! YAY! YOU GUYS ARE THE BEST! I'LL START PLANNING!
Oh, FRED! THIS COULD BE BIG TROUBLE!
I'M SURE THERE WILL BE SOME MISTAKES, BUT I THINK THIS COULD BE A GOOD LEARNING EXPERI-ENCE!
THAT WEEK-END...
EXACTLY HOW DID I GET TALKED INTO SPEND-ING MY SATURDAY CONSTRUCTING YOUR ROOM?
BECAUSE YOU'RE MY BEST FRIEND AND YOU WANT TO HELP ME OUT!
I THINK IT HAD SOME-THING TO DO WITH THE PLATE OF BURGERS YOU PROMISED HIM, TOO!
YEAH, KEVIN, THAT COULD BE PART OF IT!
OKAY, LET'S GET THIS FIRST PIECE OF DRYWALL ONTO THE BACK ATTIC WALL.
UGH! THIS STUFF IS HEAVY!
MY POOR HOUSE WILL BE COVERED IN DUST AND DIRT!
LIKE THE SONG GOES, HONEY... "LET IT GO"!
COMING THROUGH!
3

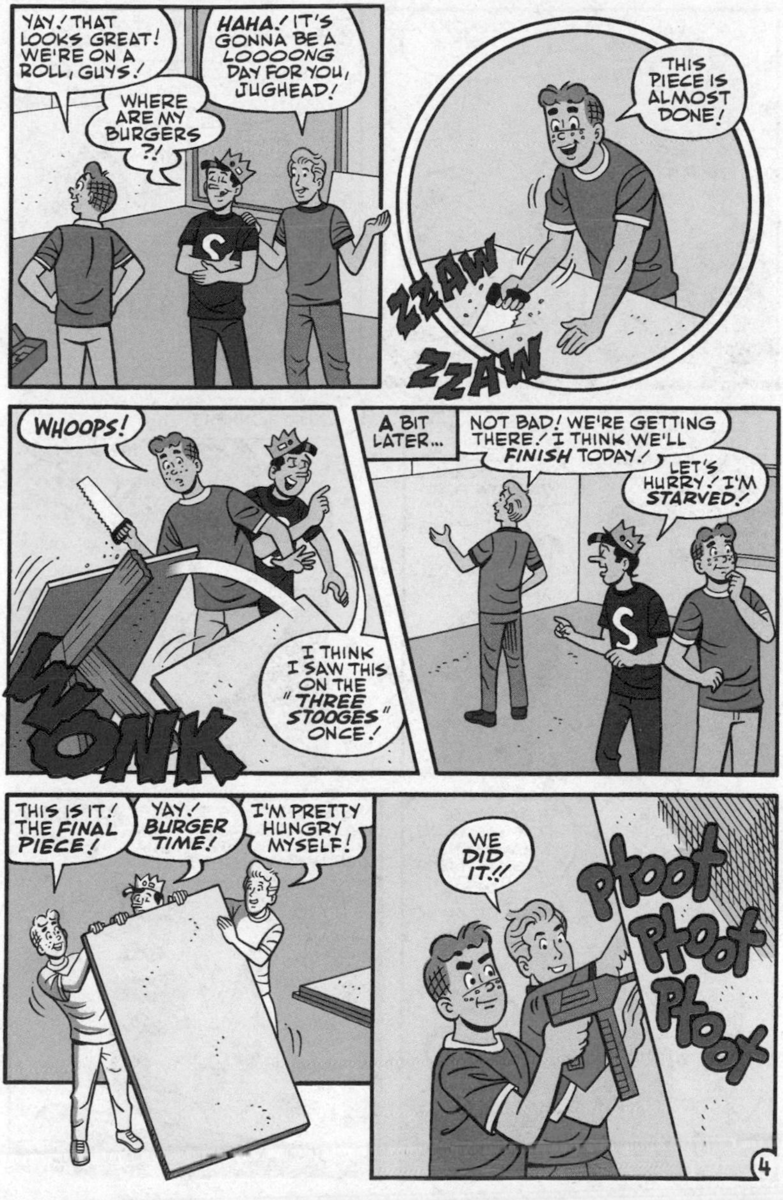
YAY! THAT LOOKS GREAT! WE'RE ON A ROLL, GUYS!
WHERE ARE MY BURGERS?!
HAHA! IT'S GONNA BE A LOOOONG DAY FOR YOU, JUGHEAD!
THIS PIECE IS ALMOST DONE!
ZZAW
ZZAW
WHOOPS!
WONK
I THINK I SAW THIS ON THE "THREE STOOGES" ONCE!
A BIT LATER...
NOT BAD! WE'RE GETTING THERE! I THINK WE'LL FINISH TODAY!
LET'S HURRY! I'M STARVED!
THIS IS IT! THE FINAL PIECE!
YAY! BURGER TIME!
I'M PRETTY HUNGRY MYSELF!
WE DID IT!!
Ptoot
Ptoot
Ptoot
Ptoot
4

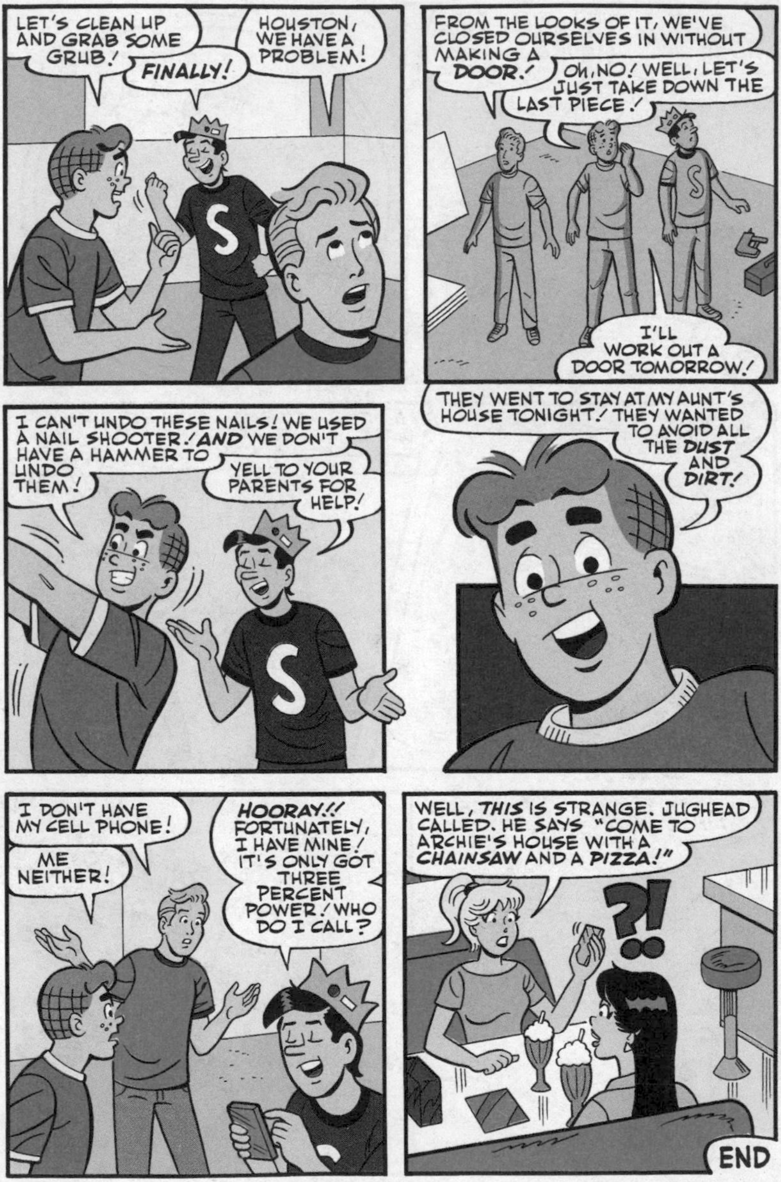

LET'S CLEAN UP AND GRAB SOME GRUB!
FINALLY!
HOUSTON, WE HAVE A PROBLEM!
FROM THE LOOKS OF IT, WE'VE CLOSED OURSELVES IN WITHOUT MAKING A DOOR.!
OH, NO! WELL, LET'S JUST TAKE DOWN THE LAST PIECE!
I'LL WORK OUT A DOOR TOMORROW!
I CAN'T UNDO THESE NAILS! WE USED A NAIL SHOOTER! AND WE DON'T HAVE A HAMMER TO UNDO THEM!
YELL TO YOUR PARENTS FOR HELP!
THEY WENT TO STAY AT MY AUNT'S HOUSE TONIGHT! THEY WANTED TO AVOID ALL THE DUST AND DIRT!
I DON'T HAVE MY CELL PHONE!
ME NEITHER!
HOORAY!! FORTUNATELY, I HAVE MINE! IT'S ONLY GOT THREE PERCENT POWER! WHO DO I CALL?
WELL, THIS IS STRANGE. JUGHEAD CALLED. HE SAYS "COME TO ARCHIE'S HOUSE WITH A CHAINSAW AND A PIZZA!"
?!
END

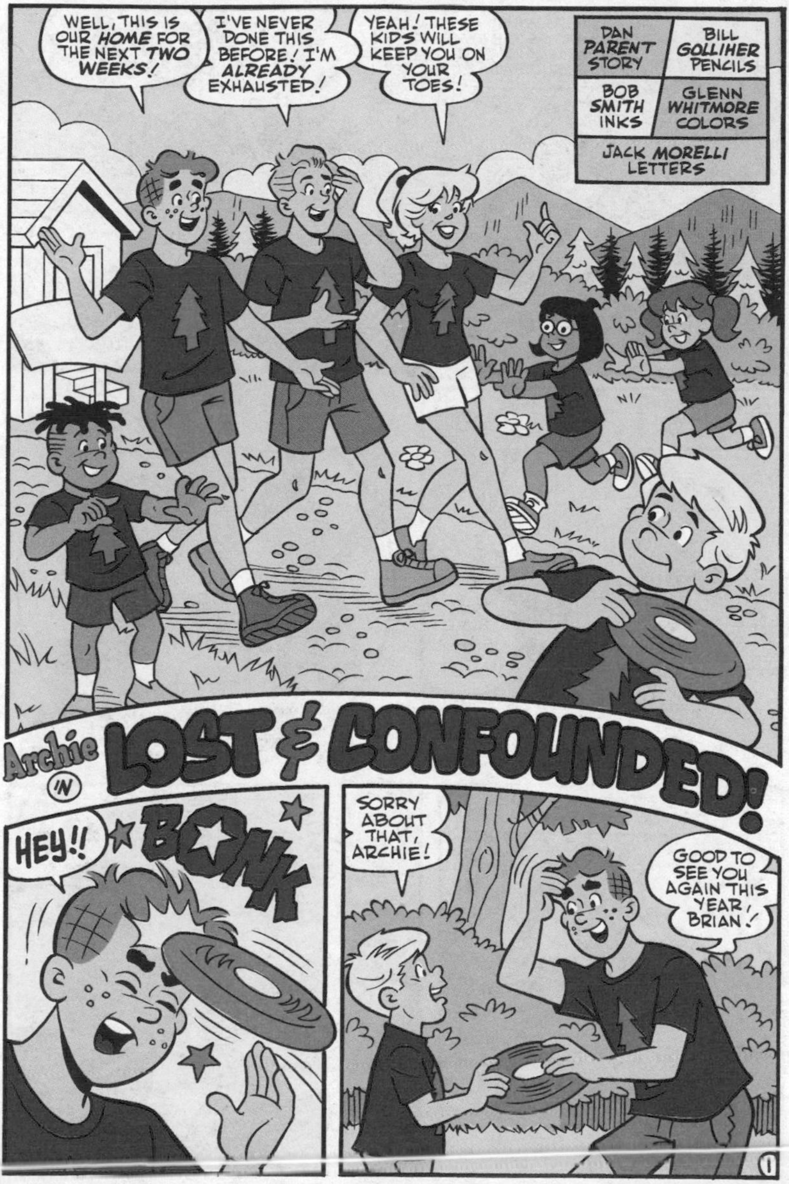
WELL, THIS IS OUR HOME FOR THE NEXT TWO WEEKS!
I'VE NEVER DONE THIS BEFORE! I'M ALREADY EXHAUSTED!
YEAH! THESE KIDS WILL KEEP YOU ON YOUR TOES!
DAN PARENT STORY
BILL GOLLIHER PENCILS
BOB SMITH INKS
GLENN WHITMORE COLORS
JACK MORELLI LETTERS
Archie IN LOST & CONFOUNDED!
HEY!!
BONK
SORRY ABOUT THAT, ARCHIE!
GOOD TO SEE YOU AGAIN THIS YEAR, BRIAN!
1

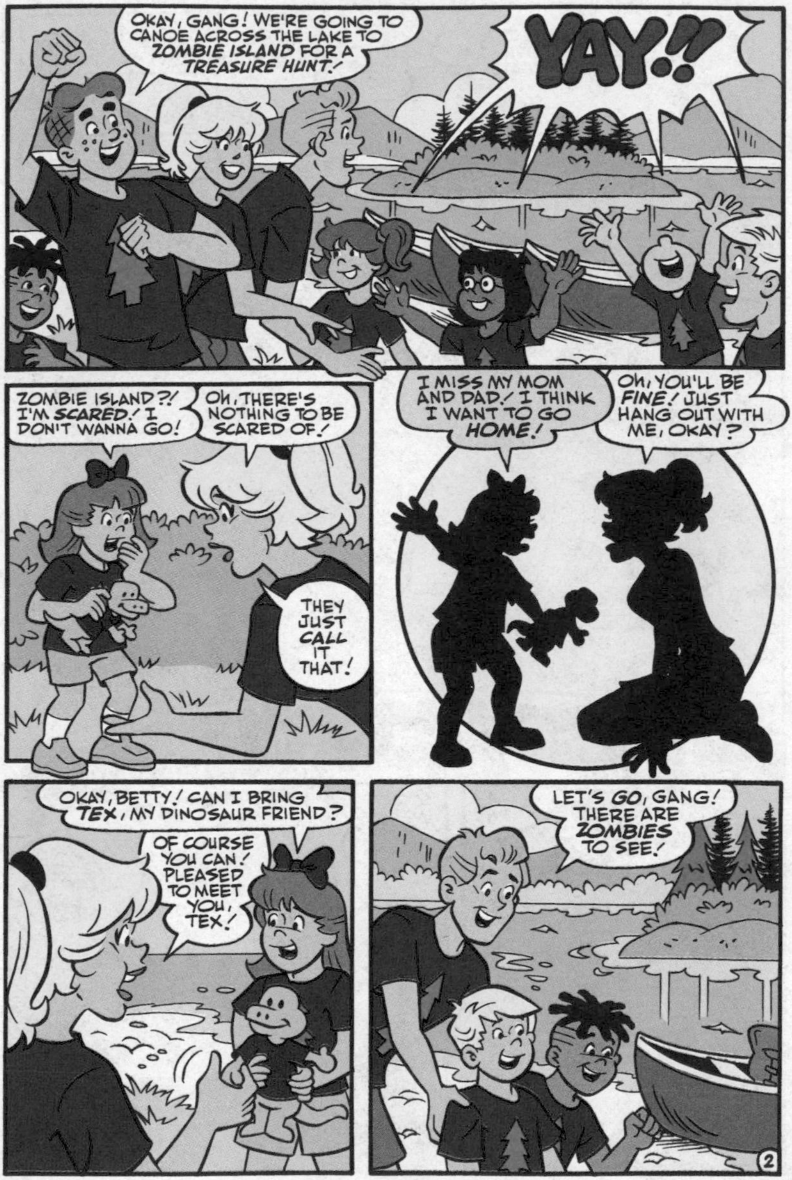
OKAY, GANG! WE'RE GOING TO CANOE ACROSS THE LAKE TO ZOMBIE ISLAND FOR A TREASURE HUNT!
YAY!!
ZOMBIE ISLAND?! I'M SCARED! I DON'T WANNA GO!
OH, THERE'S NOTHING TO BE SCARED OF!
THEY JUST CALL IT THAT!
I MISS MY MOM AND DAD! I THINK I WANT TO GO HOME!
OH, YOU'LL BE FINE! JUST HANG OUT WITH ME, OKAY?
OKAY, BETTY! CAN I BRING TEX, MY DINOSAUR FRIEND?
OF COURSE YOU CAN! PLEASED TO MEET YOU, TEX!
LET'S GO, GANG! THERE ARE ZOMBIES TO SEE!
2

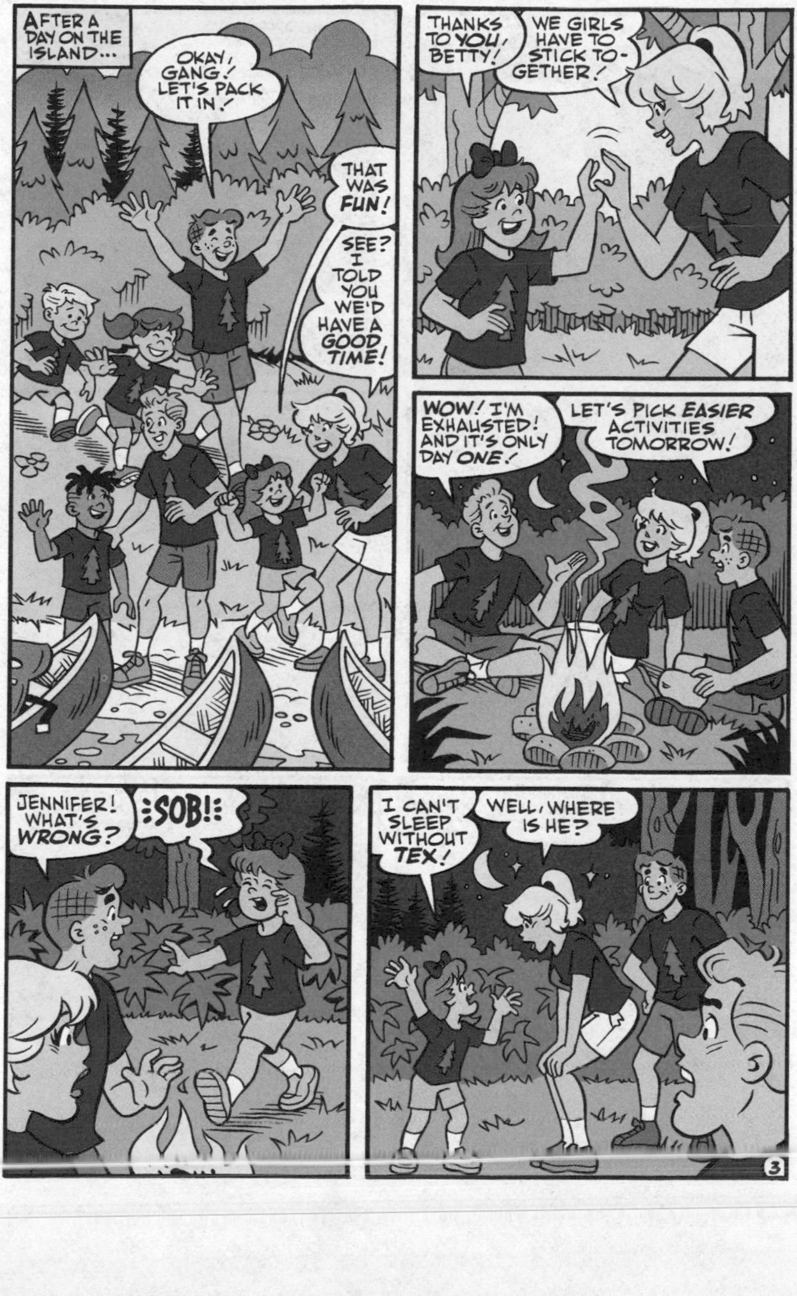
AFTER A DAY ON THE ISLAND...
OKAY, GANG! LET'S PACK IT IN!
THAT WAS FUN!
SEE? I TOLD YOU WE'D HAVE A GOOD TIME!
THANKS TO YOU, BETTY!
WE GIRLS HAVE TO STICK TO-GETHER!
WOW! I'M EXHAUSTED! AND IT'S ONLY DAY ONE!
LET'S PICK EASIER ACTIVITIES TOMORROW!
JENNIFER! WHAT'S WRONG?
SOB!
I CAN'T SLEEP WITHOUT TEX!
WELL, WHERE IS HE?
3

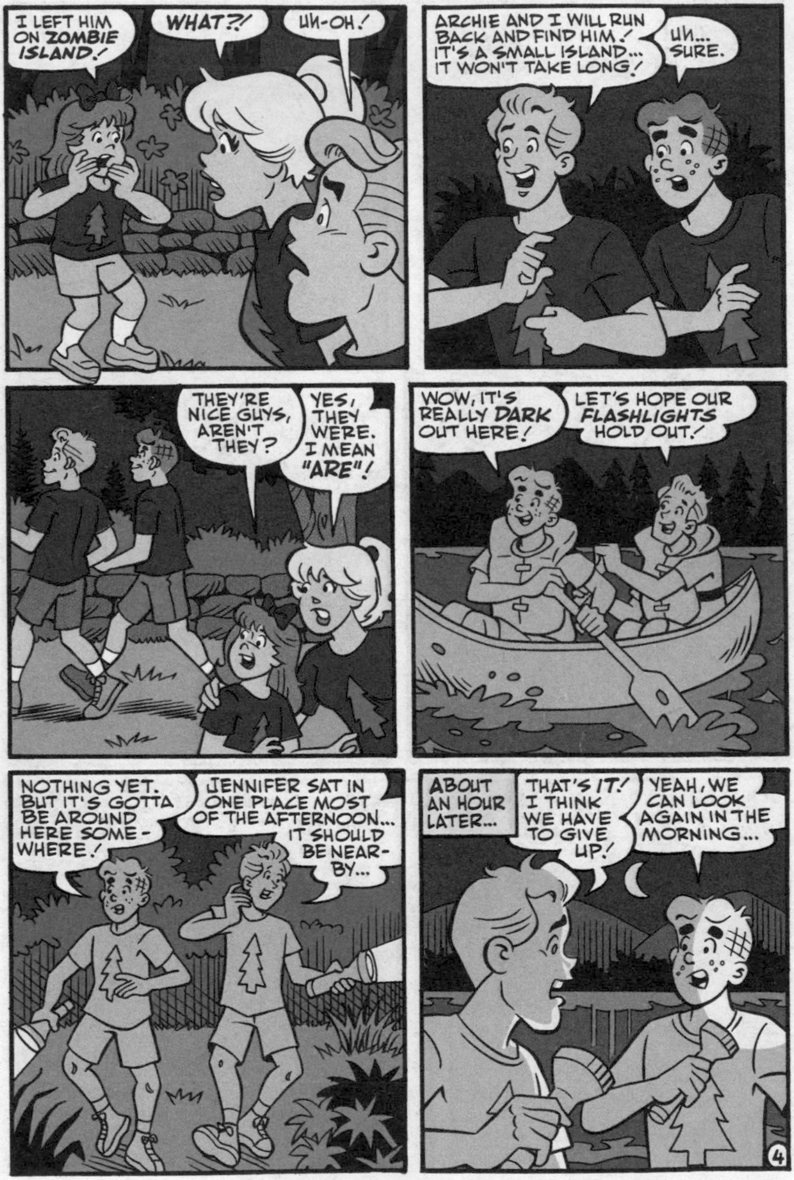
I LEFT HIM ON ZOMBIE ISLAND!
WHAT?!
UH-OH!
ARCHIE AND I WILL RUN BACK AND FIND HIM! IT'S A SMALL ISLAND... IT WON'T TAKE LONG!
UH... SURE.
THEY'RE NICE GUYS, AREN'T THEY?
YES, THEY WERE. I MEAN "ARE"!
WOW, IT'S REALLY DARK OUT HERE!
LET'S HOPE OUR FLASHLIGHTS HOLD OUT!
NOTHING YET. BUT IT'S GOTTA BE AROUND HERE SOME-WHERE!
JENNIFER SAT IN ONE PLACE MOST OF THE AFTERNOON... IT SHOULD BE NEAR-BY...
ABOUT AN HOUR LATER...
THAT'S IT! I THINK WE HAVE TO GIVE UP!
YEAH, WE CAN LOOK AGAIN IN THE MORNING...
4

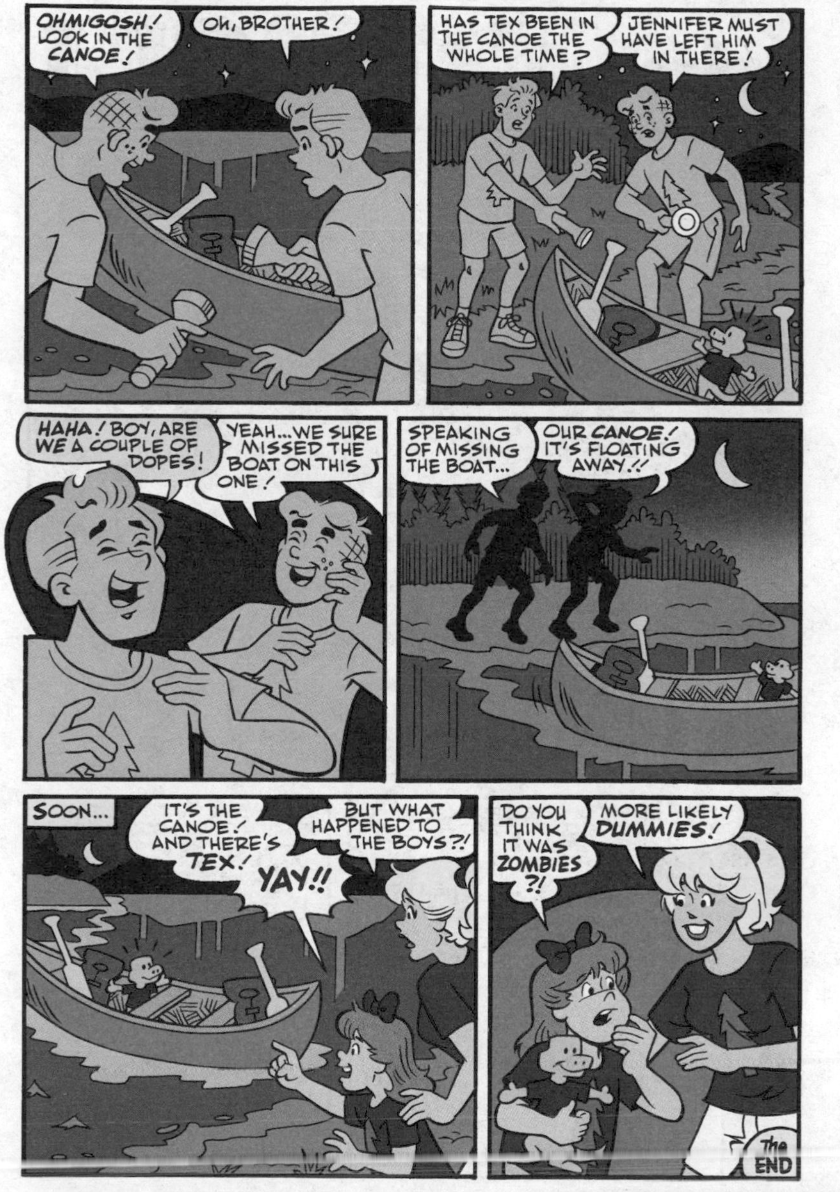
OHMIGOSH! LOOK IN THE CANOE!
Oh, BROTHER!
HAS TEX BEEN IN THE CANOE THE WHOLE TIME?
JENNIFER MUST HAVE LEFT HIM IN THERE!
HAHA! BOY, ARE WE A COUPLE OF DOPES!
YEAH...WE SURE MISSED THE BOAT ON THIS ONE!
SPEAKING OF MISSING THE BOAT...
OUR CANOE! IT'S FLOATING AWAY!!
SOON...
IT'S THE CANOE! AND THERE'S TEX!
YAY!!
BUT WHAT HAPPENED TO THE BOYS?!
DO YOU THINK IT WAS ZOMBIES?!
MORE LIKELY DUMMIES!
The END

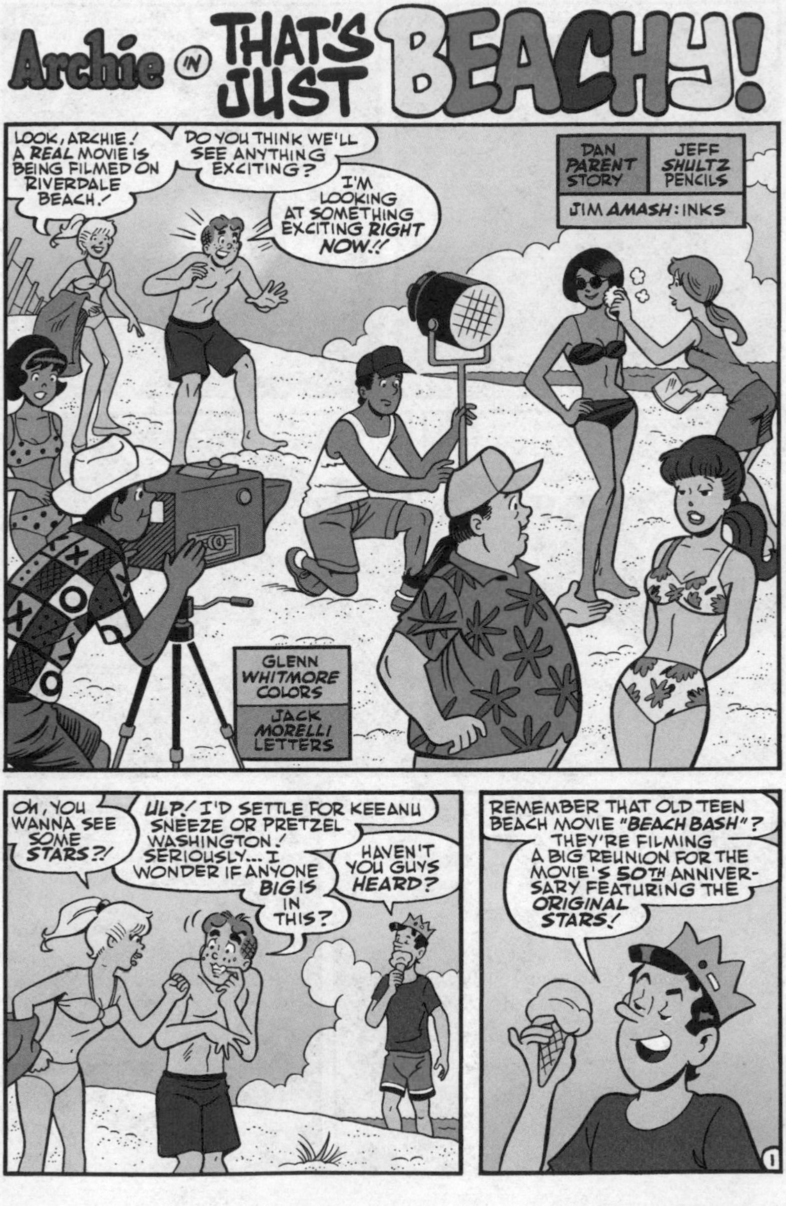
Archie IN THAT'S JUST BEACHY!
LOOK, ARCHIE! A REAL MOVIE IS BEING FILMED ON RIVERDALE BEACH!
DO YOU THINK WE'LL SEE ANYTHING EXCITING?
I'M LOOKING AT SOMETHING EXCITING RIGHT NOW!!
DAN PARENT STORY
JEFF SHULTZ PENCILS
JIM AMASH: INKS
GLENN WHITMORE COLORS
JACK MORELLI LETTERS
OH, YOU WANNA SEE SOME STARS?!
ULP! I'D SETTLE FOR KEEANU SNEEZE OR PRETZEL WASHINGTON! SERIOUSLY... I WONDER IF ANYONE BIG IS IN THIS?
HAVEN'T YOU GUYS HEARD?
REMEMBER THAT OLD TEEN BEACH MOVIE "BEACH BASH"? THEY'RE FILMING A BIG REUNION FOR THE MOVIE'S 50TH ANNIVERSARY FEATURING THE ORIGINAL STARS!
1

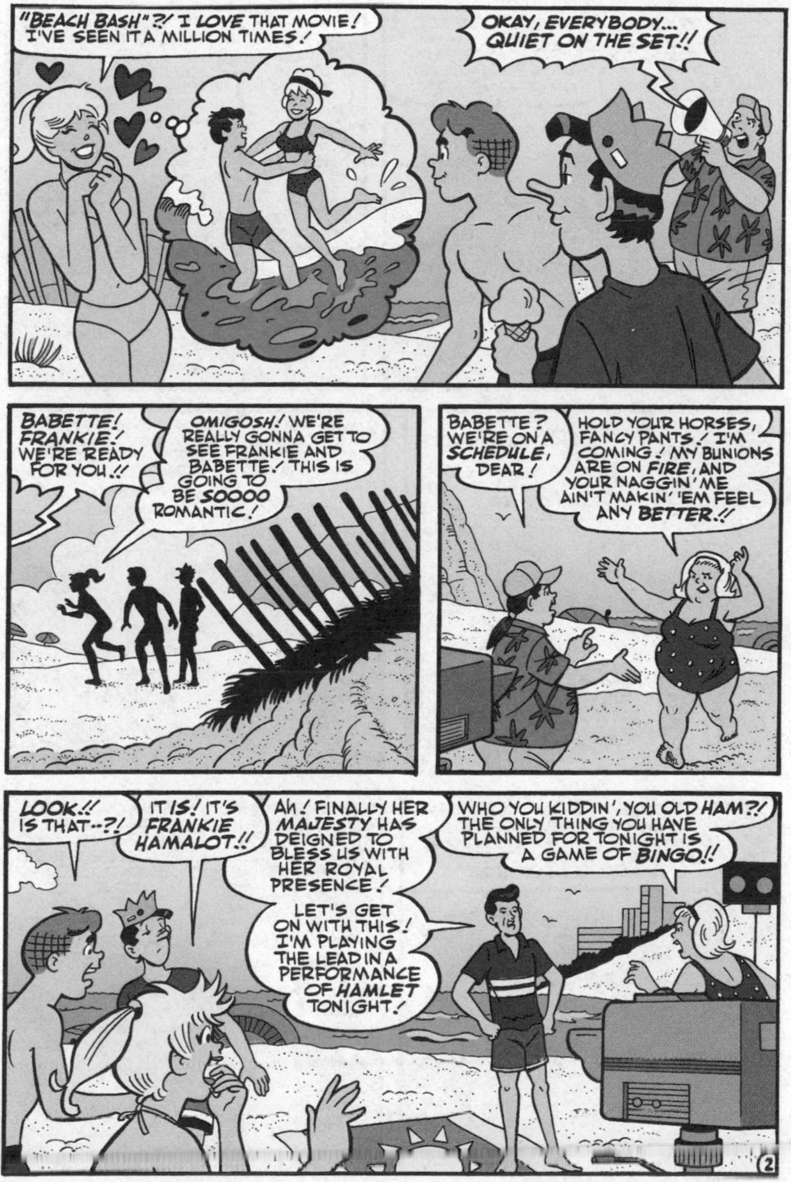
"BEACH BASH"?! I LOVE THAT MOVIE! I'VE SEEN IT A MILLION TIMES!
OKAY, EVERYBODY... QUIET ON THE SET!!
BABETTE! FRANKIE! WE'RE READY FOR YOU!!
OMIGOSH! WE'RE REALLY GONNA GET TO SEE FRANKIE AND BABETTE! THIS IS GOING TO BE SOOOO ROMANTIC!
BABETTE? WE'RE ON A SCHEDULE, DEAR!
HOLD YOUR HORSES, FANCY PANTS! I'M COMING! MY BUNIONS ARE ON FIRE, AND YOUR NAGGIN' ME AIN'T MAKIN' 'EM FEEL ANY BETTER!!
LOOK!! IS THAT--?!
IT IS! IT'S FRANKIE HAMALOT!!
Ah! FINALLY HER MAJESTY HAS DEIGNED TO BLESS US WITH HER ROYAL PRESENCE!
LET'S GET ON WITH THIS! I'M PLAYING THE LEAD IN A PERFORMANCE OF HAMLET TONIGHT!
WHO YOU KIDDIN', YOU OLD HAM?! THE ONLY THING YOU HAVE PLANNED FOR TONIGHT IS A GAME OF BINGO!!
2

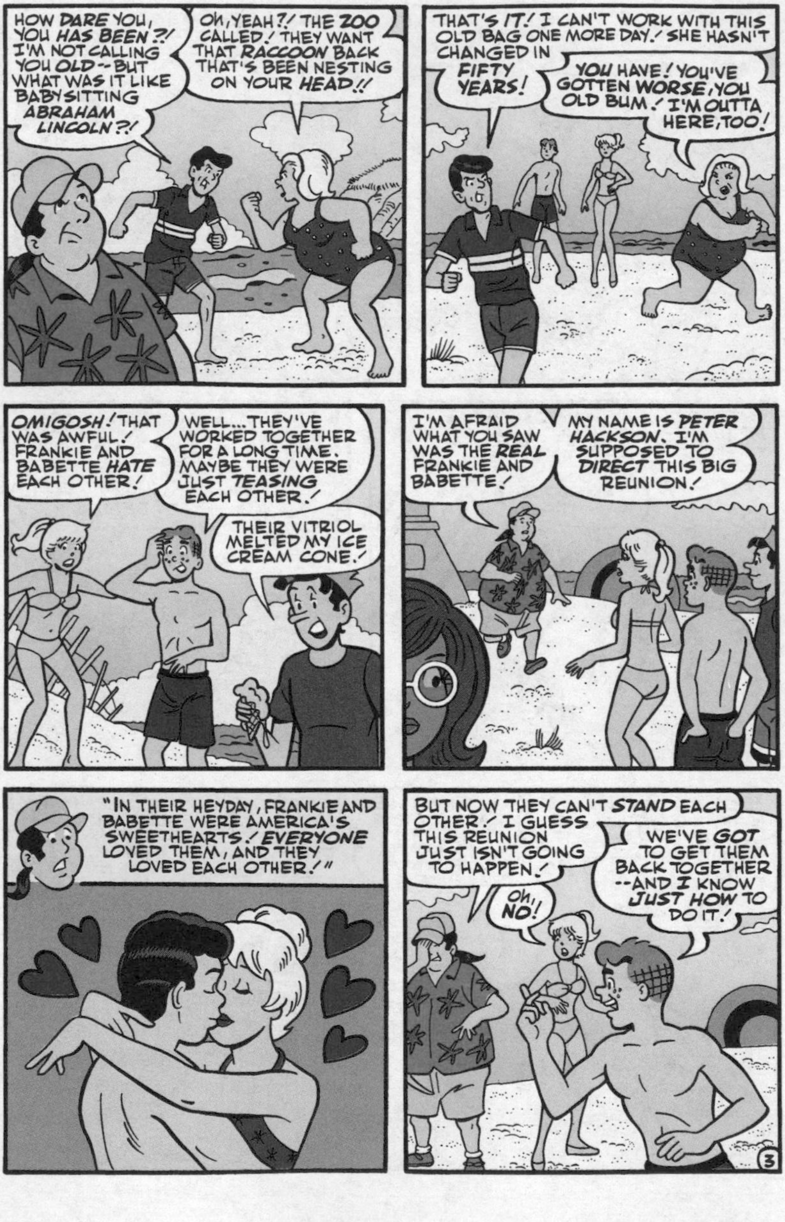
HOW DARE YOU, YOU HAS BEEN?! I'M NOT CALLING YOU OLD--BUT WHAT WAS IT LIKE BABYSITTING ABRAHAM LINCOLN?!
OH, YEAH?! THE ZOO CALLED! THEY WANT THAT RACCOON BACK THAT'S BEEN NESTING ON YOUR HEAD!!
THAT'S IT! I CAN'T WORK WITH THIS OLD BAG ONE MORE DAY! SHE HASN'T CHANGED IN FIFTY YEARS!
YOU HAVE! YOU'VE GOTTEN WORSE, YOU OLD BUM! I'M OUTTA HERE, TOO!
OMIGOSH! THAT WAS AWFUL! FRANKIE AND BABETTE HATE EACH OTHER!
WELL...THEY'VE WORKED TOGETHER FOR A LONG TIME. MAYBE THEY WERE JUST TEASING EACH OTHER!
THEIR VITRIOL MELTED MY ICE CREAM CONE!
I'M AFRAID WHAT YOU SAW WAS THE REAL FRANKIE AND BABETTE!
MY NAME IS PETER HACKSON. I'M SUPPOSED TO DIRECT THIS BIG REUNION!
"IN THEIR HEYDAY, FRANKIE AND BABETTE WERE AMERICA'S SWEETHEARTS! EVERYONE LOVED THEM, AND THEY LOVED EACH OTHER!"
BUT NOW THEY CAN'T STAND EACH OTHER! I GUESS THIS REUNION JUST ISN'T GOING TO HAPPEN!
OH, NO!
WE'VE GOT TO GET THEM BACK TOGETHER --AND I KNOW JUST HOW TO DO IT!
3

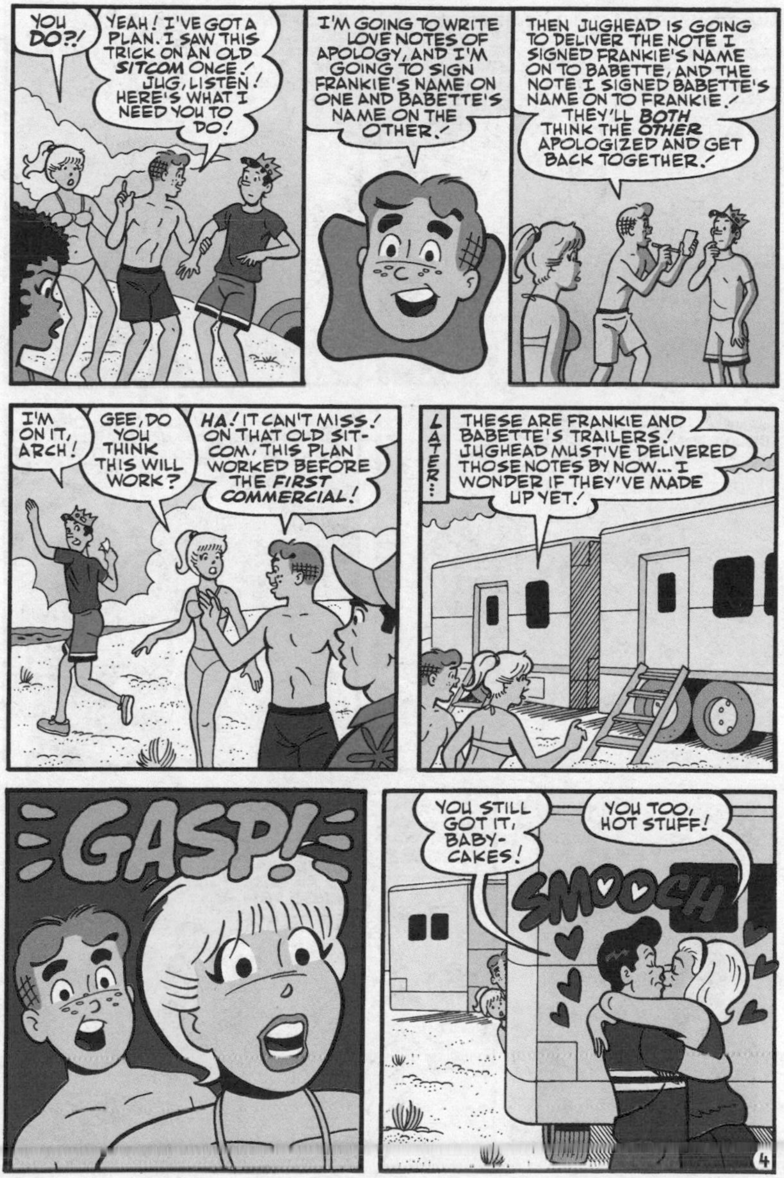
YOU DO?!
YEAH! I'VE GOT A PLAN. I SAW THIS TRICK ON AN OLD SITCOM ONCE! JUG, LISTEN! HERE'S WHAT I NEED YOU TO DO!
I'M GOING TO WRITE LOVE NOTES OF APOLOGY, AND I'M GOING TO SIGN FRANKIE'S NAME ON ONE AND BABETTE'S NAME ON THE OTHER!
THEN JUGHEAD IS GOING TO DELIVER THE NOTE I SIGNED FRANKIE'S NAME ON TO BABETTE, AND THE NOTE I SIGNED BABETTE'S NAME ON TO FRANKIE! THEY'LL BOTH THINK THE OTHER APOLOGIZED AND GET BACK TOGETHER!
I'M ON IT, ARCH!
GEE, DO YOU THINK THIS WILL WORK?
HA! IT CAN'T MISS! ON THAT OLD SIT-COM, THIS PLAN WORKED BEFORE THE FIRST COMMERCIAL!
LATER...
THESE ARE FRANKIE AND BABETTE'S TRAILERS! JUGHEAD MUST'VE DELIVERED THOSE NOTES BY NOW... I WONDER IF THEY'VE MADE UP YET!
GASP!
YOU STILL GOT IT, BABY-CAKES!
YOU TOO, HOT STUFF!
SMOOCH
4

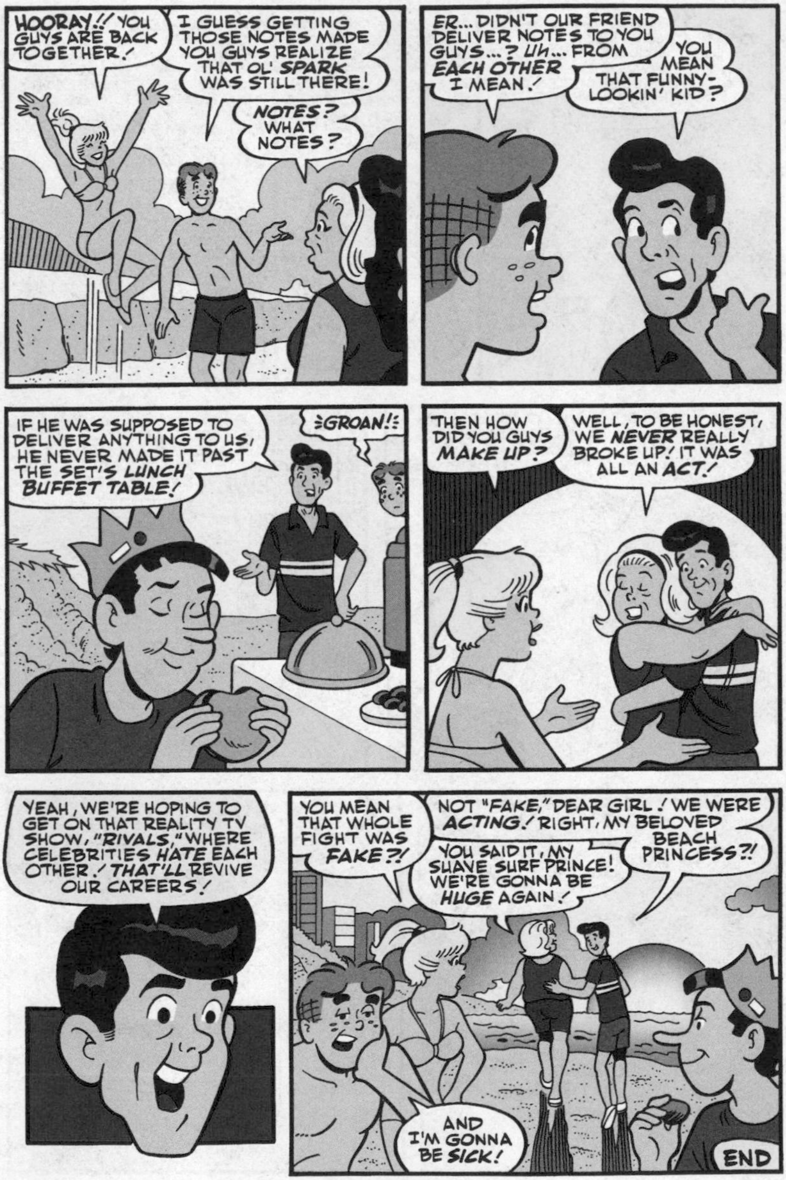
HOORAY!! YOU GUYS ARE BACK TOGETHER!
I GUESS GETTING THOSE NOTES MADE YOU GUYS REALIZE THAT OL' SPARK WAS STILL THERE!
NOTES? WHAT NOTES?
ER... DIDN'T OUR FRIEND DELIVER NOTES TO YOU GUYS...? UH... FROM EACH OTHER I MEAN!
YOU MEAN THAT FUNNY-LOOKIN' KID?
IF HE WAS SUPPOSED TO DELIVER ANYTHING TO US, HE NEVER MADE IT PAST THE SET'S LUNCH BUFFET TABLE!
GROAN!
THEN HOW DID YOU GUYS MAKE UP?
WELL, TO BE HONEST, WE NEVER REALLY BROKE UP! IT WAS ALL AN ACT!
YEAH, WE'RE HOPING TO GET ON THAT REALITY TV SHOW, "RIVALS," WHERE CELEBRITIES HATE EACH OTHER! THAT'LL REVIVE OUR CAREERS!
YOU MEAN THAT WHOLE FIGHT WAS FAKE?!
NOT "FAKE," DEAR GIRL! WE WERE ACTING! RIGHT, MY BELOVED BEACH PRINCESS?!
YOU SAID IT, MY SUAVE SURF PRINCE! WE'RE GONNA BE HUGE AGAIN!
AND I'M GONNA BE SICK!
END

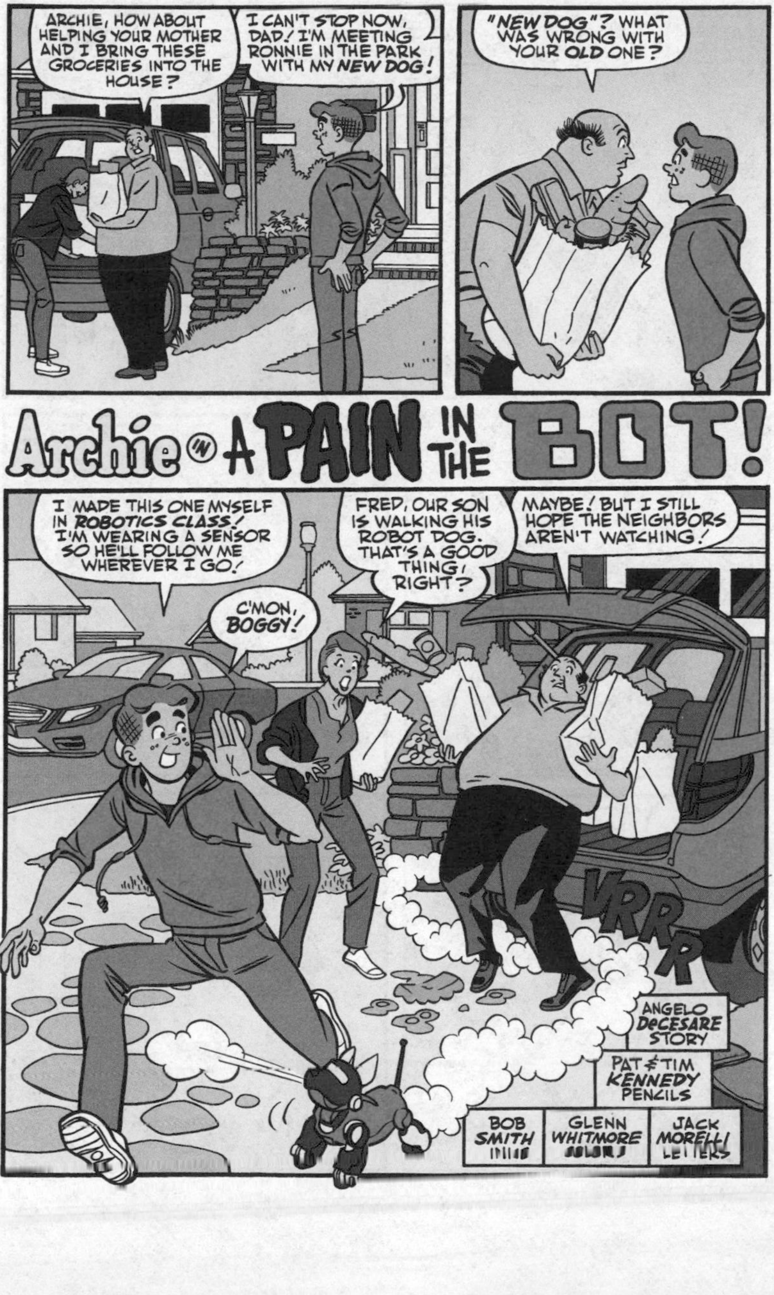
ARCHIE, HOW ABOUT HELPING YOUR MOTHER AND I BRING THESE GROCERIES INTO THE HOUSE?
I CAN'T STOP NOW, DAD! I'M MEETING RONNIE IN THE PARK WITH MY NEW DOG!
"NEW DOG"? WHAT WAS WRONG WITH YOUR OLD ONE?
Archie in A PAIN IN THE BOT!
I MADE THIS ONE MYSELF IN ROBOTICS CLASS! I'M WEARING A SENSOR SO HE'LL FOLLOW ME WHEREVER I GO!
C'MON, BOGGY!
FRED, OUR SON IS WALKING HIS ROBOT DOG. THAT'S A GOOD THING, RIGHT?
MAYBE! BUT I STILL HOPE THE NEIGHBORS AREN'T WATCHING!
VRRRR
ANGELO DeCESARE STORY
PAT & TIM KENNEDY PENCILS
BOB SMITH
GLENN WHITMORE
JACK MORELLI

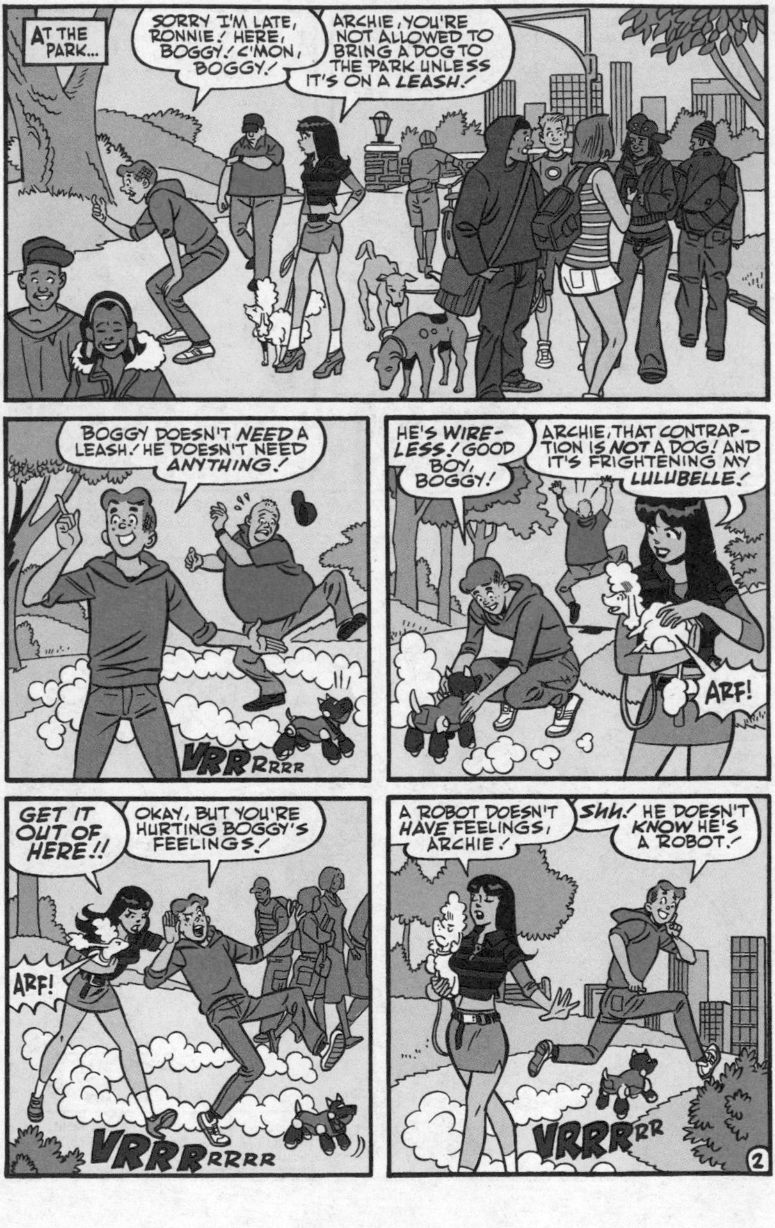
AT THE PARK...
SORRY I'M LATE, RONNIE! HERE, BOGGY! C'MON, BOGGY!
ARCHIE, YOU'RE NOT ALLOWED TO BRING A DOG TO THE PARK UNLESS IT'S ON A LEASH!
BOGGY DOESN'T NEED A LEASH! HE DOESN'T NEED ANYTHING!
VRRRrrrr
HE'S WIRE-LESS! GOOD BOY, BOGGY!
ARCHIE, THAT CONTRAP-TION IS NOT A DOG! AND IT'S FRIGHTENING MY LULUBELLE!
ARF!
GET IT OUT OF HERE!!
OKAY, BUT YOU'RE HURTING BOGGY'S FEELINGS!
ARF!
VRRRrrrrr
A ROBOT DOESN'T HAVE FEELINGS, ARCHIE!
Shh! HE DOESN'T KNOW HE'S A ROBOT!
VRRRRR
2

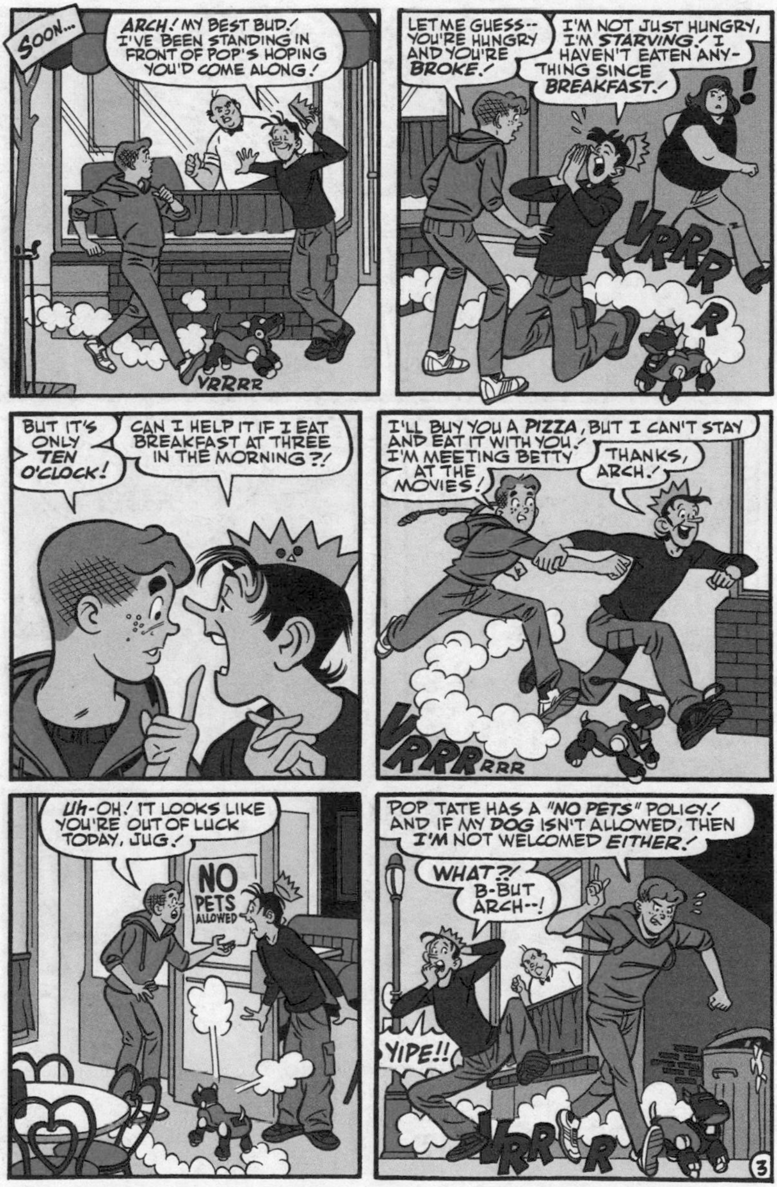
SOON...
ARCH! MY BEST BUD! I'VE BEEN STANDING IN FRONT OF POP'S HOPING YOU'D COME ALONG!
VRRRR
LET ME GUESS-- YOU'RE HUNGRY AND YOU'RE BROKE!
I'M NOT JUST HUNGRY, I'M STARVING! I HAVEN'T EATEN ANY-THING SINCE BREAKFAST!
VRRR
R
BUT IT'S ONLY TEN O'CLOCK!
CAN I HELP IT IF I EAT BREAKFAST AT THREE IN THE MORNING?!
I'LL BUY YOU A PIZZA, BUT I CAN'T STAY AND EAT IT WITH YOU! I'M MEETING BETTY AT THE MOVIES!
THANKS, ARCH!
VRRRRRR
UH-OH! IT LOOKS LIKE YOU'RE OUT OF LUCK TODAY, JUG!
NO PETS ALLOWED
POP TATE HAS A "NO PETS" POLICY! AND IF MY DOG ISN'T ALLOWED, THEN I'M NOT WELCOMED EITHER!
WHAT?! B-BUT ARCH--!
YIPE!!
VRR
R
3

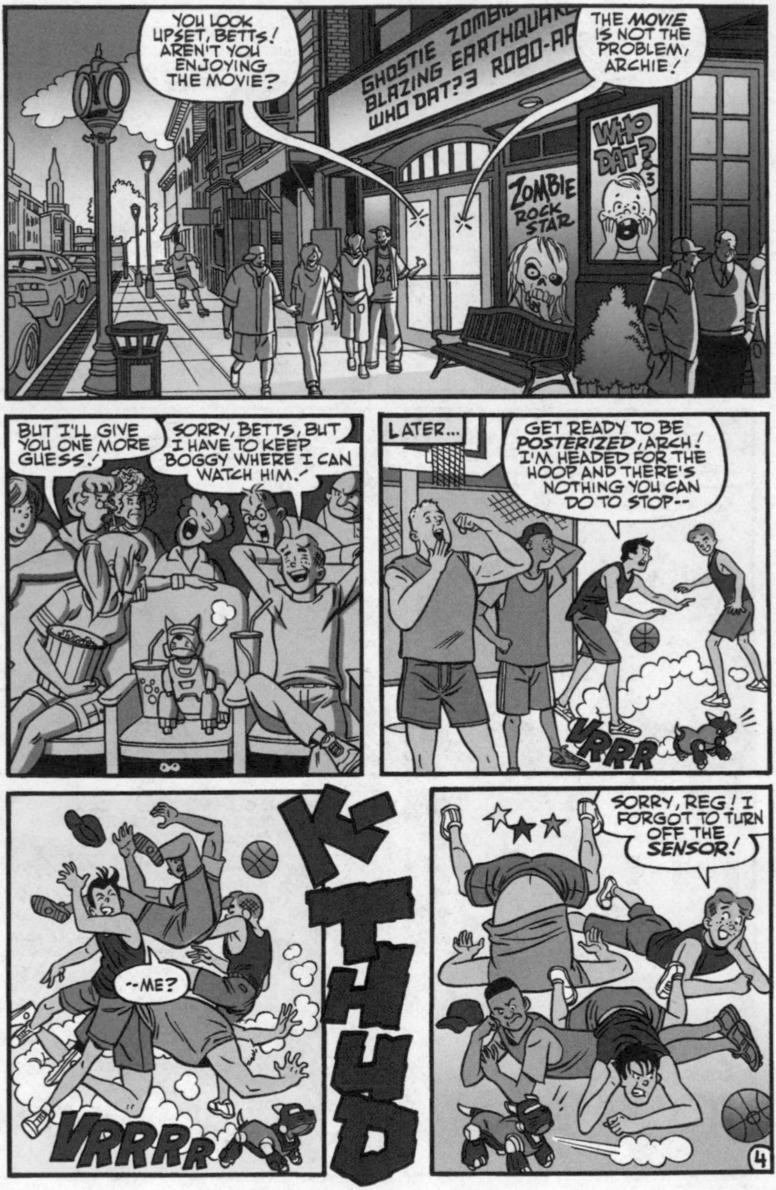
GHOSTIE ZOMBIE
BLAZING EARTHQUAKE
WHO DAT?3 ROBO-AR
YOU LOOK UPSET, BETTS! AREN'T YOU ENJOYING THE MOVIE?
THE MOVIE IS NOT THE PROBLEM, ARCHIE!
ZOMBIE ROCK STAR
WHO DAT? 3
BUT I'LL GIVE YOU ONE MORE GUESS!
SORRY, BETTS, BUT I HAVE TO KEEP BOGGY WHERE I CAN WATCH HIM.
LATER...
GET READY TO BE POSTERIZED, ARCH! I'M HEADED FOR THE HOOP AND THERE'S NOTHING YOU CAN DO TO STOP--
VRRRR
--ME?
VRRRR
K-THUD
SORRY, REG! I FORGOT TO TURN OFF THE SENSOR!
4

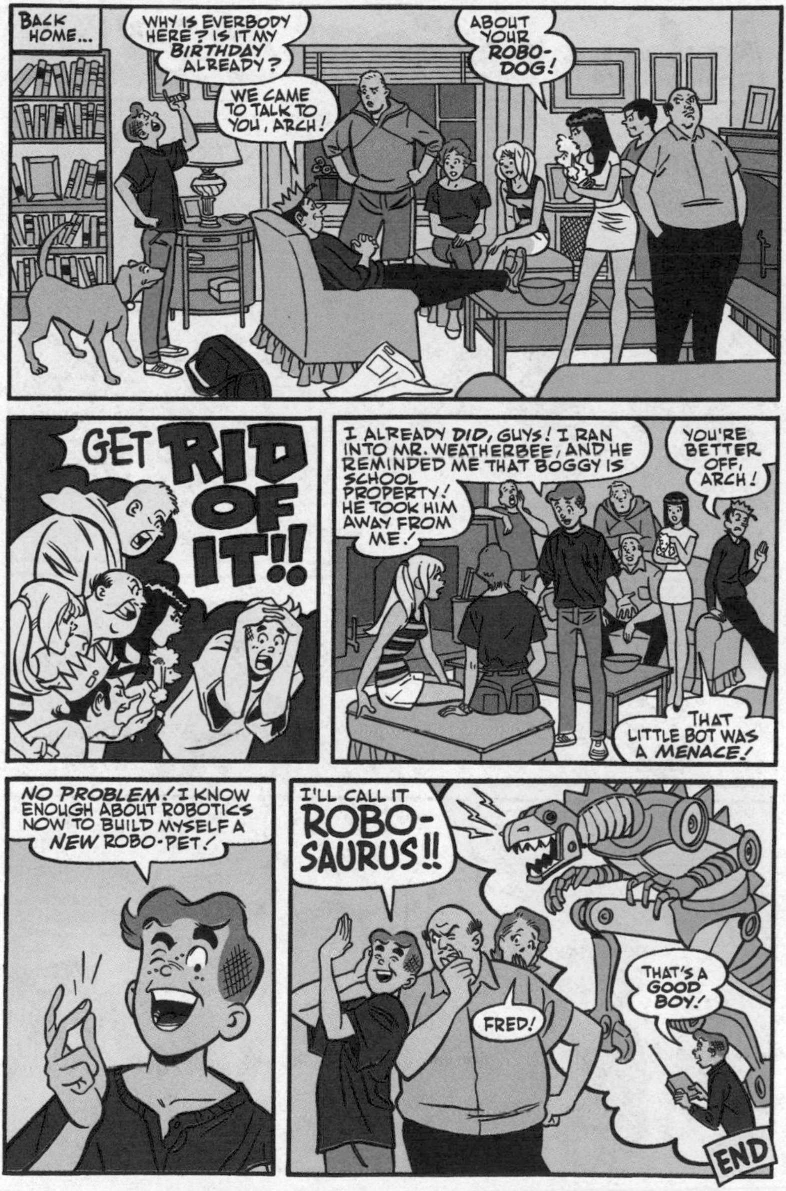
BACK HOME...
WHY IS EVERBODY HERE? IS IT MY BIRTHDAY ALREADY?
WE CAME TO TALK TO YOU, ARCH!
ABOUT YOUR ROBO-DOG!
GET RID OF IT!!
I ALREADY DID, GUYS! I RAN INTO MR. WEATHERBEE, AND HE REMINDED ME THAT BOGGY IS SCHOOL PROPERTY! HE TOOK HIM AWAY FROM ME!
YOU'RE BETTER OFF, ARCH!
THAT LITTLE BOT WAS A MENACE!
NO PROBLEM! I KNOW ENOUGH ABOUT ROBOTICS NOW TO BUILD MYSELF A NEW ROBO-PET!
I'LL CALL IT ROBO-SAURUS!!
FRED!
THAT'S A GOOD BOY!
END

Archie in Vicious Cycle!

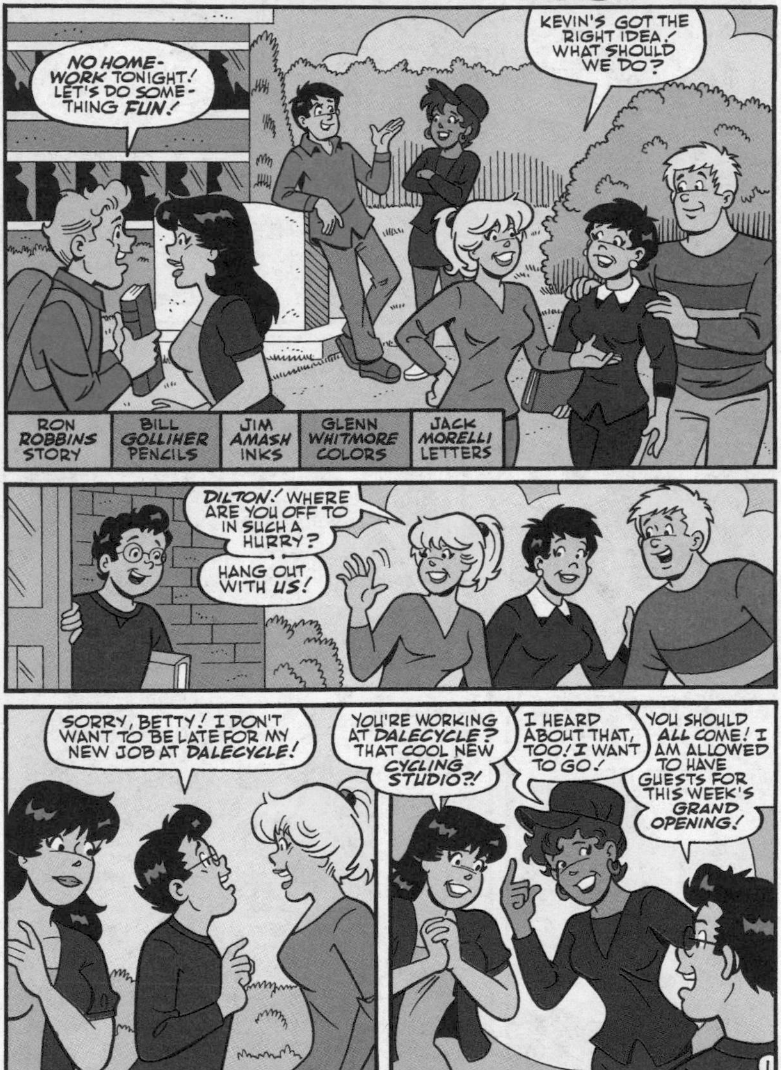
NO HOME-WORK TONIGHT! LET'S DO SOME-THING FUN!
KEVIN'S GOT THE RIGHT IDEA! WHAT SHOULD WE DO?
RON ROBBINS STORY
BILL GOLLIHER PENCILS
JIM AMASH INKS
GLENN WHITMORE COLORS
JACK MORELLI LETTERS
DILTON! WHERE ARE YOU OFF TO IN SUCH A HURRY?
HANG OUT WITH US!
SORRY, BETTY! I DON'T WANT TO BE LATE FOR MY NEW JOB AT DALECYCLE!
YOU'RE WORKING AT DALECYCLE? THAT COOL NEW CYCLING STUDIO?!
I HEARD ABOUT THAT, TOO! I WANT TO GO!
YOU SHOULD ALL COME! I AM ALLOWED TO HAVE GUESTS FOR THIS WEEK'S GRAND OPENING!
1

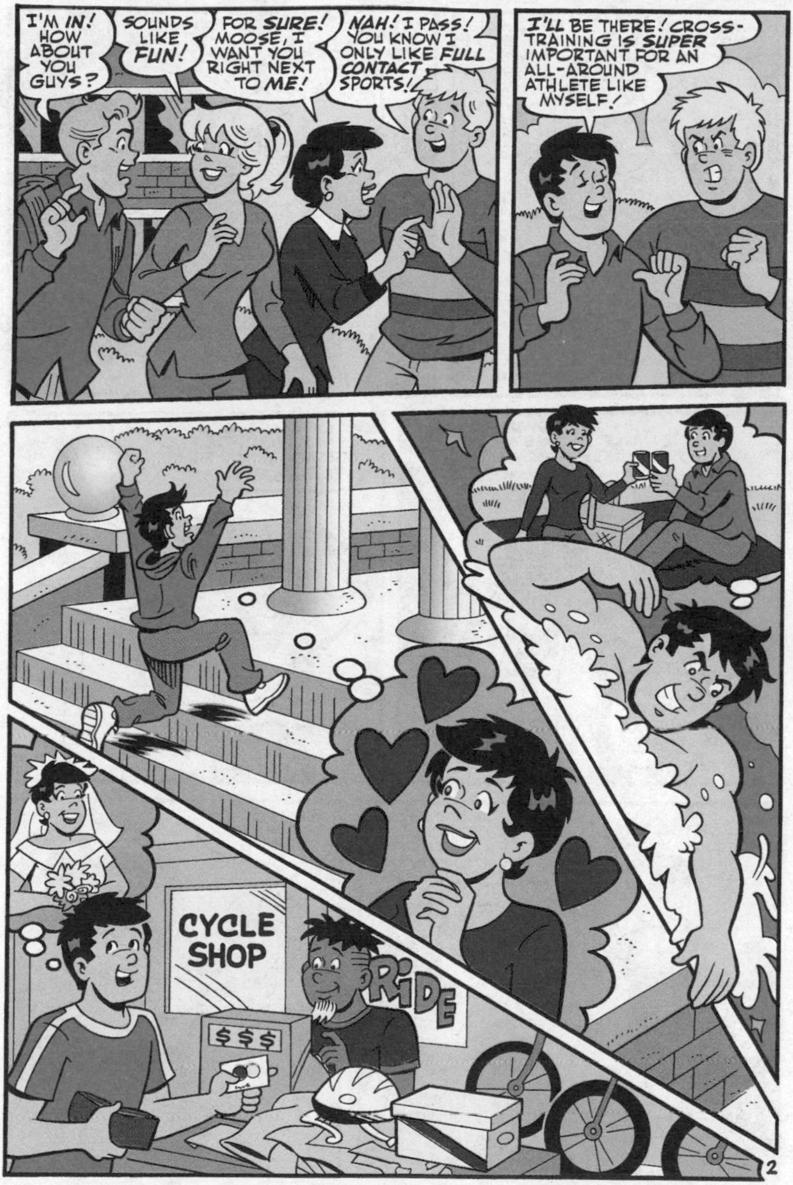
I'M IN! HOW ABOUT YOU GUYS?
SOUNDS LIKE FUN!
FOR SURE! MOOSE, I WANT YOU RIGHT NEXT TO ME!
NAH! I PASS! YOU KNOW I ONLY LIKE FULL CONTACT SPORTS!
I'LL BE THERE! CROSS-TRAINING IS SUPER IMPORTANT FOR AN ALL-AROUND ATHLETE LIKE MYSELF!
CYCLE SHOP
$ $ $
RIDE
2

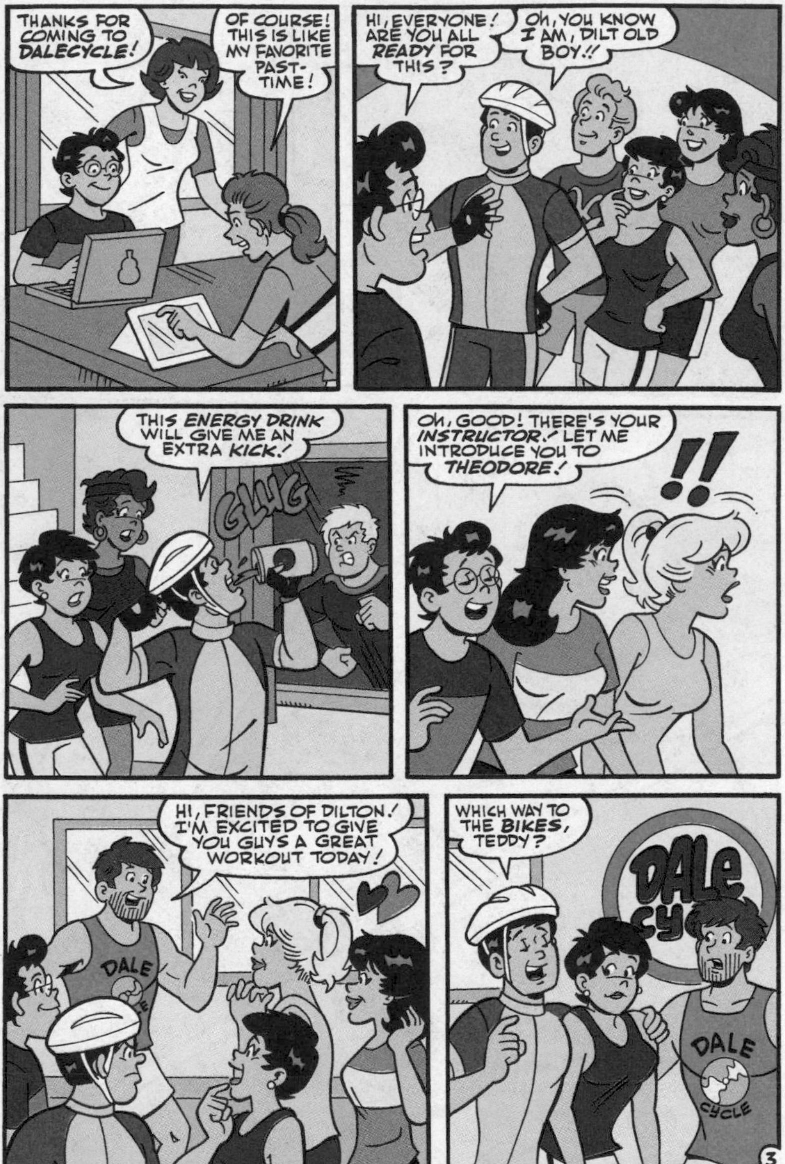
THANKS FOR COMING TO DALECYCLE!
OF COURSE! THIS IS LIKE MY FAVORITE PAST-TIME!
HI, EVERYONE! ARE YOU ALL READY FOR THIS?
Oh, YOU KNOW I AM, DILT OLD BOY!!
THIS ENERGY DRINK WILL GIVE ME AN EXTRA KICK!
GLUG
Oh, GOOD! THERE'S YOUR INSTRUCTOR! LET ME INTRODUCE YOU TO THEODORE!
!!
HI, FRIENDS OF DILTON! I'M EXCITED TO GIVE YOU GUYS A GREAT WORKOUT TODAY!
DALE
WHICH WAY TO THE BIKES, TEDDY?
DALE CY
DALE
CYCLE
3

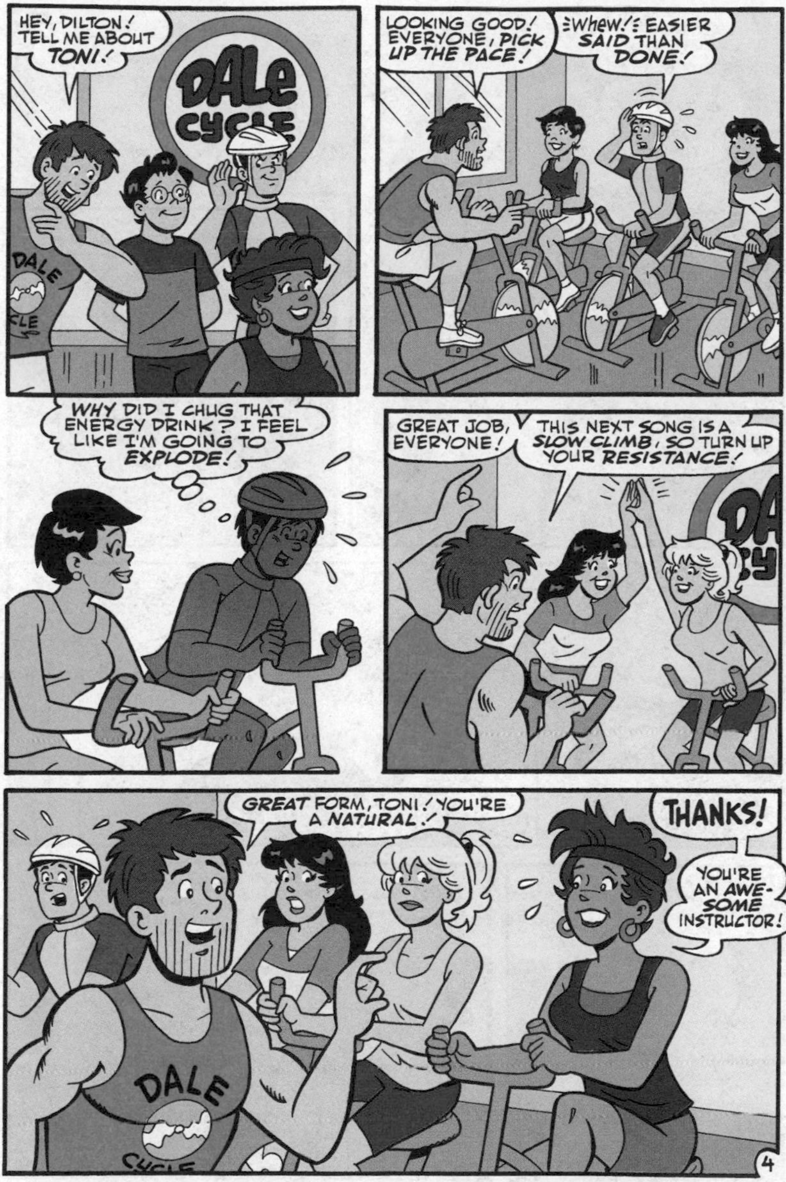
HEY, DILTON! TELL ME ABOUT TONI!
DALE CYCLE
DALE CYCLE
LOOKING GOOD! EVERYONE, PICK UP THE PACE!
WHEW! EASIER SAID THAN DONE!
WHY DID I CHUG THAT ENERGY DRINK? I FEEL LIKE I'M GOING TO EXPLODE!
GREAT JOB, EVERYONE!
THIS NEXT SONG IS A SLOW CLIMB, SO TURN UP YOUR RESISTANCE!
GREAT FORM, TONI! YOU'RE A NATURAL!
THANKS!
YOU'RE AN AWESOME INSTRUCTOR!
DALE
4

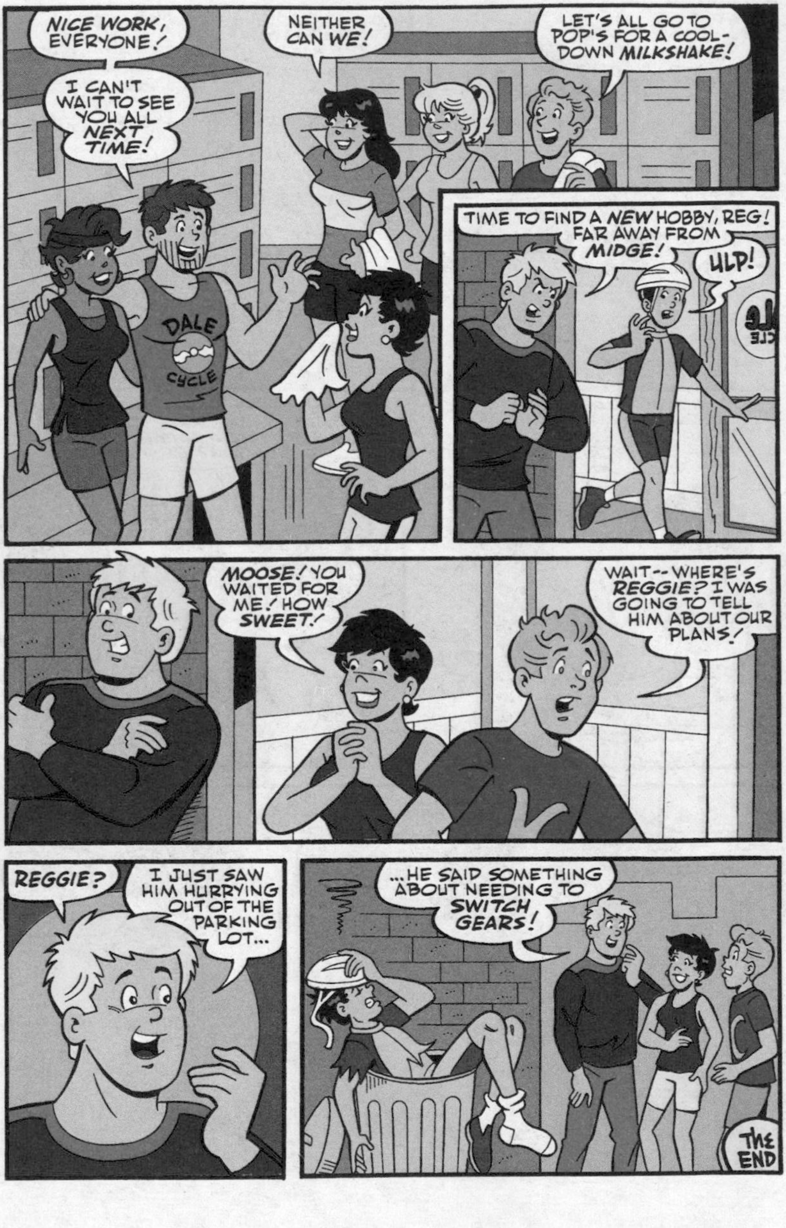
NICE WORK, EVERYONE!
I CAN'T WAIT TO SEE YOU ALL NEXT TIME!
NEITHER CAN WE!
LET'S ALL GO TO POP'S FOR A COOL-DOWN MILKSHAKE!
TIME TO FIND A NEW HOBBY, REG! FAR AWAY FROM MIDGE!
ULP!
MOOSE! YOU WAITED FOR ME! HOW SWEET!
WAIT-- WHERE'S REGGIE? I WAS GOING TO TELL HIM ABOUT OUR PLANS!
REGGIE?
I JUST SAW HIM HURRYING OUT OF THE PARKING LOT...
...HE SAID SOMETHING ABOUT NEEDING TO SWITCH GEARS!
THE END

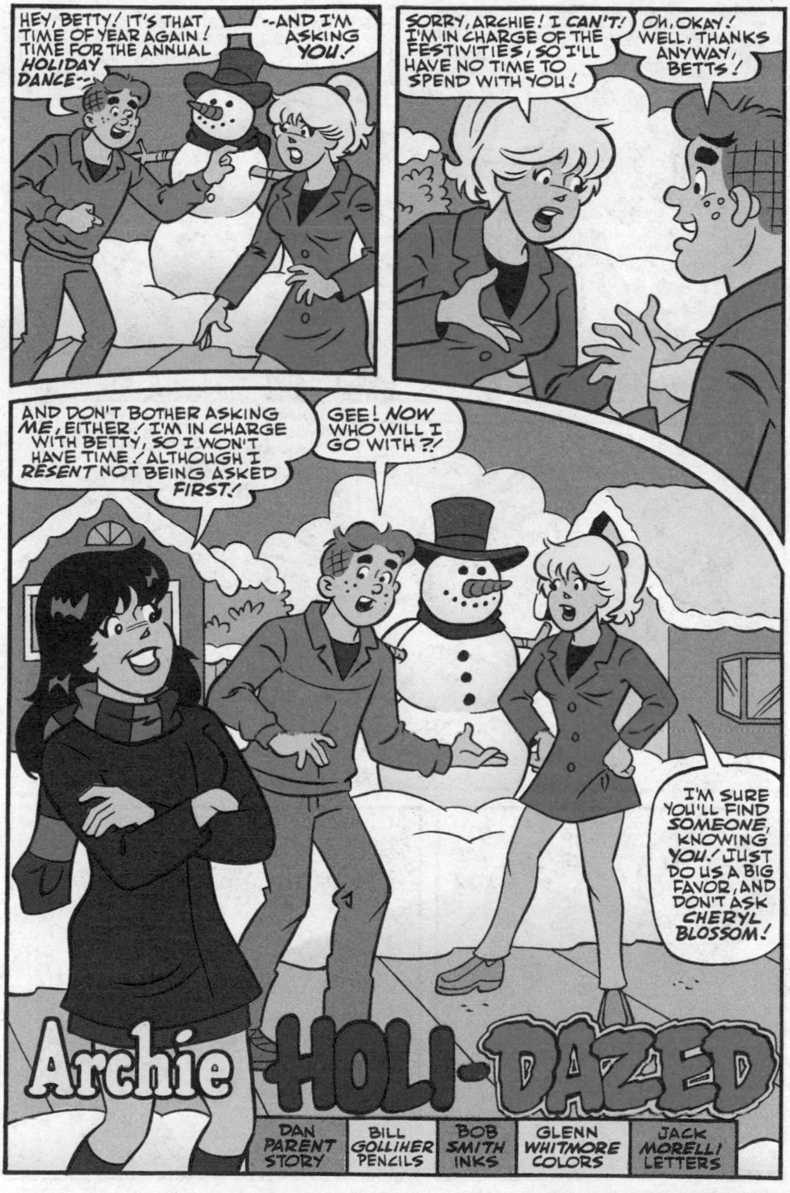

HEY, BETTY! IT'S THAT TIME OF YEAR AGAIN! TIME FOR THE ANNUAL HOLIDAY DANCE--
--AND I'M ASKING YOU!
SORRY, ARCHIE! I CAN'T! I'M IN CHARGE OF THE FESTIVITIES, SO I'LL HAVE NO TIME TO SPEND WITH YOU!
Oh, OKAY! WELL, THANKS ANYWAY, BETTS!
AND DON'T BOTHER ASKING ME, EITHER! I'M IN CHARGE WITH BETTY, SO I WON'T HAVE TIME! ALTHOUGH I RESENT NOT BEING ASKED FIRST!
GEE! NOW WHO WILL I GO WITH?!
I'M SURE YOU'LL FIND SOMEONE, KNOWING YOU! JUST DO US A BIG FAVOR, AND DON'T ASK CHERYL BLOSSOM!
Archie HOLI-DAZED
DAN PARENT STORY
BILL GOLLIHER PENCILS
BOB SMITH INKS
GLENN WHITMORE COLORS
JACK MORELLI LETTERS

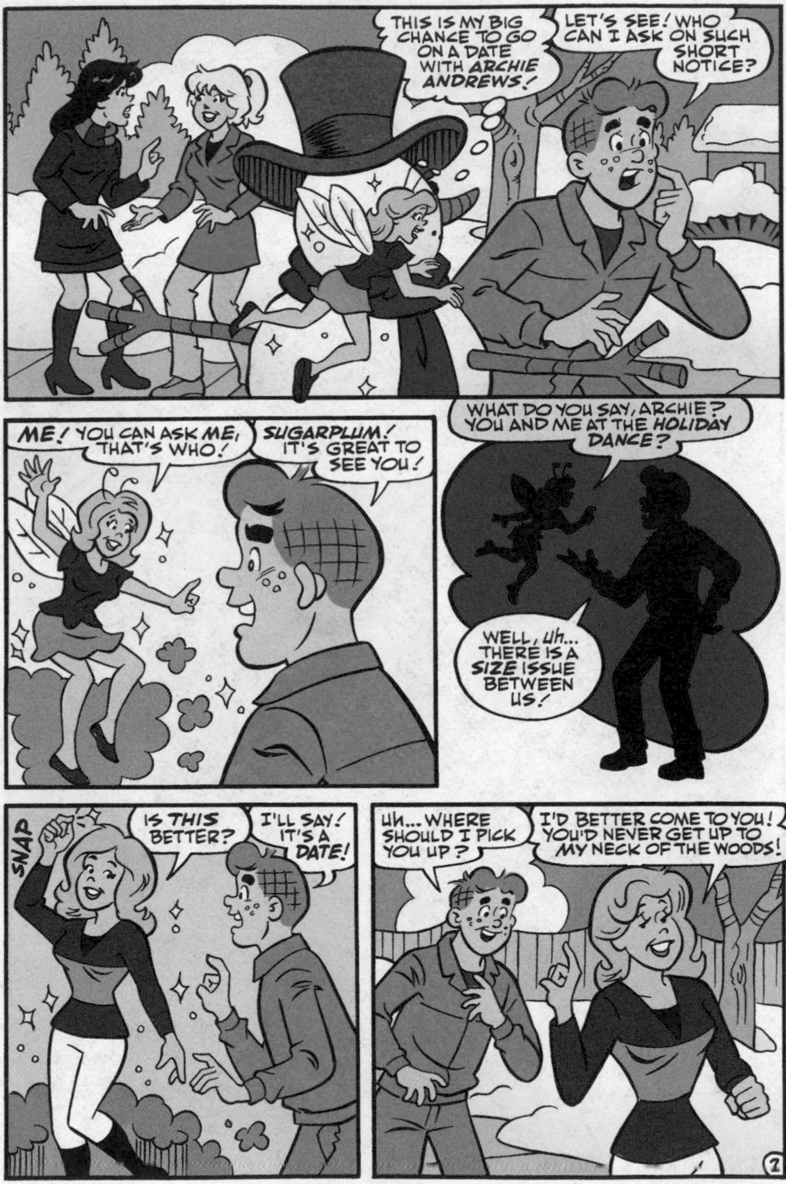
THIS IS MY BIG CHANCE TO GO ON A DATE WITH ARCHIE ANDREWS!
LET'S SEE! WHO CAN I ASK ON SUCH SHORT NOTICE?
ME! YOU CAN ASK ME, THAT'S WHO!
SUGARPLUM! IT'S GREAT TO SEE YOU!
WHAT DO YOU SAY, ARCHIE? YOU AND ME AT THE HOLIDAY DANCE?
WELL, uh... THERE IS A SIZE ISSUE BETWEEN US!
SNAP
IS THIS BETTER?
I'LL SAY! IT'S A DATE!
uh... WHERE SHOULD I PICK YOU UP?
I'D BETTER COME TO YOU! YOU'D NEVER GET UP TO MY NECK OF THE WOODS!
7

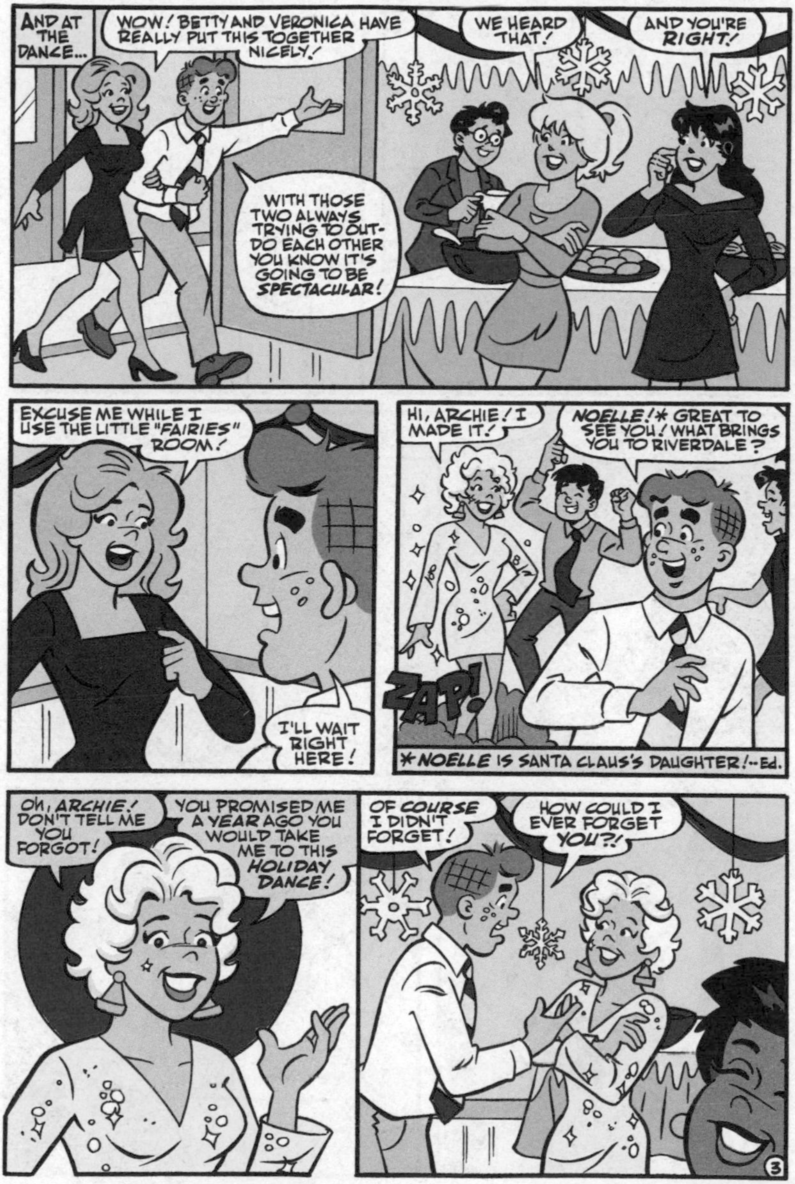
AND AT THE DANCE...
WOW! BETTY AND VERONICA HAVE REALLY PUT THIS TOGETHER NICELY!
WITH THOSE TWO ALWAYS TRYING TO OUT-DO EACH OTHER YOU KNOW IT'S GOING TO BE SPECTACULAR!
WE HEARD THAT!
AND YOU'RE RIGHT!
EXCUSE ME WHILE I USE THE LITTLE "FAIRIES" ROOM!
I'LL WAIT RIGHT HERE!
HI, ARCHIE! I MADE IT!
NOELLE!* GREAT TO SEE YOU! WHAT BRINGS YOU TO RIVERDALE?
ZAP!
*NOELLE IS SANTA CLAUS'S DAUGHTER! --Ed.
OH, ARCHIE! DON'T TELL ME YOU FORGOT!
YOU PROMISED ME A YEAR AGO YOU WOULD TAKE ME TO THIS HOLIDAY DANCE!
OF COURSE I DIDN'T FORGET!
HOW COULD I EVER FORGET YOU?!
3

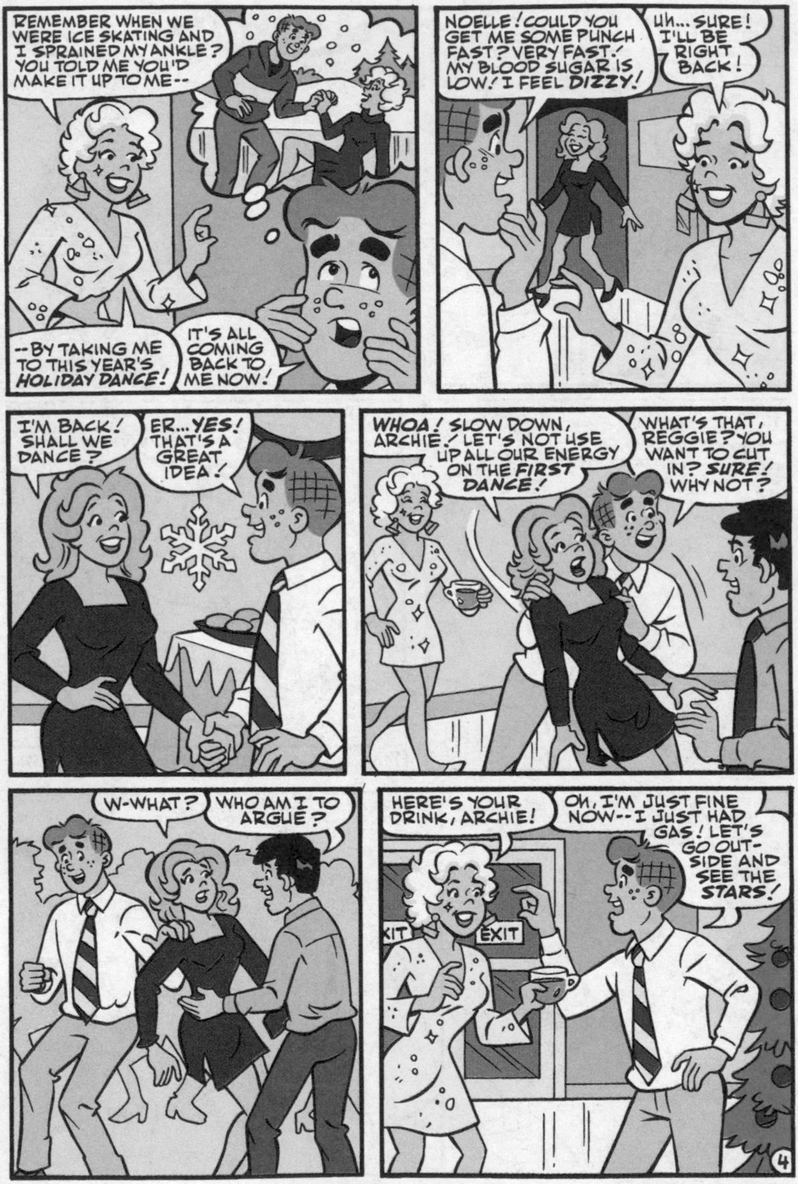
REMEMBER WHEN WE WERE ICE SKATING AND I SPRAINED MY ANKLE? YOU TOLD ME YOU'D MAKE IT UP TO ME--
--BY TAKING ME TO THIS YEAR'S HOLIDAY DANCE!
IT'S ALL COMING BACK TO ME NOW!
NOELLE! COULD YOU GET ME SOME PUNCH FAST? VERY FAST! MY BLOOD SUGAR IS LOW! I FEEL DIZZY!
UH... SURE! I'LL BE RIGHT BACK!
I'M BACK! SHALL WE DANCE?
ER... YES! THAT'S A GREAT IDEA!
WHOA! SLOW DOWN, ARCHIE! LET'S NOT USE UP ALL OUR ENERGY ON THE FIRST DANCE!
WHAT'S THAT, REGGIE? YOU WANT TO CUT IN? SURE! WHY NOT?
W-WHAT?
WHO AM I TO ARGUE?
HERE'S YOUR DRINK, ARCHIE!
OH, I'M JUST FINE NOW--I JUST HAD GAS! LET'S GO OUT-SIDE AND SEE THE STARS!
EXIT
EXIT
4

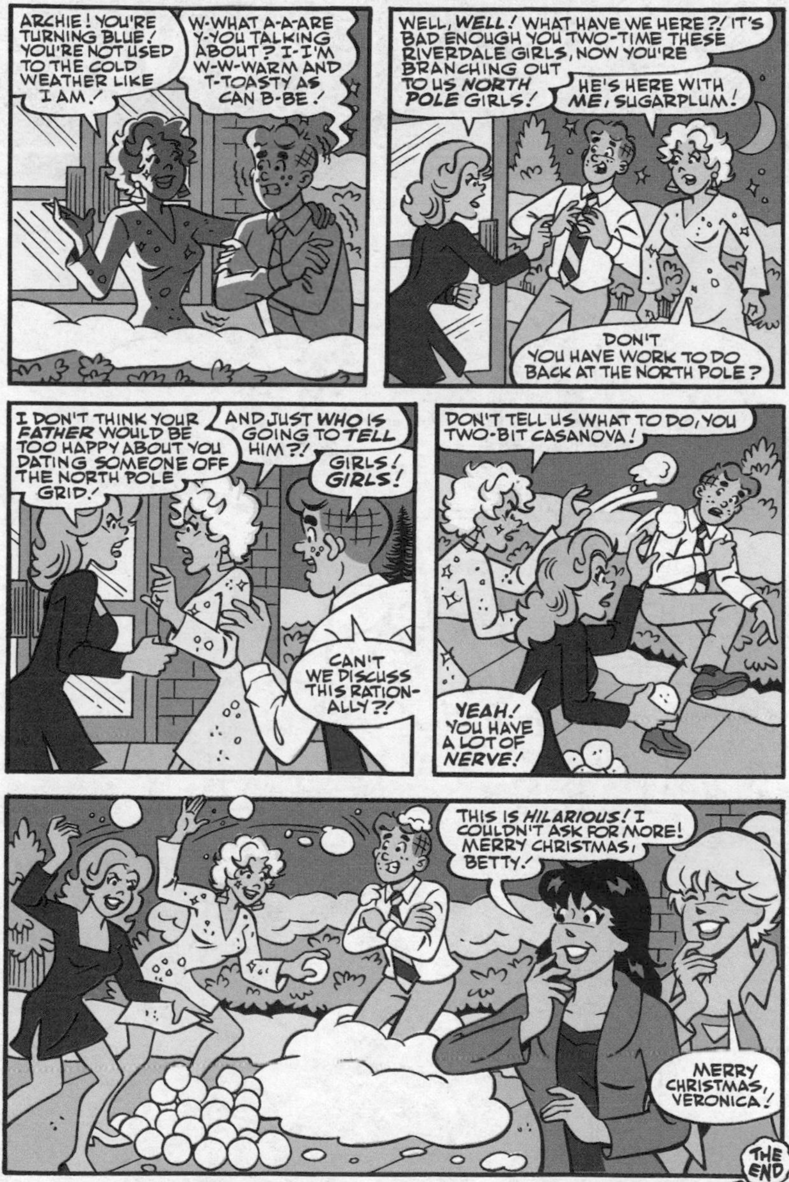
ARCHIE! YOU'RE TURNING BLUE! YOU'RE NOT USED TO THE COLD WEATHER LIKE I AM!
W-WHAT A-A-ARE Y-YOU TALKING ABOUT? I-I'M W-W-WARM AND T-TOASTY AS CAN B-BE!
WELL, WELL! WHAT HAVE WE HERE?! IT'S BAD ENOUGH YOU TWO-TIME THESE RIVERDALE GIRLS, NOW YOU'RE BRANCHING OUT TO US NORTH POLE GIRLS!
HE'S HERE WITH ME, SUGARPLUM!
DON'T YOU HAVE WORK TO DO BACK AT THE NORTH POLE?
I DON'T THINK YOUR FATHER WOULD BE TOO HAPPY ABOUT YOU DATING SOMEONE OFF THE NORTH POLE GRID!
AND JUST WHO IS GOING TO TELL HIM?!
GIRLS! GIRLS!
CAN'T WE DISCUSS THIS RATION-ALLY?!
DON'T TELL US WHAT TO DO, YOU TWO-BIT CASANOVA!
YEAH! YOU HAVE A LOT OF NERVE!
THIS IS HILARIOUS! I COULDN'T ASK FOR MORE! MERRY CHRISTMAS, BETTY!
MERRY CHRISTMAS, VERONICA!
THE END

02 BETTY & VERONICA

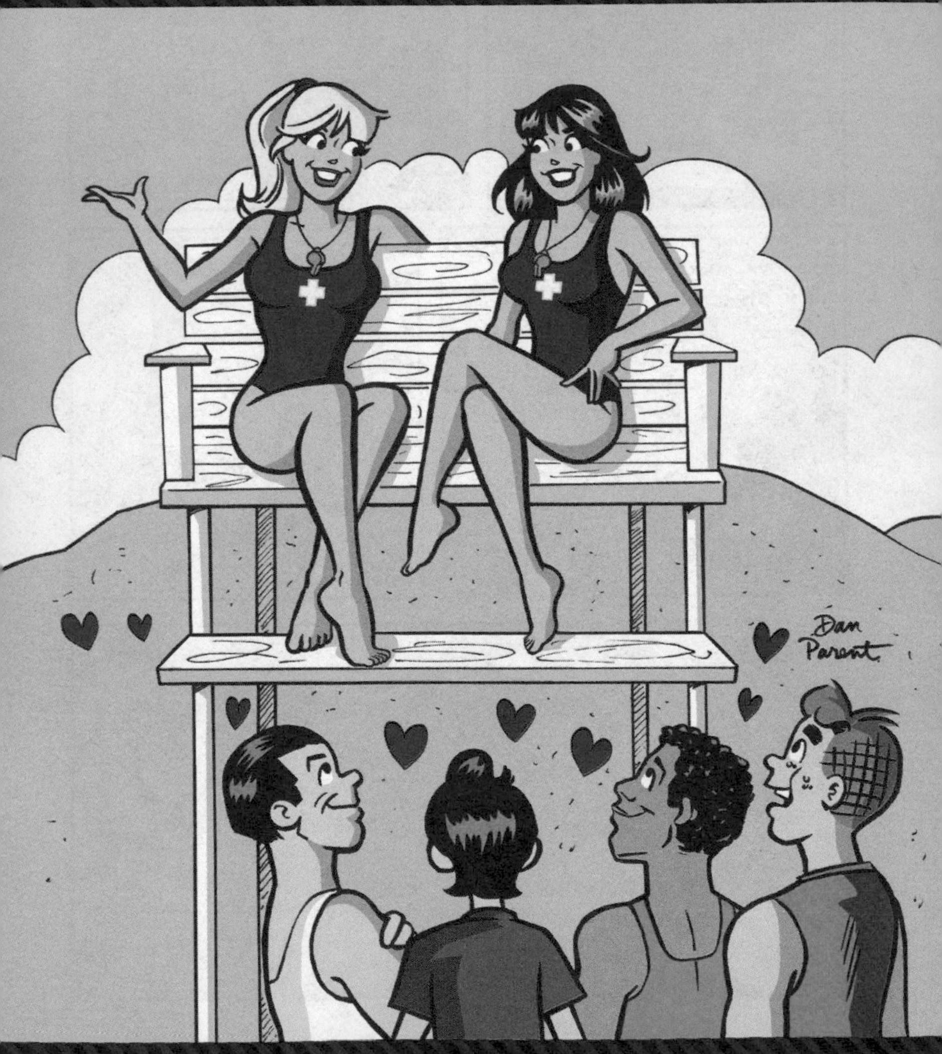

Dan Parent.

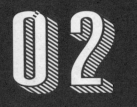

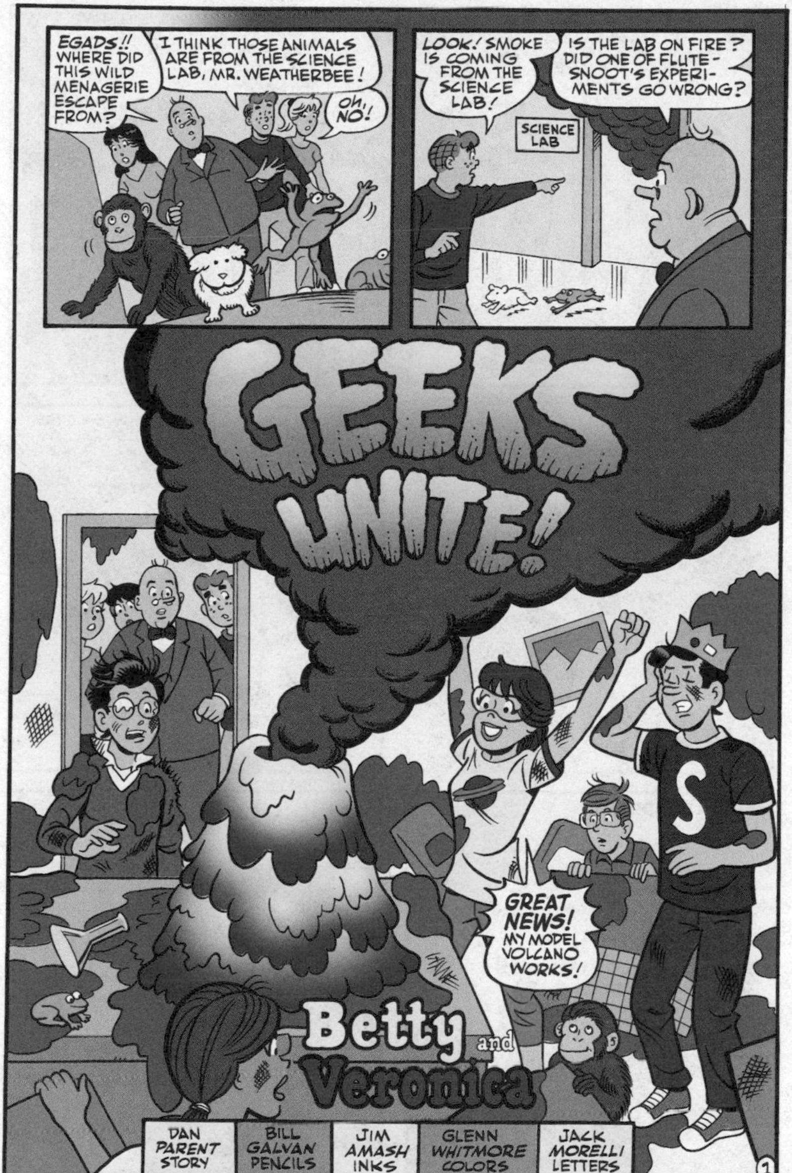
EGADS!! WHERE DID THIS WILD MENAGERIE ESCAPE FROM?
I THINK THOSE ANIMALS ARE FROM THE SCIENCE LAB, MR. WEATHERBEE!
OH, NO!
LOOK! SMOKE IS COMING FROM THE SCIENCE LAB!
IS THE LAB ON FIRE? DID ONE OF FLUTESNOOT'S EXPERIMENTS GO WRONG?
SCIENCE LAB
GEEKS UNITE!
GREAT NEWS! MY MODEL VOLCANO WORKS!
Betty and Veronica
DAN PARENT STORY
BILL GALVAN PENCILS
JIM AMASH INKS
GLENN WHITMORE COLORS
JACK MORELLI LETTERS
1

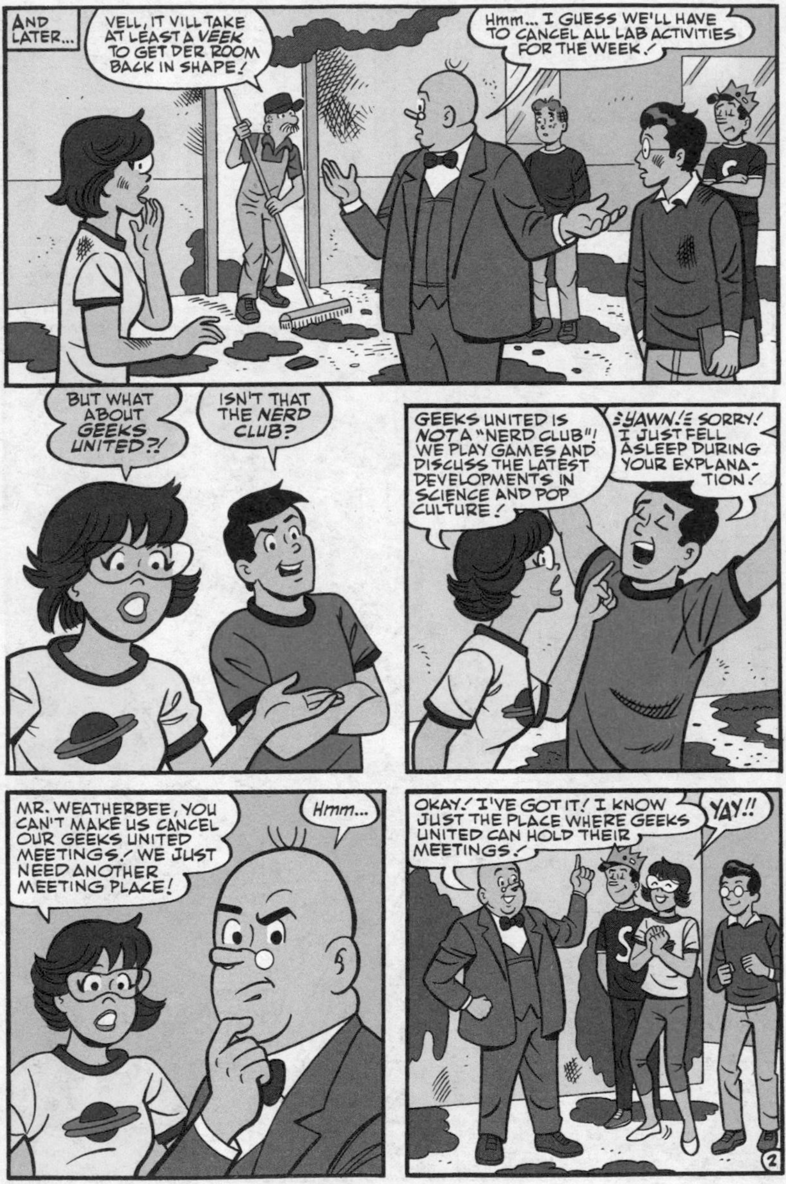
AND LATER...
VELL, IT VILL TAKE AT LEAST A VEEK TO GET DER ROOM BACK IN SHAPE!
Hmm... I GUESS WE'LL HAVE TO CANCEL ALL LAB ACTIVITIES FOR THE WEEK!
BUT WHAT ABOUT GEEKS UNITED?!
ISN'T THAT THE NERD CLUB?
GEEKS UNITED IS NOT A "NERD CLUB"! WE PLAY GAMES AND DISCUSS THE LATEST DEVELOPMENTS IN SCIENCE AND POP CULTURE!
YAWN! SORRY! I JUST FELL ASLEEP DURING YOUR EXPLANATION!
MR. WEATHERBEE, YOU CAN'T MAKE US CANCEL OUR GEEKS UNITED MEETINGS! WE JUST NEED ANOTHER MEETING PLACE!
Hmm...
OKAY! I'VE GOT IT! I KNOW JUST THE PLACE WHERE GEEKS UNITED CAN HOLD THEIR MEETINGS!
YAY!!
2

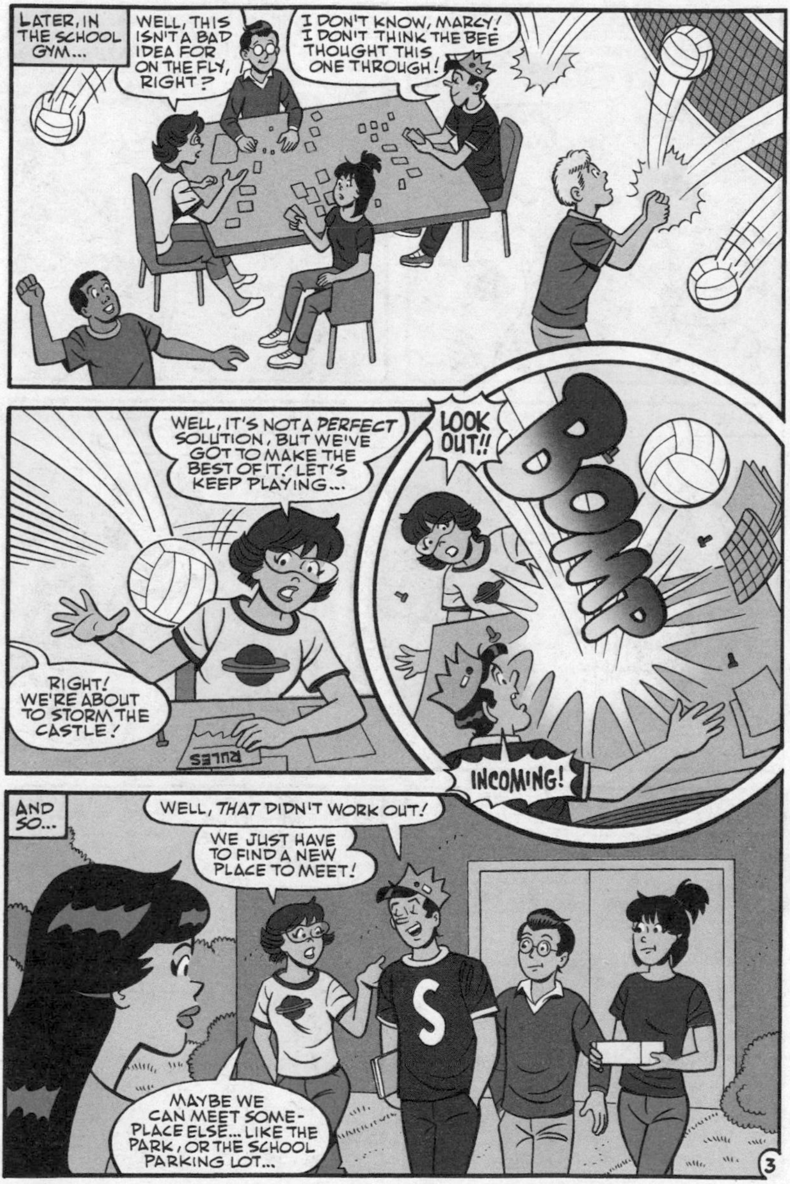
LATER, IN THE SCHOOL GYM...
WELL, THIS ISN'T A BAD IDEA FOR ON THE FLY, RIGHT?
I DON'T KNOW, MARCY! I DON'T THINK THE BEE THOUGHT THIS ONE THROUGH!
WELL, IT'S NOT A PERFECT SOLUTION, BUT WE'VE GOT TO MAKE THE BEST OF IT! LET'S KEEP PLAYING...
RIGHT! WE'RE ABOUT TO STORM THE CASTLE!
RULES
LOOK OUT!!
BOMP
INCOMING!
AND SO...
WELL, THAT DIDN'T WORK OUT!
WE JUST HAVE TO FIND A NEW PLACE TO MEET!
MAYBE WE CAN MEET SOME-PLACE ELSE... LIKE THE PARK, OR THE SCHOOL PARKING LOT...
S
3

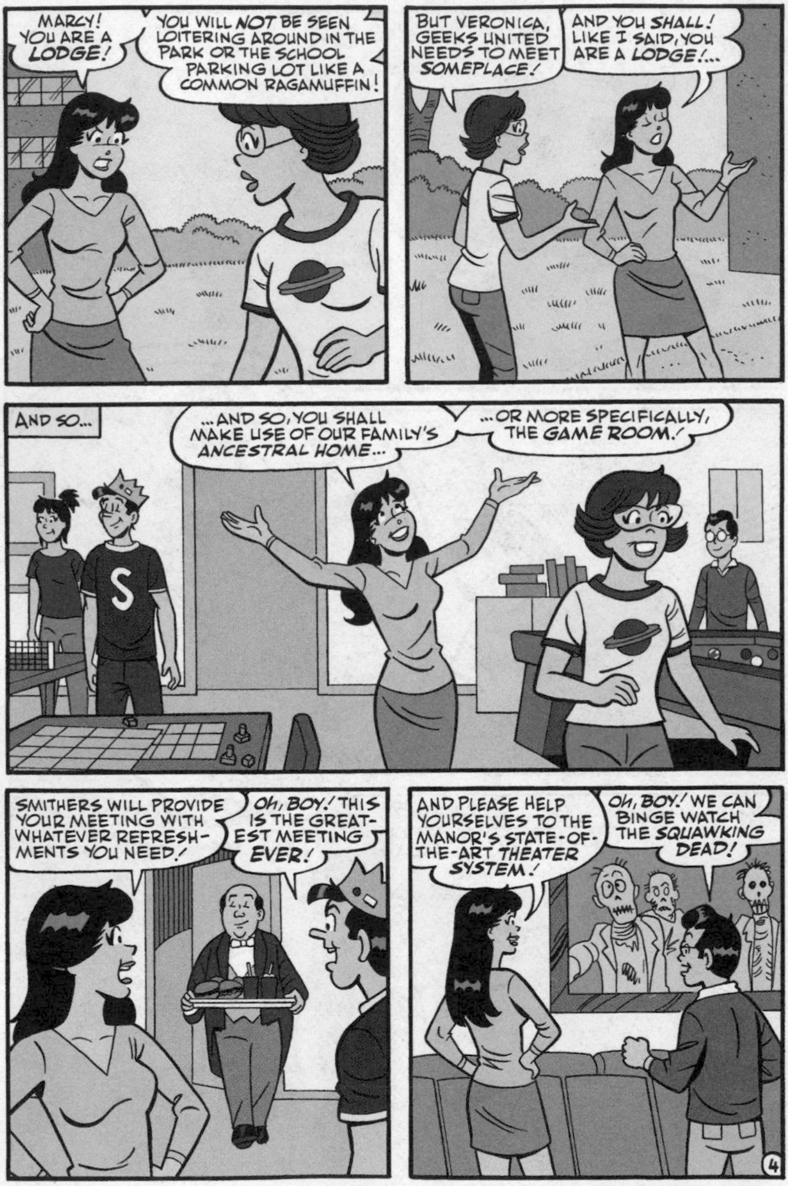
MARCY! YOU ARE A LODGE!
YOU WILL NOT BE SEEN LOITERING AROUND IN THE PARK OR THE SCHOOL PARKING LOT LIKE A COMMON RAGAMUFFIN!
BUT VERONICA, GEEKS UNITED NEEDS TO MEET SOMEPLACE!
AND YOU SHALL! LIKE I SAID, YOU ARE A LODGE!...
AND SO...
...AND SO, YOU SHALL MAKE USE OF OUR FAMILY'S ANCESTRAL HOME...
...OR MORE SPECIFICALLY, THE GAME ROOM!
S
SMITHERS WILL PROVIDE YOUR MEETING WITH WHATEVER REFRESH-MENTS YOU NEED!
OH, BOY! THIS IS THE GREAT-EST MEETING EVER!
AND PLEASE HELP YOURSELVES TO THE MANOR'S STATE-OF-THE-ART THEATER SYSTEM!
OH, BOY! WE CAN BINGE WATCH THE SQUAWKING DEAD!
4

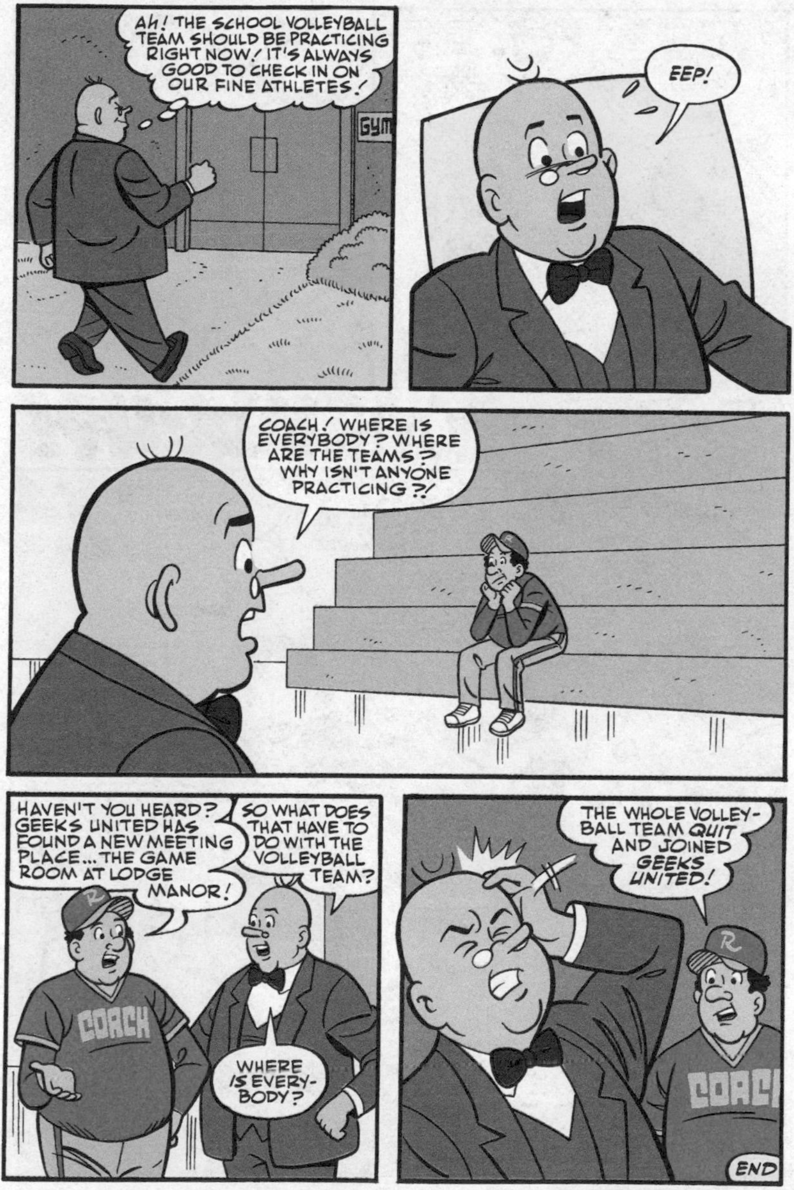
AH! THE SCHOOL VOLLEYBALL TEAM SHOULD BE PRACTICING RIGHT NOW! IT'S ALWAYS GOOD TO CHECK IN ON OUR FINE ATHLETES!
GYM
EEP!
COACH! WHERE IS EVERYBODY? WHERE ARE THE TEAMS? WHY ISN'T ANYONE PRACTICING?!
HAVEN'T YOU HEARD? GEEKS UNITED HAS FOUND A NEW MEETING PLACE... THE GAME ROOM AT LODGE MANOR!
SO WHAT DOES THAT HAVE TO DO WITH THE VOLLEYBALL TEAM?
WHERE IS EVERYBODY?
COACH
THE WHOLE VOLLEYBALL TEAM QUIT AND JOINED GEEKS UNITED!
END

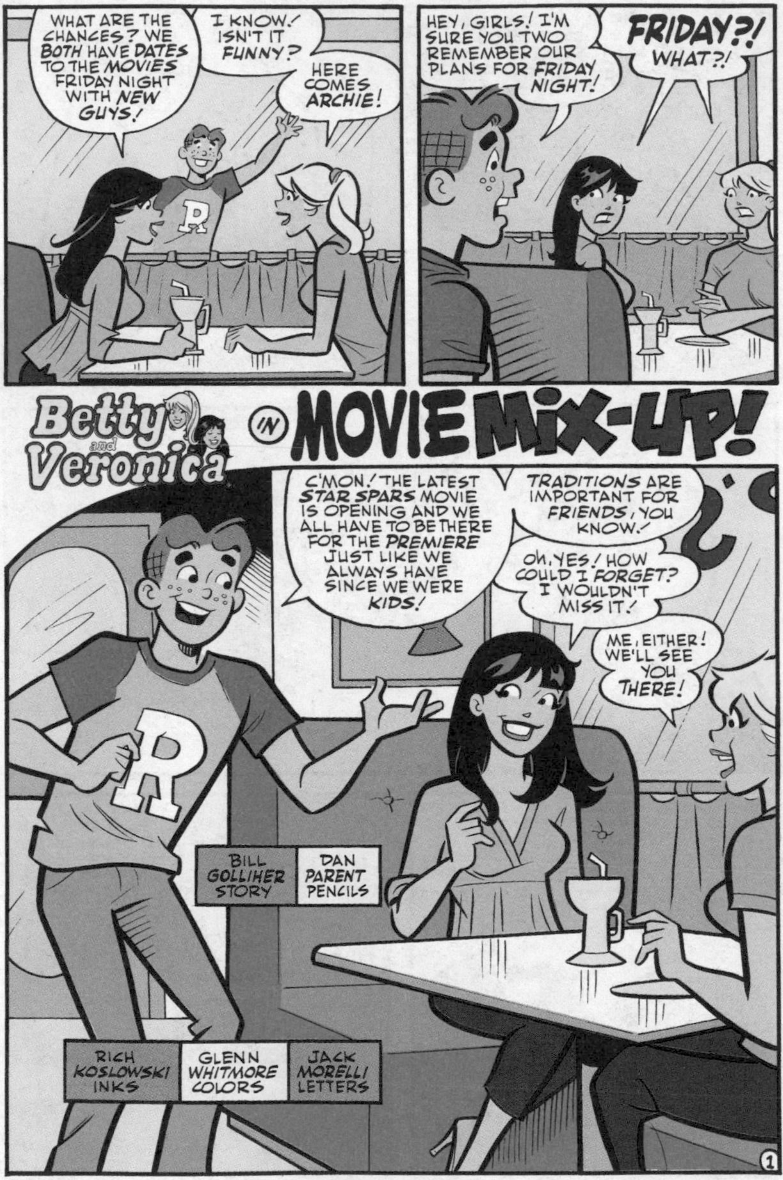
WHAT ARE THE CHANCES? WE BOTH HAVE DATES TO THE MOVIES FRIDAY NIGHT WITH NEW GUYS!
I KNOW! ISN'T IT FUNNY?
HERE COMES ARCHIE!
HEY, GIRLS! I'M SURE YOU TWO REMEMBER OUR PLANS FOR FRIDAY NIGHT!
FRIDAY?!
WHAT?!
Betty and Veronica
IN MOVIE MIX-UP!
C'MON! THE LATEST STAR SPARS MOVIE IS OPENING AND WE ALL HAVE TO BE THERE FOR THE PREMIERE JUST LIKE WE ALWAYS HAVE SINCE WE WERE KIDS!
TRADITIONS ARE IMPORTANT FOR FRIENDS, YOU KNOW!
OH, YES! HOW COULD I FORGET? I WOULDN'T MISS IT!
ME, EITHER! WE'LL SEE YOU THERE!
BILL GOLLIHER STORY
DAN PARENT PENCILS
RICH KOSLOWSKI INKS
GLENN WHITMORE COLORS
JACK MORELLI LETTERS
1

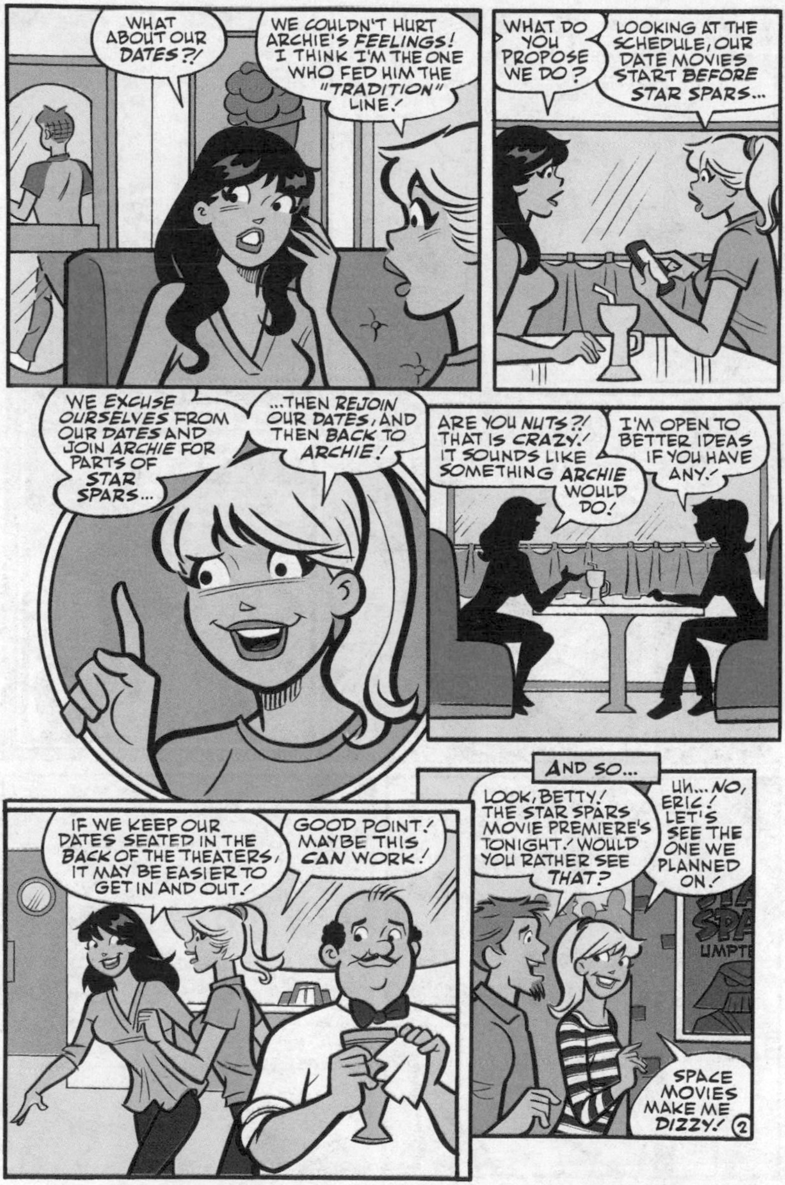
WHAT ABOUT OUR DATES?!
WE COULDN'T HURT ARCHIE'S FEELINGS! I THINK I'M THE ONE WHO FED HIM THE "TRADITION" LINE!
WHAT DO YOU PROPOSE WE DO?
LOOKING AT THE SCHEDULE, OUR DATE MOVIES START BEFORE STAR SPARS...
WE EXCUSE OURSELVES FROM OUR DATES AND JOIN ARCHIE FOR PARTS OF STAR SPARS...
...THEN REJOIN OUR DATES, AND THEN BACK TO ARCHIE!
ARE YOU NUTS?! THAT IS CRAZY! IT SOUNDS LIKE SOMETHING ARCHIE WOULD DO!
I'M OPEN TO BETTER IDEAS IF YOU HAVE ANY!
IF WE KEEP OUR DATES SEATED IN THE BACK OF THE THEATERS, IT MAY BE EASIER TO GET IN AND OUT!
GOOD POINT! MAYBE THIS CAN WORK!
AND SO...
LOOK, BETTY! THE STAR SPARS MOVIE PREMIERE'S TONIGHT! WOULD YOU RATHER SEE THAT?
UH... NO, ERIC! LET'S SEE THE ONE WE PLANNED ON!
SPACE MOVIES MAKE ME DIZZY!
2

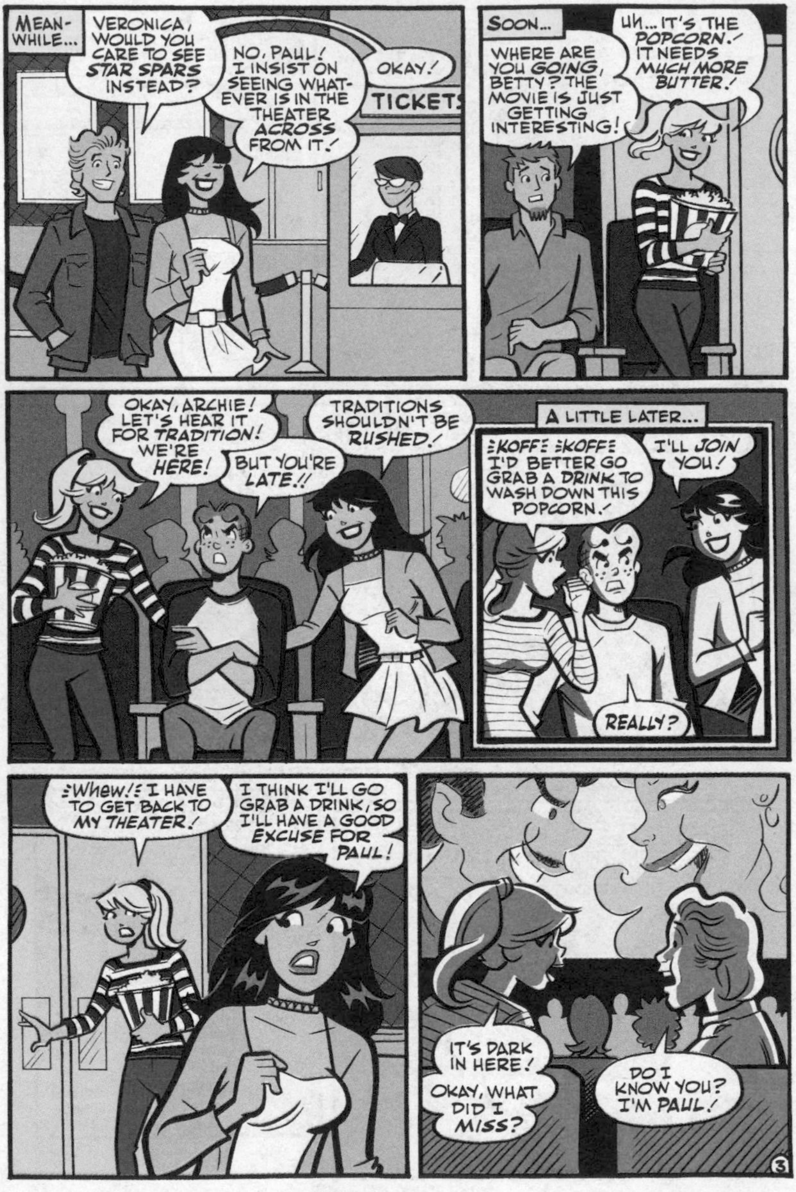
MEAN-WHILE...
VERONICA, WOULD YOU CARE TO SEE STAR SPARS INSTEAD?
NO, PAUL! I INSIST ON SEEING WHATEVER IS IN THE THEATER ACROSS FROM IT!
OKAY!
TICKETS
SOON...
WHERE ARE YOU GOING, BETTY? THE MOVIE IS JUST GETTING INTERESTING!
UH... IT'S THE POPCORN! IT NEEDS MUCH MORE BUTTER!
OKAY, ARCHIE! LET'S HEAR IT FOR TRADITION! WE'RE HERE!
BUT YOU'RE LATE!!
TRADITIONS SHOULDN'T BE RUSHED!
A LITTLE LATER...
KOFF KOFF I'D BETTER GO GRAB A DRINK TO WASH DOWN THIS POPCORN!
I'LL JOIN YOU!
REALLY?
Whew! I HAVE TO GET BACK TO MY THEATER!
I THINK I'LL GO GRAB A DRINK, SO I'LL HAVE A GOOD EXCUSE FOR PAUL!
IT'S DARK IN HERE!
OKAY, WHAT DID I MISS?
DO I KNOW YOU? I'M PAUL!
3

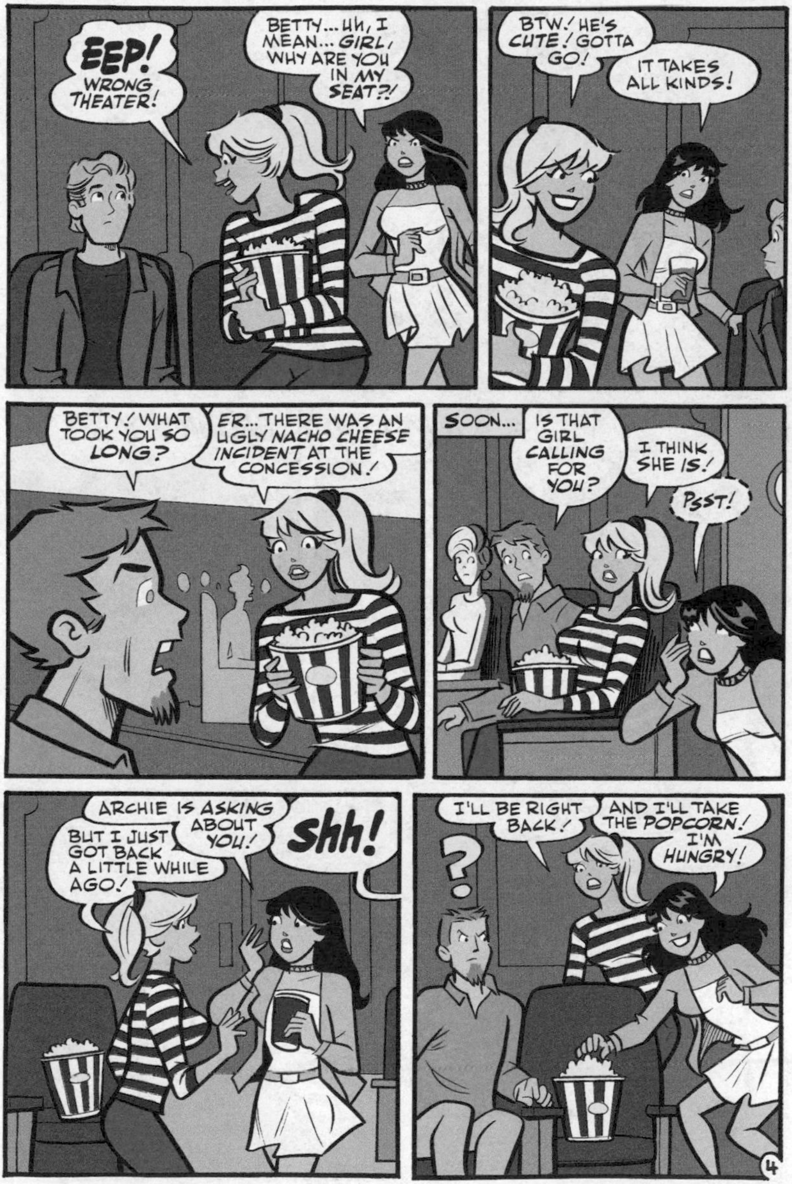
EEP! WRONG THEATER!
BETTY... UH, I MEAN... GIRL, WHY ARE YOU IN MY SEAT?!
BTW! HE'S CUTE! GOTTA GO!
IT TAKES ALL KINDS!
BETTY! WHAT TOOK YOU SO LONG?
ER... THERE WAS AN UGLY NACHO CHEESE INCIDENT AT THE CONCESSION!
SOON...
IS THAT GIRL CALLING FOR YOU?
I THINK SHE IS!
PSST!
ARCHIE IS ASKING ABOUT YOU!
BUT I JUST GOT BACK A LITTLE WHILE AGO!
SHH!
I'LL BE RIGHT BACK!
AND I'LL TAKE THE POPCORN! I'M HUNGRY!
?
4

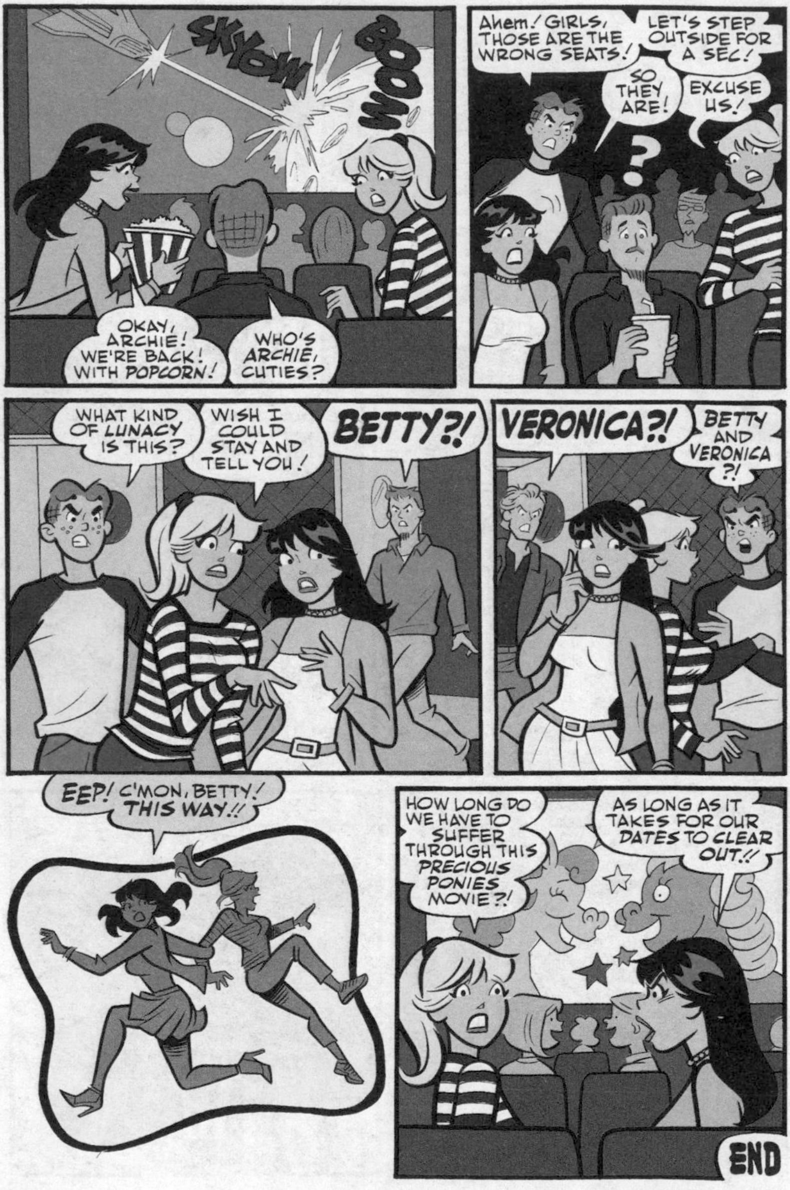
SKYOW
BOOM
OKAY, ARCHIE! WE'RE BACK! WITH POPCORN!
WHO'S ARCHIE, CUTIES?
Ahem! GIRLS, THOSE ARE THE WRONG SEATS!
LET'S STEP OUTSIDE FOR A SEC!
SO THEY ARE!
EXCUSE US!
?
WHAT KIND OF LUNACY IS THIS?
WISH I COULD STAY AND TELL YOU!
BETTY?!
VERONICA?!
BETTY AND VERONICA?!
EEP! C'MON, BETTY! THIS WAY!!
HOW LONG DO WE HAVE TO SUFFER THROUGH THIS PRECIOUS PONIES MOVIE?!
AS LONG AS IT TAKES FOR OUR DATES TO CLEAR OUT!!
END

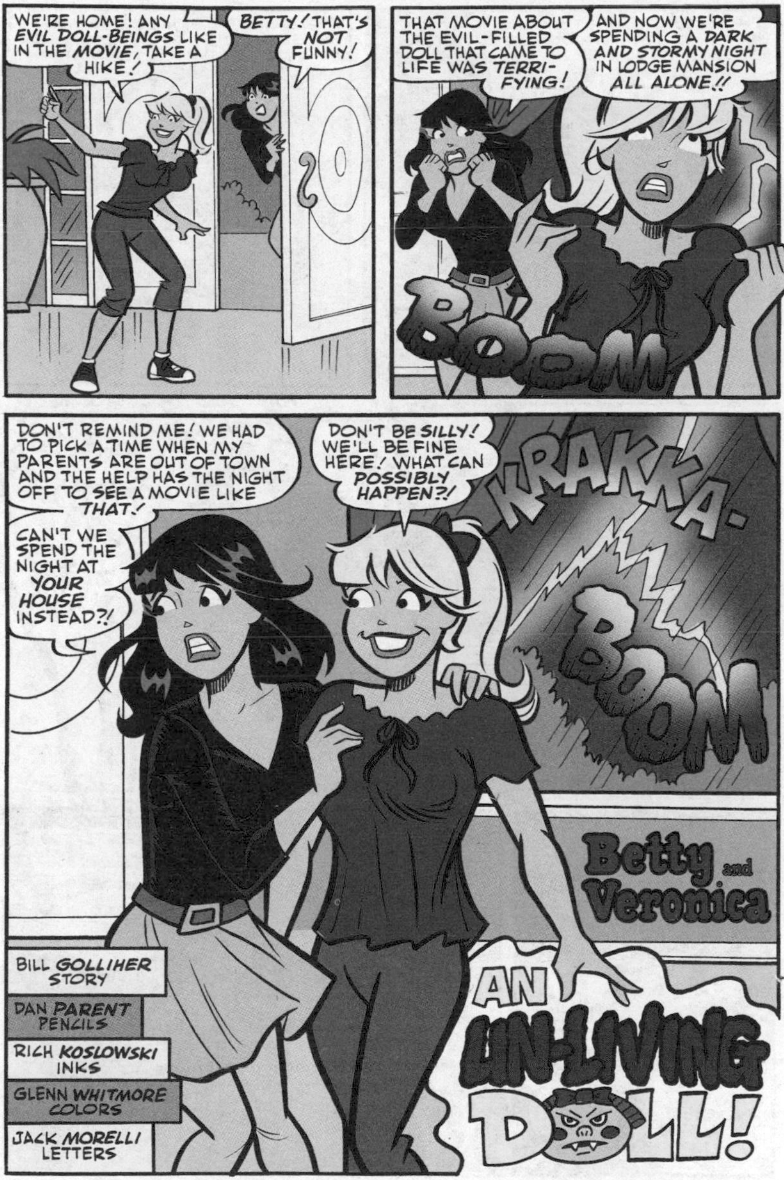
WE'RE HOME! ANY EVIL DOLL-BEINGS LIKE IN THE MOVIE, TAKE A HIKE!
BETTY! THAT'S NOT FUNNY!
THAT MOVIE ABOUT THE EVIL-FILLED DOLL THAT CAME TO LIFE WAS TERRI-FYING!
AND NOW WE'RE SPENDING A DARK AND STORMY NIGHT IN LODGE MANSION ALL ALONE!!
BOOM
DON'T REMIND ME! WE HAD TO PICK A TIME WHEN MY PARENTS ARE OUT OF TOWN AND THE HELP HAS THE NIGHT OFF TO SEE A MOVIE LIKE THAT!
CAN'T WE SPEND THE NIGHT AT YOUR HOUSE INSTEAD?!
DON'T BE SILLY! WE'LL BE FINE HERE! WHAT CAN POSSIBLY HAPPEN?!
KRAKKA-BOOM
Betty and Veronica
AN UN-LIVING DOLL!
BILL GOLLIHER STORY
DAN PARENT PENCILS
RICH KOSLOWSKI INKS
GLENN WHITMORE COLORS
JACK MORELLI LETTERS

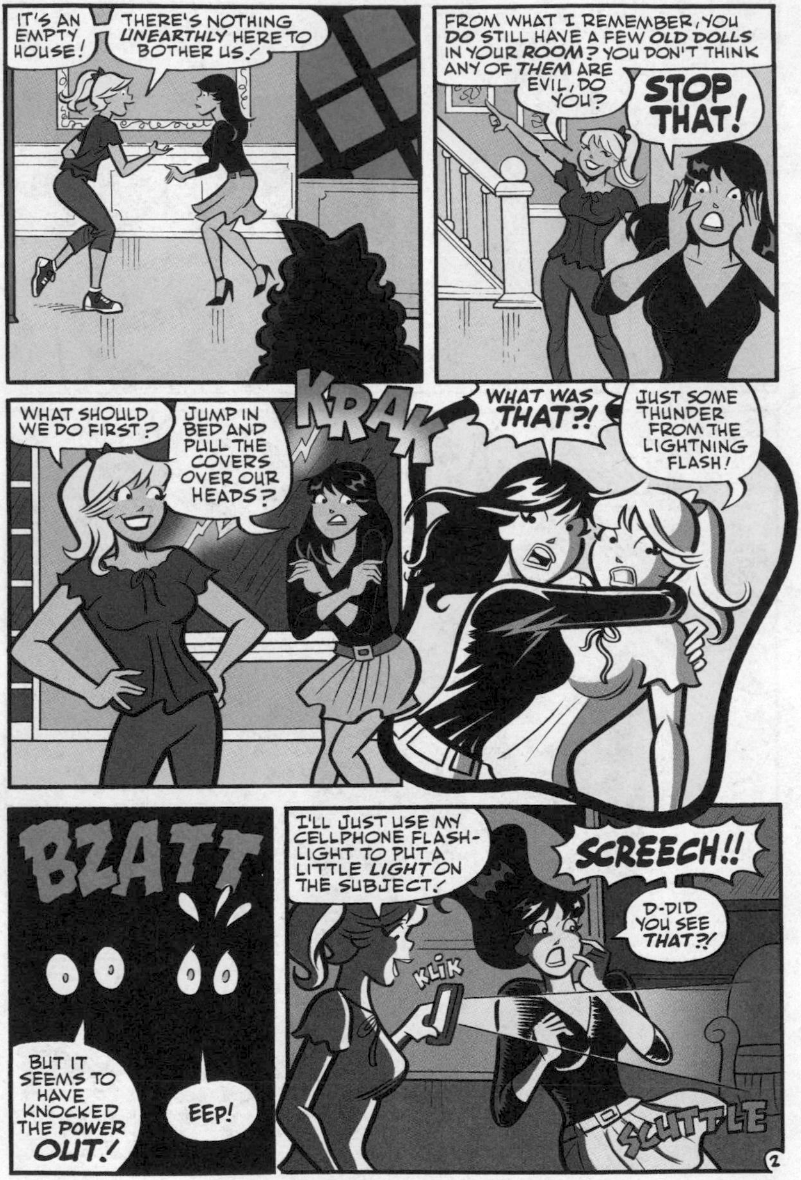
IT'S AN EMPTY HOUSE!
THERE'S NOTHING UNEARTHLY HERE TO BOTHER US!
FROM WHAT I REMEMBER, YOU DO STILL HAVE A FEW OLD DOLLS IN YOUR ROOM? YOU DON'T THINK ANY OF THEM ARE EVIL, DO YOU?
STOP THAT!
WHAT SHOULD WE DO FIRST?
JUMP IN BED AND PULL THE COVERS OVER OUR HEADS?
KRAK
WHAT WAS THAT?!
JUST SOME THUNDER FROM THE LIGHTNING FLASH!
BZATT
BUT IT SEEMS TO HAVE KNOCKED THE POWER OUT!
EEP!
I'LL JUST USE MY CELLPHONE FLASH-LIGHT TO PUT A LITTLE LIGHT ON THE SUBJECT!
SCREECH!!
D-DID YOU SEE THAT?!
KLIK
SCUTTLE
2

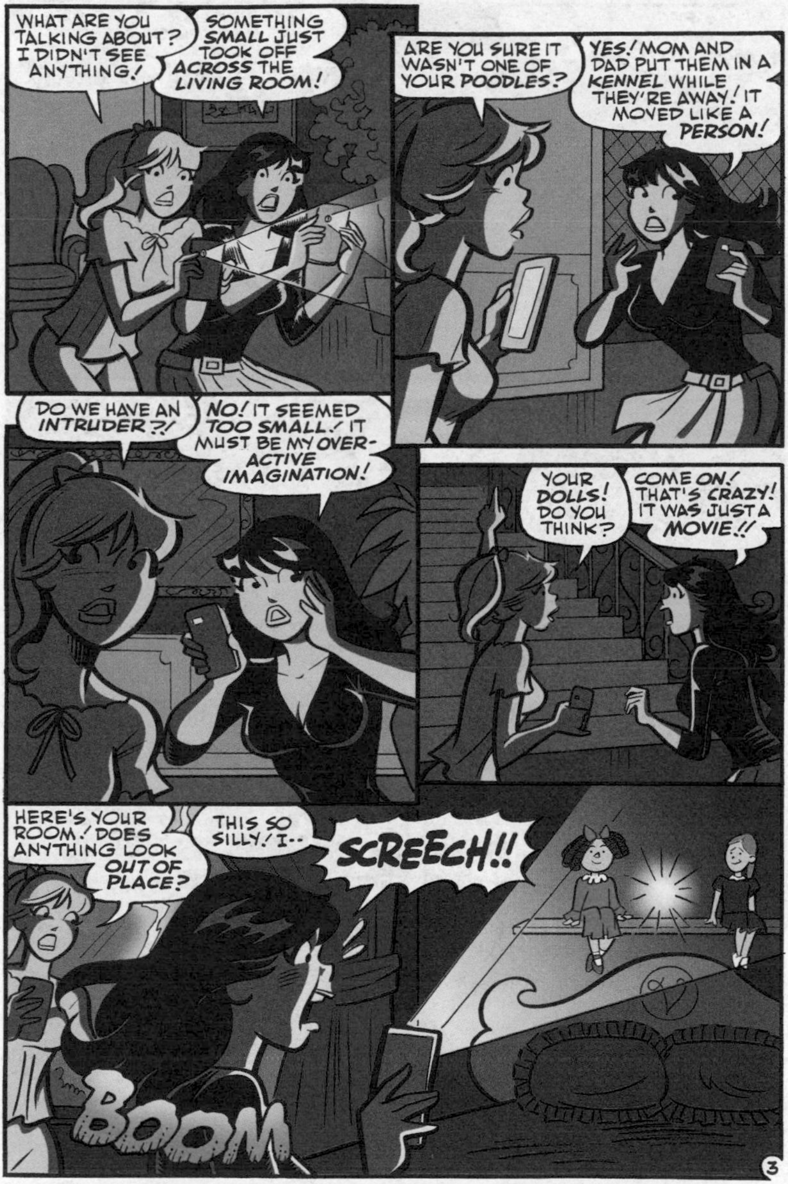
WHAT ARE YOU TALKING ABOUT? I DIDN'T SEE ANYTHING!
SOMETHING SMALL JUST TOOK OFF ACROSS THE LIVING ROOM!
ARE YOU SURE IT WASN'T ONE OF YOUR POODLES?
YES! MOM AND DAD PUT THEM IN A KENNEL WHILE THEY'RE AWAY! IT MOVED LIKE A PERSON!
DO WE HAVE AN INTRUDER?!
NO! IT SEEMED TOO SMALL! IT MUST BE MY OVER-ACTIVE IMAGINATION!
YOUR DOLLS! DO YOU THINK?
COME ON! THAT'S CRAZY! IT WAS JUST A MOVIE!!
HERE'S YOUR ROOM! DOES ANYTHING LOOK OUT OF PLACE?
THIS SO SILLY! I--
SCREECH!!
BOOM
3

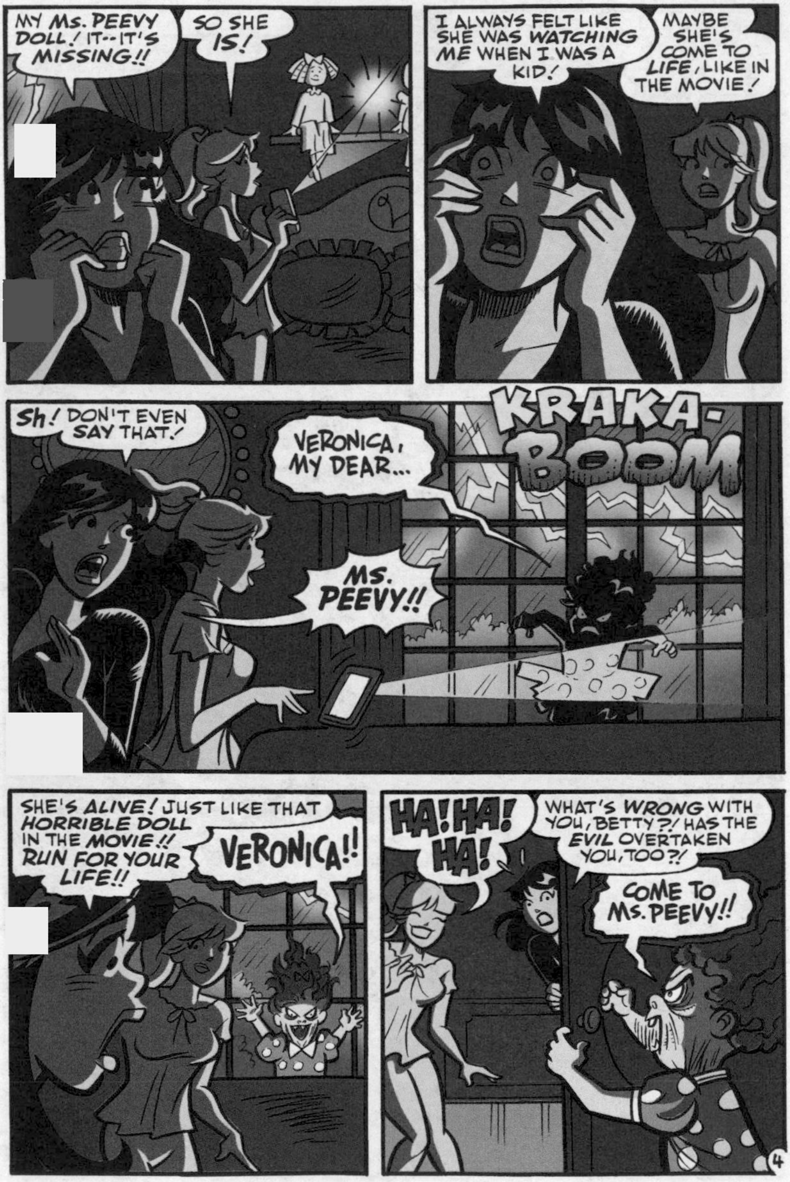
MY Ms. PEEVY DOLL! IT--IT'S MISSING!!
SO SHE IS!
I ALWAYS FELT LIKE SHE WAS WATCHING ME WHEN I WAS A KID!
MAYBE SHE'S COME TO LIFE, LIKE IN THE MOVIE!
Sh! DON'T EVEN SAY THAT!
KRAKA-BOOM
VERONICA, MY DEAR...
MS. PEEVY!!
SHE'S ALIVE! JUST LIKE THAT HORRIBLE DOLL IN THE MOVIE!! RUN FOR YOUR LIFE!!
VERONICA!!
HA! HA! HA!
WHAT'S WRONG WITH YOU, BETTY?! HAS THE EVIL OVERTAKEN YOU, TOO?!
COME TO MS. PEEVY!!
4

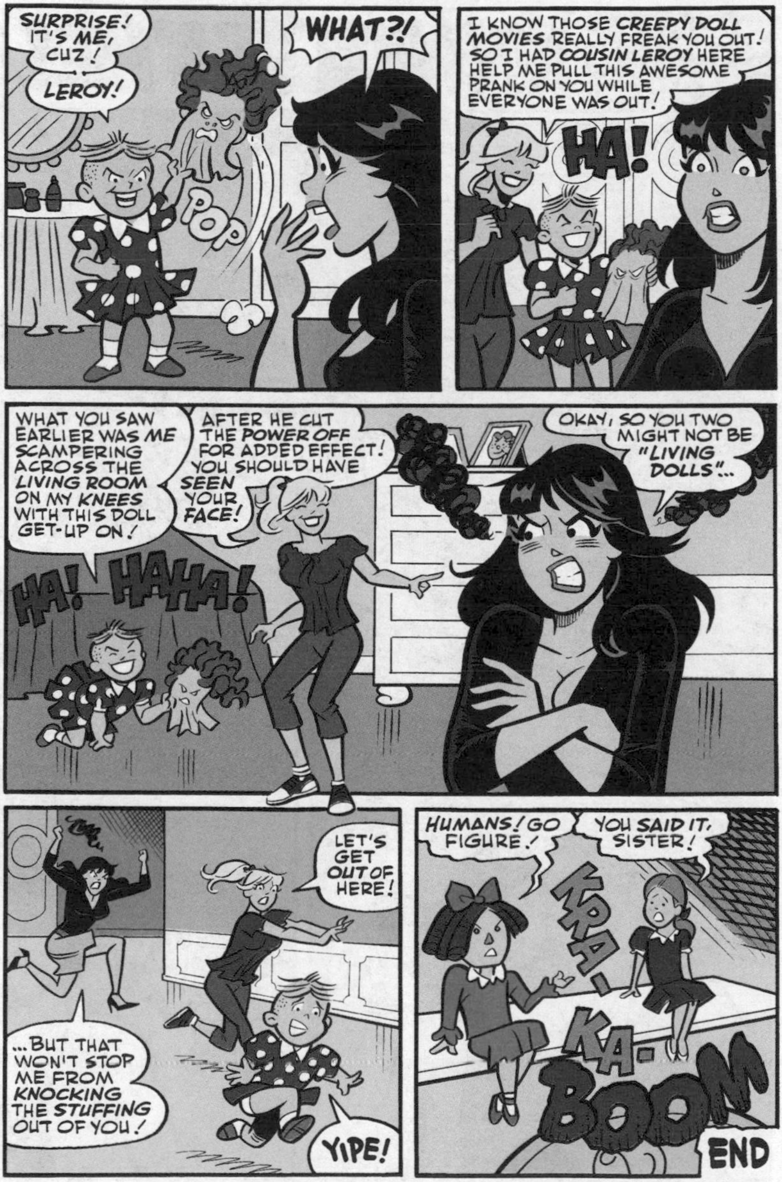
SURPRISE! IT'S ME, CUZ!
LEROY!
WHAT?!
POP
I KNOW THOSE CREEPY DOLL MOVIES REALLY FREAK YOU OUT! SO I HAD COUSIN LEROY HERE HELP ME PULL THIS AWESOME PRANK ON YOU WHILE EVERYONE WAS OUT!
HA!
WHAT YOU SAW EARLIER WAS ME SCAMPERING ACROSS THE LIVING ROOM ON MY KNEES WITH THIS DOLL GET-UP ON!
AFTER HE CUT THE POWER OFF FOR ADDED EFFECT! YOU SHOULD HAVE SEEN YOUR FACE!
HA! HAHA!
OKAY, SO YOU TWO MIGHT NOT BE "LIVING DOLLS"...
LET'S GET OUT OF HERE!
...BUT THAT WON'T STOP ME FROM KNOCKING THE STUFFING OUT OF YOU!
YIPE!
HUMANS! GO FIGURE!
YOU SAID IT, SISTER!
KRA-KA-BOOM
END

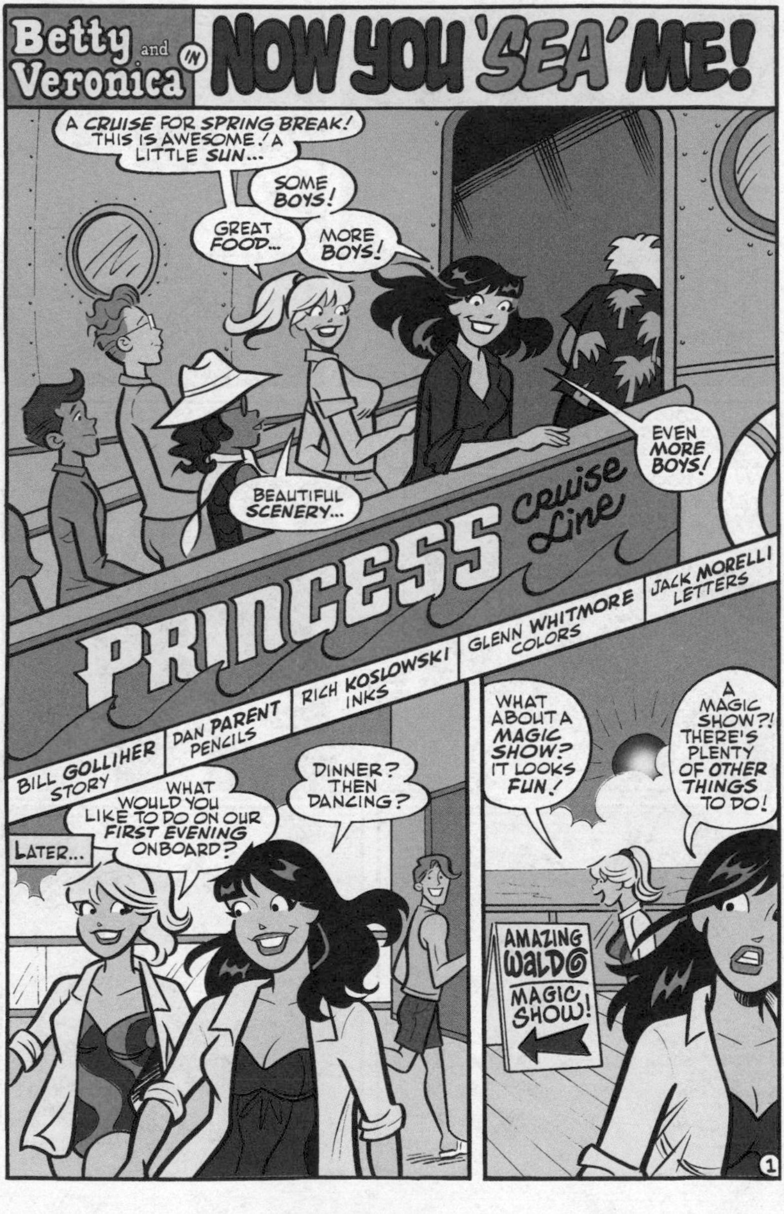
Betty and Veronica IN
NOW YOU 'SEA' ME!
A CRUISE FOR SPRING BREAK! THIS IS AWESOME! A LITTLE SUN...
SOME BOYS!
GREAT FOOD...
MORE BOYS!
BEAUTIFUL SCENERY...
EVEN MORE BOYS!
PRINCESS Cruise Line
BILL GOLLIHER STORY
DAN PARENT PENCILS
RICH KOSLOWSKI INKS
GLENN WHITMORE COLORS
JACK MORELLI LETTERS
LATER...
WHAT WOULD YOU LIKE TO DO ON OUR FIRST EVENING ONBOARD?
DINNER? THEN DANCING?
WHAT ABOUT A MAGIC SHOW? IT LOOKS FUN!
A MAGIC SHOW?! THERE'S PLENTY OF OTHER THINGS TO DO!
AMAZING WALDO MAGIC SHOW!
1

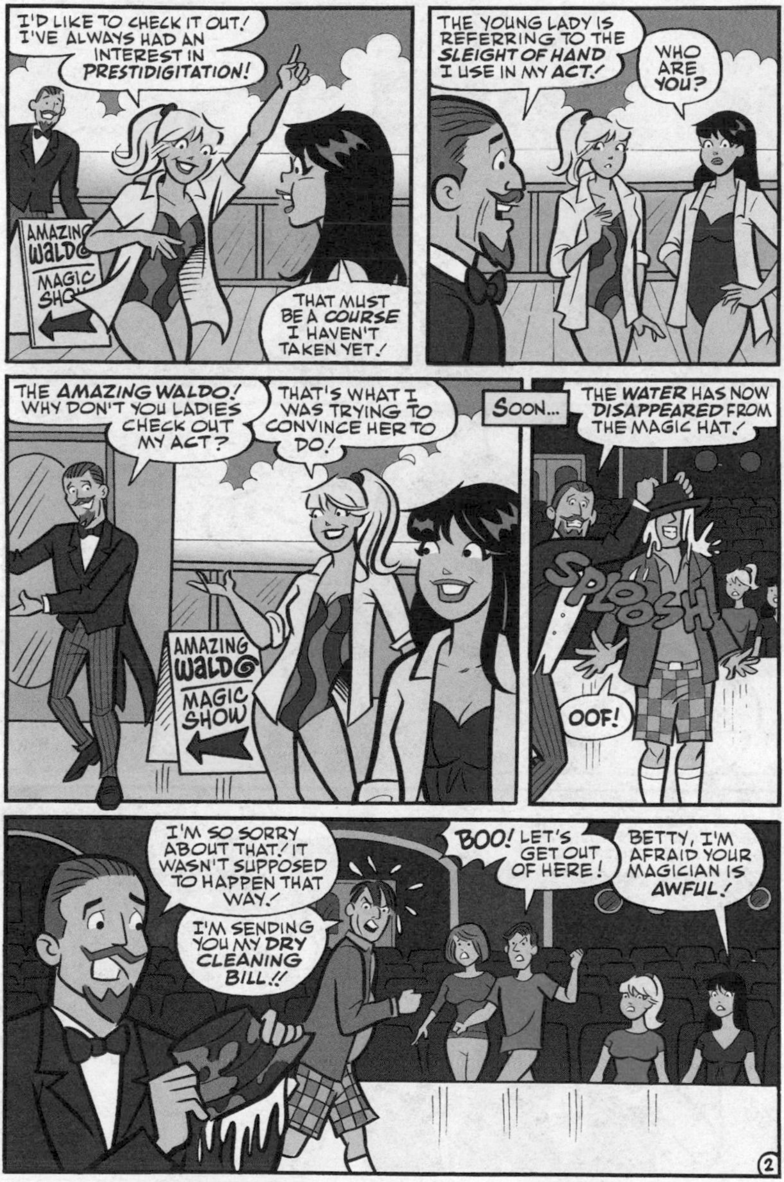
I'D LIKE TO CHECK IT OUT! I'VE ALWAYS HAD AN INTEREST IN PRESTIDIGITATION!
AMAZING WALDO MAGIC SHOW
THAT MUST BE A COURSE I HAVEN'T TAKEN YET!
THE YOUNG LADY IS REFERRING TO THE SLEIGHT OF HAND I USE IN MY ACT!
WHO ARE YOU?
THE AMAZING WALDO! WHY DON'T YOU LADIES CHECK OUT MY ACT?
THAT'S WHAT I WAS TRYING TO CONVINCE HER TO DO!
AMAZING WALDO MAGIC SHOW
SOON...
THE WATER HAS NOW DISAPPEARED FROM THE MAGIC HAT!
SPLOOSH
OOF!
I'M SO SORRY ABOUT THAT! IT WASN'T SUPPOSED TO HAPPEN THAT WAY!
I'M SENDING YOU MY DRY CLEANING BILL!!
BOO! LET'S GET OUT OF HERE!
BETTY, I'M AFRAID YOUR MAGICIAN IS AWFUL!
2

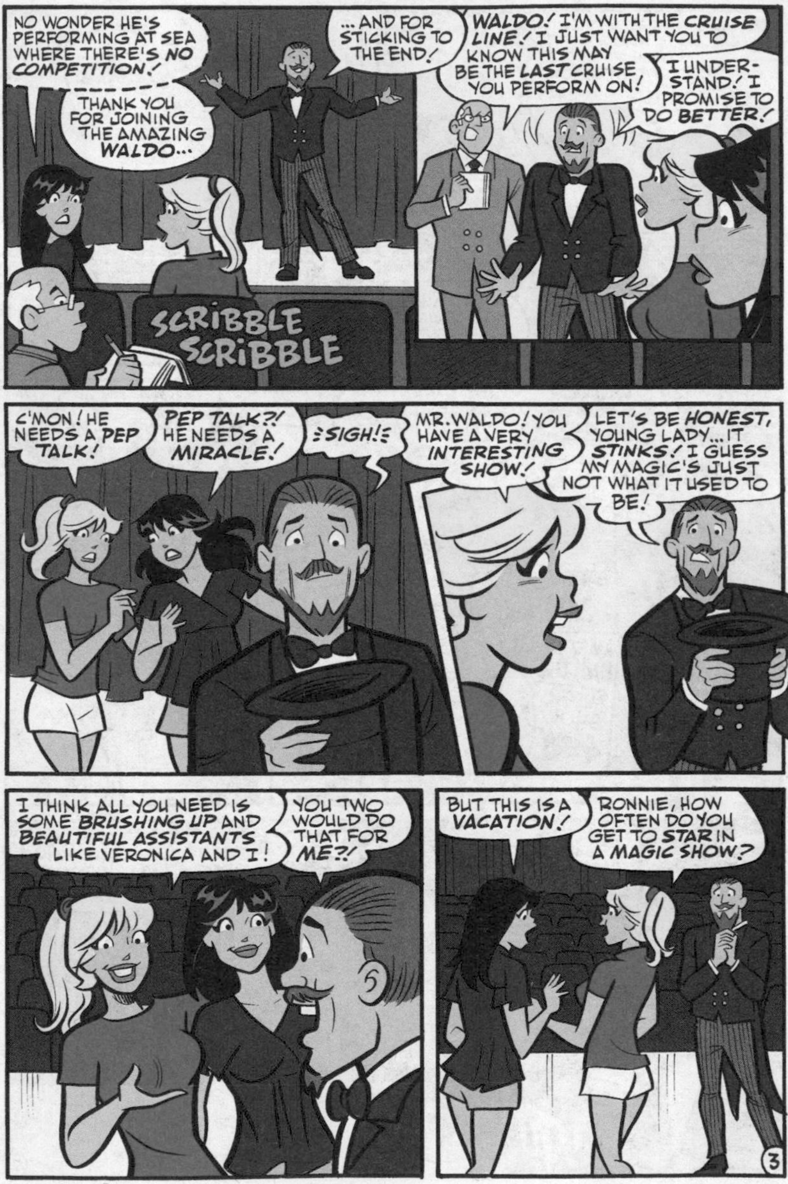
NO WONDER HE'S PERFORMING AT SEA WHERE THERE'S NO COMPETITION!
THANK YOU FOR JOINING THE AMAZING WALDO...
...AND FOR STICKING TO THE END!
SCRIBBLE SCRIBBLE
WALDO! I'M WITH THE CRUISE LINE! I JUST WANT YOU TO KNOW THIS MAY BE THE LAST CRUISE YOU PERFORM ON!
I UNDERSTAND! I PROMISE TO DO BETTER!
C'MON! HE NEEDS A PEP TALK!
PEP TALK?! HE NEEDS A MIRACLE!
SIGH!
MR. WALDO! YOU HAVE A VERY INTERESTING SHOW!
LET'S BE HONEST, YOUNG LADY... IT STINKS! I GUESS MY MAGIC'S JUST NOT WHAT IT USED TO BE!
I THINK ALL YOU NEED IS SOME BRUSHING UP AND BEAUTIFUL ASSISTANTS LIKE VERONICA AND I!
YOU TWO WOULD DO THAT FOR ME?!
BUT THIS IS A VACATION!
RONNIE, HOW OFTEN DO YOU GET TO STAR IN A MAGIC SHOW?
3

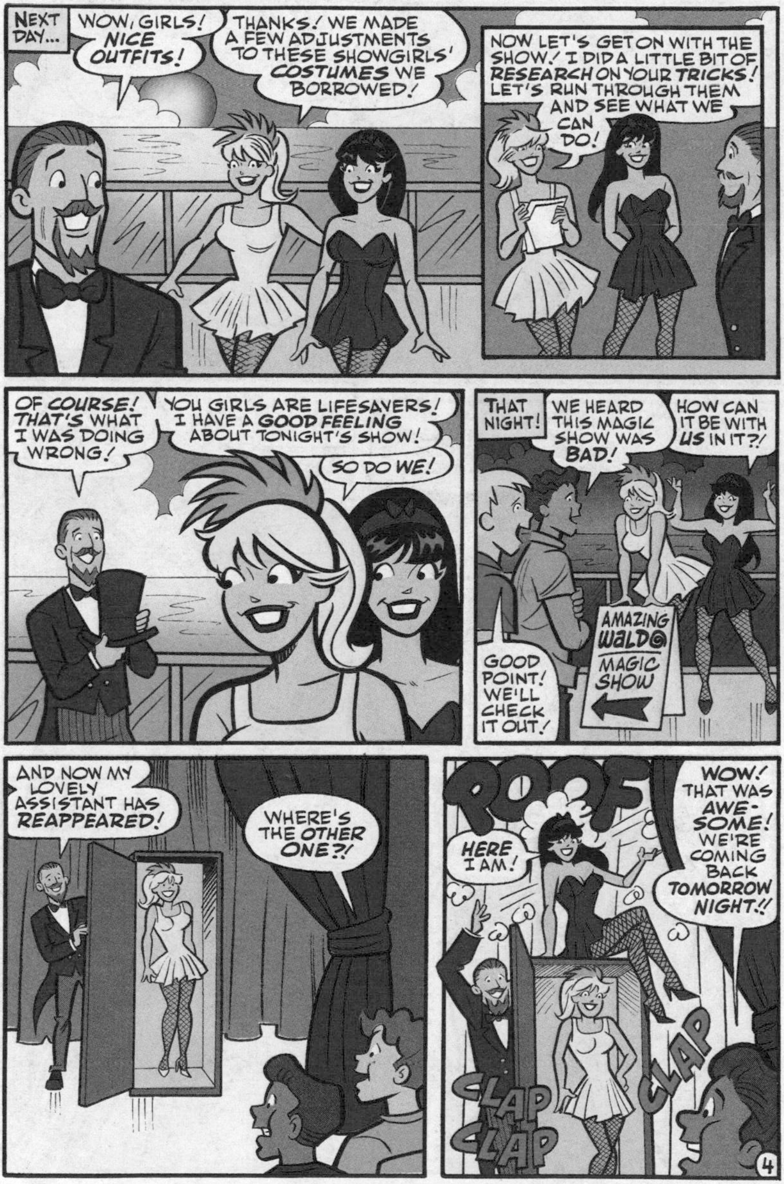
NEXT DAY...
WOW, GIRLS! NICE OUTFITS!
THANKS! WE MADE A FEW ADJUSTMENTS TO THESE SHOWGIRLS' COSTUMES WE BORROWED!
NOW LET'S GET ON WITH THE SHOW! I DID A LITTLE BIT OF RESEARCH ON YOUR TRICKS! LET'S RUN THROUGH THEM AND SEE WHAT WE CAN DO!
OF COURSE! THAT'S WHAT I WAS DOING WRONG!
YOU GIRLS ARE LIFESAVERS! I HAVE A GOOD FEELING ABOUT TONIGHT'S SHOW!
SO DO WE!
THAT NIGHT!
WE HEARD THIS MAGIC SHOW WAS BAD!
HOW CAN IT BE WITH US IN IT?!
AMAZING WALDO MAGIC SHOW
GOOD POINT! WE'LL CHECK IT OUT!
AND NOW MY LOVELY ASSISTANT HAS REAPPEARED!
WHERE'S THE OTHER ONE?!
POOF
HERE I AM!
WOW! THAT WAS AWE-SOME! WE'RE COMING BACK TOMORROW NIGHT!!
CLAP
CLAP
CLAP
4

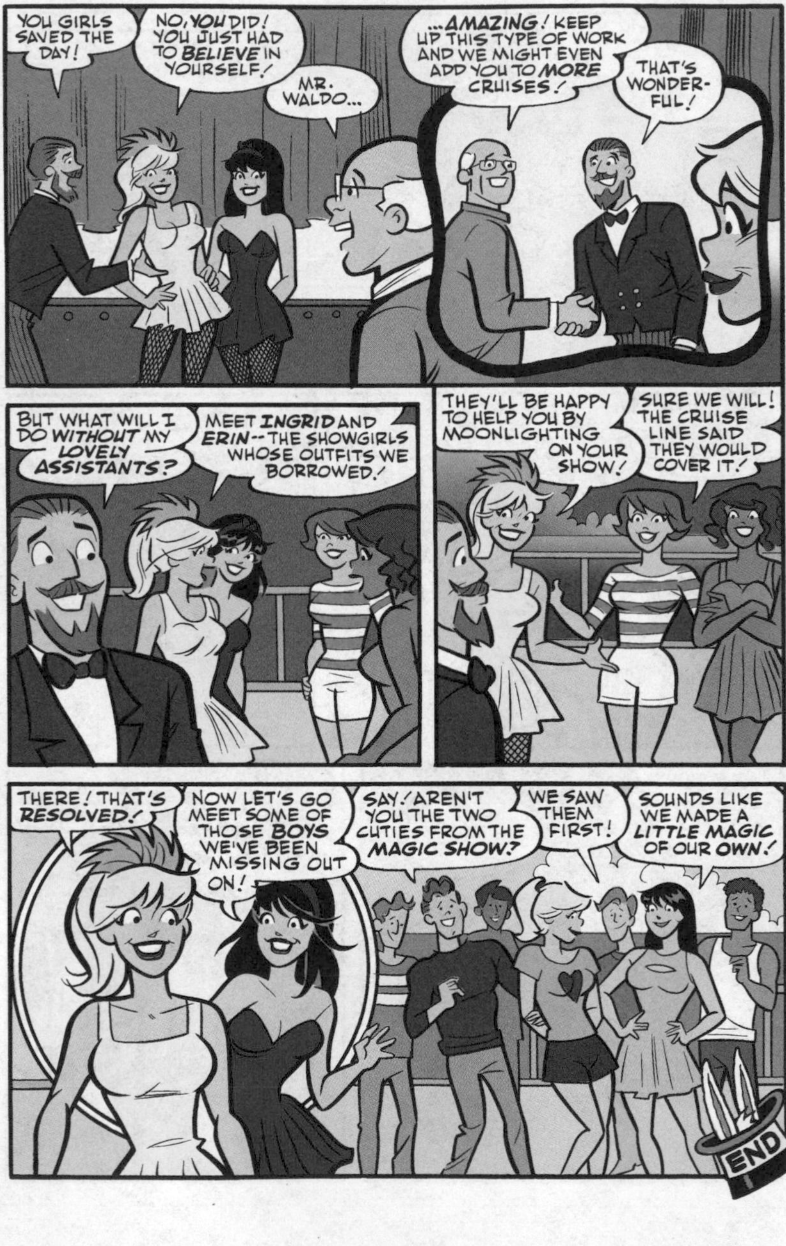
YOU GIRLS SAVED THE DAY!
NO, YOU DID! YOU JUST HAD TO BELIEVE IN YOURSELF!
MR. WALDO...
...AMAZING! KEEP UP THIS TYPE OF WORK AND WE MIGHT EVEN ADD YOU TO MORE CRUISES!
THAT'S WONDERFUL!
BUT WHAT WILL I DO WITHOUT MY LOVELY ASSISTANTS?
MEET INGRID AND ERIN--THE SHOWGIRLS WHOSE OUTFITS WE BORROWED!
THEY'LL BE HAPPY TO HELP YOU BY MOONLIGHTING ON YOUR SHOW!
SURE WE WILL! THE CRUISE LINE SAID THEY WOULD COVER IT!
THERE! THAT'S RESOLVED!
NOW LET'S GO MEET SOME OF THOSE BOYS WE'VE BEEN MISSING OUT ON!
SAY! AREN'T YOU THE TWO CUTIES FROM THE MAGIC SHOW?
WE SAW THEM FIRST!
SOUNDS LIKE WE MADE A LITTLE MAGIC OF OUR OWN!
END

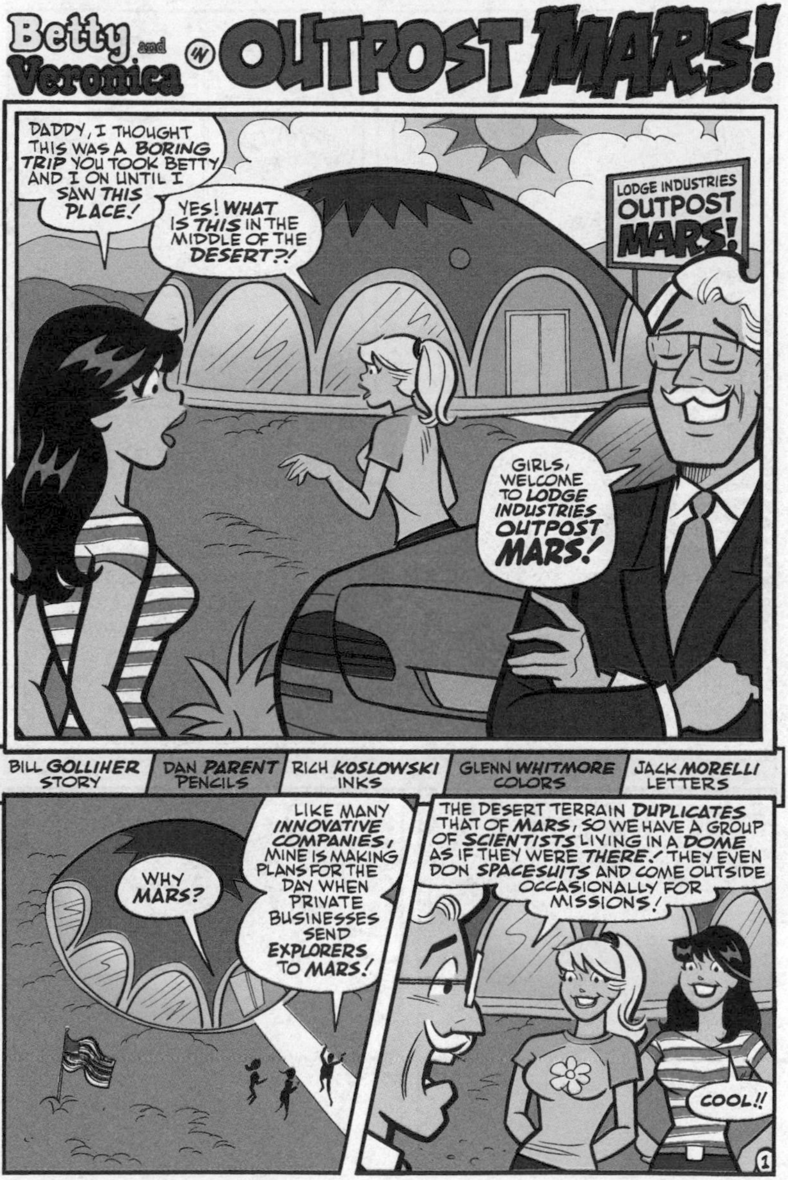

Betty and Veronica in OUTPOST MARS!
DADDY, I THOUGHT THIS WAS A BORING TRIP YOU TOOK BETTY AND I ON UNTIL I SAW THIS PLACE!
YES! WHAT IS THIS IN THE MIDDLE OF THE DESERT?!
LODGE INDUSTRIES OUTPOST MARS!
GIRLS, WELCOME TO LODGE INDUSTRIES OUTPOST MARS!
BILL GOLLIHER STORY
DAN PARENT PENCILS
RICH KOSLOWSKI INKS
GLENN WHITMORE COLORS
JACK MORELLI LETTERS
WHY MARS?
LIKE MANY INNOVATIVE COMPANIES, MINE IS MAKING PLANS FOR THE DAY WHEN PRIVATE BUSINESSES SEND EXPLORERS TO MARS!
THE DESERT TERRAIN DUPLICATES THAT OF MARS, SO WE HAVE A GROUP OF SCIENTISTS LIVING IN A DOME AS IF THEY WERE THERE! THEY EVEN DON SPACESUITS AND COME OUTSIDE OCCASIONALLY FOR MISSIONS!
COOL!!
1

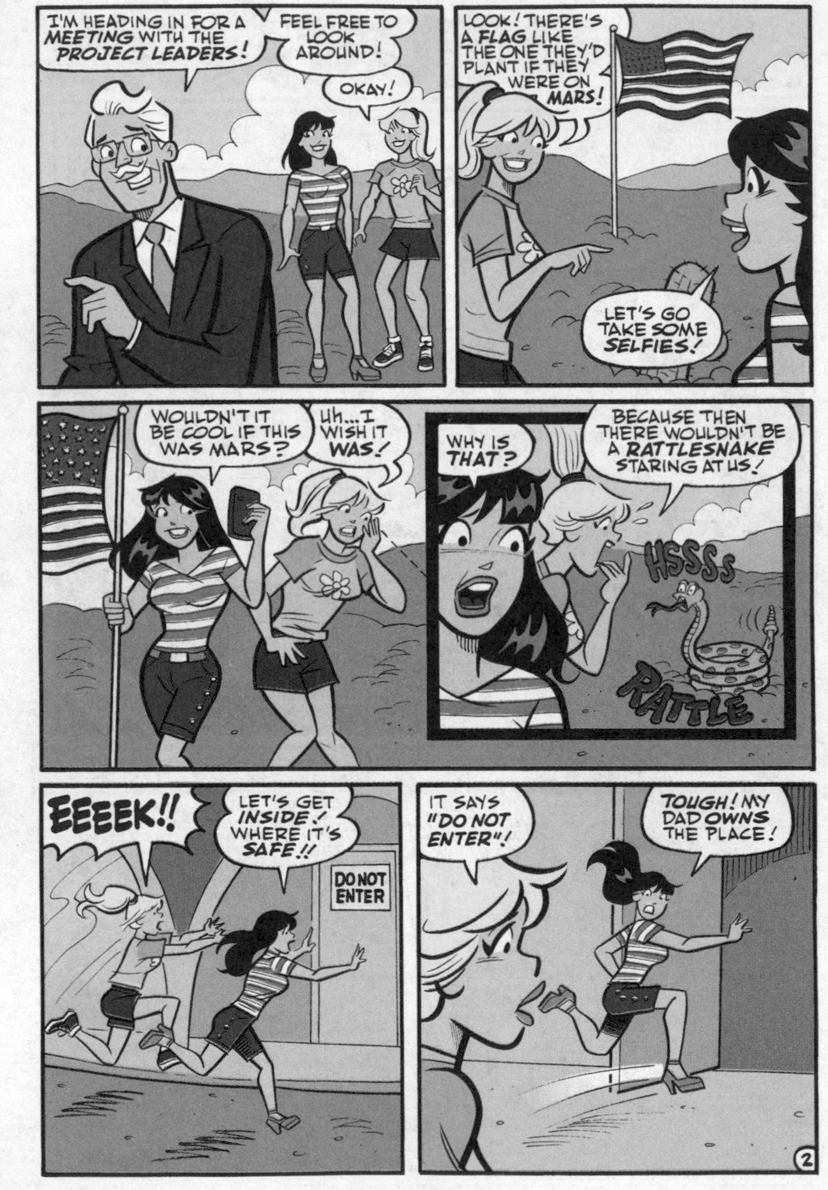

I'M HEADING IN FOR A MEETING WITH THE PROJECT LEADERS!
FEEL FREE TO LOOK AROUND!
OKAY!
LOOK! THERE'S A FLAG LIKE THE ONE THEY'D PLANT IF THEY WERE ON MARS!
LET'S GO TAKE SOME SELFIES!
WOULDN'T IT BE COOL IF THIS WAS MARS?
UH...I WISH IT WAS!
WHY IS THAT?
BECAUSE THEN THERE WOULDN'T BE A RATTLESNAKE STARING AT US!
HSSSS
RATTLE
EEEEK!!
LET'S GET INSIDE! WHERE IT'S SAFE!!
DO NOT ENTER
IT SAYS "DO NOT ENTER"!
TOUGH! MY DAD OWNS THE PLACE!
2

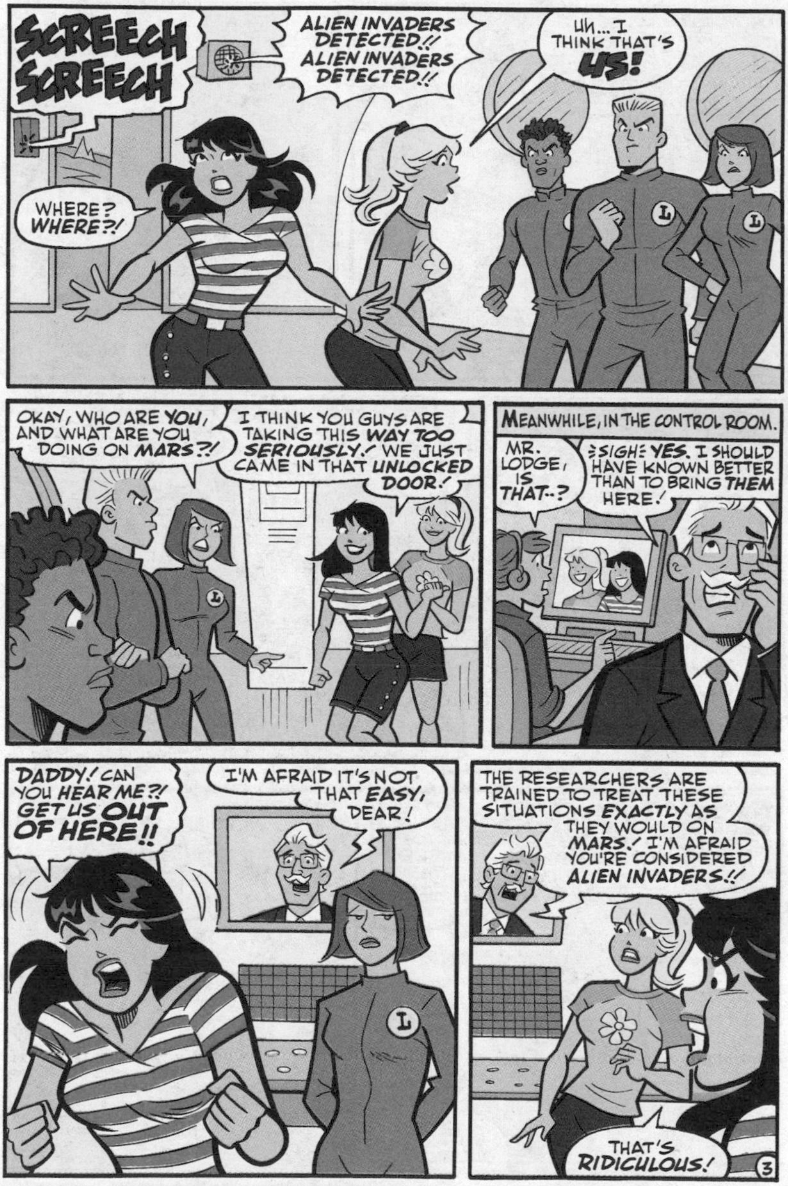
SCREECH SCREECH
ALIEN INVADERS DETECTED!! ALIEN INVADERS DETECTED!!
UH... I THINK THAT'S US!
WHERE? WHERE?!
OKAY, WHO ARE YOU, AND WHAT ARE YOU DOING ON MARS?!
I THINK YOU GUYS ARE TAKING THIS WAY TOO SERIOUSLY! WE JUST CAME IN THAT UNLOCKED DOOR!
MEANWHILE, IN THE CONTROL ROOM.
MR. LODGE, IS THAT--?
SIGH YES. I SHOULD HAVE KNOWN BETTER THAN TO BRING THEM HERE!
DADDY! CAN YOU HEAR ME?! GET US OUT OF HERE!!
I'M AFRAID IT'S NOT THAT EASY, DEAR!
THE RESEARCHERS ARE TRAINED TO TREAT THESE SITUATIONS EXACTLY AS THEY WOULD ON MARS! I'M AFRAID YOU'RE CONSIDERED ALIEN INVADERS!!
THAT'S RIDICULOUS!
3

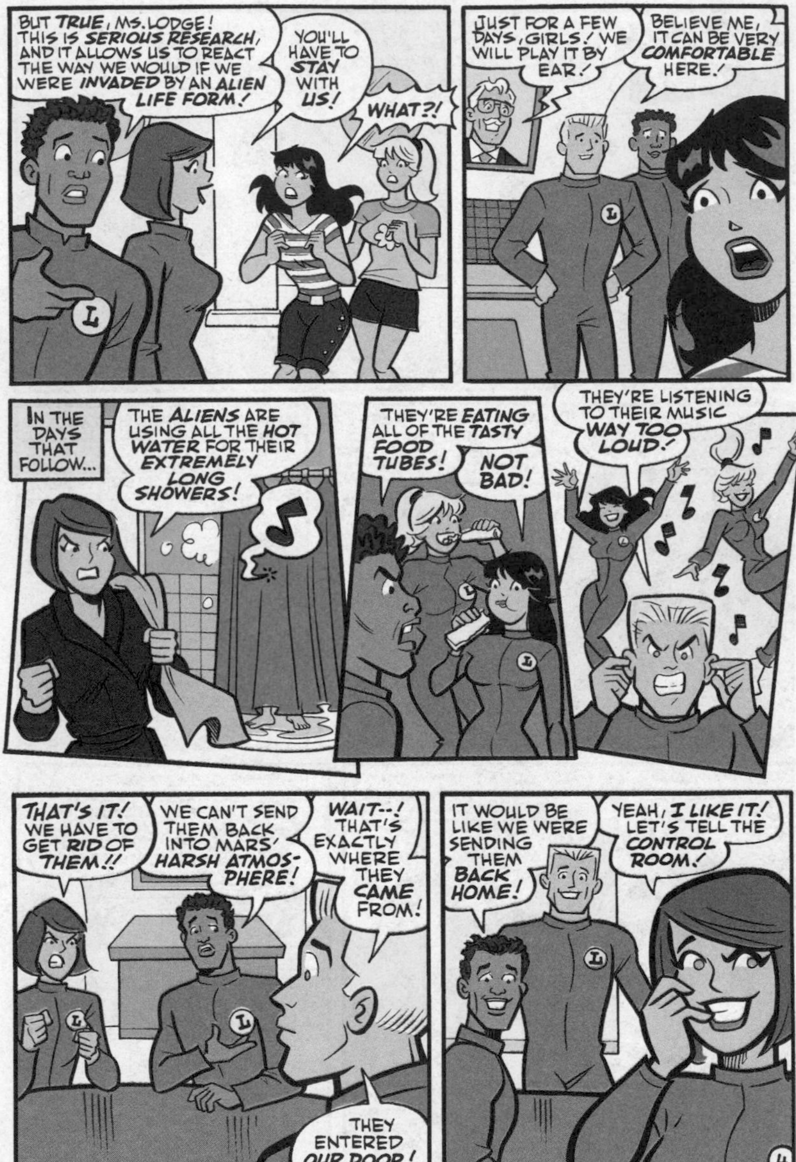
BUT TRUE, MS. LODGE! THIS IS SERIOUS RESEARCH, AND IT ALLOWS US TO REACT THE WAY WE WOULD IF WE WERE INVADED BY AN ALIEN LIFE FORM!
YOU'LL HAVE TO STAY WITH US!
WHAT?!
JUST FOR A FEW DAYS, GIRLS! WE WILL PLAY IT BY EAR!
BELIEVE ME, IT CAN BE VERY COMFORTABLE HERE!
IN THE DAYS THAT FOLLOW...
THE ALIENS ARE USING ALL THE HOT WATER FOR THEIR EXTREMELY LONG SHOWERS!
THEY'RE EATING ALL OF THE TASTY FOOD TUBES!
NOT BAD!
THEY'RE LISTENING TO THEIR MUSIC WAY TOO LOUD!
THAT'S IT! WE HAVE TO GET RID OF THEM!!
WE CAN'T SEND THEM BACK INTO MARS' HARSH ATMOS-PHERE!
WAIT--! THAT'S EXACTLY WHERE THEY CAME FROM!
THEY ENTERED OUR DOOR!
IT WOULD BE LIKE WE WERE SENDING THEM BACK HOME!
YEAH, I LIKE IT! LET'S TELL THE CONTROL ROOM!
4

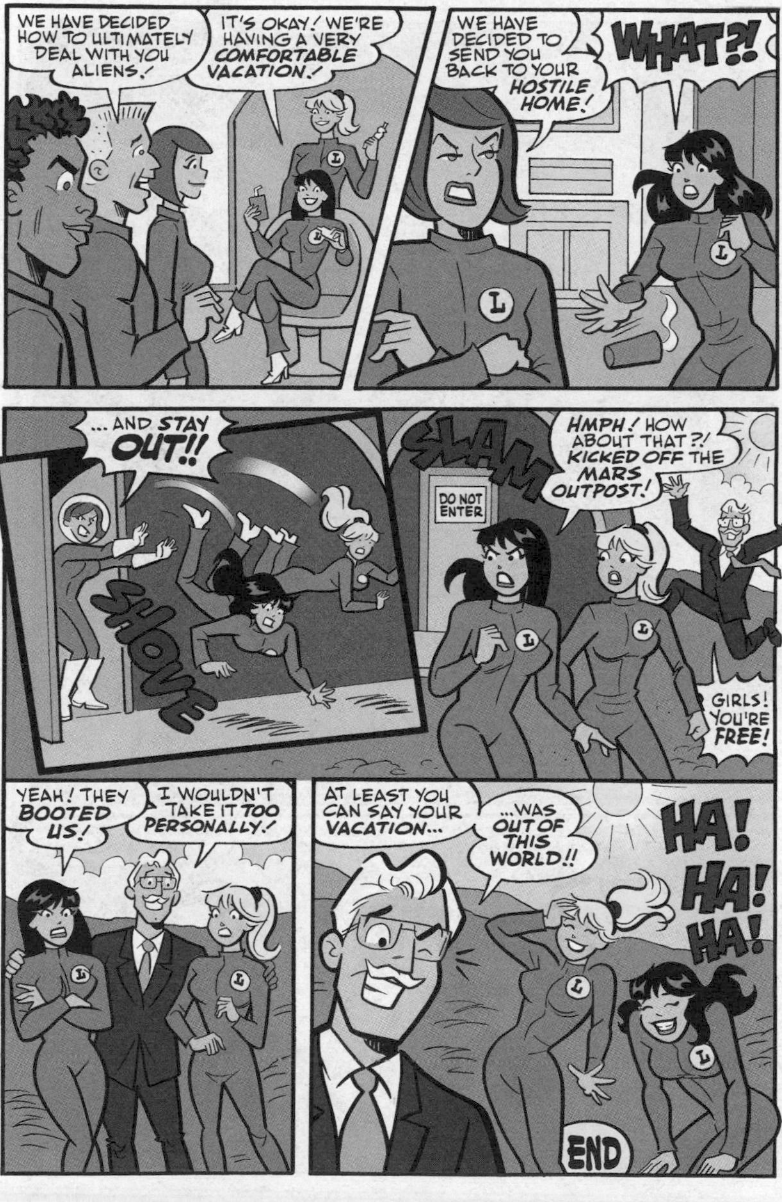
WE HAVE DECIDED HOW TO ULTIMATELY DEAL WITH YOU ALIENS.!
IT'S OKAY! WE'RE HAVING A VERY COMFORTABLE VACATION.!
WE HAVE DECIDED TO SEND YOU BACK TO YOUR HOSTILE HOME!
WHAT?!
...AND STAY OUT!!
SHOVE
SLAM
DO NOT ENTER
HMPH! HOW ABOUT THAT?! KICKED OFF THE MARS OUTPOST!
GIRLS! YOU'RE FREE!
YEAH! THEY BOOTED US!
I WOULDN'T TAKE IT TOO PERSONALLY.!
AT LEAST YOU CAN SAY YOUR VACATION...
...WAS OUT OF THIS WORLD!!
HA! HA! HA!
END

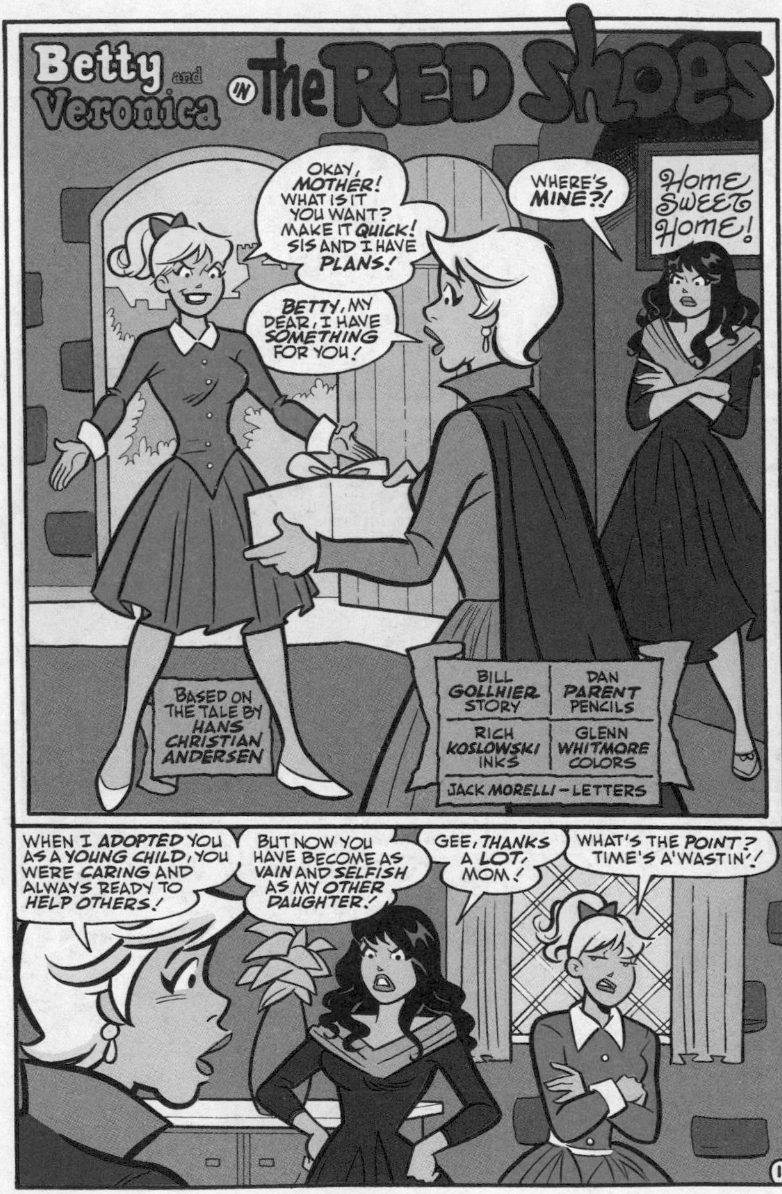
Betty and Veronica in The RED Shoes
OKAY, MOTHER! WHAT IS IT YOU WANT? MAKE IT QUICK! SIS AND I HAVE PLANS!
BETTY, MY DEAR, I HAVE SOMETHING FOR YOU!
WHERE'S MINE?!
HOME SWEET HOME!
BASED ON THE TALE BY HANS CHRISTIAN ANDERSEN
BILL GOLLHIER STORY
DAN PARENT PENCILS
RICH KOSLOWSKI INKS
GLENN WHITMORE COLORS
JACK MORELLI – LETTERS
WHEN I ADOPTED YOU AS A YOUNG CHILD, YOU WERE CARING AND ALWAYS READY TO HELP OTHERS!
BUT NOW YOU HAVE BECOME AS VAIN AND SELFISH AS MY OTHER DAUGHTER!
GEE, THANKS A LOT, MOM!
WHAT'S THE POINT? TIME'S A'WASTIN'!
1

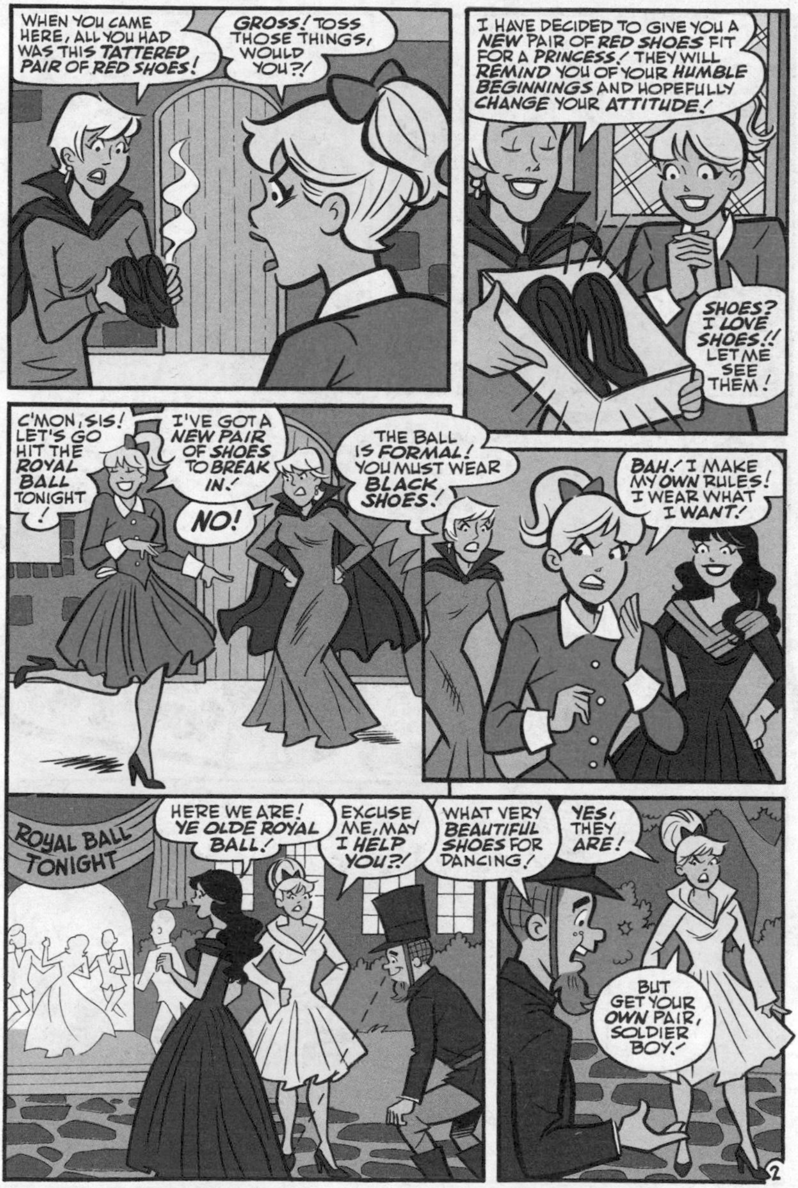
WHEN YOU CAME HERE, ALL YOU HAD WAS THIS TATTERED PAIR OF RED SHOES!
GROSS! TOSS THOSE THINGS, WOULD YOU?!
I HAVE DECIDED TO GIVE YOU A NEW PAIR OF RED SHOES FIT FOR A PRINCESS! THEY WILL REMIND YOU OF YOUR HUMBLE BEGINNINGS AND HOPEFULLY CHANGE YOUR ATTITUDE!
SHOES? I LOVE SHOES!! LET ME SEE THEM!
C'MON, SIS! LET'S GO HIT THE ROYAL BALL TONIGHT!
I'VE GOT A NEW PAIR OF SHOES TO BREAK IN!
NO!
THE BALL IS FORMAL! YOU MUST WEAR BLACK SHOES!
BAH! I MAKE MY OWN RULES! I WEAR WHAT I WANT!
ROYAL BALL TONIGHT
HERE WE ARE! YE OLDE ROYAL BALL!
EXCUSE ME, MAY I HELP YOU?!
WHAT VERY BEAUTIFUL SHOES FOR DANCING!
YES, THEY ARE!
BUT GET YOUR OWN PAIR, SOLDIER BOY!
2

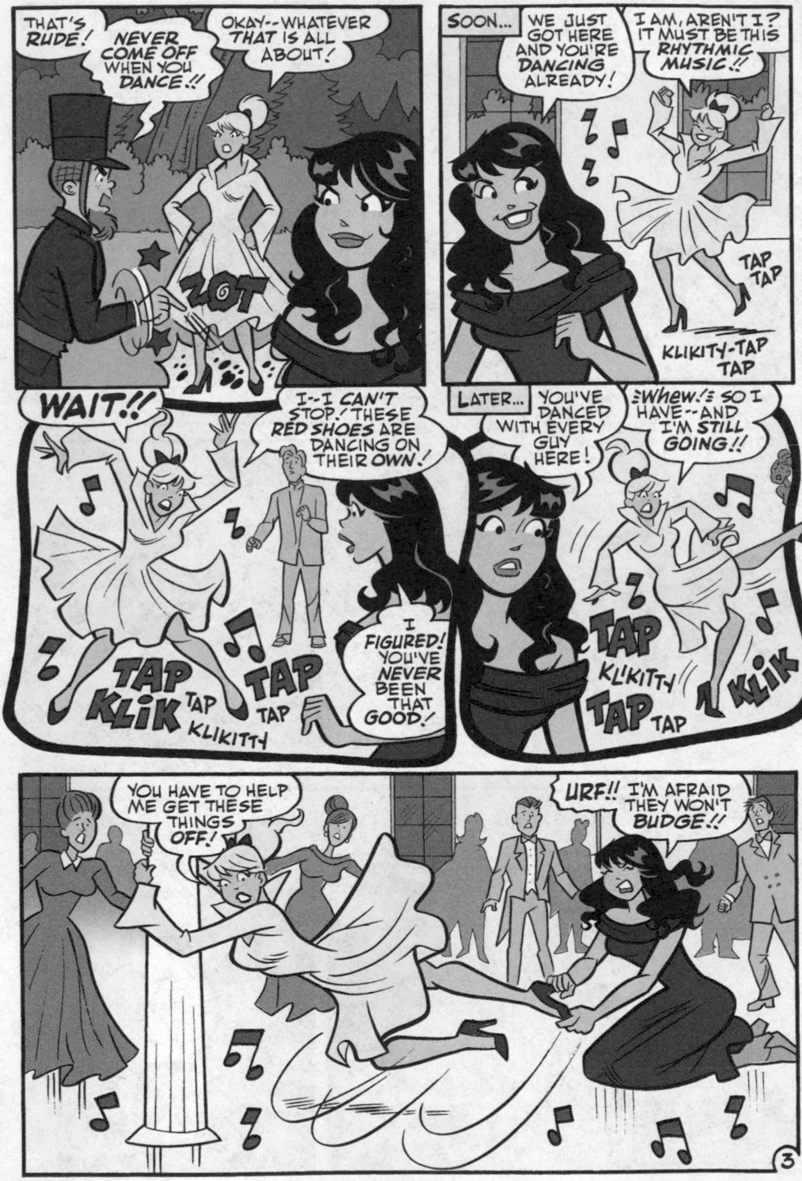
THAT'S RUDE!
NEVER COME OFF WHEN YOU DANCE!!
OKAY--WHATEVER THAT IS ALL ABOUT!
ZOT
SOON...
WE JUST GOT HERE AND YOU'RE DANCING ALREADY!
I AM, AREN'T I? IT MUST BE THIS RHYTHMIC MUSIC!!
TAP TAP
KLIKITY-TAP TAP
WAIT!!
I--I CAN'T STOP! THESE RED SHOES ARE DANCING ON THEIR OWN!
I FIGURED! YOU'VE NEVER BEEN THAT GOOD!
TAP KLIK TAP TAP TAP KLIKITTY
LATER...
YOU'VE DANCED WITH EVERY GUY HERE!
WHEW! SO I HAVE--AND I'M STILL GOING!!
TAP KLIKITTY TAP TAP KLIK
YOU HAVE TO HELP ME GET THESE THINGS OFF!
URF!! I'M AFRAID THEY WON'T BUDGE!!
3

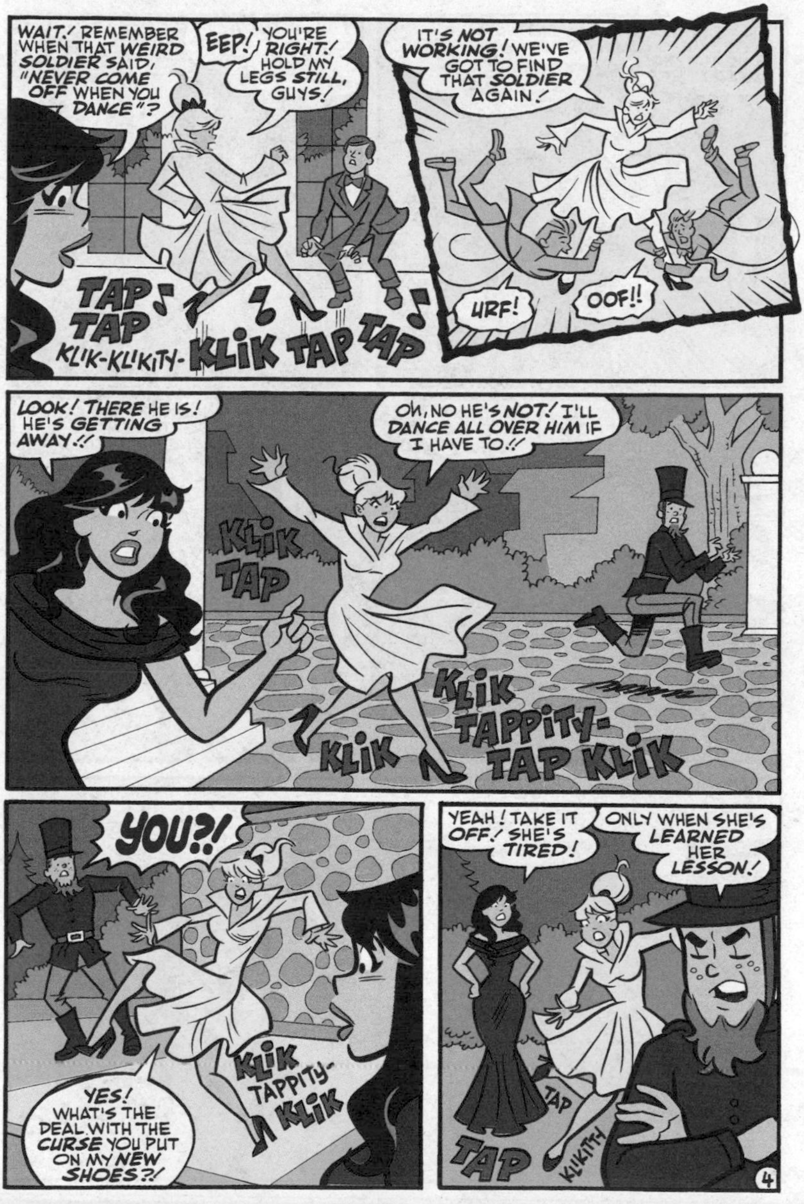
WAIT! REMEMBER WHEN THAT WEIRD SOLDIER SAID, "NEVER COME OFF WHEN YOU DANCE"?
EEP!
YOU'RE RIGHT! HOLD MY LEGS STILL, GUYS!
TAP TAP KLIK-KLIKITY-KLIK TAP TAP
IT'S NOT WORKING! WE'VE GOT TO FIND THAT SOLDIER AGAIN!
URF!
OOF!!
LOOK! THERE HE IS! HE'S GETTING AWAY!!
OH, NO HE'S NOT! I'LL DANCE ALL OVER HIM IF I HAVE TO!!
KLIK TAP
KLIK TAPPITY-TAP KLIK
KLIK
YOU?!
YES! WHAT'S THE DEAL WITH THE CURSE YOU PUT ON MY NEW SHOES?!
KLIK TAPPITY-KLIK
YEAH! TAKE IT OFF! SHE'S TIRED!
ONLY WHEN SHE'S LEARNED HER LESSON!
TAP
TAP
KLIKITY
4

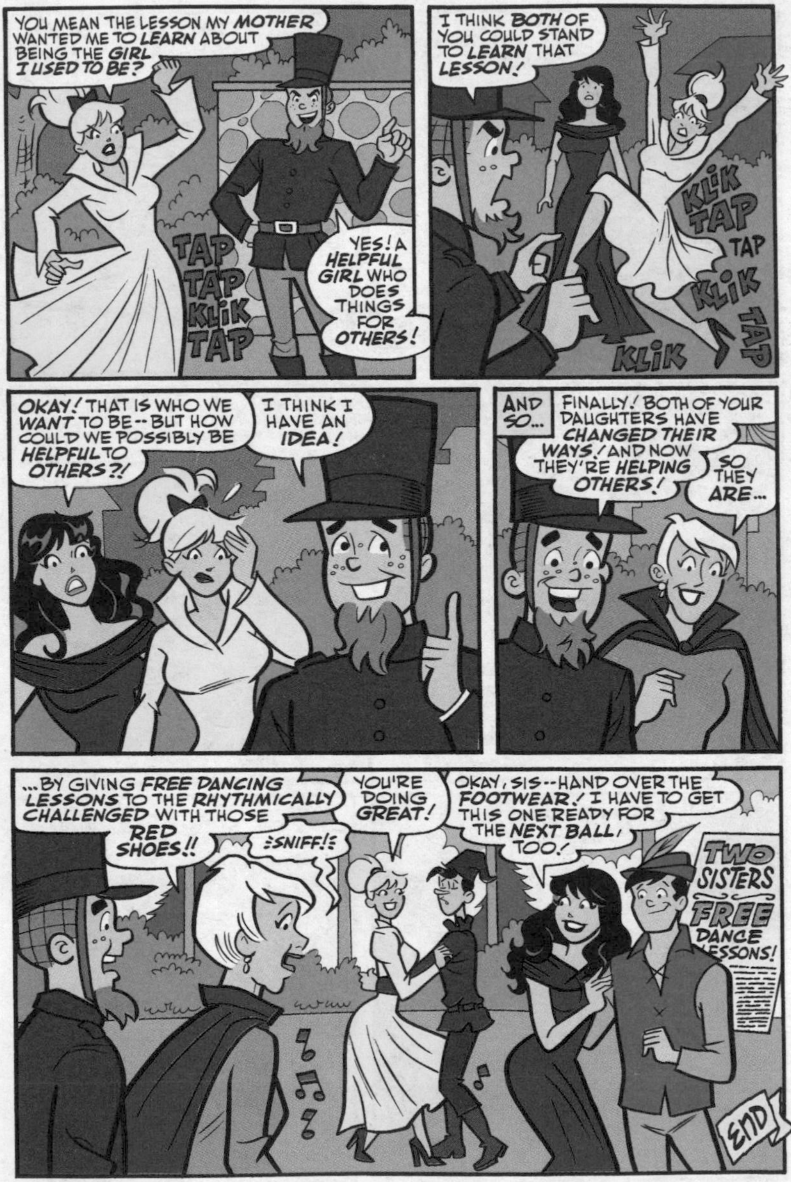
YOU MEAN THE LESSON MY MOTHER WANTED ME TO LEARN ABOUT BEING THE GIRL I USED TO BE?
YES! A HELPFUL GIRL WHO DOES THINGS FOR OTHERS!
TAP TAP KLIK TAP
I THINK BOTH OF YOU COULD STAND TO LEARN THAT LESSON!
KLIK TAP TAP KLIK TAP KLIK
OKAY! THAT IS WHO WE WANT TO BE -- BUT HOW COULD WE POSSIBLY BE HELPFUL TO OTHERS?!
I THINK I HAVE AN IDEA!
AND SO...
FINALLY! BOTH OF YOUR DAUGHTERS HAVE CHANGED THEIR WAYS! AND NOW THEY'RE HELPING OTHERS!
SO THEY ARE...
...BY GIVING FREE DANCING LESSONS TO THE RHYTHMICALLY CHALLENGED WITH THOSE RED SHOES!!
SNIFF!
YOU'RE DOING GREAT!
OKAY, SIS--HAND OVER THE FOOTWEAR! I HAVE TO GET THIS ONE READY FOR THE NEXT BALL, TOO!
TWO SISTERS FREE DANCE LESSONS!
END

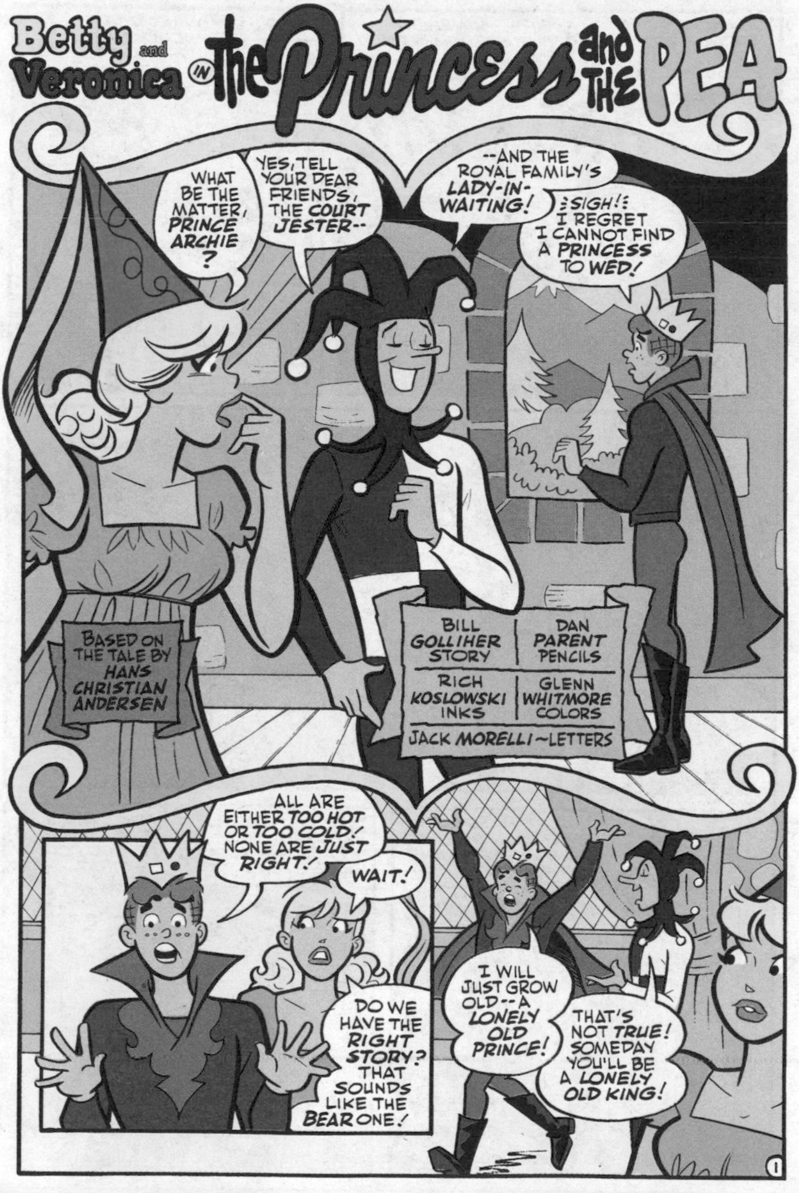
Betty and Veronica in The Princess and the Pea
WHAT BE THE MATTER, PRINCE ARCHIE?
YES, TELL YOUR DEAR FRIENDS, THE COURT JESTER--
--AND THE ROYAL FAMILY'S LADY-IN-WAITING!
SIGH! I REGRET I CANNOT FIND A PRINCESS TO WED!
BASED ON THE TALE BY HANS CHRISTIAN ANDERSEN
BILL GOLLIHER STORY
DAN PARENT PENCILS
RICH KOSLOWSKI INKS
GLENN WHITMORE COLORS
JACK MORELLI~LETTERS
ALL ARE EITHER TOO HOT OR TOO COLD! NONE ARE JUST RIGHT!
WAIT!
DO WE HAVE THE RIGHT STORY? THAT SOUNDS LIKE THE BEAR ONE!
I WILL JUST GROW OLD--A LONELY OLD PRINCE!
THAT'S NOT TRUE! SOMEDAY YOU'LL BE A LONELY OLD KING!
1

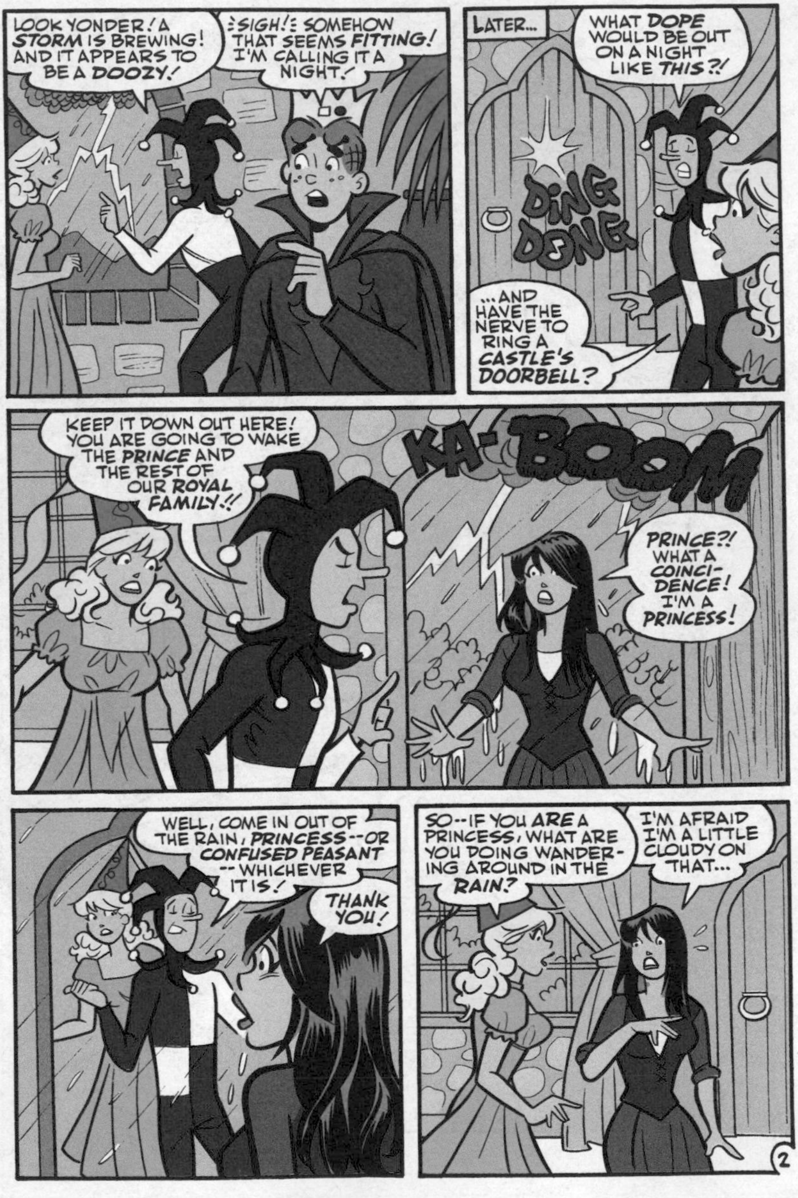

LOOK YONDER! A STORM IS BREWING! AND IT APPEARS TO BE A DOOZY!
SIGH! SOMEHOW THAT SEEMS FITTING! I'M CALLING IT A NIGHT!
LATER...
WHAT DOPE WOULD BE OUT ON A NIGHT LIKE THIS?!
DING DONG
...AND HAVE THE NERVE TO RING A CASTLE'S DOORBELL?
KEEP IT DOWN OUT HERE! YOU ARE GOING TO WAKE THE PRINCE AND THE REST OF OUR ROYAL FAMILY!!
KA-BOOM
PRINCE?! WHAT A COINCI-DENCE! I'M A PRINCESS!
WELL, COME IN OUT OF THE RAIN, PRINCESS--OR CONFUSED PEASANT --WHICHEVER IT IS!
THANK YOU!
SO--IF YOU ARE A PRINCESS, WHAT ARE YOU DOING WANDER-ING AROUND IN THE RAIN?
I'M AFRAID I'M A LITTLE CLOUDY ON THAT...
2

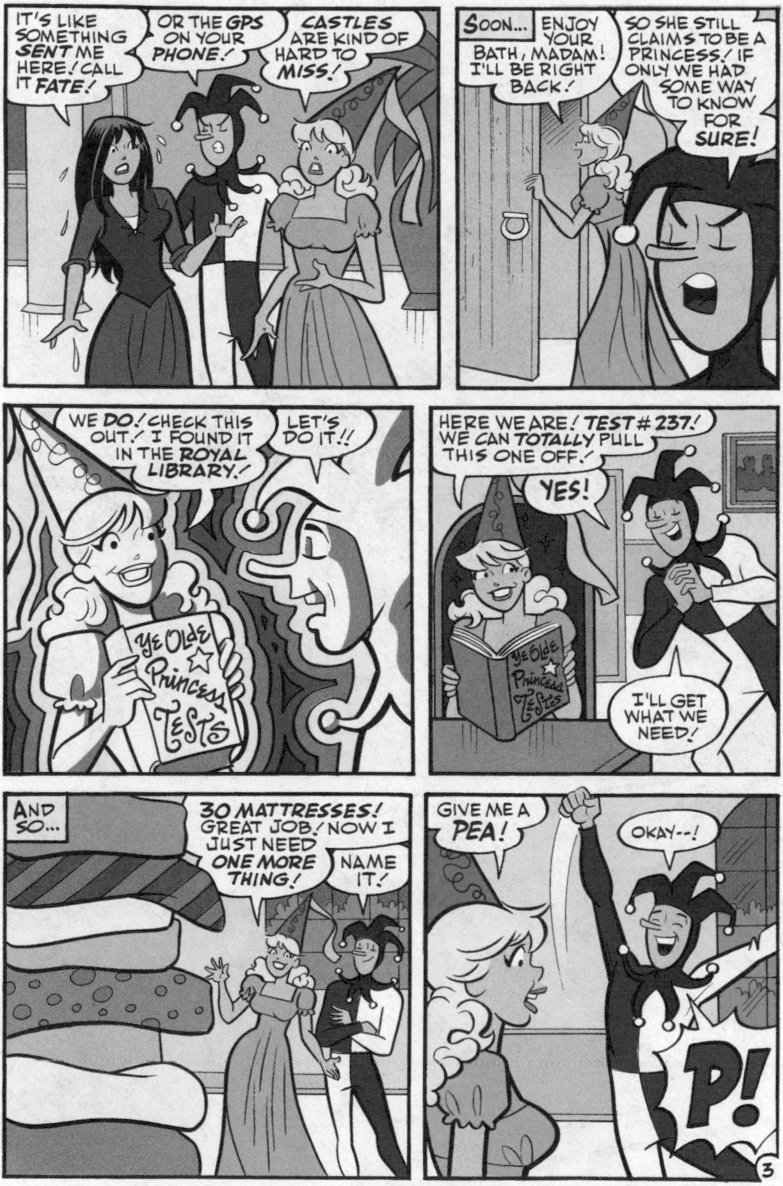
IT'S LIKE SOMETHING SENT ME HERE! CALL IT FATE!
OR THE GPS ON YOUR PHONE!
CASTLES ARE KIND OF HARD TO MISS!
SOON...
ENJOY YOUR BATH, MADAM! I'LL BE RIGHT BACK!
SO SHE STILL CLAIMS TO BE A PRINCESS! IF ONLY WE HAD SOME WAY TO KNOW FOR SURE!
WE DO! CHECK THIS OUT! I FOUND IT IN THE ROYAL LIBRARY!
LET'S DO IT!!
YE OLDE PRINCESS TESTS
HERE WE ARE! TEST # 237! WE CAN TOTALLY PULL THIS ONE OFF!
YES!
YE OLDE PRINCESS TESTS
I'LL GET WHAT WE NEED!
AND SO...
30 MATTRESSES! GREAT JOB! NOW I JUST NEED ONE MORE THING!
NAME IT!
GIVE ME A PEA!
OKAY--!
P!
3

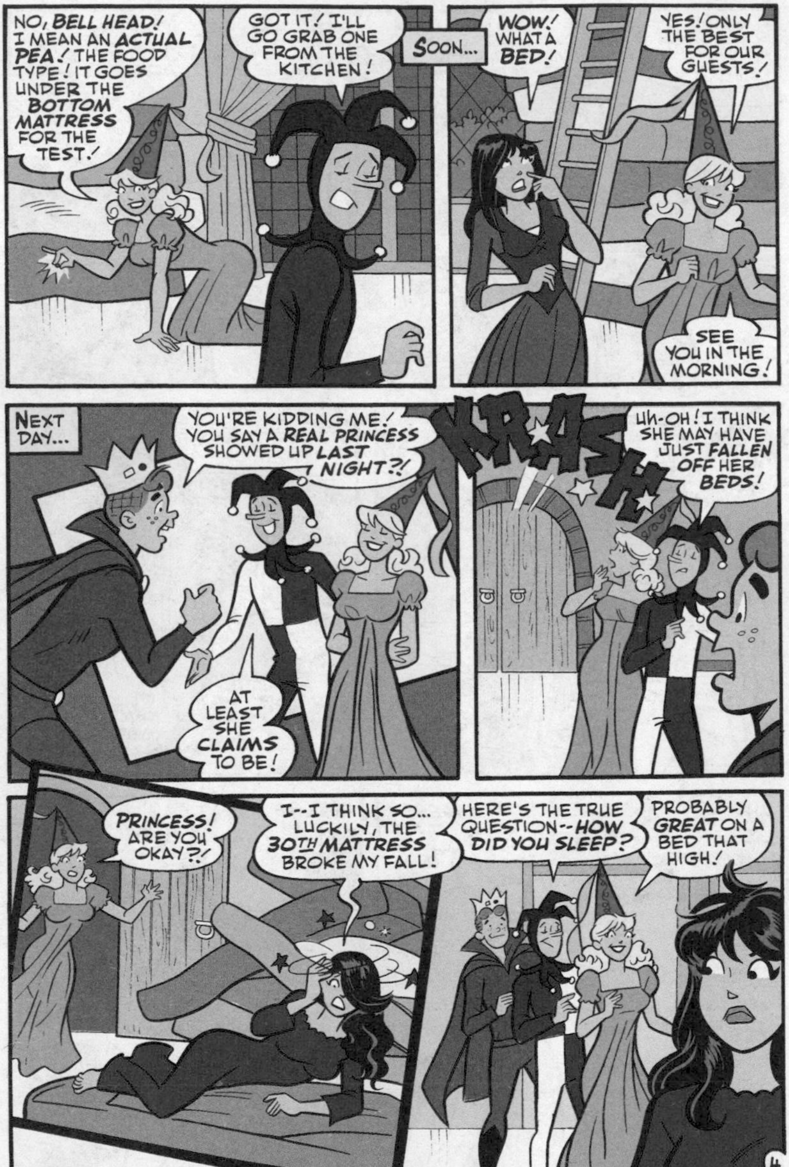
NO, BELL HEAD! I MEAN AN ACTUAL PEA! THE FOOD TYPE! IT GOES UNDER THE BOTTOM MATTRESS FOR THE TEST!
GOT IT! I'LL GO GRAB ONE FROM THE KITCHEN!
SOON...
WOW! WHAT A BED!
YES! ONLY THE BEST FOR OUR GUESTS!
SEE YOU IN THE MORNING!
NEXT DAY...
YOU'RE KIDDING ME! YOU SAY A REAL PRINCESS SHOWED UP LAST NIGHT?!
AT LEAST SHE CLAIMS TO BE!
KRASH
UH-OH! I THINK SHE MAY HAVE JUST FALLEN OFF HER BEDS!
PRINCESS! ARE YOU OKAY?!
I--I THINK SO... LUCKILY, THE 30TH MATTRESS BROKE MY FALL!
HERE'S THE TRUE QUESTION--HOW DID YOU SLEEP?
PROBABLY GREAT ON A BED THAT HIGH!
4

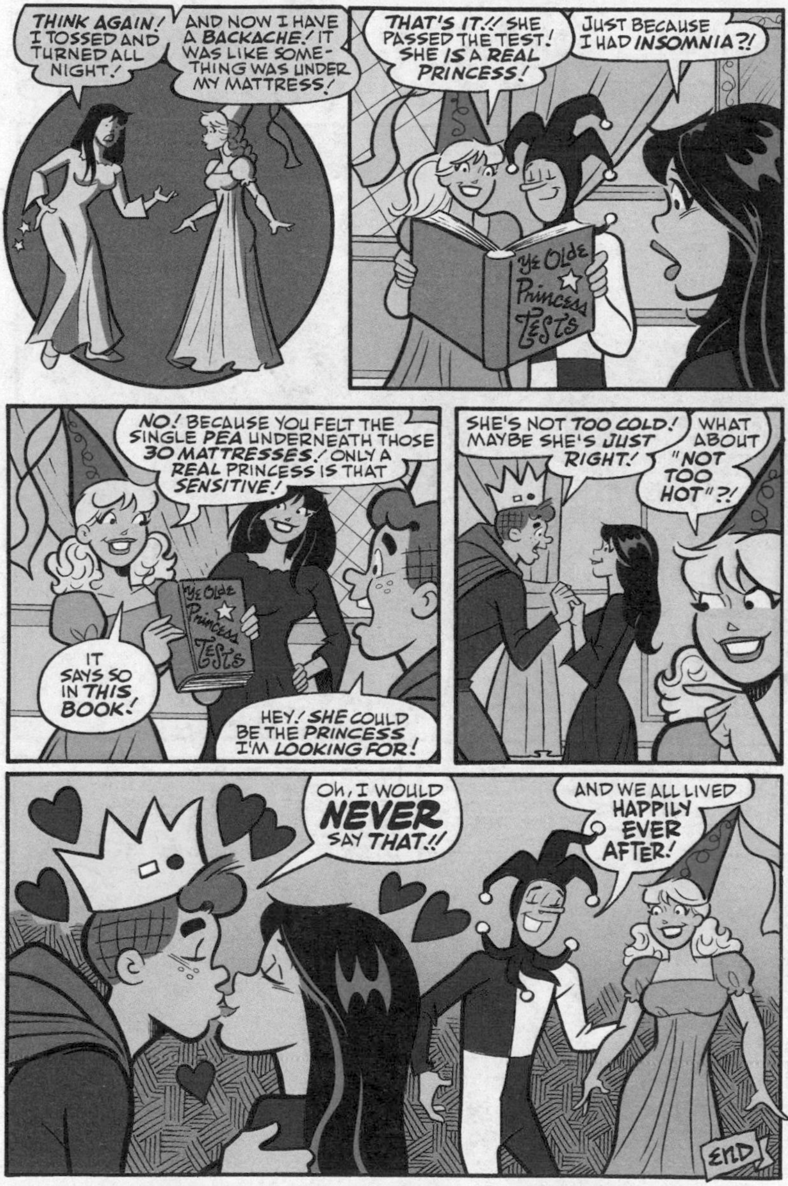
THINK AGAIN! I TOSSED AND TURNED ALL NIGHT!
AND NOW I HAVE A BACKACHE! IT WAS LIKE SOME-THING WAS UNDER MY MATTRESS!
THAT'S IT!!! SHE PASSED THE TEST! SHE IS A REAL PRINCESS!
JUST BECAUSE I HAD INSOMNIA?!
Ye Olde Princess Tests
NO! BECAUSE YOU FELT THE SINGLE PEA UNDERNEATH THOSE 30 MATTRESSES! ONLY A REAL PRINCESS IS THAT SENSITIVE!
IT SAYS SO IN THIS BOOK!
Ye Olde Princess Tests
HEY! SHE COULD BE THE PRINCESS I'M LOOKING FOR!
SHE'S NOT TOO COLD! MAYBE SHE'S JUST RIGHT!
WHAT ABOUT "NOT TOO HOT"?!
Oh, I WOULD NEVER SAY THAT!!
AND WE ALL LIVED HAPPILY EVER AFTER!
END

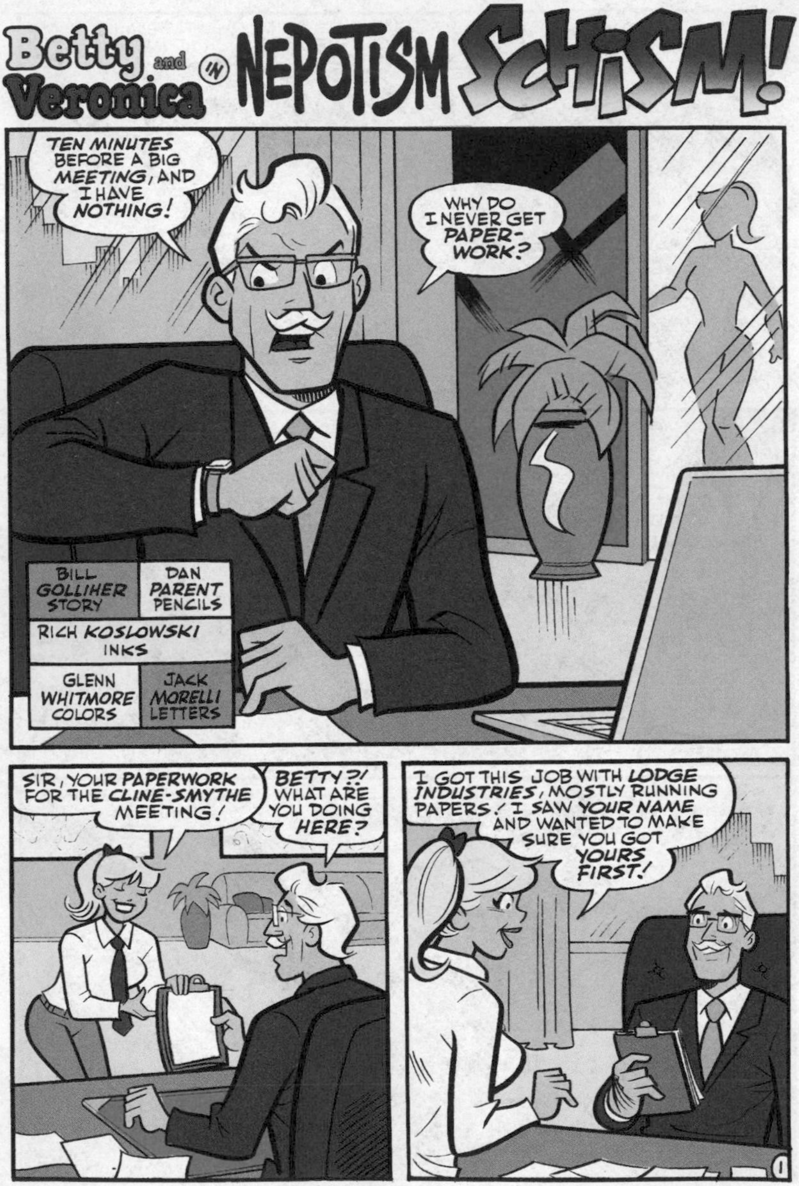
Betty and Veronica in NEPOTISM SCHISM!
TEN MINUTES BEFORE A BIG MEETING, AND I HAVE NOTHING!
WHY DO I NEVER GET PAPER-WORK?
BILL GOLLIHER STORY
DAN PARENT PENCILS
RICH KOSLOWSKI INKS
GLENN WHITMORE COLORS
JACK MORELLI LETTERS
SIR, YOUR PAPERWORK FOR THE CLINE-SMYTHE MEETING!
BETTY?! WHAT ARE YOU DOING HERE?
I GOT THIS JOB WITH LODGE INDUSTRIES, MOSTLY RUNNING PAPERS! I SAW YOUR NAME AND WANTED TO MAKE SURE YOU GOT YOURS FIRST!
1

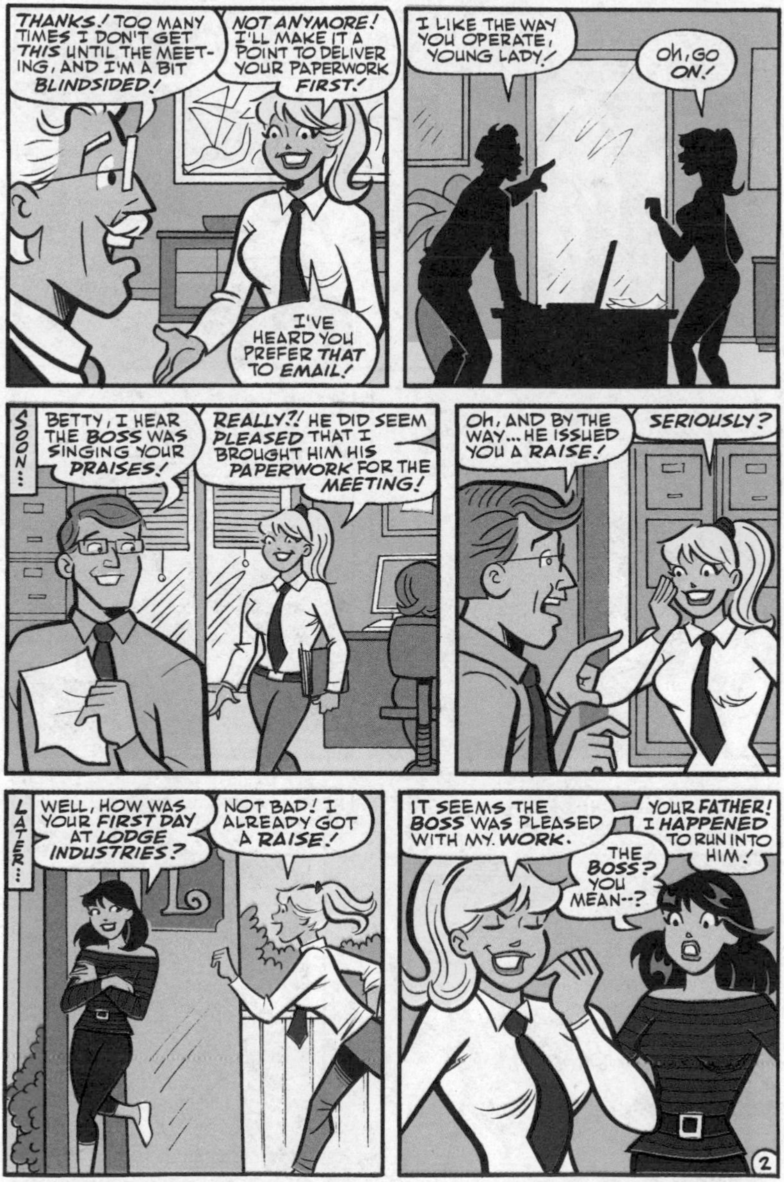
THANKS! TOO MANY TIMES I DON'T GET THIS UNTIL THE MEETING, AND I'M A BIT BLINDSIDED!
NOT ANYMORE! I'LL MAKE IT A POINT TO DELIVER YOUR PAPERWORK FIRST!
I'VE HEARD YOU PREFER THAT TO EMAIL!
I LIKE THE WAY YOU OPERATE, YOUNG LADY!
OH, GO ON!
SOON...
BETTY, I HEAR THE BOSS WAS SINGING YOUR PRAISES!
REALLY?! HE DID SEEM PLEASED THAT I BROUGHT HIM HIS PAPERWORK FOR THE MEETING!
OH, AND BY THE WAY... HE ISSUED YOU A RAISE!
SERIOUSLY?
LATER...
WELL, HOW WAS YOUR FIRST DAY AT LODGE INDUSTRIES?
NOT BAD! I ALREADY GOT A RAISE!
IT SEEMS THE BOSS WAS PLEASED WITH MY WORK.
THE BOSS? YOU MEAN--?
YOUR FATHER! I HAPPENED TO RUN INTO HIM!
2

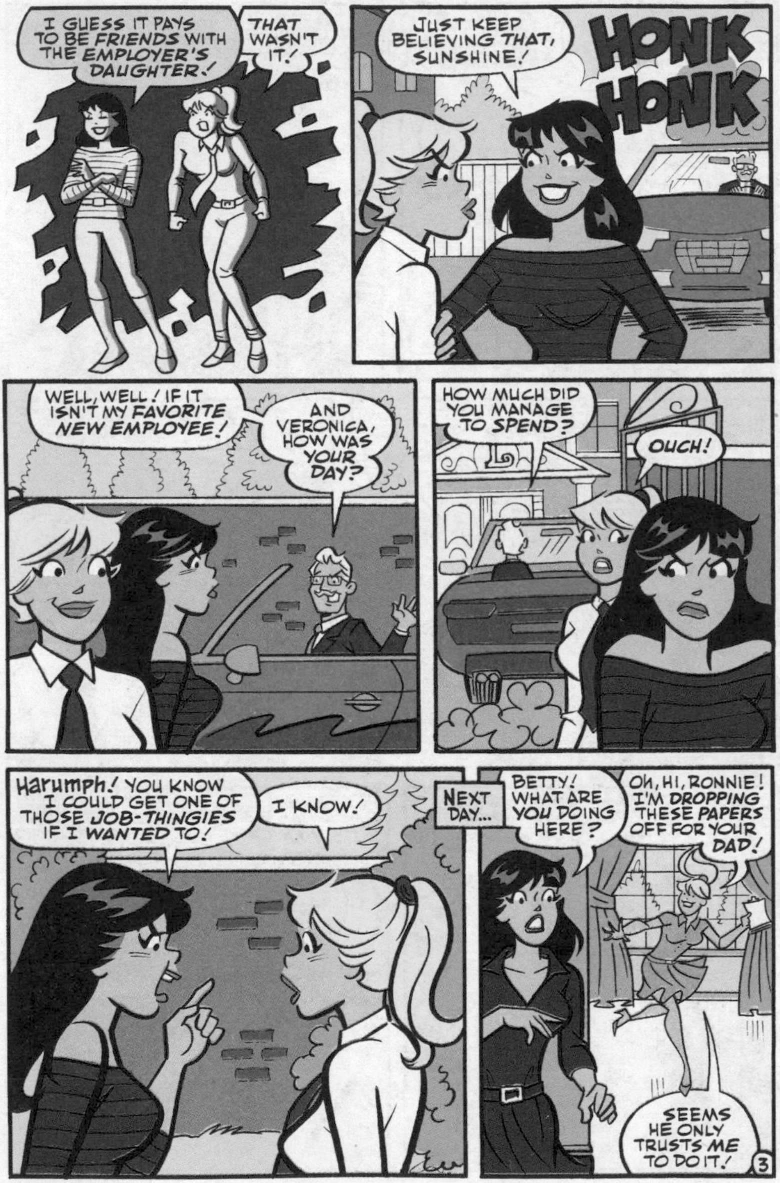
I GUESS IT PAYS TO BE FRIENDS WITH THE EMPLOYER'S DAUGHTER!
THAT WASN'T IT!
JUST KEEP BELIEVING THAT, SUNSHINE!
HONK HONK
WELL, WELL! IF IT ISN'T MY FAVORITE NEW EMPLOYEE!
AND VERONICA, HOW WAS YOUR DAY?
HOW MUCH DID YOU MANAGE TO SPEND?
OUCH!
Harumph! YOU KNOW I COULD GET ONE OF THOSE JOB-THINGIES IF I WANTED TO!
I KNOW!
NEXT DAY...
BETTY! WHAT ARE YOU DOING HERE?
Oh, HI, RONNIE! I'M DROPPING THESE PAPERS OFF FOR YOUR DAD!
SEEMS HE ONLY TRUSTS ME TO DO IT!
3

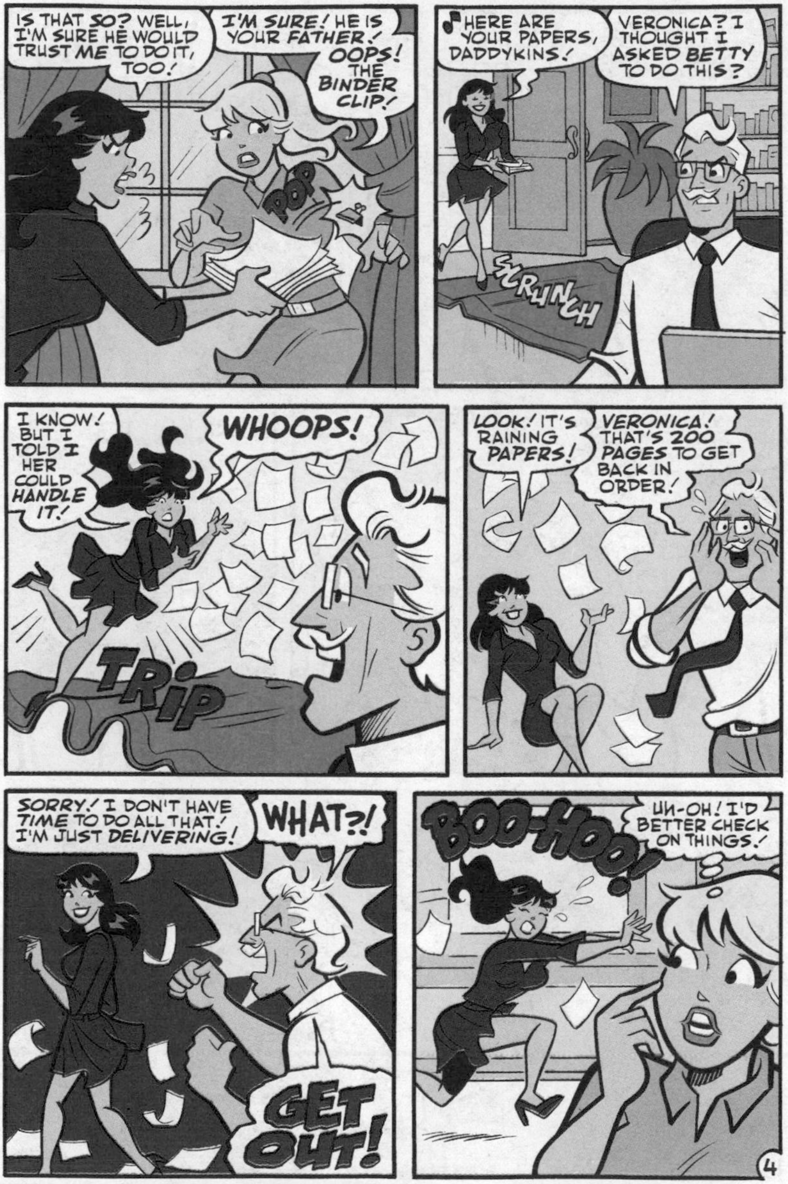
IS THAT SO? WELL, I'M SURE HE WOULD TRUST ME TO DO IT, TOO!
I'M SURE! HE IS YOUR FATHER!
OOPS! THE BINDER CLIP!
POP
HERE ARE YOUR PAPERS, DADDYKINS!
VERONICA? I THOUGHT I ASKED BETTY TO DO THIS?
SCRUNCH
I KNOW! BUT I TOLD HER I COULD HANDLE IT!
WHOOPS!
TRIP
LOOK! IT'S RAINING PAPERS!
VERONICA! THAT'S 200 PAGES TO GET BACK IN ORDER!
SORRY! I DON'T HAVE TIME TO DO ALL THAT! I'M JUST DELIVERING!
WHAT?!
GET OUT!
BOO-HOO!
UH-OH! I'D BETTER CHECK ON THINGS!
4

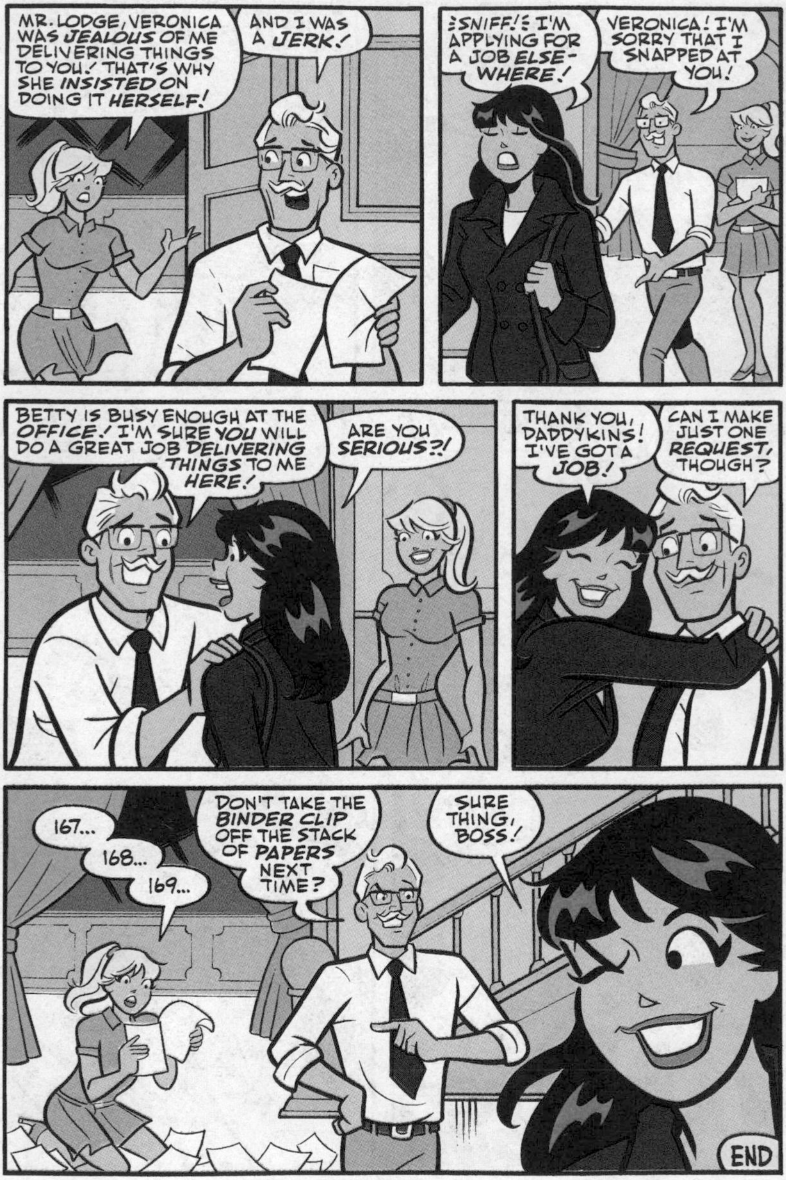
MR. LODGE, VERONICA WAS JEALOUS OF ME DELIVERING THINGS TO YOU! THAT'S WHY SHE INSISTED ON DOING IT HERSELF!
AND I WAS A JERK!
SNIFF! I'M APPLYING FOR A JOB ELSE-WHERE!
VERONICA! I'M SORRY THAT I SNAPPED AT YOU!
BETTY IS BUSY ENOUGH AT THE OFFICE! I'M SURE YOU WILL DO A GREAT JOB DELIVERING THINGS TO ME HERE!
ARE YOU SERIOUS?!
THANK YOU, DADDYKINS! I'VE GOT A JOB!
CAN I MAKE JUST ONE REQUEST, THOUGH?
167...
168...
169...
DON'T TAKE THE BINDER CLIP OFF THE STACK OF PAPERS NEXT TIME?
SURE THING, BOSS!
END

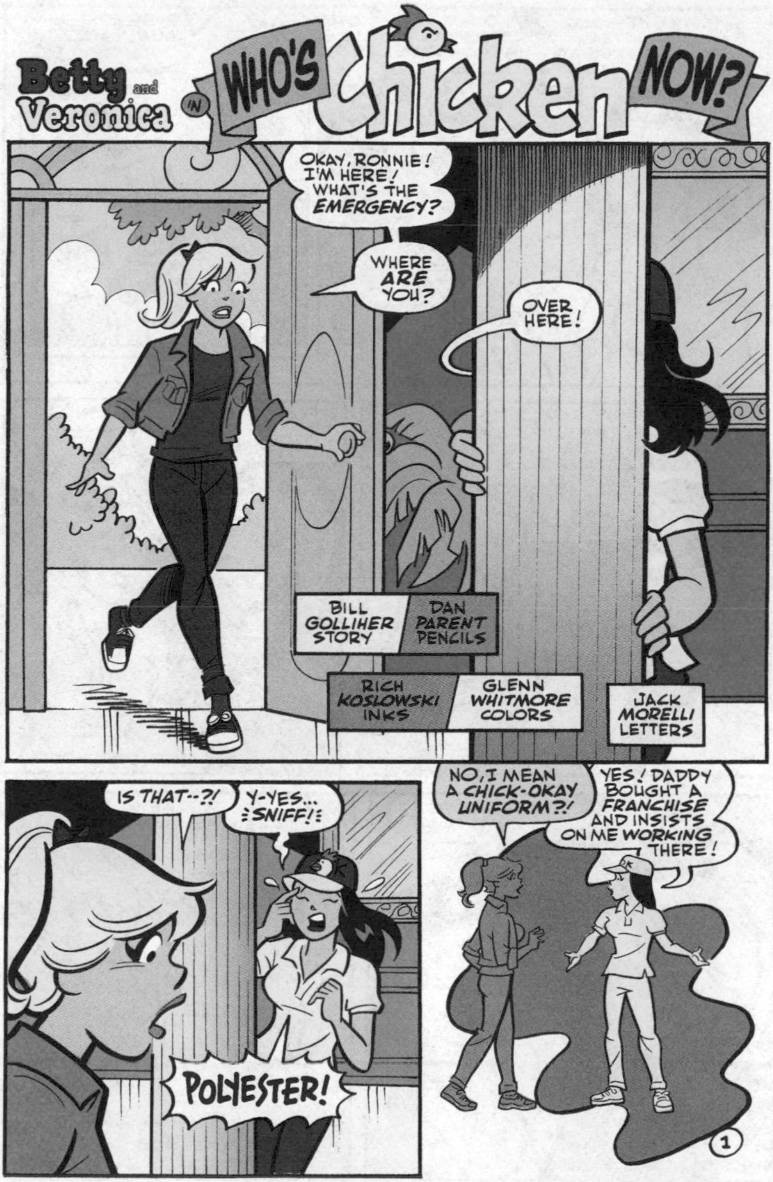
Betty and Veronica in WHO'S Chicken NOW?
OKAY, RONNIE! I'M HERE! WHAT'S THE EMERGENCY?
WHERE ARE YOU?
OVER HERE!
BILL GOLLIHER STORY
DAN PARENT PENCILS
RICH KOSLOWSKI INKS
GLENN WHITMORE COLORS
JACK MORELLI LETTERS
IS THAT--?!
Y-YES... SNIFF!
POLYESTER!
NO, I MEAN A CHICK-OKAY UNIFORM?!
YES! DADDY BOUGHT A FRANCHISE AND INSISTS ON ME WORKING THERE!
1

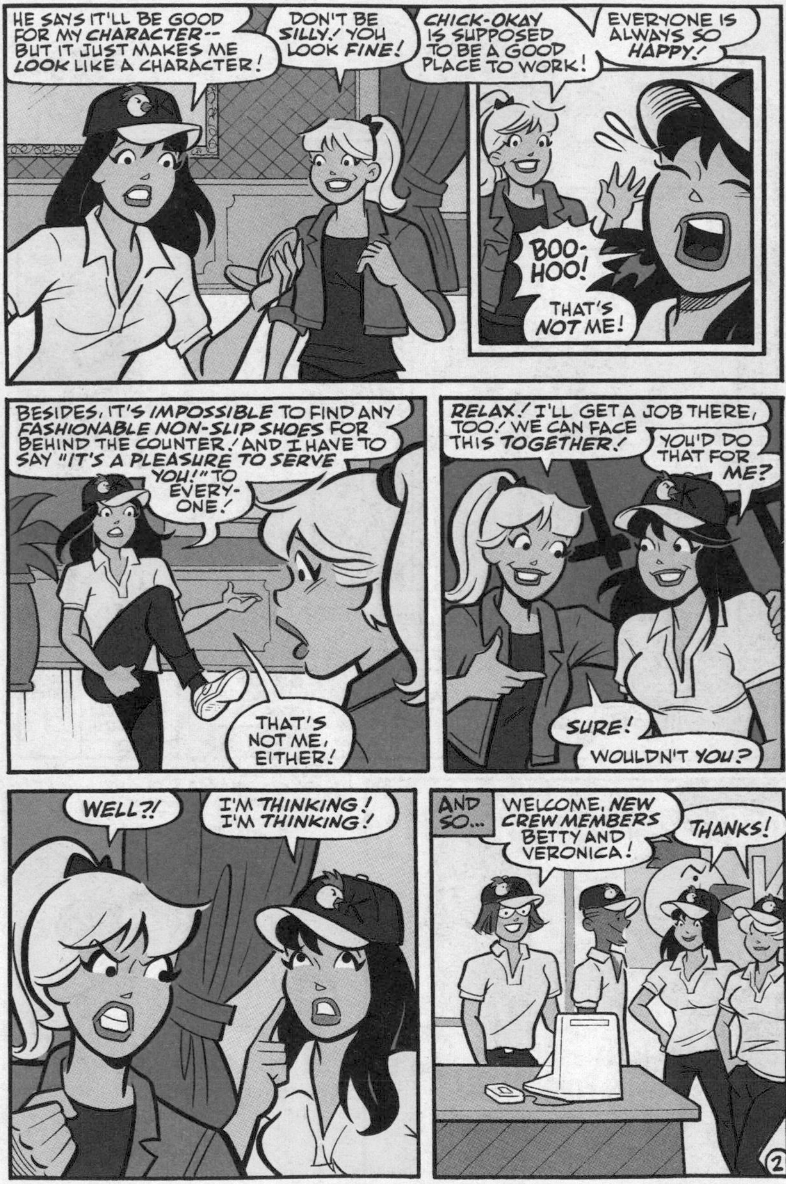
HE SAYS IT'LL BE GOOD FOR MY CHARACTER-- BUT IT JUST MAKES ME LOOK LIKE A CHARACTER!
DON'T BE SILLY! YOU LOOK FINE!
CHICK-OKAY IS SUPPOSED TO BE A GOOD PLACE TO WORK!
EVERYONE IS ALWAYS SO HAPPY!
BOO-HOO!
THAT'S NOT ME!
BESIDES, IT'S IMPOSSIBLE TO FIND ANY FASHIONABLE NON-SLIP SHOES FOR BEHIND THE COUNTER! AND I HAVE TO SAY "IT'S A PLEASURE TO SERVE YOU!" TO EVERY-ONE!
THAT'S NOT ME, EITHER!
RELAX! I'LL GET A JOB THERE, TOO! WE CAN FACE THIS TOGETHER!
YOU'D DO THAT FOR ME?
SURE!
WOULDN'T YOU?
WELL?!
I'M THINKING! I'M THINKING!
AND SO...
WELCOME, NEW CREW MEMBERS BETTY AND VERONICA!
THANKS!
2

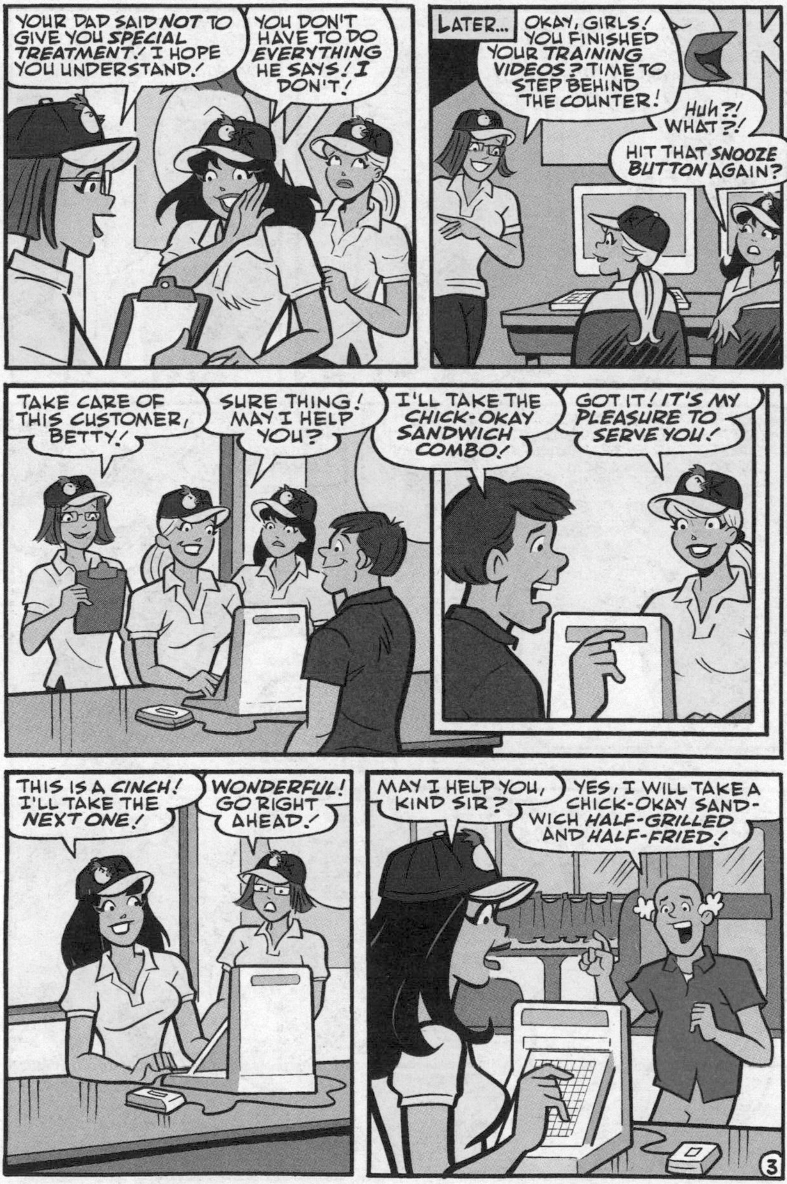
YOUR DAD SAID NOT TO GIVE YOU SPECIAL TREATMENT! I HOPE YOU UNDERSTAND!
YOU DON'T HAVE TO DO EVERYTHING HE SAYS! I DON'T!
LATER...
OKAY, GIRLS! YOU FINISHED YOUR TRAINING VIDEOS? TIME TO STEP BEHIND THE COUNTER!
HUH?! WHAT?!
HIT THAT SNOOZE BUTTON AGAIN?
TAKE CARE OF THIS CUSTOMER, BETTY!
SURE THING! MAY I HELP YOU?
I'LL TAKE THE CHICK-OKAY SANDWICH COMBO!
GOT IT! IT'S MY PLEASURE TO SERVE YOU!
THIS IS A CINCH! I'LL TAKE THE NEXT ONE!
WONDERFUL! GO RIGHT AHEAD!
MAY I HELP YOU, KIND SIR?
YES, I WILL TAKE A CHICK-OKAY SAND-WICH HALF-GRILLED AND HALF-FRIED!
3

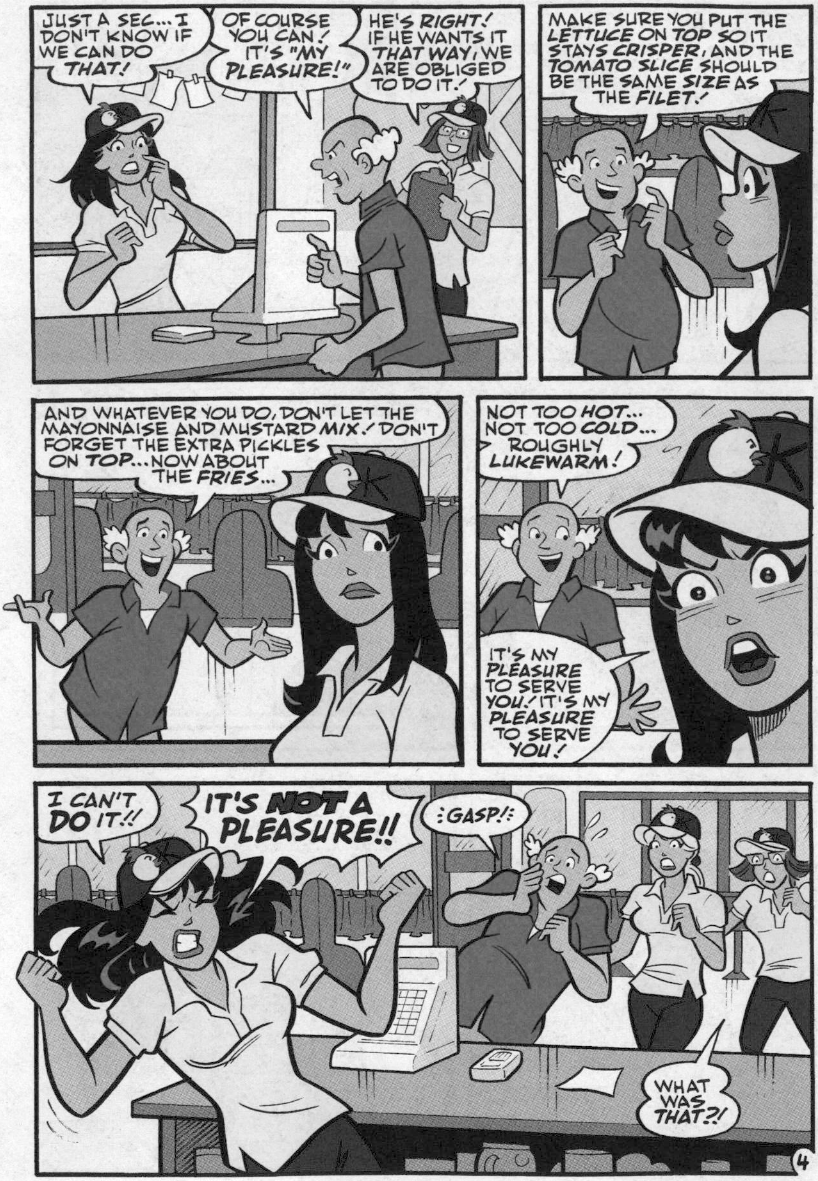
JUST A SEC... I DON'T KNOW IF WE CAN DO THAT!
OF COURSE YOU CAN! IT'S "MY PLEASURE!"
HE'S RIGHT! IF HE WANTS IT THAT WAY, WE ARE OBLIGED TO DO IT!
MAKE SURE YOU PUT THE LETTUCE ON TOP SO IT STAYS CRISPER, AND THE TOMATO SLICE SHOULD BE THE SAME SIZE AS THE FILET!
AND WHATEVER YOU DO, DON'T LET THE MAYONNAISE AND MUSTARD MIX! DON'T FORGET THE EXTRA PICKLES ON TOP... NOW ABOUT THE FRIES...
NOT TOO HOT... NOT TOO COLD... ROUGHLY LUKEWARM!
IT'S MY PLEASURE TO SERVE YOU! IT'S MY PLEASURE TO SERVE YOU!
I CAN'T DO IT!!
IT'S NOT A PLEASURE!!
GASP!
WHAT WAS THAT?!
4

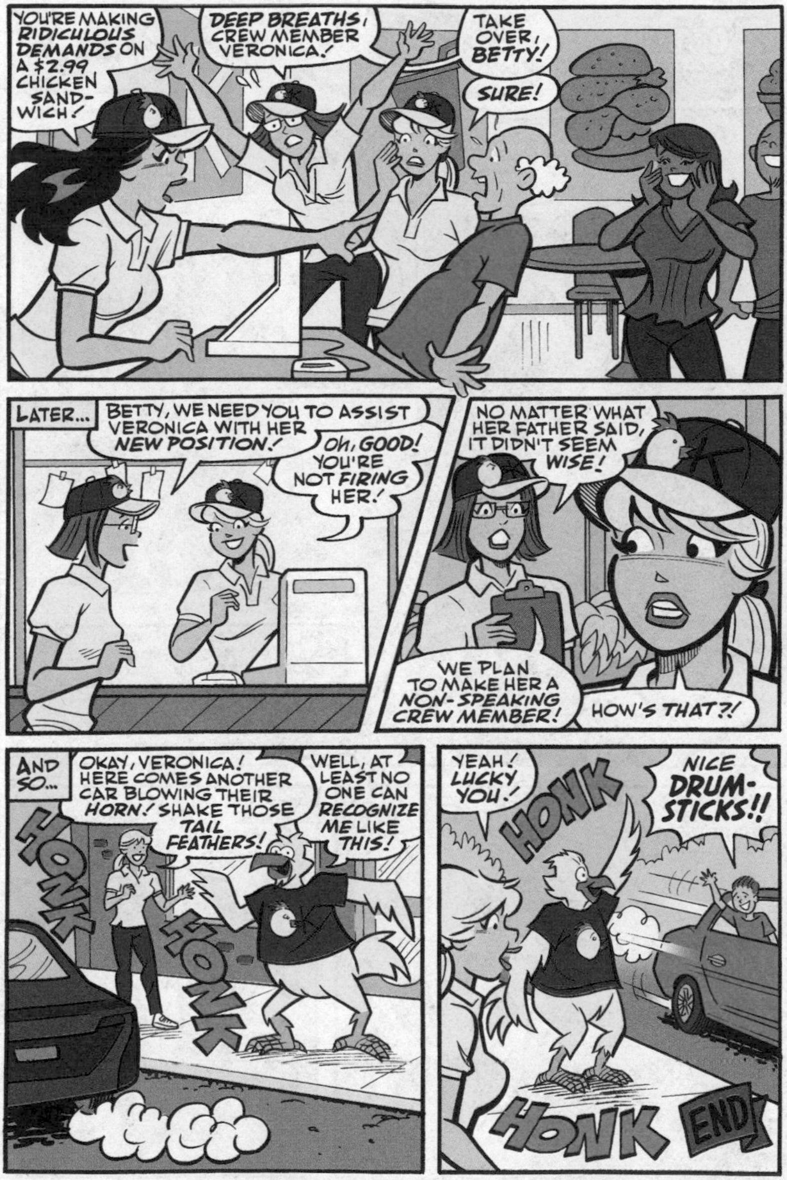
YOU'RE MAKING RIDICULOUS DEMANDS ON A $2.99 CHICKEN SAND-WICH!
DEEP BREATHS, CREW MEMBER VERONICA!
TAKE OVER, BETTY!
SURE!
LATER...
BETTY, WE NEED YOU TO ASSIST VERONICA WITH HER NEW POSITION!
Oh, GOOD! YOU'RE NOT FIRING HER!
NO MATTER WHAT HER FATHER SAID, IT DIDN'T SEEM WISE!
WE PLAN TO MAKE HER A NON-SPEAKING CREW MEMBER!
HOW'S THAT?!
AND SO...
OKAY, VERONICA! HERE COMES ANOTHER CAR BLOWING THEIR HORN! SHAKE THOSE TAIL FEATHERS!
WELL, AT LEAST NO ONE CAN RECOGNIZE ME LIKE THIS!
HONK
HONK
HONK
YEAH! LUCKY YOU!
HONK
NICE DRUMSTICKS!!
HONK
END

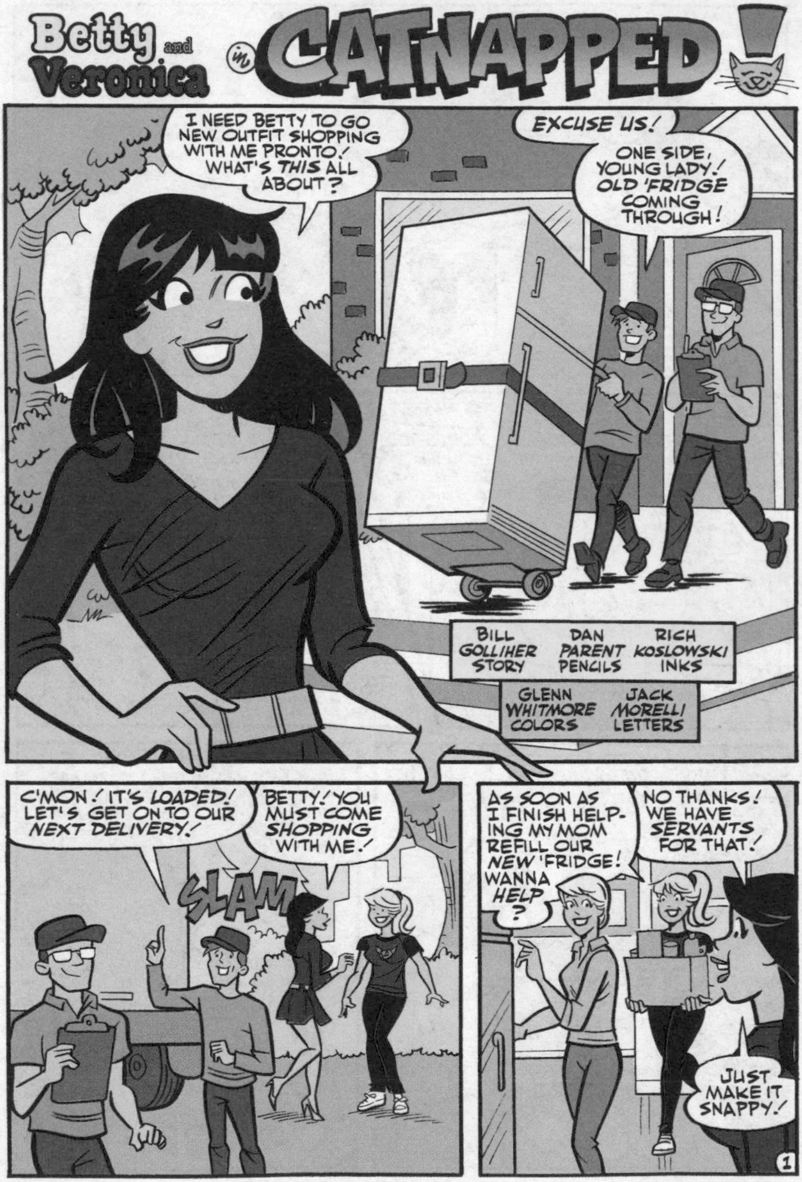

Betty and Veronica in CATNAPPED!
I NEED BETTY TO GO NEW OUTFIT SHOPPING WITH ME PRONTO! WHAT'S THIS ALL ABOUT?
EXCUSE US!
ONE SIDE, YOUNG LADY! OLD 'FRIDGE COMING THROUGH!
BILL GOLLIHER STORY
DAN PARENT PENCILS
RICH KOSLOWSKI INKS
GLENN WHITMORE COLORS
JACK MORELLI LETTERS
C'MON! IT'S LOADED! LET'S GET ON TO OUR NEXT DELIVERY!
BETTY! YOU MUST COME SHOPPING WITH ME!
SLAM
AS SOON AS I FINISH HELPING MY MOM REFILL OUR NEW 'FRIDGE! WANNA HELP?
NO THANKS! WE HAVE SERVANTS FOR THAT!
JUST MAKE IT SNAPPY!
1

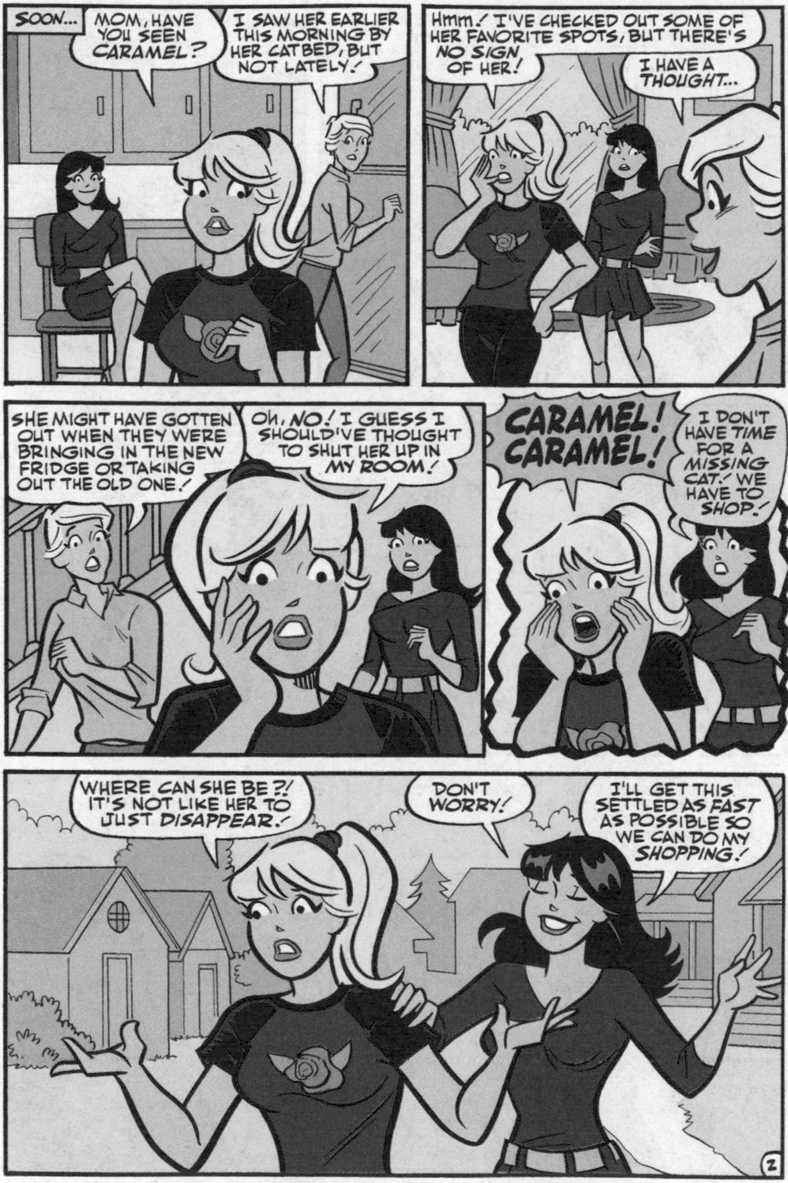
SOON...
MOM, HAVE YOU SEEN CARAMEL?
I SAW HER EARLIER THIS MORNING BY HER CAT BED, BUT NOT LATELY!
Hmm! I'VE CHECKED OUT SOME OF HER FAVORITE SPOTS, BUT THERE'S NO SIGN OF HER!
I HAVE A THOUGHT...
SHE MIGHT HAVE GOTTEN OUT WHEN THEY WERE BRINGING IN THE NEW FRIDGE OR TAKING OUT THE OLD ONE!
Oh, NO! I GUESS I SHOULD'VE THOUGHT TO SHUT HER UP IN MY ROOM!
CARAMEL! CARAMEL!
I DON'T HAVE TIME FOR A MISSING CAT! WE HAVE TO SHOP!
WHERE CAN SHE BE?! IT'S NOT LIKE HER TO JUST DISAPPEAR!
DON'T WORRY!
I'LL GET THIS SETTLED AS FAST AS POSSIBLE SO WE CAN DO MY SHOPPING!
2

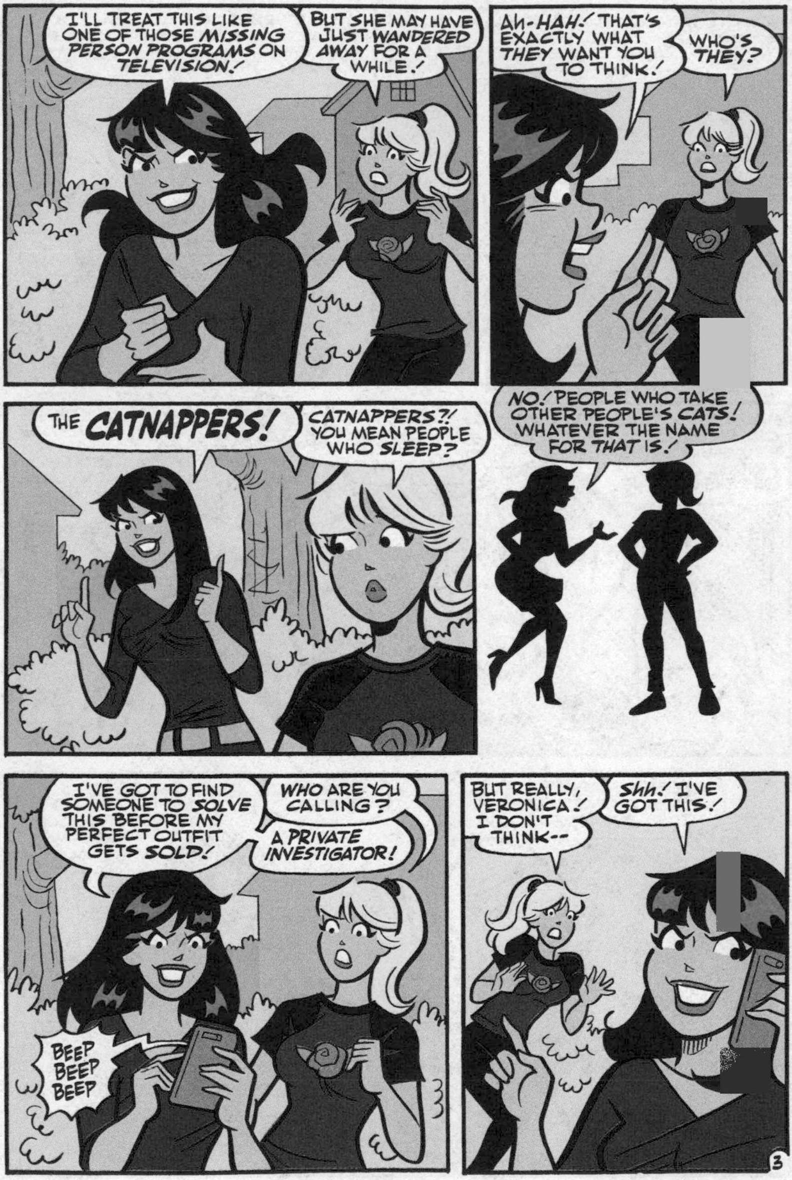

I'LL TREAT THIS LIKE ONE OF THOSE MISSING PERSON PROGRAMS ON TELEVISION!
BUT SHE MAY HAVE JUST WANDERED AWAY FOR A WHILE!
Ah-HAH! THAT'S EXACTLY WHAT THEY WANT YOU TO THINK!
WHO'S THEY?
THE CATNAPPERS!
CATNAPPERS?! YOU MEAN PEOPLE WHO SLEEP?
NO! PEOPLE WHO TAKE OTHER PEOPLE'S CATS! WHATEVER THE NAME FOR THAT IS!
I'VE GOT TO FIND SOMEONE TO SOLVE THIS BEFORE MY PERFECT OUTFIT GETS SOLD!
WHO ARE YOU CALLING?
A PRIVATE INVESTIGATOR!
BEEP BEEP BEEP
BUT REALLY, VERONICA! I DON'T THINK--
Shh! I'VE GOT THIS!
3

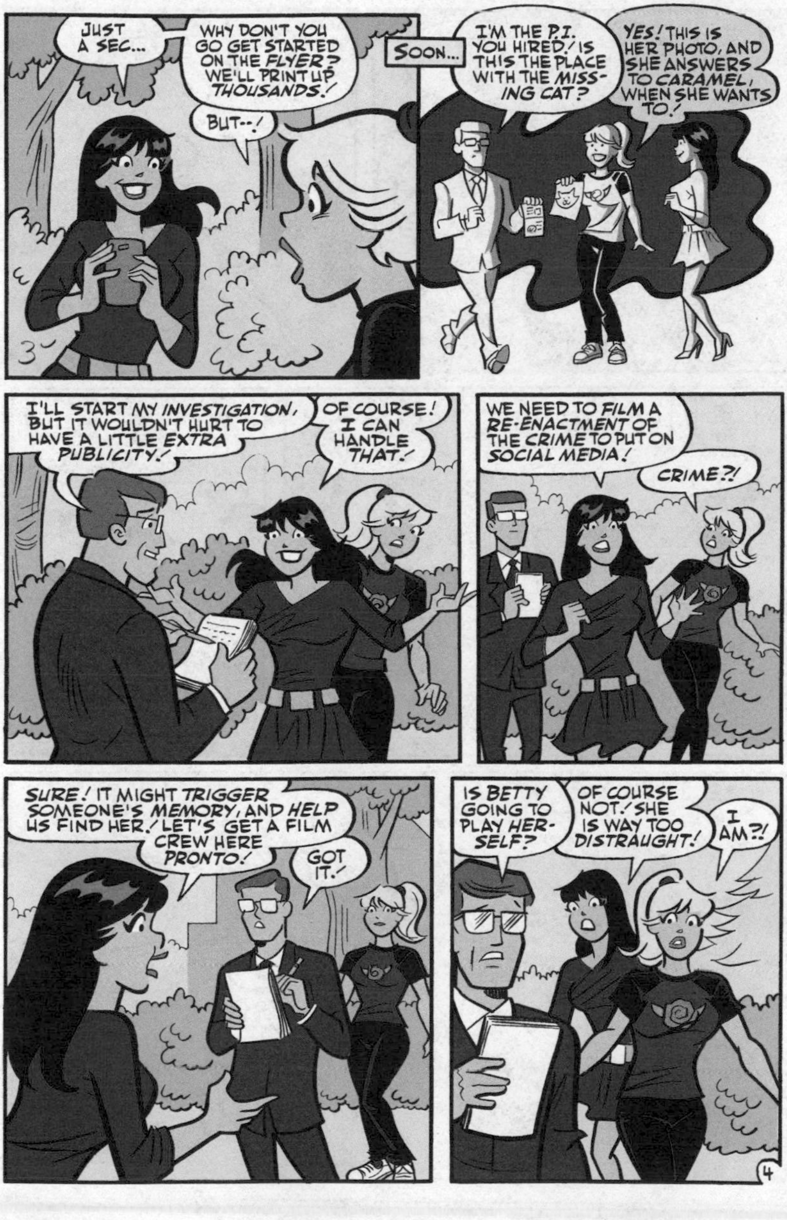
JUST A SEC...
WHY DON'T YOU GO GET STARTED ON THE FLYER? WE'LL PRINT UP THOUSANDS!
BUT--!
SOON...
I'M THE P.I. YOU HIRED! IS THIS THE PLACE WITH THE MISSING CAT?
YES! THIS IS HER PHOTO, AND SHE ANSWERS TO CARAMEL, WHEN SHE WANTS TO!
I'LL START MY INVESTIGATION, BUT IT WOULDN'T HURT TO HAVE A LITTLE EXTRA PUBLICITY!
OF COURSE! I CAN HANDLE THAT!
WE NEED TO FILM A RE-ENACTMENT OF THE CRIME TO PUT ON SOCIAL MEDIA!
CRIME?!
SURE! IT MIGHT TRIGGER SOMEONE'S MEMORY, AND HELP US FIND HER! LET'S GET A FILM CREW HERE PRONTO!
GOT IT!
IS BETTY GOING TO PLAY HER-SELF?
OF COURSE NOT! SHE IS WAY TOO DISTRAUGHT!
I AM?!
4

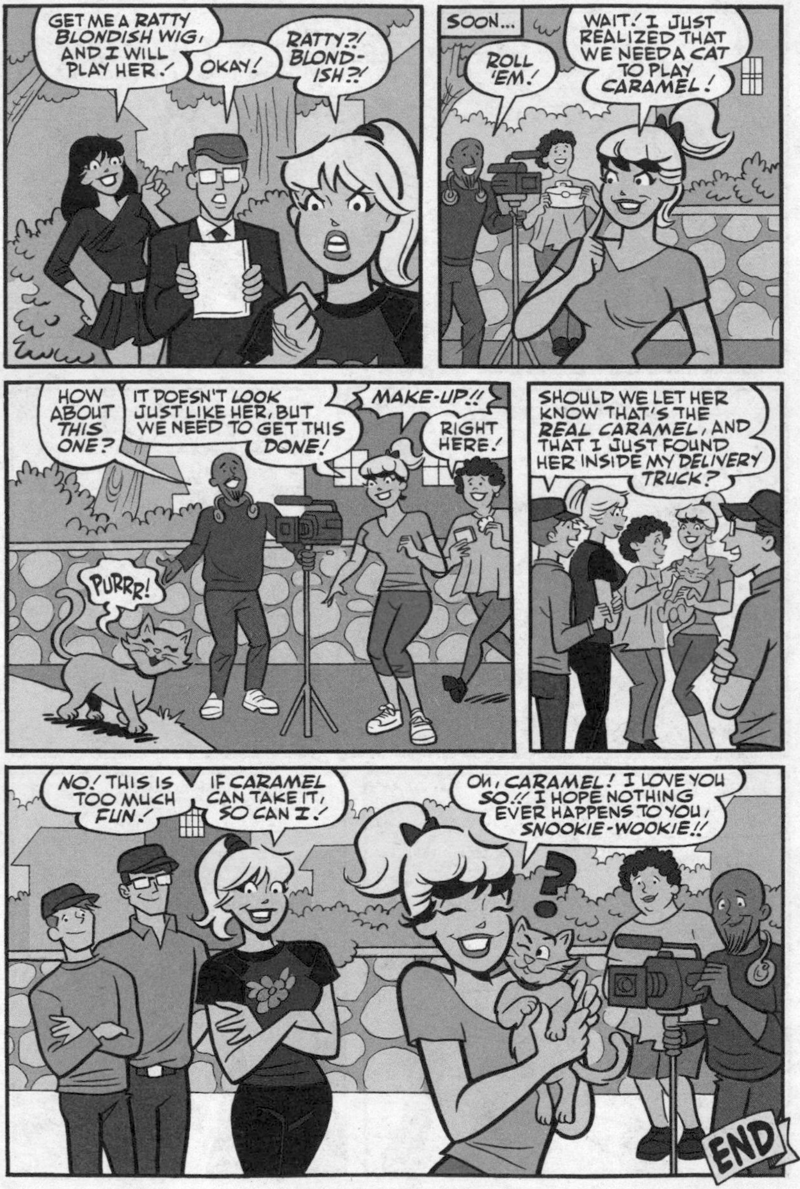
GET ME A RATTY BLONDISH WIG, AND I WILL PLAY HER!
OKAY!
RATTY?! BLOND-ISH?!
SOON...
ROLL 'EM!
WAIT! I JUST REALIZED THAT WE NEED A CAT TO PLAY CARAMEL!
HOW ABOUT THIS ONE?
IT DOESN'T LOOK JUST LIKE HER, BUT WE NEED TO GET THIS DONE!
MAKE-UP!!
RIGHT HERE!
PURRR!
SHOULD WE LET HER KNOW THAT'S THE REAL CARAMEL, AND THAT I JUST FOUND HER INSIDE MY DELIVERY TRUCK?
NO! THIS IS TOO MUCH FUN!
IF CARAMEL CAN TAKE IT, SO CAN I!
OH, CARAMEL! I LOVE YOU SO!! I HOPE NOTHING EVER HAPPENS TO YOU, SNOOKIE-WOOKIE!!
?
END

03 ARCHIE & ME

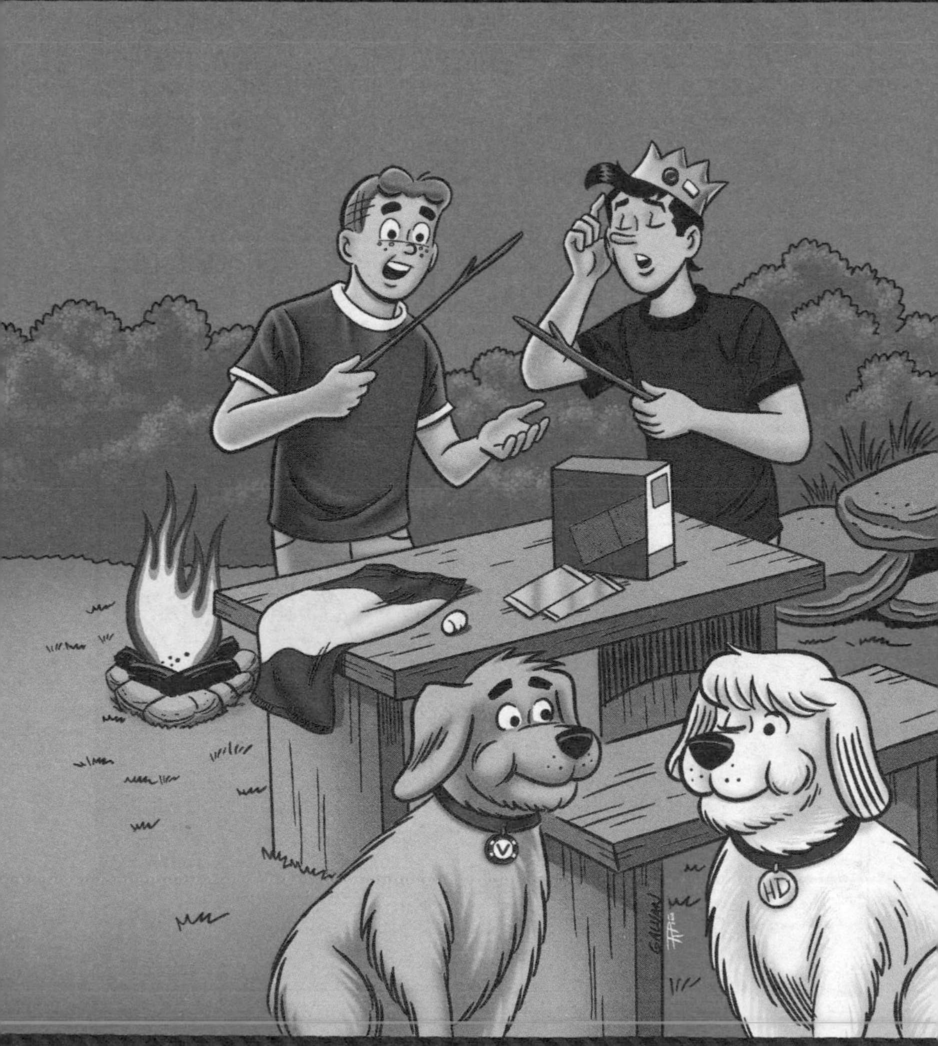

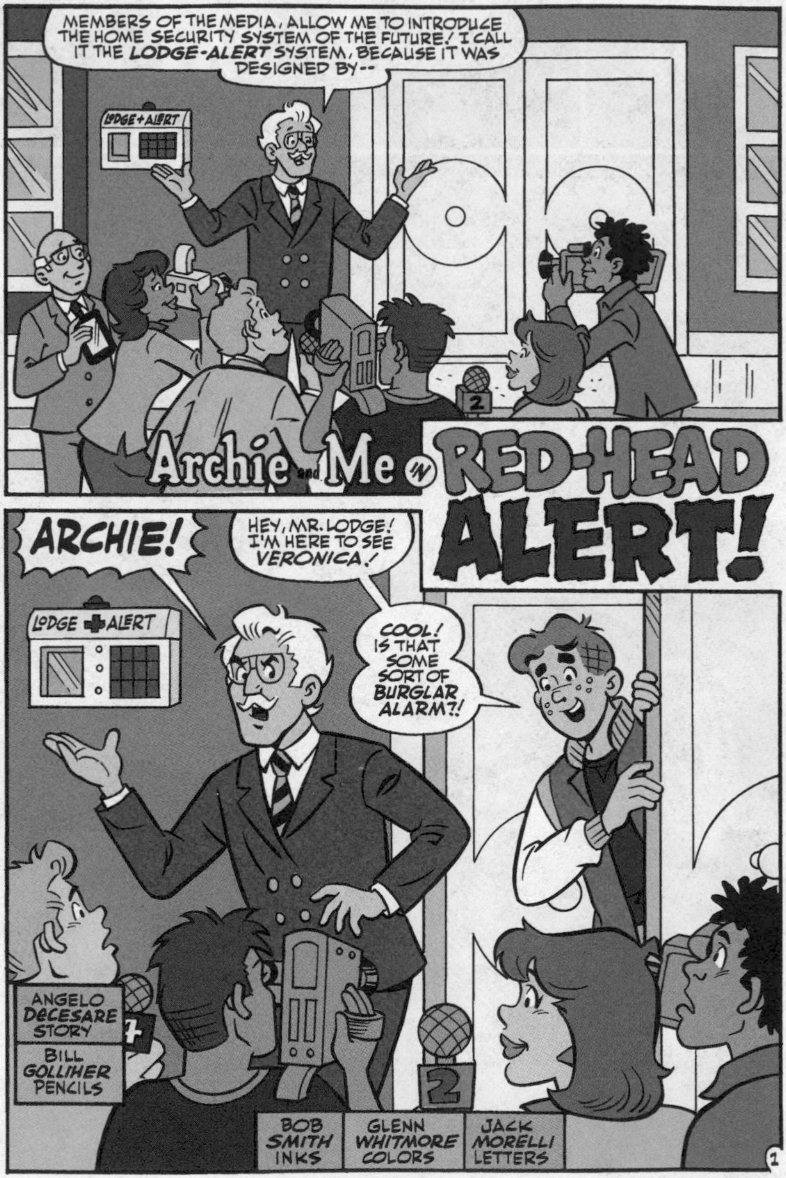
MEMBERS OF THE MEDIA, ALLOW ME TO INTRODUCE THE HOME SECURITY SYSTEM OF THE FUTURE! I CALL IT THE LODGE-ALERT SYSTEM, BECAUSE IT WAS DESIGNED BY--
LODGE+ALERT
Archie and Me in RED-HEAD ALERT!
ARCHIE!
HEY, MR. LODGE! I'M HERE TO SEE VERONICA!
COOL! IS THAT SOME SORT OF BURGLAR ALARM?!
LODGE ALERT
ANGELO DECESARE STORY
BILL GOLLIHER PENCILS
BOB SMITH INKS
GLENN WHITMORE COLORS
JACK MORELLI LETTERS
1

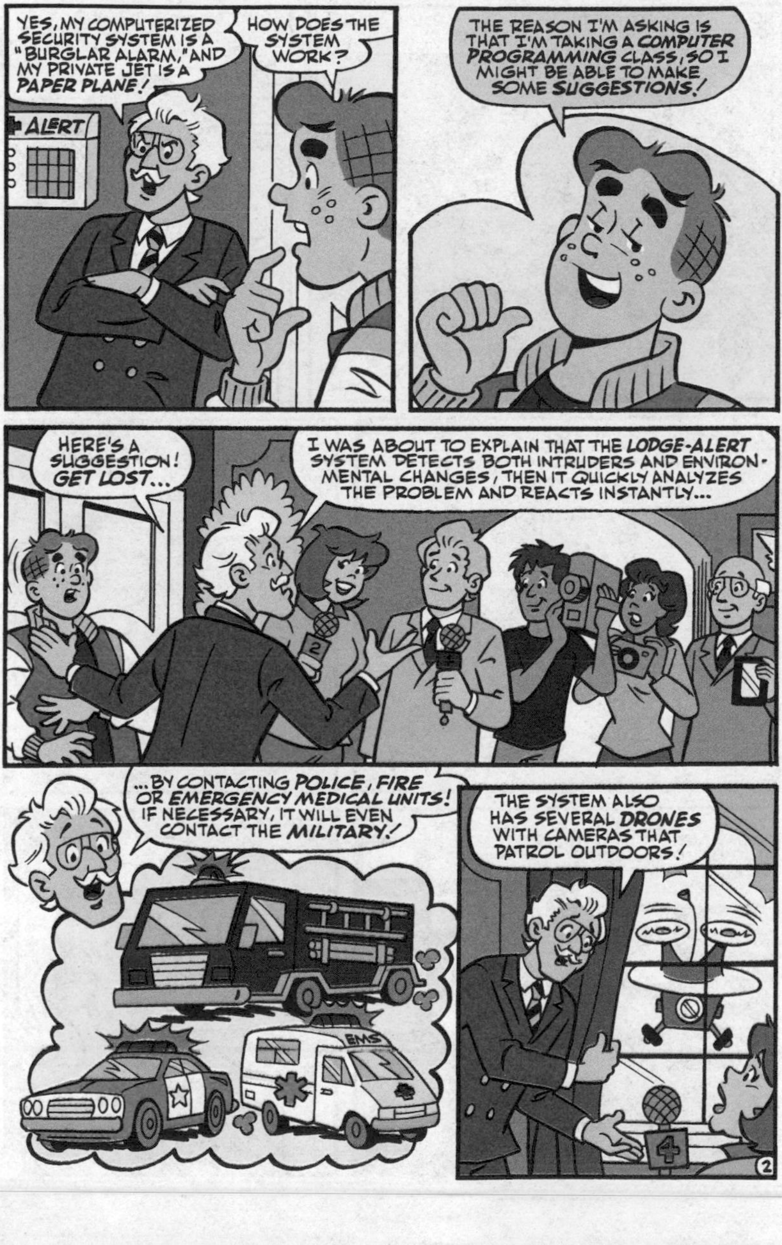
YES, MY COMPUTERIZED SECURITY SYSTEM IS A "BURGLAR ALARM," AND MY PRIVATE JET IS A PAPER PLANE!
ALERT
HOW DOES THE SYSTEM WORK?
THE REASON I'M ASKING IS THAT I'M TAKING A COMPUTER PROGRAMMING CLASS, SO I MIGHT BE ABLE TO MAKE SOME SUGGESTIONS!
HERE'S A SUGGESTION! GET LOST...
I WAS ABOUT TO EXPLAIN THAT THE LODGE-ALERT SYSTEM DETECTS BOTH INTRUDERS AND ENVIRON-MENTAL CHANGES, THEN IT QUICKLY ANALYZES THE PROBLEM AND REACTS INSTANTLY...
2
...BY CONTACTING POLICE, FIRE OR EMERGENCY MEDICAL UNITS! IF NECESSARY, IT WILL EVEN CONTACT THE MILITARY!
EMS
THE SYSTEM ALSO HAS SEVERAL DRONES WITH CAMERAS THAT PATROL OUTDOORS!
4
2

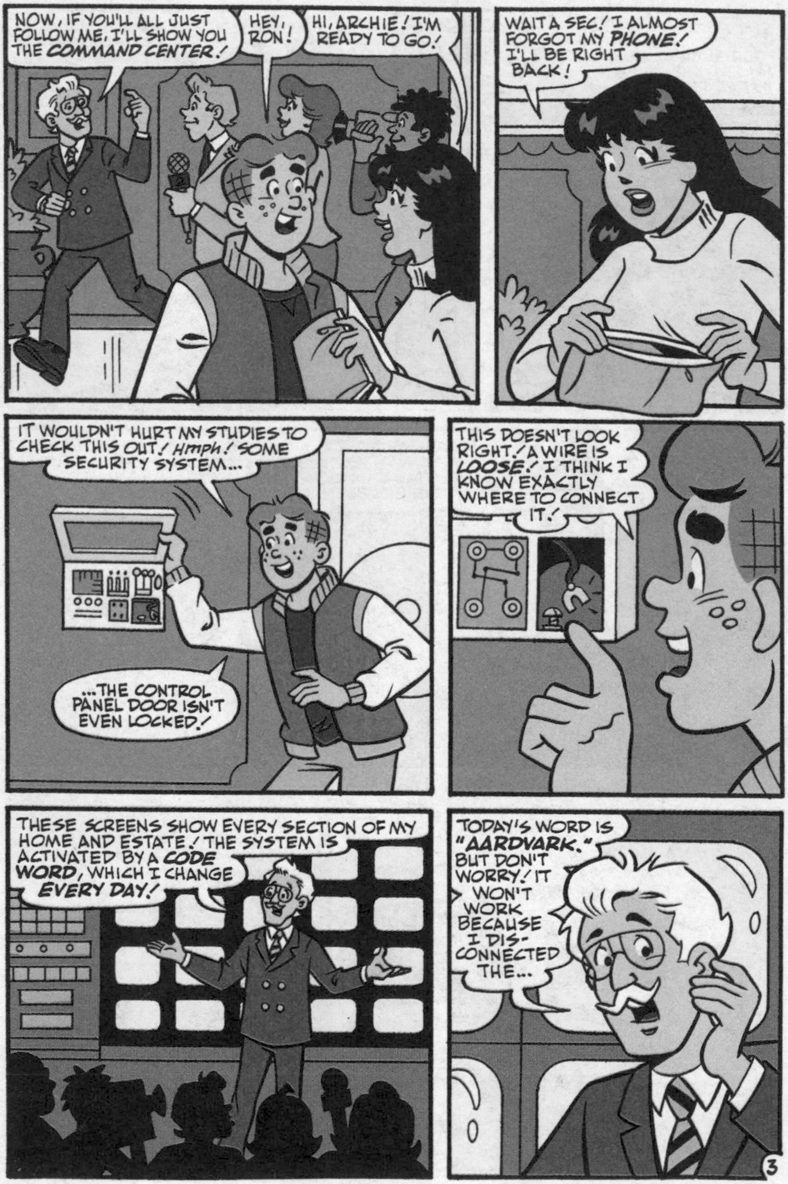
NOW, IF YOU'LL ALL JUST FOLLOW ME, I'LL SHOW YOU THE COMMAND CENTER!
HEY, RON!
HI, ARCHIE! I'M READY TO GO!
WAIT A SEC! I ALMOST FORGOT MY PHONE! I'LL BE RIGHT BACK!
IT WOULDN'T HURT MY STUDIES TO CHECK THIS OUT! Hmph! SOME SECURITY SYSTEM...
...THE CONTROL PANEL DOOR ISN'T EVEN LOCKED!
THIS DOESN'T LOOK RIGHT! A WIRE IS LOOSE! I THINK I KNOW EXACTLY WHERE TO CONNECT IT!
THESE SCREENS SHOW EVERY SECTION OF MY HOME AND ESTATE! THE SYSTEM IS ACTIVATED BY A CODE WORD, WHICH I CHANGE EVERY DAY!
TODAY'S WORD IS "AARDVARK." BUT DON'T WORRY! IT WON'T WORK BECAUSE I DIS-CONNECTED THE...
3

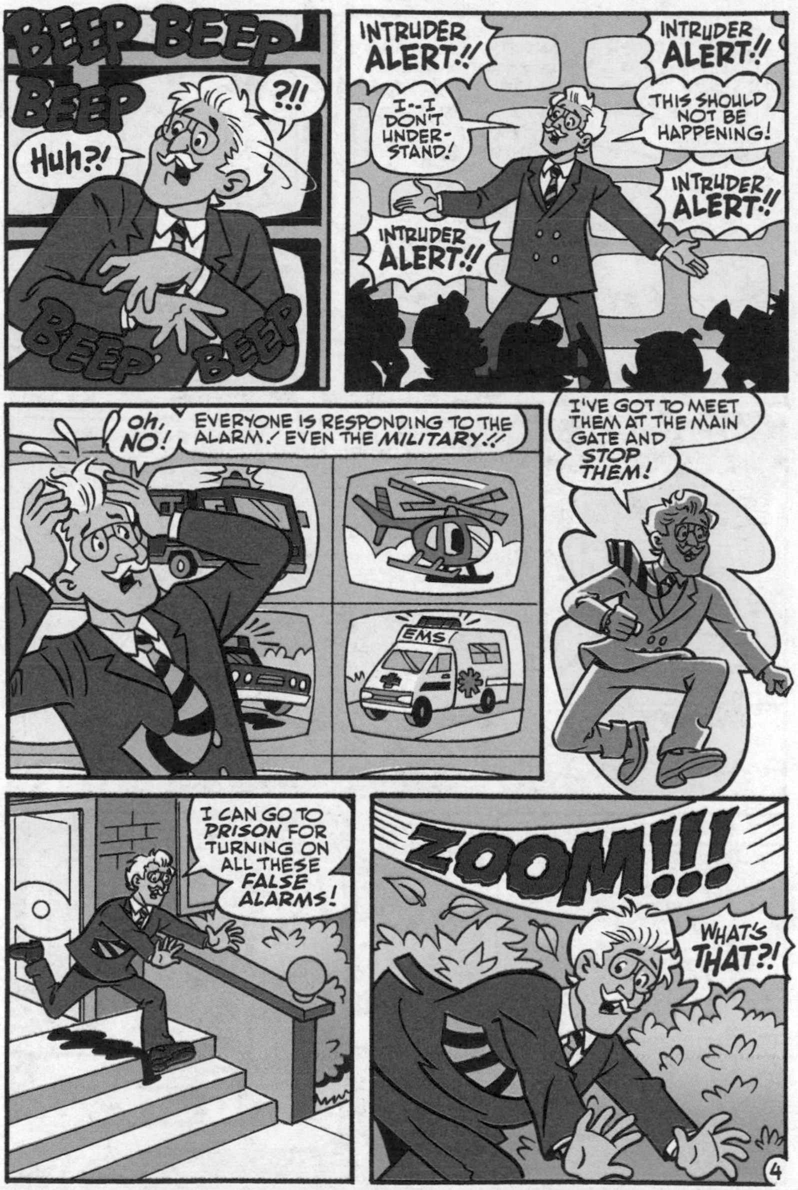
BEEP BEEP
BEEP
Huh?!
?!!
BEEP
BEEP
INTRUDER ALERT!!
I--I DON'T UNDER-STAND!
INTRUDER ALERT!!
THIS SHOULD NOT BE HAPPENING!
INTRUDER ALERT!!
INTRUDER ALERT!!
Oh, NO!
EVERYONE IS RESPONDING TO THE ALARM! EVEN THE MILITARY!!
EMS
I'VE GOT TO MEET THEM AT THE MAIN GATE AND STOP THEM!
I CAN GO TO PRISON FOR TURNING ON ALL THESE FALSE ALARMS!
ZOOM!!!
WHAT'S THAT?!
4

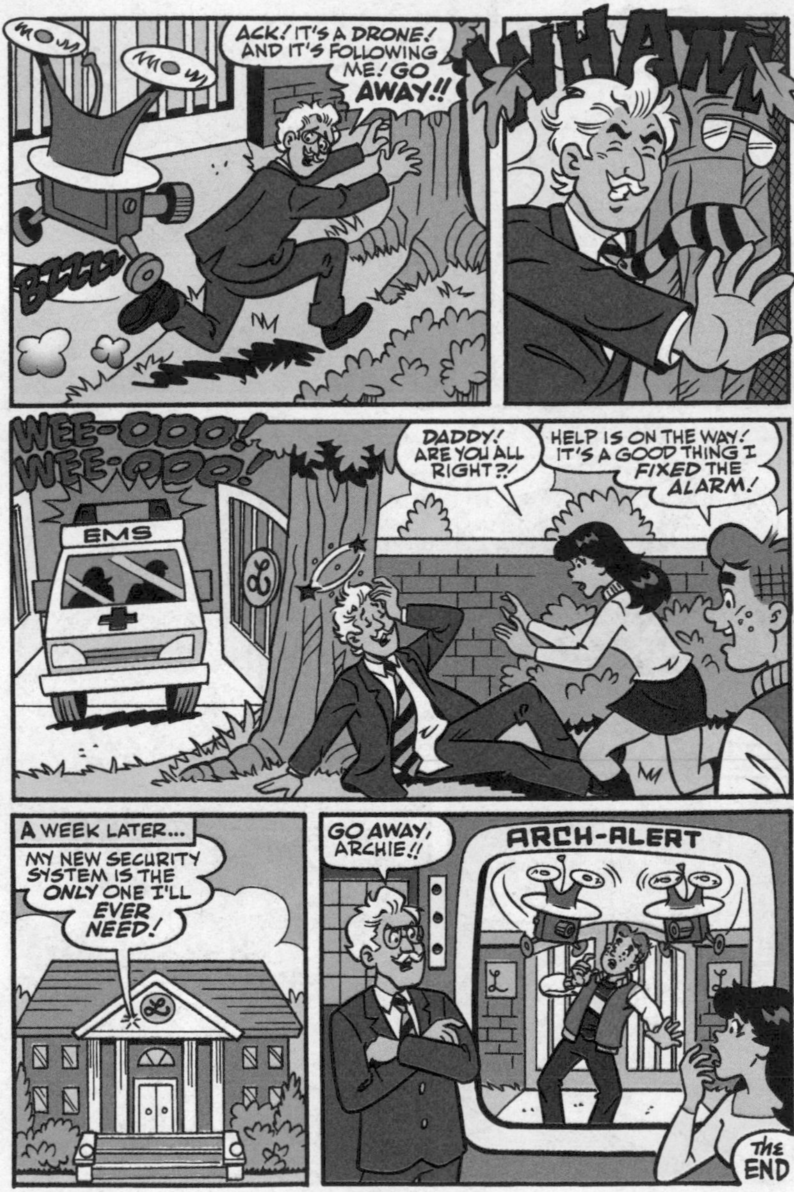
ACK! IT'S A DRONE! AND IT'S FOLLOWING ME! GO AWAY!!
BZZZZ
WHAM
WEE-OOO! WEE-OOO!
EMS
DADDY! ARE YOU ALL RIGHT?!
HELP IS ON THE WAY! IT'S A GOOD THING I FIXED THE ALARM!
A WEEK LATER...
MY NEW SECURITY SYSTEM IS THE ONLY ONE I'LL EVER NEED!
GO AWAY, ARCHIE!!
ARCH-ALERT
THE END

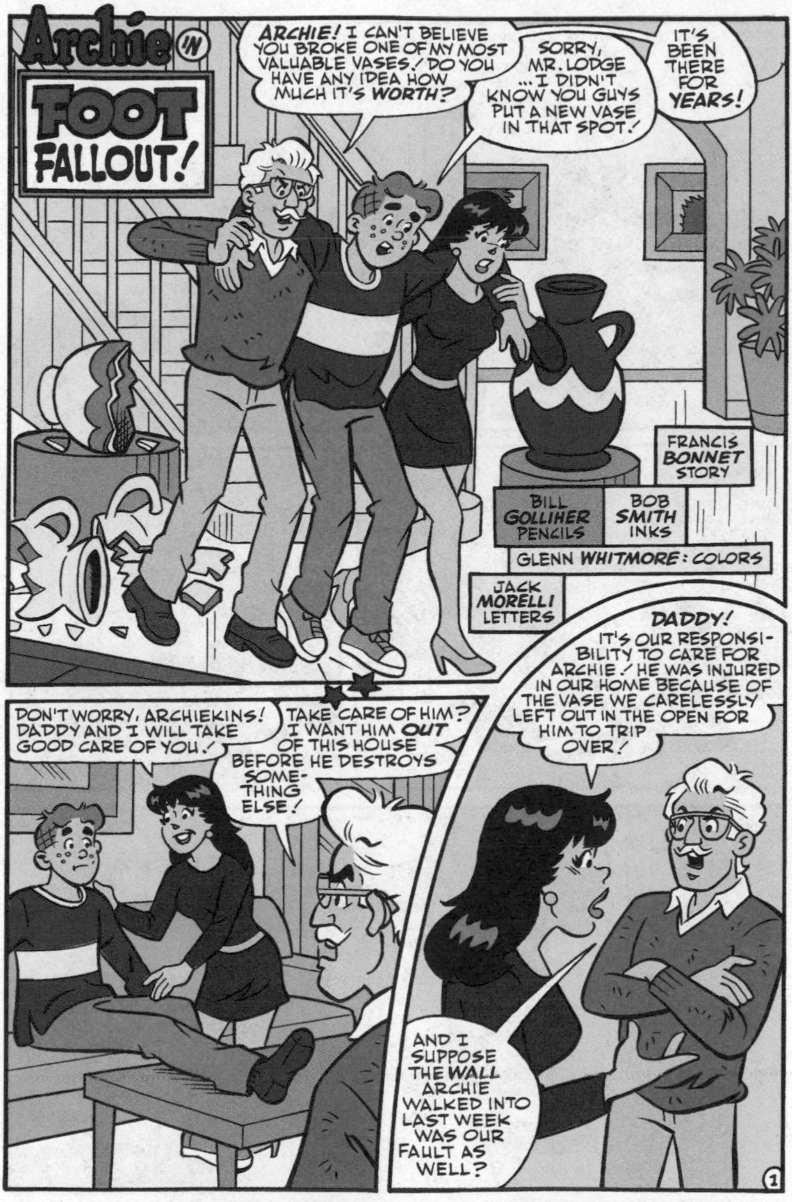

Archie IN
FOOT FALLOUT!
ARCHIE! I CAN'T BELIEVE YOU BROKE ONE OF MY MOST VALUABLE VASES! DO YOU HAVE ANY IDEA HOW MUCH IT'S WORTH?
SORRY, MR. LODGE ...I DIDN'T KNOW YOU GUYS PUT A NEW VASE IN THAT SPOT!
IT'S BEEN THERE FOR YEARS!
FRANCIS BONNET STORY
BILL GOLLIHER PENCILS
BOB SMITH INKS
GLENN WHITMORE: COLORS
JACK MORELLI LETTERS
DON'T WORRY, ARCHIEKINS! DADDY AND I WILL TAKE GOOD CARE OF YOU!
TAKE CARE OF HIM? I WANT HIM OUT OF THIS HOUSE BEFORE HE DESTROYS SOMETHING ELSE!
DADDY! IT'S OUR RESPONSIBILITY TO CARE FOR ARCHIE! HE WAS INJURED IN OUR HOME BECAUSE OF THE VASE WE CARELESSLY LEFT OUT IN THE OPEN FOR HIM TO TRIP OVER!
AND I SUPPOSE THE WALL ARCHIE WALKED INTO LAST WEEK WAS OUR FAULT AS WELL?
1

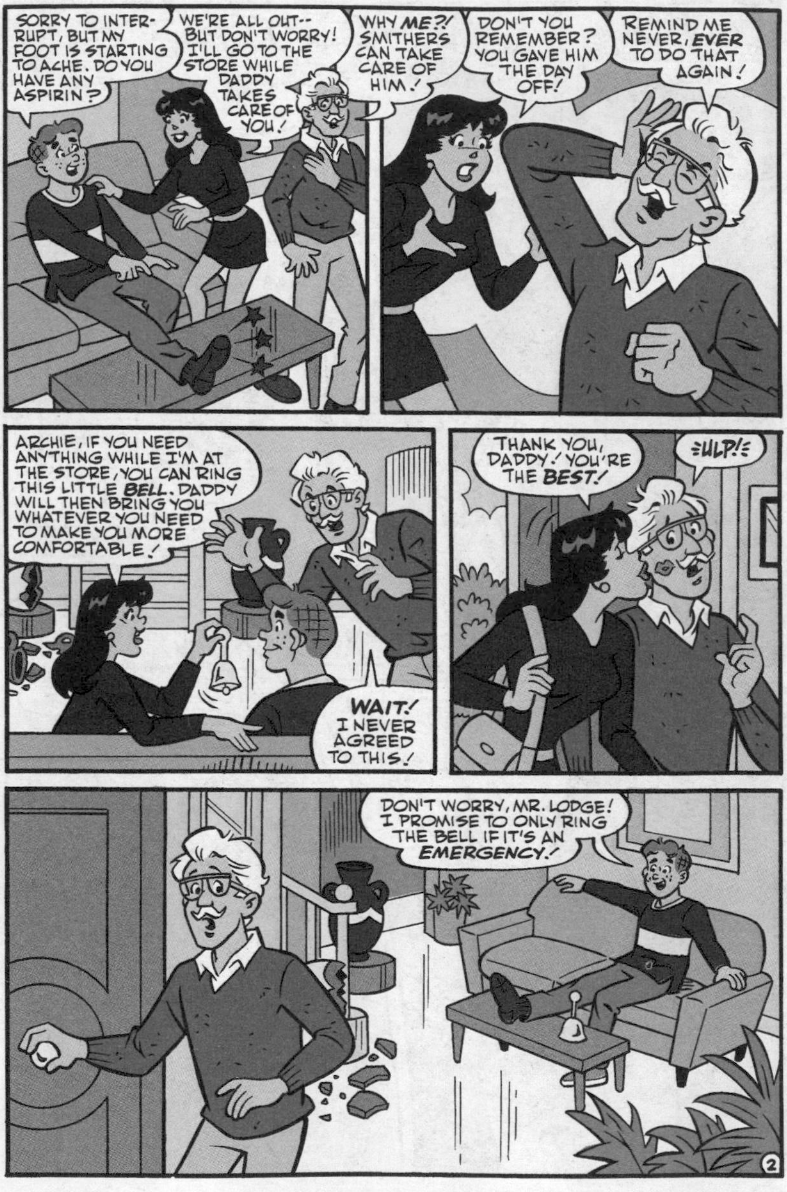
SORRY TO INTER-RUPT, BUT MY FOOT IS STARTING TO ACHE. DO YOU HAVE ANY ASPIRIN?
WE'RE ALL OUT-- BUT DON'T WORRY! I'LL GO TO THE STORE WHILE DADDY TAKES CARE OF YOU!
WHY ME?! SMITHERS CAN TAKE CARE OF HIM!
DON'T YOU REMEMBER? YOU GAVE HIM THE DAY OFF!
REMIND ME NEVER, EVER TO DO THAT AGAIN!
ARCHIE, IF YOU NEED ANYTHING WHILE I'M AT THE STORE, YOU CAN RING THIS LITTLE BELL. DADDY WILL THEN BRING YOU WHATEVER YOU NEED TO MAKE YOU MORE COMFORTABLE!
WAIT! I NEVER AGREED TO THIS!
THANK YOU, DADDY! YOU'RE THE BEST!
ULP!
DON'T WORRY, MR. LODGE! I PROMISE TO ONLY RING THE BELL IF IT'S AN EMERGENCY!
2

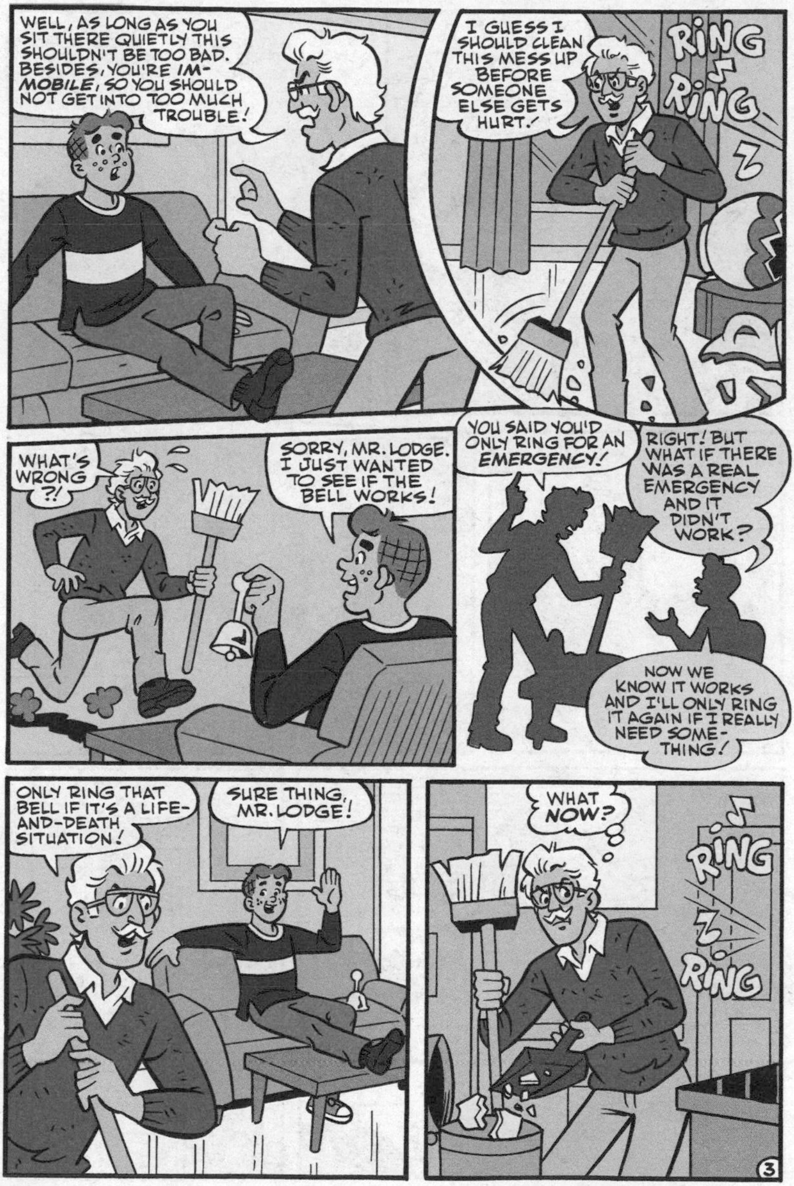
WELL, AS LONG AS YOU SIT THERE QUIETLY THIS SHOULDN'T BE TOO BAD. BESIDES, YOU'RE IM-MOBILE, SO YOU SHOULD NOT GET INTO TOO MUCH TROUBLE!
I GUESS I SHOULD CLEAN THIS MESS UP BEFORE SOMEONE ELSE GETS HURT!
RING RING
WHAT'S WRONG ?!
SORRY, MR. LODGE. I JUST WANTED TO SEE IF THE BELL WORKS!
YOU SAID YOU'D ONLY RING FOR AN EMERGENCY!
RIGHT! BUT WHAT IF THERE WAS A REAL EMERGENCY AND IT DIDN'T WORK?
NOW WE KNOW IT WORKS AND I'LL ONLY RING IT AGAIN IF I REALLY NEED SOME-THING!
ONLY RING THAT BELL IF IT'S A LIFE-AND-DEATH SITUATION!
SURE THING, MR. LODGE!
WHAT NOW?
RING RING
3

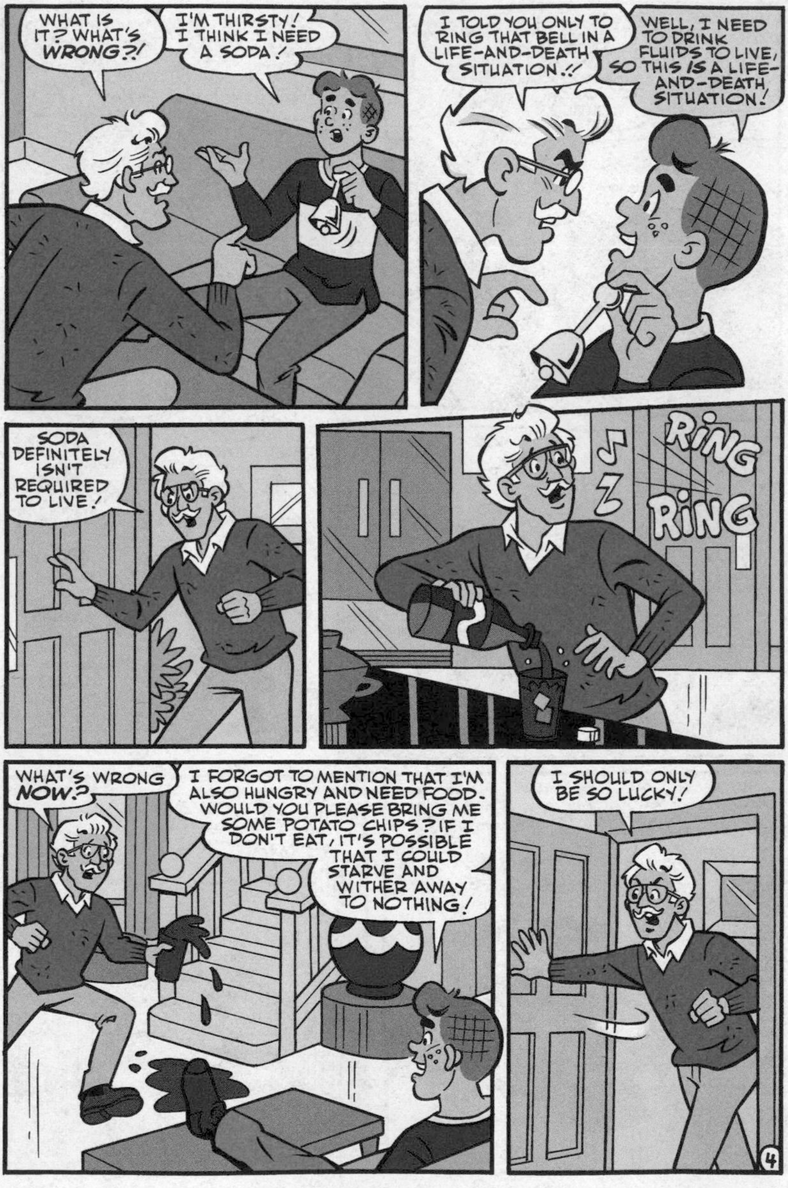
WHAT IS IT? WHAT'S WRONG?!
I'M THIRSTY! I THINK I NEED A SODA!
I TOLD YOU ONLY TO RING THAT BELL IN A LIFE-AND-DEATH SITUATION.!!
WELL, I NEED TO DRINK FLUIDS TO LIVE, SO THIS IS A LIFE-AND-DEATH SITUATION!
SODA DEFINITELY ISN'T REQUIRED TO LIVE!
RING RING
WHAT'S WRONG NOW?
I FORGOT TO MENTION THAT I'M ALSO HUNGRY AND NEED FOOD. WOULD YOU PLEASE BRING ME SOME POTATO CHIPS? IF I DON'T EAT, IT'S POSSIBLE THAT I COULD STARVE AND WITHER AWAY TO NOTHING!
I SHOULD ONLY BE SO LUCKY!
4

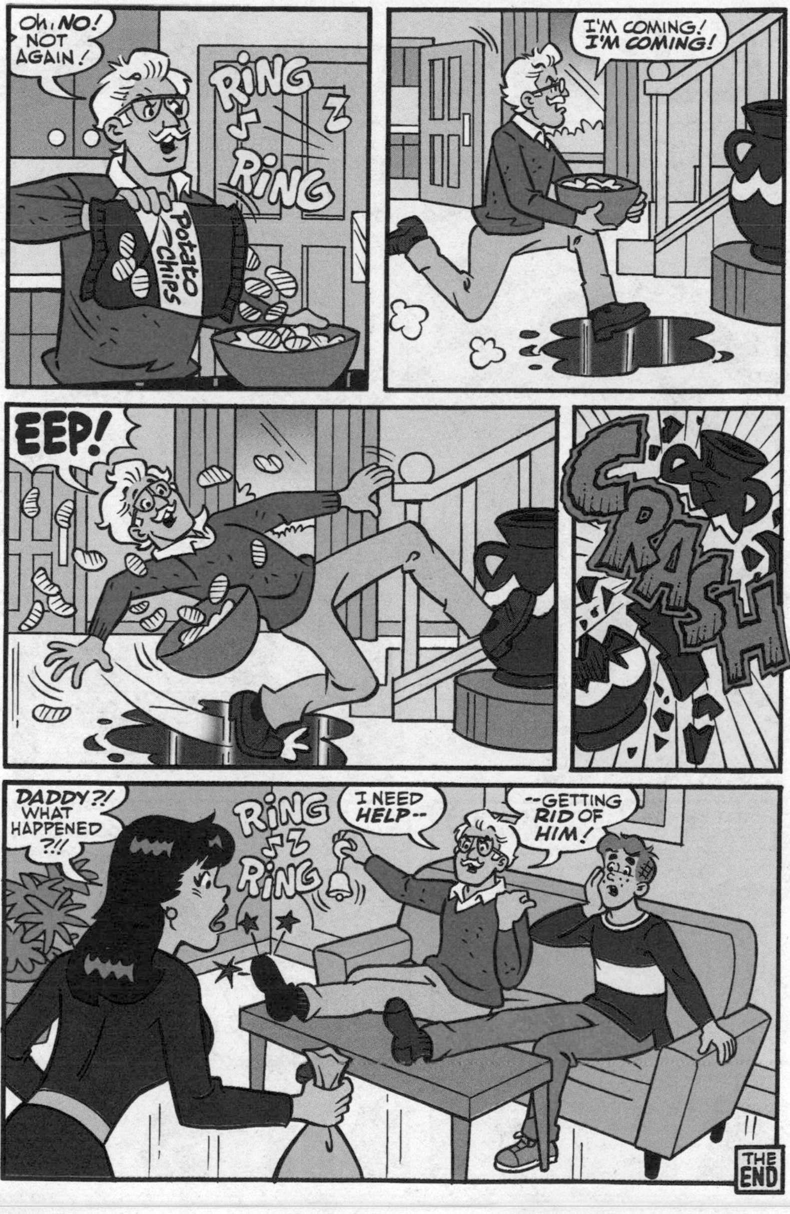
Oh, NO! NOT AGAIN!
RING
RING
Potato Chips
I'M COMING! I'M COMING!
EEP!
CRASH
DADDY?! WHAT HAPPENED?!!
RING
RING
I NEED HELP--
--GETTING RID OF HIM!
THE END

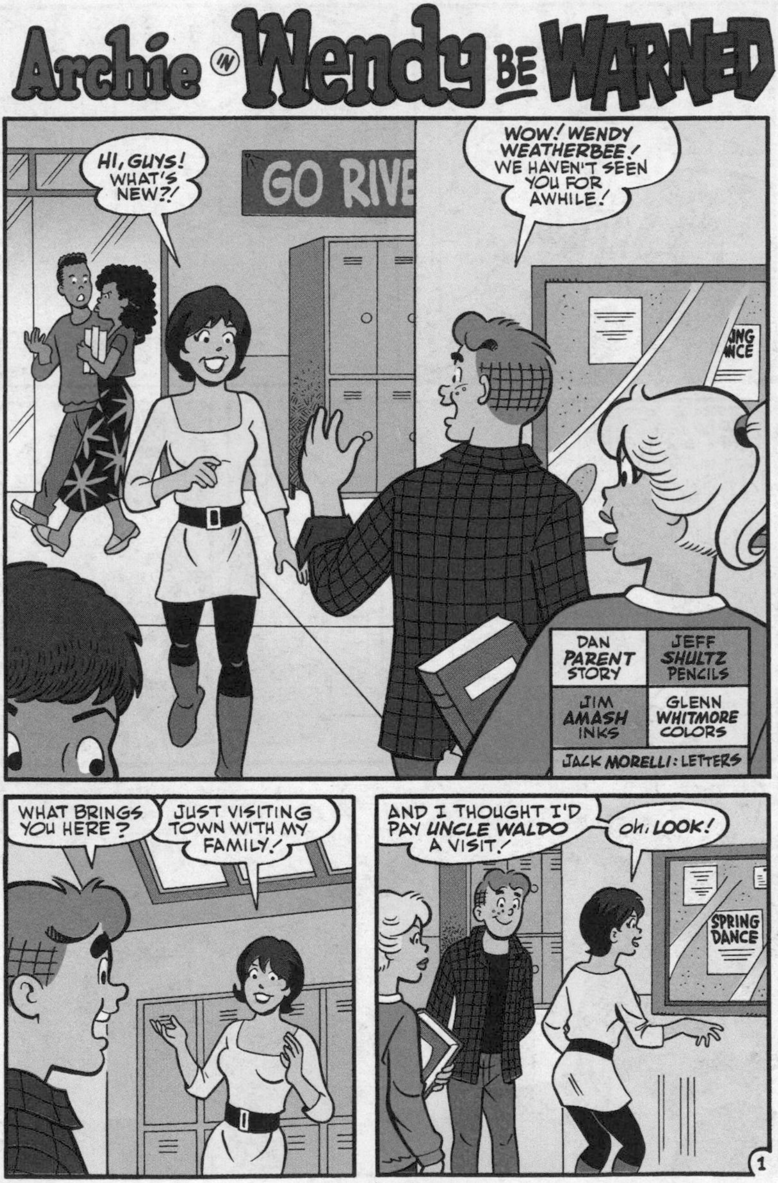

Archie in Wendy Be Warned
HI, GUYS! WHAT'S NEW?!
GO RIVE
WOW! WENDY WEATHERBEE! WE HAVEN'T SEEN YOU FOR AWHILE!
DAN PARENT STORY
JEFF SHULTZ PENCILS
JIM AMASH INKS
GLENN WHITMORE COLORS
JACK MORELLI: LETTERS
WHAT BRINGS YOU HERE?
JUST VISITING TOWN WITH MY FAMILY!
AND I THOUGHT I'D PAY UNCLE WALDO A VISIT!
oh, LOOK!
SPRING DANCE
1

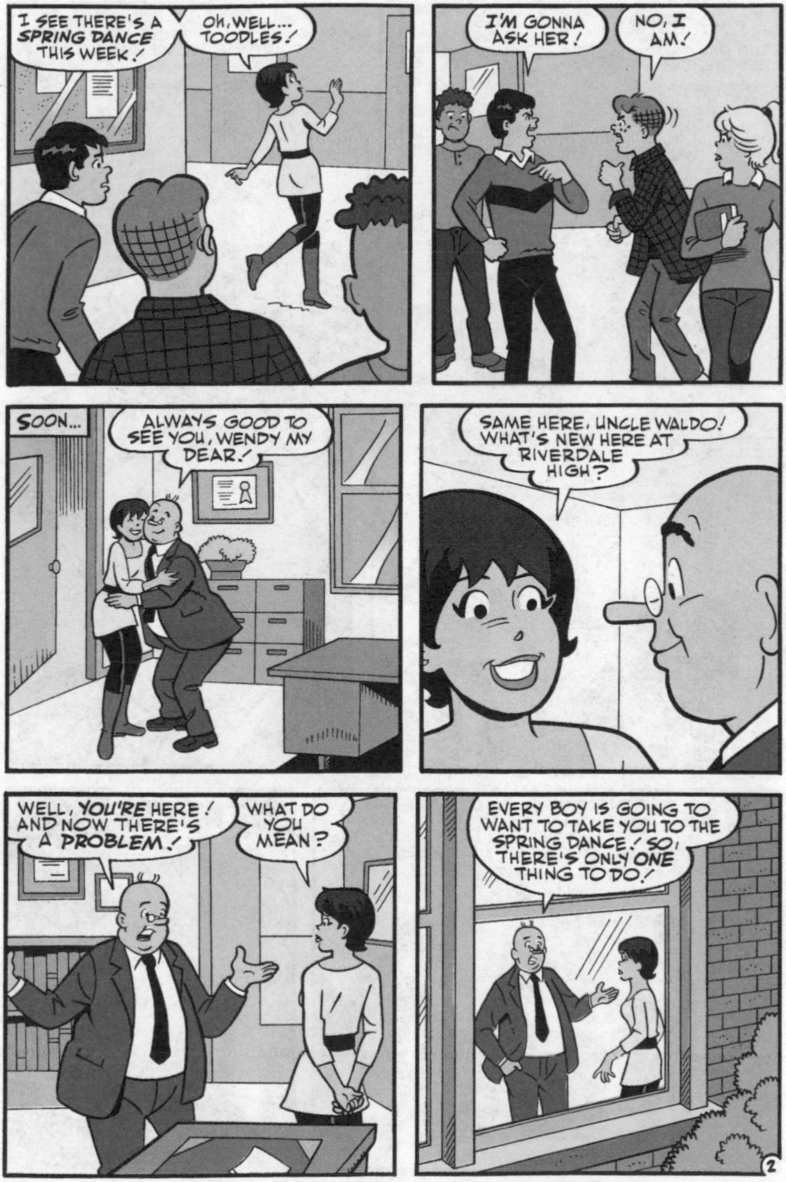
I SEE THERE'S A SPRING DANCE THIS WEEK!
Oh, WELL... TOODLES!
I'M GONNA ASK HER!
NO, I AM!
SOON...
ALWAYS GOOD TO SEE YOU, WENDY MY DEAR!
SAME HERE, UNCLE WALDO! WHAT'S NEW HERE AT RIVERDALE HIGH?
WELL, YOU'RE HERE! AND NOW THERE'S A PROBLEM!
WHAT DO YOU MEAN?
EVERY BOY IS GOING TO WANT TO TAKE YOU TO THE SPRING DANCE! SO, THERE'S ONLY ONE THING TO DO!
2

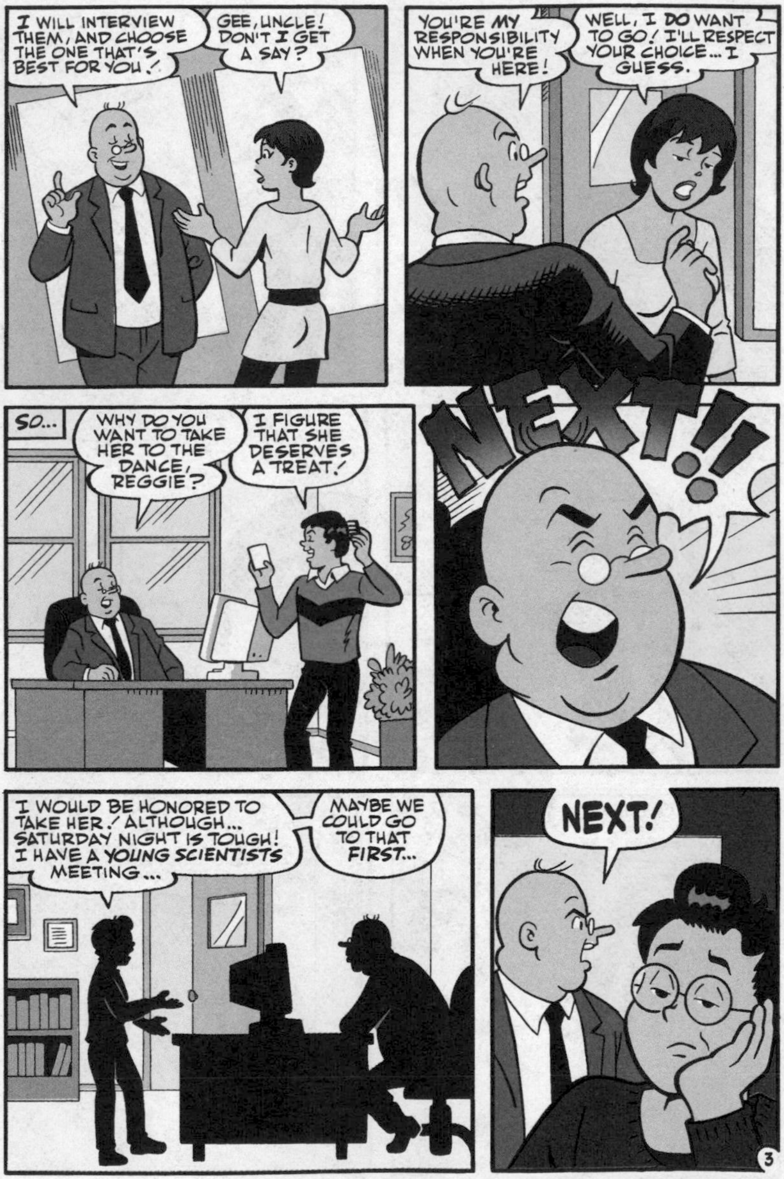
I WILL INTERVIEW THEM, AND CHOOSE THE ONE THAT'S BEST FOR YOU!
GEE, UNCLE! DON'T I GET A SAY?
YOU'RE MY RESPONSIBILITY WHEN YOU'RE HERE!
WELL, I DO WANT TO GO! I'LL RESPECT YOUR CHOICE... I GUESS.
SO...
WHY DO YOU WANT TO TAKE HER TO THE DANCE, REGGIE?
I FIGURE THAT SHE DESERVES A TREAT!
NEXT!!
I WOULD BE HONORED TO TAKE HER! ALTHOUGH... SATURDAY NIGHT IS TOUGH! I HAVE A YOUNG SCIENTISTS MEETING...
MAYBE WE COULD GO TO THAT FIRST...
NEXT!
3

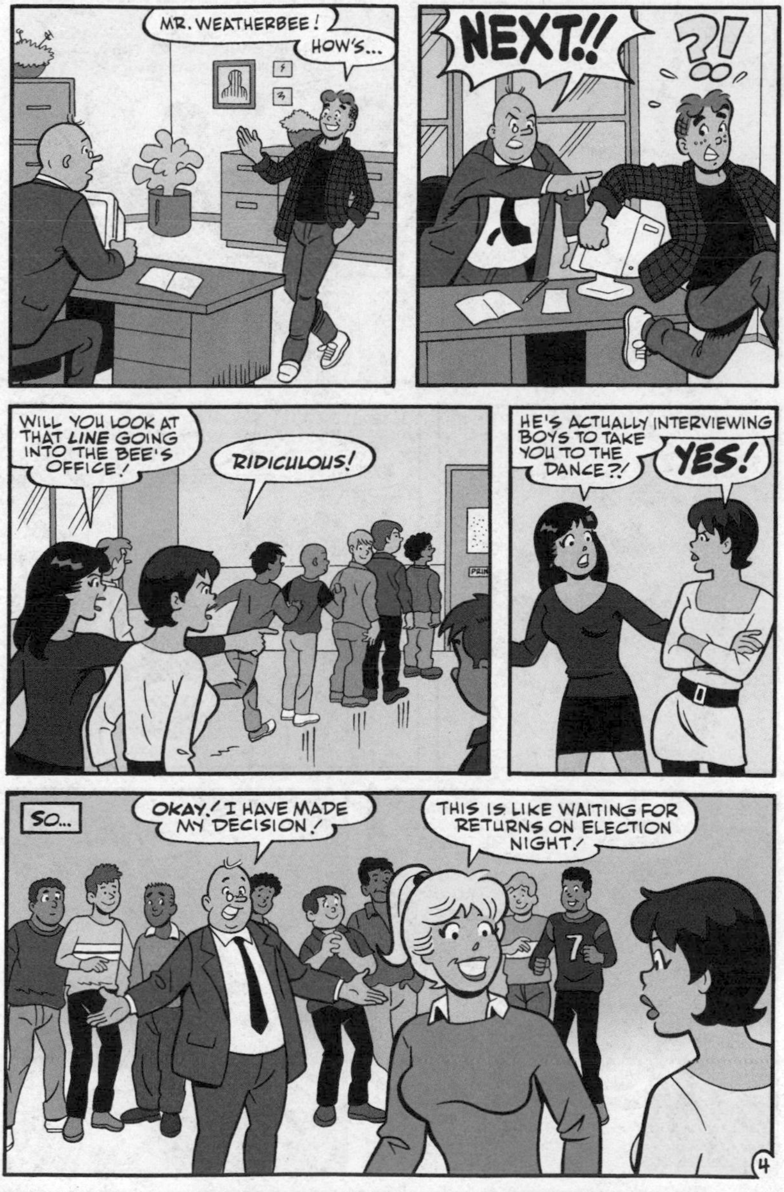
MR. WEATHERBEE!
HOW'S...
NEXT!!
?!
WILL YOU LOOK AT THAT LINE GOING INTO THE BEE'S OFFICE!
RIDICULOUS!
HE'S ACTUALLY INTERVIEWING BOYS TO TAKE YOU TO THE DANCE?!
YES!
SO...
OKAY! I HAVE MADE MY DECISION!
THIS IS LIKE WAITING FOR RETURNS ON ELECTION NIGHT!
4

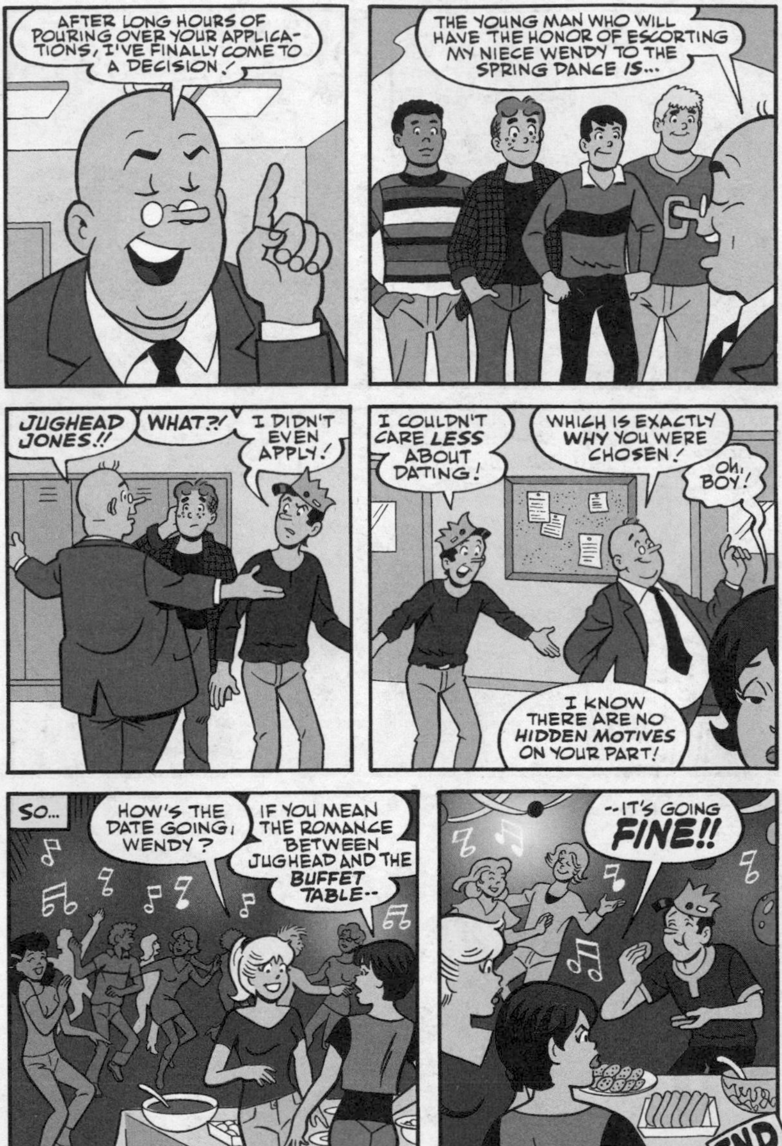
AFTER LONG HOURS OF POURING OVER YOUR APPLICA-TIONS, I'VE FINALLY COME TO A DECISION!
THE YOUNG MAN WHO WILL HAVE THE HONOR OF ESCORTING MY NIECE WENDY TO THE SPRING DANCE IS...
JUGHEAD JONES!!
WHAT?!
I DIDN'T EVEN APPLY!
I COULDN'T CARE LESS ABOUT DATING!
WHICH IS EXACTLY WHY YOU WERE CHOSEN!
OH, BOY!
I KNOW THERE ARE NO HIDDEN MOTIVES ON YOUR PART!
SO...
HOW'S THE DATE GOING, WENDY?
IF YOU MEAN THE ROMANCE BETWEEN JUGHEAD AND THE BUFFET TABLE--
--IT'S GOING FINE!!
END

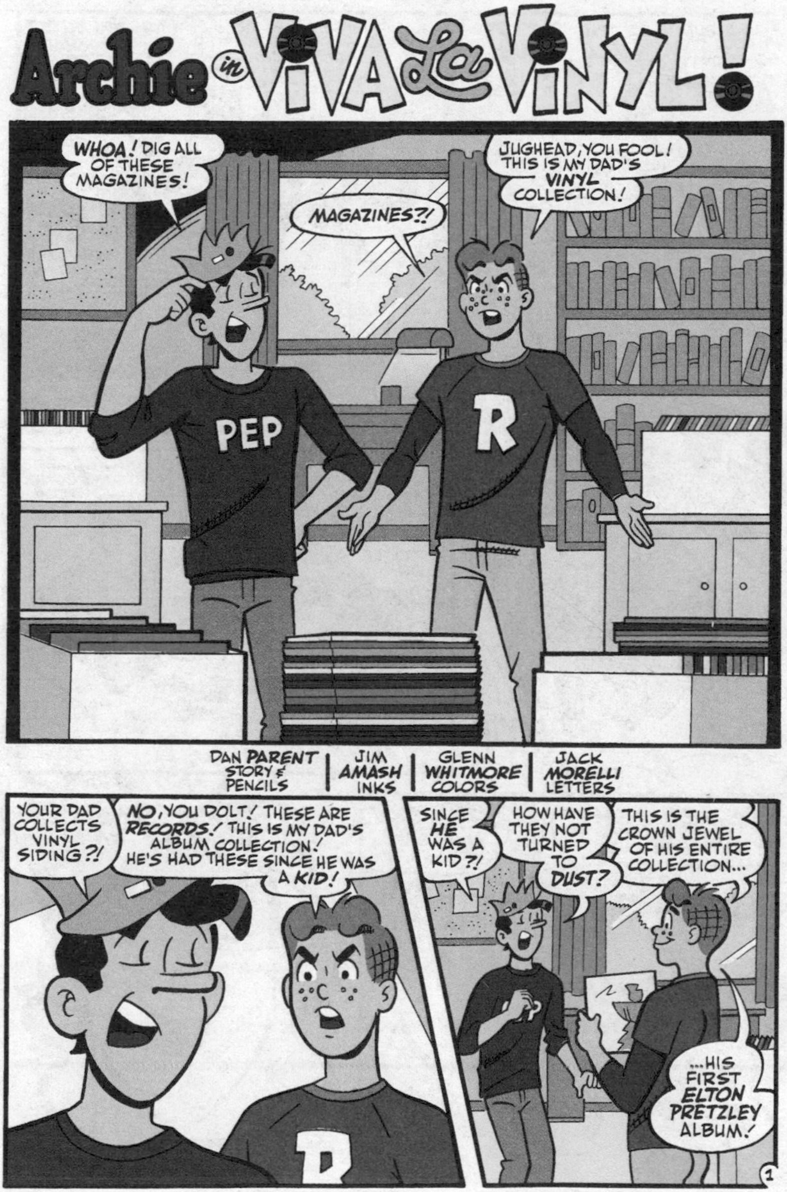
Archie in VIVA La VINYL!
WHOA! DIG ALL OF THESE MAGAZINES!
MAGAZINES?!
JUGHEAD, YOU FOOL! THIS IS MY DAD'S VINYL COLLECTION!
PEP
R
DAN PARENT STORY & PENCILS
JIM AMASH INKS
GLENN WHITMORE COLORS
JACK MORELLI LETTERS
YOUR DAD COLLECTS VINYL SIDING?!
NO, YOU DOLT! THESE ARE RECORDS! THIS IS MY DAD'S ALBUM COLLECTION! HE'S HAD THESE SINCE HE WAS A KID!
SINCE HE WAS A KID?!
HOW HAVE THEY NOT TURNED TO DUST?
THIS IS THE CROWN JEWEL OF HIS ENTIRE COLLECTION...
...HIS FIRST ELTON PRETZLEY ALBUM!
1

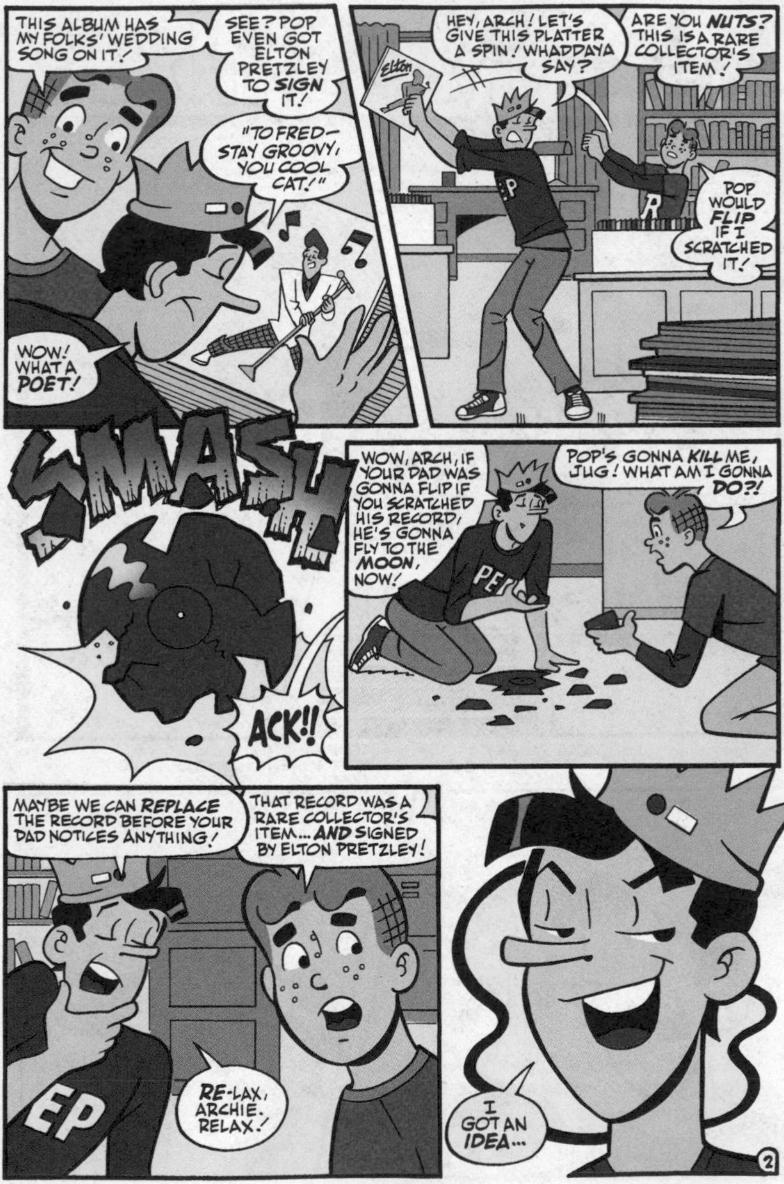
THIS ALBUM HAS MY FOLKS' WEDDING SONG ON IT!
SEE? POP EVEN GOT ELTON PRETZLEY TO SIGN IT!
"TO FRED— STAY GROOVY, YOU COOL CAT!"
WOW! WHAT A POET!
Elton
HEY, ARCH! LET'S GIVE THIS PLATTER A SPIN! WHADDAYA SAY?
ARE YOU NUTS? THIS IS A RARE COLLECTOR'S ITEM!
POP WOULD FLIP IF I SCRATCHED IT!
SMASH
ACK!!
WOW, ARCH, IF YOUR DAD WAS GONNA FLIP IF YOU SCRATCHED HIS RECORD, HE'S GONNA FLY TO THE MOON, NOW!
POP'S GONNA KILL ME, JUG! WHAT AM I GONNA DO?!
MAYBE WE CAN REPLACE THE RECORD BEFORE YOUR DAD NOTICES ANYTHING!
THAT RECORD WAS A RARE COLLECTOR'S ITEM... AND SIGNED BY ELTON PRETZLEY!
RE-LAX, ARCHIE. RELAX.!
I GOT AN IDEA...
2

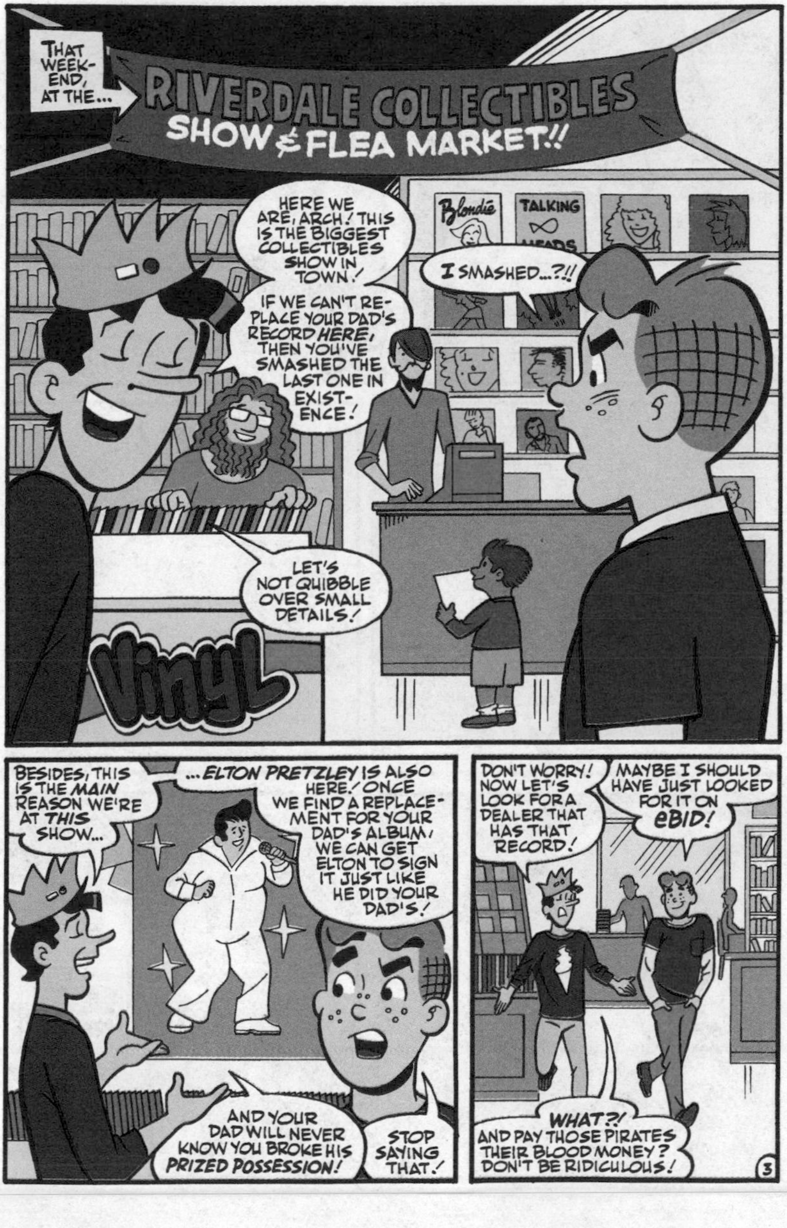
THAT WEEK-END, AT THE...
RIVERDALE COLLECTIBLES SHOW & FLEA MARKET!!
Blondie
TALKING HEADS
HERE WE ARE, ARCH! THIS IS THE BIGGEST COLLECTIBLES SHOW IN TOWN!
IF WE CAN'T RE-PLACE YOUR DAD'S RECORD HERE, THEN YOU'VE SMASHED THE LAST ONE IN EXIST-ENCE!
I SMASHED...?!!
LET'S NOT QUIBBLE OVER SMALL DETAILS!
VINYL
BESIDES, THIS IS THE MAIN REASON WE'RE AT THIS SHOW...
...ELTON PRETZLEY IS ALSO HERE! ONCE WE FIND A REPLACE-MENT FOR YOUR DAD'S ALBUM, WE CAN GET ELTON TO SIGN IT JUST LIKE HE DID YOUR DAD'S!
AND YOUR DAD WILL NEVER KNOW YOU BROKE HIS PRIZED POSSESSION!
STOP SAYING THAT!
DON'T WORRY! NOW LET'S LOOK FOR A DEALER THAT HAS THAT RECORD!
MAYBE I SHOULD HAVE JUST LOOKED FOR IT ON eBID!
WHAT?! AND PAY THOSE PIRATES THEIR BLOOD MONEY? DON'T BE RIDICULOUS!
3

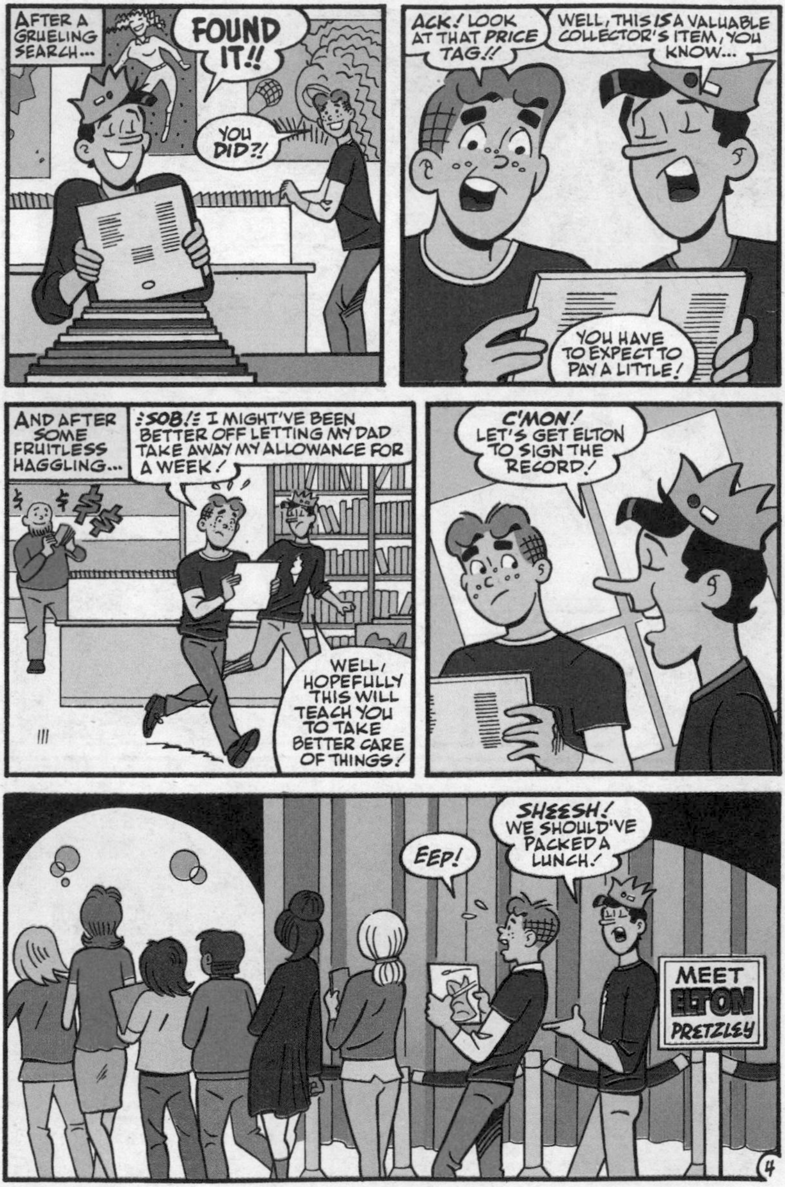
AFTER A GRUELING SEARCH...
FOUND IT!!
YOU DID?!
ACK! LOOK AT THAT PRICE TAG!!
WELL, THIS IS A VALUABLE COLLECTOR'S ITEM, YOU KNOW...
YOU HAVE TO EXPECT TO PAY A LITTLE!
AND AFTER SOME FRUITLESS HAGGLING...
SOB! I MIGHT'VE BEEN BETTER OFF LETTING MY DAD TAKE AWAY MY ALLOWANCE FOR A WEEK!
WELL, HOPEFULLY THIS WILL TEACH YOU TO TAKE BETTER CARE OF THINGS!
C'MON! LET'S GET ELTON TO SIGN THE RECORD!
EEP!
SHEESH! WE SHOULD'VE PACKED A LUNCH!
MEET ELTON PRETZLEY
4

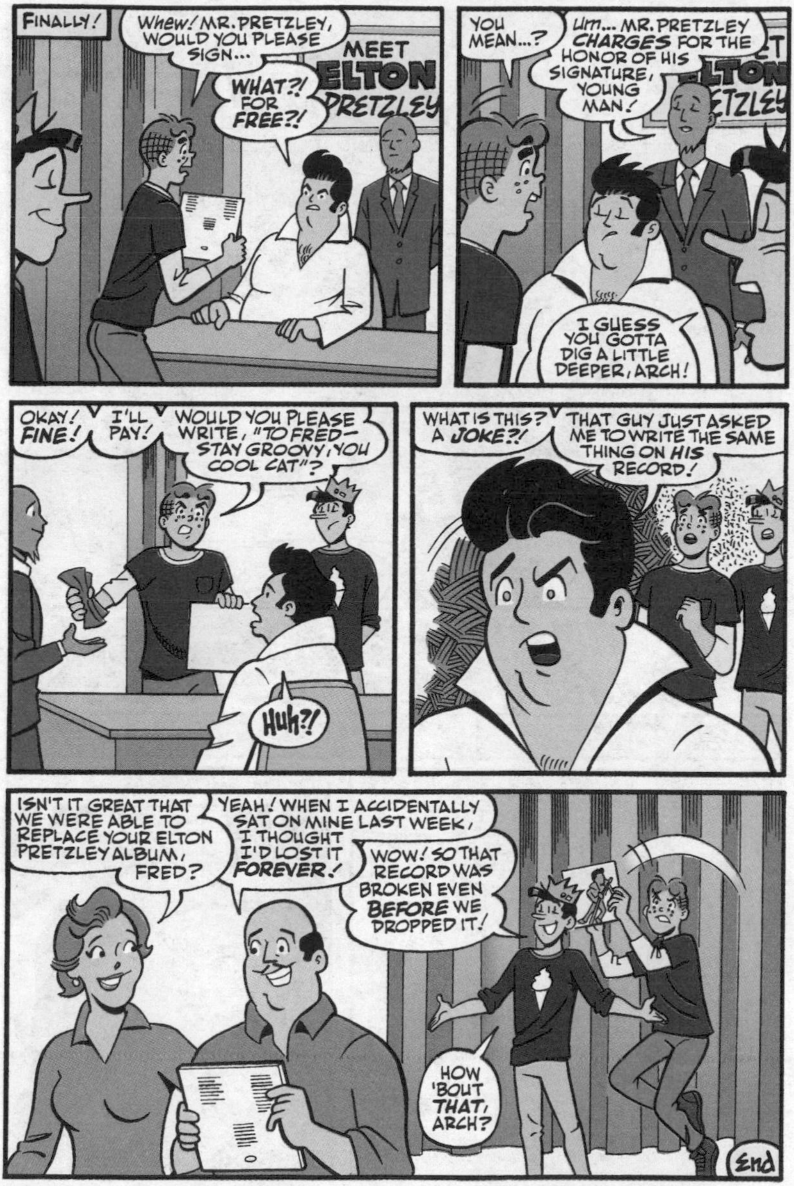
FINALLY!
Whew! MR. PRETZLEY, WOULD YOU PLEASE SIGN...
WHAT?! FOR FREE?!
MEET ELTON PRETZLEY
YOU MEAN...?
Um... MR. PRETZLEY CHARGES FOR THE HONOR OF HIS SIGNATURE, YOUNG MAN!
I GUESS YOU GOTTA DIG A LITTLE DEEPER, ARCH!
OKAY! FINE!
I'LL PAY!
WOULD YOU PLEASE WRITE, "TO FRED— STAY GROOVY, YOU COOL CAT"?
HUH?!
WHAT IS THIS? A JOKE?!
THAT GUY JUST ASKED ME TO WRITE THE SAME THING ON HIS RECORD!
ISN'T IT GREAT THAT WE WERE ABLE TO REPLACE YOUR ELTON PRETZLEY ALBUM, FRED?
YEAH! WHEN I ACCIDENTALLY SAT ON MINE LAST WEEK, I THOUGHT I'D LOST IT FOREVER!
WOW! SO THAT RECORD WAS BROKEN EVEN BEFORE WE DROPPED IT!
HOW 'BOUT THAT, ARCH?
End

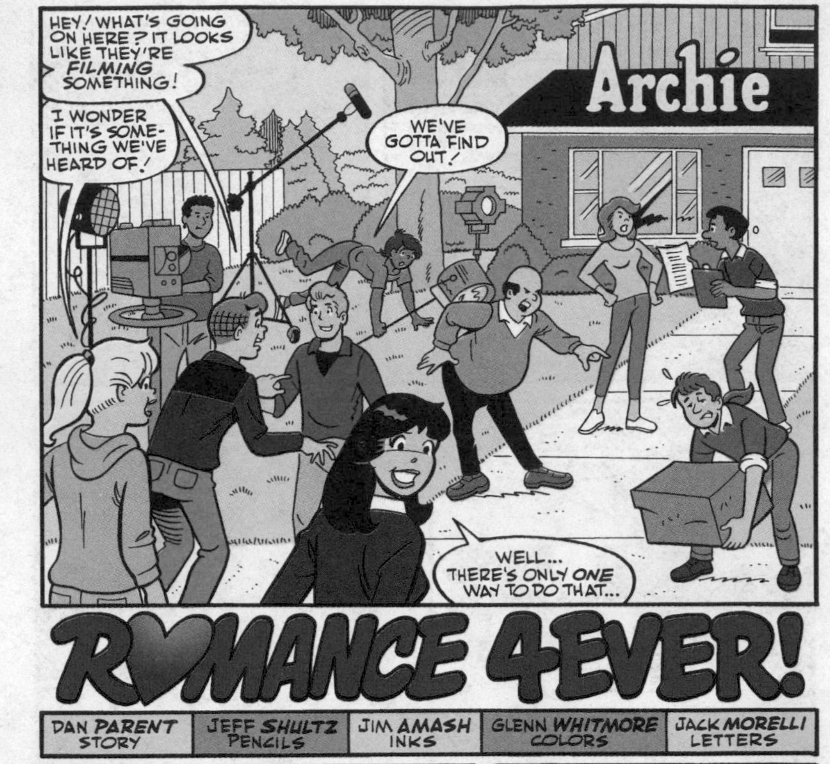
HEY! WHAT'S GOING ON HERE? IT LOOKS LIKE THEY'RE FILMING SOMETHING!
I WONDER IF IT'S SOMETHING WE'VE HEARD OF!
WE'VE GOTTA FIND OUT!
Archie
WELL... THERE'S ONLY ONE WAY TO DO THAT...

ROMANCE 4EVER!

DAN PARENT STORY	JEFF SHULTZ PENCILS	JIM AMASH INKS	GLENN WHITMORE COLORS	JACK MORELLI LETTERS

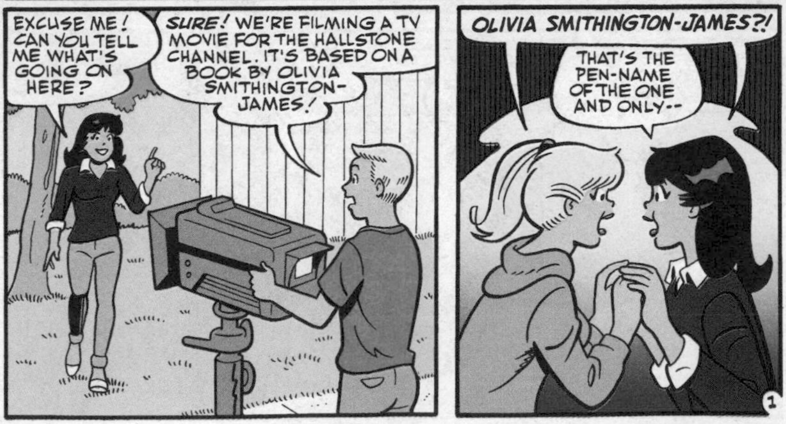
EXCUSE ME! CAN YOU TELL ME WHAT'S GOING ON HERE?
SURE! WE'RE FILMING A TV MOVIE FOR THE HALLSTONE CHANNEL. IT'S BASED ON A BOOK BY OLIVIA SMITHINGTON-JAMES!
OLIVIA SMITHINGTON-JAMES?!
THAT'S THE PEN-NAME OF THE ONE AND ONLY--
1

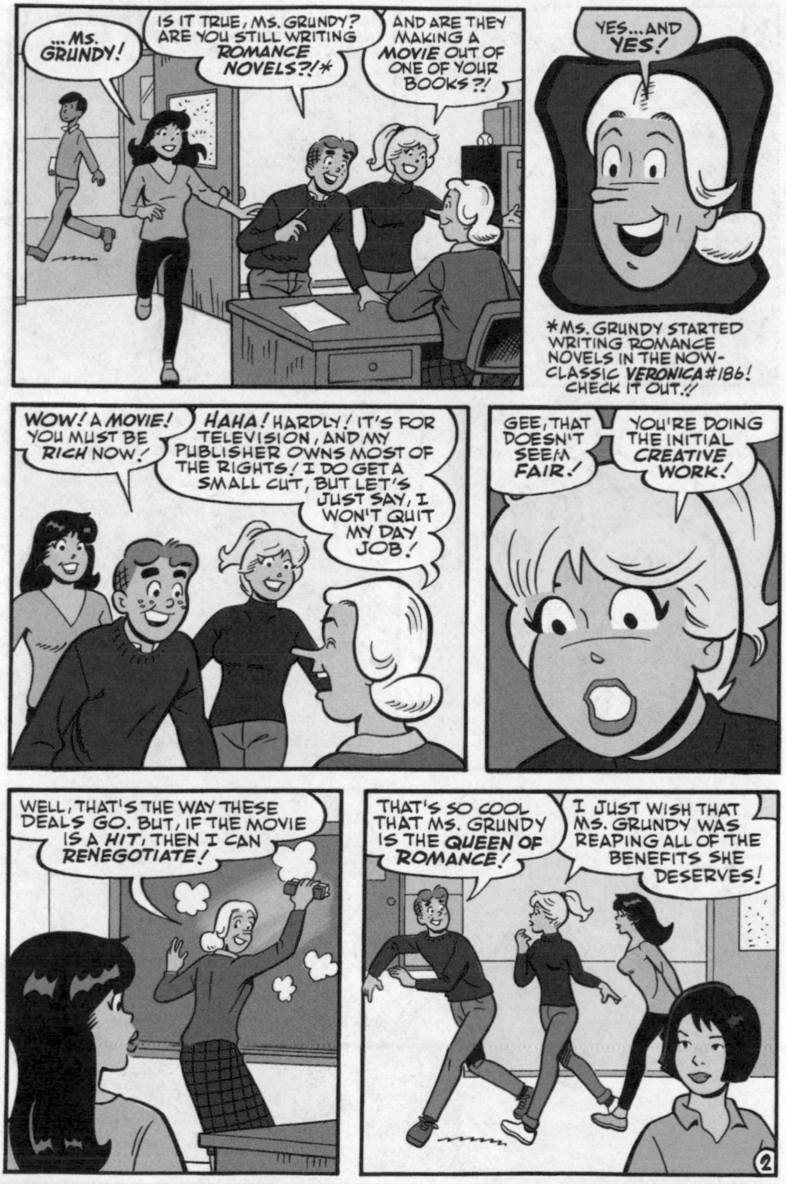
...MS. GRUNDY!
IS IT TRUE, MS. GRUNDY? ARE YOU STILL WRITING ROMANCE NOVELS?!*
AND ARE THEY MAKING A MOVIE OUT OF ONE OF YOUR BOOKS?!
YES...AND YES!
*MS. GRUNDY STARTED WRITING ROMANCE NOVELS IN THE NOW-CLASSIC VERONICA #186! CHECK IT OUT.!!
WOW! A MOVIE! YOU MUST BE RICH NOW!
HAHA! HARDLY! IT'S FOR TELEVISION, AND MY PUBLISHER OWNS MOST OF THE RIGHTS! I DO GET A SMALL CUT, BUT LET'S JUST SAY, I WON'T QUIT MY DAY JOB!
GEE, THAT DOESN'T SEEM FAIR!
YOU'RE DOING THE INITIAL CREATIVE WORK!
WELL, THAT'S THE WAY THESE DEALS GO. BUT, IF THE MOVIE IS A HIT, THEN I CAN RENEGOTIATE!
THAT'S SO COOL THAT MS. GRUNDY IS THE QUEEN OF ROMANCE!
I JUST WISH THAT MS. GRUNDY WAS REAPING ALL OF THE BENEFITS SHE DESERVES!
2

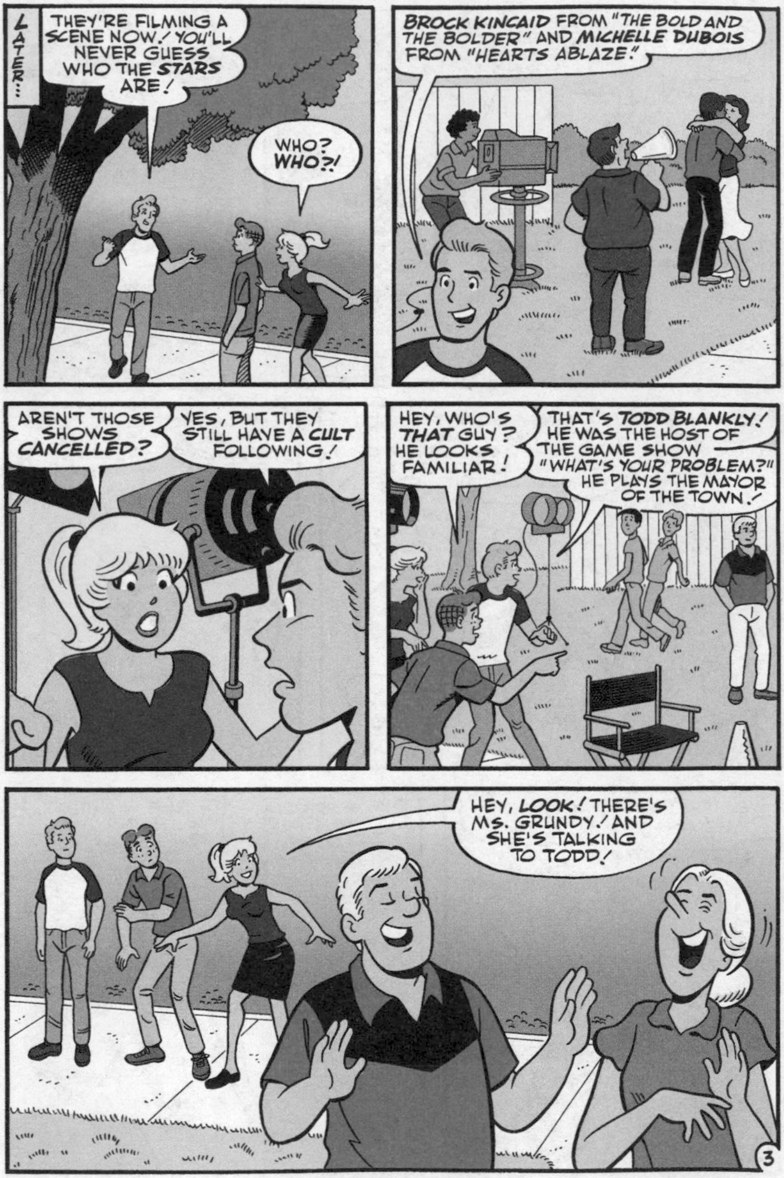
LATER...
THEY'RE FILMING A SCENE NOW! YOU'LL NEVER GUESS WHO THE STARS ARE!
WHO? WHO?!
BROCK KINCAID FROM "THE BOLD AND THE BOLDER" AND MICHELLE DUBOIS FROM "HEARTS ABLAZE."
AREN'T THOSE SHOWS CANCELLED?
YES, BUT THEY STILL HAVE A CULT FOLLOWING!
HEY, WHO'S THAT GUY? HE LOOKS FAMILIAR!
THAT'S TODD BLANKLY! HE WAS THE HOST OF THE GAME SHOW "WHAT'S YOUR PROBLEM?" HE PLAYS THE MAYOR OF THE TOWN.
HEY, LOOK! THERE'S MS. GRUNDY! AND SHE'S TALKING TO TODD!
3

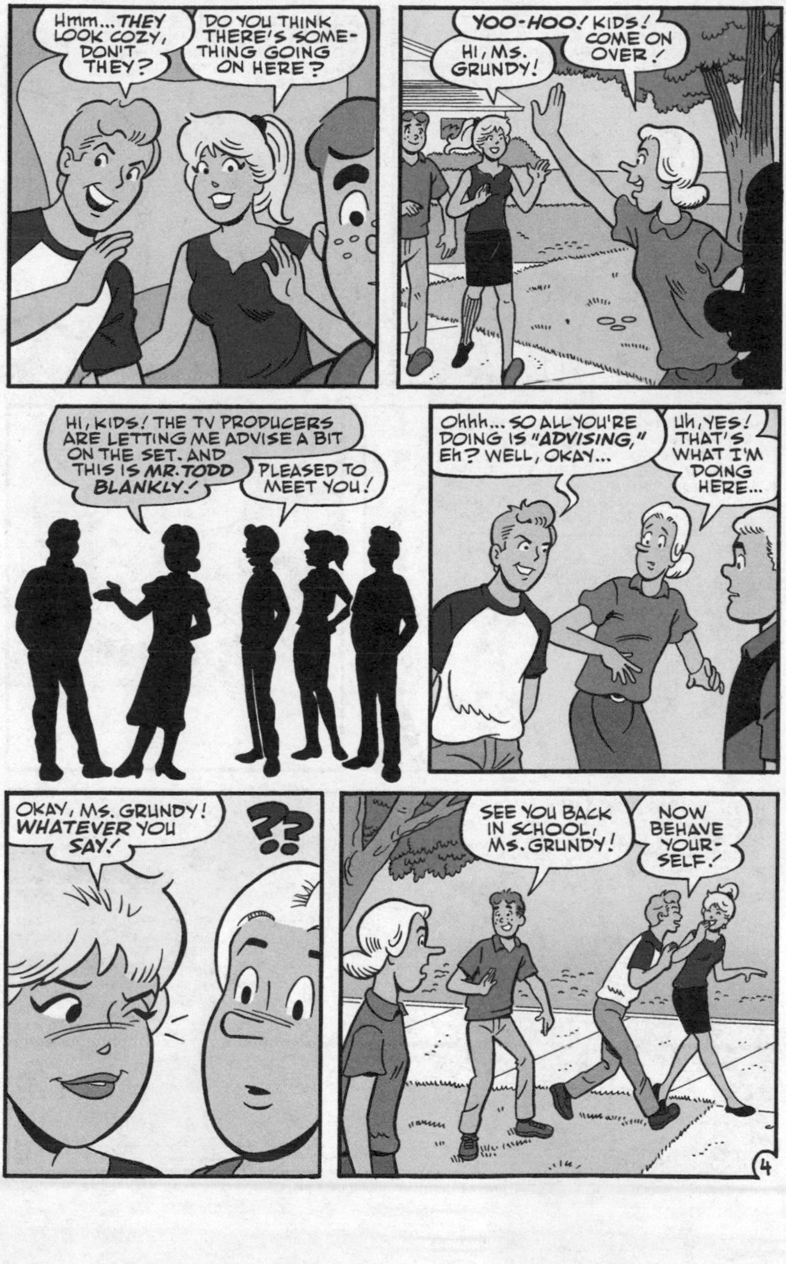
Hmm... THEY LOOK COZY, DON'T THEY?
DO YOU THINK THERE'S SOME-THING GOING ON HERE?
YOO-HOO! KIDS! COME ON OVER!
HI, MS. GRUNDY!
HI, KIDS! THE TV PRODUCERS ARE LETTING ME ADVISE A BIT ON THE SET. AND THIS IS MR. TODD BLANKLY!
PLEASED TO MEET YOU!
Ohhh... SO ALL YOU'RE DOING IS "ADVISING," Eh? WELL, OKAY...
Uh, YES! THAT'S WHAT I'M DOING HERE...
OKAY, MS. GRUNDY! WHATEVER YOU SAY!
??
SEE YOU BACK IN SCHOOL, MS. GRUNDY!
NOW BEHAVE YOUR-SELF!
4

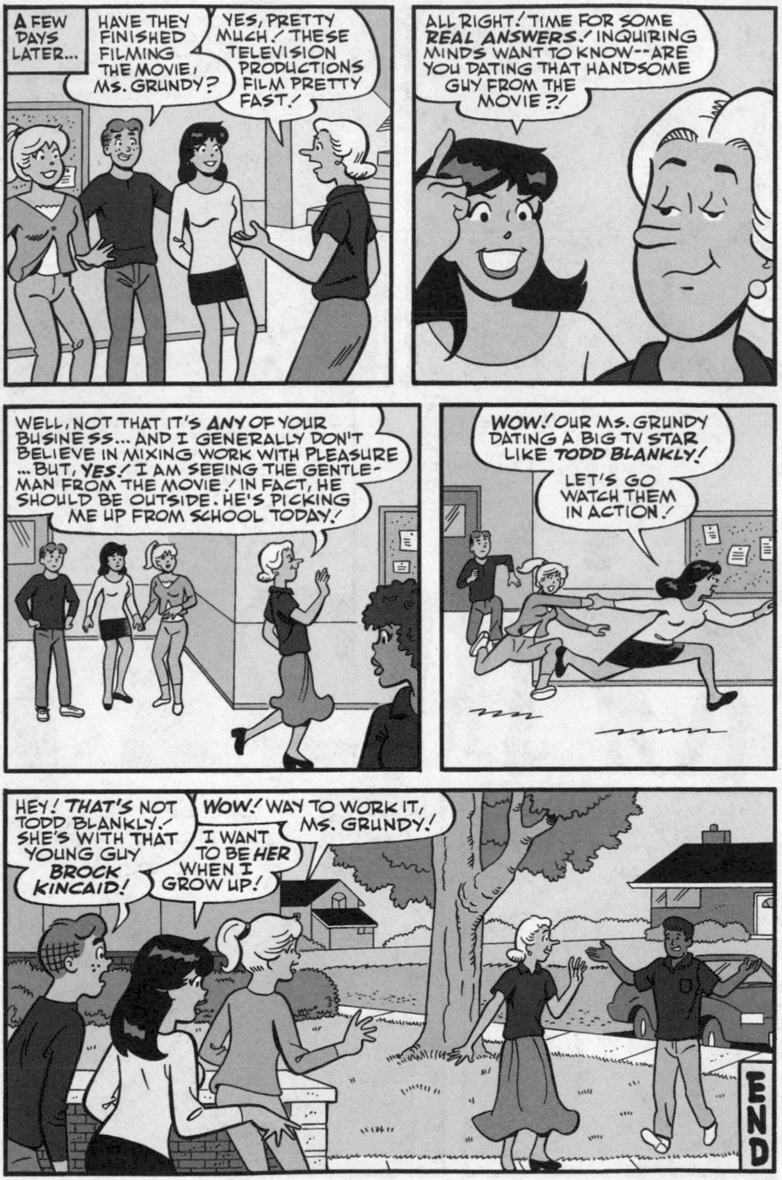
A FEW DAYS LATER...
HAVE THEY FINISHED FILMING THE MOVIE, MS. GRUNDY?
YES, PRETTY MUCH! THESE TELEVISION PRODUCTIONS FILM PRETTY FAST!
ALL RIGHT! TIME FOR SOME REAL ANSWERS! INQUIRING MINDS WANT TO KNOW--ARE YOU DATING THAT HANDSOME GUY FROM THE MOVIE?!
WELL, NOT THAT IT'S ANY OF YOUR BUSINESS... AND I GENERALLY DON'T BELIEVE IN MIXING WORK WITH PLEASURE ...BUT, YES! I AM SEEING THE GENTLEMAN FROM THE MOVIE! IN FACT, HE SHOULD BE OUTSIDE. HE'S PICKING ME UP FROM SCHOOL TODAY!
WOW! OUR MS. GRUNDY DATING A BIG TV STAR LIKE TODD BLANKLY!
LET'S GO WATCH THEM IN ACTION!
HEY! THAT'S NOT TODD BLANKLY! SHE'S WITH THAT YOUNG GUY BROCK KINCAID!
WOW! WAY TO WORK IT, MS. GRUNDY!
I WANT TO BE HER WHEN I GROW UP!
END

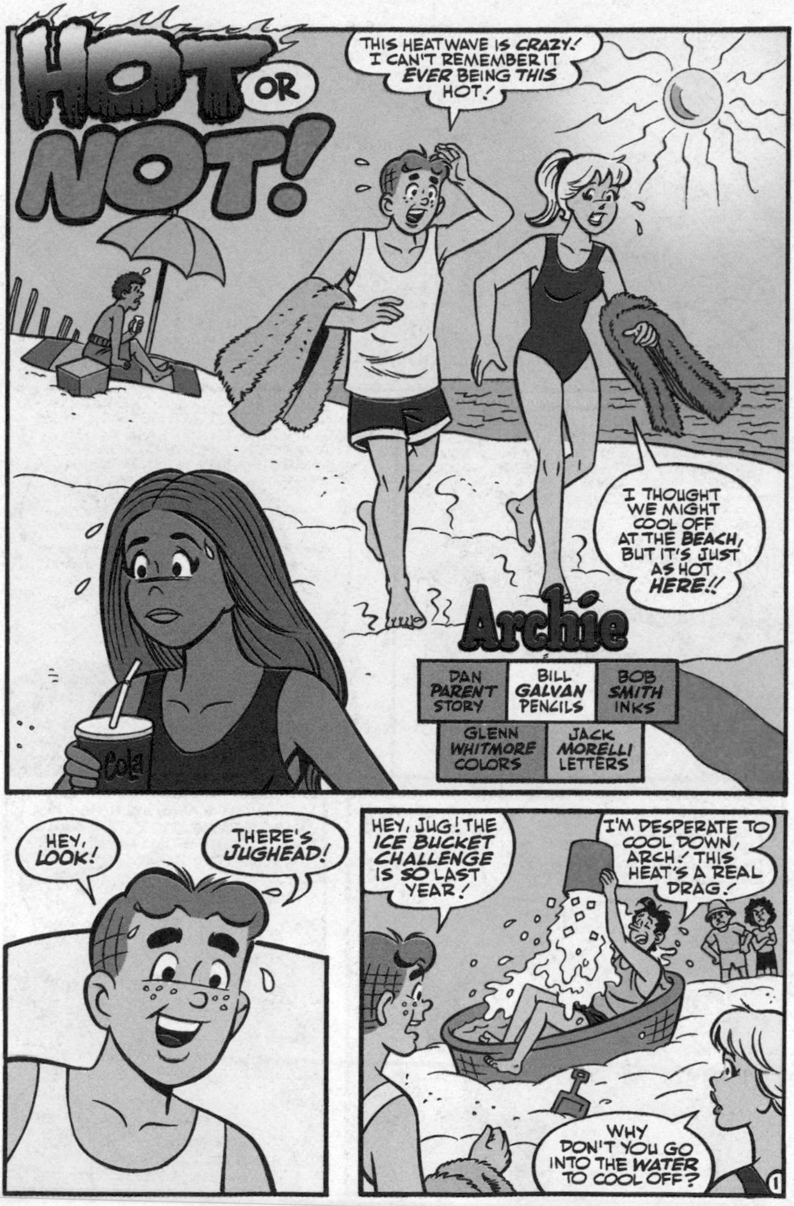
HOT OR NOT!
THIS HEATWAVE IS CRAZY! I CAN'T REMEMBER IT EVER BEING THIS HOT!
I THOUGHT WE MIGHT COOL OFF AT THE BEACH, BUT IT'S JUST AS HOT HERE!!
Archie
DAN PARENT STORY
BILL GALVAN PENCILS
BOB SMITH INKS
GLENN WHITMORE COLORS
JACK MORELLI LETTERS
Cola
HEY, LOOK!
THERE'S JUGHEAD!
HEY, JUG! THE ICE BUCKET CHALLENGE IS SO LAST YEAR!
I'M DESPERATE TO COOL DOWN, ARCH! THIS HEAT'S A REAL DRAG!
WHY DON'T YOU GO INTO THE WATER TO COOL OFF?
1

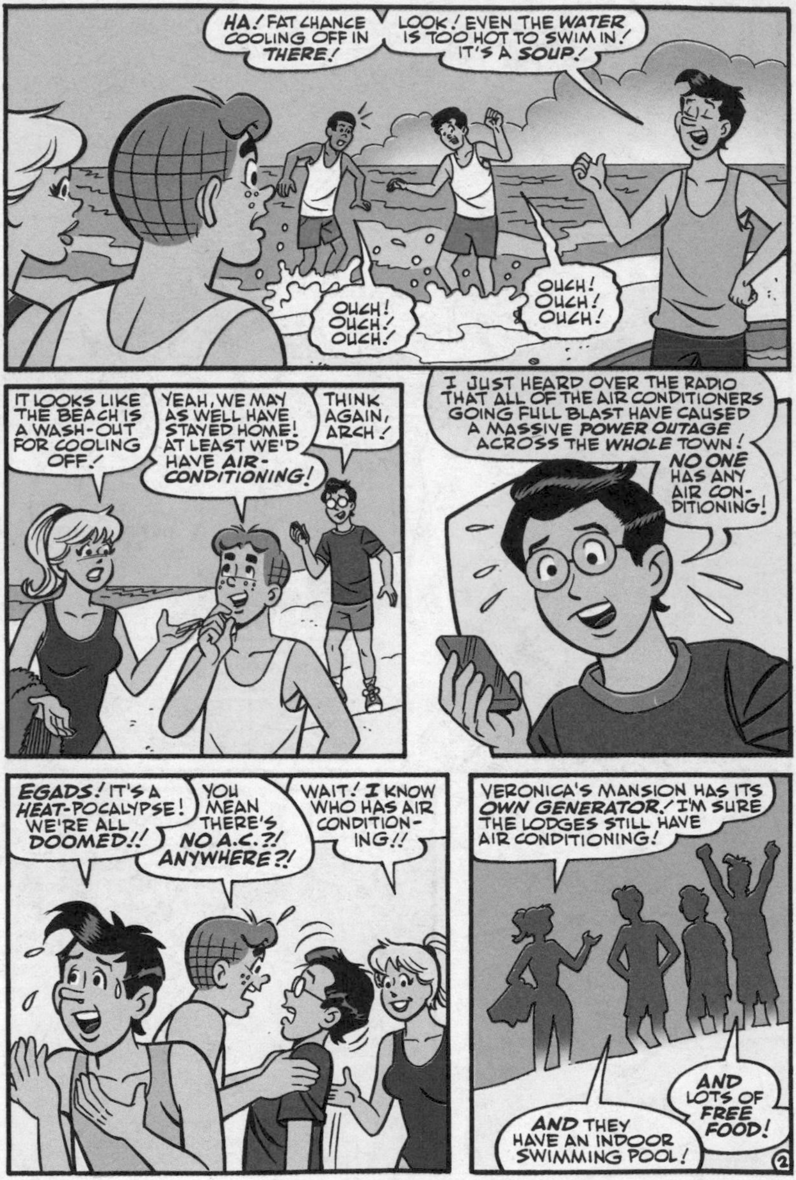
HA! FAT CHANCE COOLING OFF IN THERE!
LOOK! EVEN THE WATER IS TOO HOT TO SWIM IN! IT'S A SOUP!
OUCH! OUCH! OUCH!
OUCH! OUCH! OUCH!
IT LOOKS LIKE THE BEACH IS A WASH-OUT FOR COOLING OFF!
YEAH, WE MAY AS WELL HAVE STAYED HOME! AT LEAST WE'D HAVE AIR-CONDITIONING!
THINK AGAIN, ARCH!
I JUST HEARD OVER THE RADIO THAT ALL OF THE AIR CONDITIONERS GOING FULL BLAST HAVE CAUSED A MASSIVE POWER OUTAGE ACROSS THE WHOLE TOWN! NO ONE HAS ANY AIR CONDITIONING!
EGADS! IT'S A HEAT-POCALYPSE! WE'RE ALL DOOMED!!
YOU MEAN THERE'S NO A.C.?! ANYWHERE?!
WAIT! I KNOW WHO HAS AIR CONDITIONING!!
VERONICA'S MANSION HAS ITS OWN GENERATOR! I'M SURE THE LODGES STILL HAVE AIR CONDITIONING!
AND THEY HAVE AN INDOOR SWIMMING POOL!
AND LOTS OF FREE FOOD!
2

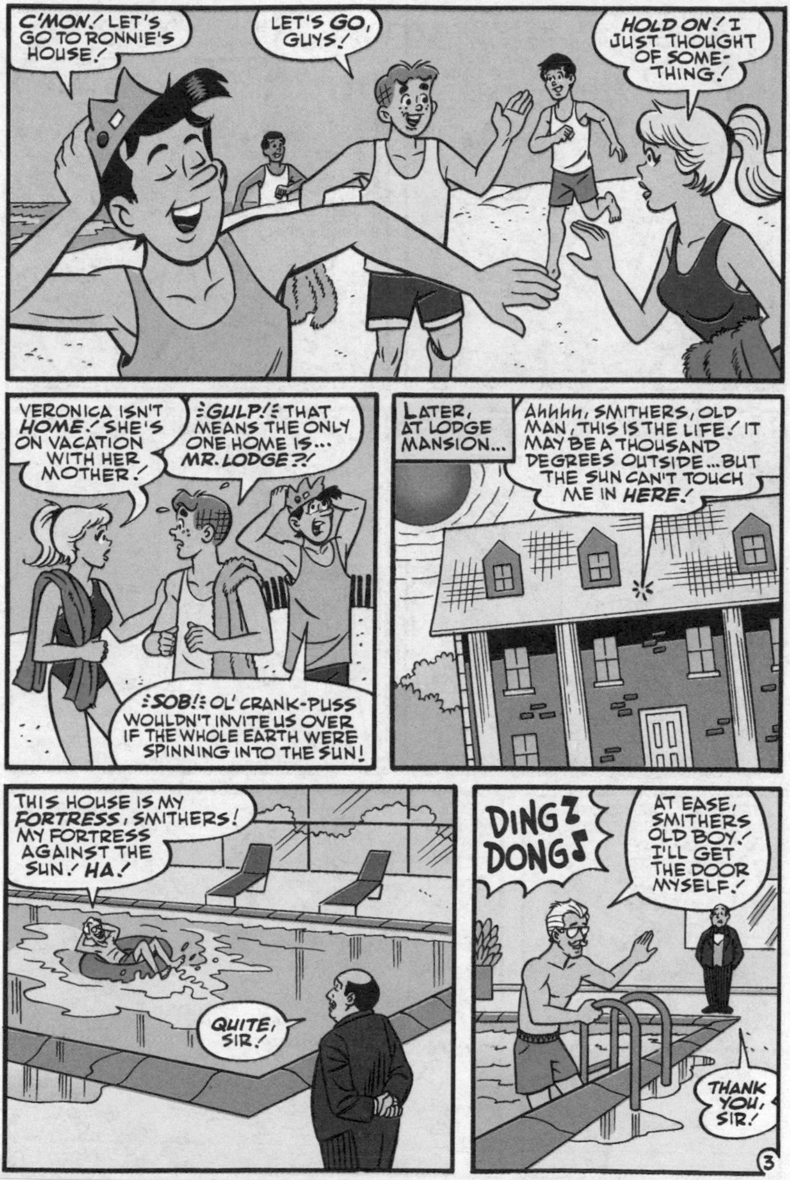
C'MON! LET'S GO TO RONNIE'S HOUSE!
LET'S GO, GUYS!
HOLD ON! I JUST THOUGHT OF SOME-THING!
VERONICA ISN'T HOME! SHE'S ON VACATION WITH HER MOTHER!
GULP! THAT MEANS THE ONLY ONE HOME IS... MR. LODGE?!
SOB! OL' CRANK-PUSS WOULDN'T INVITE US OVER IF THE WHOLE EARTH WERE SPINNING INTO THE SUN!
LATER, AT LODGE MANSION...
Ahhhh, SMITHERS, OLD MAN, THIS IS THE LIFE! IT MAY BE A THOUSAND DEGREES OUTSIDE...BUT THE SUN CAN'T TOUCH ME IN HERE!
THIS HOUSE IS MY FORTRESS, SMITHERS! MY FORTRESS AGAINST THE SUN! HA!
QUITE, SIR!
DING DONG
AT EASE, SMITHERS OLD BOY! I'LL GET THE DOOR MYSELF!
THANK YOU, SIR!
3

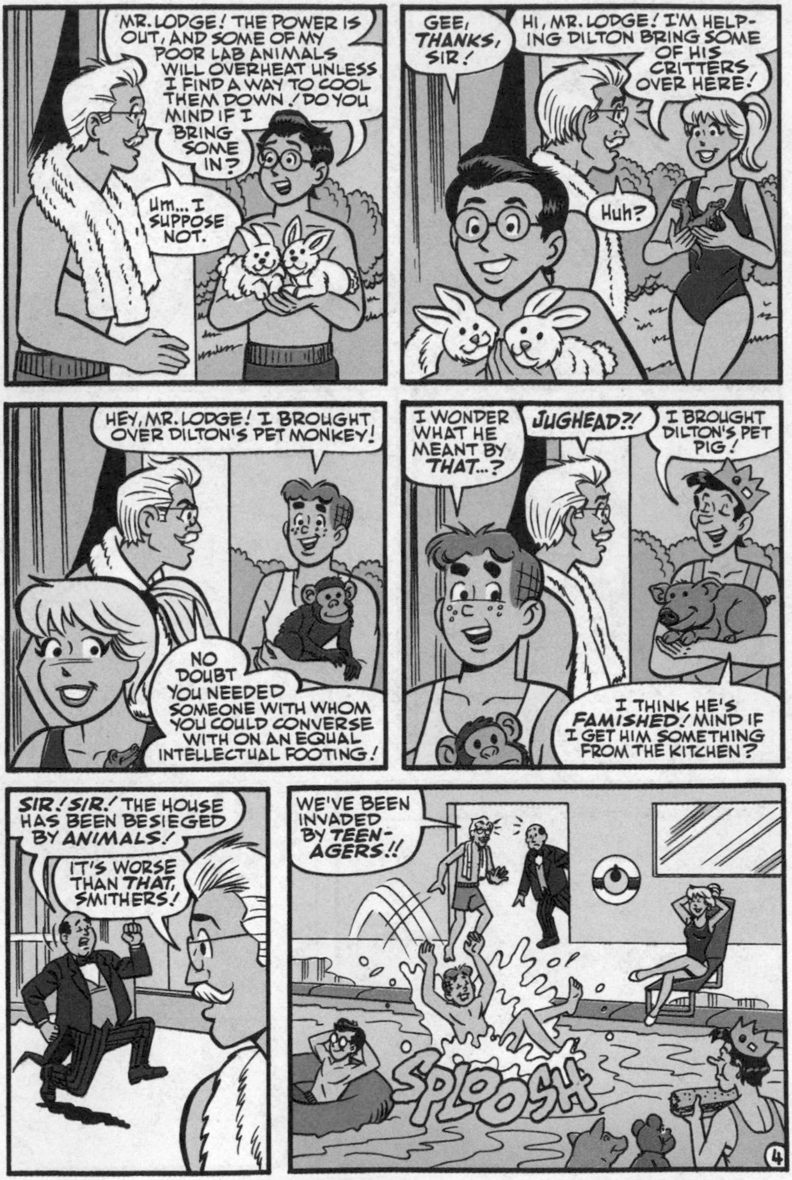
MR. LODGE! THE POWER IS OUT, AND SOME OF MY POOR LAB ANIMALS WILL OVERHEAT UNLESS I FIND A WAY TO COOL THEM DOWN! DO YOU MIND IF I BRING SOME IN?
Um... I SUPPOSE NOT.
GEE, THANKS, SIR!
HI, MR. LODGE! I'M HELPING DILTON BRING SOME OF HIS CRITTERS OVER HERE!
Huh?
HEY, MR. LODGE! I BROUGHT OVER DILTON'S PET MONKEY!
NO DOUBT YOU NEEDED SOMEONE WITH WHOM YOU COULD CONVERSE WITH ON AN EQUAL INTELLECTUAL FOOTING!
I WONDER WHAT HE MEANT BY THAT...?
JUGHEAD?!
I BROUGHT DILTON'S PET PIG!
I THINK HE'S FAMISHED! MIND IF I GET HIM SOMETHING FROM THE KITCHEN?
SIR! SIR! THE HOUSE HAS BEEN BESIEGED BY ANIMALS!
IT'S WORSE THAN THAT, SMITHERS!
WE'VE BEEN INVADED BY TEEN-AGERS!!
SPLOOSH
4

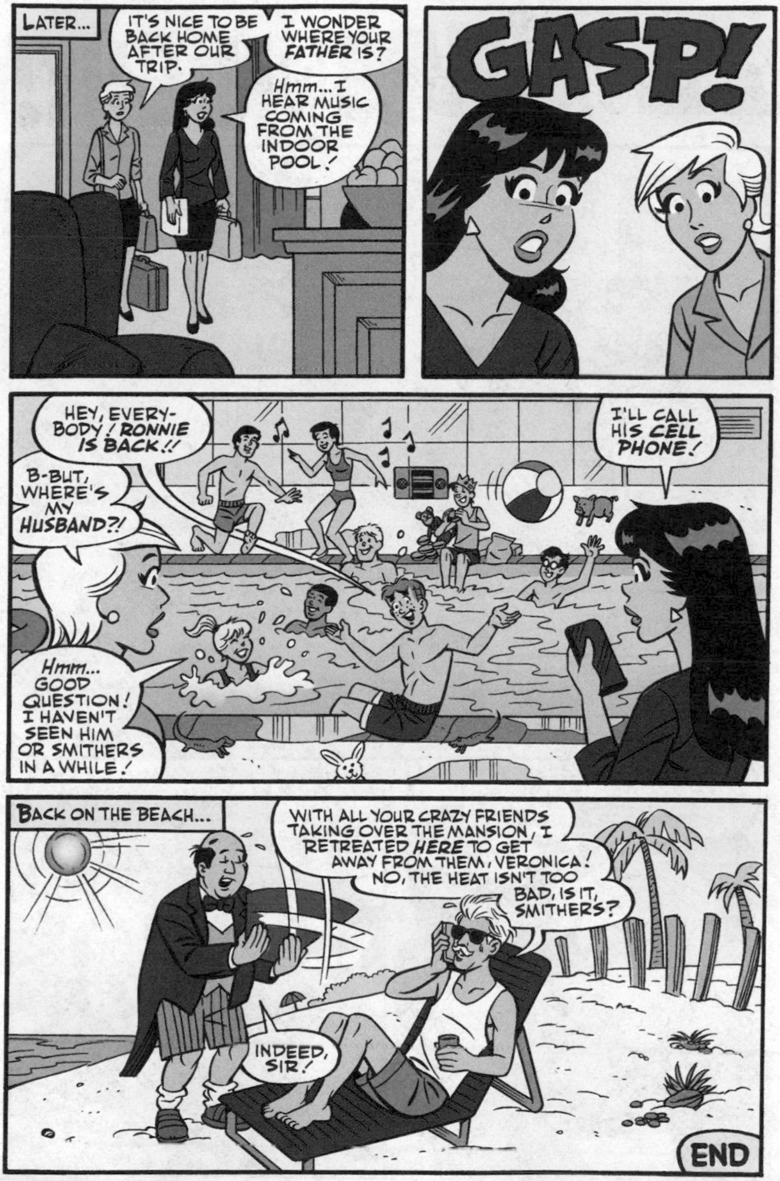
LATER...
IT'S NICE TO BE BACK HOME AFTER OUR TRIP.
I WONDER WHERE YOUR FATHER IS?
Hmm... I HEAR MUSIC COMING FROM THE INDOOR POOL!
GASP!
HEY, EVERY-BODY! RONNIE IS BACK!!
B-BUT, WHERE'S MY HUSBAND?!
I'LL CALL HIS CELL PHONE!
Hmm... GOOD QUESTION! I HAVEN'T SEEN HIM OR SMITHERS IN A WHILE!
BACK ON THE BEACH...
WITH ALL YOUR CRAZY FRIENDS TAKING OVER THE MANSION, I RETREATED HERE TO GET AWAY FROM THEM, VERONICA! NO, THE HEAT ISN'T TOO BAD, IS IT, SMITHERS?
INDEED, SIR!
END

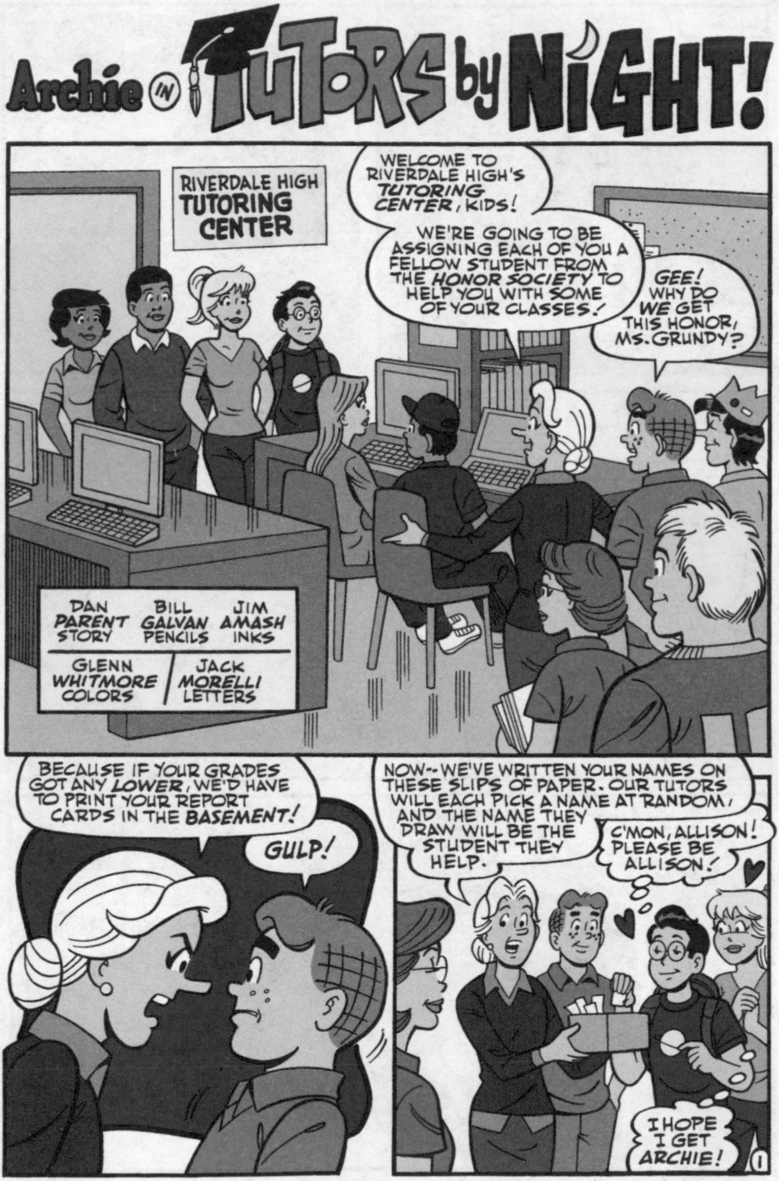
Archie in TUTORS by NIGHT!
RIVERDALE HIGH TUTORING CENTER
WELCOME TO RIVERDALE HIGH'S TUTORING CENTER, KIDS!
WE'RE GOING TO BE ASSIGNING EACH OF YOU A FELLOW STUDENT FROM THE HONOR SOCIETY TO HELP YOU WITH SOME OF YOUR CLASSES!
GEE! WHY DO WE GET THIS HONOR, MS. GRUNDY?
DAN PARENT STORY
BILL GALVAN PENCILS
JIM AMASH INKS
GLENN WHITMORE COLORS
JACK MORELLI LETTERS
BECAUSE IF YOUR GRADES GOT ANY LOWER, WE'D HAVE TO PRINT YOUR REPORT CARDS IN THE BASEMENT!
GULP!
NOW-- WE'VE WRITTEN YOUR NAMES ON THESE SLIPS OF PAPER. OUR TUTORS WILL EACH PICK A NAME AT RANDOM, AND THE NAME THEY DRAW WILL BE THE STUDENT THEY HELP.
C'MON, ALLISON! PLEASE BE ALLISON!
I HOPE I GET ARCHIE!
1

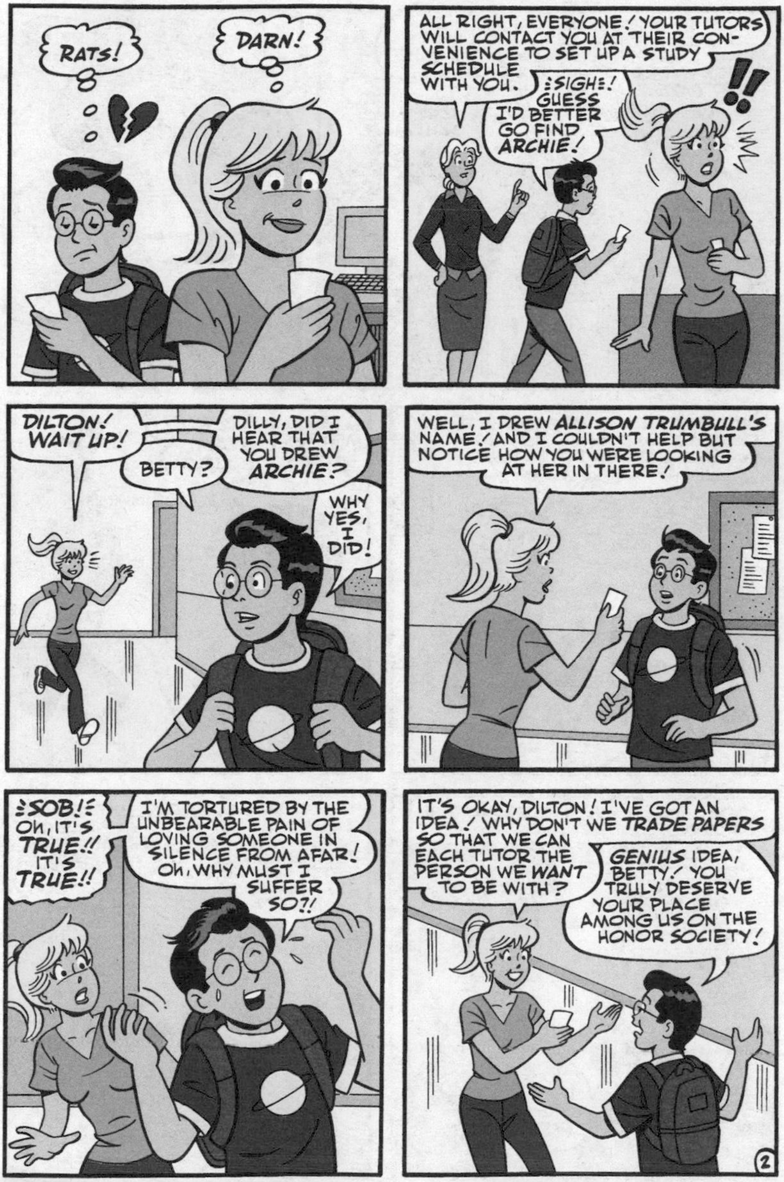
RATS!
DARN!
ALL RIGHT, EVERYONE! YOUR TUTORS WILL CONTACT YOU AT THEIR CON-VENIENCE TO SET UP A STUDY SCHEDULE WITH YOU.
SIGH! GUESS I'D BETTER GO FIND ARCHIE!
!!
DILTON! WAIT UP!
BETTY?
DILLY, DID I HEAR THAT YOU DREW ARCHIE?
WHY YES, I DID!
WELL, I DREW ALLISON TRUMBULL'S NAME! AND I COULDN'T HELP BUT NOTICE HOW YOU WERE LOOKING AT HER IN THERE!
SOB! OH, IT'S TRUE!! IT'S TRUE!!
I'M TORTURED BY THE UNBEARABLE PAIN OF LOVING SOMEONE IN SILENCE FROM AFAR! OH, WHY MUST I SUFFER SO?!
IT'S OKAY, DILTON! I'VE GOT AN IDEA! WHY DON'T WE TRADE PAPERS SO THAT WE CAN EACH TUTOR THE PERSON WE WANT TO BE WITH?
GENIUS IDEA, BETTY! YOU TRULY DESERVE YOUR PLACE AMONG US ON THE HONOR SOCIETY!
2

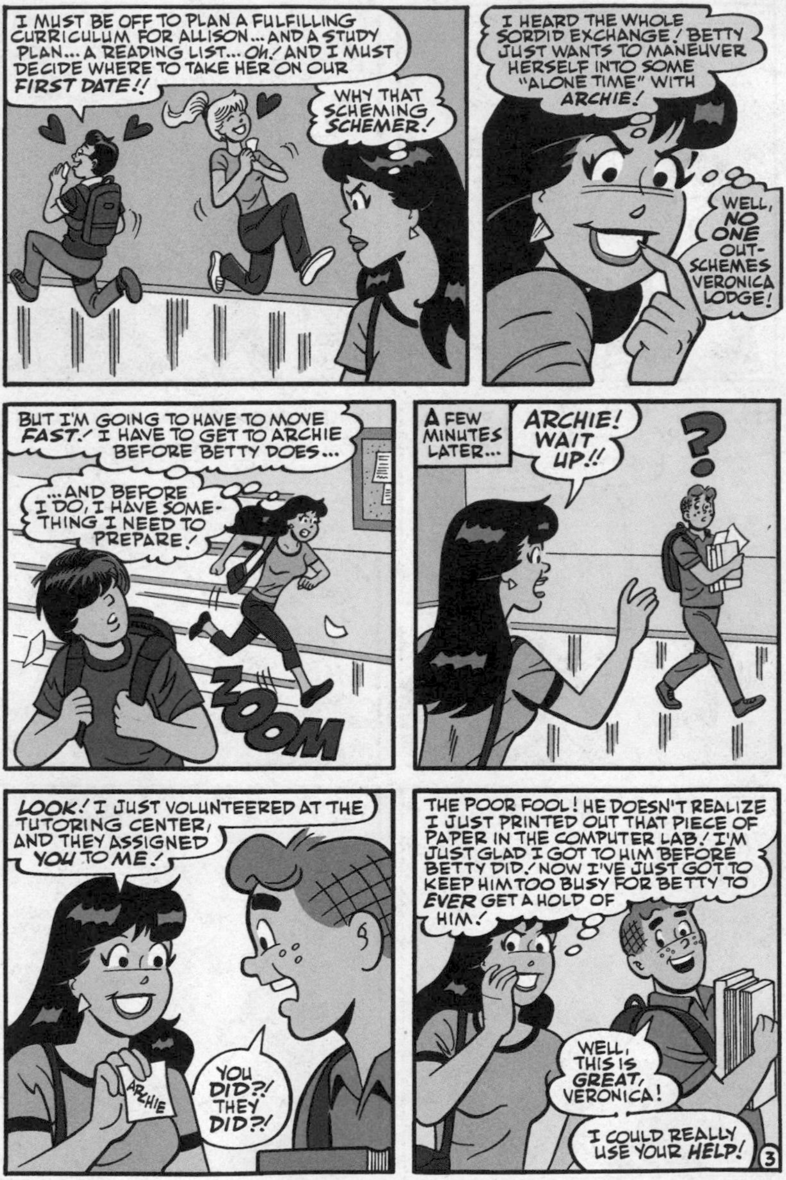
I MUST BE OFF TO PLAN A FULFILLING CURRICULUM FOR ALLISON... AND A STUDY PLAN... A READING LIST... OH! AND I MUST DECIDE WHERE TO TAKE HER ON OUR FIRST DATE!!
WHY THAT SCHEMING SCHEMER!
I HEARD THE WHOLE SORDID EXCHANGE! BETTY JUST WANTS TO MANEUVER HERSELF INTO SOME "ALONE TIME" WITH ARCHIE!
WELL, NO ONE OUT-SCHEMES VERONICA LODGE!
BUT I'M GOING TO HAVE TO MOVE FAST! I HAVE TO GET TO ARCHIE BEFORE BETTY DOES...
...AND BEFORE I DO, I HAVE SOMETHING I NEED TO PREPARE!
ZOOM
A FEW MINUTES LATER...
ARCHIE! WAIT UP!!
?
LOOK! I JUST VOLUNTEERED AT THE TUTORING CENTER, AND THEY ASSIGNED YOU TO ME!
ARCHIE
YOU DID?! THEY DID?!
THE POOR FOOL! HE DOESN'T REALIZE I JUST PRINTED OUT THAT PIECE OF PAPER IN THE COMPUTER LAB! I'M JUST GLAD I GOT TO HIM BEFORE BETTY DID! NOW I'VE JUST GOT TO KEEP HIM TOO BUSY FOR BETTY TO EVER GET A HOLD OF HIM!
WELL, THIS IS GREAT, VERONICA!
I COULD REALLY USE YOUR HELP!
3

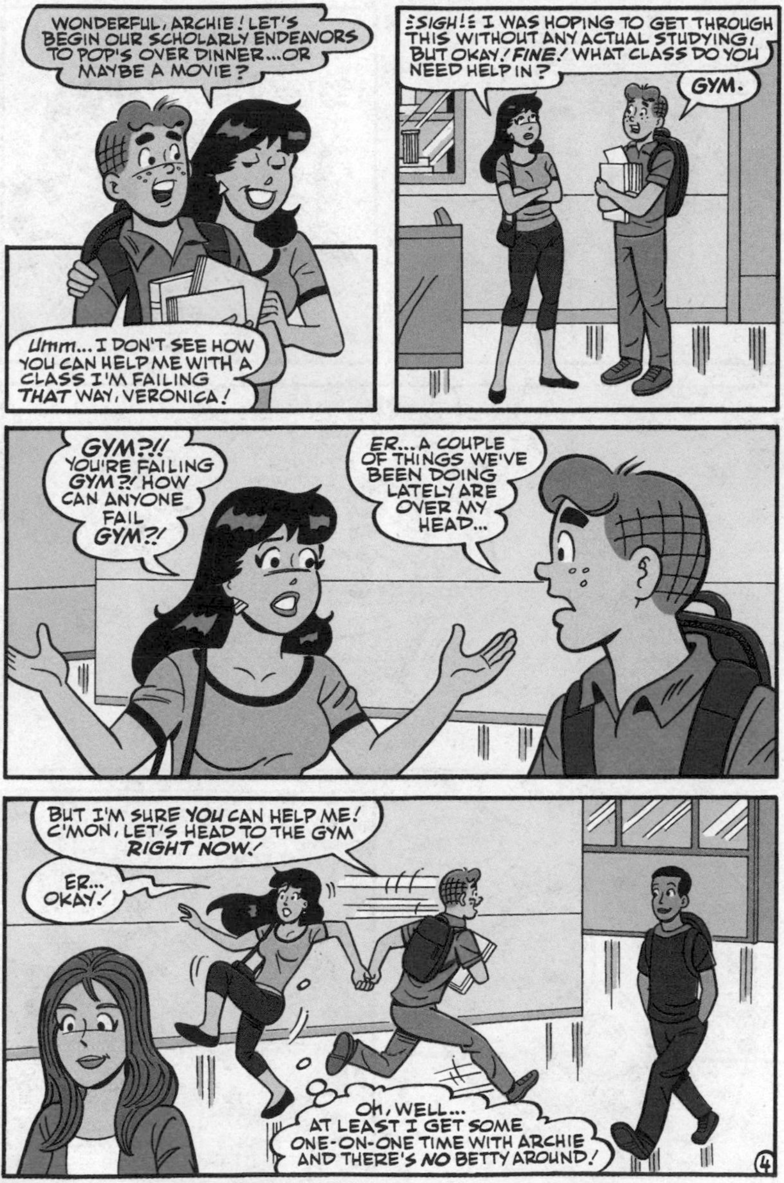
WONDERFUL, ARCHIE! LET'S BEGIN OUR SCHOLARLY ENDEAVORS TO POP'S OVER DINNER...OR MAYBE A MOVIE?
UMM... I DON'T SEE HOW YOU CAN HELP ME WITH A CLASS I'M FAILING THAT WAY, VERONICA!
SIGH! I WAS HOPING TO GET THROUGH THIS WITHOUT ANY ACTUAL STUDYING, BUT OKAY! FINE! WHAT CLASS DO YOU NEED HELP IN?
GYM.
GYM?!! YOU'RE FAILING GYM?! HOW CAN ANYONE FAIL GYM?!
ER... A COUPLE OF THINGS WE'VE BEEN DOING LATELY ARE OVER MY HEAD...
BUT I'M SURE YOU CAN HELP ME! C'MON, LET'S HEAD TO THE GYM RIGHT NOW!
ER... OKAY!
OH, WELL... AT LEAST I GET SOME ONE-ON-ONE TIME WITH ARCHIE AND THERE'S NO BETTY AROUND!
4

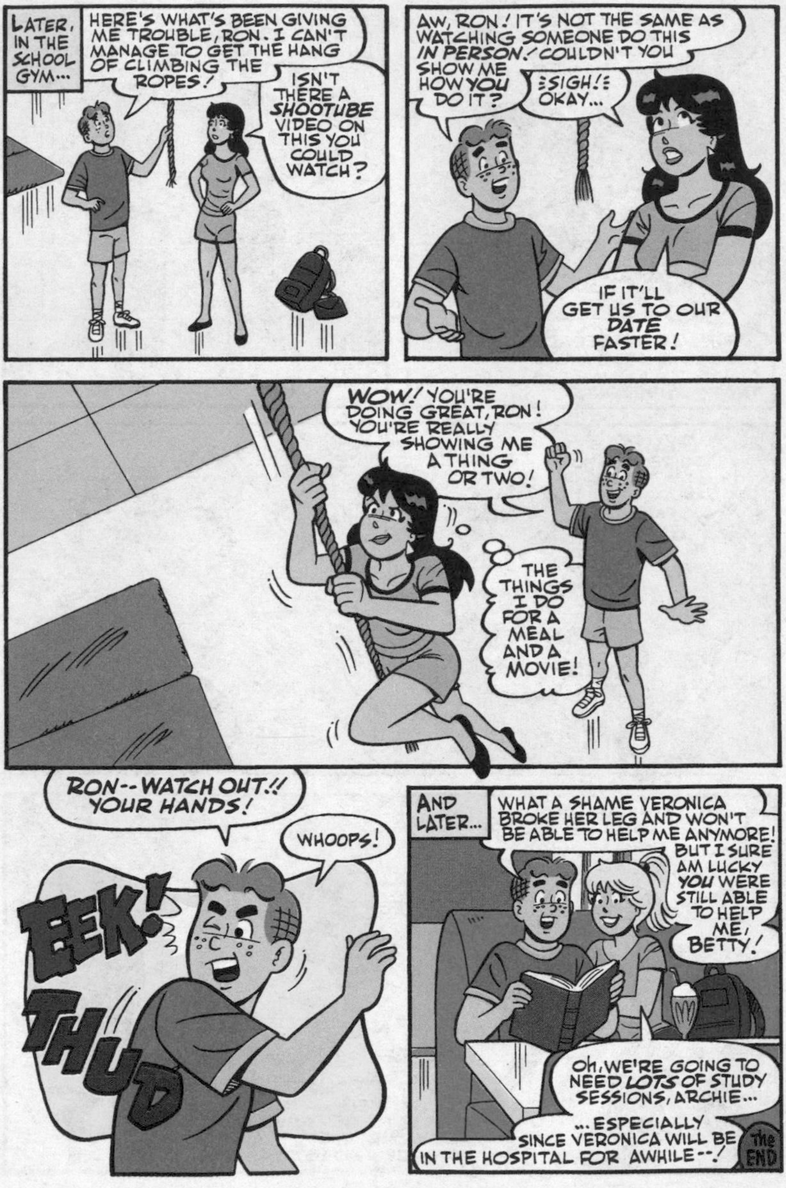
LATER, IN THE SCHOOL GYM...
HERE'S WHAT'S BEEN GIVING ME TROUBLE, RON. I CAN'T MANAGE TO GET THE HANG OF CLIMBING THE ROPES!
ISN'T THERE A SHOOTUBE VIDEO ON THIS YOU COULD WATCH?
AW, RON! IT'S NOT THE SAME AS WATCHING SOMEONE DO THIS IN PERSON! COULDN'T YOU SHOW ME HOW YOU DO IT?
SIGH! OKAY...
IF IT'LL GET US TO OUR DATE FASTER!
WOW! YOU'RE DOING GREAT, RON! YOU'RE REALLY SHOWING ME A THING OR TWO!
THE THINGS I DO FOR A MEAL AND A MOVIE!
RON--WATCH OUT!! YOUR HANDS!
WHOOPS!
EEK!
THUD
AND LATER...
WHAT A SHAME VERONICA BROKE HER LEG AND WON'T BE ABLE TO HELP ME ANYMORE! BUT I SURE AM LUCKY YOU WERE STILL ABLE TO HELP ME, BETTY!
Oh, WE'RE GOING TO NEED LOTS OF STUDY SESSIONS, ARCHIE...
...ESPECIALLY SINCE VERONICA WILL BE IN THE HOSPITAL FOR AWHILE--!
The END

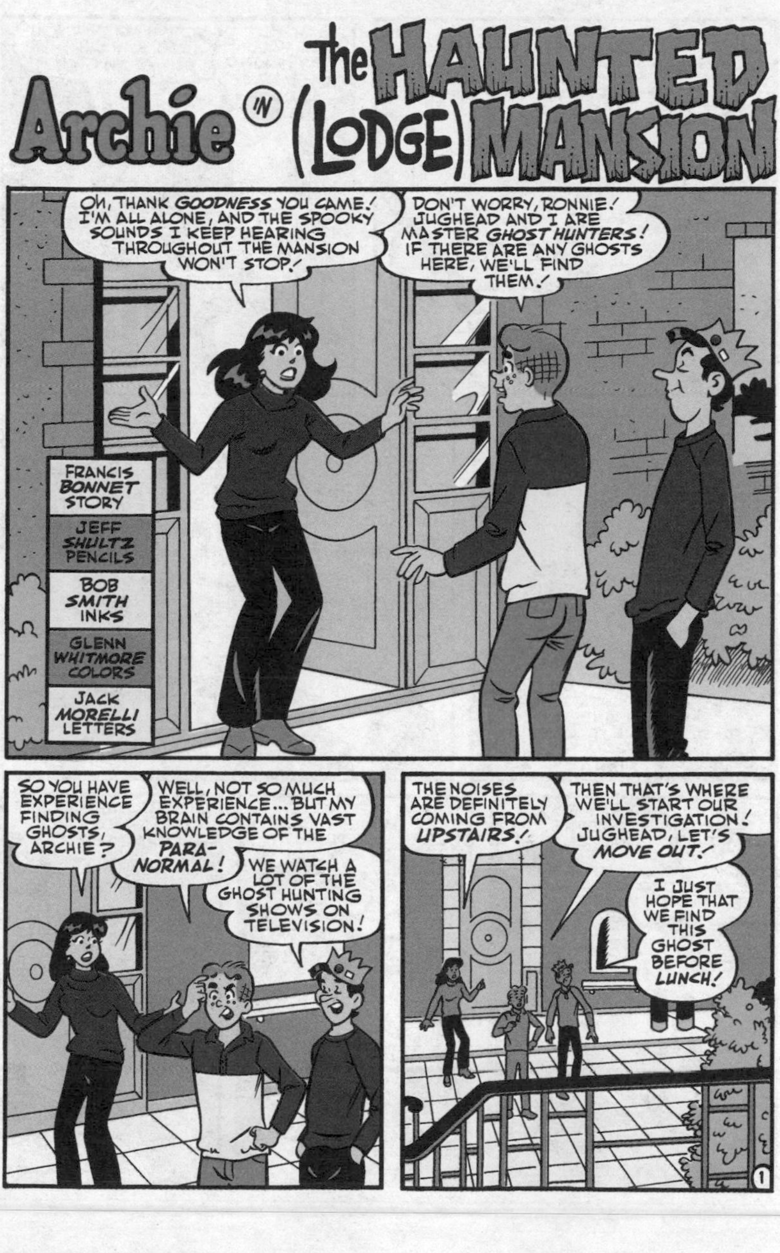

Archie in The HAUNTED (LODGE) MANSION
OH, THANK GOODNESS YOU CAME! I'M ALL ALONE, AND THE SPOOKY SOUNDS I KEEP HEARING THROUGHOUT THE MANSION WON'T STOP!
DON'T WORRY, RONNIE! JUGHEAD AND I ARE MASTER GHOST HUNTERS! IF THERE ARE ANY GHOSTS HERE, WE'LL FIND THEM!
FRANCIS BONNET STORY
JEFF SHULTZ PENCILS
BOB SMITH INKS
GLENN WHITMORE COLORS
JACK MORELLI LETTERS
SO YOU HAVE EXPERIENCE FINDING GHOSTS, ARCHIE?
WELL, NOT SO MUCH EXPERIENCE... BUT MY BRAIN CONTAINS VAST KNOWLEDGE OF THE PARA-NORMAL!
WE WATCH A LOT OF THE GHOST HUNTING SHOWS ON TELEVISION!
THE NOISES ARE DEFINITELY COMING FROM UPSTAIRS!
THEN THAT'S WHERE WE'LL START OUR INVESTIGATION! JUGHEAD, LET'S MOVE OUT!
I JUST HOPE THAT WE FIND THIS GHOST BEFORE LUNCH!
1

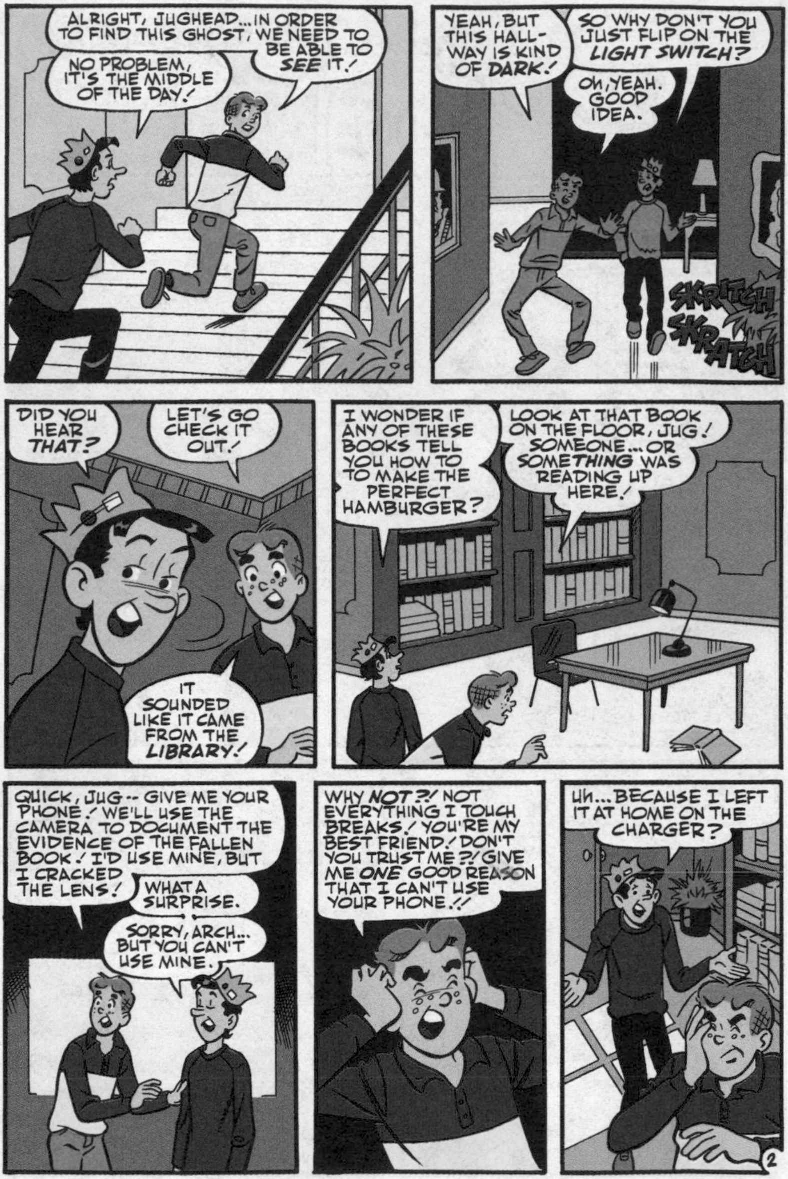
ALRIGHT, JUGHEAD... IN ORDER TO FIND THIS GHOST, WE NEED TO BE ABLE TO SEE IT.!
NO PROBLEM, IT'S THE MIDDLE OF THE DAY.!
YEAH, BUT THIS HALL-WAY IS KIND OF DARK.!
SO WHY DON'T YOU JUST FLIP ON THE LIGHT SWITCH?
OH, YEAH. GOOD IDEA.
SKRITCH
SKRATCH
DID YOU HEAR THAT?
LET'S GO CHECK IT OUT.!
IT SOUNDED LIKE IT CAME FROM THE LIBRARY.!
I WONDER IF ANY OF THESE BOOKS TELL YOU HOW TO TO MAKE THE PERFECT HAMBURGER?
LOOK AT THAT BOOK ON THE FLOOR, JUG.! SOMEONE... OR SOMETHING WAS READING UP HERE.!
QUICK, JUG -- GIVE ME YOUR PHONE.! WE'LL USE THE CAMERA TO DOCUMENT THE EVIDENCE OF THE FALLEN BOOK.! I'D USE MINE, BUT I CRACKED THE LENS.!
WHAT A SURPRISE.
SORRY, ARCH... BUT YOU CAN'T USE MINE.
WHY NOT?!! NOT EVERYTHING I TOUCH BREAKS.! YOU'RE MY BEST FRIEND.! DON'T YOU TRUST ME?!! GIVE ME ONE GOOD REASON THAT I CAN'T USE YOUR PHONE.!!
UH... BECAUSE I LEFT IT AT HOME ON THE CHARGER?
2

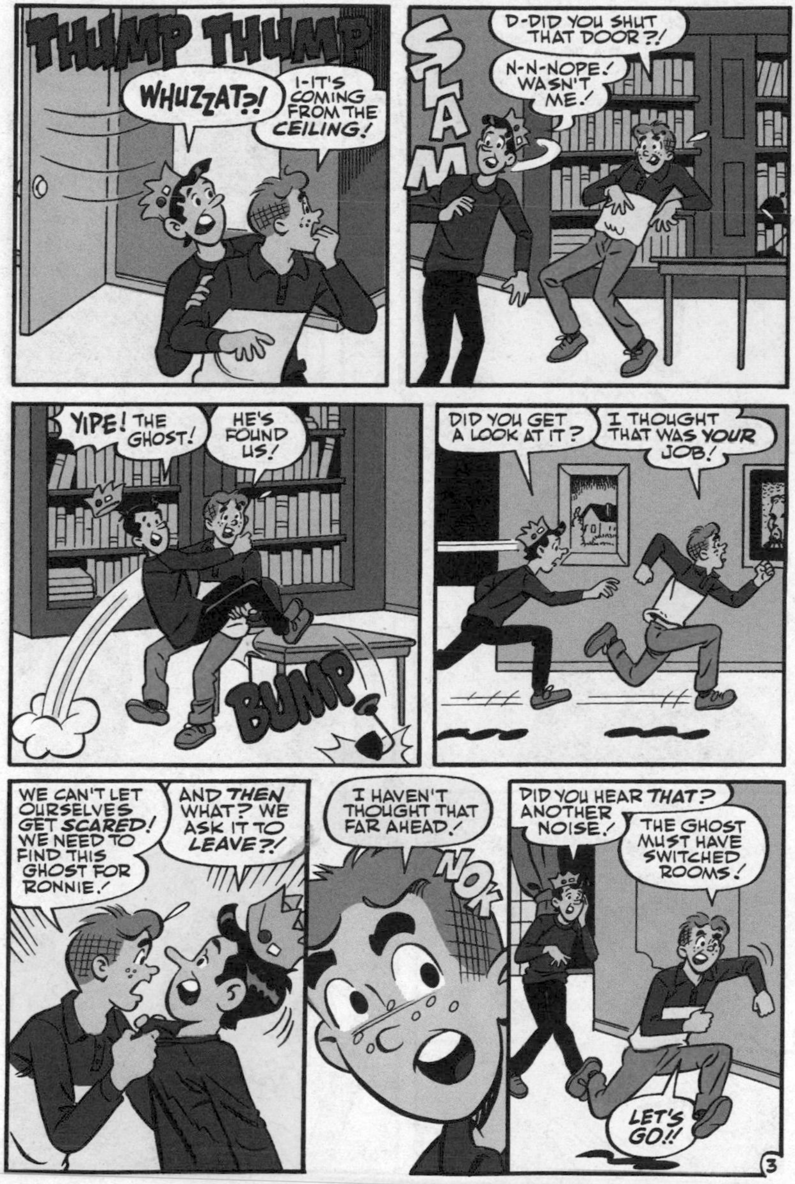
THUMP THUMP
WHUZZAT?!
I-IT'S COMING FROM THE CEILING!
SLAM
D-DID YOU SHUT THAT DOOR?!
N-N-NOPE! WASN'T ME!
YIPE! THE GHOST!
HE'S FOUND US!
BUMP
DID YOU GET A LOOK AT IT?
I THOUGHT THAT WAS YOUR JOB!
WE CAN'T LET OURSELVES GET SCARED! WE NEED TO FIND THIS GHOST FOR RONNIE!
AND THEN WHAT? WE ASK IT TO LEAVE?!
I HAVEN'T THOUGHT THAT FAR AHEAD!
NOK
DID YOU HEAR THAT? ANOTHER NOISE!
THE GHOST MUST HAVE SWITCHED ROOMS!
LET'S GO!!
3

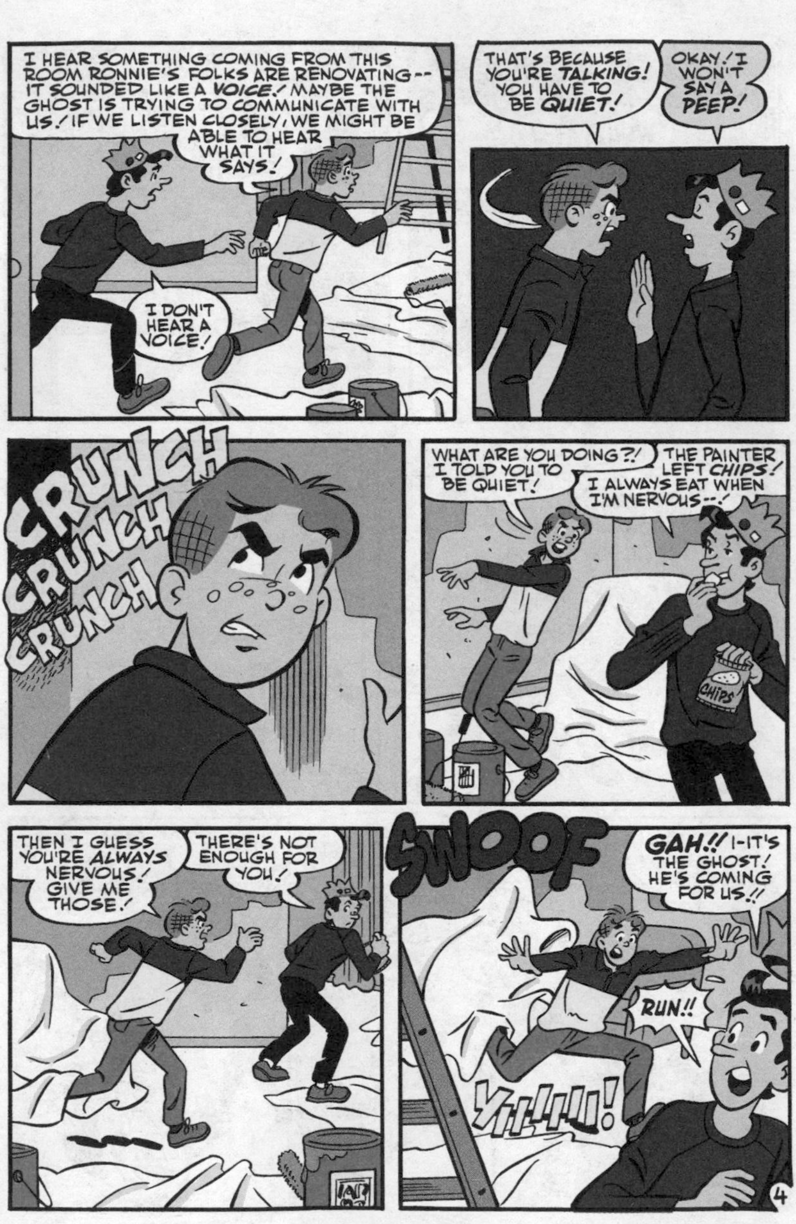
I HEAR SOMETHING COMING FROM THIS ROOM RONNIE'S FOLKS ARE RENOVATING-- IT SOUNDED LIKE A VOICE! MAYBE THE GHOST IS TRYING TO COMMUNICATE WITH US! IF WE LISTEN CLOSELY, WE MIGHT BE ABLE TO HEAR WHAT IT SAYS!
I DON'T HEAR A VOICE!
THAT'S BECAUSE YOU'RE TALKING! YOU HAVE TO BE QUIET!
OKAY! I WON'T SAY A PEEP!
CRUNCH CRUNCH CRUNCH CRUNCH
WHAT ARE YOU DOING?! I TOLD YOU TO BE QUIET!
THE PAINTER LEFT CHIPS! I ALWAYS EAT WHEN I'M NERVOUS--!
CHIPS
THEN I GUESS YOU'RE ALWAYS NERVOUS! GIVE ME THOSE!
THERE'S NOT ENOUGH FOR YOU!
SWOOF
GAH!! I-IT'S THE GHOST! HE'S COMING FOR US!!
RUN!!
YIIIIIII!
4

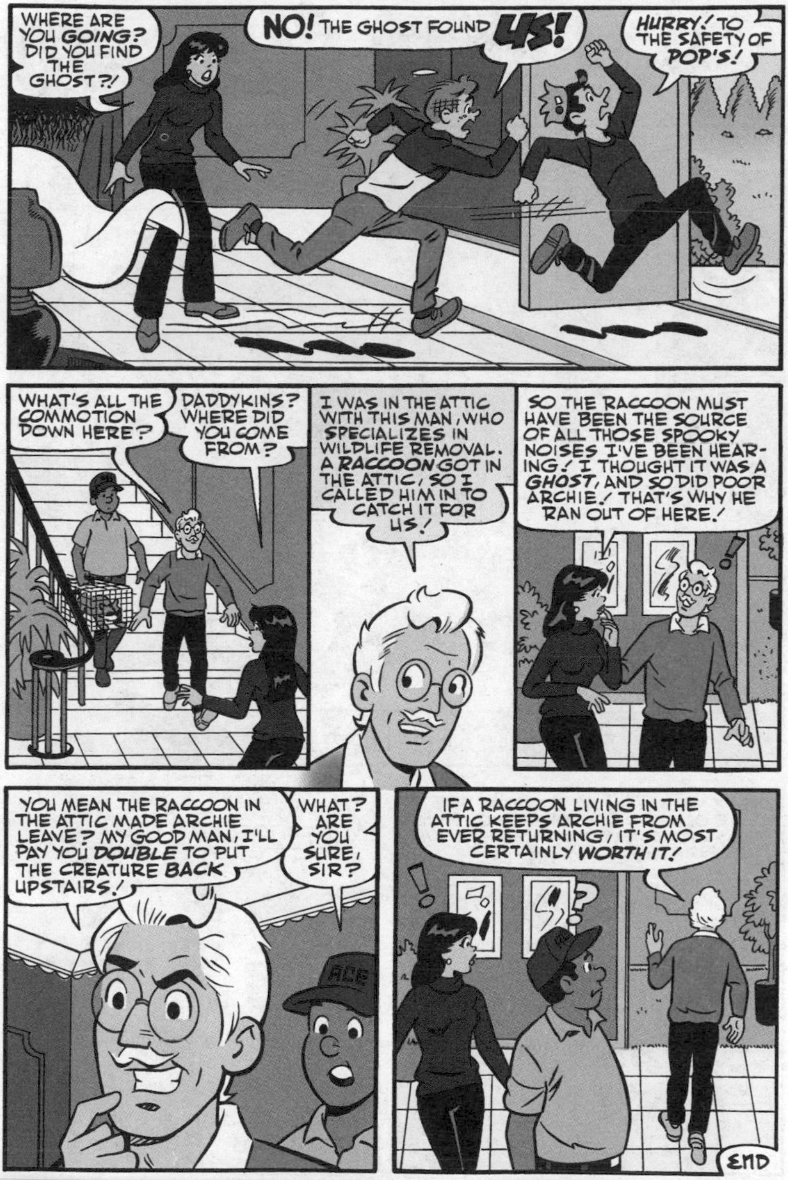
WHERE ARE YOU GOING? DID YOU FIND THE GHOST?!
NO! THE GHOST FOUND US!
HURRY! TO THE SAFETY OF POP'S!
WHAT'S ALL THE COMMOTION DOWN HERE?
DADDYKINS? WHERE DID YOU COME FROM?
I WAS IN THE ATTIC WITH THIS MAN, WHO SPECIALIZES IN WILDLIFE REMOVAL. A RACCOON GOT IN THE ATTIC, SO I CALLED HIM IN TO CATCH IT FOR US!
SO THE RACCOON MUST HAVE BEEN THE SOURCE OF ALL THOSE SPOOKY NOISES I'VE BEEN HEARING! I THOUGHT IT WAS A GHOST, AND SO DID POOR ARCHIE! THAT'S WHY HE RAN OUT OF HERE!
YOU MEAN THE RACCOON IN THE ATTIC MADE ARCHIE LEAVE? MY GOOD MAN, I'LL PAY YOU DOUBLE TO PUT THE CREATURE BACK UPSTAIRS!
WHAT? ARE YOU SURE, SIR?
ACE
IF A RACCOON LIVING IN THE ATTIC KEEPS ARCHIE FROM EVER RETURNING, IT'S MOST CERTAINLY WORTH IT!
END

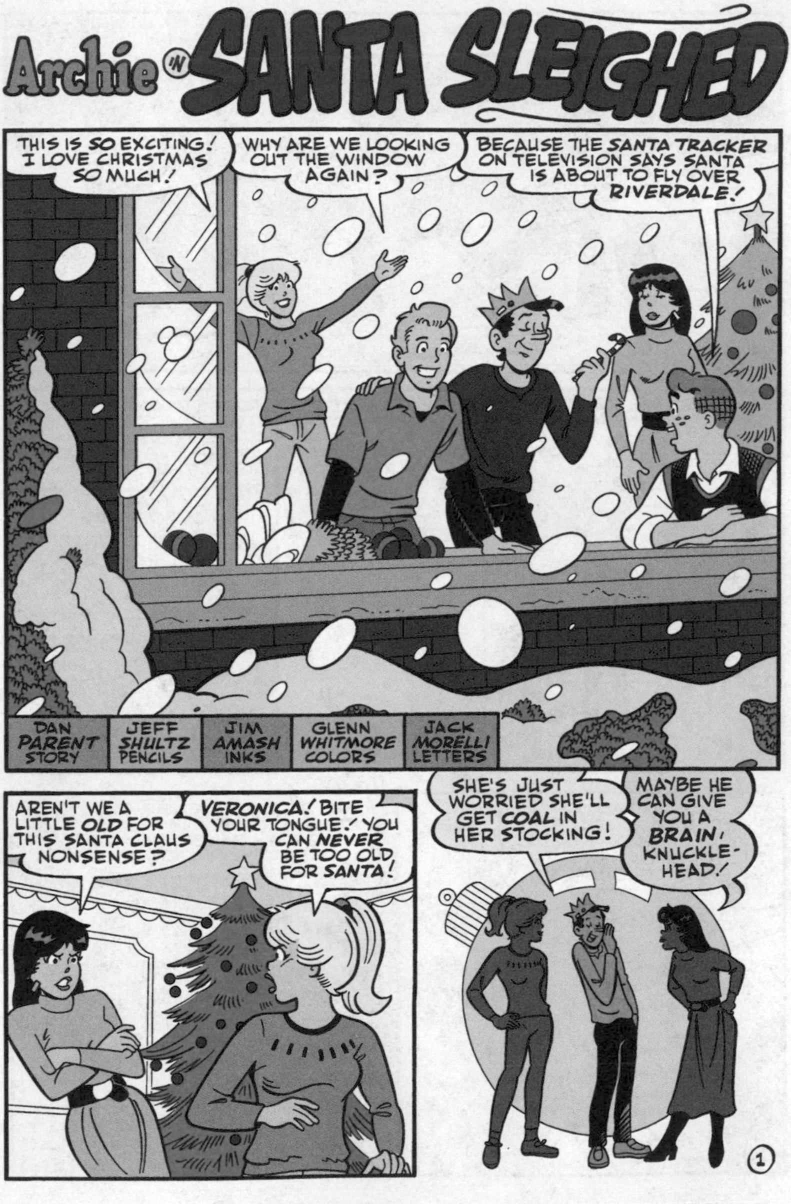
Archie 'N SANTA SLEIGHED
THIS IS SO EXCITING! I LOVE CHRISTMAS SO MUCH!
WHY ARE WE LOOKING OUT THE WINDOW AGAIN?
BECAUSE THE SANTA TRACKER ON TELEVISION SAYS SANTA IS ABOUT TO FLY OVER RIVERDALE!
DAN PARENT STORY
JEFF SHULTZ PENCILS
JIM AMASH INKS
GLENN WHITMORE COLORS
JACK MORELLI LETTERS
AREN'T WE A LITTLE OLD FOR THIS SANTA CLAUS NONSENSE?
VERONICA! BITE YOUR TONGUE! YOU CAN NEVER BE TOO OLD FOR SANTA!
SHE'S JUST WORRIED SHE'LL GET COAL IN HER STOCKING!
MAYBE HE CAN GIVE YOU A BRAIN, KNUCKLE-HEAD!
1

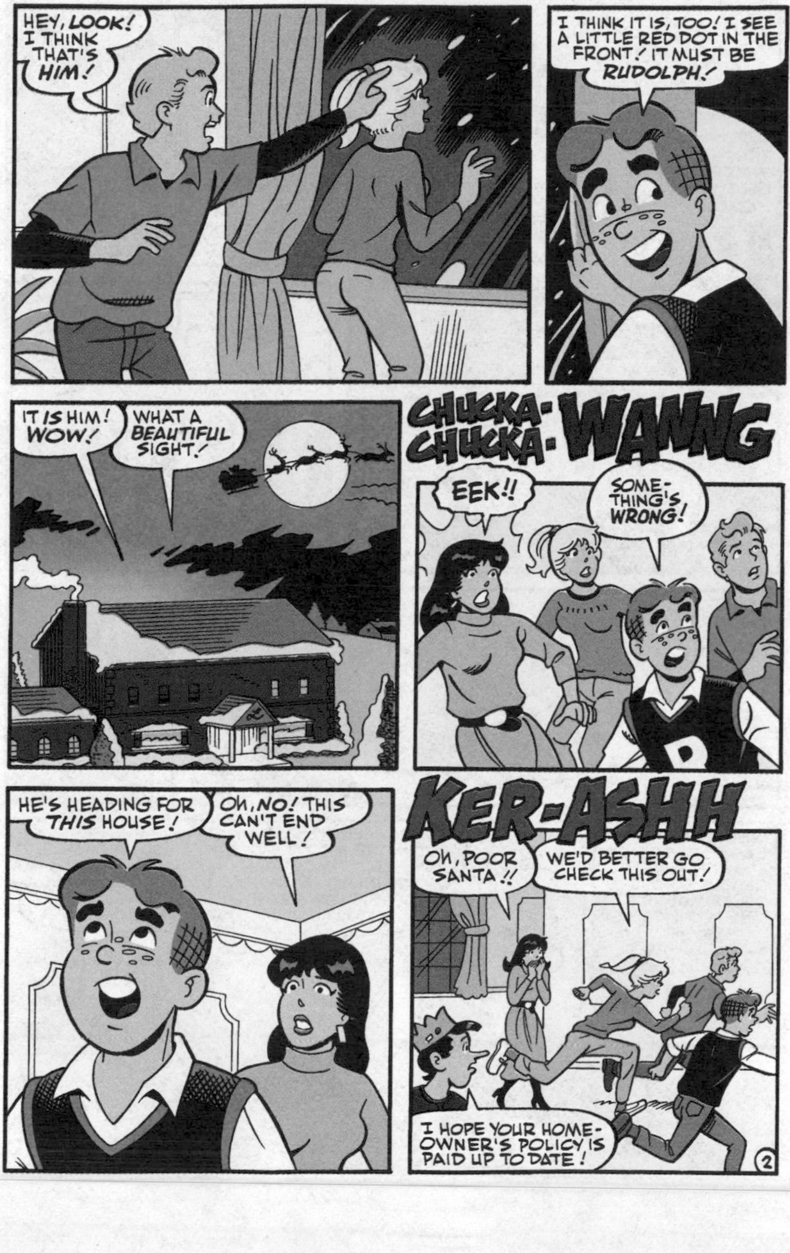
HEY, LOOK! I THINK THAT'S HIM!
I THINK IT IS, TOO! I SEE A LITTLE RED DOT IN THE FRONT! IT MUST BE RUDOLPH!
IT IS HIM! WOW!
WHAT A BEAUTIFUL SIGHT!
CHUCKA-CHUCKA-WANNG
EEK!!
SOME-THING'S WRONG!
HE'S HEADING FOR THIS HOUSE!
OH, NO! THIS CAN'T END WELL!
KER-ASHH
OH, POOR SANTA!!
WE'D BETTER GO CHECK THIS OUT!
I HOPE YOUR HOME-OWNER'S POLICY IS PAID UP TO DATE!
2

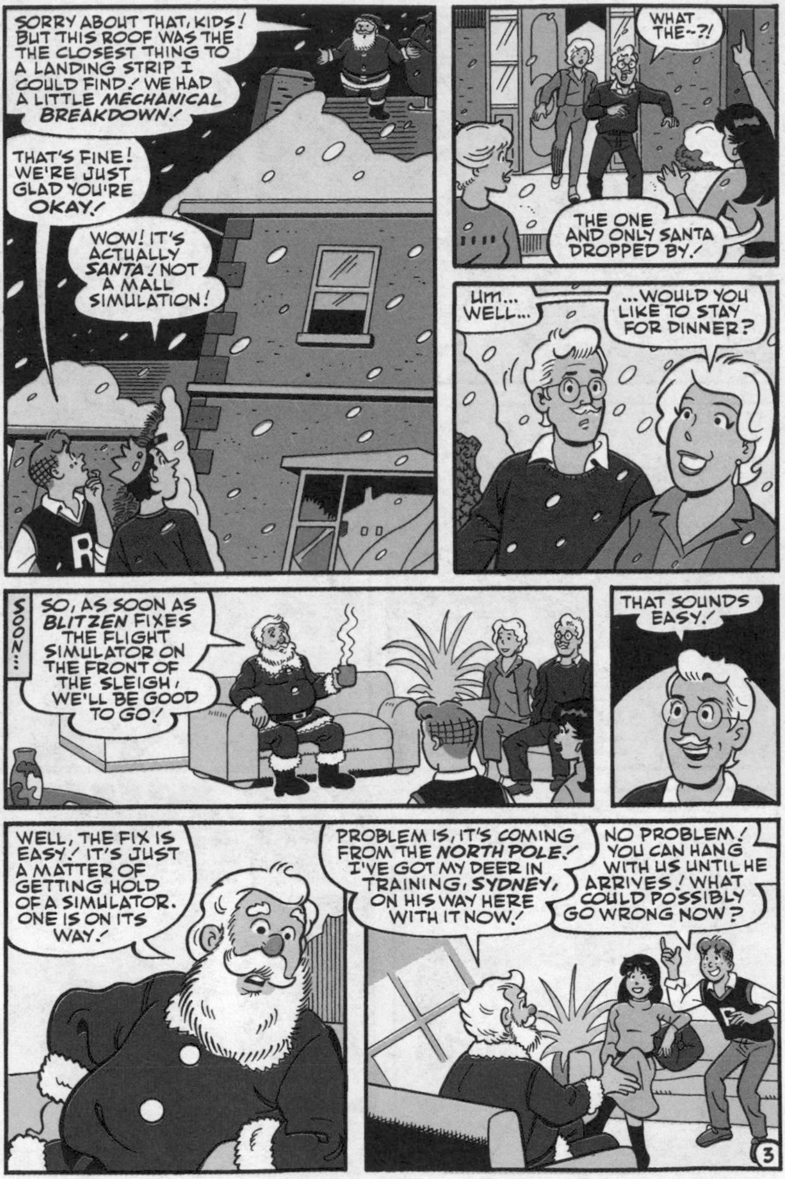
SORRY ABOUT THAT, KIDS! BUT THIS ROOF WAS THE THE CLOSEST THING TO A LANDING STRIP I COULD FIND! WE HAD A LITTLE MECHANICAL BREAKDOWN!
THAT'S FINE! WE'RE JUST GLAD YOU'RE OKAY!
WOW! IT'S ACTUALLY SANTA! NOT A MALL SIMULATION!
WHAT THE--?!
THE ONE AND ONLY SANTA DROPPED BY!
UM... WELL...
...WOULD YOU LIKE TO STAY FOR DINNER?
SOON...
SO, AS SOON AS BLITZEN FIXES THE FLIGHT SIMULATOR ON THE FRONT OF THE SLEIGH, WE'LL BE GOOD TO GO!
THAT SOUNDS EASY!
WELL, THE FIX IS EASY! IT'S JUST A MATTER OF GETTING HOLD OF A SIMULATOR. ONE IS ON ITS WAY!
PROBLEM IS, IT'S COMING FROM THE NORTH POLE! I'VE GOT MY DEER IN TRAINING, SYDNEY, ON HIS WAY HERE WITH IT NOW!
NO PROBLEM! YOU CAN HANG WITH US UNTIL HE ARRIVES! WHAT COULD POSSIBLY GO WRONG NOW?
3

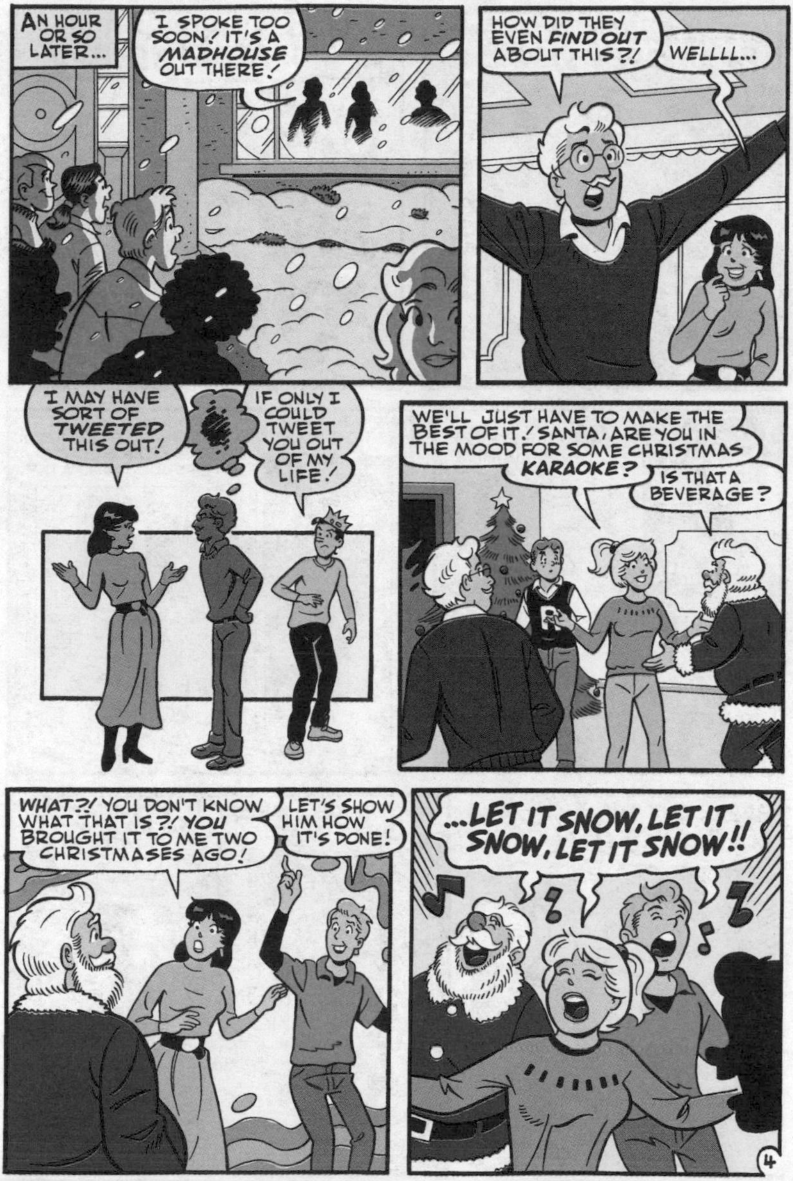
AN HOUR OR SO LATER...
I SPOKE TOO SOON! IT'S A MADHOUSE OUT THERE!
HOW DID THEY EVEN FIND OUT ABOUT THIS?!
WELLLL...
I MAY HAVE SORT OF TWEETED THIS OUT!
IF ONLY I COULD TWEET YOU OUT OF MY LIFE!
WE'LL JUST HAVE TO MAKE THE BEST OF IT! SANTA, ARE YOU IN THE MOOD FOR SOME CHRISTMAS KARAOKE?
IS THAT A BEVERAGE?
WHAT?! YOU DON'T KNOW WHAT THAT IS?! YOU BROUGHT IT TO ME TWO CHRISTMASES AGO!
LET'S SHOW HIM HOW IT'S DONE!
...LET IT SNOW, LET IT SNOW, LET IT SNOW!!
4

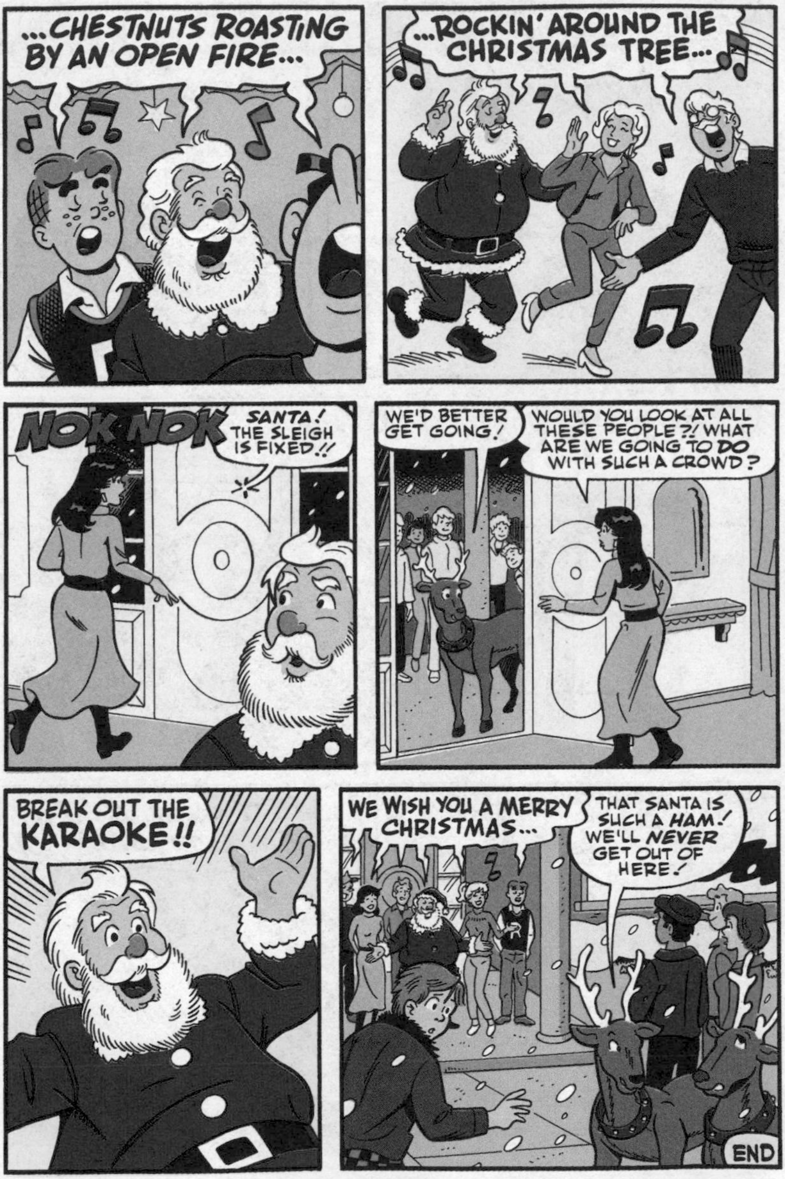
...CHESTNUTS ROASTING BY AN OPEN FIRE...
...ROCKIN' AROUND THE CHRISTMAS TREE...
NOK NOK
SANTA! THE SLEIGH IS FIXED!!
WE'D BETTER GET GOING!
WOULD YOU LOOK AT ALL THESE PEOPLE?! WHAT ARE WE GOING TO DO WITH SUCH A CROWD?
BREAK OUT THE KARAOKE!!
WE WISH YOU A MERRY CHRISTMAS...
THAT SANTA IS SUCH A HAM! WE'LL NEVER GET OUT OF HERE!
END

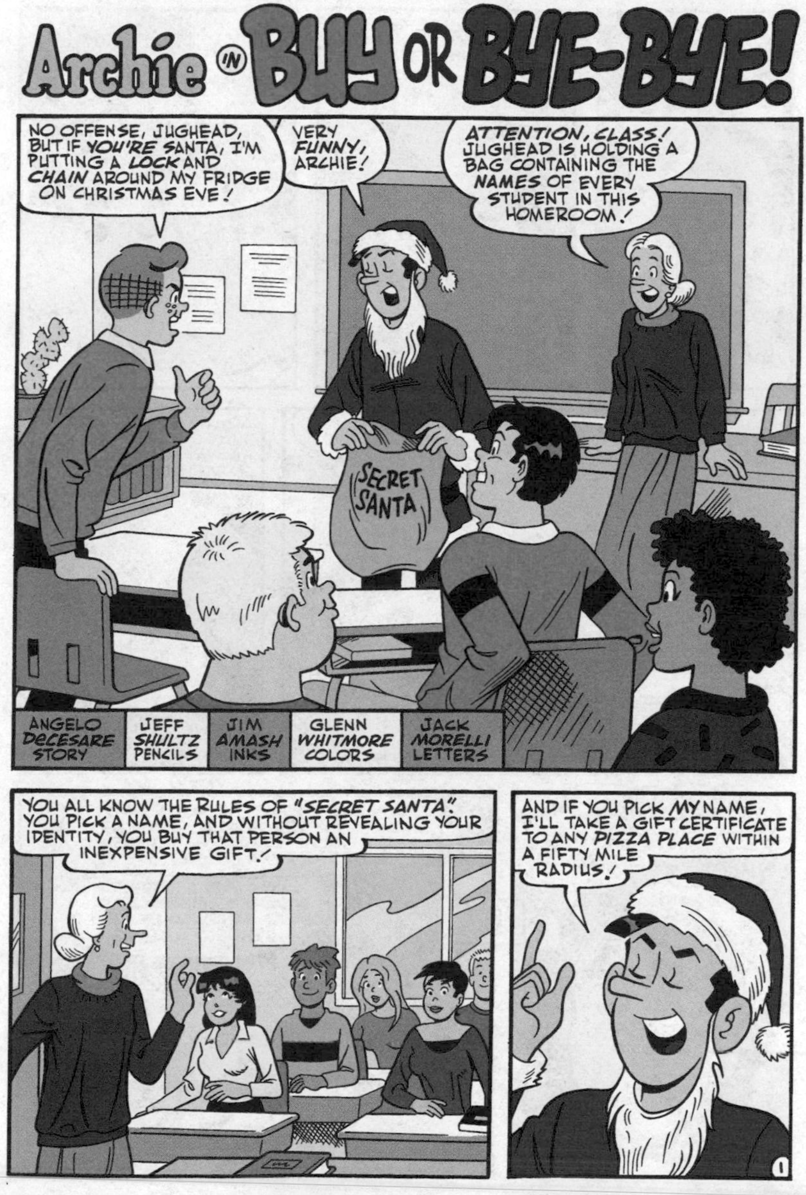
Archie in BUY OR BYE-BYE!
NO OFFENSE, JUGHEAD, BUT IF YOU'RE SANTA, I'M PUTTING A LOCK AND CHAIN AROUND MY FRIDGE ON CHRISTMAS EVE!
VERY FUNNY, ARCHIE!
ATTENTION, CLASS! JUGHEAD IS HOLDING A BAG CONTAINING THE NAMES OF EVERY STUDENT IN THIS HOMEROOM!
SECRET SANTA
ANGELO DECESARE STORY
JEFF SHULTZ PENCILS
JIM AMASH INKS
GLENN WHITMORE COLORS
JACK MORELLI LETTERS
YOU ALL KNOW THE RULES OF "SECRET SANTA". YOU PICK A NAME, AND WITHOUT REVEALING YOUR IDENTITY, YOU BUY THAT PERSON AN INEXPENSIVE GIFT!
AND IF YOU PICK MY NAME, I'LL TAKE A GIFT CERTIFICATE TO ANY PIZZA PLACE WITHIN A FIFTY MILE RADIUS!
1

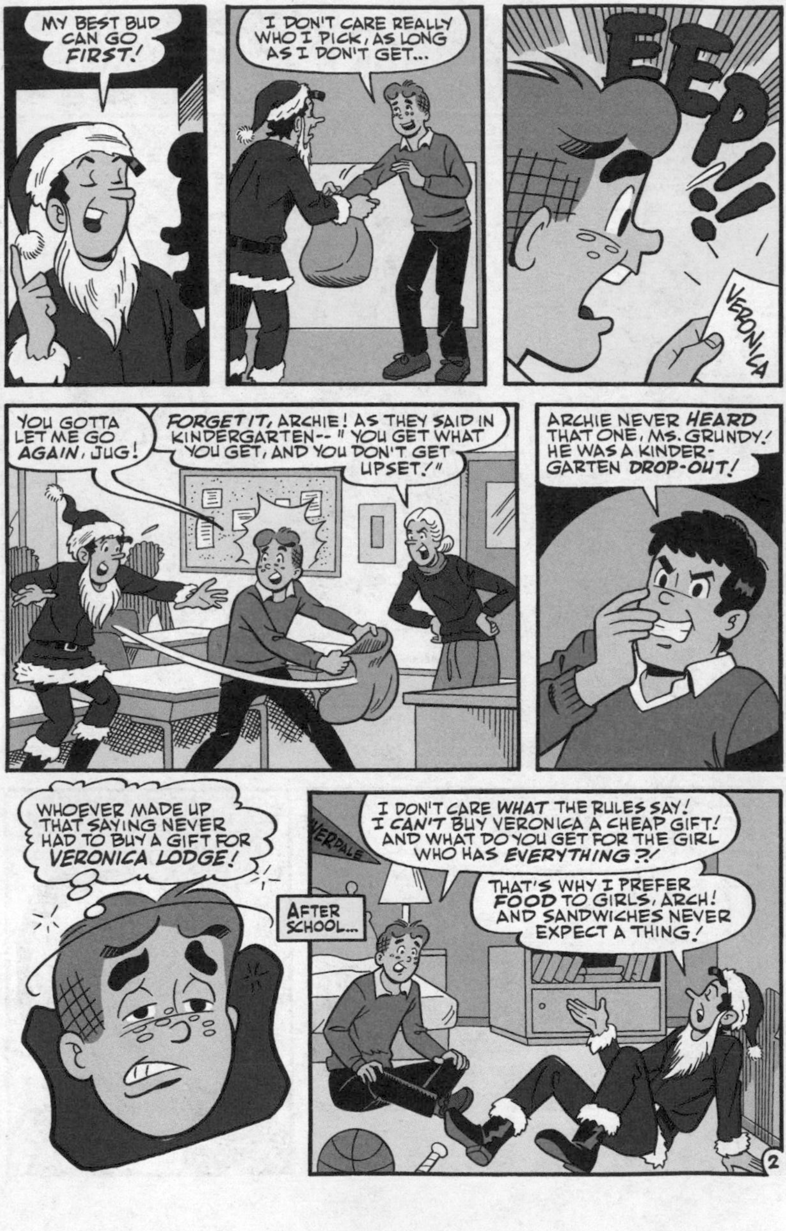
MY BEST BUD CAN GO FIRST!
I DON'T CARE REALLY WHO I PICK, AS LONG AS I DON'T GET...
EEP!!!
VERONICA
YOU GOTTA LET ME GO AGAIN, JUG!
FORGET IT, ARCHIE! AS THEY SAID IN KINDERGARTEN-- "YOU GET WHAT YOU GET, AND YOU DON'T GET UPSET!"
ARCHIE NEVER HEARD THAT ONE, MS. GRUNDY! HE WAS A KINDER-GARTEN DROP-OUT!
WHOEVER MADE UP THAT SAYING NEVER HAD TO BUY A GIFT FOR VERONICA LODGE!
AFTER SCHOOL...
I DON'T CARE WHAT THE RULES SAY! I CAN'T BUY VERONICA A CHEAP GIFT! AND WHAT DO YOU GET FOR THE GIRL WHO HAS EVERYTHING?!
THAT'S WHY I PREFER FOOD TO GIRLS, ARCH! AND SANDWICHES NEVER EXPECT A THING!
2

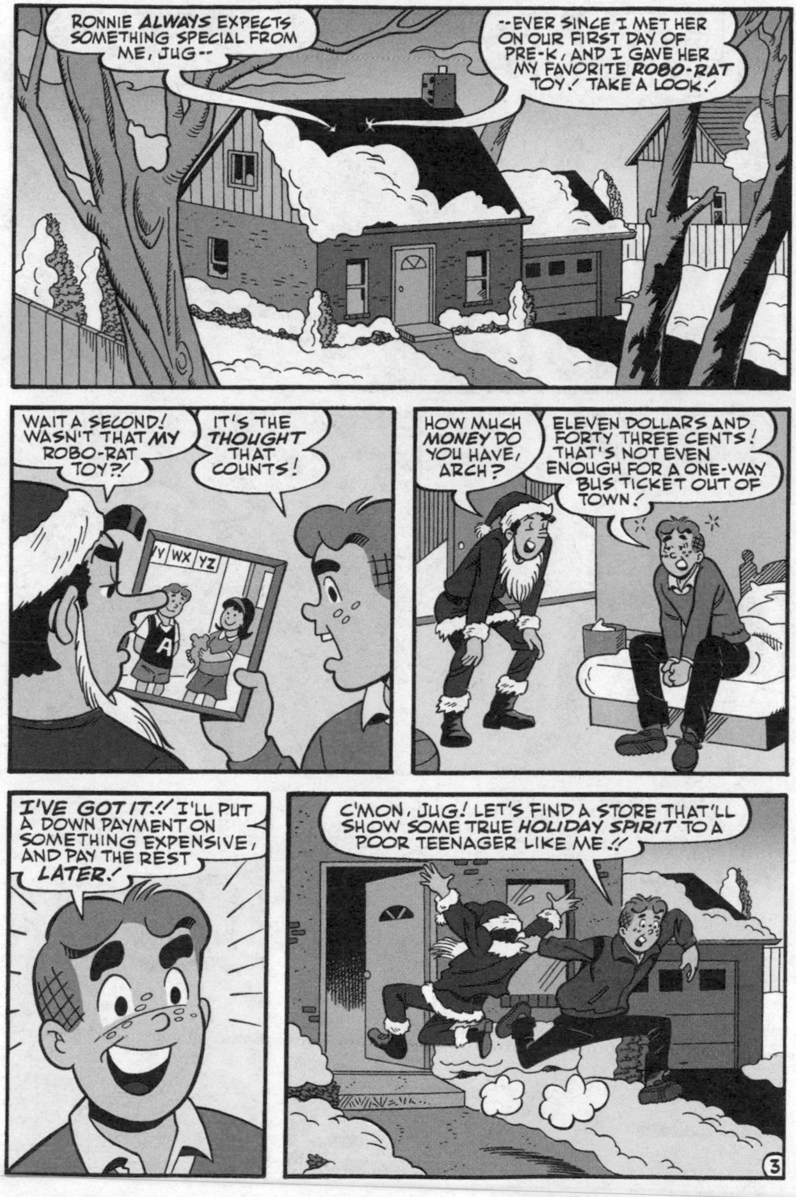
RONNIE ALWAYS EXPECTS SOMETHING SPECIAL FROM ME, JUG--
--EVER SINCE I MET HER ON OUR FIRST DAY OF PRE-K, AND I GAVE HER MY FAVORITE ROBO-RAT TOY! TAKE A LOOK!
WAIT A SECOND! WASN'T THAT MY ROBO-RAT TOY?!
IT'S THE THOUGHT THAT COUNTS!
HOW MUCH MONEY DO YOU HAVE, ARCH?
ELEVEN DOLLARS AND FORTY THREE CENTS! THAT'S NOT EVEN ENOUGH FOR A ONE-WAY BUS TICKET OUT OF TOWN!
I'VE GOT IT!! I'LL PUT A DOWN PAYMENT ON SOMETHING EXPENSIVE, AND PAY THE REST LATER!
C'MON, JUG! LET'S FIND A STORE THAT'LL SHOW SOME TRUE HOLIDAY SPIRIT TO A POOR TEENAGER LIKE ME!!
3

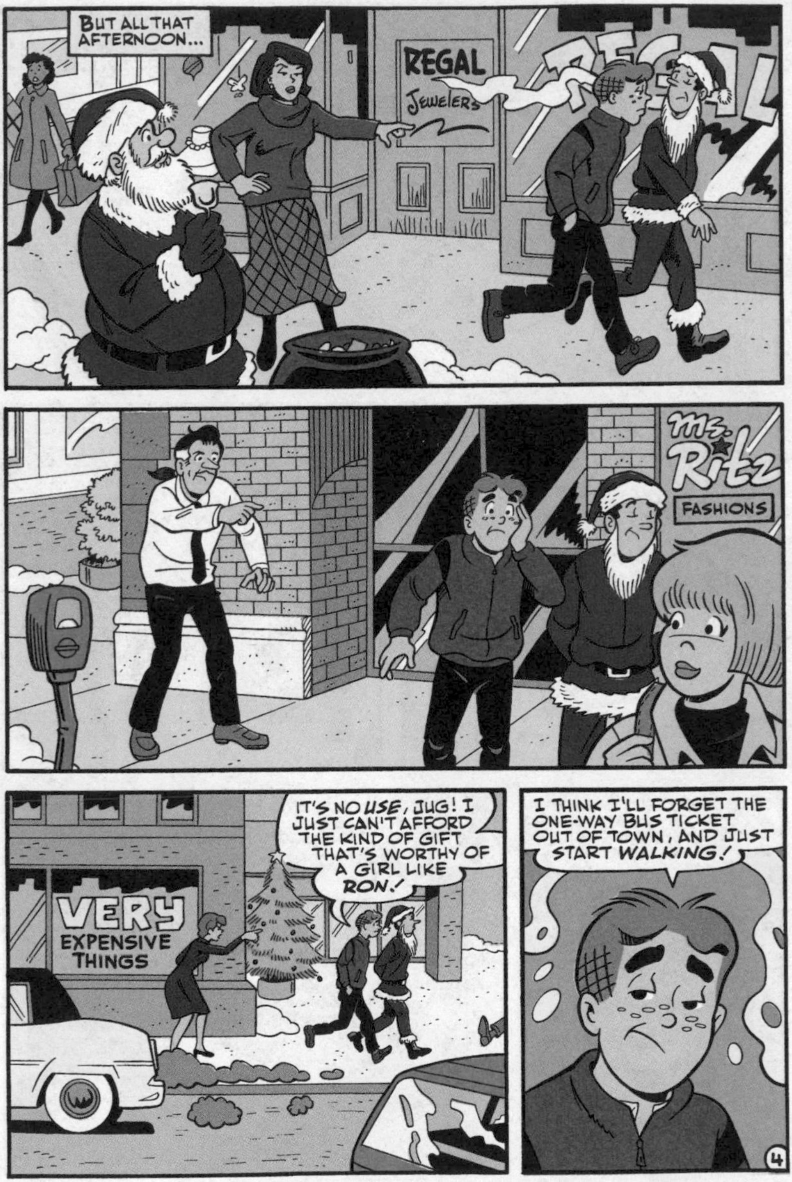
BUT ALL THAT AFTERNOON...
REGAL
Jewelers
Ms. Ritz
FASHIONS
VERY
EXPENSIVE THINGS
IT'S NO USE, JUG! I JUST CAN'T AFFORD THE KIND OF GIFT THAT'S WORTHY OF A GIRL LIKE RON!
I THINK I'LL FORGET THE ONE-WAY BUS TICKET OUT OF TOWN, AND JUST START WALKING!
4

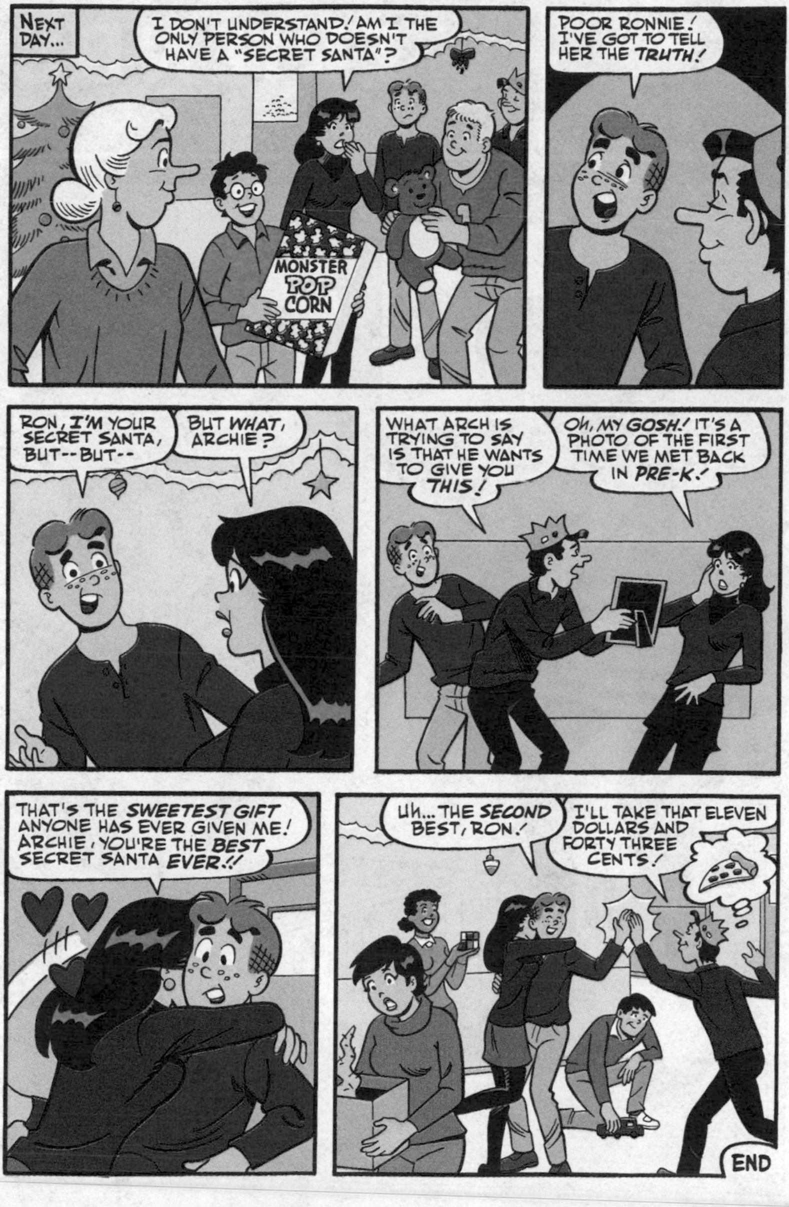
NEXT DAY...
I DON'T UNDERSTAND! AM I THE ONLY PERSON WHO DOESN'T HAVE A "SECRET SANTA"?
MONSTER POP CORN
POOR RONNIE! I'VE GOT TO TELL HER THE TRUTH!
RON, I'M YOUR SECRET SANTA, BUT--BUT--
BUT WHAT, ARCHIE?
WHAT ARCH IS TRYING TO SAY IS THAT HE WANTS TO GIVE YOU THIS!
OH, MY GOSH! IT'S A PHOTO OF THE FIRST TIME WE MET BACK IN PRE-K!
THAT'S THE SWEETEST GIFT ANYONE HAS EVER GIVEN ME! ARCHIE, YOU'RE THE BEST SECRET SANTA EVER!!
UH... THE SECOND BEST, RON!
I'LL TAKE THAT ELEVEN DOLLARS AND FORTY THREE CENTS!
END

04 B&V FRIENDS

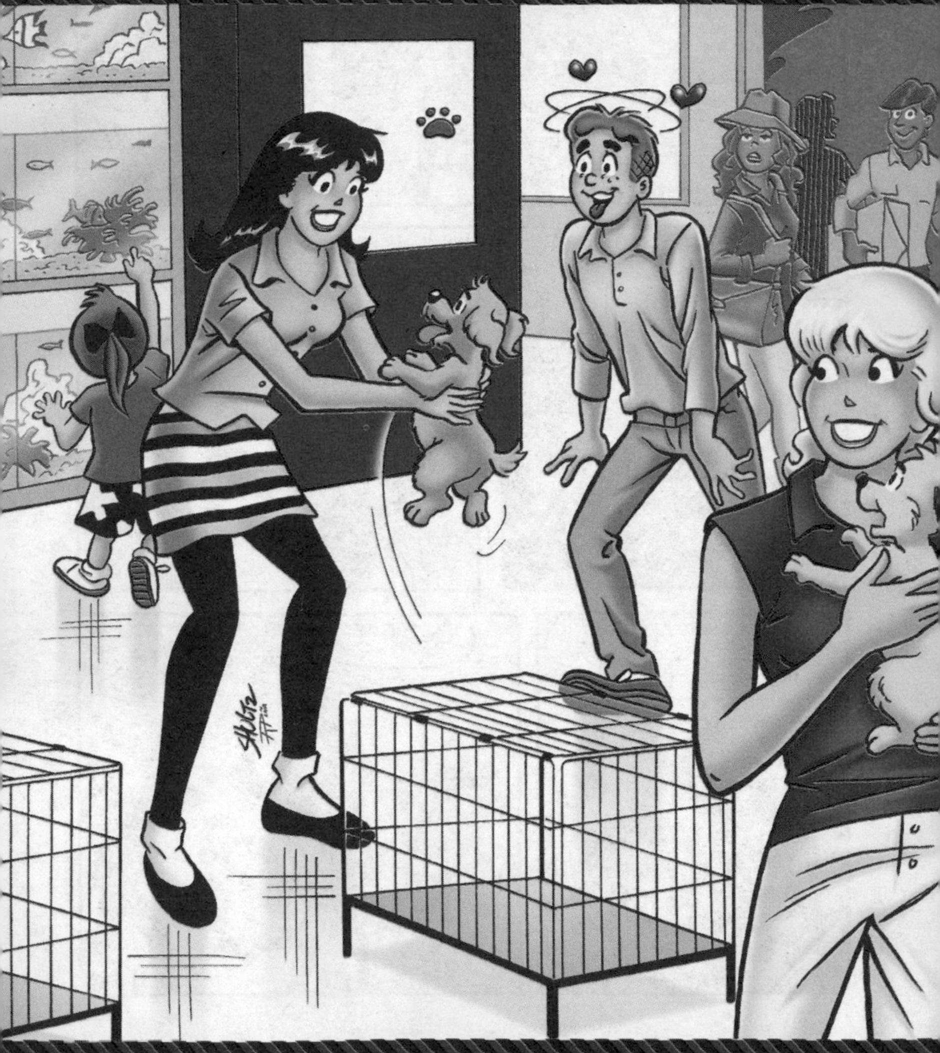

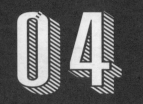

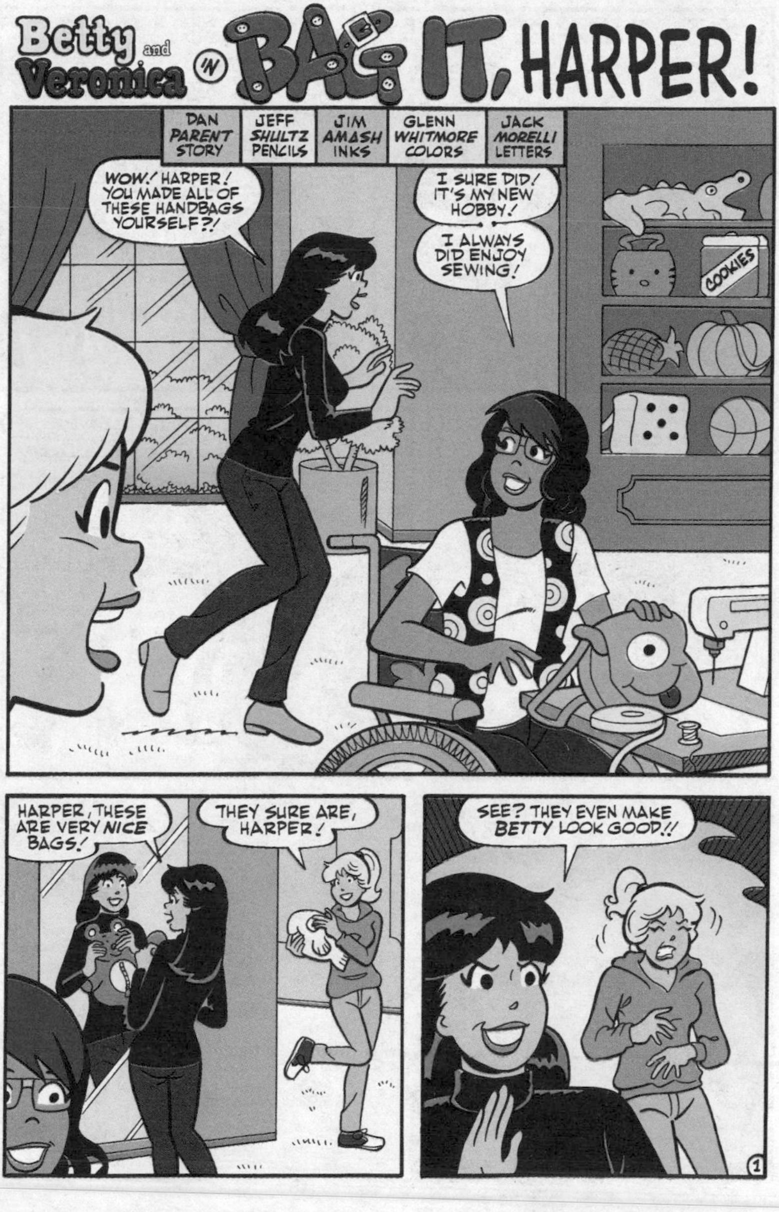
Betty and Veronica in BAG IT, HARPER!
DAN PARENT STORY
JEFF SHULTZ PENCILS
JIM AMASH INKS
GLENN WHITMORE COLORS
JACK MORELLI LETTERS
WOW! HARPER! YOU MADE ALL OF THESE HANDBAGS YOURSELF?!
I SURE DID! IT'S MY NEW HOBBY!
I ALWAYS DID ENJOY SEWING!
COOKIES
HARPER, THESE ARE VERY NICE BAGS!
THEY SURE ARE, HARPER!
SEE? THEY EVEN MAKE BETTY LOOK GOOD!!
1

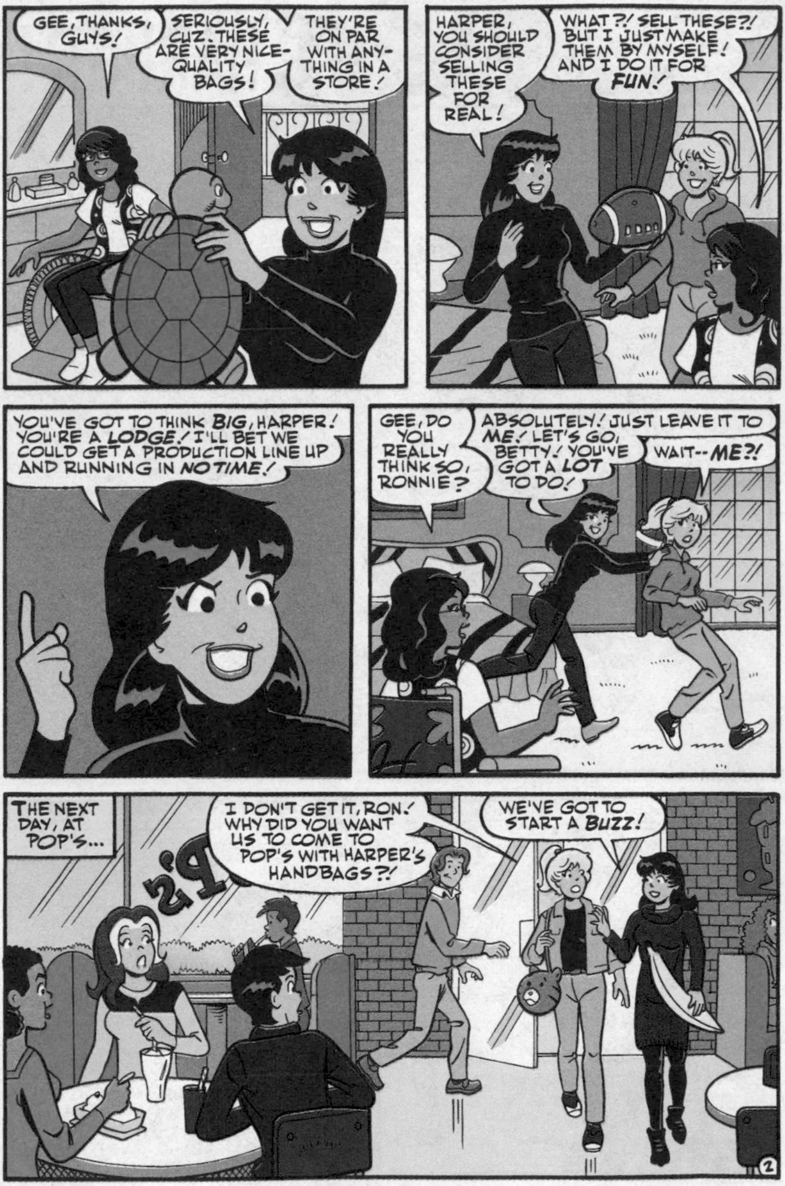
GEE, THANKS, GUYS!
SERIOUSLY, CUZ. THESE ARE VERY NICE-QUALITY BAGS!
THEY'RE ON PAR WITH ANY-THING IN A STORE!
HARPER, YOU SHOULD CONSIDER SELLING THESE FOR REAL!
WHAT?! SELL THESE?! BUT I JUST MAKE THEM BY MYSELF! AND I DO IT FOR FUN!
YOU'VE GOT TO THINK BIG, HARPER! YOU'RE A LODGE! I'LL BET WE COULD GET A PRODUCTION LINE UP AND RUNNING IN NO TIME!
GEE, DO YOU REALLY THINK SO, RONNIE?
ABSOLUTELY! JUST LEAVE IT TO ME! LET'S GO, BETTY! YOU'VE GOT A LOT TO DO!
WAIT--ME?!
THE NEXT DAY, AT POP'S...
I DON'T GET IT, RON! WHY DID YOU WANT US TO COME TO POP'S WITH HARPER'S HANDBAGS?!
WE'VE GOT TO START A BUZZ!
2

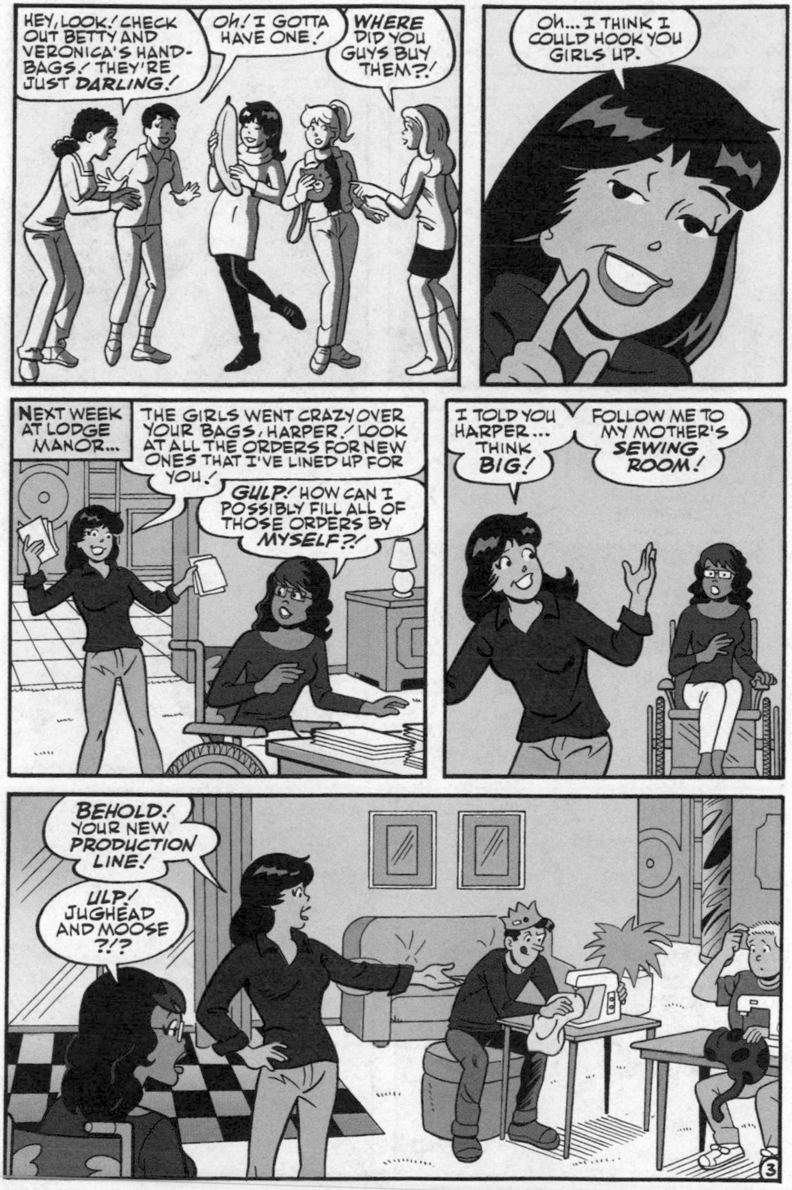

HEY, LOOK! CHECK OUT BETTY AND VERONICA'S HAND-BAGS! THEY'RE JUST DARLING!
OH! I GOTTA HAVE ONE!
WHERE DID YOU GUYS BUY THEM?!
OH... I THINK I COULD HOOK YOU GIRLS UP.
NEXT WEEK AT LODGE MANOR...
THE GIRLS WENT CRAZY OVER YOUR BAGS, HARPER! LOOK AT ALL THE ORDERS FOR NEW ONES THAT I'VE LINED UP FOR YOU!
GULP! HOW CAN I POSSIBLY FILL ALL OF THOSE ORDERS BY MYSELF?!
I TOLD YOU HARPER... THINK BIG!
FOLLOW ME TO MY MOTHER'S SEWING ROOM!
BEHOLD! YOUR NEW PRODUCTION LINE!
ULP! JUGHEAD AND MOOSE ?!?
3

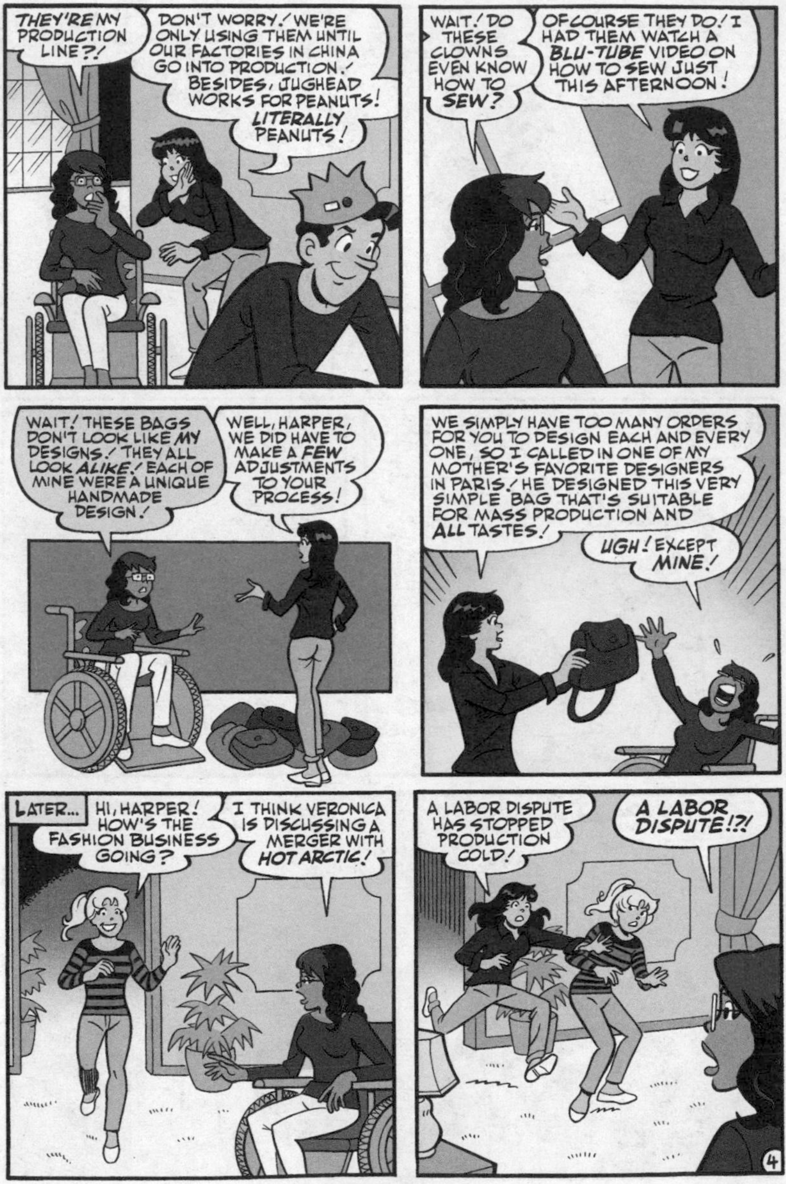
THEY'RE MY PRODUCTION LINE?!
DON'T WORRY! WE'RE ONLY USING THEM UNTIL OUR FACTORIES IN CHINA GO INTO PRODUCTION! BESIDES, JUGHEAD WORKS FOR PEANUTS! LITERALLY PEANUTS!
WAIT! DO THESE CLOWNS EVEN KNOW HOW TO SEW?
OF COURSE THEY DO! I HAD THEM WATCH A BLU-TUBE VIDEO ON HOW TO SEW JUST THIS AFTERNOON!
WAIT! THESE BAGS DON'T LOOK LIKE MY DESIGNS! THEY ALL LOOK ALIKE! EACH OF MINE WERE A UNIQUE HANDMADE DESIGN!
WELL, HARPER, WE DID HAVE TO MAKE A FEW ADJUSTMENTS TO YOUR PROCESS!
WE SIMPLY HAVE TOO MANY ORDERS FOR YOU TO DESIGN EACH AND EVERY ONE, SO I CALLED IN ONE OF MY MOTHER'S FAVORITE DESIGNERS IN PARIS! HE DESIGNED THIS VERY SIMPLE BAG THAT'S SUITABLE FOR MASS PRODUCTION AND ALL TASTES!
UGH! EXCEPT MINE!
LATER...
HI, HARPER! HOW'S THE FASHION BUSINESS GOING?
I THINK VERONICA IS DISCUSSING A MERGER WITH HOT ARCTIC!
A LABOR DISPUTE HAS STOPPED PRODUCTION COLD!
A LABOR DISPUTE!?!
4

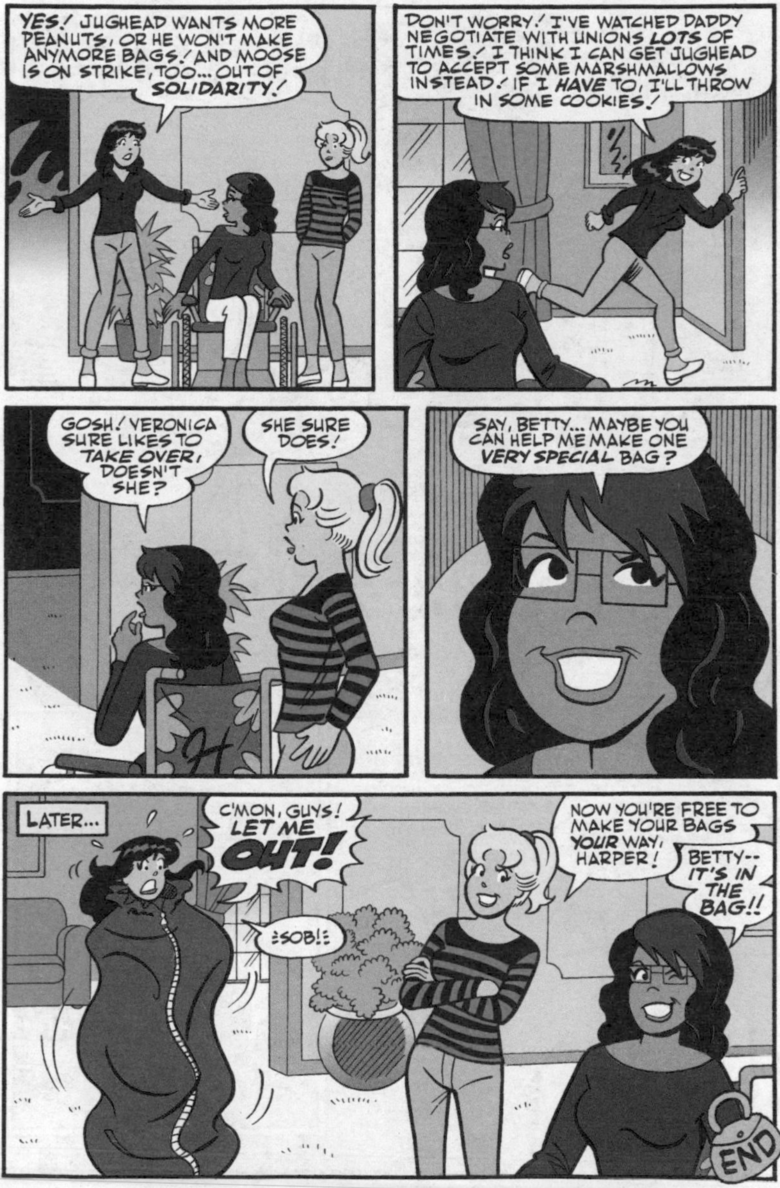
YES! JUGHEAD WANTS MORE PEANUTS, OR HE WON'T MAKE ANYMORE BAGS! AND MOOSE IS ON STRIKE, TOO... OUT OF SOLIDARITY!
DON'T WORRY! I'VE WATCHED DADDY NEGOTIATE WITH UNIONS LOTS OF TIMES! I THINK I CAN GET JUGHEAD TO ACCEPT SOME MARSHMALLOWS INSTEAD! IF I HAVE TO, I'LL THROW IN SOME COOKIES!
GOSH! VERONICA SURE LIKES TO TAKE OVER, DOESN'T SHE?
SHE SURE DOES!
SAY, BETTY... MAYBE YOU CAN HELP ME MAKE ONE VERY SPECIAL BAG?
LATER...
C'MON, GUYS! LET ME OUT!
SOB!
NOW YOU'RE FREE TO MAKE YOUR BAGS YOUR WAY, HARPER!
BETTY-- IT'S IN THE BAG!!
END

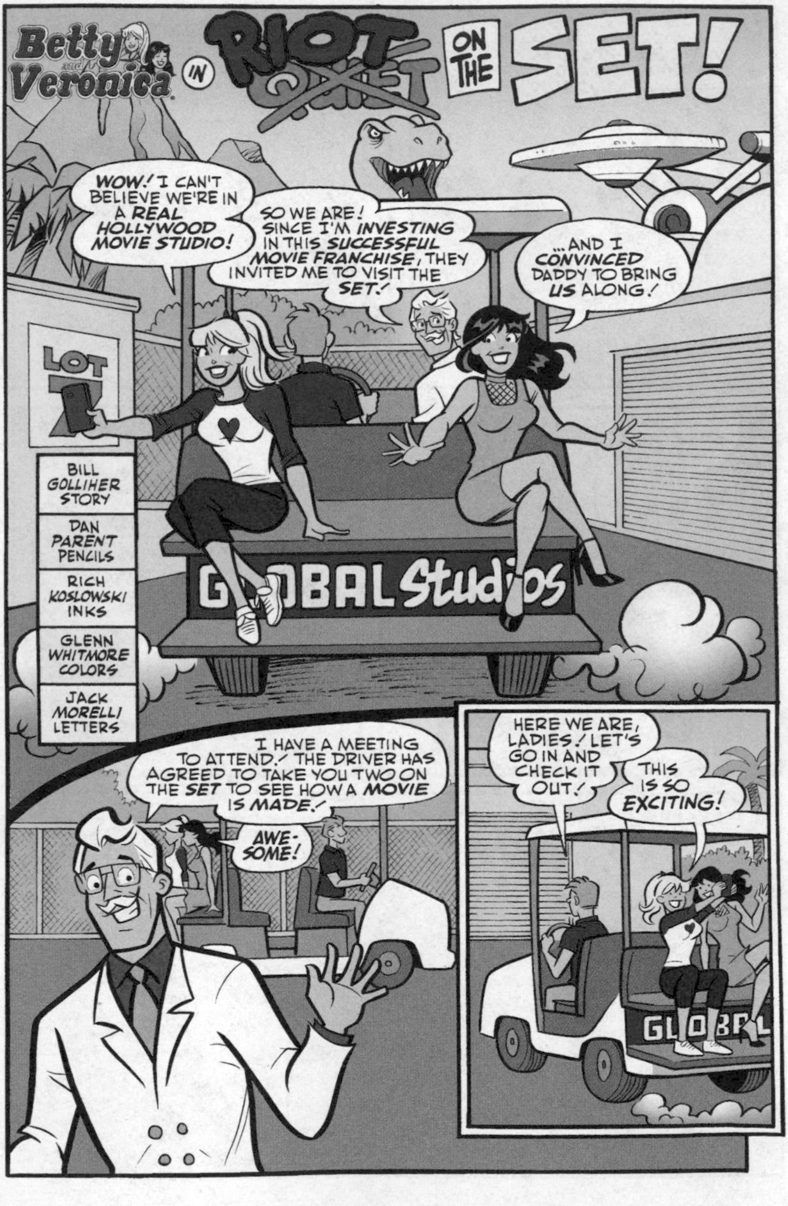

Betty and Veronica
IN
RIOT QUIET ON THE SET!
WOW! I CAN'T BELIEVE WE'RE IN A REAL HOLLYWOOD MOVIE STUDIO!
SO WE ARE! SINCE I'M INVESTING IN THIS SUCCESSFUL MOVIE FRANCHISE, THEY INVITED ME TO VISIT THE SET!
...AND I CONVINCED DADDY TO BRING US ALONG!
LOT 7
BILL GOLLIHER STORY
DAN PARENT PENCILS
RICH KOSLOWSKI INKS
GLENN WHITMORE COLORS
JACK MORELLI LETTERS
GLOBAL Studios
I HAVE A MEETING TO ATTEND! THE DRIVER HAS AGREED TO TAKE YOU TWO ON THE SET TO SEE HOW A MOVIE IS MADE!
AWE-SOME!
HERE WE ARE, LADIES! LET'S GO IN AND CHECK IT OUT!
THIS IS SO EXCITING!
GLOBAL

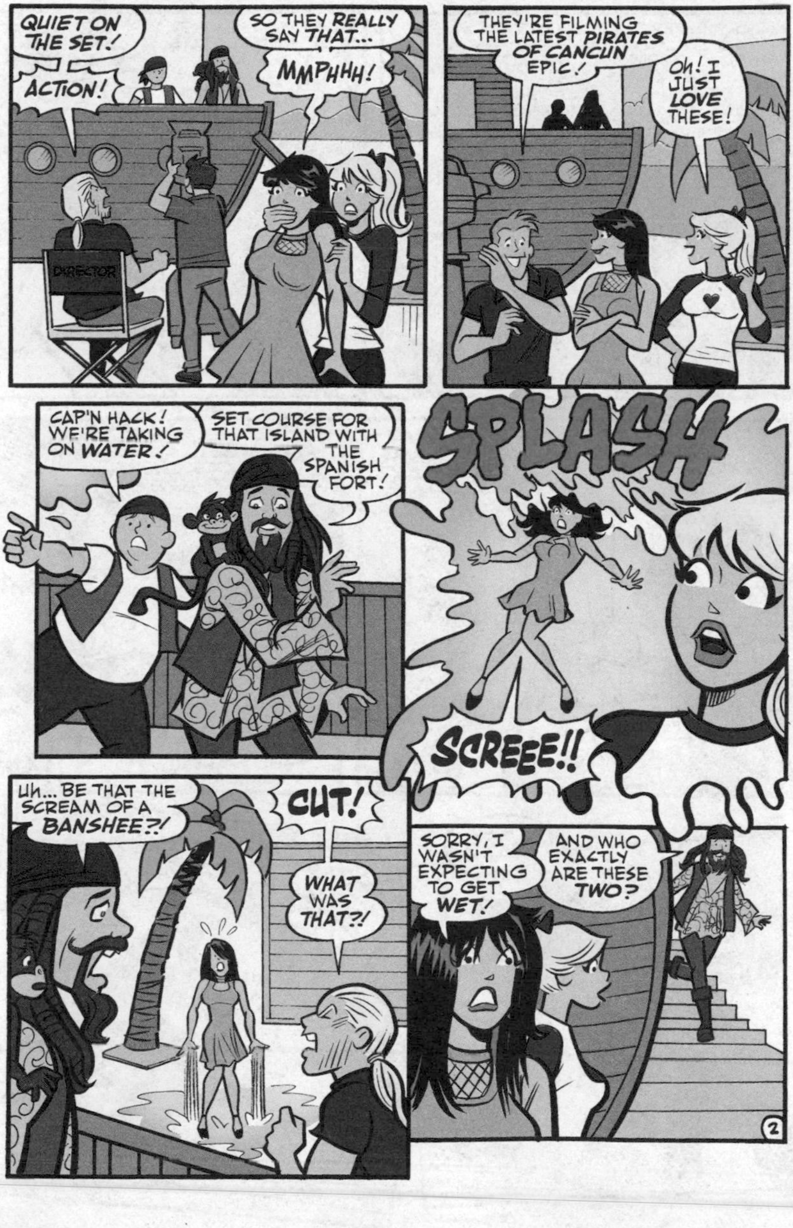
QUIET ON THE SET!
ACTION!
SO THEY REALLY SAY THAT...
MMPHHH!
DIRECTOR
THEY'RE FILMING THE LATEST PIRATES OF CANCUN EPIC!
Oh! I JUST LOVE THESE!
CAP'N HACK! WE'RE TAKING ON WATER!
SET COURSE FOR THAT ISLAND WITH THE SPANISH FORT!
SPLASH
SCREEE!!
Uh... BE THAT THE SCREAM OF A BANSHEE?!
CUT!
WHAT WAS THAT?!
SORRY, I WASN'T EXPECTING TO GET WET!
AND WHO EXACTLY ARE THESE TWO?
2

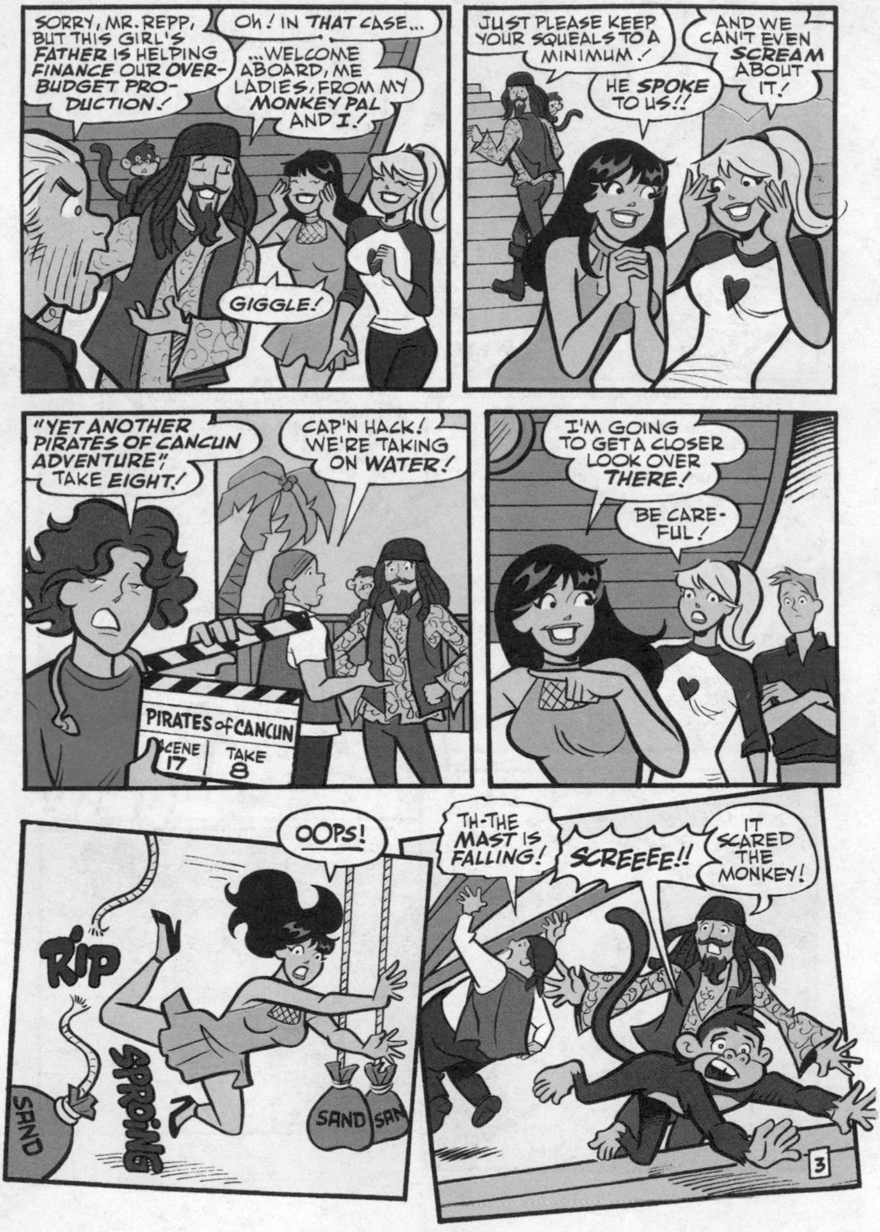
SORRY, MR. REPP, BUT THIS GIRL'S FATHER IS HELPING FINANCE OUR OVER-BUDGET PRO-DUCTION!
Oh! IN THAT CASE...
...WELCOME ABOARD, ME LADIES, FROM MY MONKEY PAL AND I!
GIGGLE!
JUST PLEASE KEEP YOUR SQUEALS TO A MINIMUM!
HE SPOKE TO US!!
AND WE CAN'T EVEN SCREAM ABOUT IT!
"YET ANOTHER PIRATES OF CANCUN ADVENTURE", TAKE EIGHT!
PIRATES of CANCUN
SCENE 17
TAKE 8
CAP'N HACK! WE'RE TAKING ON WATER!
I'M GOING TO GET A CLOSER LOOK OVER THERE!
BE CARE-FUL!
OOPS!
RIP
SPROING
SAND
SAND
TH-THE MAST IS FALLING!
SCREEEE!!
IT SCARED THE MONKEY!
3

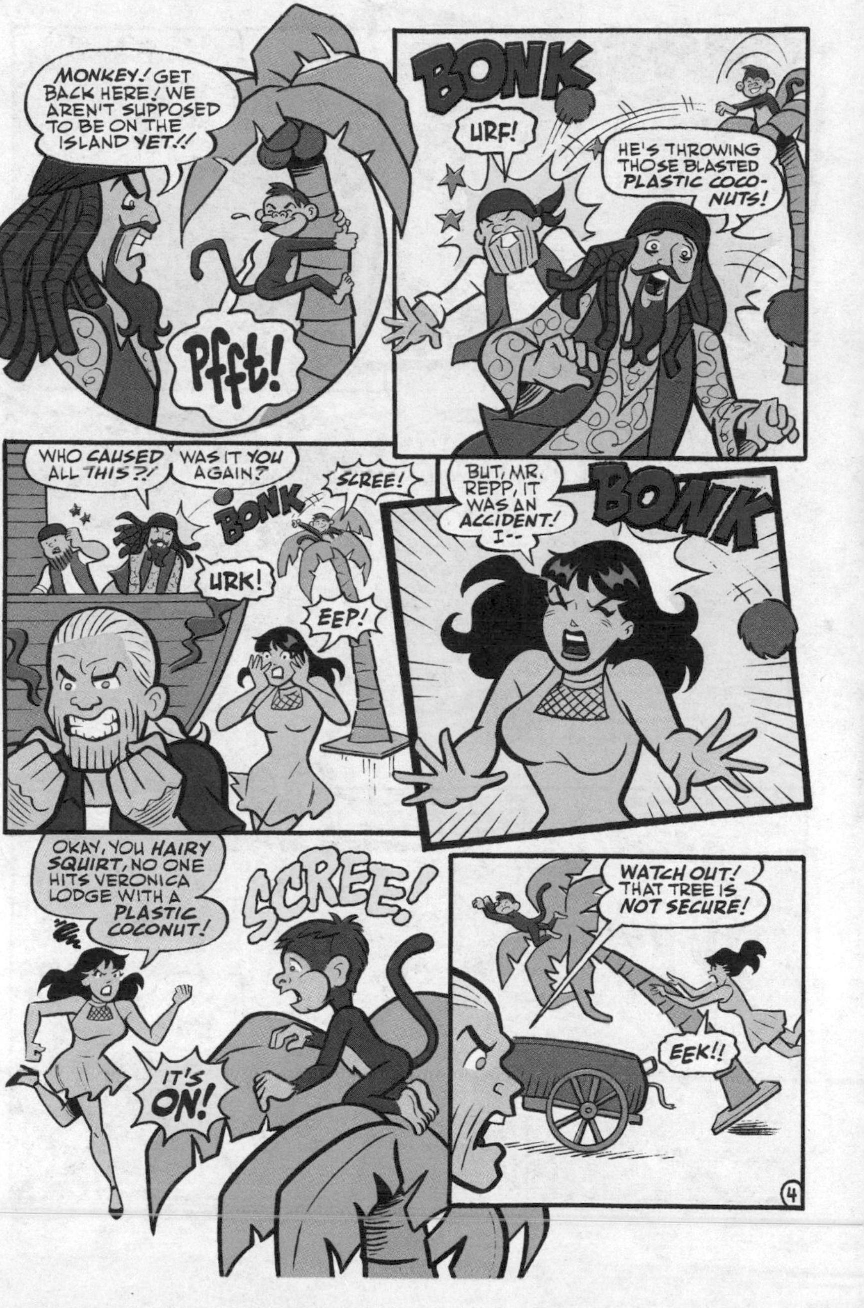
MONKEY! GET BACK HERE! WE AREN'T SUPPOSED TO BE ON THE ISLAND YET!!
Pfft!
BONK
URF!
HE'S THROWING THOSE BLASTED PLASTIC COCO- NUTS!
WHO CAUSED ALL THIS?!
WAS IT YOU AGAIN?
BONK
SCREE!
URK!
EEP!
BUT, MR. REPP, IT WAS AN ACCIDENT! I--
BONK
OKAY, YOU HAIRY SQUIRT, NO ONE HITS VERONICA LODGE WITH A PLASTIC COCONUT!
SCREE!
IT'S ON!
WATCH OUT! THAT TREE IS NOT SECURE!
EEK!!
4

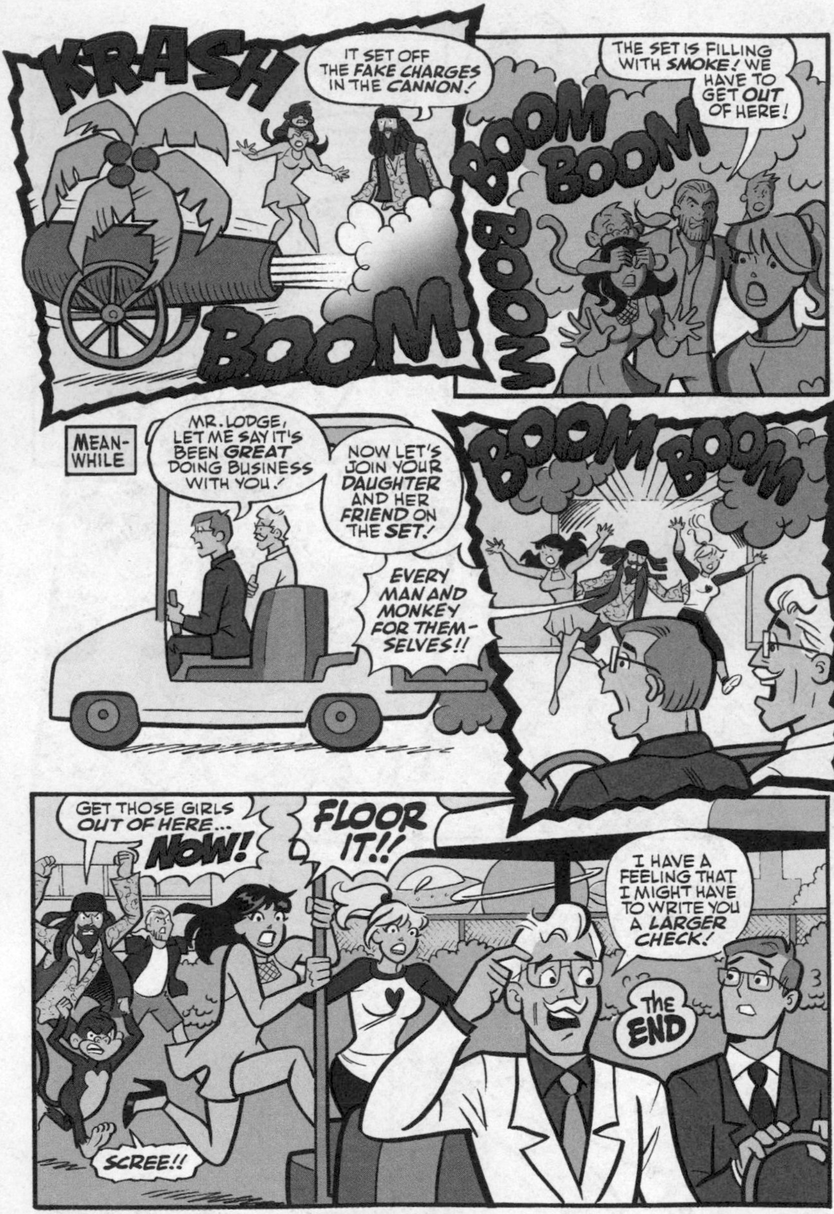
KRASH
IT SET OFF THE FAKE CHARGES IN THE CANNON!
BOOM
THE SET IS FILLING WITH SMOKE! WE HAVE TO GET OUT OF HERE!
BOOM BOOM BOOM
MEAN-WHILE
MR. LODGE, LET ME SAY IT'S BEEN GREAT DOING BUSINESS WITH YOU!
NOW LET'S JOIN YOUR DAUGHTER AND HER FRIEND ON THE SET!
BOOM BOOM
EVERY MAN AND MONKEY FOR THEM-SELVES!!
GET THOSE GIRLS OUT OF HERE... NOW!
FLOOR IT!!
I HAVE A FEELING THAT I MIGHT HAVE TO WRITE YOU A LARGER CHECK!
THE END
SCREE!!

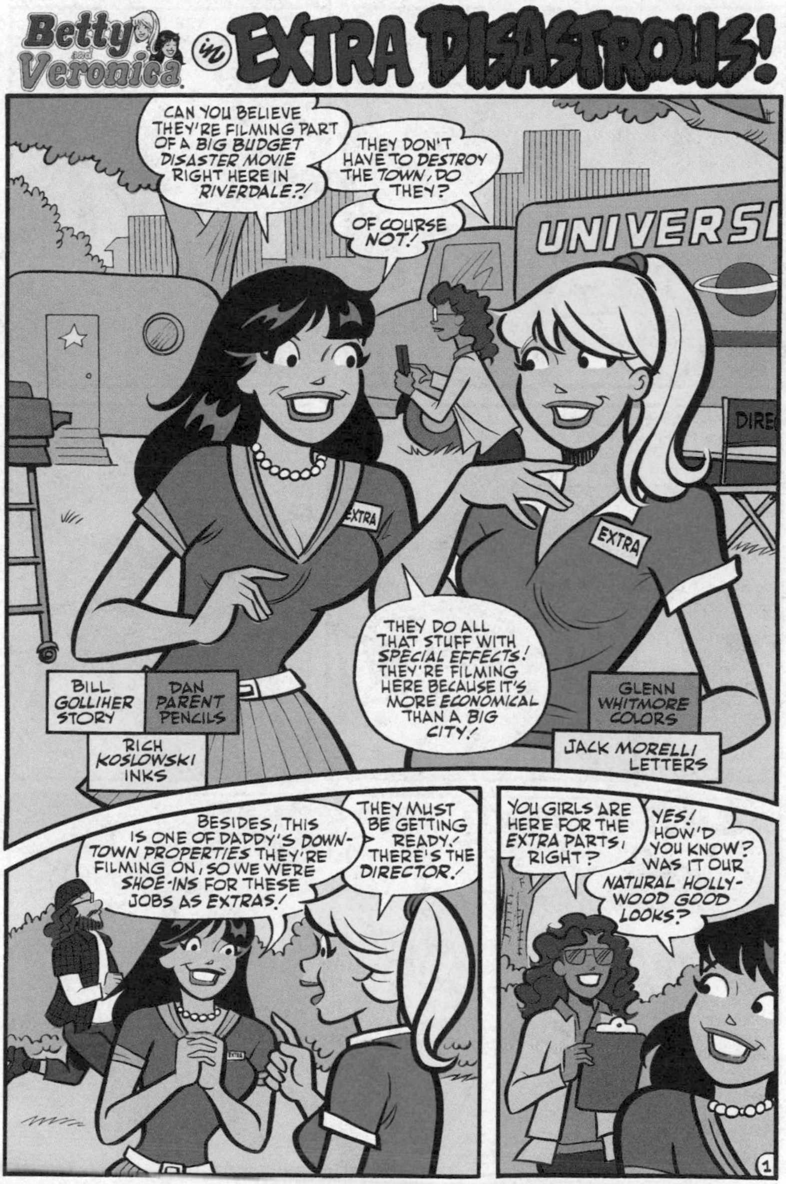
Betty and Veronica in EXTRA DISASTROUS!
CAN YOU BELIEVE THEY'RE FILMING PART OF A BIG BUDGET DISASTER MOVIE RIGHT HERE IN RIVERDALE?!
THEY DON'T HAVE TO DESTROY THE TOWN, DO THEY?
OF COURSE NOT!
UNIVERSI
DIREC
EXTRA
EXTRA
THEY DO ALL THAT STUFF WITH SPECIAL EFFECTS! THEY'RE FILMING HERE BECAUSE IT'S MORE ECONOMICAL THAN A BIG CITY!
BILL GOLLIHER STORY
DAN PARENT PENCILS
RICH KOSLOWSKI INKS
GLENN WHITMORE COLORS
JACK MORELLI LETTERS
BESIDES, THIS IS ONE OF DADDY'S DOWNTOWN PROPERTIES THEY'RE FILMING ON, SO WE WERE SHOE-INS FOR THESE JOBS AS EXTRAS!
THEY MUST BE GETTING READY! THERE'S THE DIRECTOR!
YOU GIRLS ARE HERE FOR THE EXTRA PARTS, RIGHT?
YES! HOW'D YOU KNOW? WAS IT OUR NATURAL HOLLYWOOD GOOD LOOKS?
1

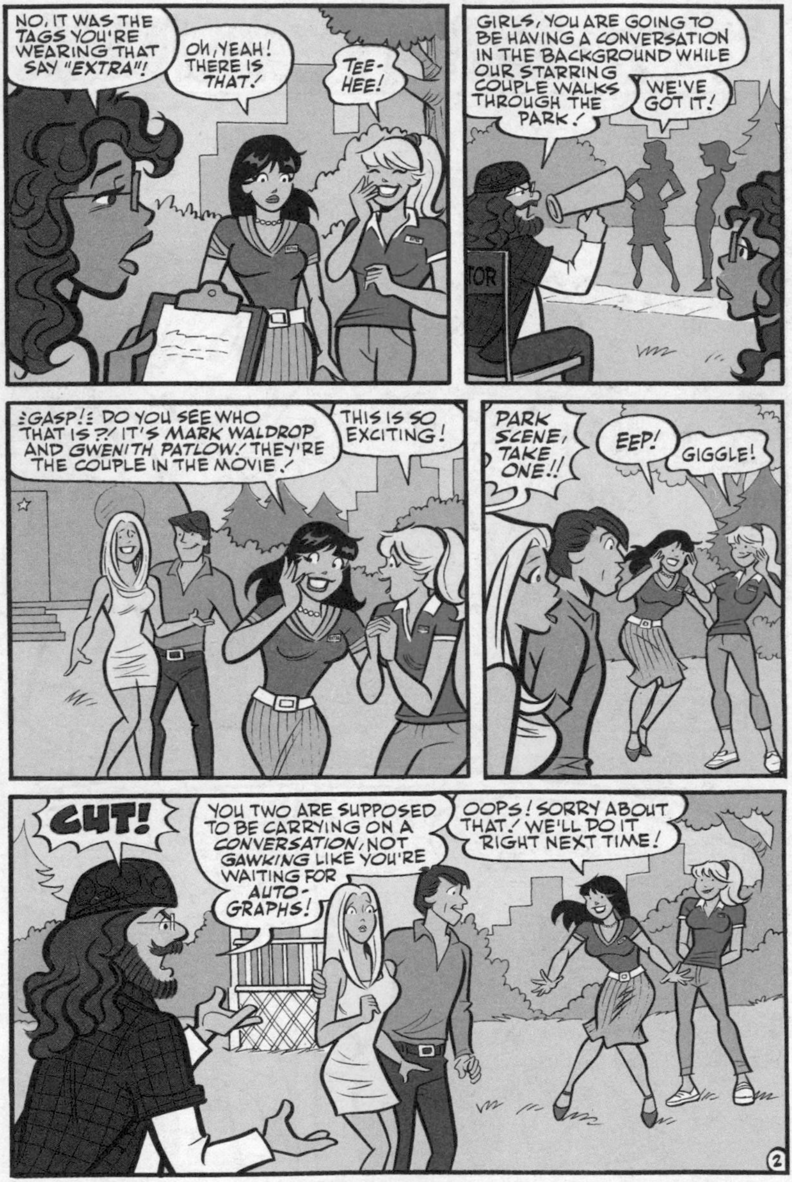
NO, IT WAS THE TAGS YOU'RE WEARING THAT SAY "EXTRA"!
OH, YEAH! THERE IS THAT!
TEE-HEE!
GIRLS, YOU ARE GOING TO BE HAVING A CONVERSATION IN THE BACKGROUND WHILE OUR STARRING COUPLE WALKS THROUGH THE PARK!
WE'VE GOT IT!
:GASP!: DO YOU SEE WHO THAT IS?! IT'S MARK WALDROP AND GWENITH PATLOW! THEY'RE THE COUPLE IN THE MOVIE!
THIS IS SO EXCITING!
PARK SCENE, TAKE ONE!!
EEP!
GIGGLE!
CUT!
YOU TWO ARE SUPPOSED TO BE CARRYING ON A CONVERSATION, NOT GAWKING LIKE YOU'RE WAITING FOR AUTO-GRAPHS!
OOPS! SORRY ABOUT THAT! WE'LL DO IT RIGHT NEXT TIME!
2

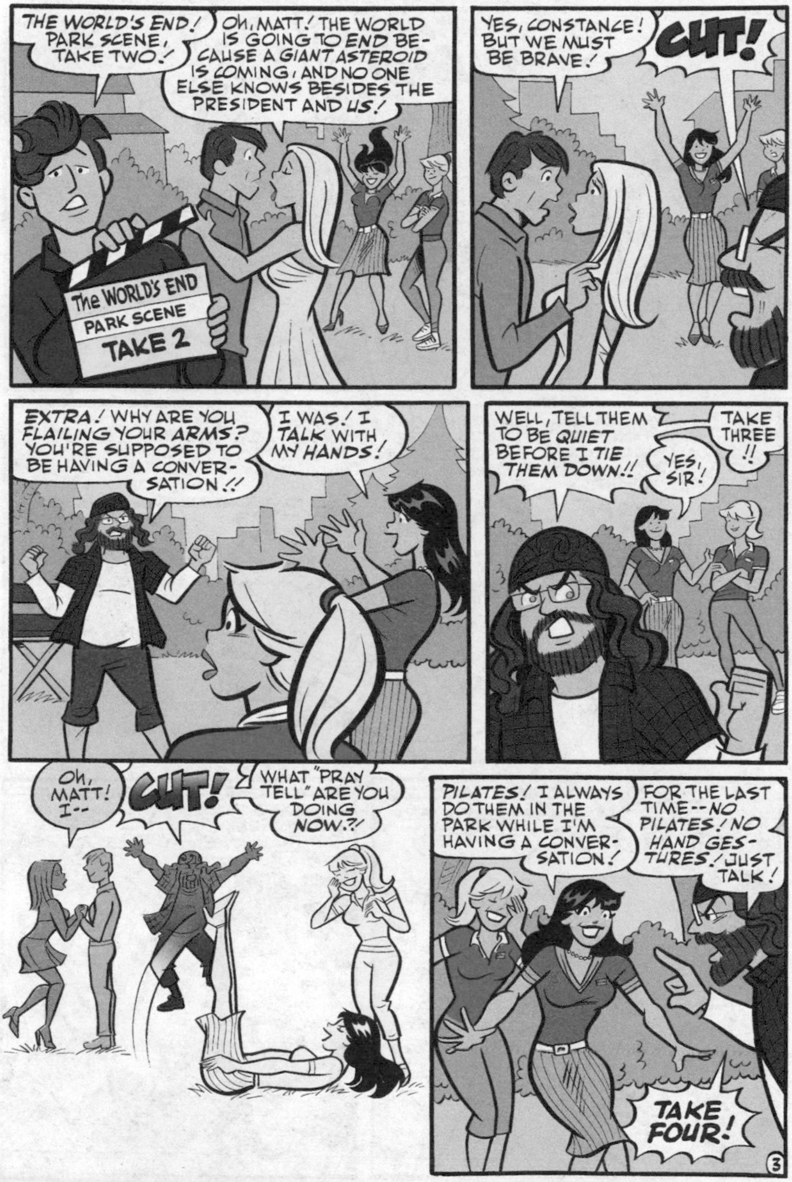
THE WORLD'S END! PARK SCENE, TAKE TWO!
OH, MATT! THE WORLD IS GOING TO END BECAUSE A GIANT ASTEROID IS COMING, AND NO ONE ELSE KNOWS BESIDES THE PRESIDENT AND US!
The WORLD'S END
PARK SCENE
TAKE 2
YES, CONSTANCE! BUT WE MUST BE BRAVE!
CUT!
EXTRA! WHY ARE YOU FLAILING YOUR ARMS? YOU'RE SUPPOSED TO BE HAVING A CONVERSATION!!
I WAS! I TALK WITH MY HANDS!
WELL, TELL THEM TO BE QUIET BEFORE I TIE THEM DOWN!!
YES, SIR!
TAKE THREE!!
OH, MATT! I--
CUT!
WHAT "PRAY TELL" ARE YOU DOING NOW?!
PILATES! I ALWAYS DO THEM IN THE PARK WHILE I'M HAVING A CONVERSATION!
FOR THE LAST TIME--NO PILATES! NO HAND GESTURES! JUST TALK!
TAKE FOUR!
3

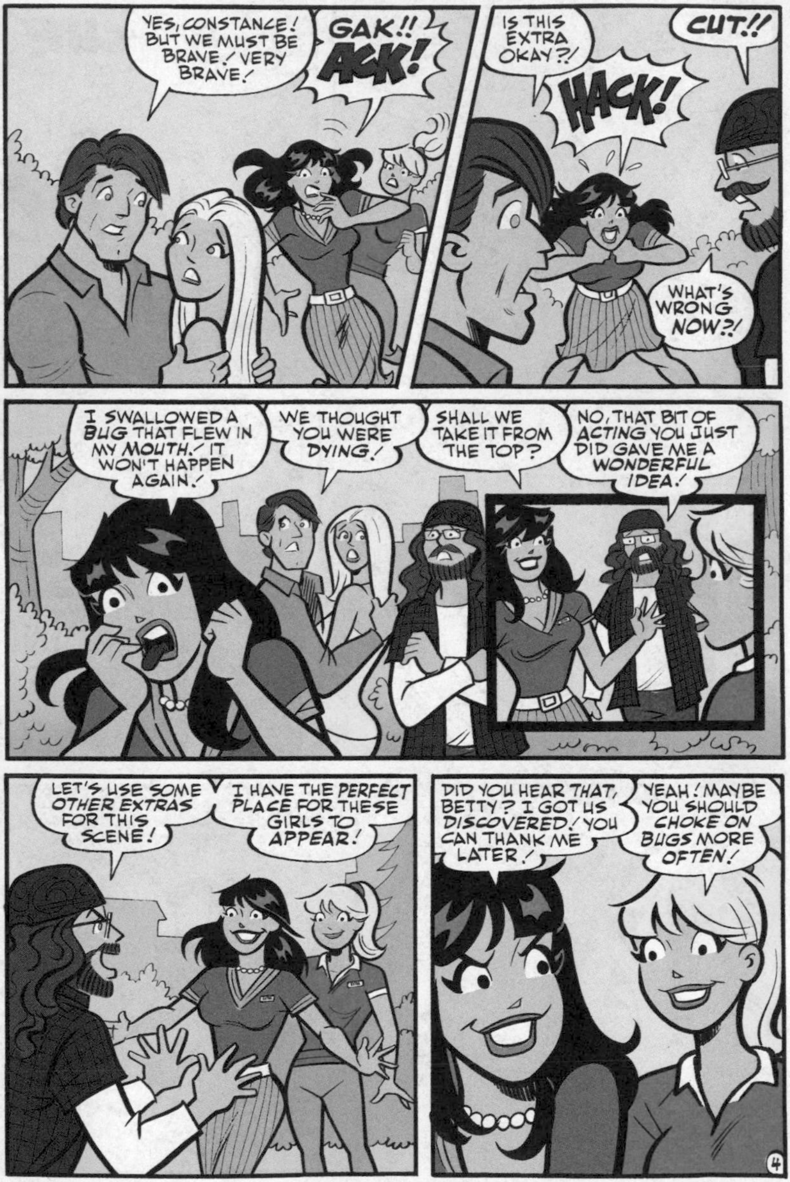
YES, CONSTANCE! BUT WE MUST BE BRAVE! VERY BRAVE!
GAK!! ACK!
IS THIS EXTRA OKAY?!
HACK!
CUT!!
WHAT'S WRONG NOW?!
I SWALLOWED A BUG THAT FLEW IN MY MOUTH! IT WON'T HAPPEN AGAIN!
WE THOUGHT YOU WERE DYING!
SHALL WE TAKE IT FROM THE TOP?
NO, THAT BIT OF ACTING YOU JUST DID GAVE ME A WONDERFUL IDEA!
LET'S USE SOME OTHER EXTRAS FOR THIS SCENE!
I HAVE THE PERFECT PLACE FOR THESE GIRLS TO APPEAR!
DID YOU HEAR THAT, BETTY? I GOT US DISCOVERED! YOU CAN THANK ME LATER!
YEAH! MAYBE YOU SHOULD CHOKE ON BUGS MORE OFTEN!
4

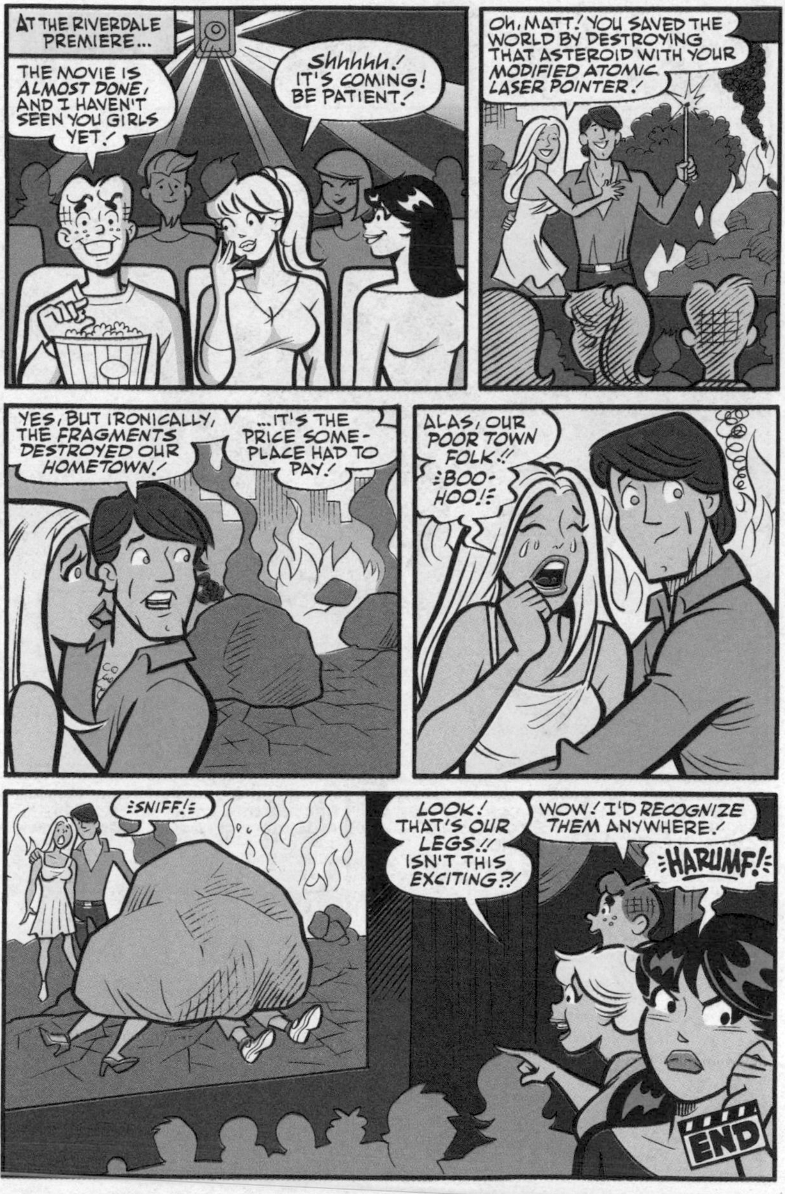
AT THE RIVERDALE PREMIERE...
THE MOVIE IS ALMOST DONE, AND I HAVEN'T SEEN YOU GIRLS YET!
Shhhhh! IT'S COMING! BE PATIENT!
Oh, MATT! YOU SAVED THE WORLD BY DESTROYING THAT ASTEROID WITH YOUR MODIFIED ATOMIC LASER POINTER!
YES, BUT IRONICALLY, THE FRAGMENTS DESTROYED OUR HOMETOWN!
...IT'S THE PRICE SOME-PLACE HAD TO PAY!
ALAS, OUR POOR TOWN FOLK!!
BOO-HOO!
SNIFF!
LOOK! THAT'S OUR LEGS!! ISN'T THIS EXCITING?!
WOW! I'D RECOGNIZE THEM ANYWHERE!
HARUMF!
END

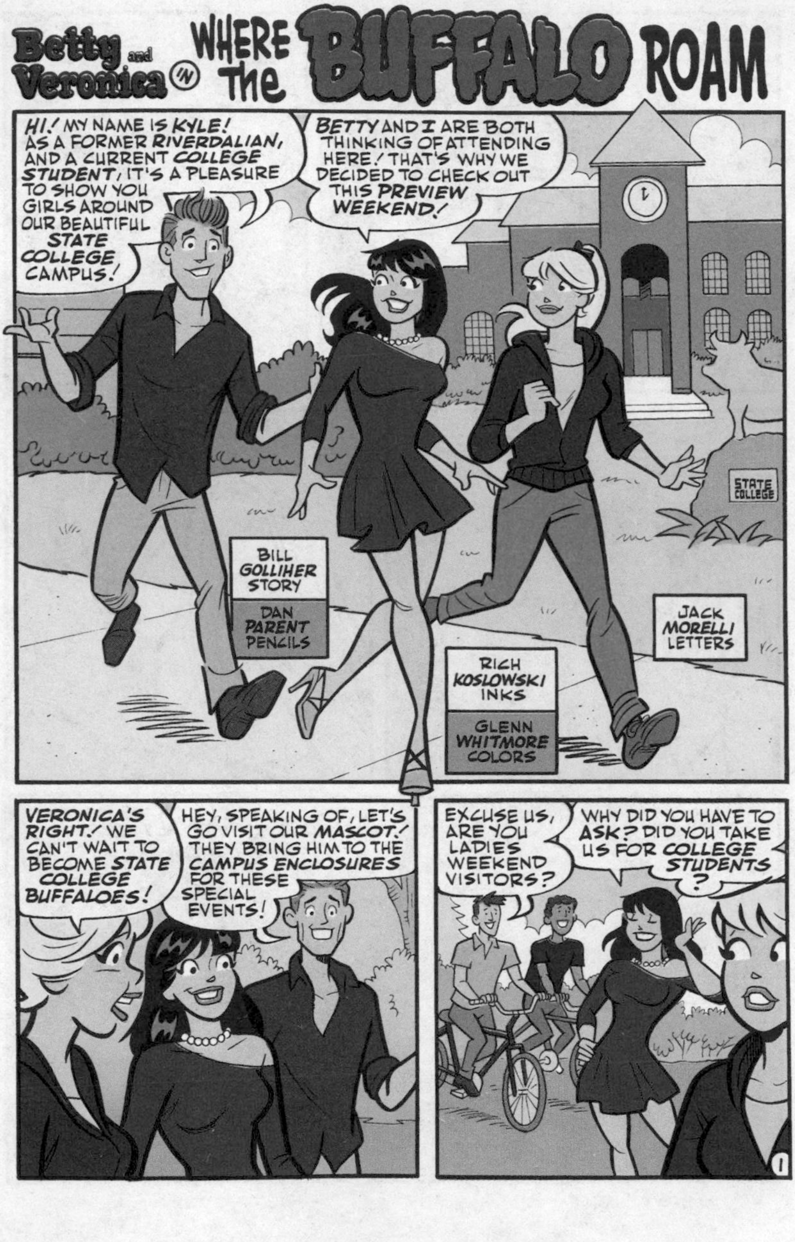
Betty and Veronica in WHERE the BUFFALO ROAM
HI! MY NAME IS KYLE! AS A FORMER RIVERDALIAN, AND A CURRENT COLLEGE STUDENT, IT'S A PLEASURE TO SHOW YOU GIRLS AROUND OUR BEAUTIFUL STATE COLLEGE CAMPUS!
BETTY AND I ARE BOTH THINKING OF ATTENDING HERE! THAT'S WHY WE DECIDED TO CHECK OUT THIS PREVIEW WEEKEND!
STATE COLLEGE
BILL GOLLIHER STORY
DAN PARENT PENCILS
RICH KOSLOWSKI INKS
GLENN WHITMORE COLORS
JACK MORELLI LETTERS
VERONICA'S RIGHT! WE CAN'T WAIT TO BECOME STATE COLLEGE BUFFALOES!
HEY, SPEAKING OF, LET'S GO VISIT OUR MASCOT! THEY BRING HIM TO THE CAMPUS ENCLOSURES FOR THESE SPECIAL EVENTS!
EXCUSE US, ARE YOU LADIES WEEKEND VISITORS?
WHY DID YOU HAVE TO ASK? DID YOU TAKE US FOR COLLEGE STUDENTS?
1

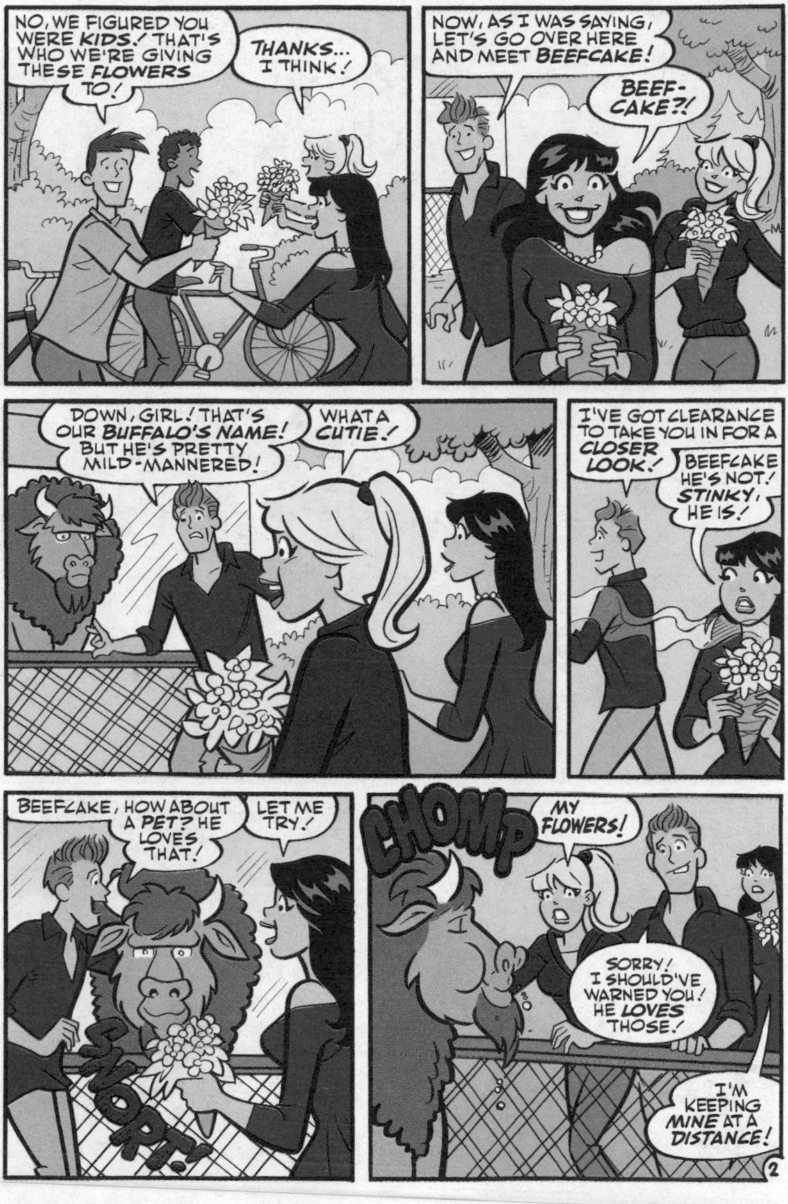
NO, WE FIGURED YOU WERE KIDS! THAT'S WHO WE'RE GIVING THESE FLOWERS TO!
THANKS... I THINK!
NOW, AS I WAS SAYING, LET'S GO OVER HERE AND MEET BEEFCAKE!
BEEF-CAKE?!
DOWN, GIRL! THAT'S OUR BUFFALO'S NAME! BUT HE'S PRETTY MILD-MANNERED!
WHAT A CUTIE!
I'VE GOT CLEARANCE TO TAKE YOU IN FOR A CLOSER LOOK!
BEEFCAKE HE'S NOT! STINKY, HE IS!
BEEFCAKE, HOW ABOUT A PET? HE LOVES THAT!
LET ME TRY!
SNORT!
CHOMP
MY FLOWERS!
SORRY! I SHOULD'VE WARNED YOU! HE LOVES THOSE!
I'M KEEPING MINE AT A DISTANCE!
2

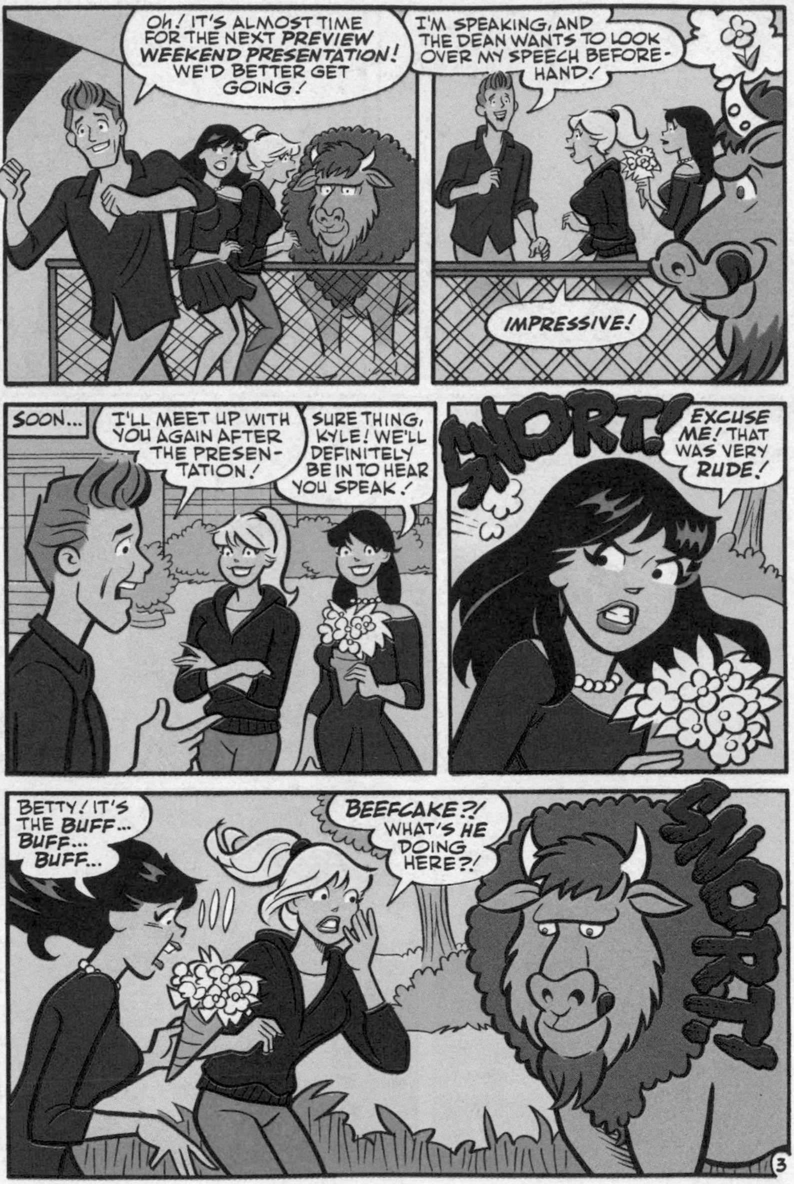
Oh! IT'S ALMOST TIME FOR THE NEXT PREVIEW WEEKEND PRESENTATION! WE'D BETTER GET GOING!
I'M SPEAKING, AND THE DEAN WANTS TO LOOK OVER MY SPEECH BEFORE-HAND!
IMPRESSIVE!
SOON...
I'LL MEET UP WITH YOU AGAIN AFTER THE PRESEN-TATION!
SURE THING, KYLE! WE'LL DEFINITELY BE IN TO HEAR YOU SPEAK!
SNORT!
EXCUSE ME! THAT WAS VERY RUDE!
BETTY! IT'S THE BUFF... BUFF... BUFF...
BEEFCAKE?! WHAT'S HE DOING HERE?!
SNORT!
3

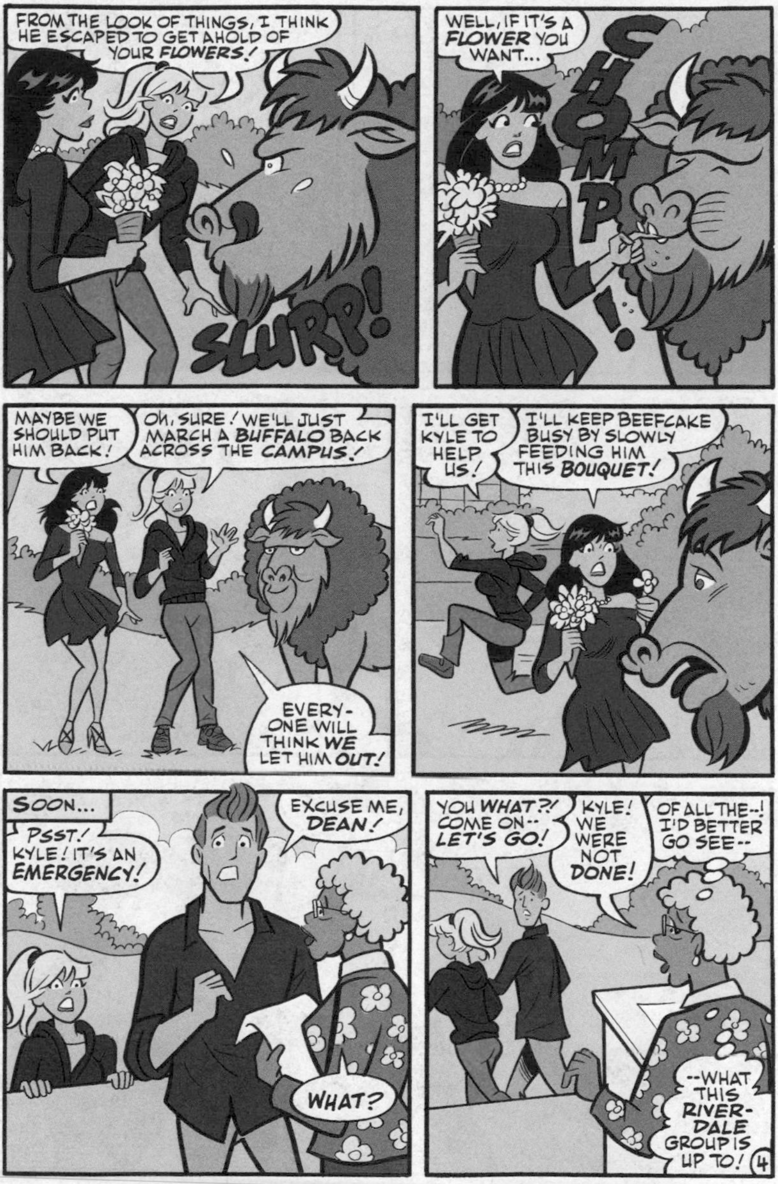
FROM THE LOOK OF THINGS, I THINK HE ESCAPED TO GET AHOLD OF YOUR FLOWERS!
SLURP!
WELL, IF IT'S A FLOWER YOU WANT...
CHOMP!!
MAYBE WE SHOULD PUT HIM BACK!
OH, SURE! WE'LL JUST MARCH A BUFFALO BACK ACROSS THE CAMPUS!
EVERY-ONE WILL THINK WE LET HIM OUT!
I'LL GET KYLE TO HELP US!
I'LL KEEP BEEFCAKE BUSY BY SLOWLY FEEDING HIM THIS BOUQUET!
SOON...
PSST! KYLE! IT'S AN EMERGENCY!
EXCUSE ME, DEAN!
WHAT?
YOU WHAT?!! COME ON-- LET'S GO!
KYLE! WE WERE NOT DONE!
OF ALL THE--! I'D BETTER GO SEE--
--WHAT THIS RIVER-DALE GROUP IS UP TO!
4

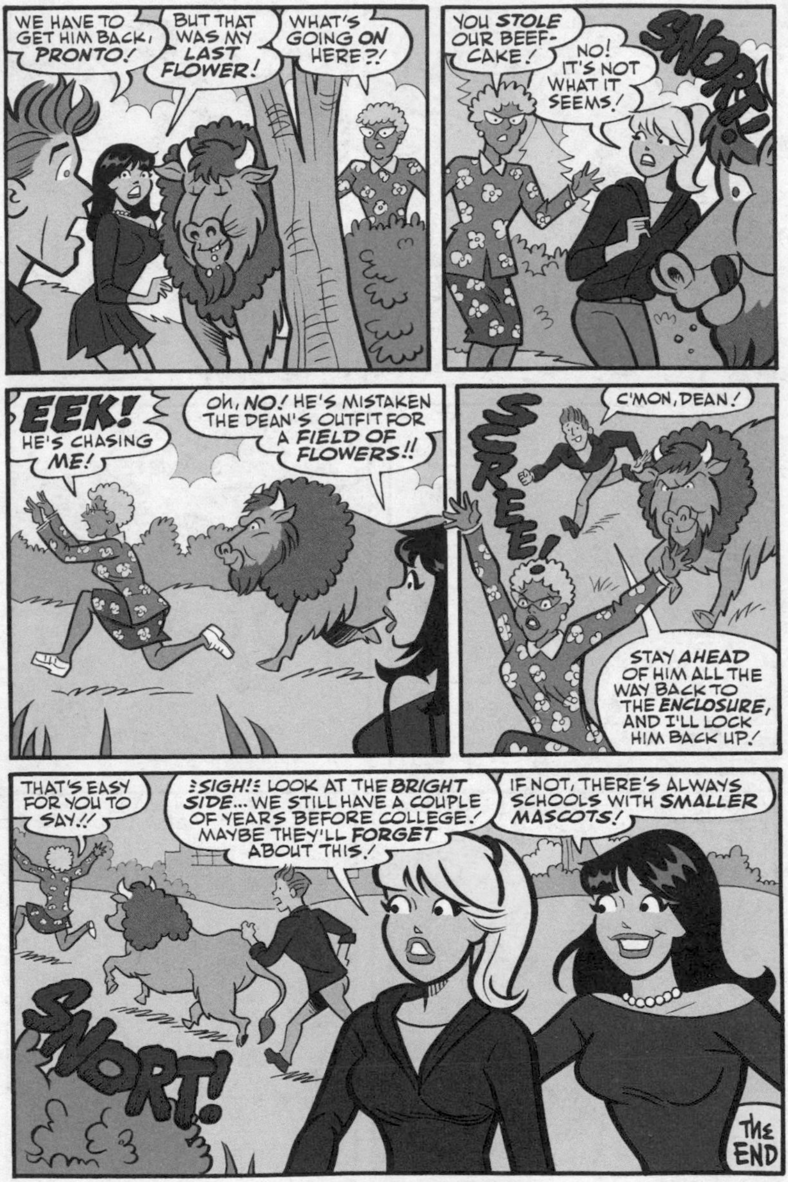
WE HAVE TO GET HIM BACK, PRONTO!
BUT THAT WAS MY LAST FLOWER!
WHAT'S GOING ON HERE?!
YOU STOLE OUR BEEF-CAKE!
NO! IT'S NOT WHAT IT SEEMS!
SNORT!!
EEK! HE'S CHASING ME!
Oh, NO! HE'S MISTAKEN THE DEAN'S OUTFIT FOR A FIELD OF FLOWERS!!
SCREEE!
C'MON, DEAN!
STAY AHEAD OF HIM ALL THE WAY BACK TO THE ENCLOSURE, AND I'LL LOCK HIM BACK UP!
THAT'S EASY FOR YOU TO SAY!!
SIGH! LOOK AT THE BRIGHT SIDE... WE STILL HAVE A COUPLE OF YEARS BEFORE COLLEGE! MAYBE THEY'LL FORGET ABOUT THIS!
IF NOT, THERE'S ALWAYS SCHOOLS WITH SMALLER MASCOTS!
SNORT!
THE END

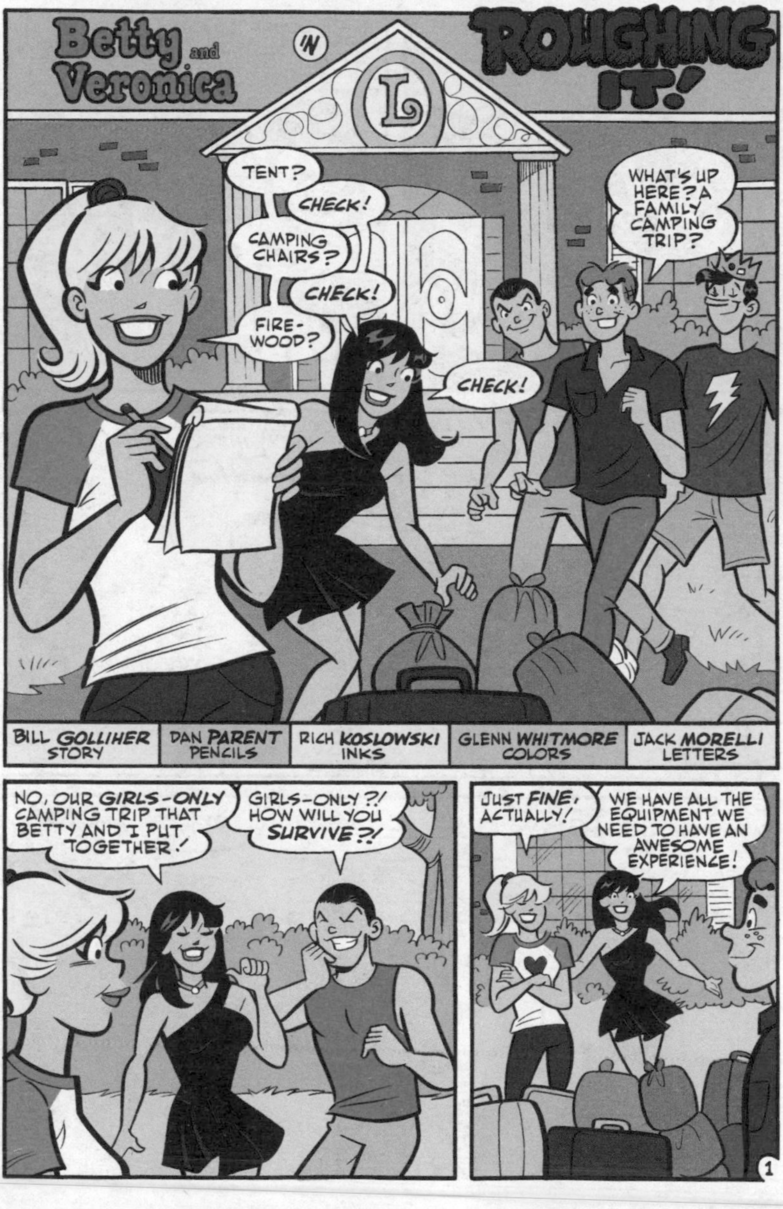
Betty and Veronica
IN
ROUGHING IT!
TENT?
CHECK!
CAMPING CHAIRS?
CHECK!
FIRE-WOOD?
CHECK!
WHAT'S UP HERE? A FAMILY CAMPING TRIP?
BILL GOLLIHER STORY
DAN PARENT PENCILS
RICH KOSLOWSKI INKS
GLENN WHITMORE COLORS
JACK MORELLI LETTERS
NO, OUR GIRLS-ONLY CAMPING TRIP THAT BETTY AND I PUT TOGETHER!
GIRLS-ONLY?! HOW WILL YOU SURVIVE?!
JUST FINE, ACTUALLY!
WE HAVE ALL THE EQUIPMENT WE NEED TO HAVE AN AWESOME EXPERIENCE!
1

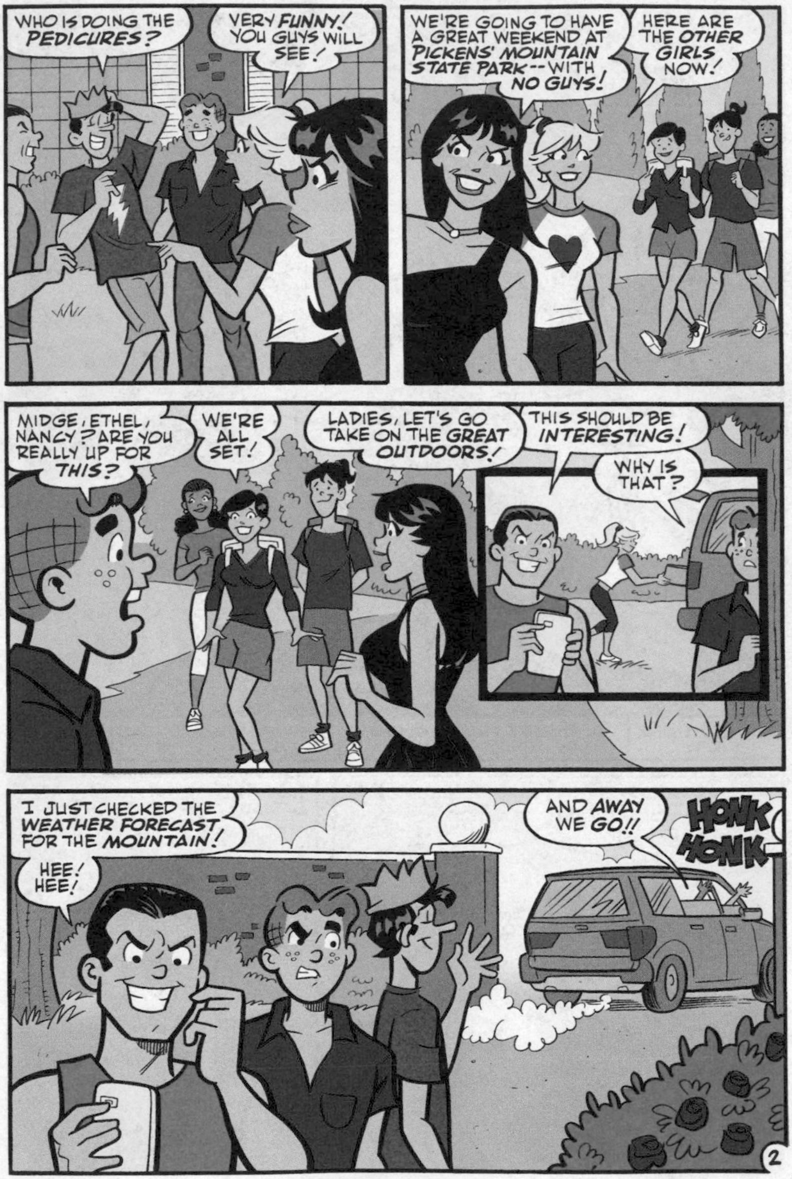
WHO IS DOING THE PEDICURES?
VERY FUNNY! YOU GUYS WILL SEE!
WE'RE GOING TO HAVE A GREAT WEEKEND AT PICKENS' MOUNTAIN STATE PARK -- WITH NO GUYS!
HERE ARE THE OTHER GIRLS, NOW!
MIDGE, ETHEL, NANCY? ARE YOU REALLY UP FOR THIS?
WE'RE ALL SET!
LADIES, LET'S GO TAKE ON THE GREAT OUTDOORS!
THIS SHOULD BE INTERESTING!
WHY IS THAT?
I JUST CHECKED THE WEATHER FORECAST FOR THE MOUNTAIN!
HEE! HEE!
AND AWAY WE GO!!
HONK HONK
2

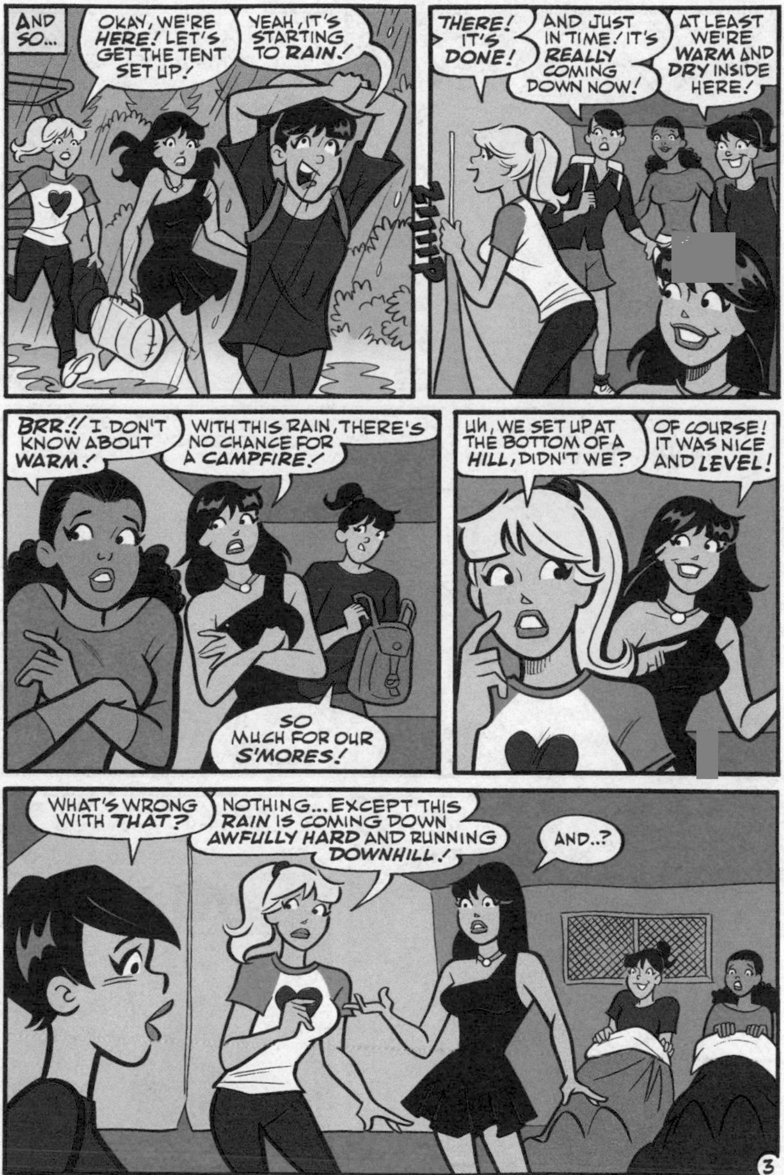
AND SO...
OKAY, WE'RE HERE! LET'S GET THE TENT SET UP!
YEAH, IT'S STARTING TO RAIN!
ZZZIIIP
THERE! IT'S DONE!
AND JUST IN TIME! IT'S REALLY COMING DOWN NOW!
AT LEAST WE'RE WARM AND DRY INSIDE HERE!
BRR!! I DON'T KNOW ABOUT WARM!
WITH THIS RAIN, THERE'S NO CHANCE FOR A CAMPFIRE!
SO MUCH FOR OUR S'MORES!
UH, WE SET UP AT THE BOTTOM OF A HILL, DIDN'T WE?
OF COURSE! IT WAS NICE AND LEVEL!
WHAT'S WRONG WITH THAT?
NOTHING... EXCEPT THIS RAIN IS COMING DOWN AWFULLY HARD AND RUNNING DOWNHILL!
AND..?
3

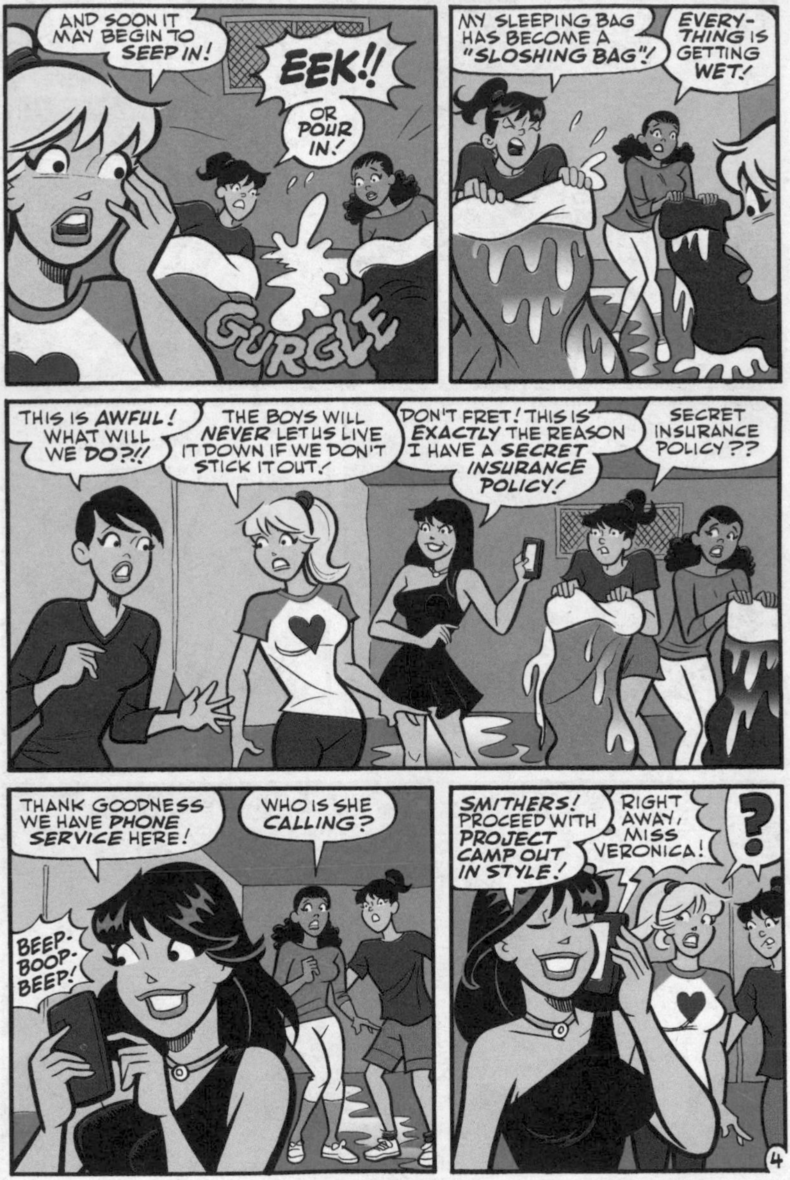

AND SOON IT MAY BEGIN TO SEEP IN!
EEK!!
OR POUR IN!
GURGLE
MY SLEEPING BAG HAS BECOME A "SLOSHING BAG"!
EVERY-THING IS GETTING WET!
THIS IS AWFUL! WHAT WILL WE DO?!!
THE BOYS WILL NEVER LET US LIVE IT DOWN IF WE DON'T STICK IT OUT!
DON'T FRET! THIS IS EXACTLY THE REASON I HAVE A SECRET INSURANCE POLICY!
SECRET INSURANCE POLICY??
THANK GOODNESS WE HAVE PHONE SERVICE HERE!
WHO IS SHE CALLING?
BEEP-BOOP-BEEP!
SMITHERS! PROCEED WITH PROJECT CAMP OUT IN STYLE!
RIGHT AWAY, MISS VERONICA!
?
4

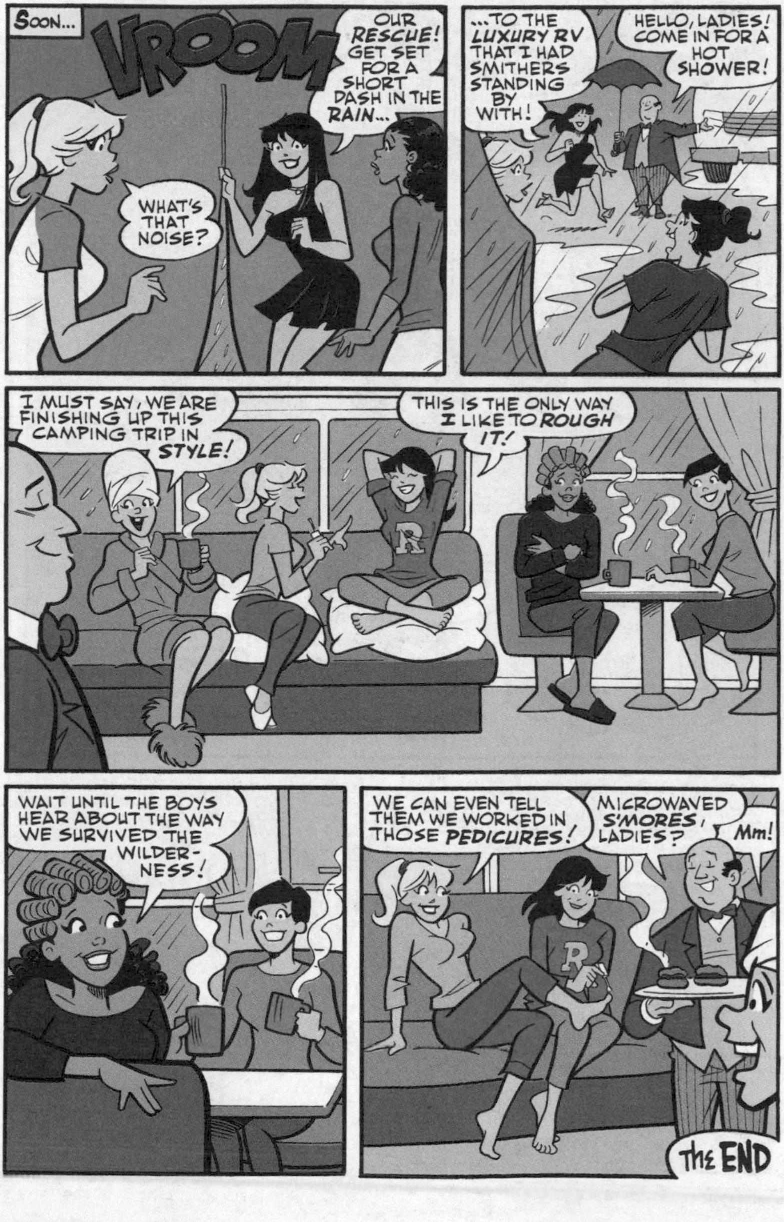
Soon...
VROOM
OUR RESCUE! GET SET FOR A SHORT DASH IN THE RAIN...
WHAT'S THAT NOISE?
...TO THE LUXURY RV THAT I HAD SMITHERS STANDING BY WITH!
HELLO, LADIES! COME IN FOR A HOT SHOWER!
I MUST SAY, WE ARE FINISHING UP THIS CAMPING TRIP IN STYLE!
THIS IS THE ONLY WAY I LIKE TO ROUGH IT!
WAIT UNTIL THE BOYS HEAR ABOUT THE WAY WE SURVIVED THE WILDER-NESS!
WE CAN EVEN TELL THEM WE WORKED IN THOSE PEDICURES!
MICROWAVED S'MORES, LADIES?
Mm!
THE END

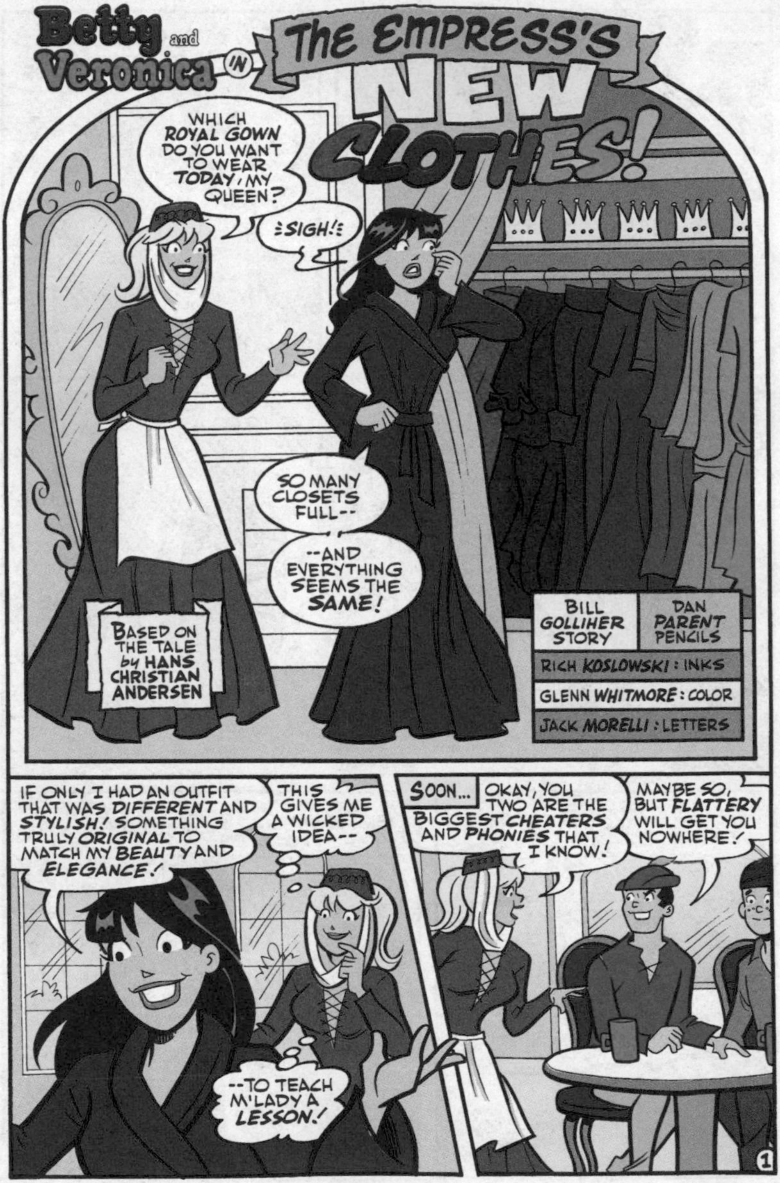
Betty and Veronica
IN
THE EMPRESS'S NEW CLOTHES!
WHICH ROYAL GOWN DO YOU WANT TO WEAR TODAY, MY QUEEN?
SIGH!
SO MANY CLOSETS FULL--
--AND EVERYTHING SEEMS THE SAME!
BASED ON THE TALE by HANS CHRISTIAN ANDERSEN
BILL GOLLIHER STORY
DAN PARENT PENCILS
RICH KOSLOWSKI : INKS
GLENN WHITMORE : COLOR
JACK MORELLI : LETTERS
IF ONLY I HAD AN OUTFIT THAT WAS DIFFERENT AND STYLISH! SOMETHING TRULY ORIGINAL TO MATCH MY BEAUTY AND ELEGANCE!
THIS GIVES ME A WICKED IDEA--
--TO TEACH M'LADY A LESSON!
SOON...
OKAY, YOU TWO ARE THE BIGGEST CHEATERS AND PHONIES THAT I KNOW!
MAYBE SO, BUT FLATTERY WILL GET YOU NOWHERE!
1

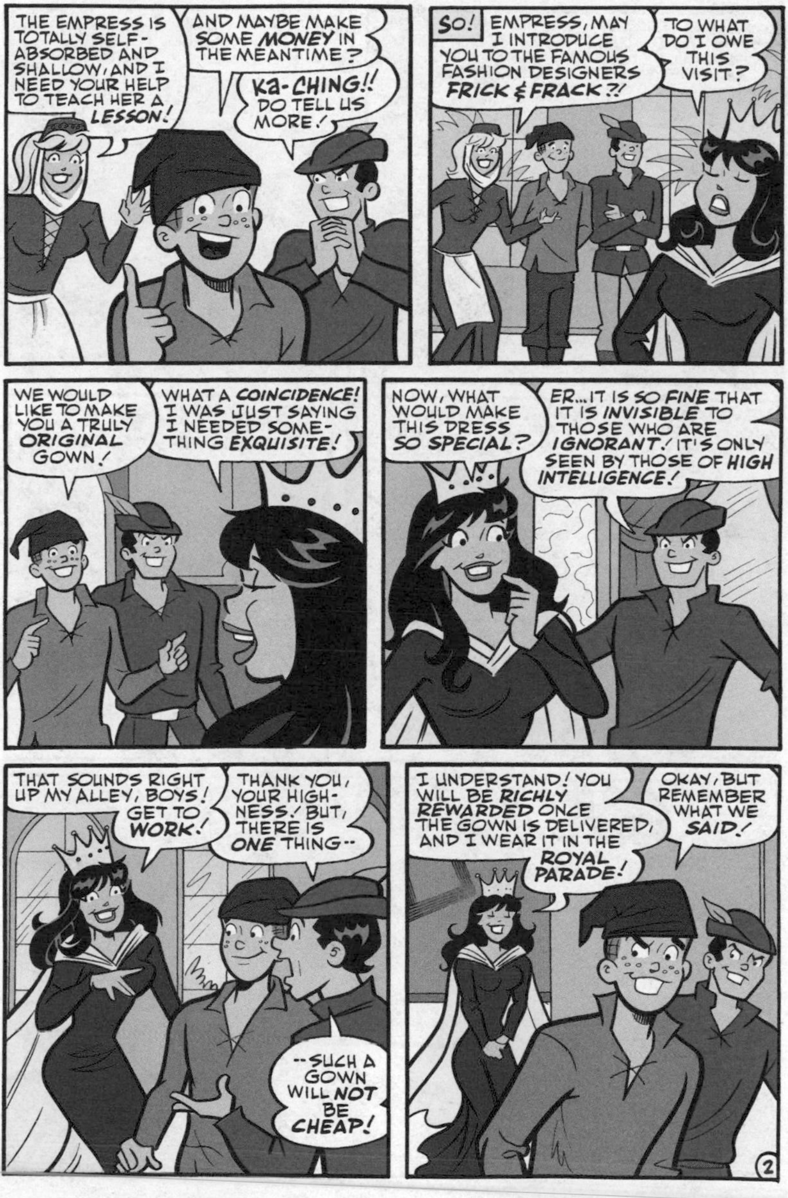
THE EMPRESS IS TOTALLY SELF-ABSORBED AND SHALLOW, AND I NEED YOUR HELP TO TEACH HER A LESSON!
AND MAYBE MAKE SOME MONEY IN THE MEANTIME?
KA-CHING!! DO TELL US MORE!
SO!
EMPRESS, MAY I INTRODUCE YOU TO THE FAMOUS FASHION DESIGNERS FRICK & FRACK?!
TO WHAT DO I OWE THIS VISIT?
WE WOULD LIKE TO MAKE YOU A TRULY ORIGINAL GOWN!
WHAT A COINCIDENCE! I WAS JUST SAYING I NEEDED SOMETHING EXQUISITE!
NOW, WHAT WOULD MAKE THIS DRESS SO SPECIAL?
ER...IT IS SO FINE THAT IT IS INVISIBLE TO THOSE WHO ARE IGNORANT! IT'S ONLY SEEN BY THOSE OF HIGH INTELLIGENCE!
THAT SOUNDS RIGHT UP MY ALLEY, BOYS! GET TO WORK!
THANK YOU, YOUR HIGHNESS! BUT, THERE IS ONE THING--
--SUCH A GOWN WILL NOT BE CHEAP!
I UNDERSTAND! YOU WILL BE RICHLY REWARDED ONCE THE GOWN IS DELIVERED, AND I WEAR IT IN THE ROYAL PARADE!
OKAY, BUT REMEMBER WHAT WE SAID!
2

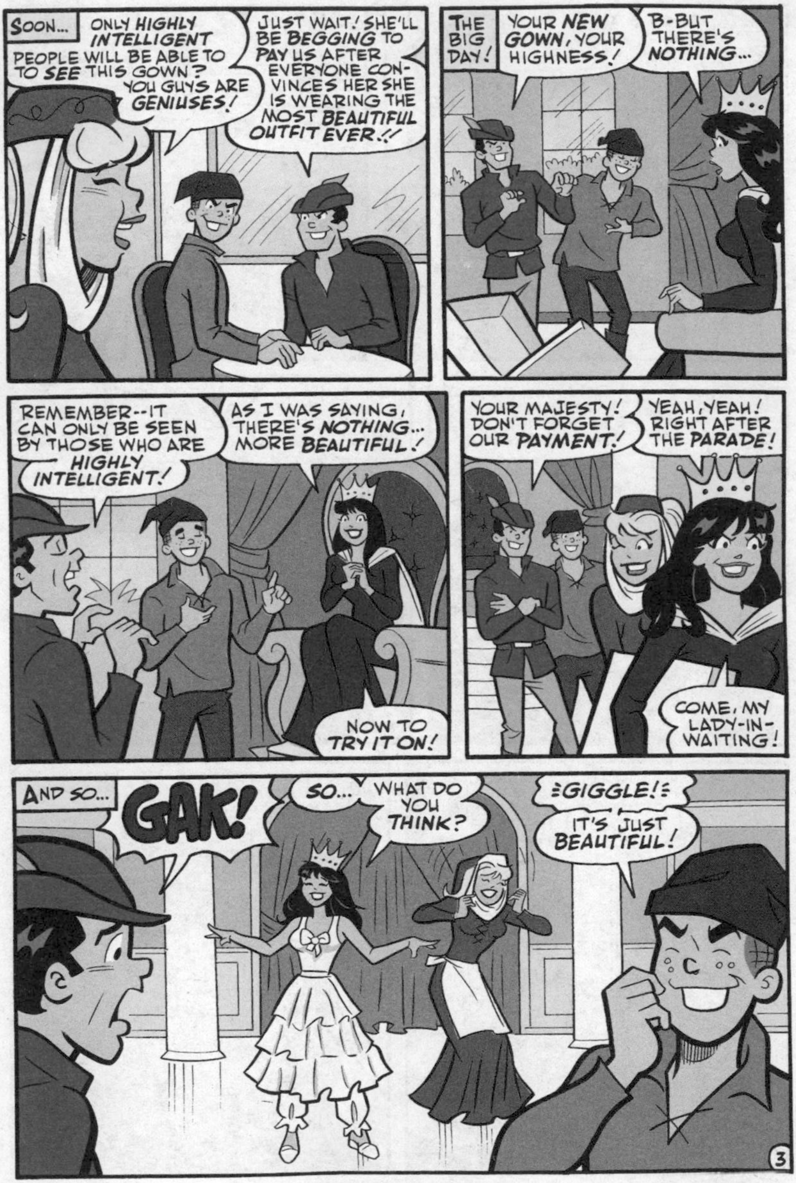
SOON...
ONLY HIGHLY INTELLIGENT PEOPLE WILL BE ABLE TO TO SEE THIS GOWN? YOU GUYS ARE GENIUSES!
JUST WAIT! SHE'LL BE BEGGING TO PAY US AFTER EVERYONE CONVINCES HER SHE IS WEARING THE MOST BEAUTIFUL OUTFIT EVER!!
THE BIG DAY!
YOUR NEW GOWN, YOUR HIGHNESS!
B-BUT THERE'S NOTHING...
REMEMBER--IT CAN ONLY BE SEEN BY THOSE WHO ARE HIGHLY INTELLIGENT!
AS I WAS SAYING, THERE'S NOTHING... MORE BEAUTIFUL!
NOW TO TRY IT ON!
YOUR MAJESTY! DON'T FORGET OUR PAYMENT!
YEAH, YEAH! RIGHT AFTER THE PARADE!
COME, MY LADY-IN-WAITING!
AND SO...
GAK!
SO... WHAT DO YOU THINK?
GIGGLE!
IT'S JUST BEAUTIFUL!
3

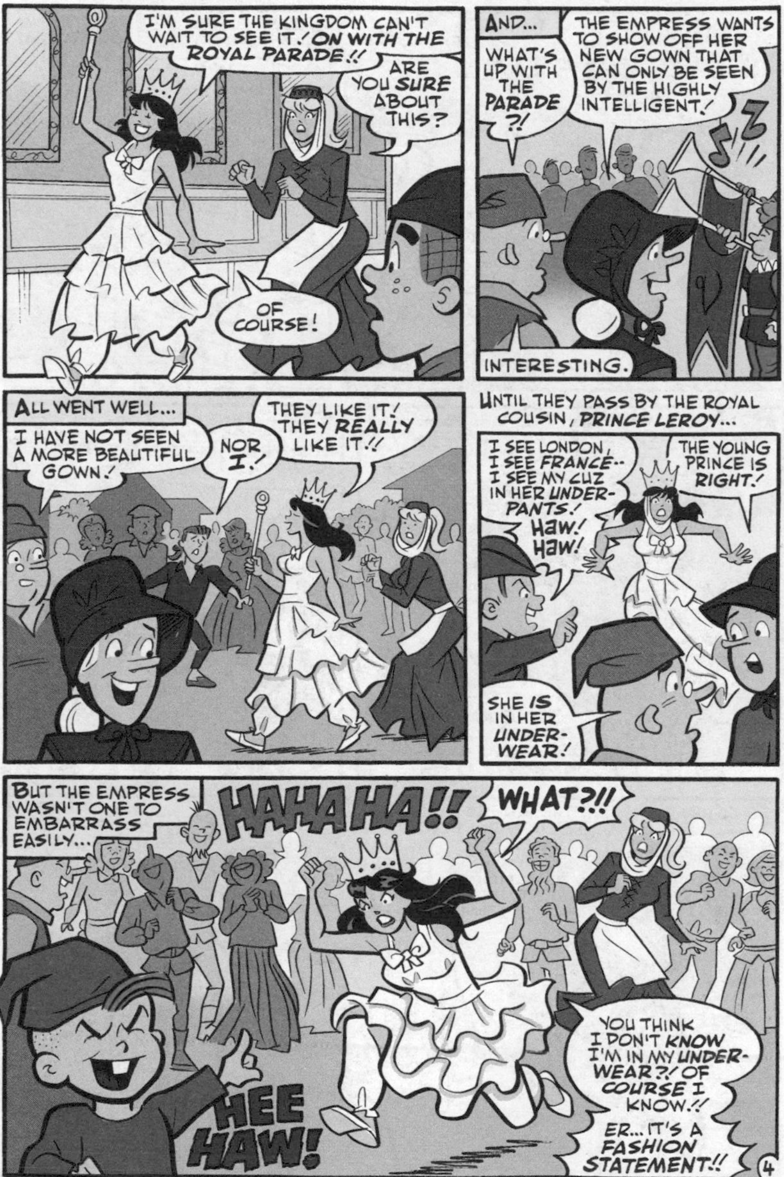
I'M SURE THE KINGDOM CAN'T WAIT TO SEE IT.! ON WITH THE ROYAL PARADE.!!
ARE YOU SURE ABOUT THIS?
OF COURSE!
AND...
WHAT'S UP WITH THE PARADE?!
THE EMPRESS WANTS TO SHOW OFF HER NEW GOWN THAT CAN ONLY BE SEEN BY THE HIGHLY INTELLIGENT.!
INTERESTING.
ALL WENT WELL...
I HAVE NOT SEEN A MORE BEAUTIFUL GOWN.!
NOR I.!
THEY LIKE IT.! THEY REALLY LIKE IT.!!
UNTIL THEY PASS BY THE ROYAL COUSIN, PRINCE LEROY...
I SEE LONDON, I SEE FRANCE-- I SEE MY CUZ IN HER UNDER-PANTS.!
HAW! HAW!
THE YOUNG PRINCE IS RIGHT.!
SHE IS IN HER UNDER-WEAR.!
BUT THE EMPRESS WASN'T ONE TO EMBARRASS EASILY...
HAHAHA!!
WHAT?!!
HEE HAW!
YOU THINK I DON'T KNOW I'M IN MY UNDER-WEAR?! OF COURSE I KNOW.!!
ER... IT'S A FASHION STATEMENT.!!
4

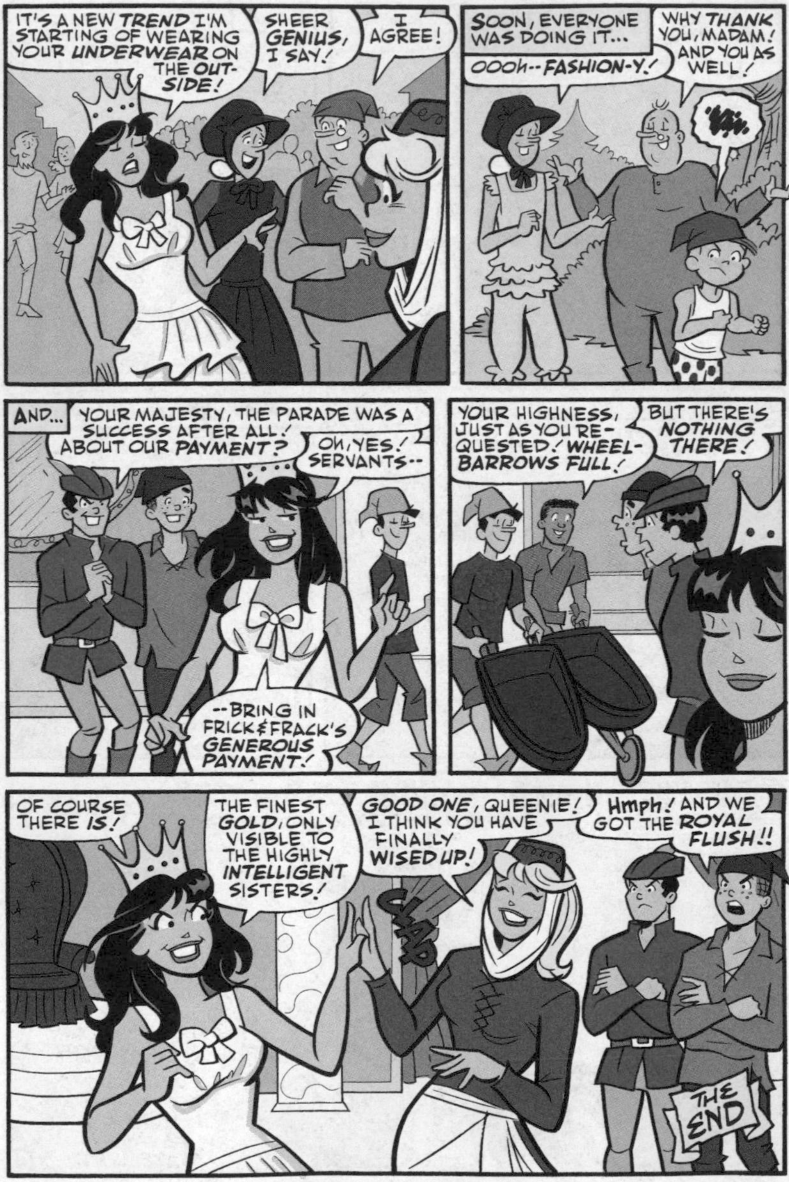
IT'S A NEW TREND I'M STARTING OF WEARING YOUR UNDERWEAR ON THE OUT-SIDE!
SHEER GENIUS, I SAY!
I AGREE!
SOON, EVERYONE WAS DOING IT...
OOOh--FASHION-Y!
WHY THANK YOU, MADAM! AND YOU AS WELL!
AND...
YOUR MAJESTY, THE PARADE WAS A SUCCESS AFTER ALL! ABOUT OUR PAYMENT?
OH, YES! SERVANTS--
--BRING IN FRICK & FRACK'S GENEROUS PAYMENT!
YOUR HIGHNESS, JUST AS YOU RE-QUESTED! WHEEL-BARROWS FULL!
BUT THERE'S NOTHING THERE!
OF COURSE THERE IS!
THE FINEST GOLD, ONLY VISIBLE TO THE HIGHLY INTELLIGENT SISTERS!
GOOD ONE, QUEENIE! I THINK YOU HAVE FINALLY WISED UP!
CLAP
Hmph! AND WE GOT THE ROYAL FLUSH!!
THE END

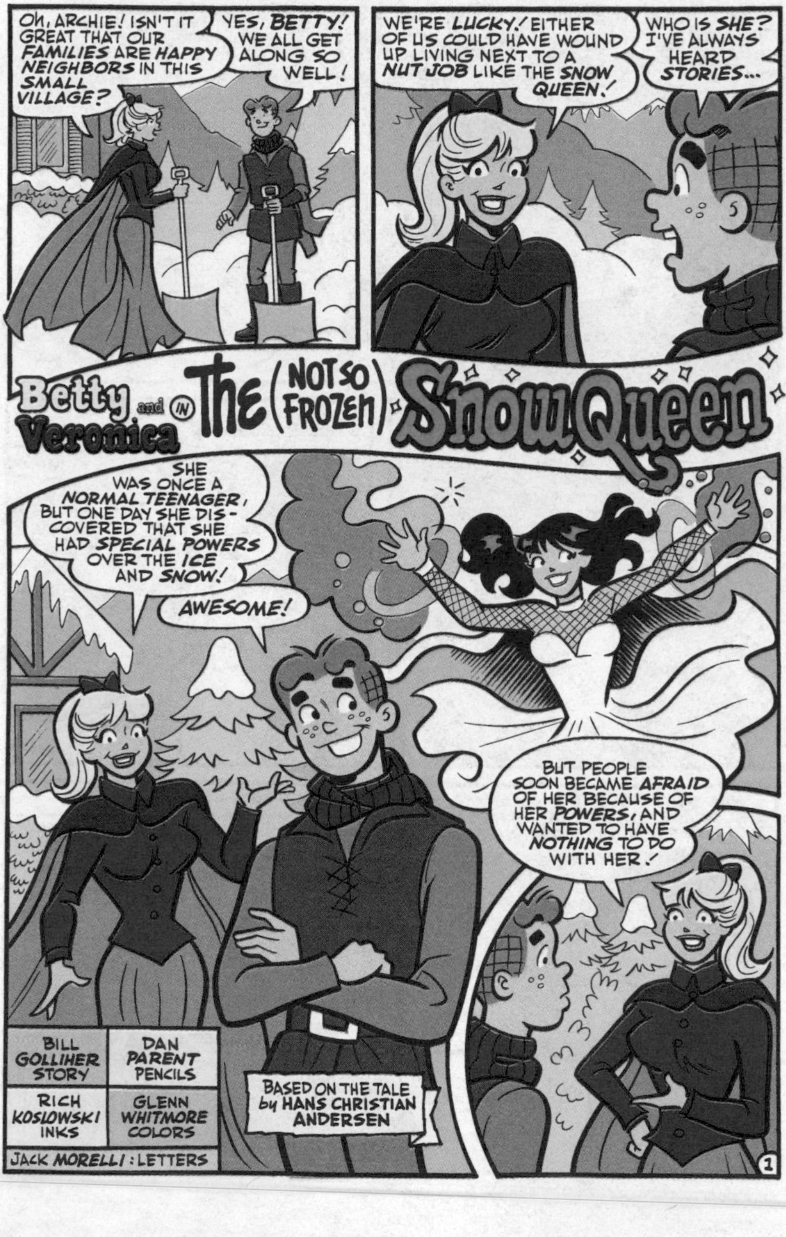
OH, ARCHIE! ISN'T IT GREAT THAT OUR FAMILIES ARE HAPPY NEIGHBORS IN THIS SMALL VILLAGE?
YES, BETTY! WE ALL GET ALONG SO WELL!
WE'RE LUCKY! EITHER OF US COULD HAVE WOUND UP LIVING NEXT TO A NUT JOB LIKE THE SNOW QUEEN!
WHO IS SHE? I'VE ALWAYS HEARD STORIES...
Betty and Veronica in The (NOT SO FROZEN) Snow Queen
SHE WAS ONCE A NORMAL TEENAGER, BUT ONE DAY SHE DIS-COVERED THAT SHE HAD SPECIAL POWERS OVER THE ICE AND SNOW!
AWESOME!
BUT PEOPLE SOON BECAME AFRAID OF HER BECAUSE OF HER POWERS, AND WANTED TO HAVE NOTHING TO DO WITH HER!
BILL GOLLIHER STORY
DAN PARENT PENCILS
RICH KOSLOWSKI INKS
GLENN WHITMORE COLORS
JACK MORELLI : LETTERS
BASED ON THE TALE by HANS CHRISTIAN ANDERSEN
1

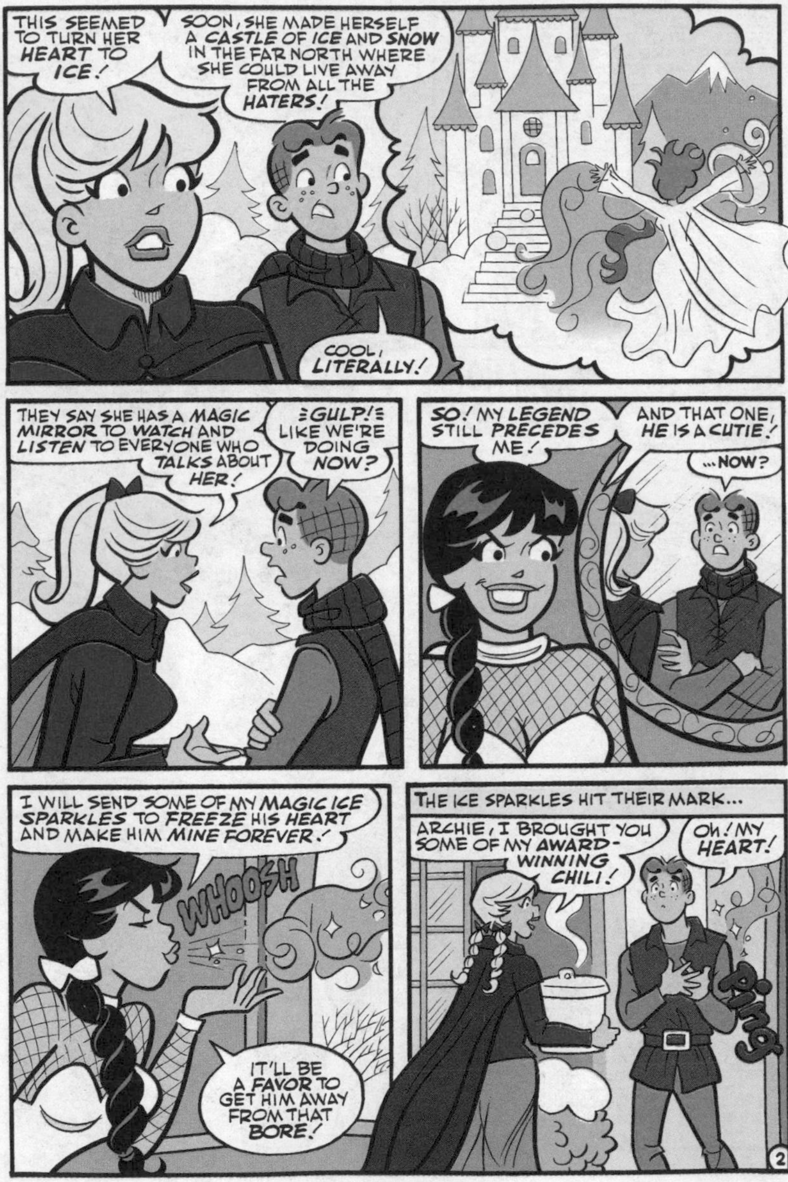
THIS SEEMED TO TURN HER HEART TO ICE!
SOON, SHE MADE HERSELF A CASTLE OF ICE AND SNOW IN THE FAR NORTH WHERE SHE COULD LIVE AWAY FROM ALL THE HATERS!
COOL, LITERALLY!
THEY SAY SHE HAS A MAGIC MIRROR TO WATCH AND LISTEN TO EVERYONE WHO TALKS ABOUT HER!
GULP! LIKE WE'RE DOING NOW?
SO! MY LEGEND STILL PRECEDES ME!
AND THAT ONE, HE IS A CUTIE!
...NOW?
I WILL SEND SOME OF MY MAGIC ICE SPARKLES TO FREEZE HIS HEART AND MAKE HIM MINE FOREVER!
WHOOSH
IT'LL BE A FAVOR TO GET HIM AWAY FROM THAT BORE!
THE ICE SPARKLES HIT THEIR MARK...
ARCHIE, I BROUGHT YOU SOME OF MY AWARD-WINNING CHILI!
OH! MY HEART!
PING
2

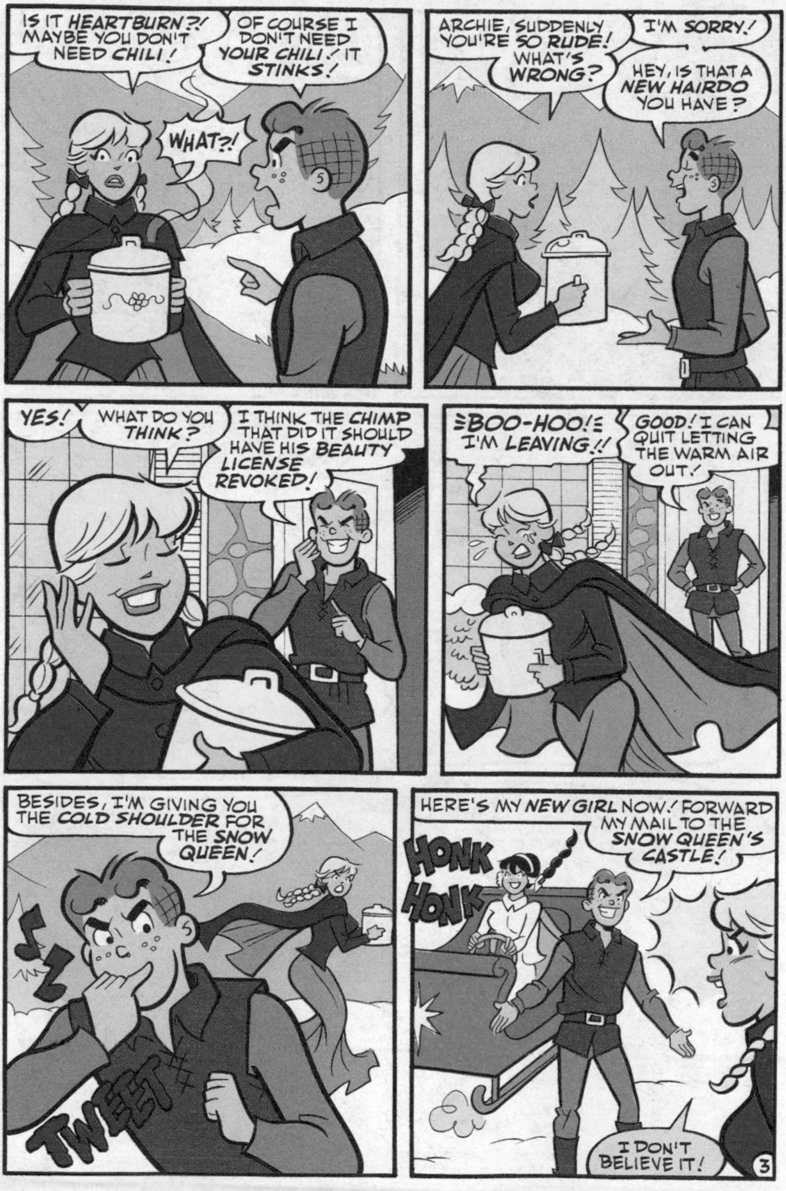
IS IT HEARTBURN?! MAYBE YOU DON'T NEED CHILI!
OF COURSE I DON'T NEED YOUR CHILI! IT STINKS!
WHAT?!
ARCHIE, SUDDENLY YOU'RE SO RUDE! WHAT'S WRONG?
I'M SORRY!
HEY, IS THAT A NEW HAIRDO YOU HAVE?
YES!
WHAT DO YOU THINK?
I THINK THE CHIMP THAT DID IT SHOULD HAVE HIS BEAUTY LICENSE REVOKED!
BOO-HOO! I'M LEAVING!!
GOOD! I CAN QUIT LETTING THE WARM AIR OUT!
BESIDES, I'M GIVING YOU THE COLD SHOULDER FOR THE SNOW QUEEN!
TWEET
HERE'S MY NEW GIRL NOW! FORWARD MY MAIL TO THE SNOW QUEEN'S CASTLE!
HONK
HONK
I DON'T BELIEVE IT!
3

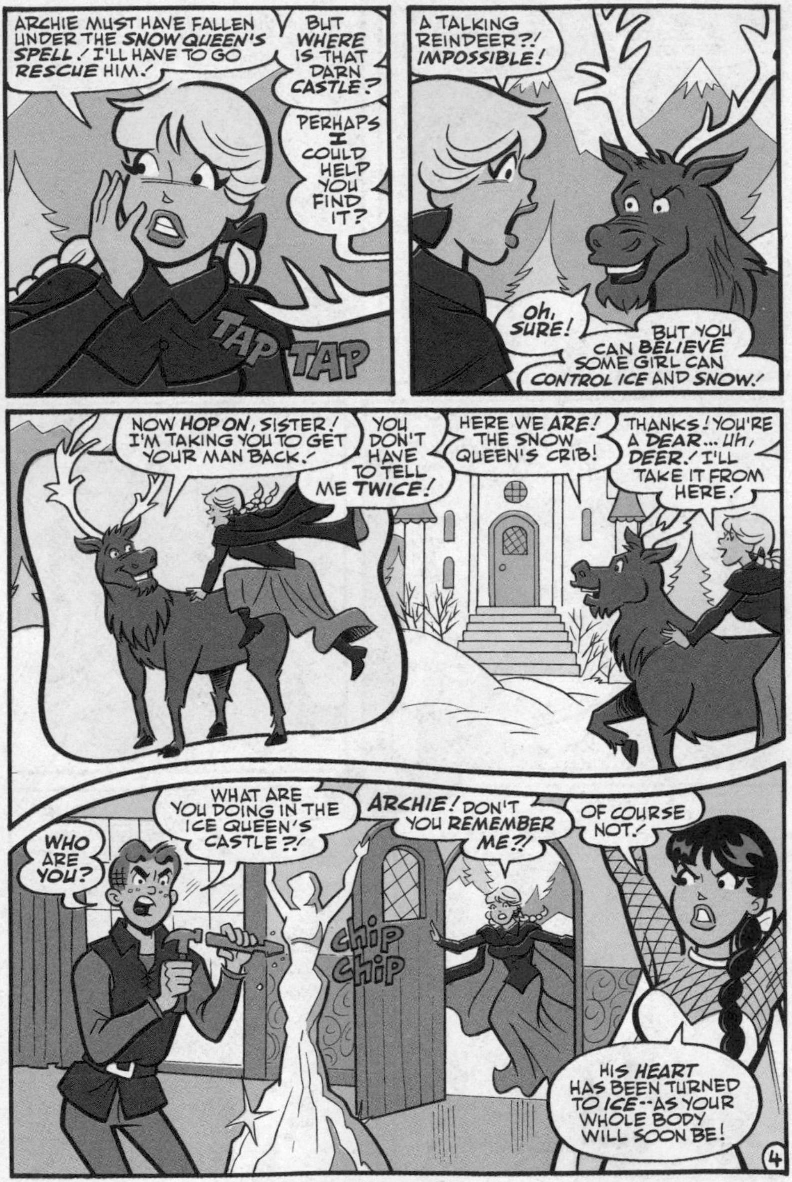
ARCHIE MUST HAVE FALLEN UNDER THE SNOW QUEEN'S SPELL! I'LL HAVE TO GO RESCUE HIM!
BUT WHERE IS THAT DARN CASTLE?
PERHAPS I COULD HELP YOU FIND IT?
TAP TAP
A TALKING REINDEER?! IMPOSSIBLE!
Oh, SURE!
BUT YOU CAN BELIEVE SOME GIRL CAN CONTROL ICE AND SNOW!
NOW HOP ON, SISTER! I'M TAKING YOU TO GET YOUR MAN BACK!
YOU DON'T HAVE TO TELL ME TWICE!
HERE WE ARE! THE SNOW QUEEN'S CRIB!
THANKS! YOU'RE A DEAR... Uh, DEER! I'LL TAKE IT FROM HERE!
WHO ARE YOU?
WHAT ARE YOU DOING IN THE ICE QUEEN'S CASTLE?!
ARCHIE! DON'T YOU REMEMBER ME?!
OF COURSE NOT!
CHIP CHIP
HIS HEART HAS BEEN TURNED TO ICE--AS YOUR WHOLE BODY WILL SOON BE!
4

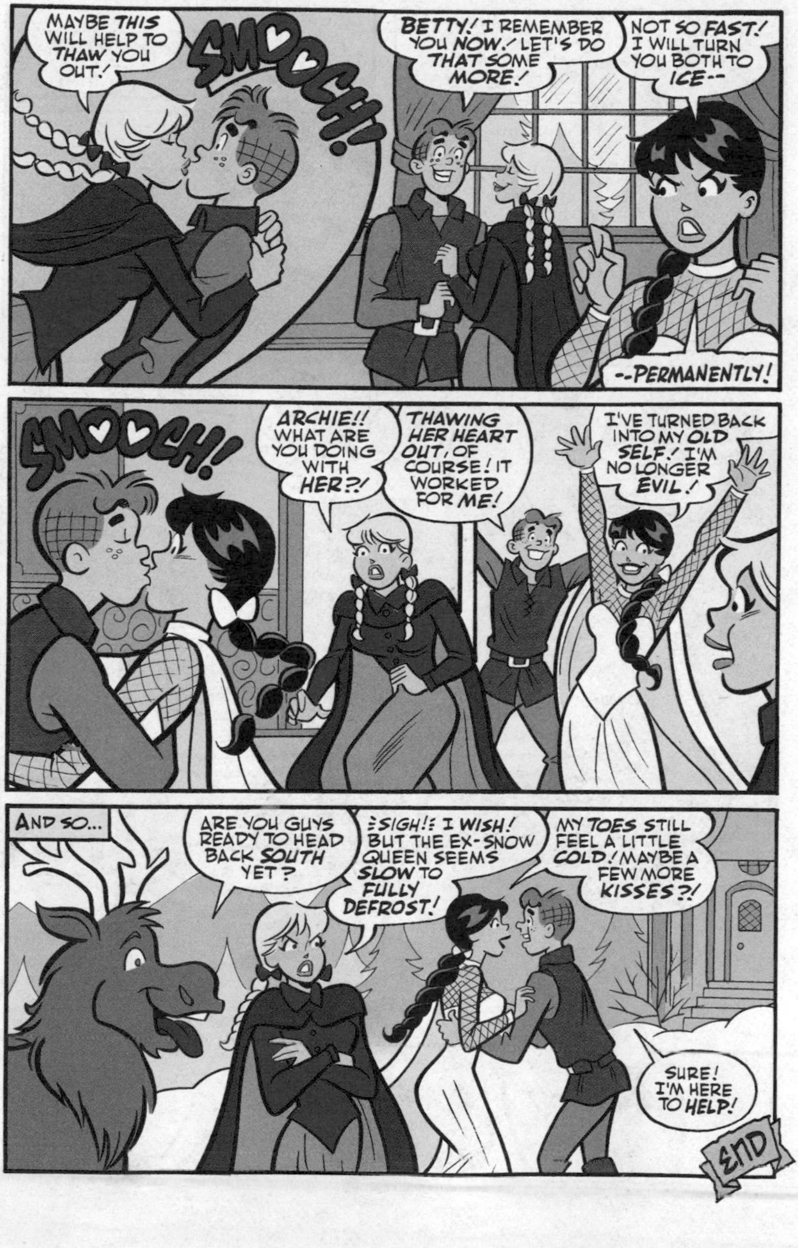
MAYBE THIS WILL HELP TO THAW YOU OUT!
SMOOCH!
BETTY! I REMEMBER YOU NOW! LET'S DO THAT SOME MORE!
NOT SO FAST! I WILL TURN YOU BOTH TO ICE--
--PERMANENTLY!
SMOOCH!
ARCHIE!! WHAT ARE YOU DOING WITH HER?!
THAWING HER HEART OUT, OF COURSE! IT WORKED FOR ME!
I'VE TURNED BACK INTO MY OLD SELF! I'M NO LONGER EVIL!
AND SO...
ARE YOU GUYS READY TO HEAD BACK SOUTH YET?
SIGH! I WISH! BUT THE EX-SNOW QUEEN SEEMS SLOW TO FULLY DEFROST!
MY TOES STILL FEEL A LITTLE COLD! MAYBE A FEW MORE KISSES?!
SURE! I'M HERE TO HELP!
END

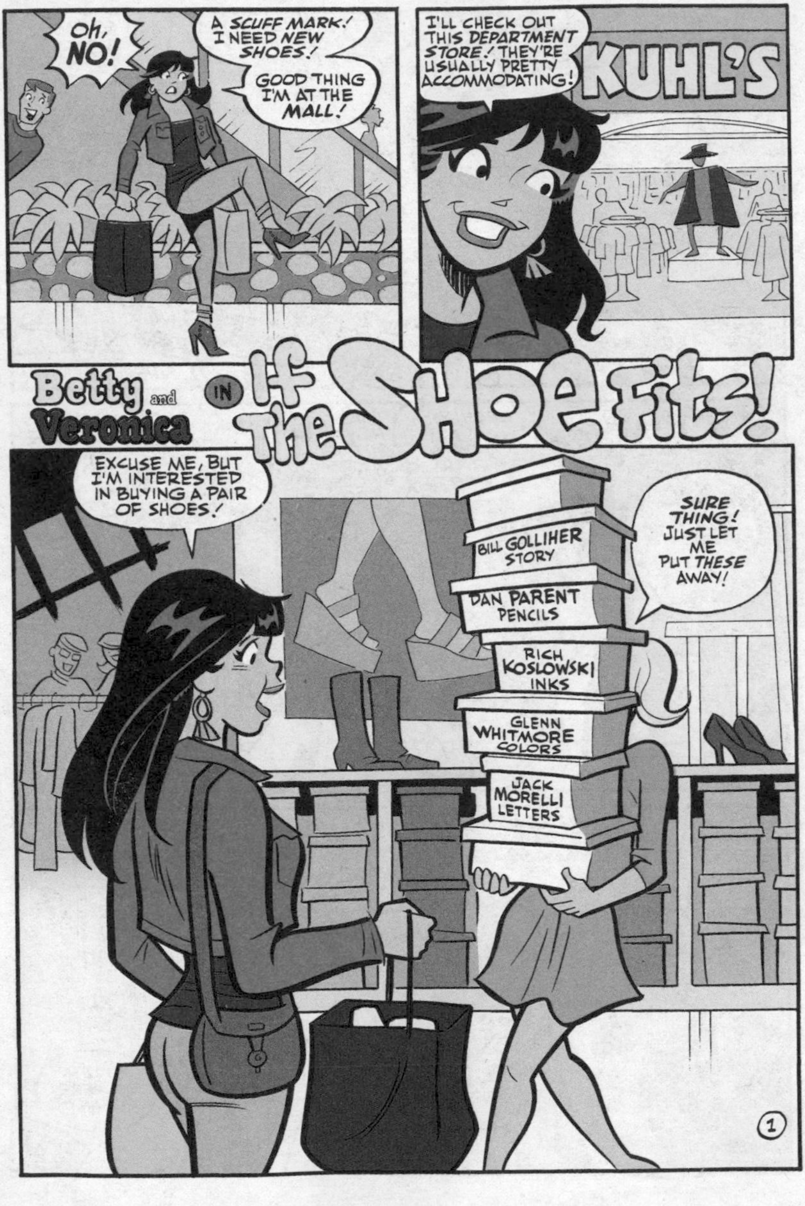
Oh, NO!
A SCUFF MARK! I NEED NEW SHOES!
GOOD THING I'M AT THE MALL!
I'LL CHECK OUT THIS DEPARTMENT STORE! THEY'RE USUALLY PRETTY ACCOMMODATING!
KUHL'S
Betty and Veronica IN If the SHOE Fits!
EXCUSE ME, BUT I'M INTERESTED IN BUYING A PAIR OF SHOES!
SURE THING! JUST LET ME PUT THESE AWAY!
BILL GOLLIHER STORY
DAN PARENT PENCILS
RICH KOSLOWSKI INKS
GLENN WHITMORE COLORS
JACK MORELLI LETTERS
1

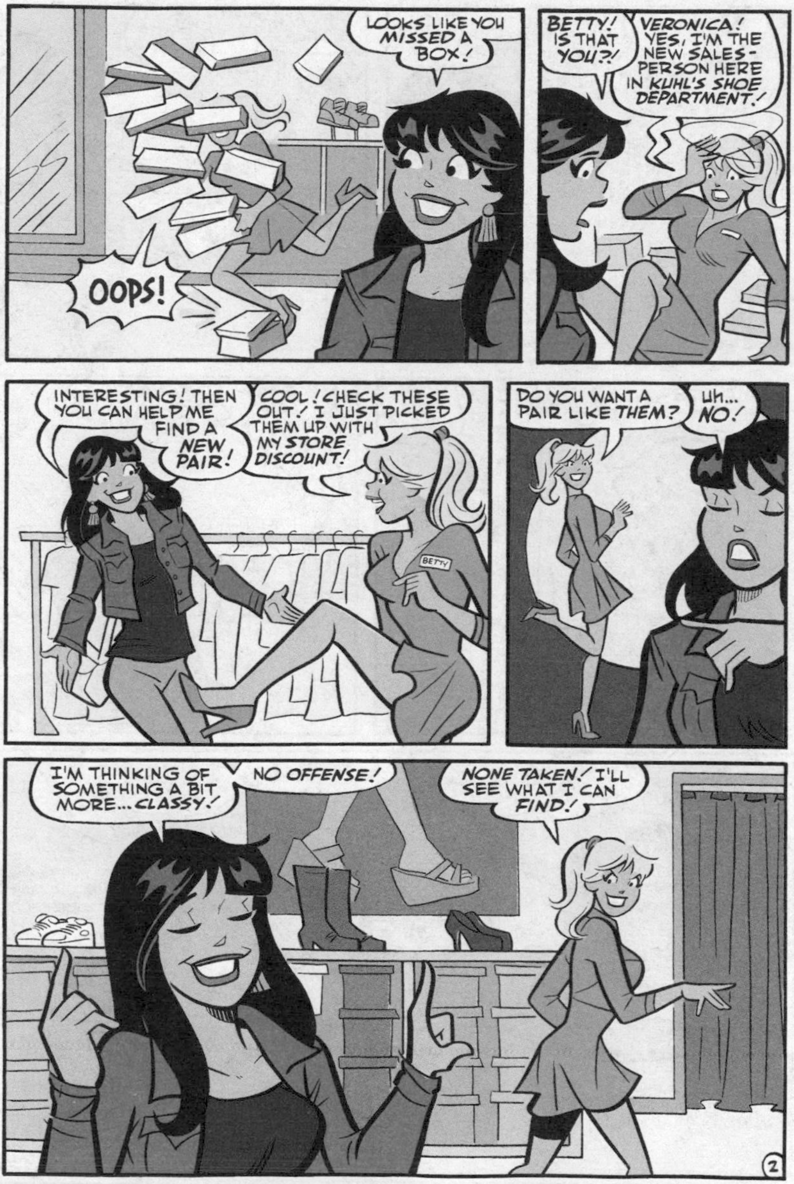
LOOKS LIKE YOU MISSED A BOX!
OOPS!
BETTY! IS THAT YOU?!
VERONICA! YES, I'M THE NEW SALES-PERSON HERE IN KUHL'S SHOE DEPARTMENT!
INTERESTING! THEN YOU CAN HELP ME FIND A NEW PAIR!
COOL! CHECK THESE OUT! I JUST PICKED THEM UP WITH MY STORE DISCOUNT!
BETTY
DO YOU WANT A PAIR LIKE THEM?
uh... NO!
I'M THINKING OF SOMETHING A BIT MORE... CLASSY!
NO OFFENSE!
NONE TAKEN! I'LL SEE WHAT I CAN FIND!
2

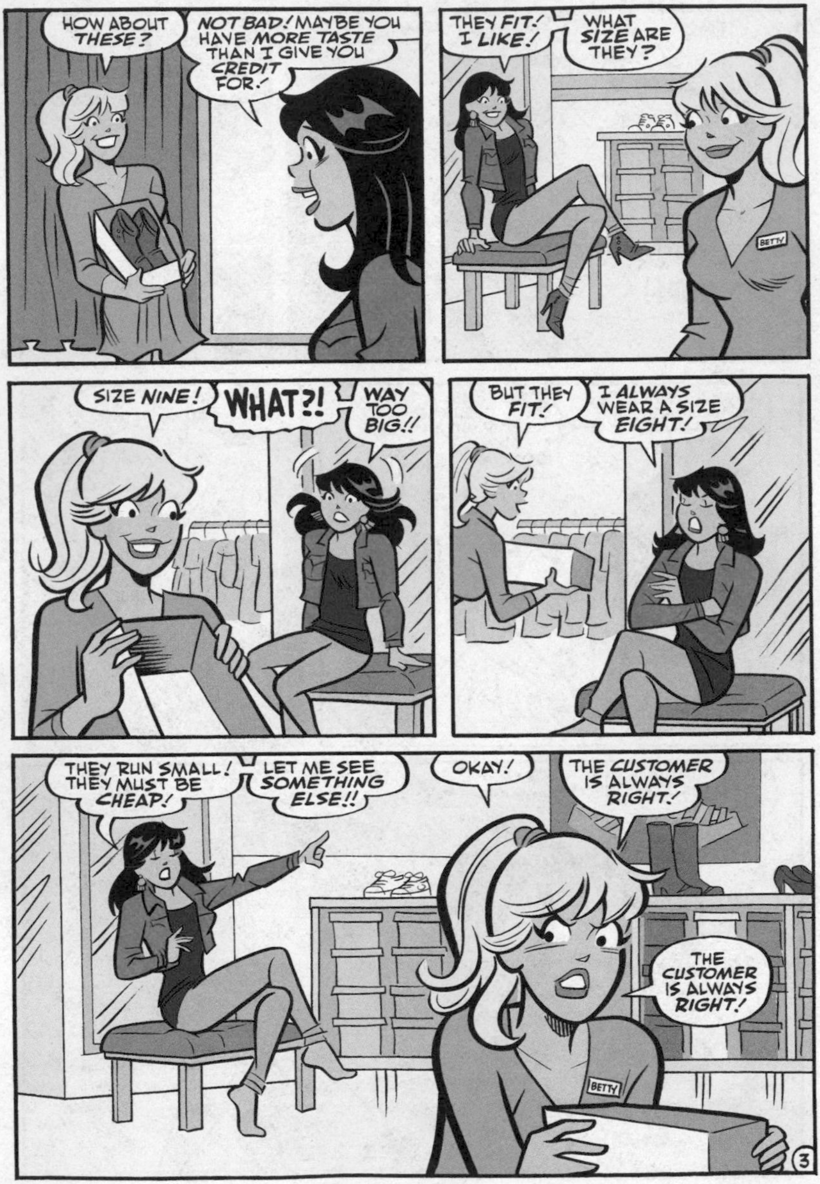
HOW ABOUT THESE?
NOT BAD! MAYBE YOU HAVE MORE TASTE THAN I GIVE YOU CREDIT FOR!
THEY FIT! I LIKE!
WHAT SIZE ARE THEY?
BETTY
SIZE NINE!
WHAT?!
WAY TOO BIG!!
BUT THEY FIT!
I ALWAYS WEAR A SIZE EIGHT!
THEY RUN SMALL! THEY MUST BE CHEAP!
LET ME SEE SOMETHING ELSE!!
OKAY!
THE CUSTOMER IS ALWAYS RIGHT!
THE CUSTOMER IS ALWAYS RIGHT!
BETTY
3

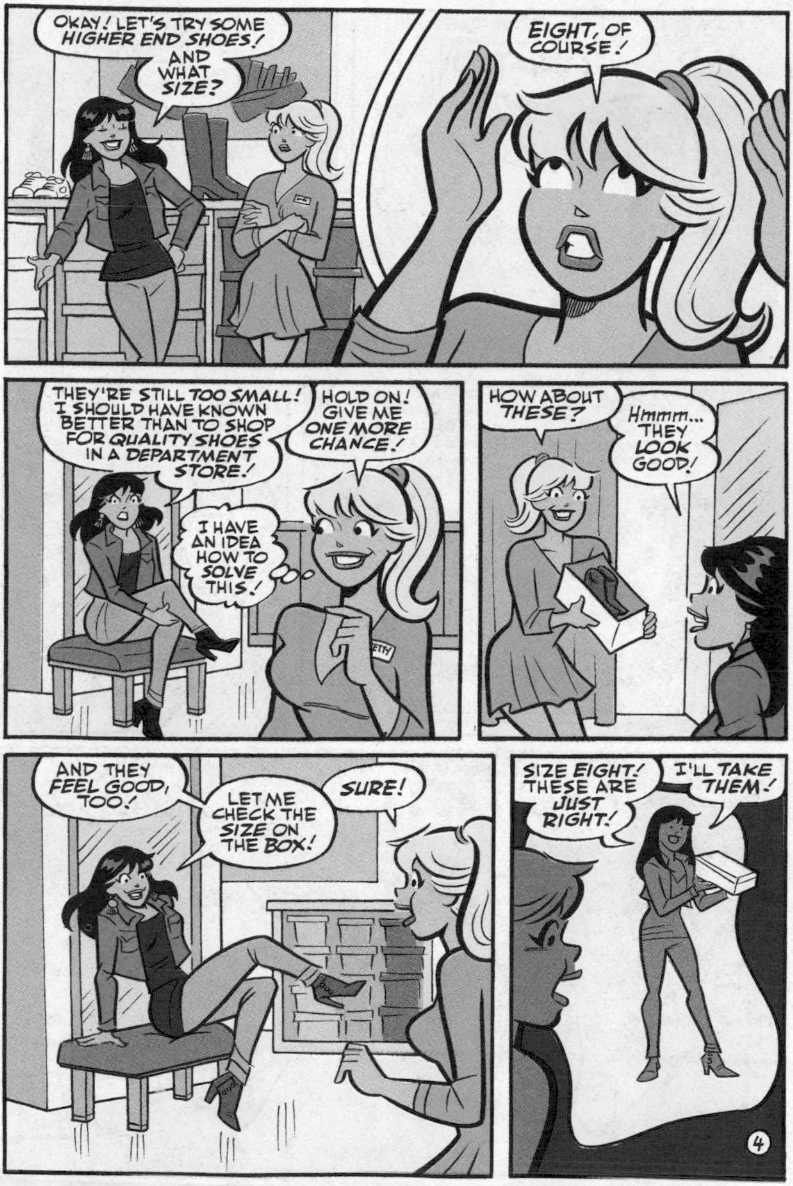
OKAY! LET'S TRY SOME HIGHER END SHOES!
AND WHAT SIZE?
EIGHT, OF COURSE!
THEY'RE STILL TOO SMALL! I SHOULD HAVE KNOWN BETTER THAN TO SHOP FOR QUALITY SHOES IN A DEPARTMENT STORE!
HOLD ON! GIVE ME ONE MORE CHANCE!
I HAVE AN IDEA HOW TO SOLVE THIS!
BETTY
HOW ABOUT THESE?
Hmmm... THEY LOOK GOOD!
AND THEY FEEL GOOD, TOO!
LET ME CHECK THE SIZE ON THE BOX!
SURE!
SIZE EIGHT! THESE ARE JUST RIGHT!
I'LL TAKE THEM!
4

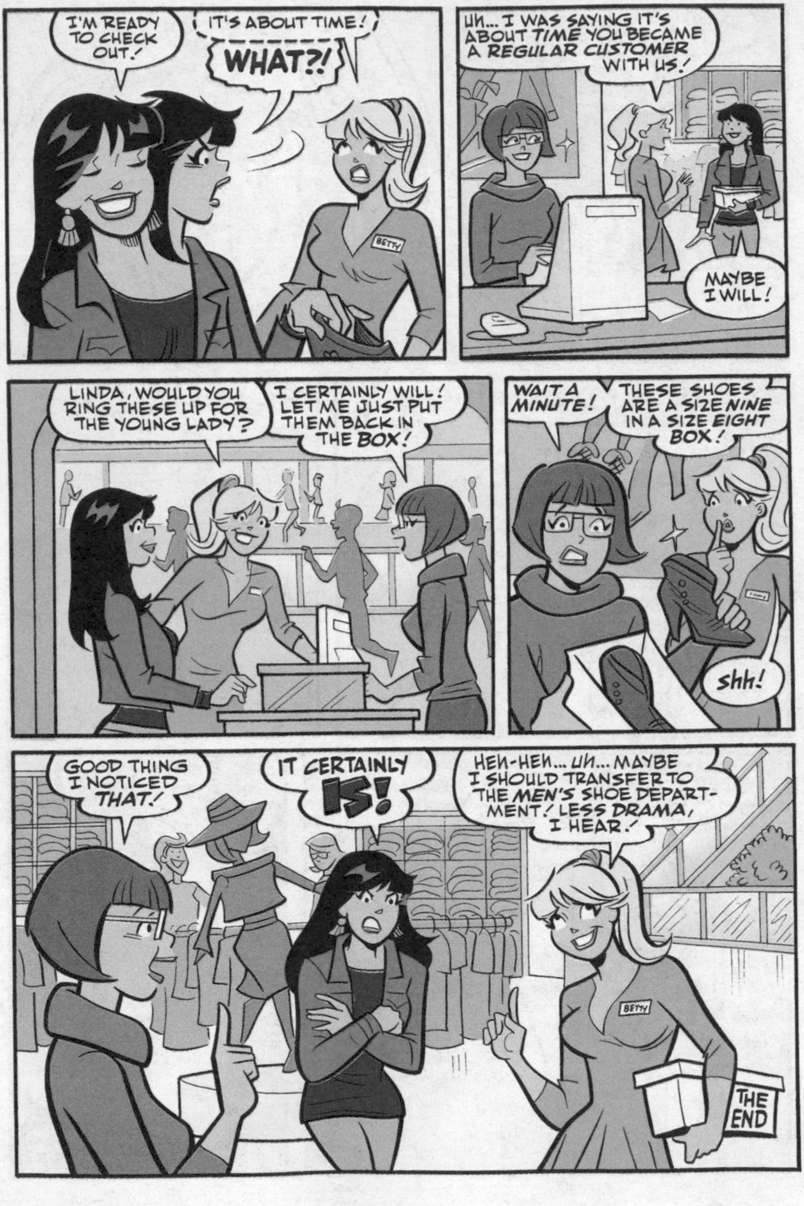
I'M READY TO CHECK OUT!
IT'S ABOUT TIME!
WHAT?!
UH... I WAS SAYING IT'S ABOUT TIME YOU BECAME A REGULAR CUSTOMER WITH US!
MAYBE I WILL!
BETTY
LINDA, WOULD YOU RING THESE UP FOR THE YOUNG LADY?
I CERTAINLY WILL! LET ME JUST PUT THEM BACK IN THE BOX!
WAIT A MINUTE!
THESE SHOES ARE A SIZE NINE IN A SIZE EIGHT BOX!
shh!
GOOD THING I NOTICED THAT!
IT CERTAINLY IS!
HEH-HEH... UH... MAYBE I SHOULD TRANSFER TO THE MEN'S SHOE DEPARTMENT! LESS DRAMA, I HEAR!
BETTY
THE END

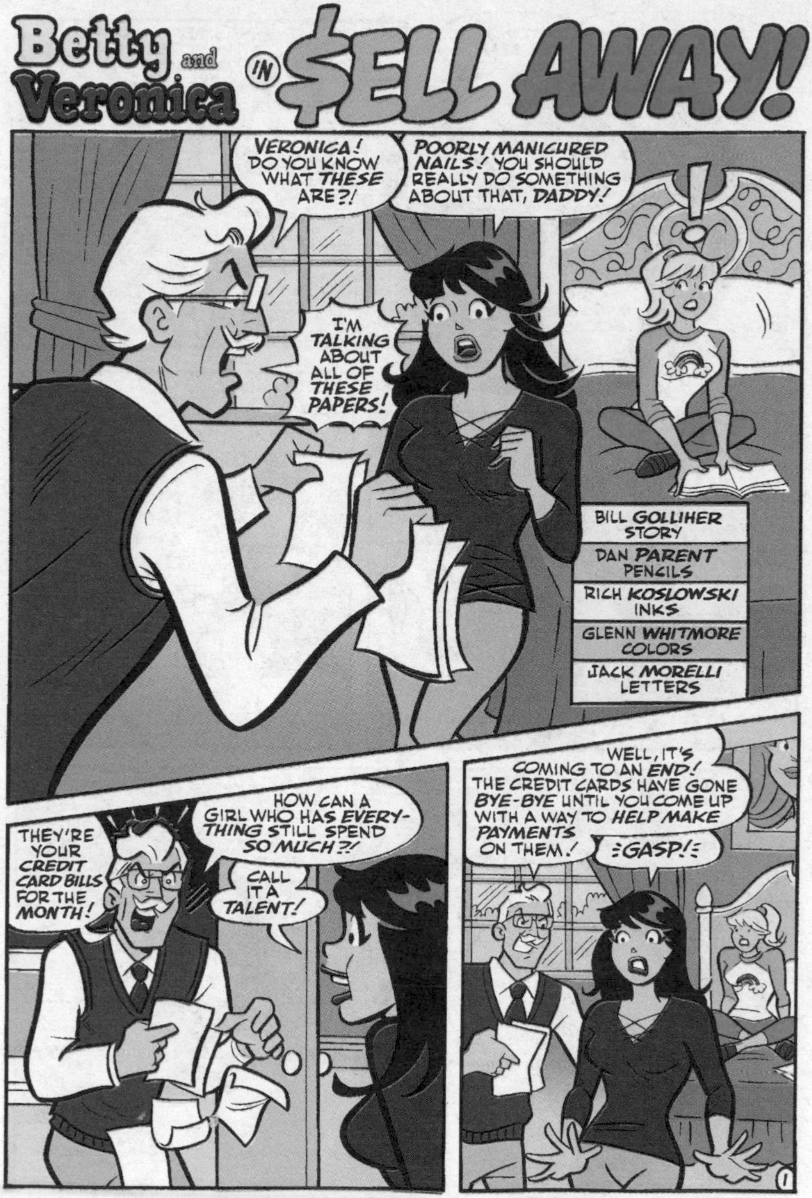
Betty and Veronica
IN
$ELL AWAY!
VERONICA! DO YOU KNOW WHAT THESE ARE?!
POORLY MANICURED NAILS! YOU SHOULD REALLY DO SOMETHING ABOUT THAT, DADDY!
!
I'M TALKING ABOUT ALL OF THESE PAPERS!
BILL GOLLIHER STORY
DAN PARENT PENCILS
RICH KOSLOWSKI INKS
GLENN WHITMORE COLORS
JACK MORELLI LETTERS
THEY'RE YOUR CREDIT CARD BILLS FOR THE MONTH!
HOW CAN A GIRL WHO HAS EVERY-THING STILL SPEND SO MUCH?!
CALL IT A TALENT!
WELL, IT'S COMING TO AN END! THE CREDIT CARDS HAVE GONE BYE-BYE UNTIL YOU COME UP WITH A WAY TO HELP MAKE PAYMENTS ON THEM!
GASP!
1

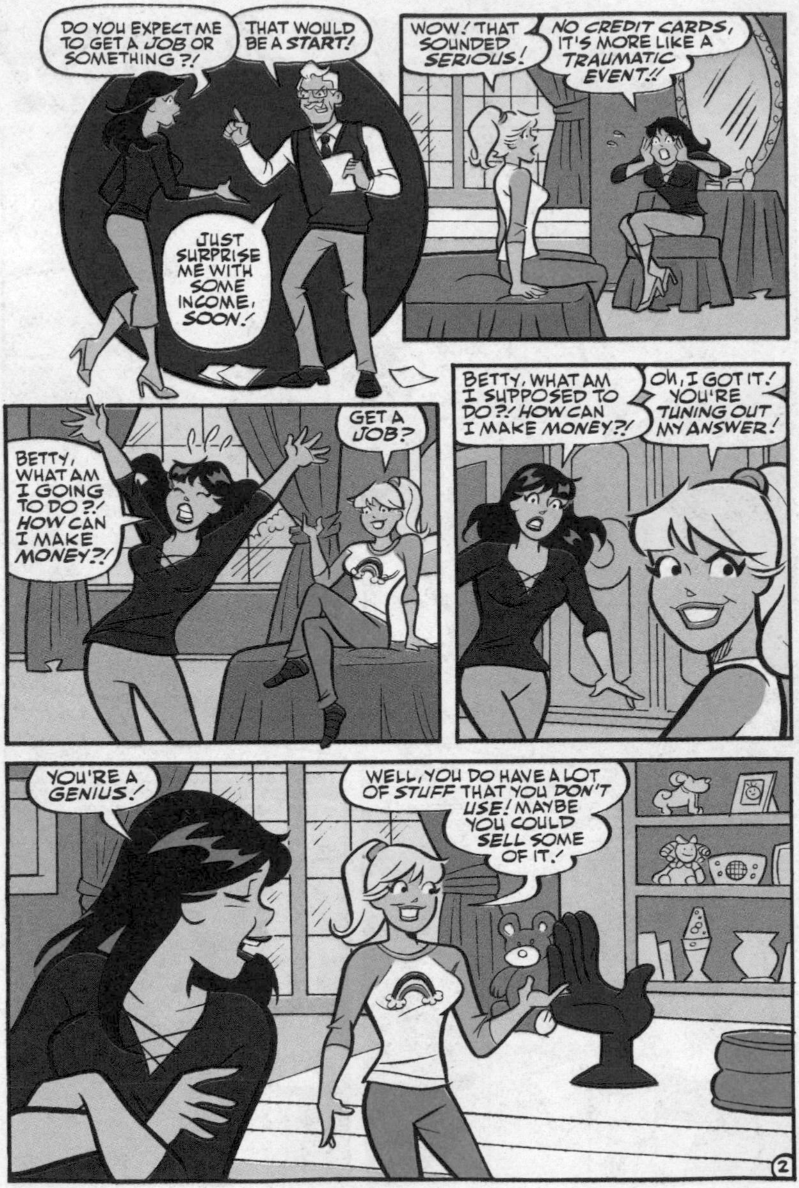
DO YOU EXPECT ME TO GET A JOB OR SOMETHING?!
THAT WOULD BE A START!
JUST SURPRISE ME WITH SOME INCOME, SOON!
WOW! THAT SOUNDED SERIOUS!
NO CREDIT CARDS, IT'S MORE LIKE A TRAUMATIC EVENT!!
BETTY, WHAT AM I GOING TO DO?! HOW CAN I MAKE MONEY?!
GET A JOB?
BETTY, WHAT AM I SUPPOSED TO DO?! HOW CAN I MAKE MONEY?!
OH, I GOT IT! YOU'RE TUNING OUT MY ANSWER!
YOU'RE A GENIUS!
WELL, YOU DO HAVE A LOT OF STUFF THAT YOU DON'T USE! MAYBE YOU COULD SELL SOME OF IT!
2

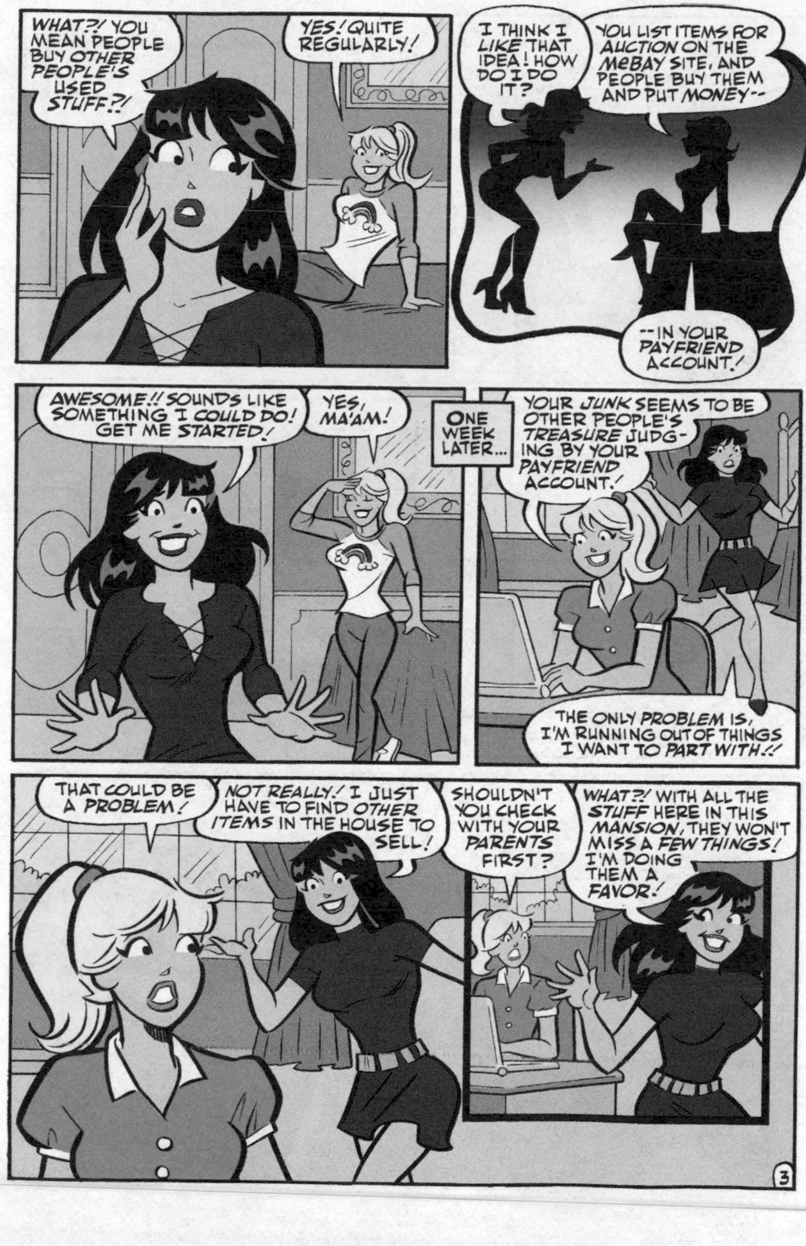
WHAT?! YOU MEAN PEOPLE BUY OTHER PEOPLE'S USED STUFF?!
YES! QUITE REGULARLY!
I THINK I LIKE THAT IDEA! HOW DO I DO IT?
YOU LIST ITEMS FOR AUCTION ON THE MEBAY SITE, AND PEOPLE BUY THEM AND PUT MONEY--
--IN YOUR PAYFRIEND ACCOUNT!
AWESOME!! SOUNDS LIKE SOMETHING I COULD DO! GET ME STARTED!
YES, MA'AM!
ONE WEEK LATER...
YOUR JUNK SEEMS TO BE OTHER PEOPLE'S TREASURE JUDGING BY YOUR PAYFRIEND ACCOUNT!
THE ONLY PROBLEM IS, I'M RUNNING OUT OF THINGS I WANT TO PART WITH!!
THAT COULD BE A PROBLEM!
NOT REALLY! I JUST HAVE TO FIND OTHER ITEMS IN THE HOUSE TO SELL!
SHOULDN'T YOU CHECK WITH YOUR PARENTS FIRST?
WHAT?! WITH ALL THE STUFF HERE IN THIS MANSION, THEY WON'T MISS A FEW THINGS! I'M DOING THEM A FAVOR!
3

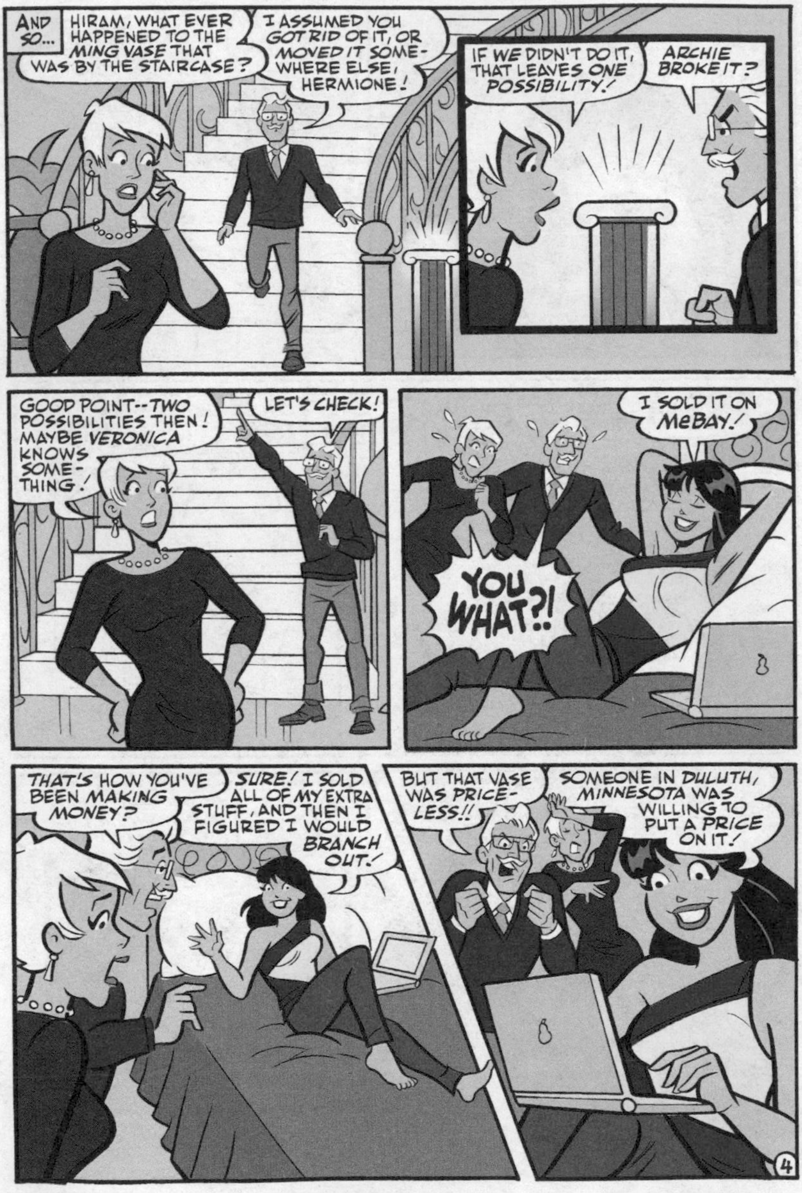
AND SO...
HIRAM, WHAT EVER HAPPENED TO THE MING VASE THAT WAS BY THE STAIRCASE?
I ASSUMED YOU GOT RID OF IT, OR MOVED IT SOMEWHERE ELSE, HERMIONE!
IF WE DIDN'T DO IT, THAT LEAVES ONE POSSIBILITY!
ARCHIE BROKE IT?
GOOD POINT--TWO POSSIBILITIES THEN! MAYBE VERONICA KNOWS SOMETHING!
LET'S CHECK!
I SOLD IT ON MeBAY!
YOU WHAT?!
THAT'S HOW YOU'VE BEEN MAKING MONEY?
SURE! I SOLD ALL OF MY EXTRA STUFF, AND THEN I FIGURED I WOULD BRANCH OUT!
BUT THAT VASE WAS PRICELESS!!
SOMEONE IN DULUTH, MINNESOTA WAS WILLING TO PUT A PRICE ON IT!
4

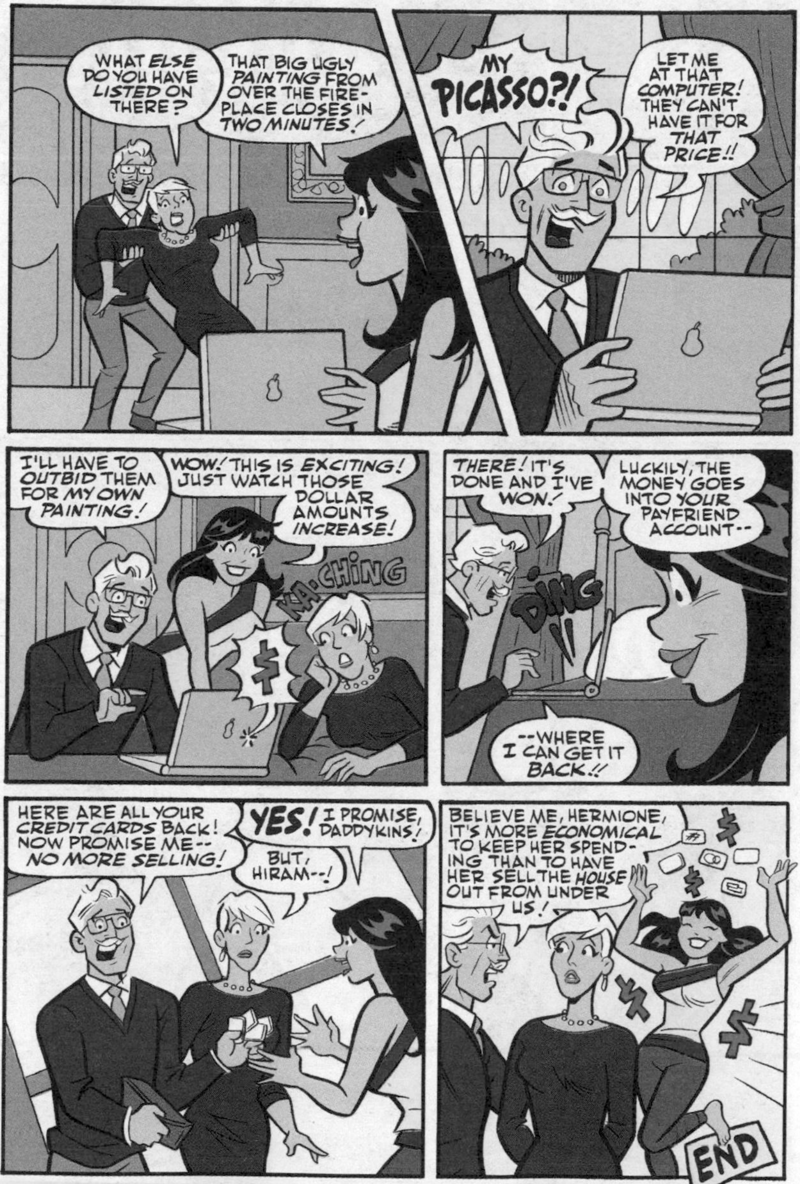
WHAT ELSE DO YOU HAVE LISTED ON THERE?
THAT BIG UGLY PAINTING FROM OVER THE FIRE-PLACE CLOSES IN TWO MINUTES!
MY PICASSO?!
LET ME AT THAT COMPUTER! THEY CAN'T HAVE IT FOR THAT PRICE!!
I'LL HAVE TO OUTBID THEM FOR MY OWN PAINTING!
WOW! THIS IS EXCITING! JUST WATCH THOSE DOLLAR AMOUNTS INCREASE!
KA-CHING
$
THERE! IT'S DONE AND I'VE WON!
LUCKILY, THE MONEY GOES INTO YOUR PAYFRIEND ACCOUNT--
DING
--WHERE I CAN GET IT BACK!!
HERE ARE ALL YOUR CREDIT CARDS BACK! NOW PROMISE ME-- NO MORE SELLING!
YES! I PROMISE, DADDYKINS!
BUT, HIRAM--!
BELIEVE ME, HERMIONE, IT'S MORE ECONOMICAL TO KEEP HER SPENDING THAN TO HAVE HER SELL THE HOUSE OUT FROM UNDER US!
END

05 WORLD OF ARCHIE

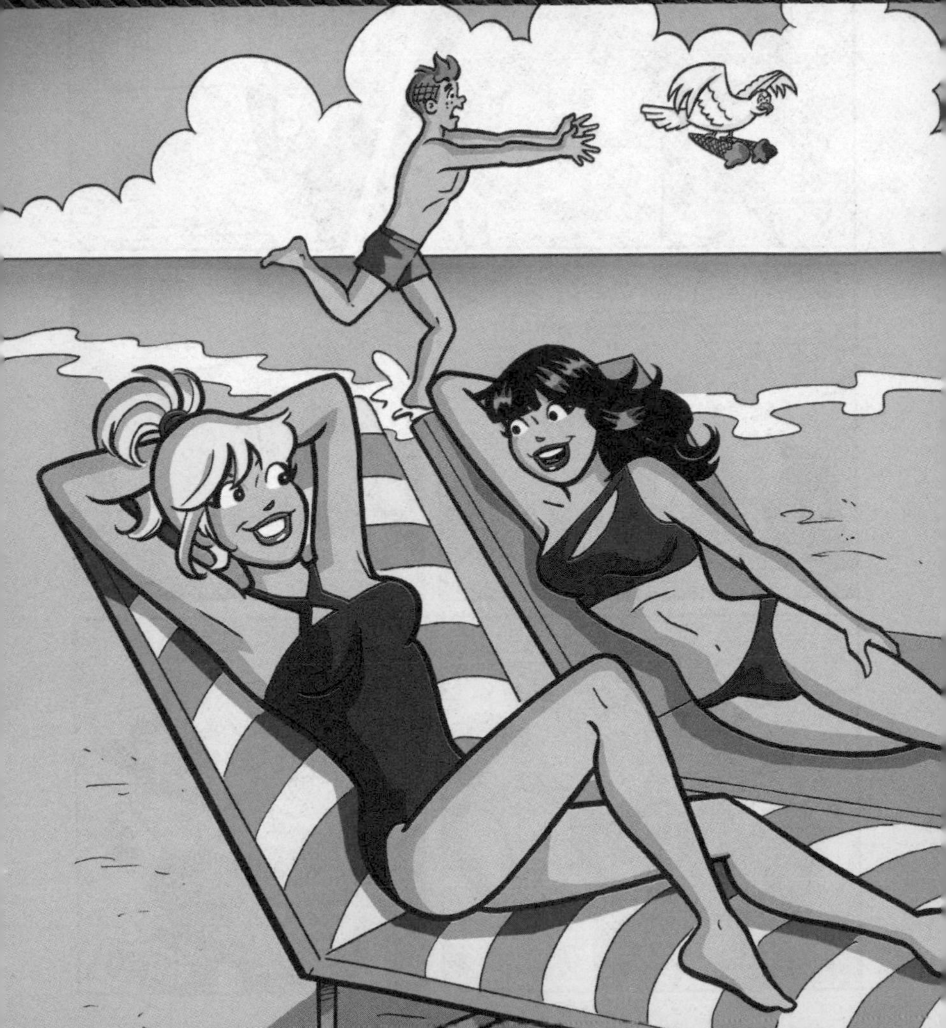

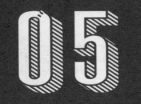

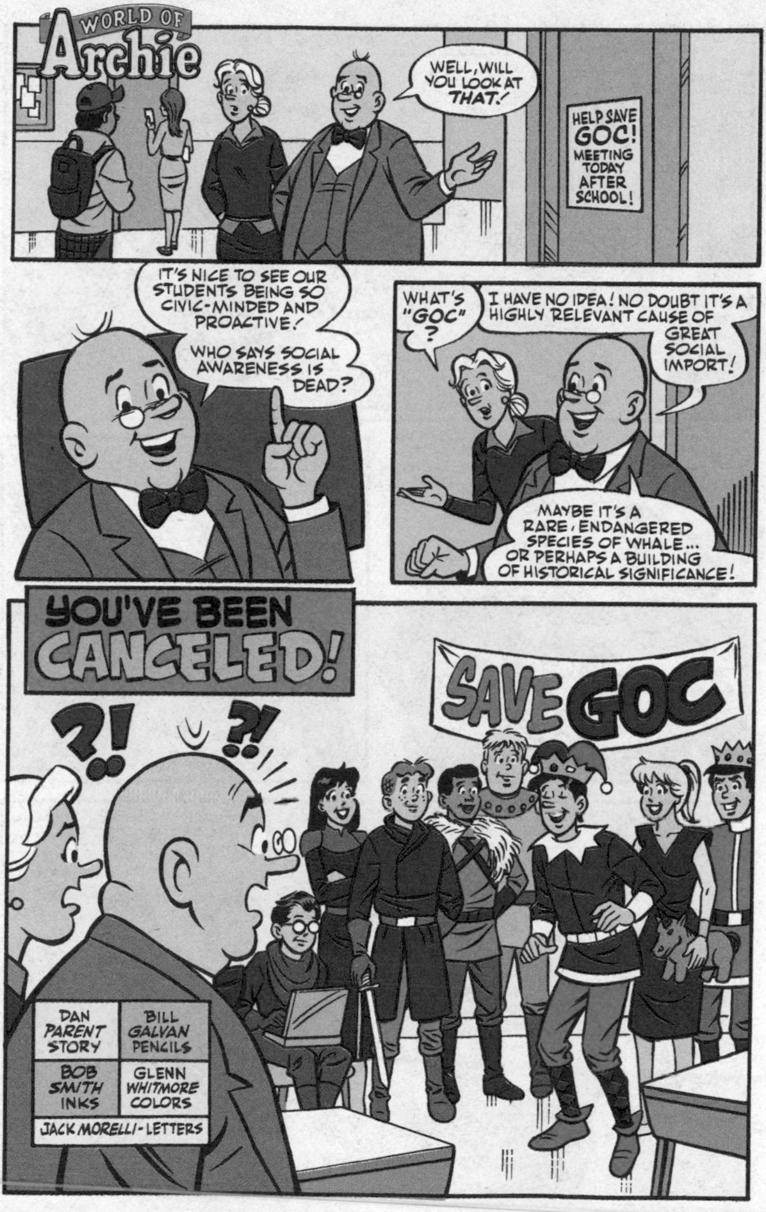
WORLD OF Archie
WELL, WILL YOU LOOK AT THAT!
HELP SAVE GOC! MEETING TODAY AFTER SCHOOL!
IT'S NICE TO SEE OUR STUDENTS BEING SO CIVIC-MINDED AND PROACTIVE!
WHO SAYS SOCIAL AWARENESS IS DEAD?
WHAT'S "GOC"?
I HAVE NO IDEA! NO DOUBT IT'S A HIGHLY RELEVANT CAUSE OF GREAT SOCIAL IMPORT!
MAYBE IT'S A RARE, ENDANGERED SPECIES OF WHALE... OR PERHAPS A BUILDING OF HISTORICAL SIGNIFICANCE!
YOU'VE BEEN CANCELED!
SAVE GOC
?!
?!
DAN PARENT STORY
BILL GALVAN PENCILS
BOB SMITH INKS
GLENN WHITMORE COLORS
JACK MORELLI - LETTERS

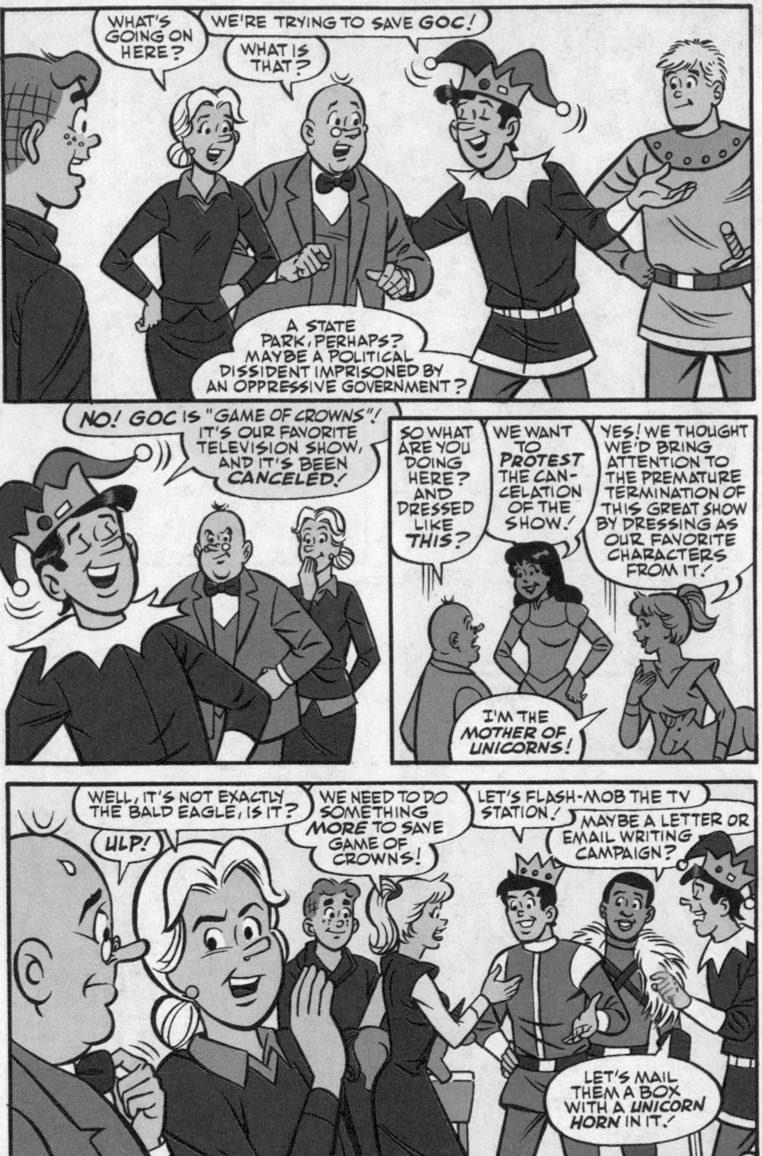
WHAT'S GOING ON HERE?
WE'RE TRYING TO SAVE GOC!
WHAT IS THAT?
A STATE PARK, PERHAPS? MAYBE A POLITICAL DISSIDENT IMPRISONED BY AN OPPRESSIVE GOVERNMENT?
NO! GOC IS "GAME OF CROWNS"! IT'S OUR FAVORITE TELEVISION SHOW, AND IT'S BEEN CANCELED!
SO WHAT ARE YOU DOING HERE? AND DRESSED LIKE THIS?
WE WANT TO PROTEST THE CAN-CELATION OF THE SHOW!
YES! WE THOUGHT WE'D BRING ATTENTION TO THE PREMATURE TERMINATION OF THIS GREAT SHOW BY DRESSING AS OUR FAVORITE CHARACTERS FROM IT!
I'M THE MOTHER OF UNICORNS!
WELL, IT'S NOT EXACTLY THE BALD EAGLE, IS IT?
ULP!
WE NEED TO DO SOMETHING MORE TO SAVE GAME OF CROWNS!
LET'S FLASH-MOB THE TV STATION!
MAYBE A LETTER OR EMAIL WRITING CAMPAIGN?
LET'S MAIL THEM A BOX WITH A UNICORN HORN IN IT!
2

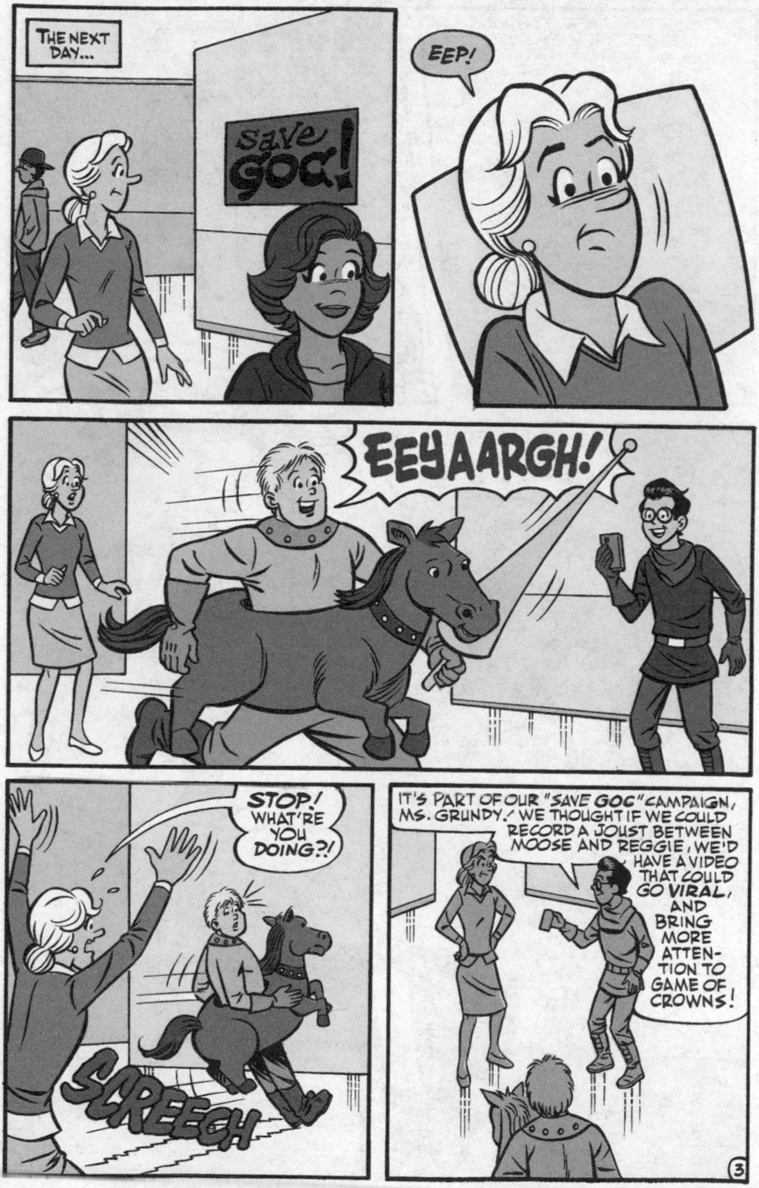
THE NEXT DAY...
SAVE GOC!
EEP!
EEYAARGH!
STOP! WHAT'RE YOU DOING?!
SCREECH
IT'S PART OF OUR "SAVE GOC" CAMPAIGN, MS. GRUNDY! WE THOUGHT IF WE COULD RECORD A JOUST BETWEEN MOOSE AND REGGIE, WE'D HAVE A VIDEO THAT COULD GO VIRAL, AND BRING MORE ATTENTION TO GAME OF CROWNS!
3

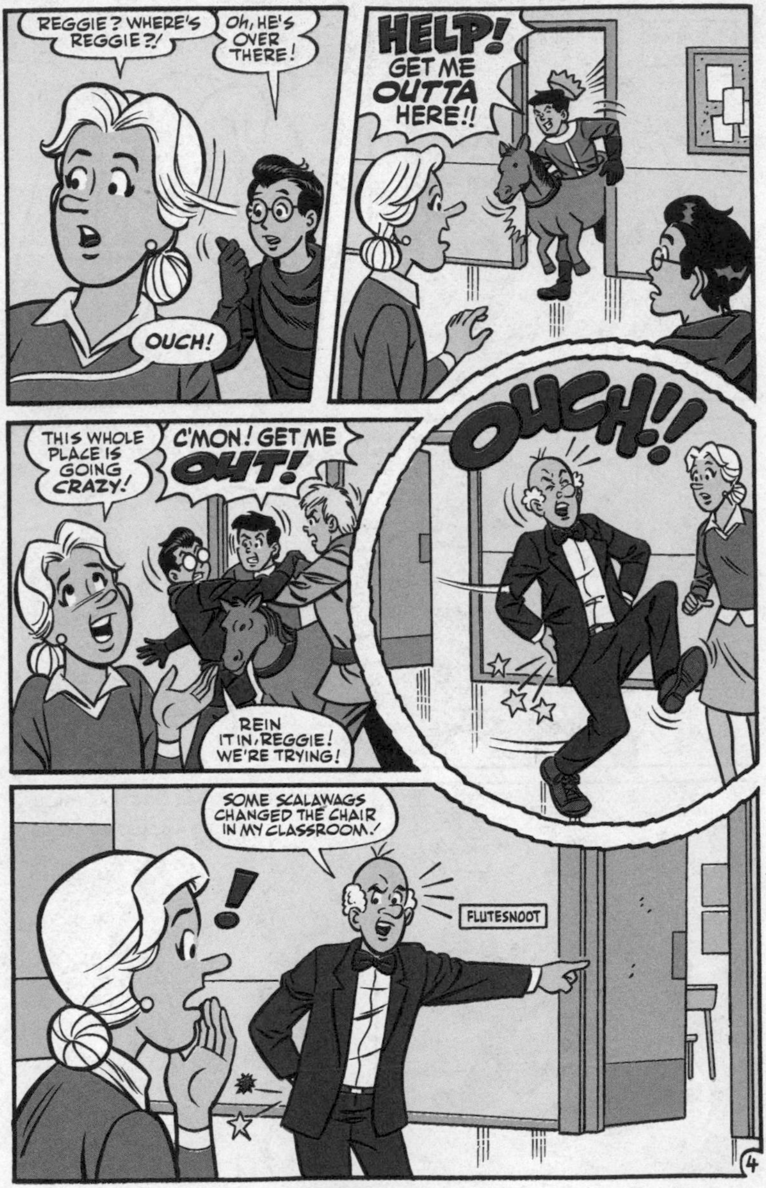
REGGIE? WHERE'S REGGIE?!
Oh, HE'S OVER THERE!
OUCH!
HELP! GET ME OUTTA HERE!!
THIS WHOLE PLACE IS GOING CRAZY!
C'MON! GET ME OUT!
REIN IT IN, REGGIE! WE'RE TRYING!
OUCH!!
SOME SCALAWAGS CHANGED THE CHAIR IN MY CLASSROOM!
!
FLUTESNOOT
4

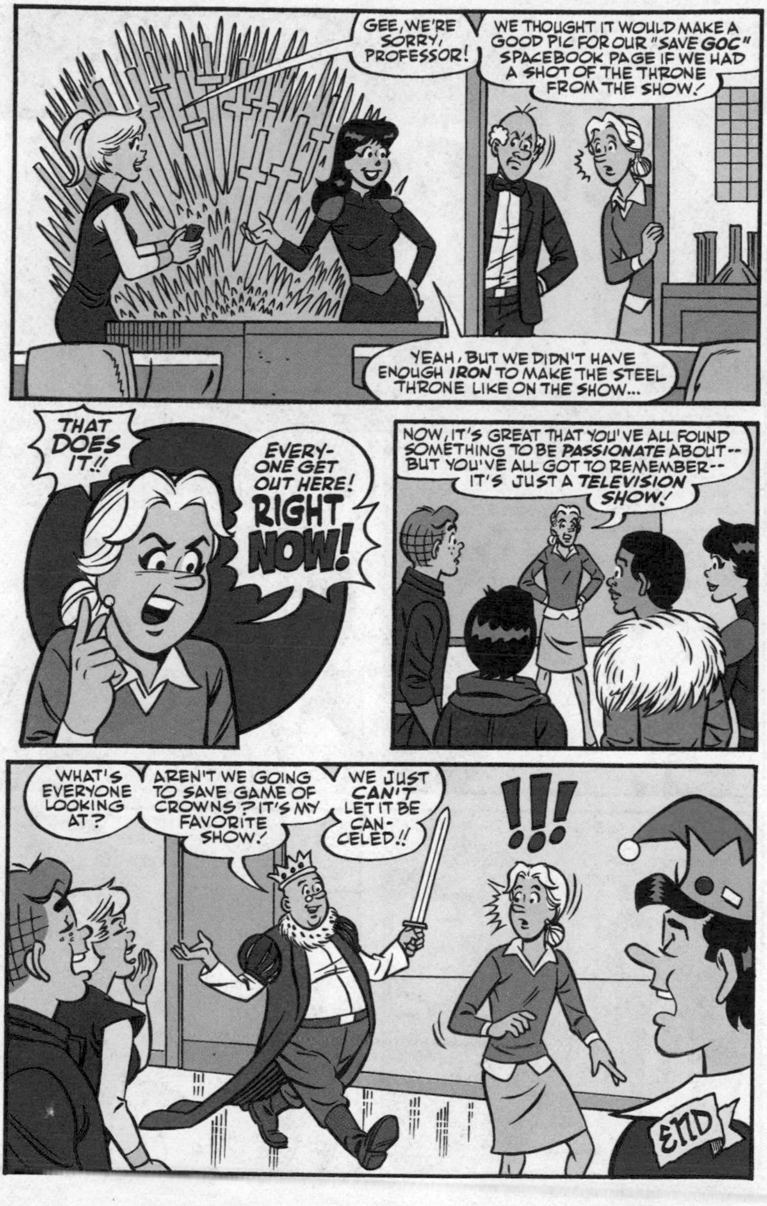
GEE, WE'RE SORRY, PROFESSOR!
WE THOUGHT IT WOULD MAKE A GOOD PIC FOR OUR "SAVE GOC" SPACEBOOK PAGE IF WE HAD A SHOT OF THE THRONE FROM THE SHOW!
YEAH, BUT WE DIDN'T HAVE ENOUGH IRON TO MAKE THE STEEL THRONE LIKE ON THE SHOW...
THAT DOES IT!!
EVERY-ONE GET OUT HERE! RIGHT NOW!
NOW, IT'S GREAT THAT YOU'VE ALL FOUND SOMETHING TO BE PASSIONATE ABOUT-- BUT YOU'VE ALL GOT TO REMEMBER-- IT'S JUST A TELEVISION SHOW!
WHAT'S EVERYONE LOOKING AT?
AREN'T WE GOING TO SAVE GAME OF CROWNS? IT'S MY FAVORITE SHOW!
WE JUST CAN'T LET IT BE CAN-CELED!!
!!!
END

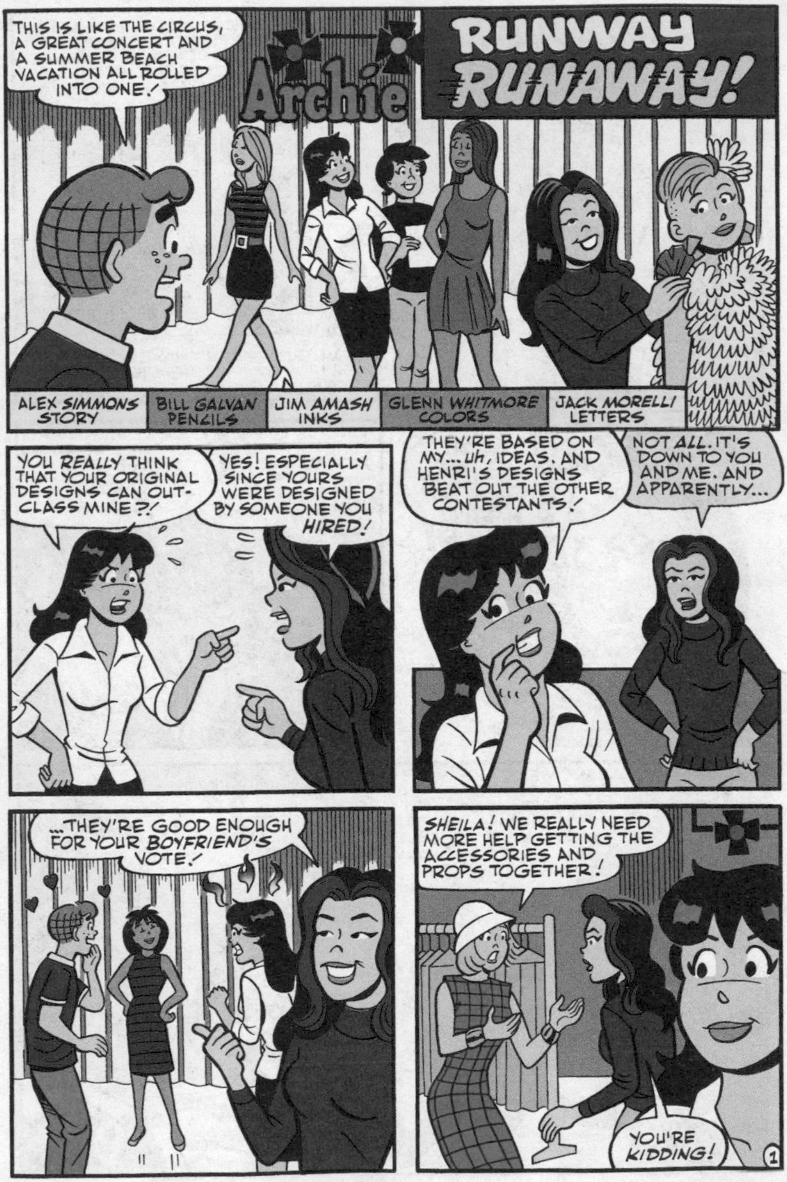
THIS IS LIKE THE CIRCUS, A GREAT CONCERT AND A SUMMER BEACH VACATION ALL ROLLED INTO ONE!
Archie
RUNWAY RUNAWAY!
ALEX SIMMONS STORY
BILL GALVAN PENCILS
JIM AMASH INKS
GLENN WHITMORE COLORS
JACK MORELLI LETTERS
YOU REALLY THINK THAT YOUR ORIGINAL DESIGNS CAN OUT-CLASS MINE?!
YES! ESPECIALLY SINCE YOURS WERE DESIGNED BY SOMEONE YOU HIRED!
THEY'RE BASED ON MY... uh, IDEAS. AND HENRI'S DESIGNS BEAT OUT THE OTHER CONTESTANTS!
NOT ALL. IT'S DOWN TO YOU AND ME. AND APPARENTLY...
...THEY'RE GOOD ENOUGH FOR YOUR BOYFRIEND'S VOTE!
SHEILA! WE REALLY NEED MORE HELP GETTING THE ACCESSORIES AND PROPS TOGETHER!
YOU'RE KIDDING!
1

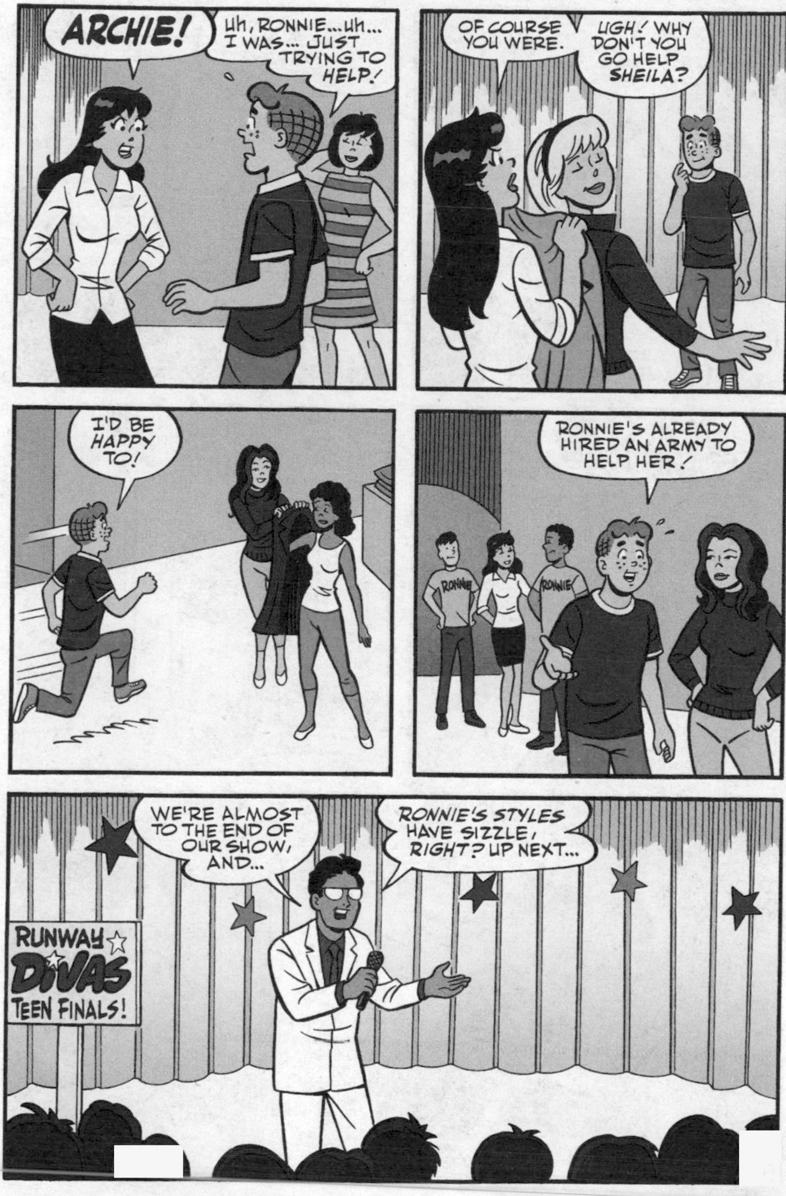
ARCHIE!
UH, RONNIE...UH... I WAS... JUST TRYING TO HELP!
OF COURSE YOU WERE.
UGH! WHY DON'T YOU GO HELP SHEILA?
I'D BE HAPPY TO!
RONNIE'S ALREADY HIRED AN ARMY TO HELP HER!
RONNIE
RONNIE
WE'RE ALMOST TO THE END OF OUR SHOW, AND...
RONNIE'S STYLES HAVE SIZZLE, RIGHT? UP NEXT...
RUNWAY DIVAS TEEN FINALS!

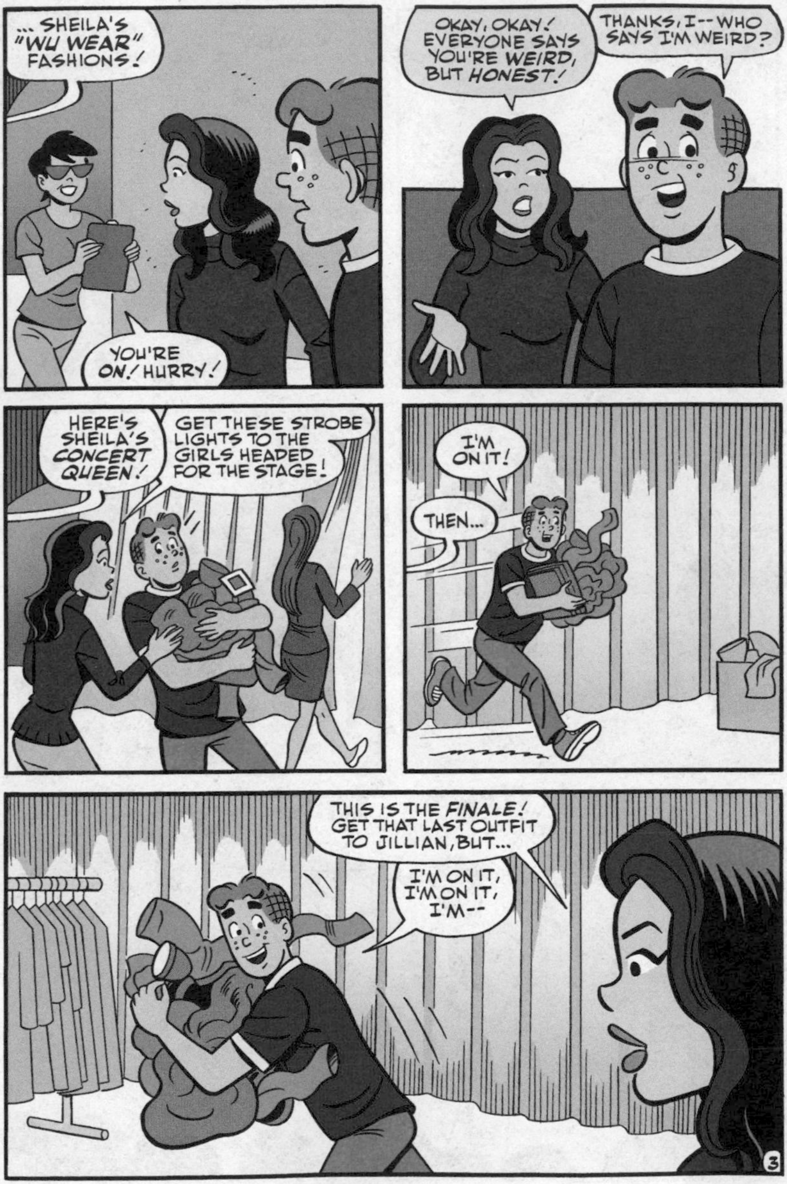
... SHEILA'S "WU WEAR" FASHIONS!
YOU'RE ON! HURRY!
OKAY, OKAY! EVERYONE SAYS YOU'RE WEIRD, BUT HONEST!
THANKS, I-- WHO SAYS I'M WEIRD?
HERE'S SHEILA'S CONCERT QUEEN!
GET THESE STROBE LIGHTS TO THE GIRLS HEADED FOR THE STAGE!
I'M ON IT!
THEN...
THIS IS THE FINALE! GET THAT LAST OUTFIT TO JILLIAN, BUT...
I'M ON IT, I'M ON IT, I'M--
3

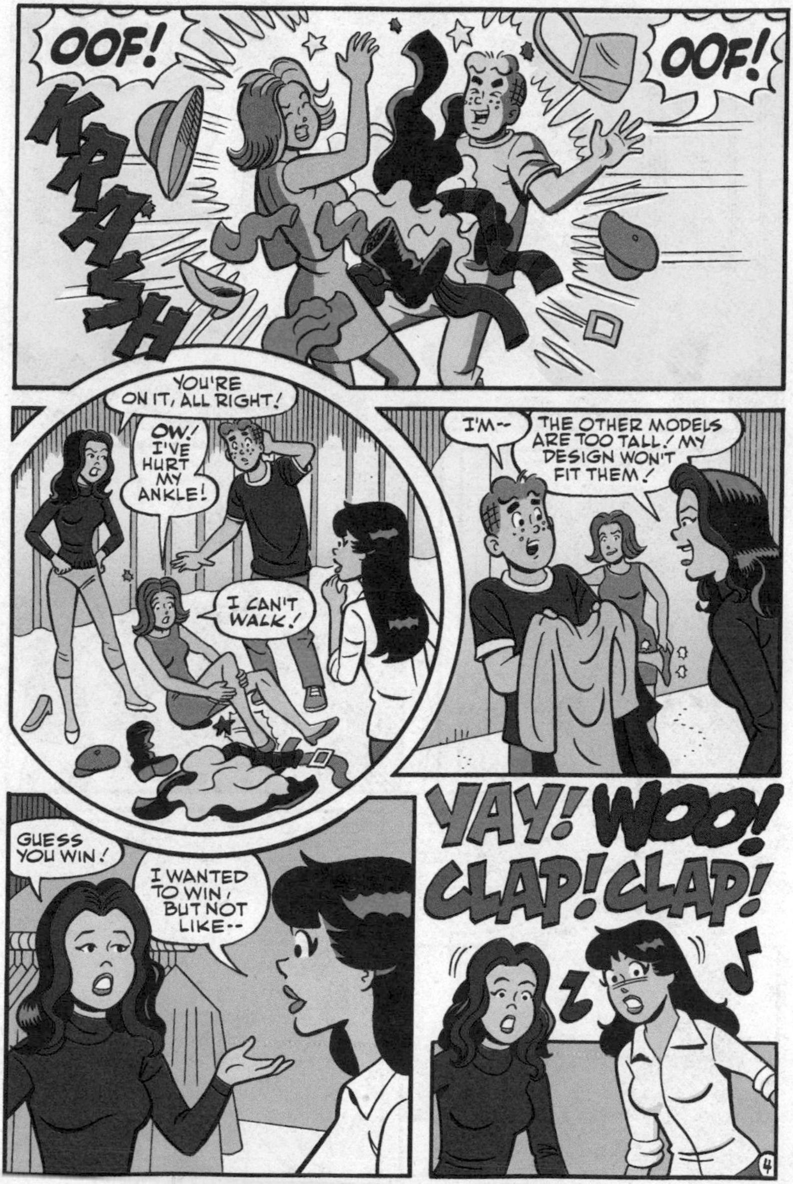
OOF!
KRASH
OOF!
YOU'RE ON IT, ALL RIGHT!
OW! I'VE HURT MY ANKLE!
I CAN'T WALK!
I'M--
THE OTHER MODELS ARE TOO TALL! MY DESIGN WON'T FIT THEM!
GUESS YOU WIN!
I WANTED TO WIN, BUT NOT LIKE--
YAY! WOO!
CLAP! CLAP!
4

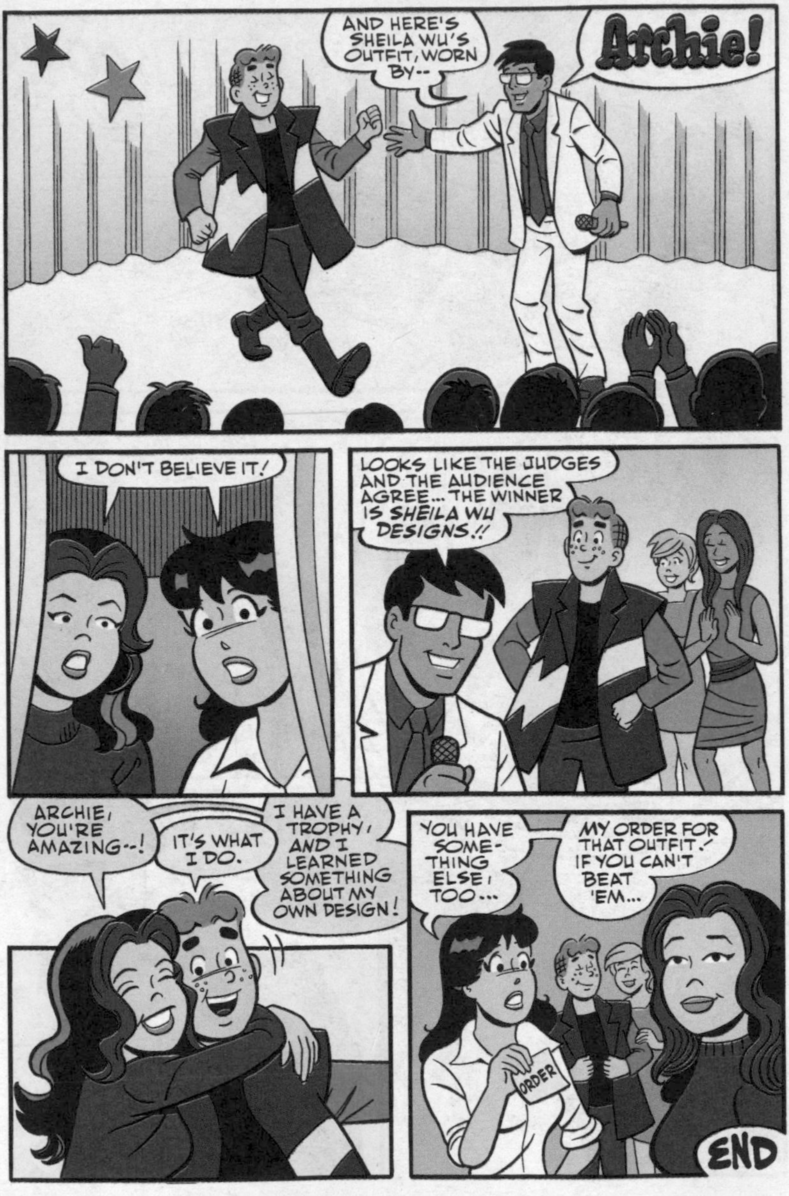
AND HERE'S SHEILA WU'S OUTFIT, WORN BY--
Archie!
I DON'T BELIEVE IT!
LOOKS LIKE THE JUDGES AND THE AUDIENCE AGREE... THE WINNER IS SHEILA WU DESIGNS!!
ARCHIE, YOU'RE AMAZING--!
IT'S WHAT I DO.
I HAVE A TROPHY, AND I LEARNED SOMETHING ABOUT MY OWN DESIGN!
YOU HAVE SOME-THING ELSE, TOO...
MY ORDER FOR THAT OUTFIT! IF YOU CAN'T BEAT 'EM...
ORDER
END

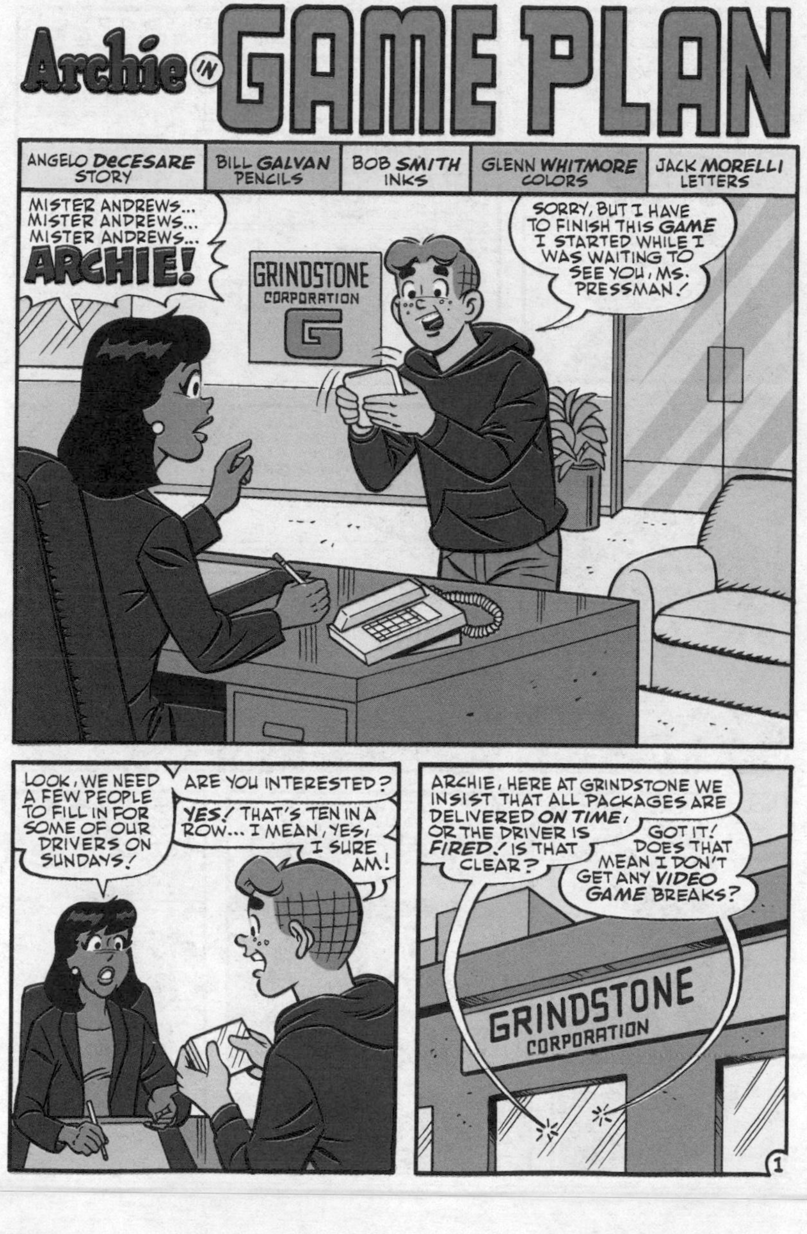
Archie in GAME PLAN
ANGELO DeCESARE STORY
BILL GALVAN PENCILS
BOB SMITH INKS
GLENN WHITMORE COLORS
JACK MORELLI LETTERS
MISTER ANDREWS... MISTER ANDREWS... MISTER ANDREWS... ARCHIE!
SORRY, BUT I HAVE TO FINISH THIS GAME I STARTED WHILE I WAS WAITING TO SEE YOU, MS. PRESSMAN!
GRINDSTONE CORPORATION G
LOOK, WE NEED A FEW PEOPLE TO FILL IN FOR SOME OF OUR DRIVERS ON SUNDAYS!
ARE YOU INTERESTED?
YES! THAT'S TEN IN A ROW... I MEAN, YES, I SURE AM!
ARCHIE, HERE AT GRINDSTONE WE INSIST THAT ALL PACKAGES ARE DELIVERED ON TIME, OR THE DRIVER IS FIRED! IS THAT CLEAR?
GOT IT! DOES THAT MEAN I DON'T GET ANY VIDEO GAME BREAKS?
GRINDSTONE CORPORATION
1

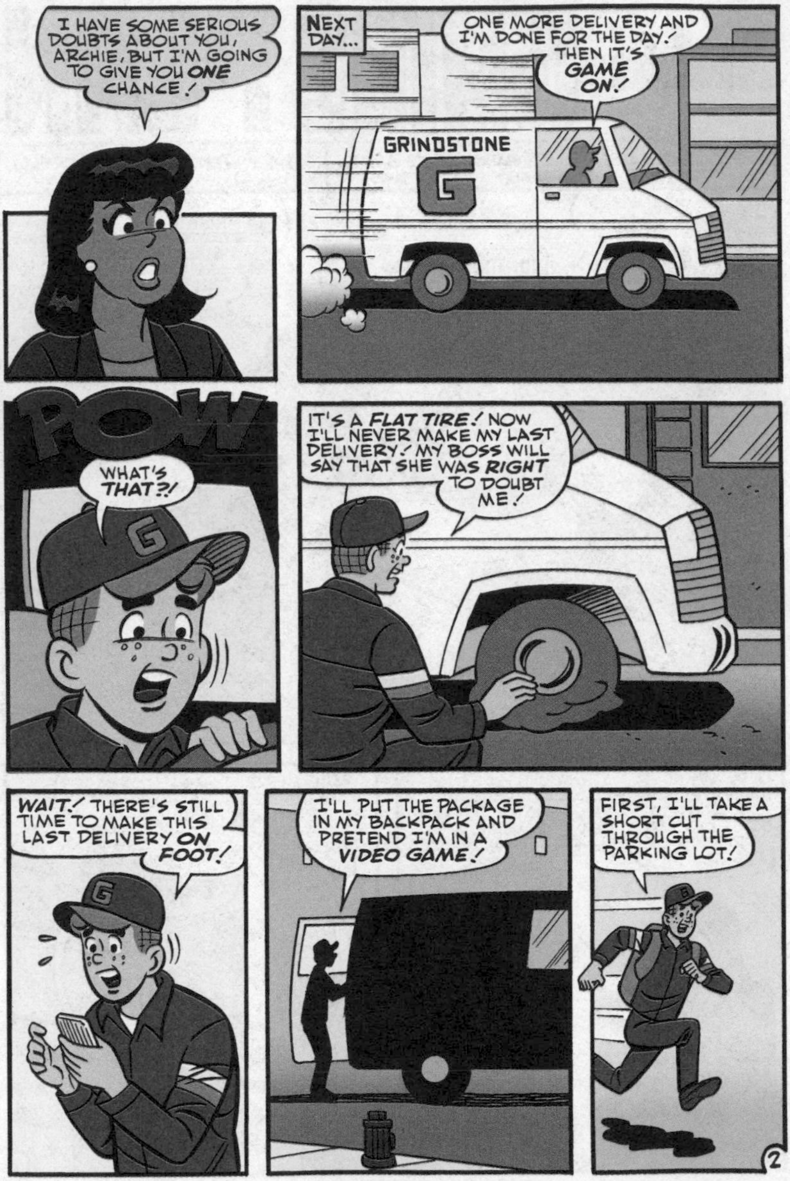
I HAVE SOME SERIOUS DOUBTS ABOUT YOU, ARCHIE, BUT I'M GOING TO GIVE YOU ONE CHANCE!
NEXT DAY...
ONE MORE DELIVERY AND I'M DONE FOR THE DAY! THEN IT'S GAME ON!
GRINDSTONE
G
POW
WHAT'S THAT?!
G
IT'S A FLAT TIRE! NOW I'LL NEVER MAKE MY LAST DELIVERY! MY BOSS WILL SAY THAT SHE WAS RIGHT TO DOUBT ME!
WAIT! THERE'S STILL TIME TO MAKE THIS LAST DELIVERY ON FOOT!
G
I'LL PUT THE PACKAGE IN MY BACKPACK AND PRETEND I'M IN A VIDEO GAME!
FIRST, I'LL TAKE A SHORT CUT THROUGH THE PARKING LOT!
2

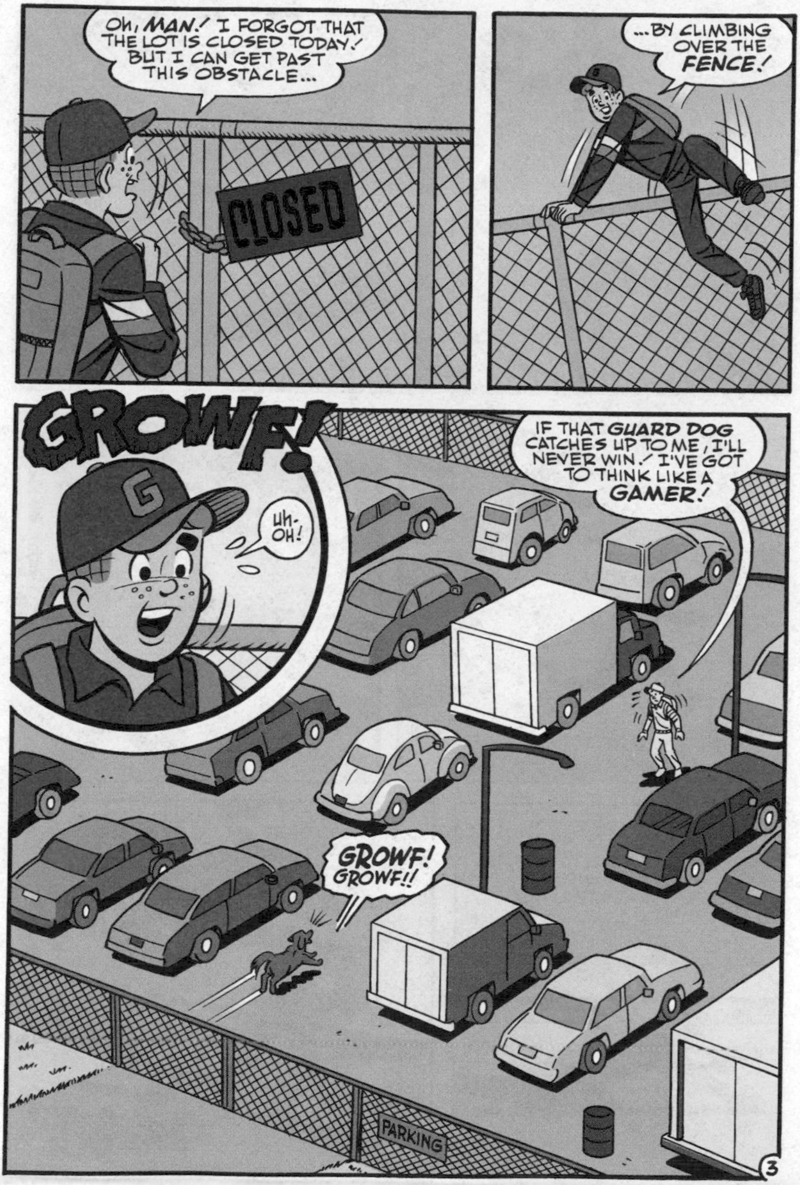
OH, MAN! I FORGOT THAT THE LOT IS CLOSED TODAY! BUT I CAN GET PAST THIS OBSTACLE...
CLOSED
...BY CLIMBING OVER THE FENCE!
GROWF!
UH-OH!
IF THAT GUARD DOG CATCHES UP TO ME, I'LL NEVER WIN.! I'VE GOT TO THINK LIKE A GAMER!
GROWF! GROWF!!
PARKING
3

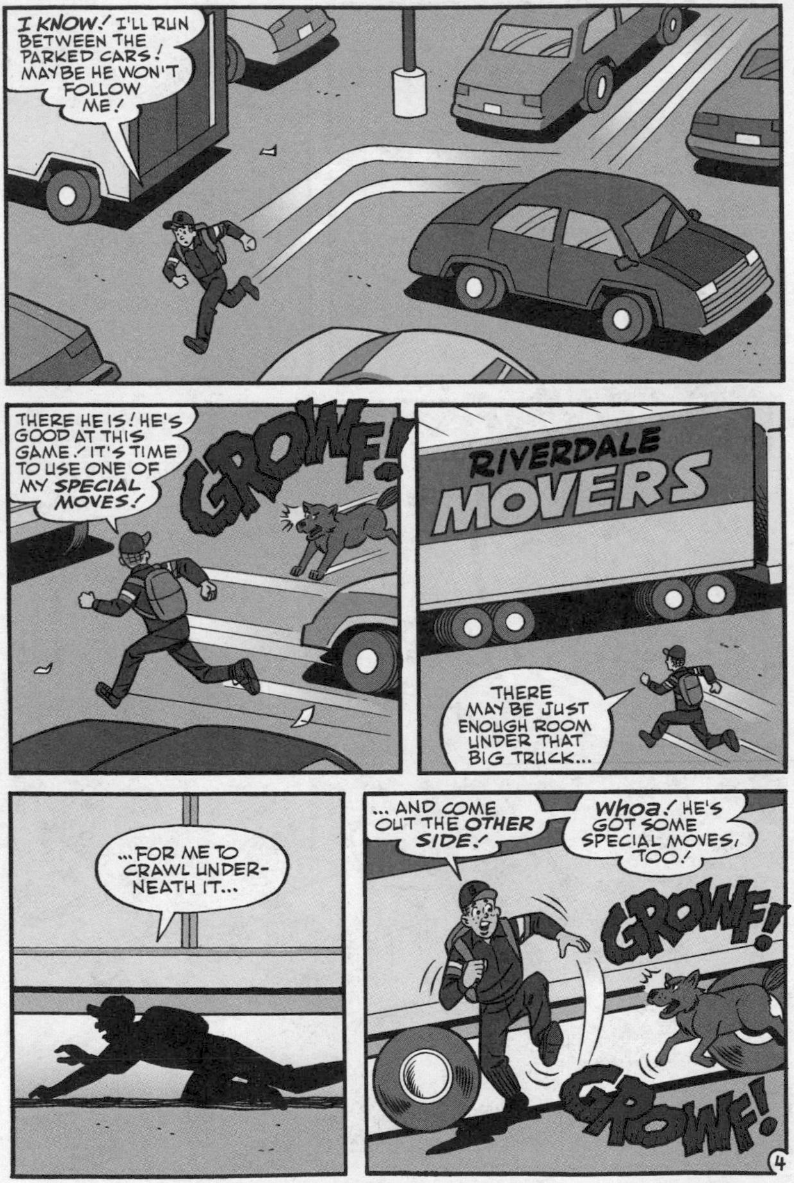
I KNOW! I'LL RUN BETWEEN THE PARKED CARS! MAYBE HE WON'T FOLLOW ME!
THERE HE IS! HE'S GOOD AT THIS GAME! IT'S TIME TO USE ONE OF MY SPECIAL MOVES!
GROWF!
RIVERDALE MOVERS
THERE MAY BE JUST ENOUGH ROOM UNDER THAT BIG TRUCK...
...FOR ME TO CRAWL UNDERNEATH IT...
... AND COME OUT THE OTHER SIDE!
Whoa! HE'S GOT SOME SPECIAL MOVES, TOO!
GROWF!
GROWF!
4

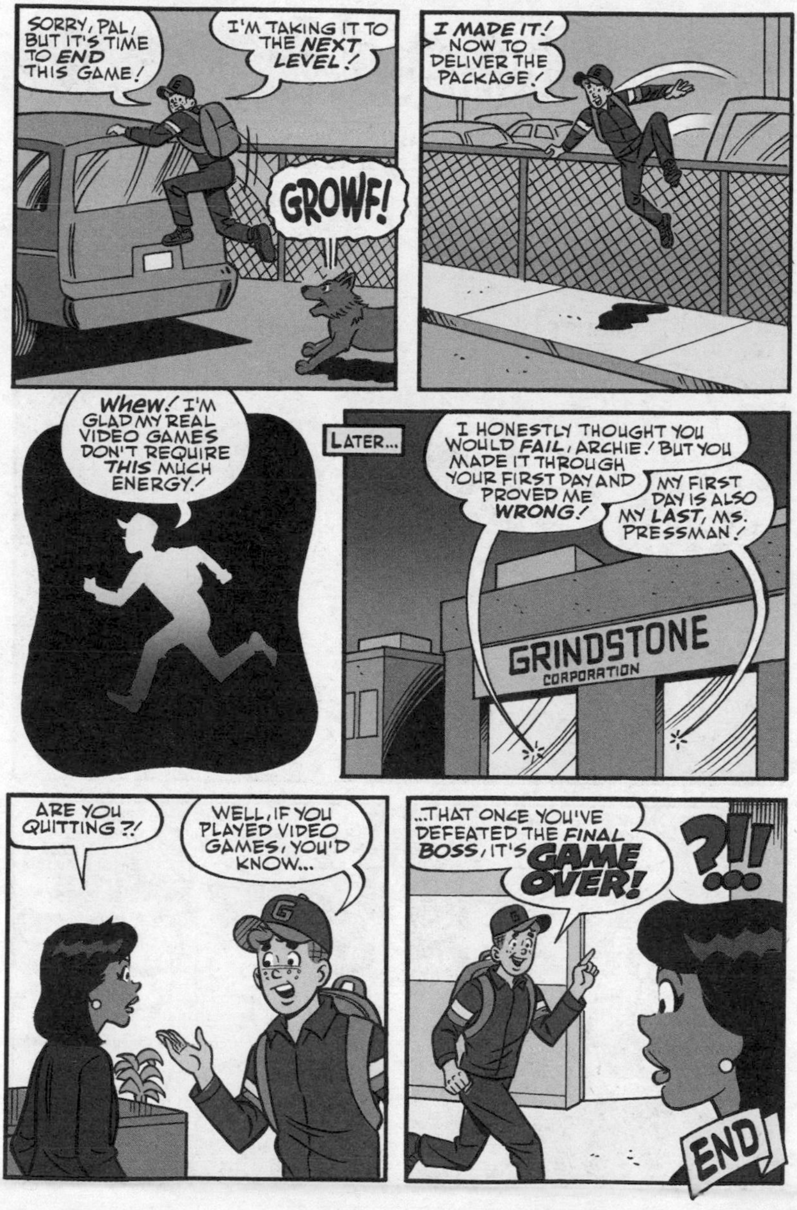
SORRY, PAL, BUT IT'S TIME TO END THIS GAME!
I'M TAKING IT TO THE NEXT LEVEL!
GROWF!
I MADE IT! NOW TO DELIVER THE PACKAGE!
Whew! I'M GLAD MY REAL VIDEO GAMES DON'T REQUIRE THIS MUCH ENERGY!
LATER...
I HONESTLY THOUGHT YOU WOULD FAIL, ARCHIE! BUT YOU MADE IT THROUGH YOUR FIRST DAY AND PROVED ME WRONG!
MY FIRST DAY IS ALSO MY LAST, MS. PRESSMAN!
GRINDSTONE CORPORATION
ARE YOU QUITTING?!
WELL, IF YOU PLAYED VIDEO GAMES, YOU'D KNOW...
...THAT ONCE YOU'VE DEFEATED THE FINAL BOSS, IT'S GAME OVER!
?!!...
END

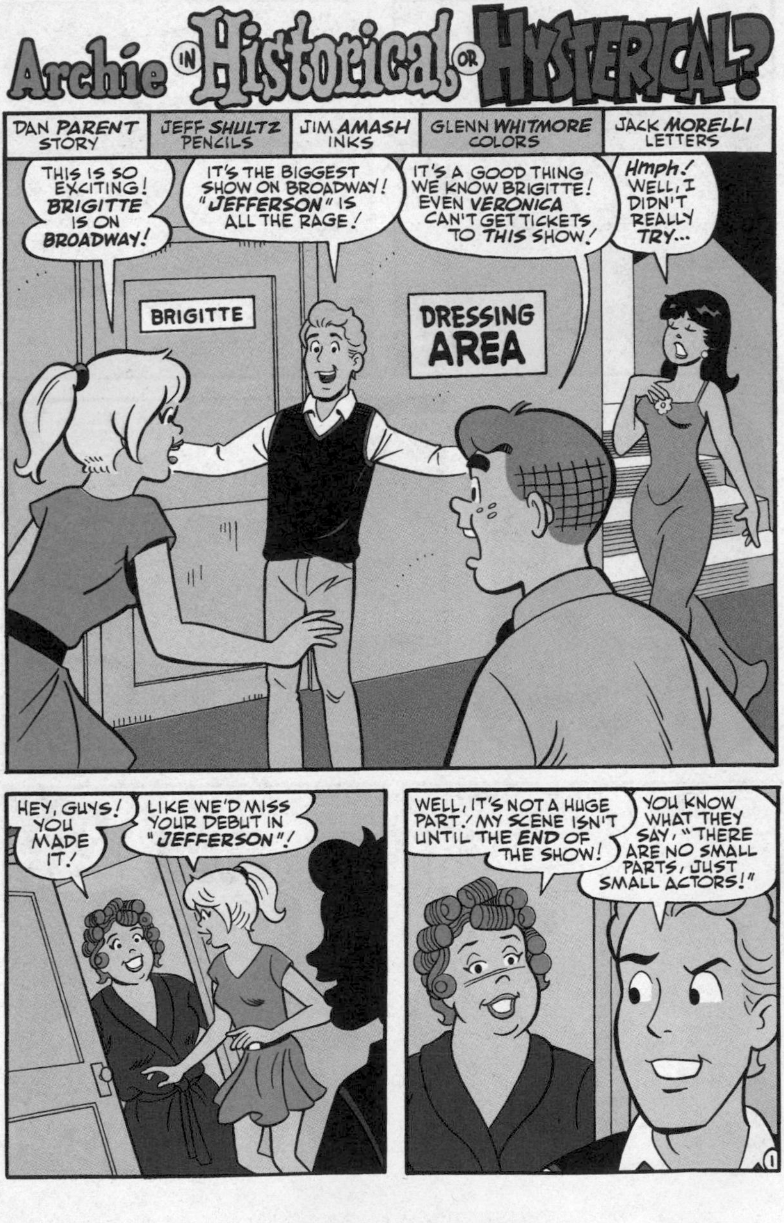

Archie in Historical or Hysterical?
DAN PARENT STORY
JEFF SHULTZ PENCILS
JIM AMASH INKS
GLENN WHITMORE COLORS
JACK MORELLI LETTERS
THIS IS SO EXCITING! BRIGITTE IS ON BROADWAY!
IT'S THE BIGGEST SHOW ON BROADWAY! "JEFFERSON" IS ALL THE RAGE!
IT'S A GOOD THING WE KNOW BRIGITTE! EVEN VERONICA CAN'T GET TICKETS TO THIS SHOW!
Hmph! WELL, I DIDN'T REALLY TRY...
BRIGITTE
DRESSING AREA
HEY, GUYS! YOU MADE IT!
LIKE WE'D MISS YOUR DEBUT IN "JEFFERSON"!
WELL, IT'S NOT A HUGE PART! MY SCENE ISN'T UNTIL THE END OF THE SHOW!
YOU KNOW WHAT THEY SAY, "THERE ARE NO SMALL PARTS, JUST SMALL ACTORS!"
1

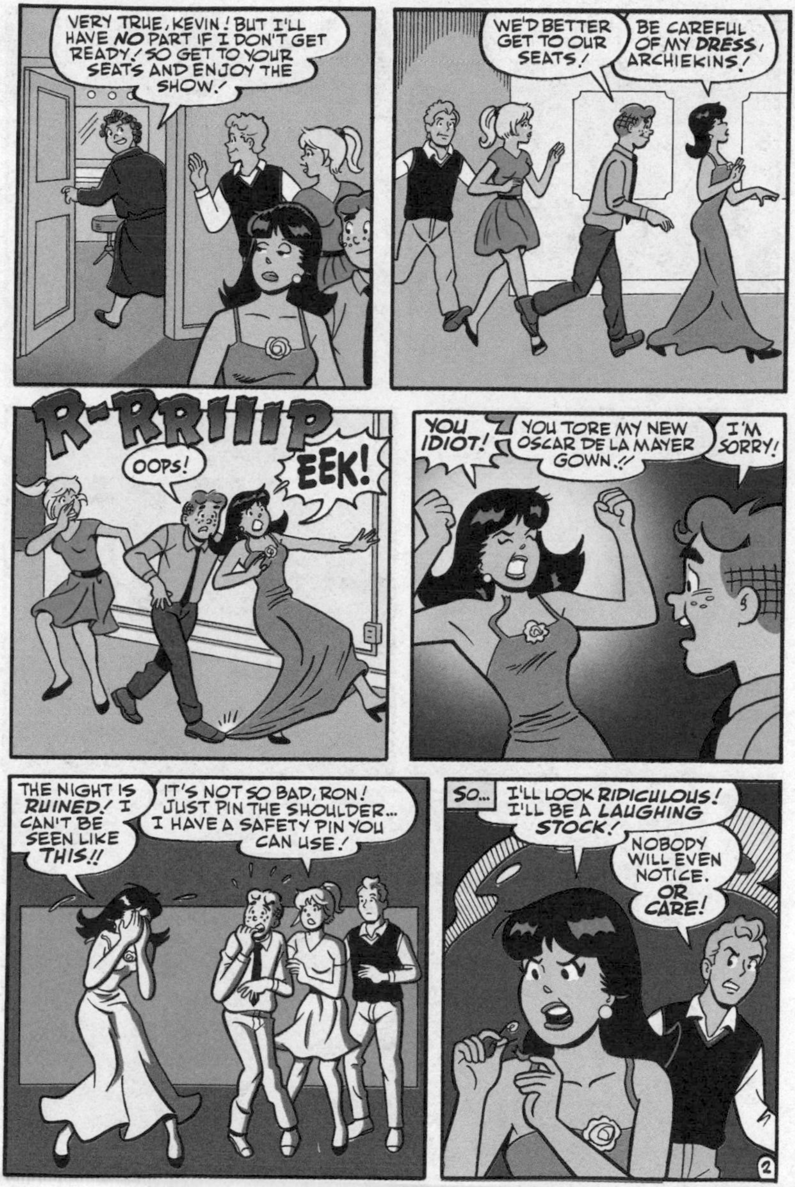
VERY TRUE, KEVIN! BUT I'LL HAVE NO PART IF I DON'T GET READY! SO GET TO YOUR SEATS AND ENJOY THE SHOW!
WE'D BETTER GET TO OUR SEATS!
BE CAREFUL OF MY DRESS, ARCHIEKINS!
R-RRIIIP
OOPS!
EEK!
YOU IDIOT!
YOU TORE MY NEW OSCAR DE LA MAYER GOWN!!
I'M SORRY!
THE NIGHT IS RUINED! I CAN'T BE SEEN LIKE THIS!!
IT'S NOT SO BAD, RON! JUST PIN THE SHOULDER... I HAVE A SAFETY PIN YOU CAN USE!
SO...
I'LL LOOK RIDICULOUS! I'LL BE A LAUGHING STOCK!
NOBODY WILL EVEN NOTICE. OR CARE!
2

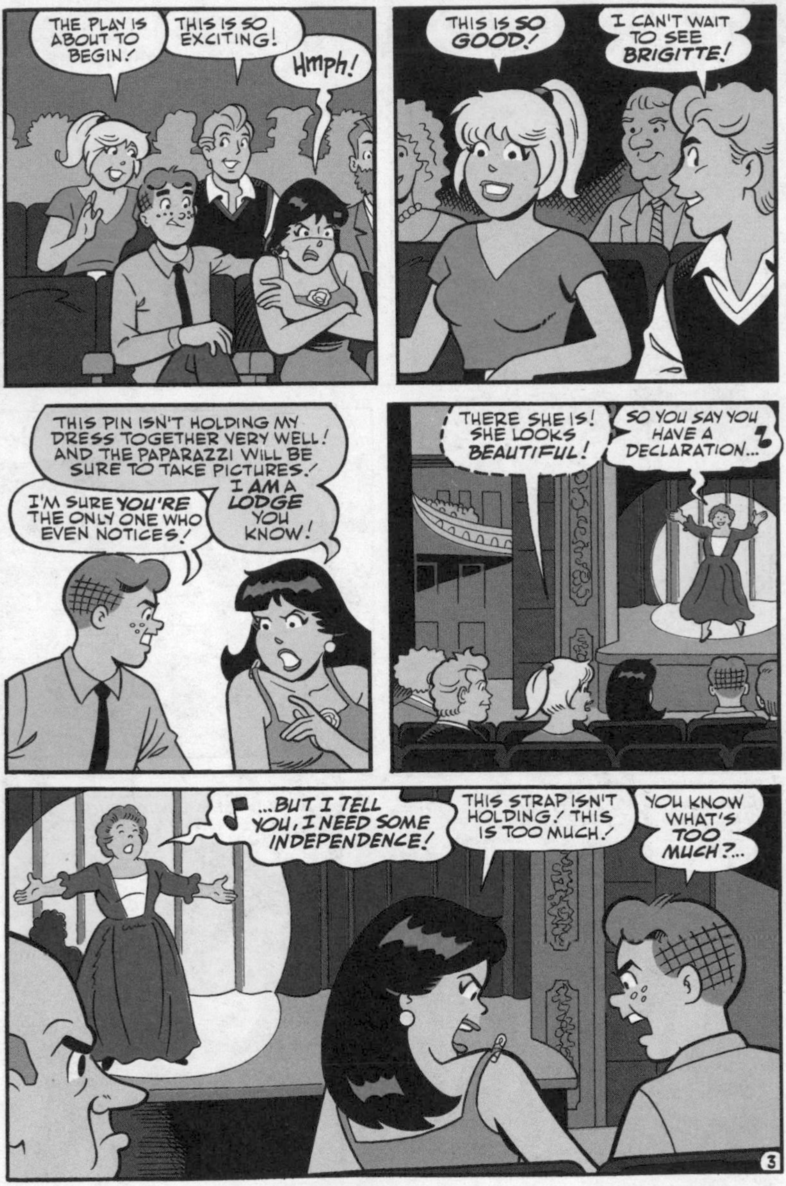
THE PLAY IS ABOUT TO BEGIN!
THIS IS SO EXCITING!
Hmph!
THIS IS SO GOOD!
I CAN'T WAIT TO SEE BRIGITTE!
THIS PIN ISN'T HOLDING MY DRESS TOGETHER VERY WELL! AND THE PAPARAZZI WILL BE SURE TO TAKE PICTURES!
I AM A LODGE YOU KNOW!
I'M SURE YOU'RE THE ONLY ONE WHO EVEN NOTICES!
THERE SHE IS! SHE LOOKS BEAUTIFUL!
SO YOU SAY YOU HAVE A DECLARATION...
...BUT I TELL YOU, I NEED SOME INDEPENDENCE!
THIS STRAP ISN'T HOLDING! THIS IS TOO MUCH!
YOU KNOW WHAT'S TOO MUCH?...
3

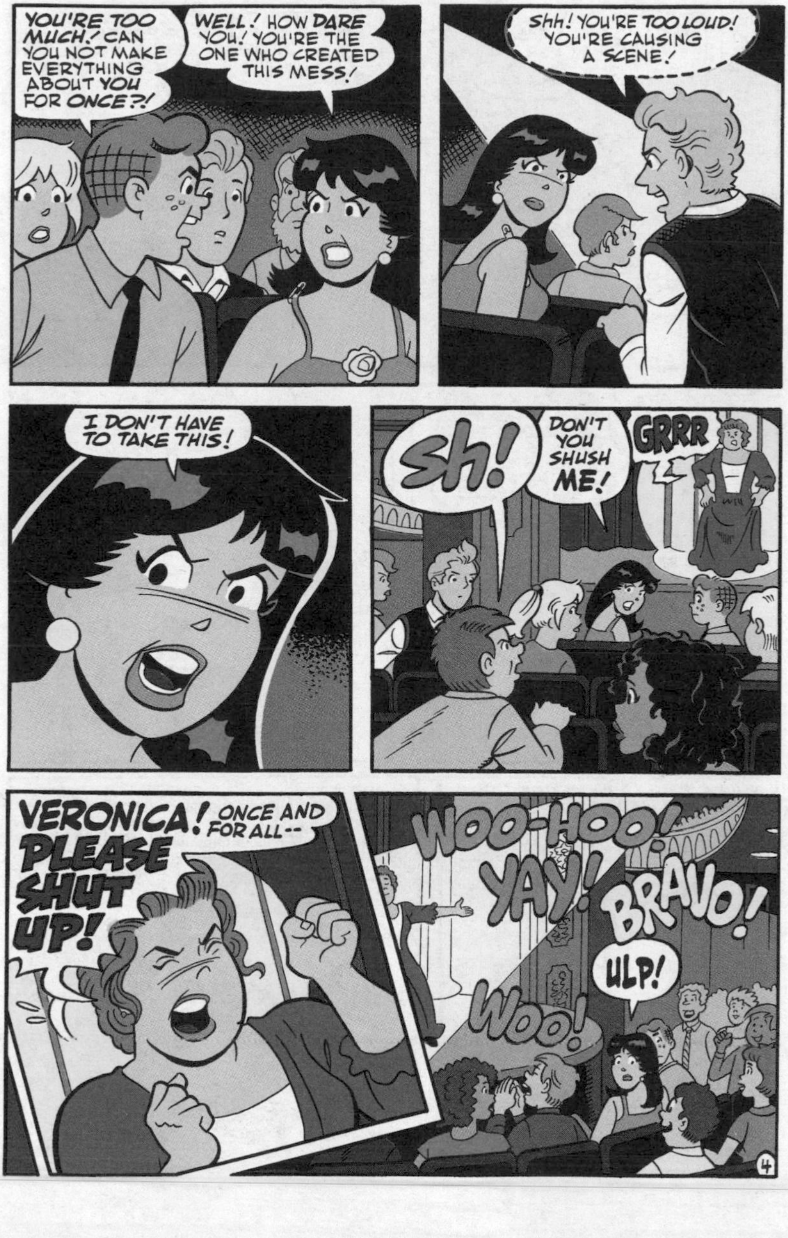
YOU'RE TOO MUCH! CAN YOU NOT MAKE EVERYTHING ABOUT YOU FOR ONCE?!
WELL! HOW DARE YOU! YOU'RE THE ONE WHO CREATED THIS MESS!
Shh! YOU'RE TOO LOUD! YOU'RE CAUSING A SCENE!
I DON'T HAVE TO TAKE THIS!
Sh!
DON'T YOU SHUSH ME!
GRRR
VERONICA! ONCE AND FOR ALL--
PLEASE SHUT UP!
WOO-HOO!
YAY!
BRAVO!
ULP!
WOO!
4

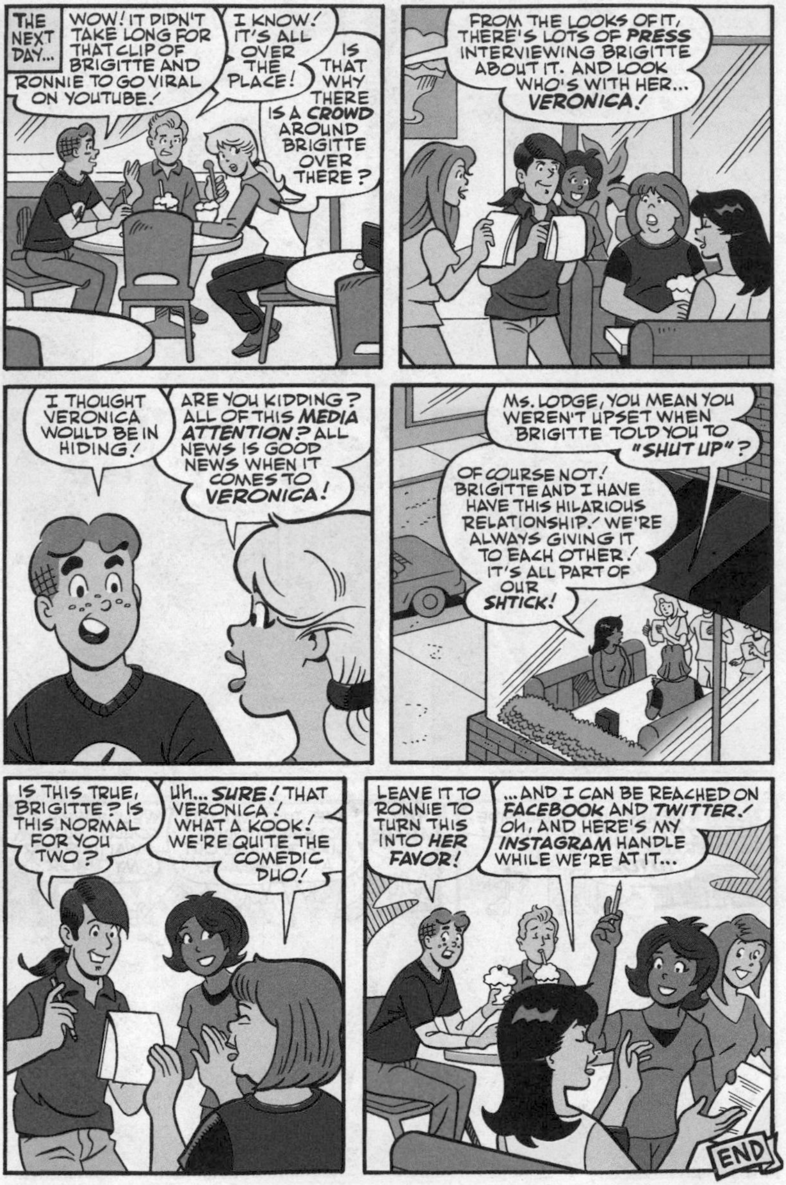
THE NEXT DAY...
WOW! IT DIDN'T TAKE LONG FOR THAT CLIP OF BRIGITTE AND RONNIE TO GO VIRAL ON YOUTUBE!
I KNOW! IT'S ALL OVER THE PLACE!
IS THAT WHY THERE IS A CROWD AROUND BRIGITTE OVER THERE?
FROM THE LOOKS OF IT, THERE'S LOTS OF PRESS INTERVIEWING BRIGITTE ABOUT IT. AND LOOK WHO'S WITH HER... VERONICA!
I THOUGHT VERONICA WOULD BE IN HIDING!
ARE YOU KIDDING? ALL OF THIS MEDIA ATTENTION? ALL NEWS IS GOOD NEWS WHEN IT COMES TO VERONICA!
MS. LODGE, YOU MEAN YOU WEREN'T UPSET WHEN BRIGITTE TOLD YOU TO "SHUT UP"?
OF COURSE NOT! BRIGITTE AND I HAVE HAVE THIS HILARIOUS RELATIONSHIP! WE'RE ALWAYS GIVING IT TO EACH OTHER! IT'S ALL PART OF OUR SHTICK!
IS THIS TRUE, BRIGITTE? IS THIS NORMAL FOR YOU TWO?
UH... SURE! THAT VERONICA! WHAT A KOOK! WE'RE QUITE THE COMEDIC DUO!
LEAVE IT TO RONNIE TO TURN THIS INTO HER FAVOR!
...AND I CAN BE REACHED ON FACEBOOK AND TWITTER! OH, AND HERE'S MY INSTAGRAM HANDLE WHILE WE'RE AT IT...
END

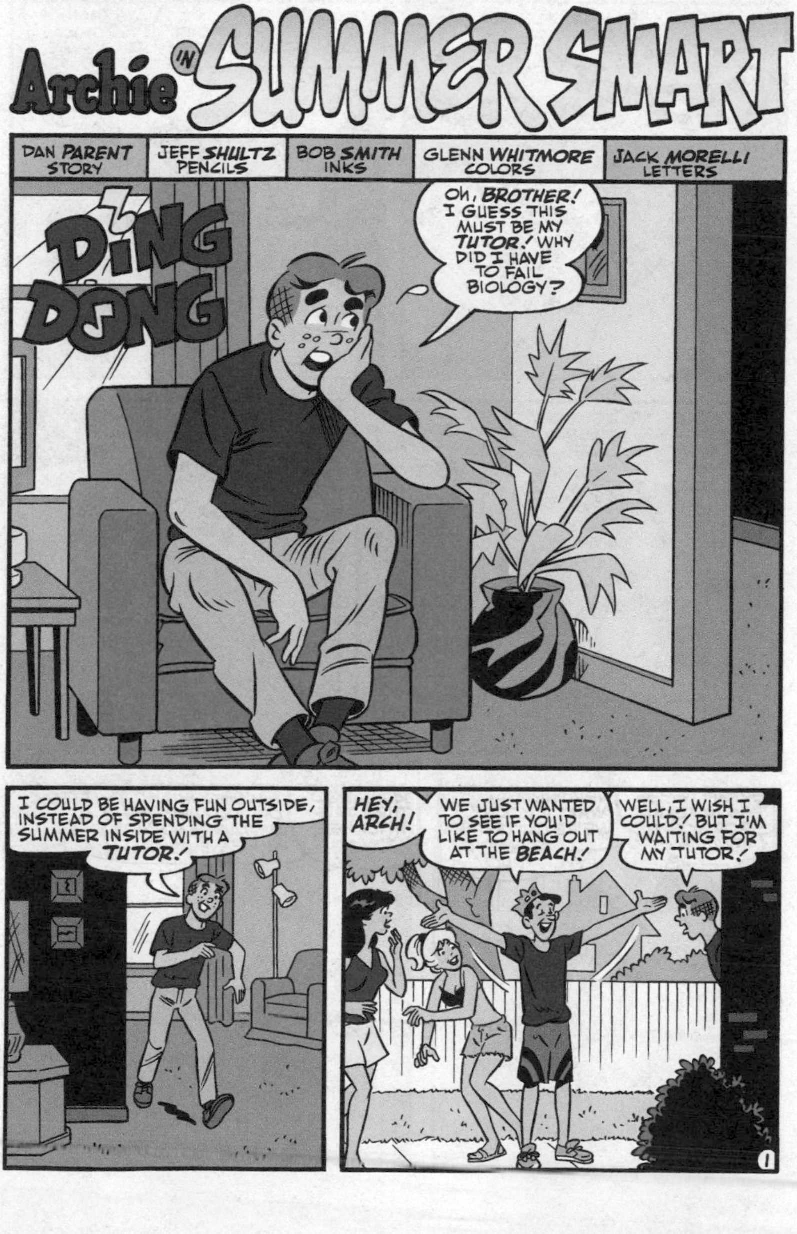
Archie in SUMMER SMART
DAN PARENT STORY
JEFF SHULTZ PENCILS
BOB SMITH INKS
GLENN WHITMORE COLORS
JACK MORELLI LETTERS
DING DONG
Oh, BROTHER! I GUESS THIS MUST BE MY TUTOR! WHY DID I HAVE TO FAIL BIOLOGY?
I COULD BE HAVING FUN OUTSIDE, INSTEAD OF SPENDING THE SUMMER INSIDE WITH A TUTOR!
HEY, ARCH!
WE JUST WANTED TO SEE IF YOU'D LIKE TO HANG OUT AT THE BEACH!
WELL, I WISH I COULD! BUT I'M WAITING FOR MY TUTOR!
1

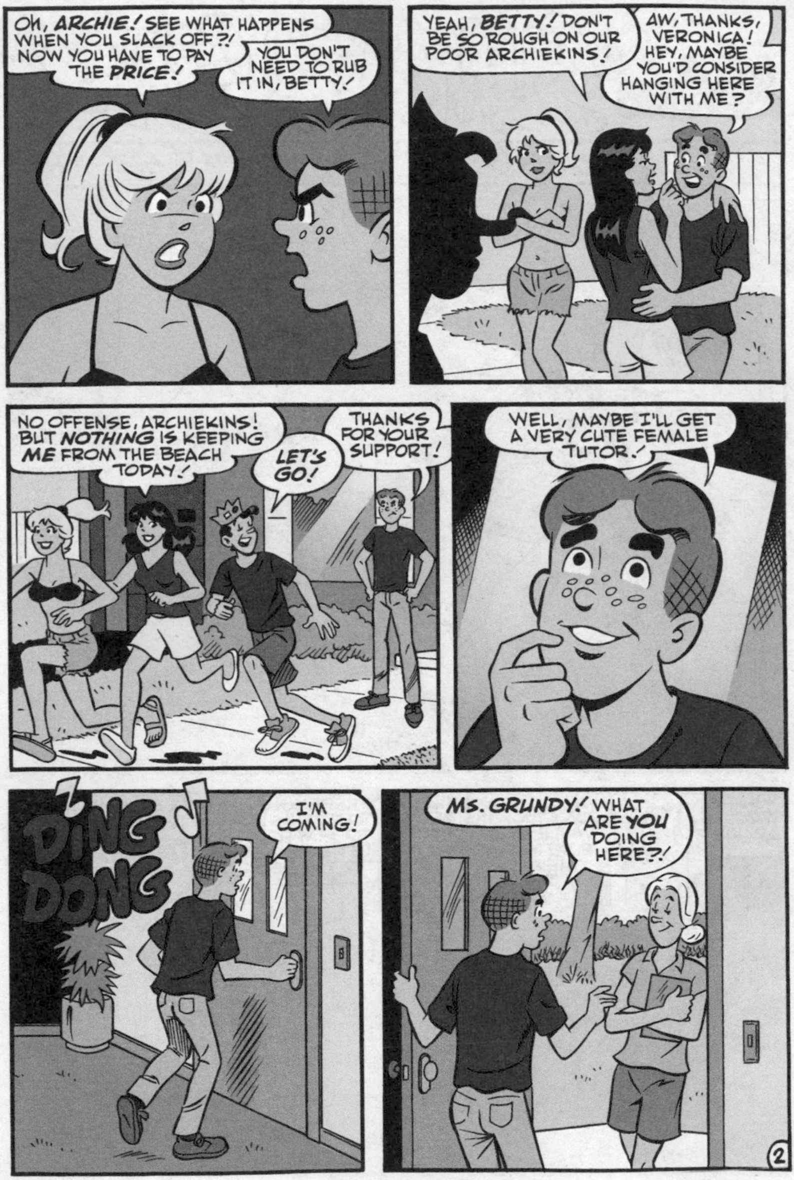
OH, ARCHIE! SEE WHAT HAPPENS WHEN YOU SLACK OFF?! NOW YOU HAVE TO PAY THE PRICE!
YOU DON'T NEED TO RUB IT IN, BETTY!
YEAH, BETTY! DON'T BE SO ROUGH ON OUR POOR ARCHIEKINS!
AW, THANKS, VERONICA! HEY, MAYBE YOU'D CONSIDER HANGING HERE WITH ME?
NO OFFENSE, ARCHIEKINS! BUT NOTHING IS KEEPING ME FROM THE BEACH TODAY!
LET'S GO!
THANKS FOR YOUR SUPPORT!
WELL, MAYBE I'LL GET A VERY CUTE FEMALE TUTOR!
DING DONG
I'M COMING!
MS. GRUNDY! WHAT ARE YOU DOING HERE?!
2

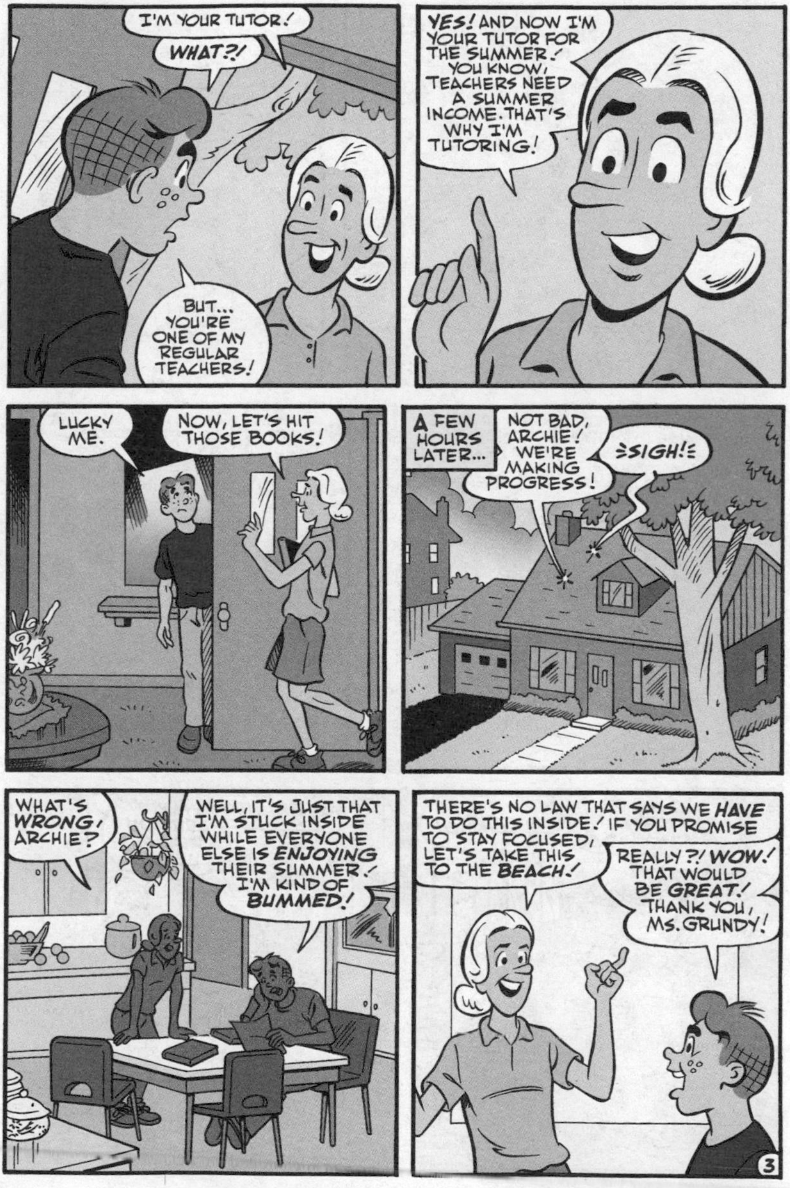
I'M YOUR TUTOR!
WHAT?!
BUT... YOU'RE ONE OF MY REGULAR TEACHERS!
YES! AND NOW I'M YOUR TUTOR FOR THE SUMMER! YOU KNOW, TEACHERS NEED A SUMMER INCOME. THAT'S WHY I'M TUTORING!
LUCKY ME.
NOW, LET'S HIT THOSE BOOKS!
A FEW HOURS LATER...
NOT BAD, ARCHIE! WE'RE MAKING PROGRESS!
SIGH!
WHAT'S WRONG, ARCHIE?
WELL, IT'S JUST THAT I'M STUCK INSIDE WHILE EVERYONE ELSE IS ENJOYING THEIR SUMMER! I'M KIND OF BUMMED!
THERE'S NO LAW THAT SAYS WE HAVE TO DO THIS INSIDE! IF YOU PROMISE TO STAY FOCUSED, LET'S TAKE THIS TO THE BEACH!
REALLY?! WOW! THAT WOULD BE GREAT! THANK YOU, MS. GRUNDY!
3

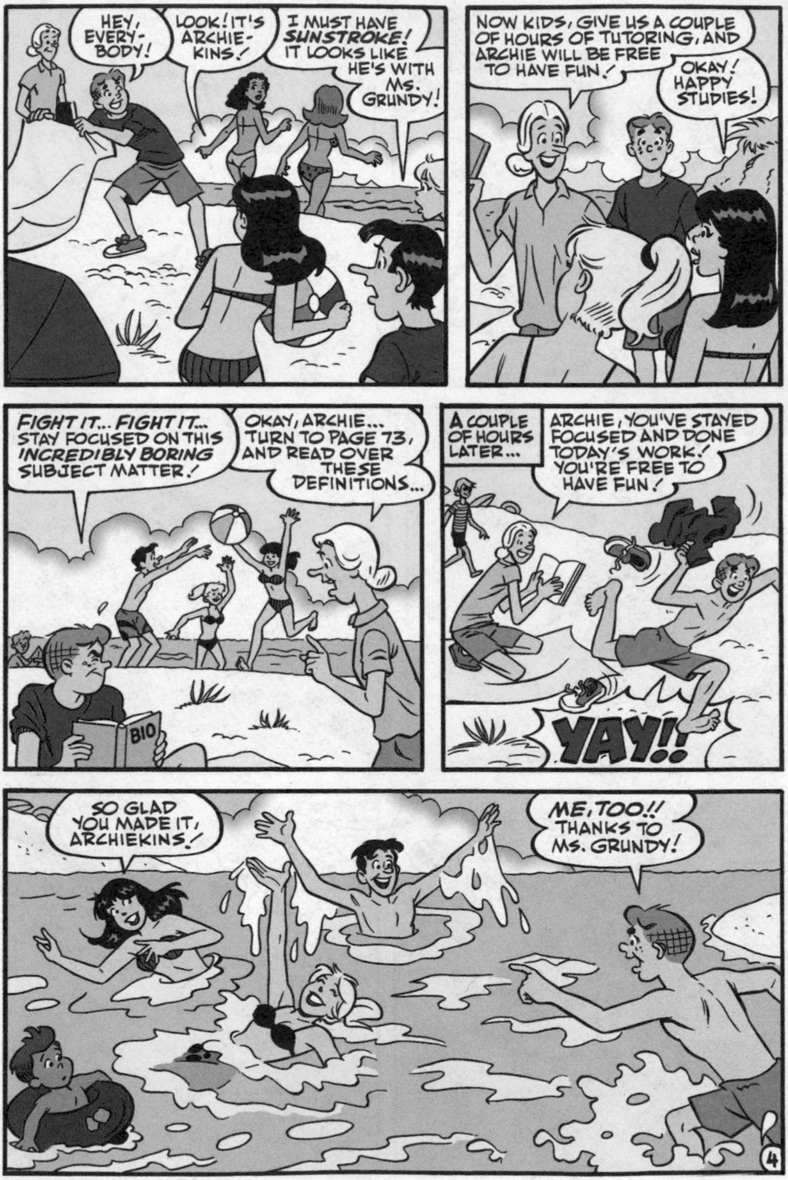
HEY, EVERY-BODY!
LOOK! IT'S ARCHIE-KINS!
I MUST HAVE SUNSTROKE! IT LOOKS LIKE HE'S WITH MS. GRUNDY!
NOW KIDS, GIVE US A COUPLE OF HOURS OF TUTORING, AND ARCHIE WILL BE FREE TO HAVE FUN!
OKAY! HAPPY STUDIES!
FIGHT IT... FIGHT IT... STAY FOCUSED ON THIS INCREDIBLY BORING SUBJECT MATTER!
OKAY, ARCHIE... TURN TO PAGE 73, AND READ OVER THESE DEFINITIONS...
BIO
A COUPLE OF HOURS LATER...
ARCHIE, YOU'VE STAYED FOCUSED AND DONE TODAY'S WORK! YOU'RE FREE TO HAVE FUN!
YAY!!
SO GLAD YOU MADE IT, ARCHIEKINS!
ME, TOO!! THANKS TO MS. GRUNDY!
4

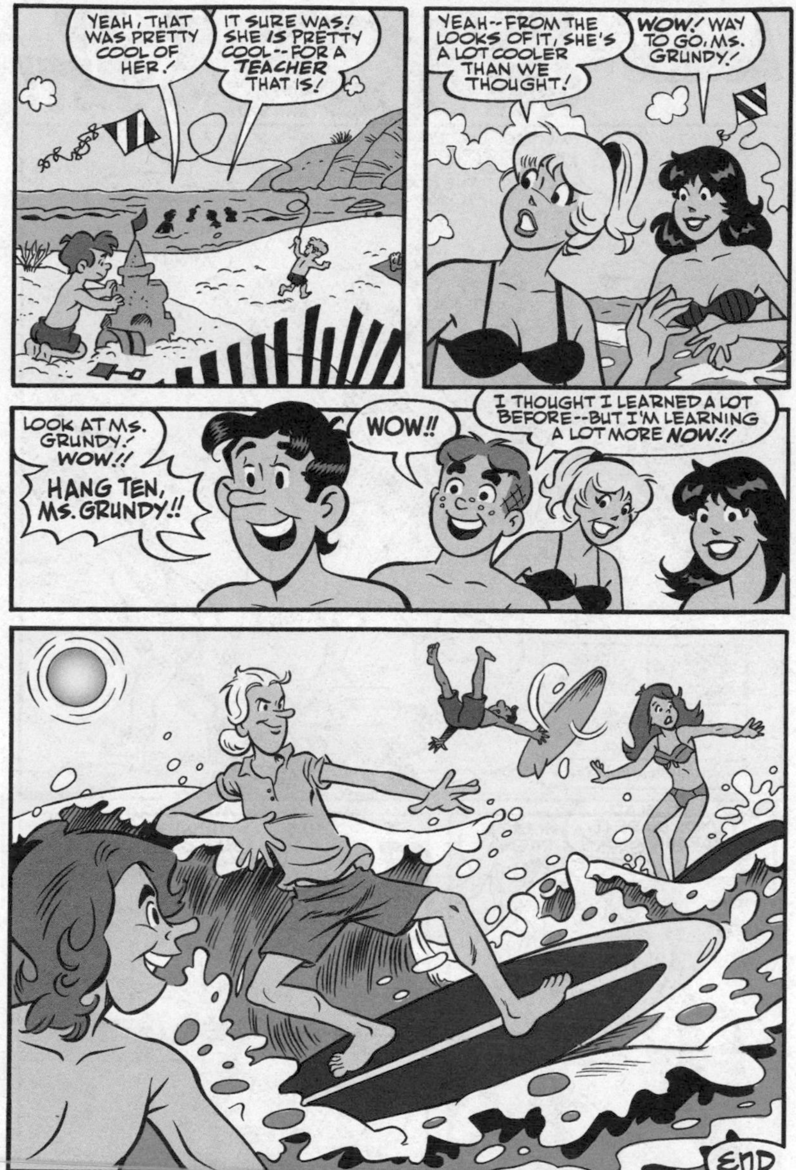
YEAH, THAT WAS PRETTY COOL OF HER!
IT SURE WAS! SHE IS PRETTY COOL--FOR A TEACHER THAT IS!
YEAH--FROM THE LOOKS OF IT, SHE'S A LOT COOLER THAN WE THOUGHT!
WOW! WAY TO GO, MS. GRUNDY!
LOOK AT MS. GRUNDY! WOW!!
HANG TEN, MS. GRUNDY!!
WOW!!
I THOUGHT I LEARNED A LOT BEFORE--BUT I'M LEARNING A LOT MORE NOW!!
END

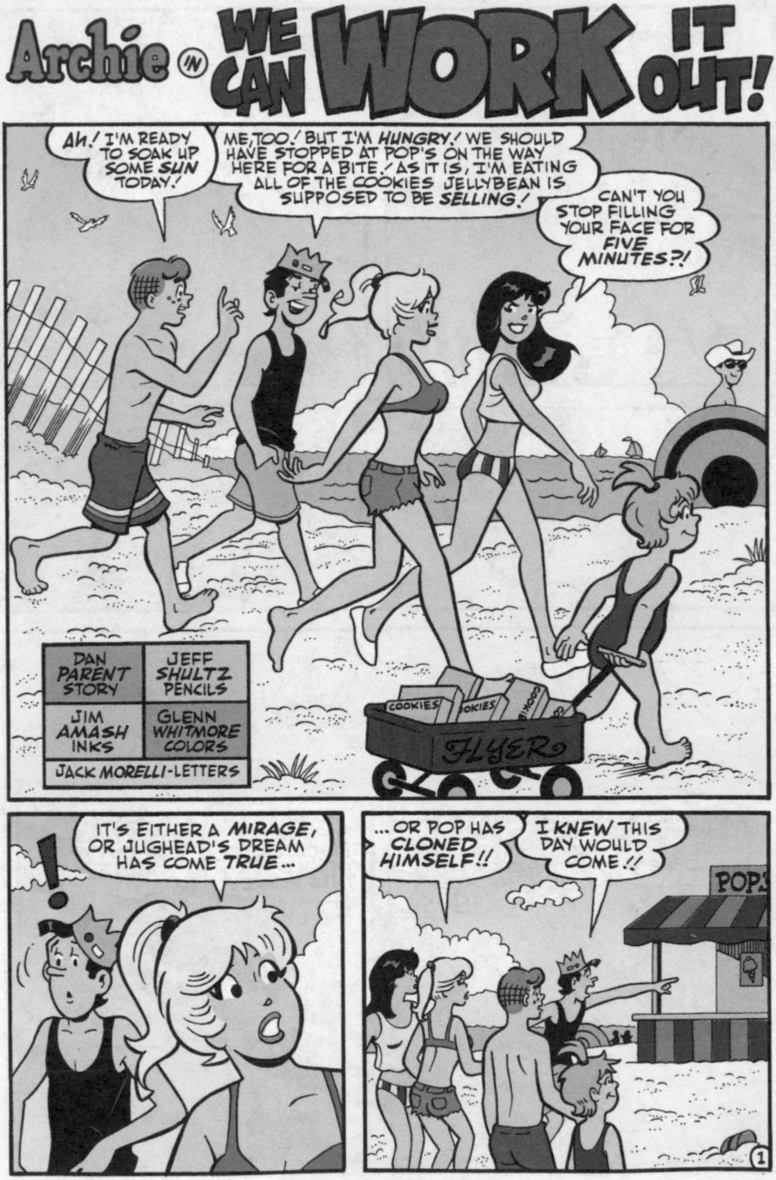
Archie in
WE CAN WORK IT OUT!
Ah! I'M READY TO SOAK UP SOME SUN TODAY!
ME, TOO! BUT I'M HUNGRY! WE SHOULD HAVE STOPPED AT POP'S ON THE WAY HERE FOR A BITE! AS IT IS, I'M EATING ALL OF THE COOKIES JELLYBEAN IS SUPPOSED TO BE SELLING!
CAN'T YOU STOP FILLING YOUR FACE FOR FIVE MINUTES?!
DAN PARENT STORY
JEFF SHULTZ PENCILS
JIM AMASH INKS
GLENN WHITMORE COLORS
JACK MORELLI-LETTERS
COOKIES
FLYER
!
IT'S EITHER A MIRAGE, OR JUGHEAD'S DREAM HAS COME TRUE...
...OR POP HAS CLONED HIMSELF!!
I KNEW THIS DAY WOULD COME!!
POP'S
1

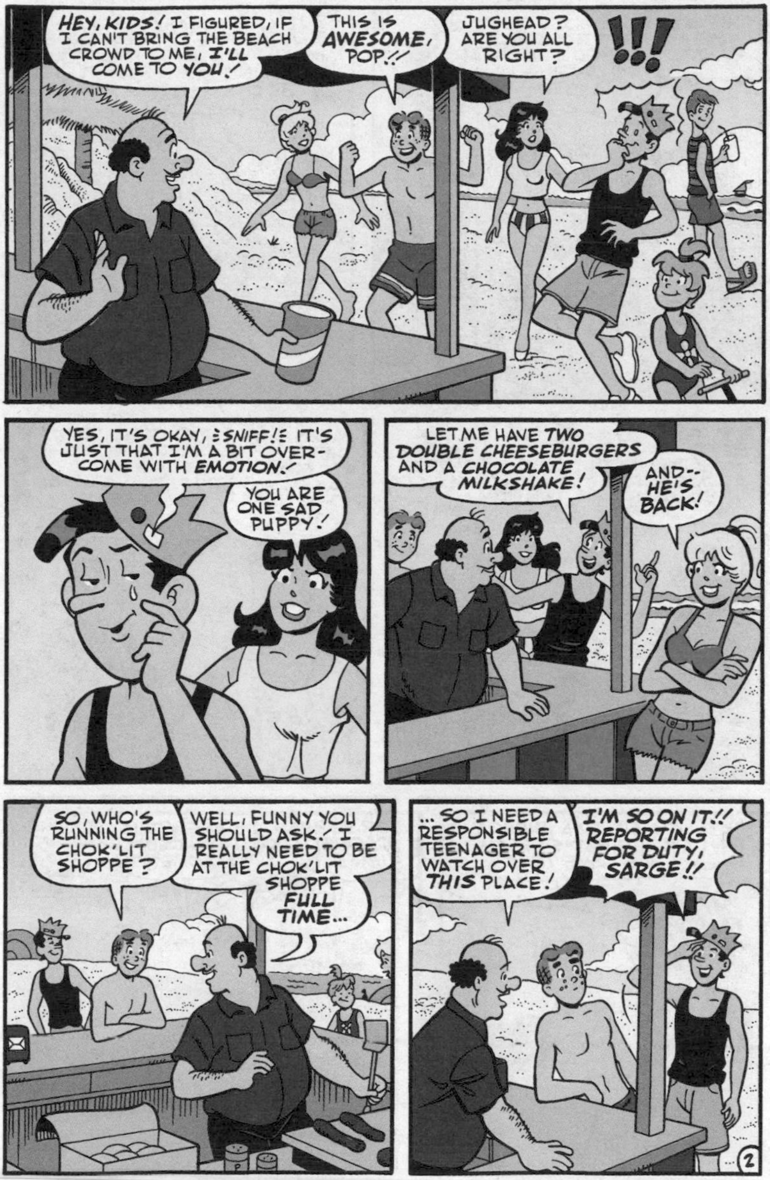
HEY, KIDS! I FIGURED, IF I CAN'T BRING THE BEACH CROWD TO ME, I'LL COME TO YOU!
THIS IS AWESOME, POP!!
JUGHEAD? ARE YOU ALL RIGHT?
!!!
YES, IT'S OKAY, SNIFF! IT'S JUST THAT I'M A BIT OVER-COME WITH EMOTION!
YOU ARE ONE SAD PUPPY!
LET ME HAVE TWO DOUBLE CHEESEBURGERS AND A CHOCOLATE MILKSHAKE!
AND-- HE'S BACK!
SO, WHO'S RUNNING THE CHOK'LIT SHOPPE?
WELL, FUNNY YOU SHOULD ASK! I REALLY NEED TO BE AT THE CHOK'LIT SHOPPE FULL TIME...
... SO I NEED A RESPONSIBLE TEENAGER TO WATCH OVER THIS PLACE!
I'M SO ON IT!! REPORTING FOR DUTY, SARGE!!
...2

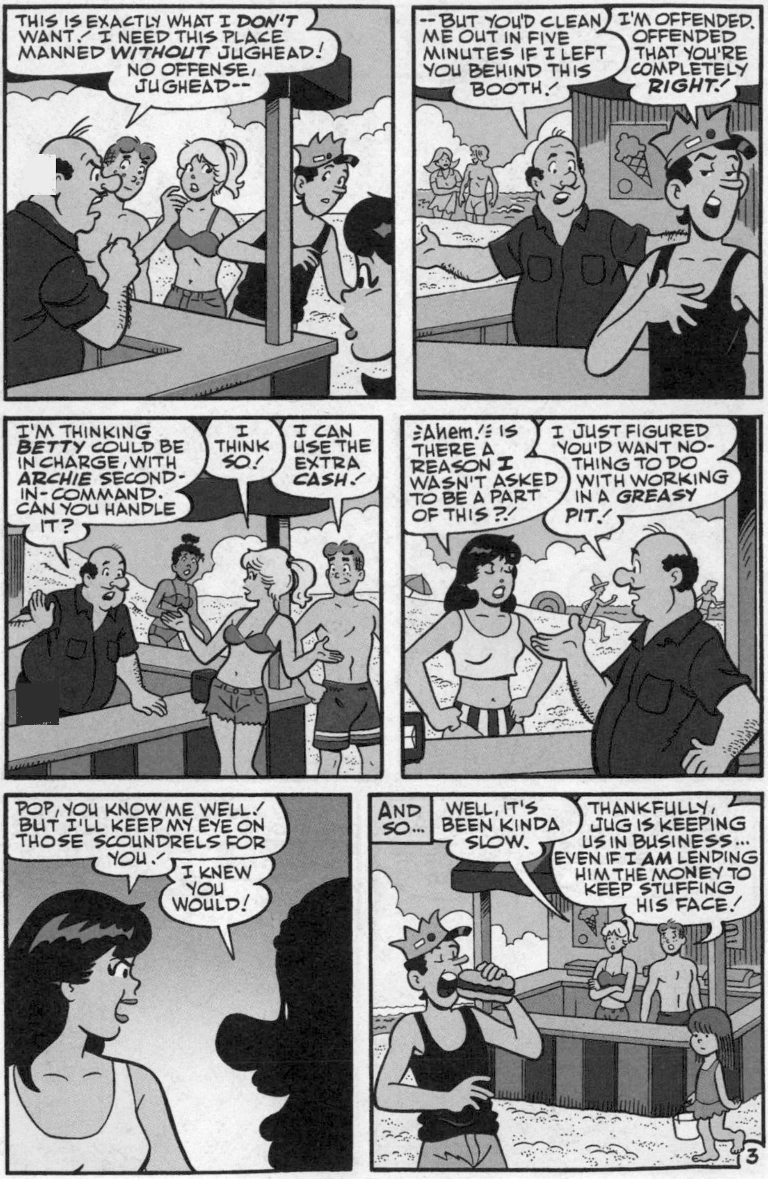
THIS IS EXACTLY WHAT I DON'T WANT.! I NEED THIS PLACE MANNED WITHOUT JUGHEAD!
NO OFFENSE, JUGHEAD--
--BUT YOU'D CLEAN ME OUT IN FIVE MINUTES IF I LEFT YOU BEHIND THIS BOOTH.!
I'M OFFENDED. OFFENDED THAT YOU'RE COMPLETELY RIGHT.!
I'M THINKING BETTY COULD BE IN CHARGE, WITH ARCHIE SECOND-IN-COMMAND. CAN YOU HANDLE IT?
I THINK SO!
I CAN USE THE EXTRA CASH.!
Ahem.! IS THERE A REASON I WASN'T ASKED TO BE A PART OF THIS?!
I JUST FIGURED YOU'D WANT NOTHING TO DO WITH WORKING IN A GREASY PIT.!
POP, YOU KNOW ME WELL.! BUT I'LL KEEP MY EYE ON THOSE SCOUNDRELS FOR YOU.!
I KNEW YOU WOULD!
AND SO...
WELL, IT'S BEEN KINDA SLOW.
THANKFULLY, JUG IS KEEPING US IN BUSINESS... EVEN IF I AM LENDING HIM THE MONEY TO KEEP STUFFING HIS FACE!
3

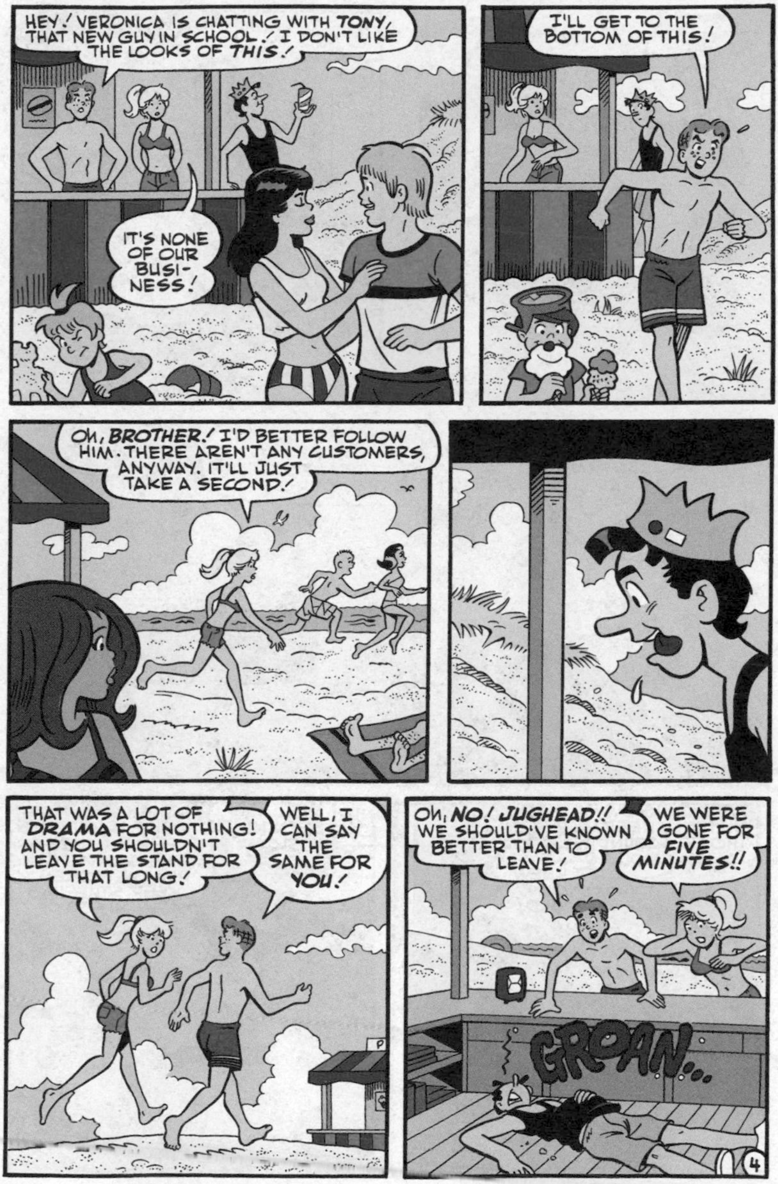
HEY! VERONICA IS CHATTING WITH TONY, THAT NEW GUY IN SCHOOL! I DON'T LIKE THE LOOKS OF THIS!
IT'S NONE OF OUR BUSI- NESS!
I'LL GET TO THE BOTTOM OF THIS!
OH, BROTHER! I'D BETTER FOLLOW HIM. THERE AREN'T ANY CUSTOMERS, ANYWAY. IT'LL JUST TAKE A SECOND!
THAT WAS A LOT OF DRAMA FOR NOTHING! AND YOU SHOULDN'T LEAVE THE STAND FOR THAT LONG!
WELL, I CAN SAY THE SAME FOR YOU!
OH, NO! JUGHEAD!! WE SHOULD'VE KNOWN BETTER THAN TO LEAVE!
WE WERE GONE FOR FIVE MINUTES!!
GROAN...
4

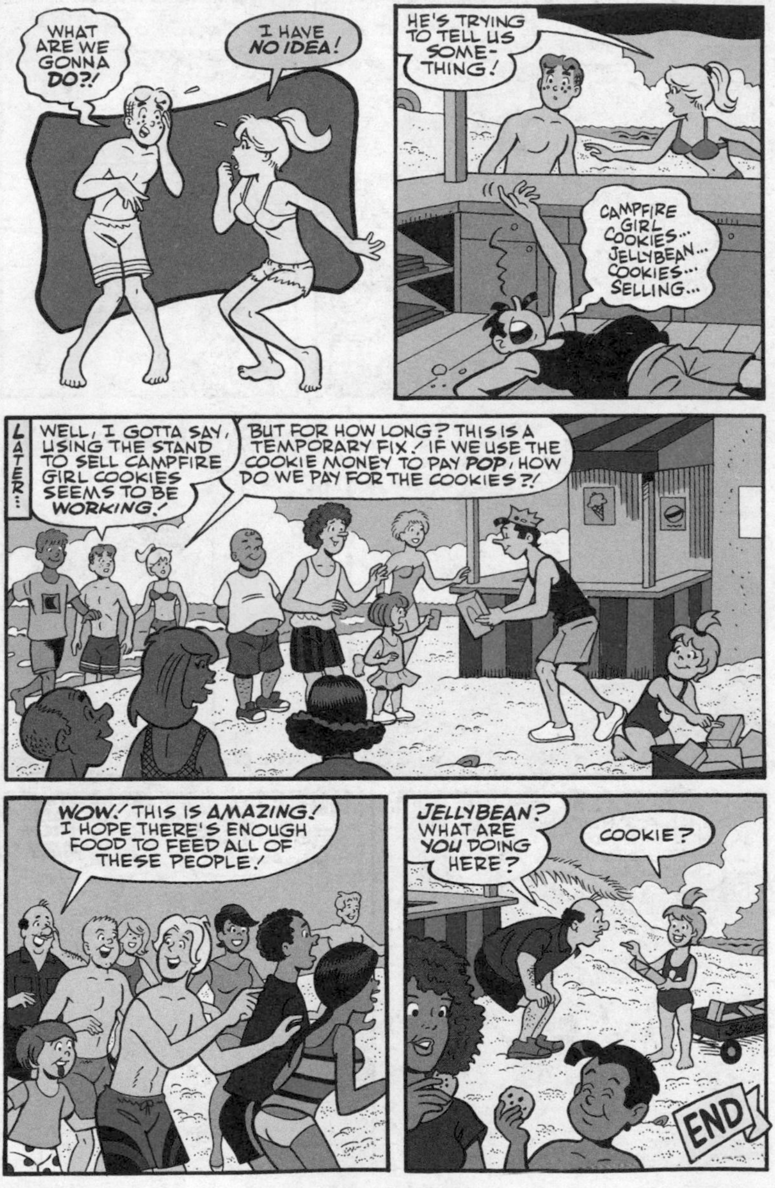

WHAT ARE WE GONNA DO?!
I HAVE NO IDEA!
HE'S TRYING TO TELL US SOME-THING!
CAMPFIRE GIRL COOKIES... JELLYBEAN... COOKIES... SELLING...
LATER...
WELL, I GOTTA SAY, USING THE STAND TO SELL CAMPFIRE GIRL COOKIES SEEMS TO BE WORKING!
BUT FOR HOW LONG? THIS IS A TEMPORARY FIX! IF WE USE THE COOKIE MONEY TO PAY POP, HOW DO WE PAY FOR THE COOKIES?!
WOW! THIS IS AMAZING! I HOPE THERE'S ENOUGH FOOD TO FEED ALL OF THESE PEOPLE!
JELLYBEAN? WHAT ARE YOU DOING HERE?
COOKIE?
END

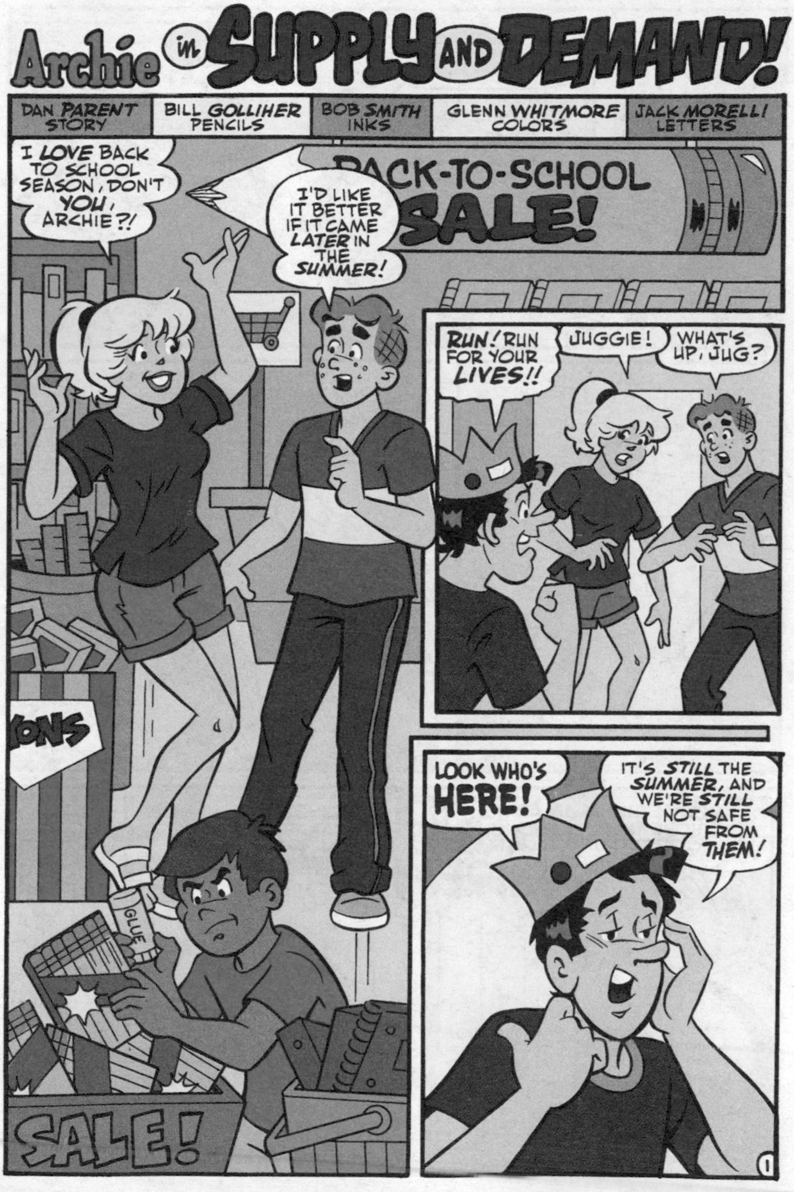
Archie in SUPPLY AND DEMAND!
DAN PARENT STORY
BILL GOLLIHER PENCILS
BOB SMITH INKS
GLENN WHITMORE COLORS
JACK MORELLI LETTERS
BACK-TO-SCHOOL SALE!
I LOVE BACK TO SCHOOL SEASON, DON'T YOU, ARCHIE?!
I'D LIKE IT BETTER IF IT CAME LATER IN THE SUMMER!
GLUE
SALE!
RUN! RUN FOR YOUR LIVES!!
JUGGIE!
WHAT'S UP, JUG?
LOOK WHO'S HERE!
IT'S STILL THE SUMMER, AND WE'RE STILL NOT SAFE FROM THEM!
1

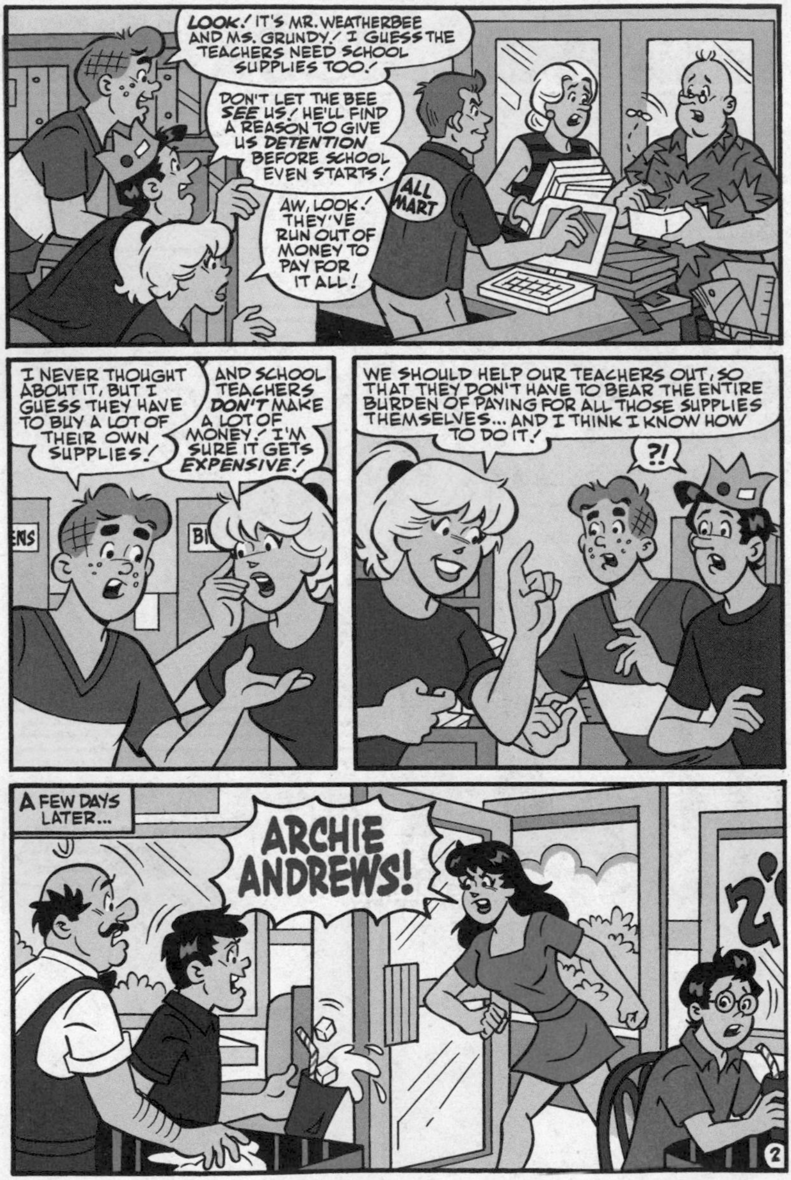
LOOK! IT'S MR. WEATHERBEE AND MS. GRUNDY! I GUESS THE TEACHERS NEED SCHOOL SUPPLIES TOO!
DON'T LET THE BEE SEE US! HE'LL FIND A REASON TO GIVE US DETENTION BEFORE SCHOOL EVEN STARTS!
AW, LOOK! THEY'VE RUN OUT OF MONEY TO PAY FOR IT ALL!
ALL MART
I NEVER THOUGHT ABOUT IT, BUT I GUESS THEY HAVE TO BUY A LOT OF THEIR OWN SUPPLIES!
AND SCHOOL TEACHERS DON'T MAKE A LOT OF MONEY! I'M SURE IT GETS EXPENSIVE!
WE SHOULD HELP OUR TEACHERS OUT, SO THAT THEY DON'T HAVE TO BEAR THE ENTIRE BURDEN OF PAYING FOR ALL THOSE SUPPLIES THEMSELVES... AND I THINK I KNOW HOW TO DO IT!
?!
A FEW DAYS LATER...
ARCHIE ANDREWS!
2

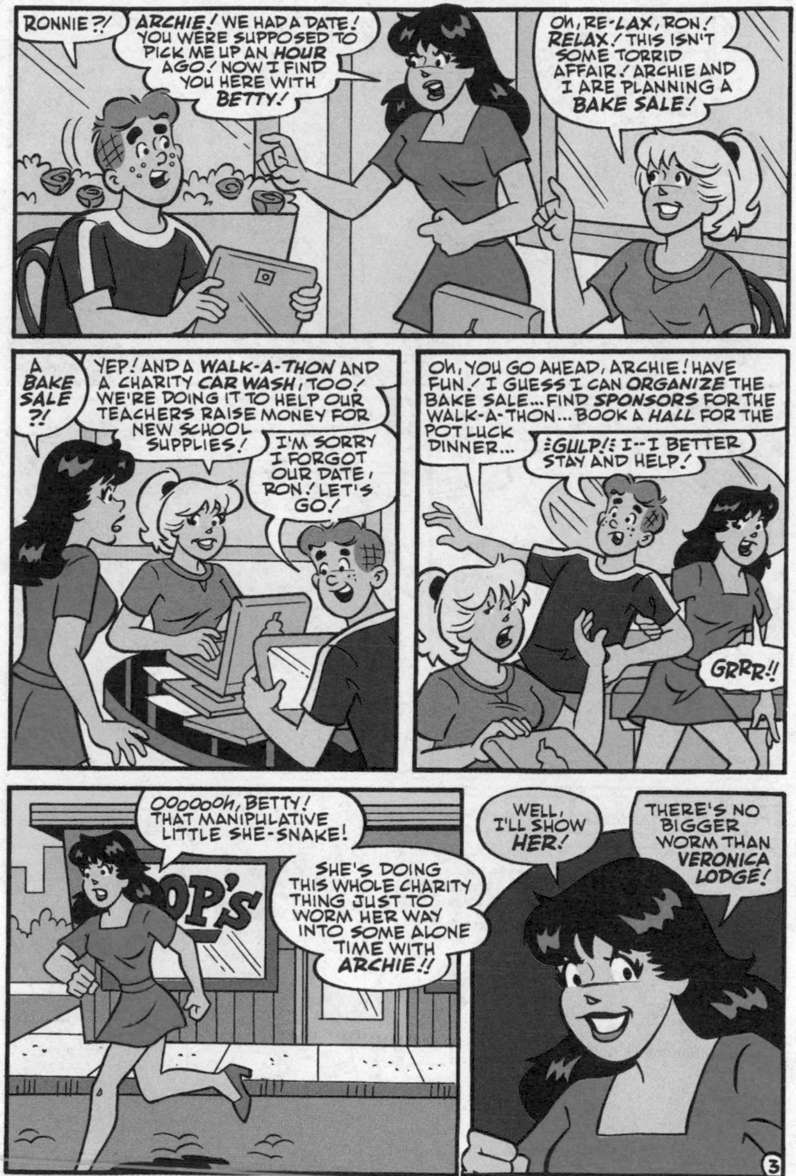
RONNIE?!
ARCHIE! WE HAD A DATE! YOU WERE SUPPOSED TO PICK ME UP AN HOUR AGO! NOW I FIND YOU HERE WITH BETTY!
OH, RE-LAX, RON! RELAX! THIS ISN'T SOME TORRID AFFAIR! ARCHIE AND I ARE PLANNING A BAKE SALE!
A BAKE SALE?!
YEP! AND A WALK-A-THON AND A CHARITY CAR WASH, TOO! WE'RE DOING IT TO HELP OUR TEACHERS RAISE MONEY FOR NEW SCHOOL SUPPLIES!
I'M SORRY I FORGOT OUR DATE, RON! LET'S GO!
OH, YOU GO AHEAD, ARCHIE! HAVE FUN! I GUESS I CAN ORGANIZE THE BAKE SALE... FIND SPONSORS FOR THE WALK-A-THON... BOOK A HALL FOR THE POT LUCK DINNER...
GULP! I--I BETTER STAY AND HELP!
GRRR!!
OOOOOOH, BETTY! THAT MANIPULATIVE LITTLE SHE-SNAKE!
SHE'S DOING THIS WHOLE CHARITY THING JUST TO WORM HER WAY INTO SOME ALONE TIME WITH ARCHIE!!
WELL, I'LL SHOW HER!
THERE'S NO BIGGER WORM THAN VERONICA LODGE!
3

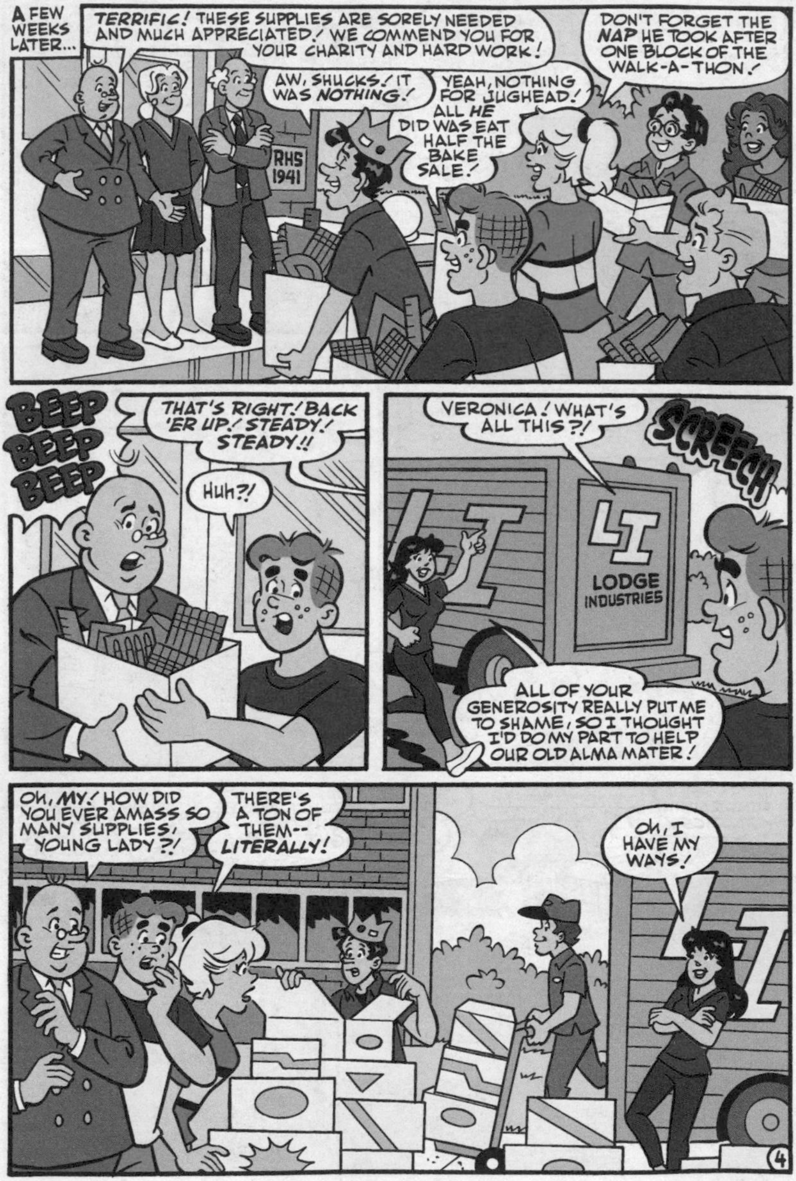
A FEW WEEKS LATER...
TERRIFIC! THESE SUPPLIES ARE SORELY NEEDED AND MUCH APPRECIATED! WE COMMEND YOU FOR YOUR CHARITY AND HARD WORK!
AW, SHUCKS! IT WAS NOTHING!
YEAH, NOTHING FOR JUGHEAD! ALL HE DID WAS EAT HALF THE BAKE SALE!
DON'T FORGET THE NAP HE TOOK AFTER ONE BLOCK OF THE WALK-A-THON!
RHS 1941
BEEP BEEP BEEP
THAT'S RIGHT! BACK 'ER UP! STEADY! STEADY!!
Huh?!
VERONICA! WHAT'S ALL THIS?!
SCREECH
LI
LODGE INDUSTRIES
ALL OF YOUR GENEROSITY REALLY PUT ME TO SHAME, SO I THOUGHT I'D DO MY PART TO HELP OUR OLD ALMA MATER!
Oh, MY! HOW DID YOU EVER AMASS SO MANY SUPPLIES, YOUNG LADY?!
THERE'S A TON OF THEM-- LITERALLY!
Oh, I HAVE MY WAYS!
4

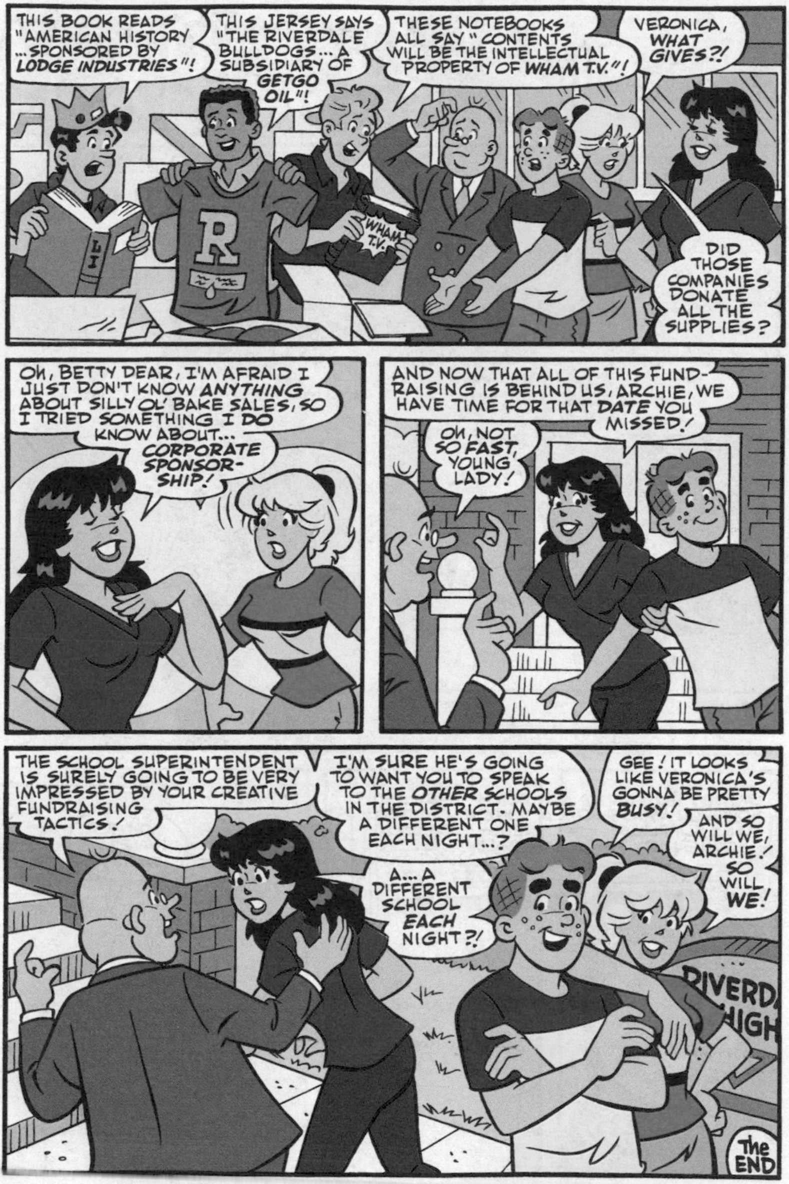
THIS BOOK READS "AMERICAN HISTORY ...SPONSORED BY LODGE INDUSTRIES"!
THIS JERSEY SAYS "THE RIVERDALE BULLDOGS... A SUBSIDIARY OF GETGO OIL"!
THESE NOTEBOOKS ALL SAY "CONTENTS WILL BE THE INTELLECTUAL PROPERTY OF WHAM T.V."!
VERONICA, WHAT GIVES?!
WHAM T.V.
DID THOSE COMPANIES DONATE ALL THE SUPPLIES?
OH, BETTY DEAR, I'M AFRAID I JUST DON'T KNOW ANYTHING ABOUT SILLY OL' BAKE SALES, SO I TRIED SOMETHING I DO KNOW ABOUT... CORPORATE SPONSORSHIP!
AND NOW THAT ALL OF THIS FUND-RAISING IS BEHIND US, ARCHIE, WE HAVE TIME FOR THAT DATE YOU MISSED!
OH, NOT SO FAST, YOUNG LADY!
THE SCHOOL SUPERINTENDENT IS SURELY GOING TO BE VERY IMPRESSED BY YOUR CREATIVE FUNDRAISING TACTICS!
I'M SURE HE'S GOING TO WANT YOU TO SPEAK TO THE OTHER SCHOOLS IN THE DISTRICT. MAYBE A DIFFERENT ONE EACH NIGHT...?
A... A DIFFERENT SCHOOL EACH NIGHT?!
GEE! IT LOOKS LIKE VERONICA'S GONNA BE PRETTY BUSY!
AND SO WILL WE, ARCHIE! SO WILL WE!
RIVERDA HIGH
The END

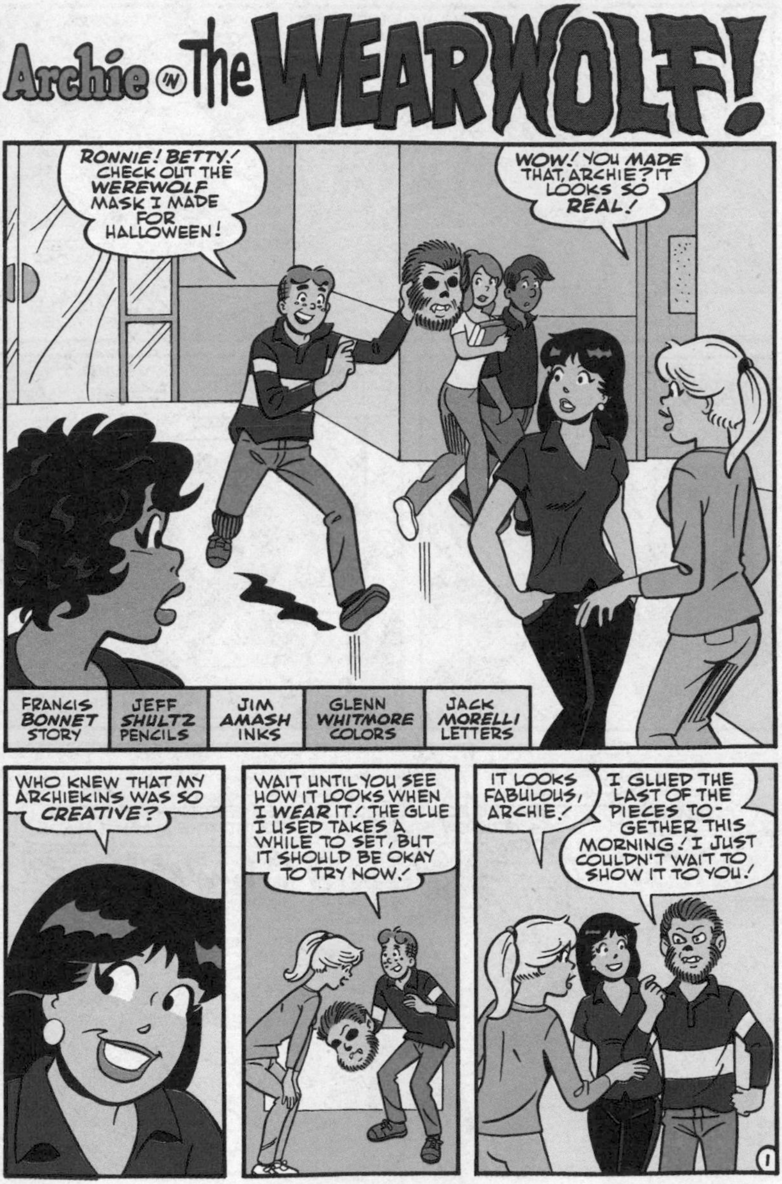
Archie in The WEARWOLF!
RONNIE! BETTY! CHECK OUT THE WEREWOLF MASK I MADE FOR HALLOWEEN!
WOW! YOU MADE THAT, ARCHIE? IT LOOKS SO REAL!
FRANCIS BONNET STORY
JEFF SHULTZ PENCILS
JIM AMASH INKS
GLENN WHITMORE COLORS
JACK MORELLI LETTERS
WHO KNEW THAT MY ARCHIEKINS WAS SO CREATIVE?
WAIT UNTIL YOU SEE HOW IT LOOKS WHEN I WEAR IT! THE GLUE I USED TAKES A WHILE TO SET, BUT IT SHOULD BE OKAY TO TRY NOW!
IT LOOKS FABULOUS, ARCHIE!
I GLUED THE LAST OF THE PIECES TO-GETHER THIS MORNING! I JUST COULDN'T WAIT TO SHOW IT TO YOU!
1

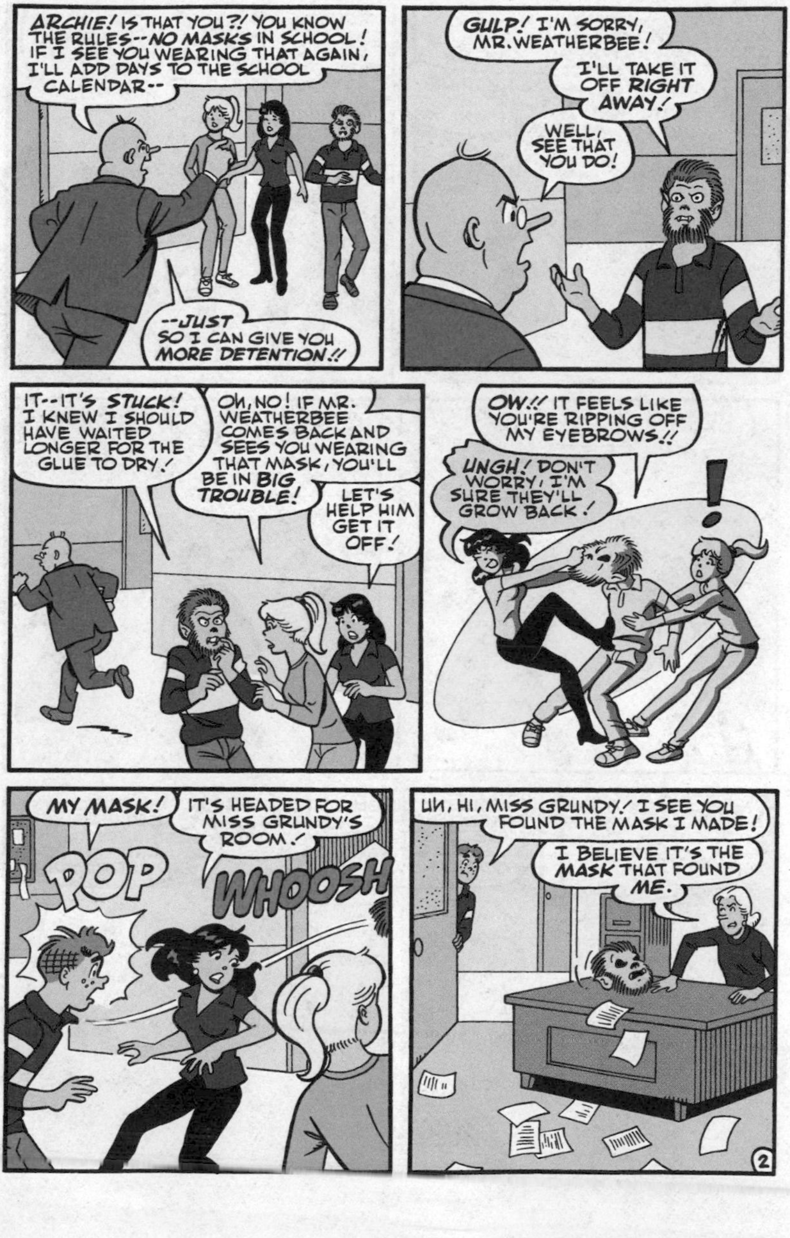
ARCHIE! IS THAT YOU?! YOU KNOW THE RULES--NO MASKS IN SCHOOL! IF I SEE YOU WEARING THAT AGAIN, I'LL ADD DAYS TO THE SCHOOL CALENDAR--
--JUST SO I CAN GIVE YOU MORE DETENTION!!
GULP! I'M SORRY, MR. WEATHERBEE!
I'LL TAKE IT OFF RIGHT AWAY!
WELL, SEE THAT YOU DO!
IT--IT'S STUCK! I KNEW I SHOULD HAVE WAITED LONGER FOR THE GLUE TO DRY!
OH, NO! IF MR. WEATHERBEE COMES BACK AND SEES YOU WEARING THAT MASK, YOU'LL BE IN BIG TROUBLE!
LET'S HELP HIM GET IT OFF!
OW!! IT FEELS LIKE YOU'RE RIPPING OFF MY EYEBROWS!!
UNGH! DON'T WORRY, I'M SURE THEY'LL GROW BACK!
!
MY MASK!
IT'S HEADED FOR MISS GRUNDY'S ROOM!
POP
WHOOSH
UH, HI, MISS GRUNDY! I SEE YOU FOUND THE MASK I MADE!
I BELIEVE IT'S THE MASK THAT FOUND ME.
2

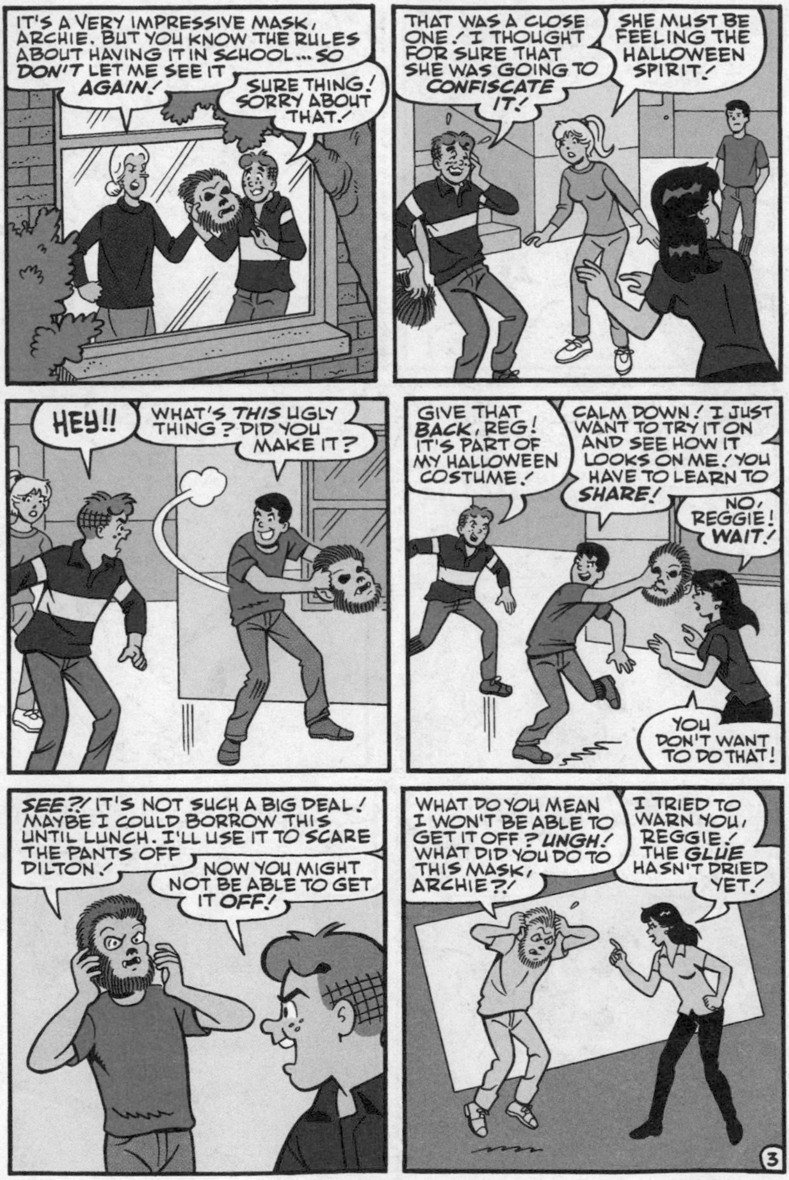
IT'S A VERY IMPRESSIVE MASK, ARCHIE. BUT YOU KNOW THE RULES ABOUT HAVING IT IN SCHOOL... SO DON'T LET ME SEE IT AGAIN!
SURE THING! SORRY ABOUT THAT!
THAT WAS A CLOSE ONE! I THOUGHT FOR SURE THAT SHE WAS GOING TO CONFISCATE IT!
SHE MUST BE FEELING THE HALLOWEEN SPIRIT!
HEY!!
WHAT'S THIS UGLY THING? DID YOU MAKE IT?
GIVE THAT BACK, REG! IT'S PART OF MY HALLOWEEN COSTUME!
CALM DOWN! I JUST WANT TO TRY IT ON AND SEE HOW IT LOOKS ON ME! YOU HAVE TO LEARN TO SHARE!
NO, REGGIE! WAIT!
YOU DON'T WANT TO DO THAT!
SEE?! IT'S NOT SUCH A BIG DEAL! MAYBE I COULD BORROW THIS UNTIL LUNCH. I'LL USE IT TO SCARE THE PANTS OFF DILTON!
NOW YOU MIGHT NOT BE ABLE TO GET IT OFF!
WHAT DO YOU MEAN I WON'T BE ABLE TO GET IT OFF? UNGH! WHAT DID YOU DO TO THIS MASK, ARCHIE?!
I TRIED TO WARN YOU, REGGIE! THE GLUE HASN'T DRIED YET!
3

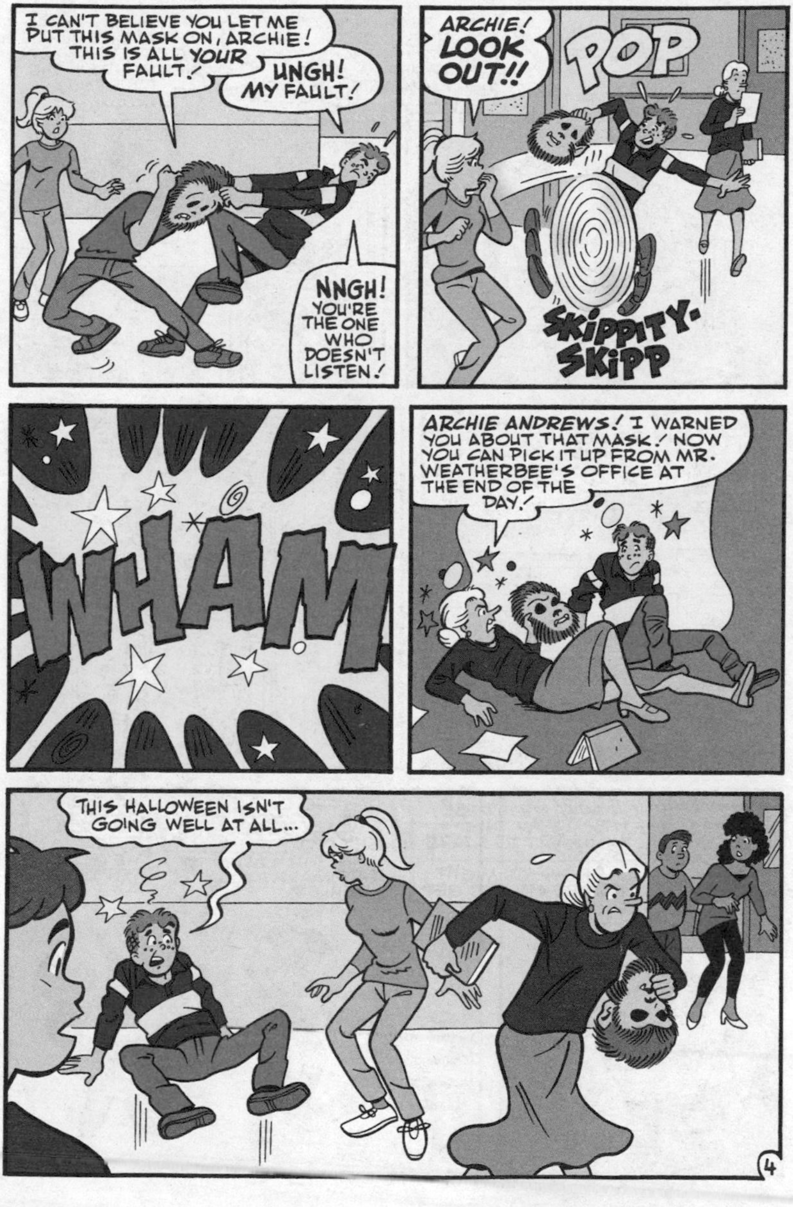

I CAN'T BELIEVE YOU LET ME PUT THIS MASK ON, ARCHIE! THIS IS ALL YOUR FAULT!
UNGH! MY FAULT!
NNGH! YOU'RE THE ONE WHO DOESN'T LISTEN!
ARCHIE! LOOK OUT!!
POP
SKIPPITY-SKIPP
WHAM
ARCHIE ANDREWS! I WARNED YOU ABOUT THAT MASK! NOW YOU CAN PICK IT UP FROM MR. WEATHERBEE'S OFFICE AT THE END OF THE DAY!
THIS HALLOWEEN ISN'T GOING WELL AT ALL...
4

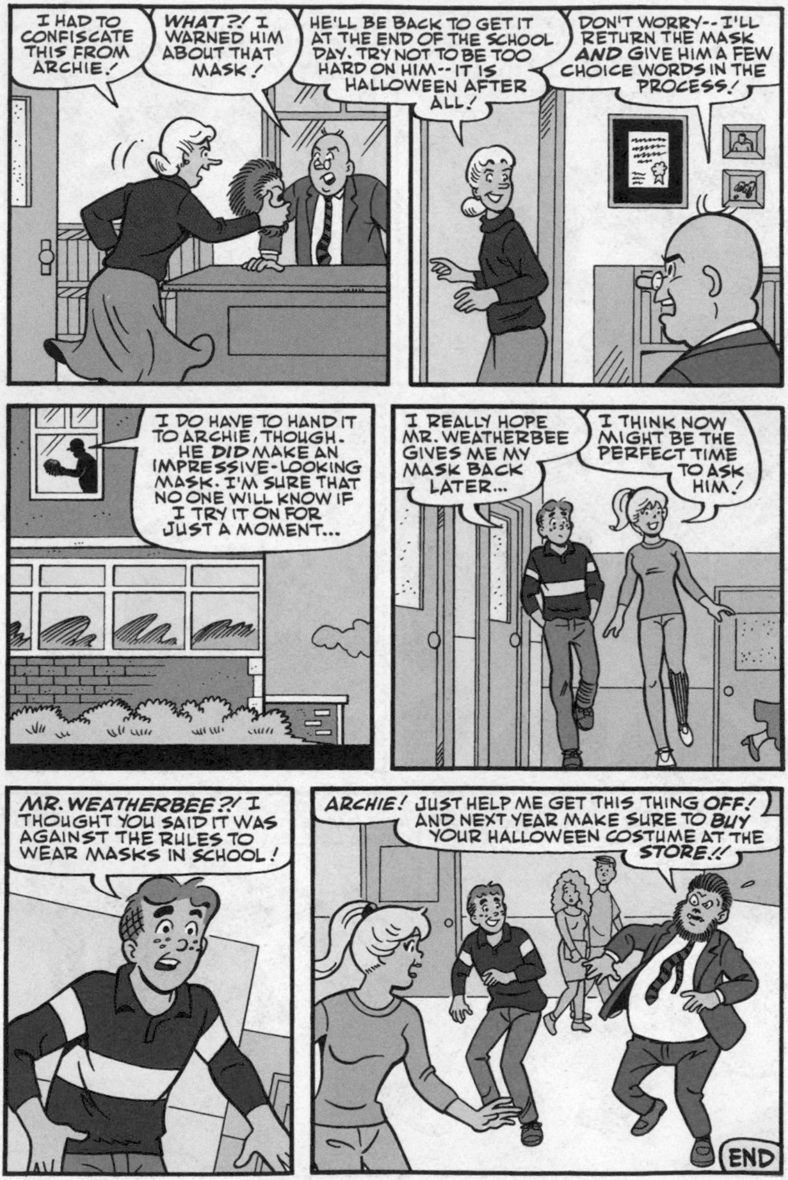
I HAD TO CONFISCATE THIS FROM ARCHIE!
WHAT?! I WARNED HIM ABOUT THAT MASK!
HE'LL BE BACK TO GET IT AT THE END OF THE SCHOOL DAY. TRY NOT TO BE TOO HARD ON HIM-- IT IS HALLOWEEN AFTER ALL!
DON'T WORRY-- I'LL RETURN THE MASK AND GIVE HIM A FEW CHOICE WORDS IN THE PROCESS!
I DO HAVE TO HAND IT TO ARCHIE, THOUGH. HE DID MAKE AN IMPRESSIVE-LOOKING MASK. I'M SURE THAT NO ONE WILL KNOW IF I TRY IT ON FOR JUST A MOMENT...
I REALLY HOPE MR. WEATHERBEE GIVES ME MY MASK BACK LATER...
I THINK NOW MIGHT BE THE PERFECT TIME TO ASK HIM!
MR. WEATHERBEE?! I THOUGHT YOU SAID IT WAS AGAINST THE RULES TO WEAR MASKS IN SCHOOL!
ARCHIE! JUST HELP ME GET THIS THING OFF! AND NEXT YEAR MAKE SURE TO BUY YOUR HALLOWEEN COSTUME AT THE STORE!!
END

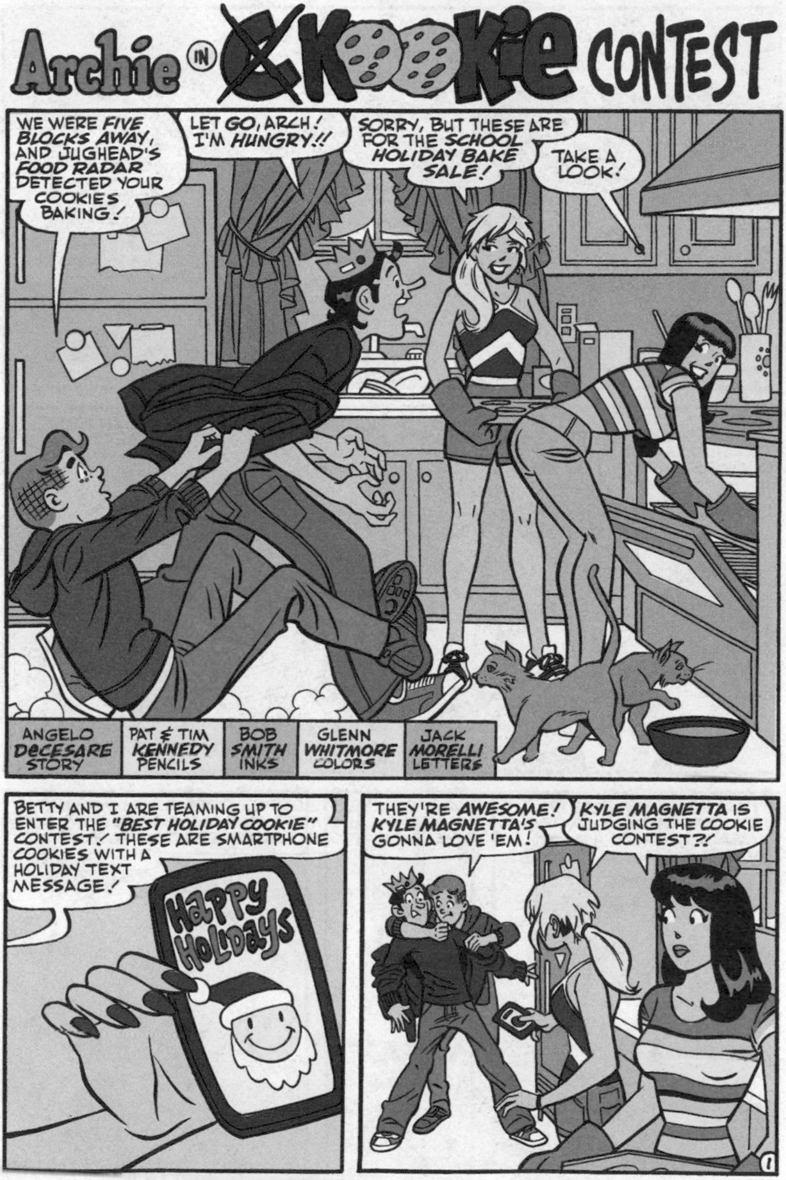
Archie IN ~~C~~KooKie CONTEST
WE WERE FIVE BLOCKS AWAY, AND JUGHEAD'S FOOD RADAR DETECTED YOUR COOKIES BAKING!
LET GO, ARCH! I'M HUNGRY!!
SORRY, BUT THESE ARE FOR THE SCHOOL HOLIDAY BAKE SALE!
TAKE A LOOK!
ANGELO DECESARE STORY
PAT & TIM KENNEDY PENCILS
BOB SMITH INKS
GLENN WHITMORE COLORS
JACK MORELLI LETTERS
BETTY AND I ARE TEAMING UP TO ENTER THE "BEST HOLIDAY COOKIE" CONTEST! THESE ARE SMARTPHONE COOKIES WITH A HOLIDAY TEXT MESSAGE!
Happy Holidays
THEY'RE AWESOME! KYLE MAGNETTA'S GONNA LOVE 'EM!
KYLE MAGNETTA IS JUDGING THE COOKIE CONTEST?!
1

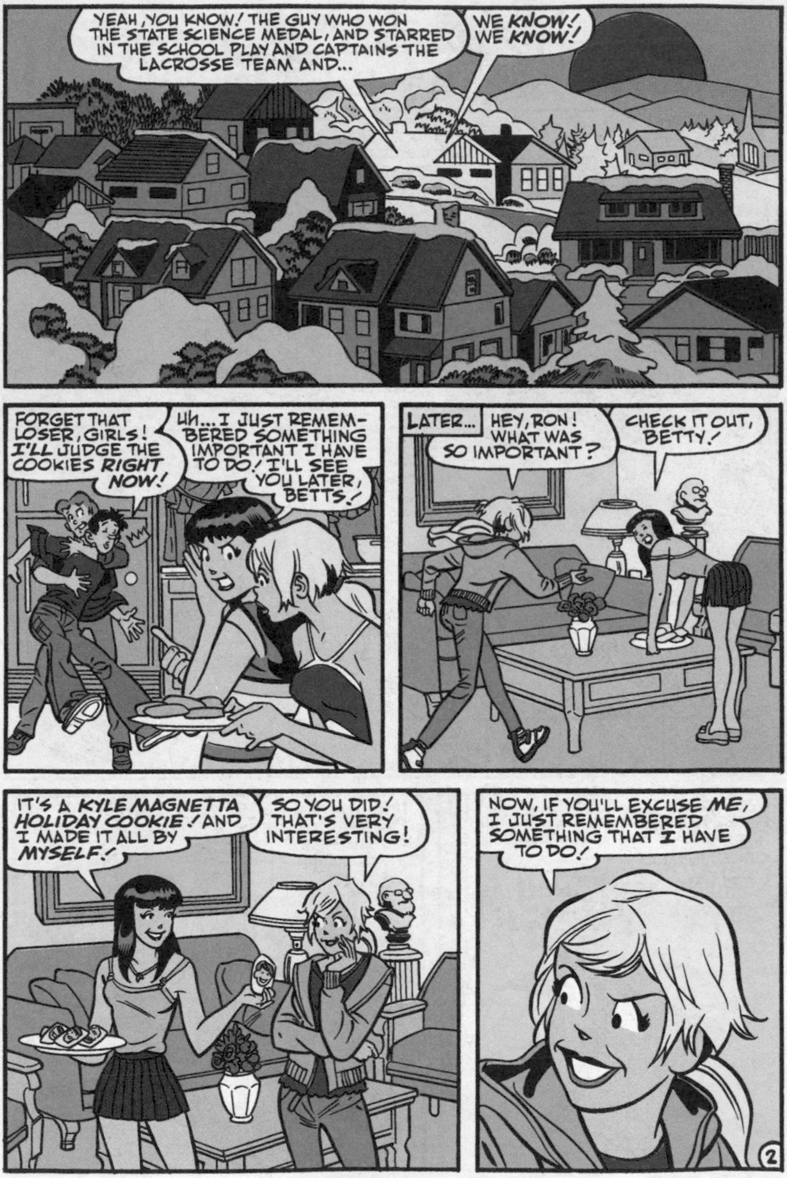
YEAH, YOU KNOW! THE GUY WHO WON THE STATE SCIENCE MEDAL, AND STARRED IN THE SCHOOL PLAY AND CAPTAINS THE LACROSSE TEAM AND...
WE KNOW! WE KNOW!
FORGET THAT LOSER, GIRLS! I'LL JUDGE THE COOKIES RIGHT NOW!
UH... I JUST REMEMBERED SOMETHING IMPORTANT I HAVE TO DO! I'LL SEE YOU LATER, BETTS!
LATER...
HEY, RON! WHAT WAS SO IMPORTANT?
CHECK IT OUT, BETTY!
IT'S A KYLE MAGNETTA HOLIDAY COOKIE! AND I MADE IT ALL BY MYSELF!
SO YOU DID! THAT'S VERY INTERESTING!
NOW, IF YOU'LL EXCUSE ME, I JUST REMEMBERED SOMETHING THAT I HAVE TO DO!
2

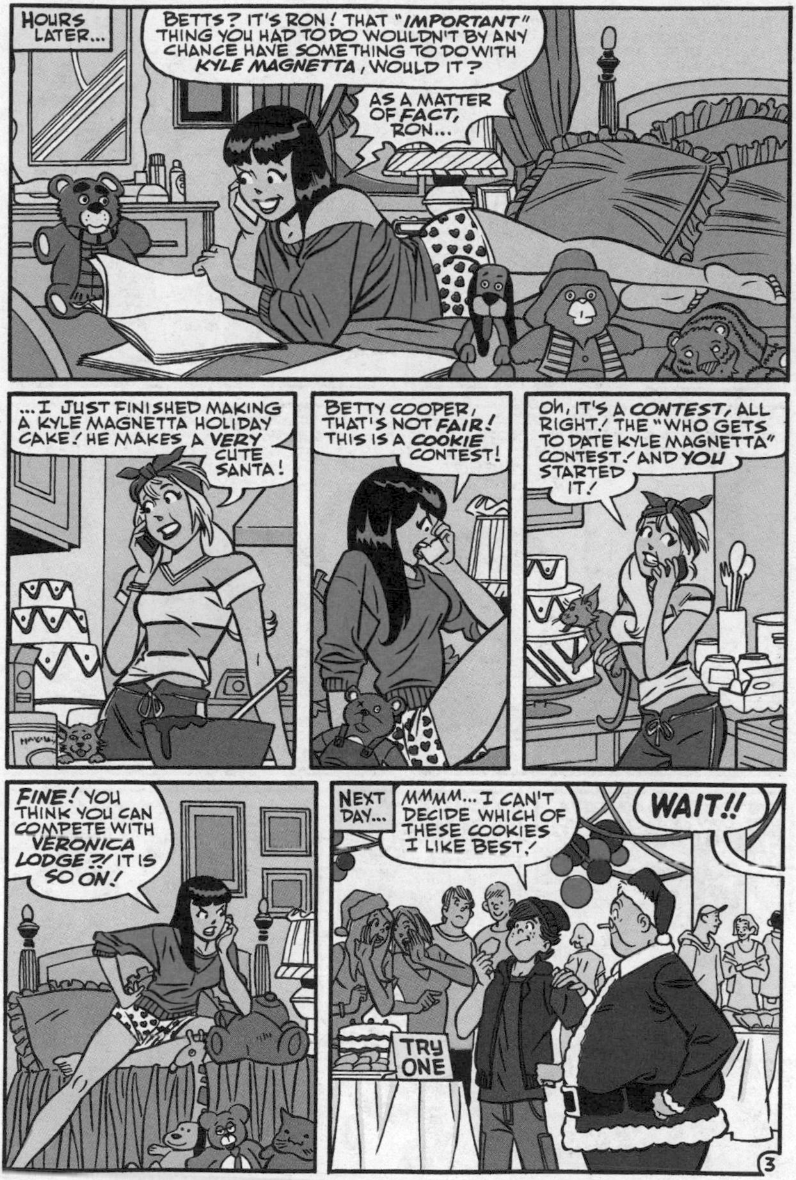
HOURS LATER...
BETTS? IT'S RON! THAT "IMPORTANT" THING YOU HAD TO DO WOULDN'T BY ANY CHANCE HAVE SOMETHING TO DO WITH KYLE MAGNETTA, WOULD IT?
AS A MATTER OF FACT, RON...
...I JUST FINISHED MAKING A KYLE MAGNETTA HOLIDAY CAKE! HE MAKES A VERY CUTE SANTA!
BETTY COOPER, THAT'S NOT FAIR! THIS IS A COOKIE CONTEST!
OH, IT'S A CONTEST, ALL RIGHT! THE "WHO GETS TO DATE KYLE MAGNETTA" CONTEST! AND YOU STARTED IT!
FINE! YOU THINK YOU CAN COMPETE WITH VERONICA LODGE?! IT IS SO ON!
NEXT DAY...
MMMM... I CAN'T DECIDE WHICH OF THESE COOKIES I LIKE BEST!
WAIT!!
TRY ONE
3

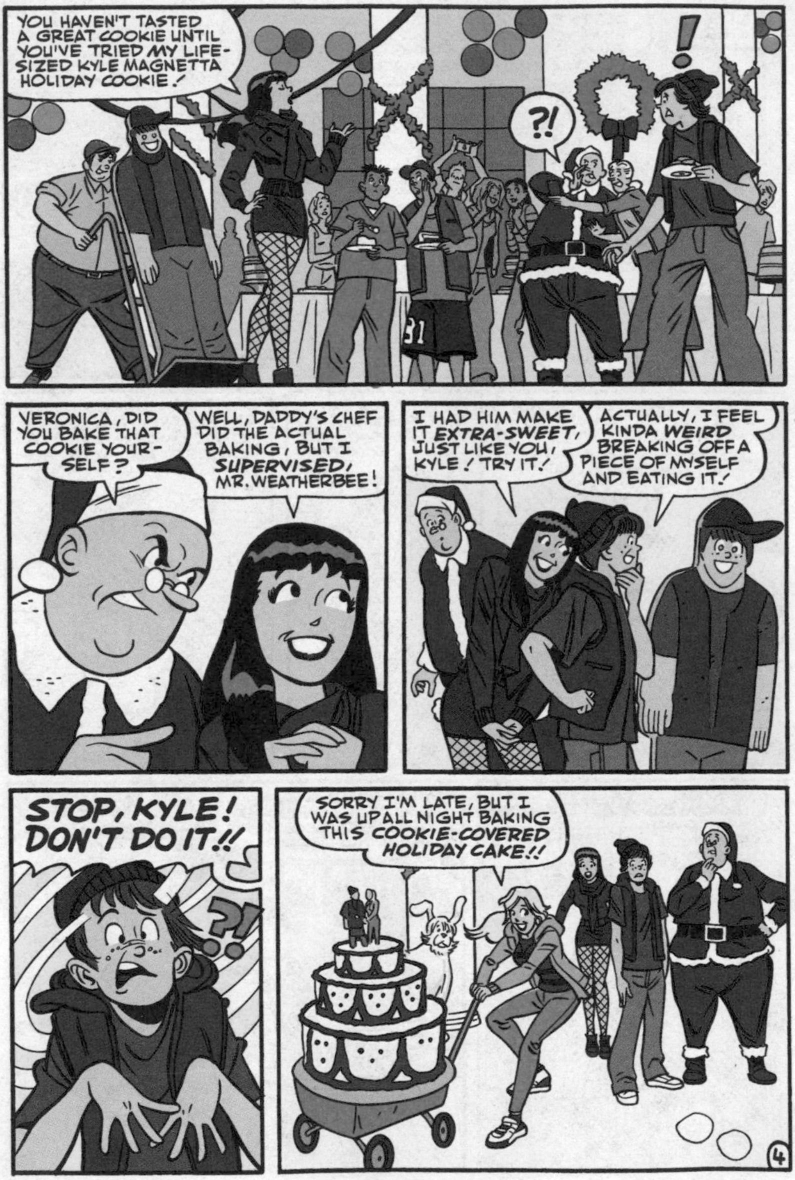
YOU HAVEN'T TASTED A GREAT COOKIE UNTIL YOU'VE TRIED MY LIFE-SIZED KYLE MAGNETTA HOLIDAY COOKIE!
?!
!
VERONICA, DID YOU BAKE THAT COOKIE YOURSELF?
WELL, DADDY'S CHEF DID THE ACTUAL BAKING, BUT I SUPERVISED, MR. WEATHERBEE!
I HAD HIM MAKE IT EXTRA-SWEET, JUST LIKE YOU, KYLE! TRY IT!
ACTUALLY, I FEEL KINDA WEIRD BREAKING OFF A PIECE OF MYSELF AND EATING IT!
STOP, KYLE! DON'T DO IT!!
?!
SORRY I'M LATE, BUT I WAS UP ALL NIGHT BAKING THIS COOKIE-COVERED HOLIDAY CAKE!!
4

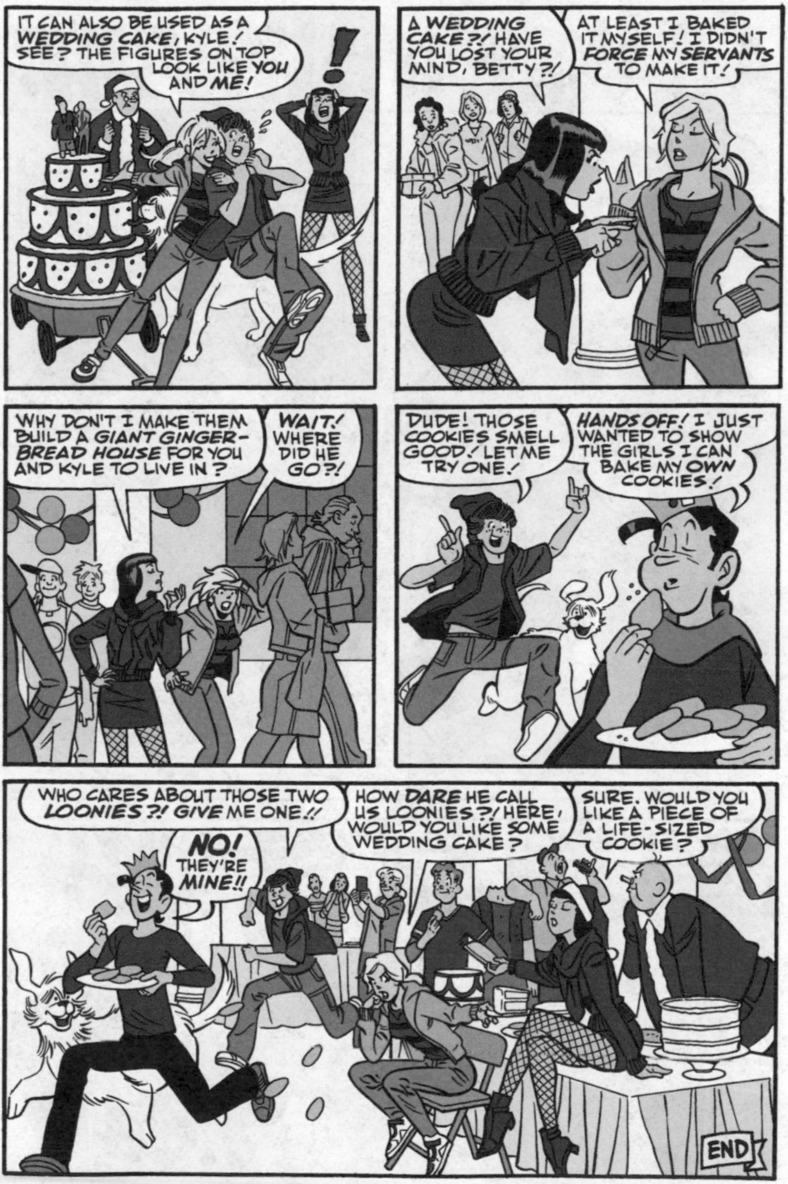
IT CAN ALSO BE USED AS A WEDDING CAKE, KYLE! SEE? THE FIGURES ON TOP LOOK LIKE YOU AND ME!
!
A WEDDING CAKE?! HAVE YOU LOST YOUR MIND, BETTY?!
AT LEAST I BAKED IT MYSELF! I DIDN'T FORCE MY SERVANTS TO MAKE IT!
WHY DON'T I MAKE THEM BUILD A GIANT GINGER-BREAD HOUSE FOR YOU AND KYLE TO LIVE IN?
WAIT! WHERE DID HE GO?!
DUDE! THOSE COOKIES SMELL GOOD! LET ME TRY ONE!
HANDS OFF! I JUST WANTED TO SHOW THE GIRLS I CAN BAKE MY OWN COOKIES!
WHO CARES ABOUT THOSE TWO LOONIES?! GIVE ME ONE!!
NO! THEY'RE MINE!!
HOW DARE HE CALL US LOONIES?! HERE, WOULD YOU LIKE SOME WEDDING CAKE?
SURE. WOULD YOU LIKE A PIECE OF A LIFE-SIZED COOKIE?
END

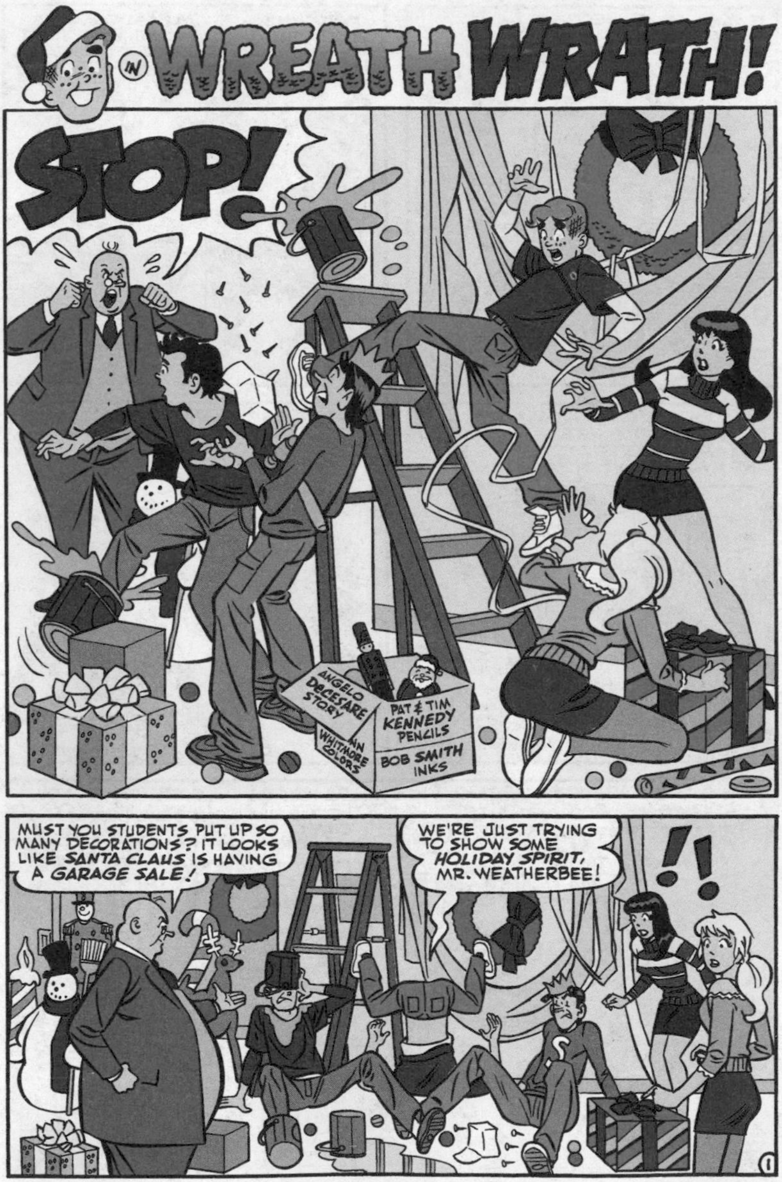

IN
WREATH WRATH!
STOP!
ANGELO DECESARE STORY
PAT & TIM KENNEDY PENCILS
BOB SMITH INKS
ANN WHITMORE COLORS
MUST YOU STUDENTS PUT UP SO MANY DECORATIONS? IT LOOKS LIKE SANTA CLAUS IS HAVING A GARAGE SALE!
WE'RE JUST TRYING TO SHOW SOME HOLIDAY SPIRIT, MR. WEATHERBEE!
!!
1

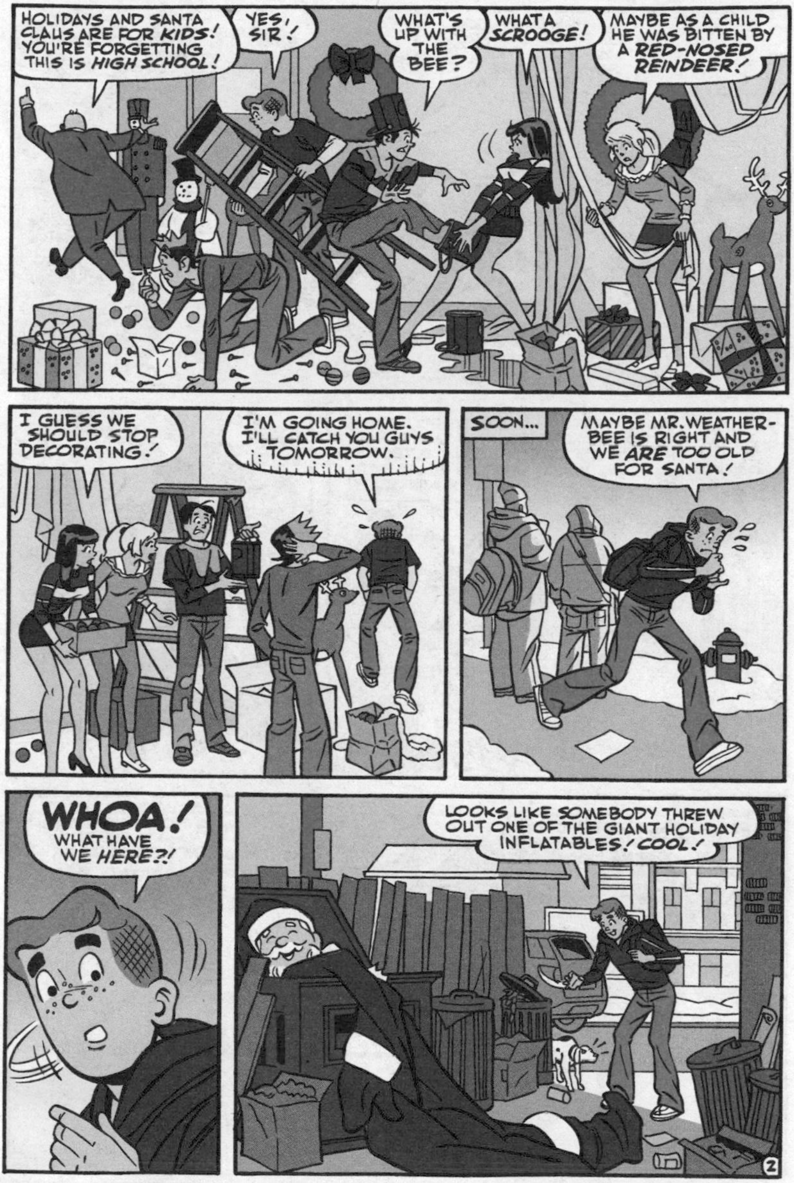
HOLIDAYS AND SANTA CLAUS ARE FOR KIDS! YOU'RE FORGETTING THIS IS HIGH SCHOOL!
YES, SIR!
WHAT'S UP WITH THE BEE?
WHAT A SCROOGE!
MAYBE AS A CHILD HE WAS BITTEN BY A RED-NOSED REINDEER!
I GUESS WE SHOULD STOP DECORATING!
I'M GOING HOME. I'LL CATCH YOU GUYS TOMORROW.
SOON...
MAYBE MR. WEATHERBEE IS RIGHT AND WE ARE TOO OLD FOR SANTA!
WHOA! WHAT HAVE WE HERE?!
LOOKS LIKE SOMEBODY THREW OUT ONE OF THE GIANT HOLIDAY INFLATABLES! COOL!
2

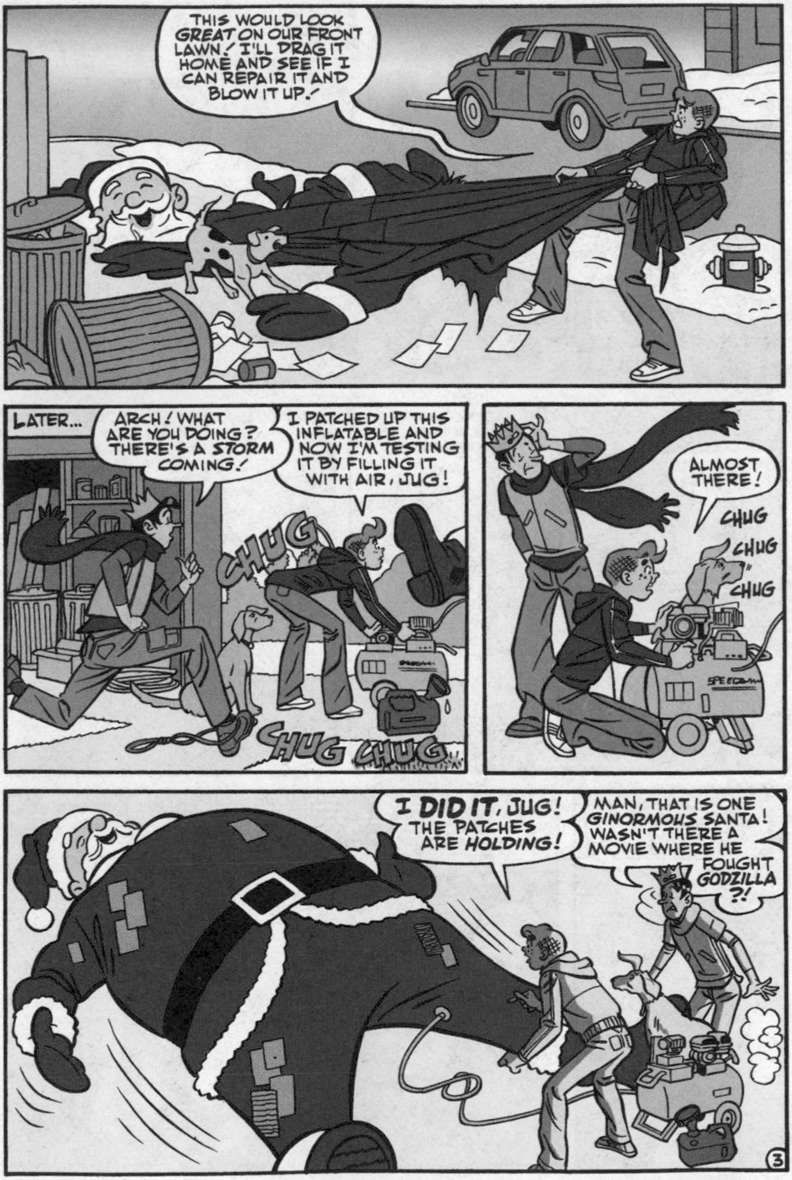
THIS WOULD LOOK GREAT ON OUR FRONT LAWN! I'LL DRAG IT HOME AND SEE IF I CAN REPAIR IT AND BLOW IT UP!
LATER...
ARCH! WHAT ARE YOU DOING? THERE'S A STORM COMING!
I PATCHED UP THIS INFLATABLE AND NOW I'M TESTING IT BY FILLING IT WITH AIR, JUG!
CHUG
CHUG CHUG
ALMOST THERE!
CHUG
CHUG
CHUG
I DID IT, JUG! THE PATCHES ARE HOLDING!
MAN, THAT IS ONE GINORMOUS SANTA! WASN'T THERE A MOVIE WHERE HE FOUGHT GODZILLA?!
3

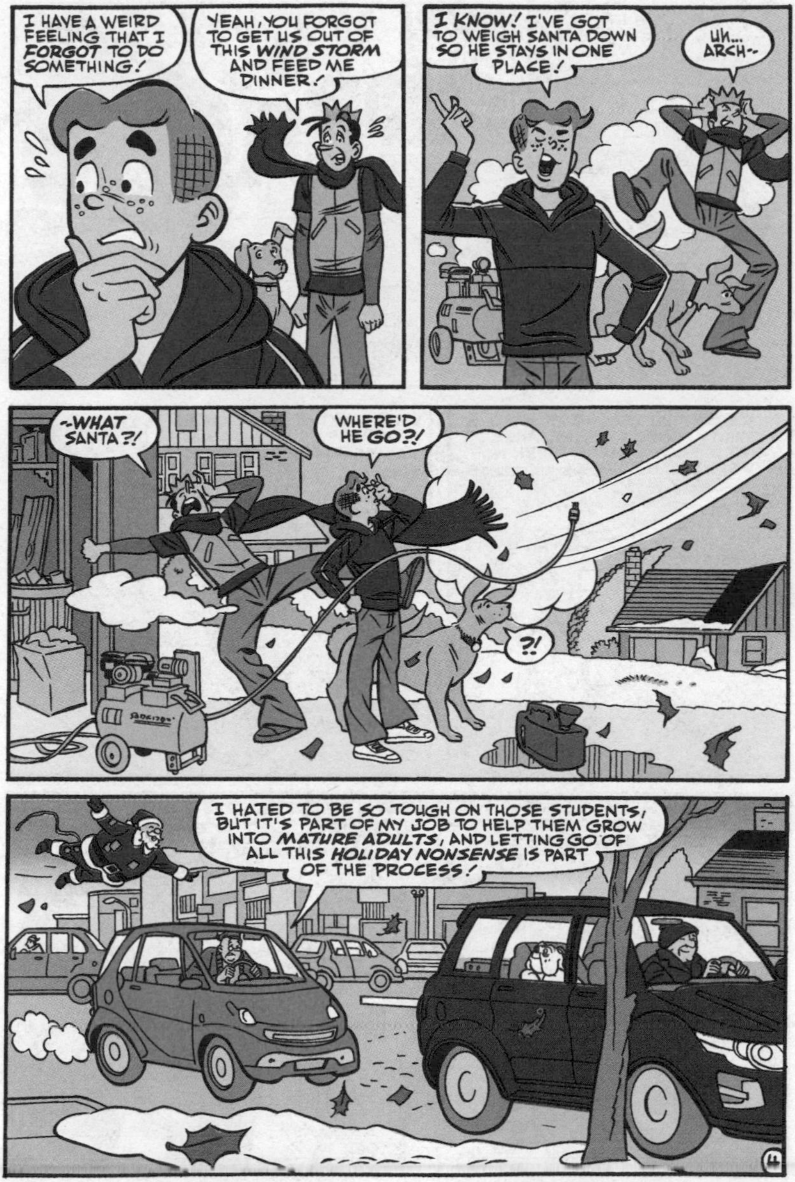
I HAVE A WEIRD FEELING THAT I FORGOT TO DO SOMETHING!
YEAH, YOU FORGOT TO GET US OUT OF THIS WIND STORM AND FEED ME DINNER!
I KNOW! I'VE GOT TO WEIGH SANTA DOWN SO HE STAYS IN ONE PLACE!
UH... ARCH--
--WHAT SANTA?!
WHERE'D HE GO?!
?!
I HATED TO BE SO TOUGH ON THOSE STUDENTS, BUT IT'S PART OF MY JOB TO HELP THEM GROW INTO MATURE ADULTS, AND LETTING GO OF ALL THIS HOLIDAY NONSENSE IS PART OF THE PROCESS!

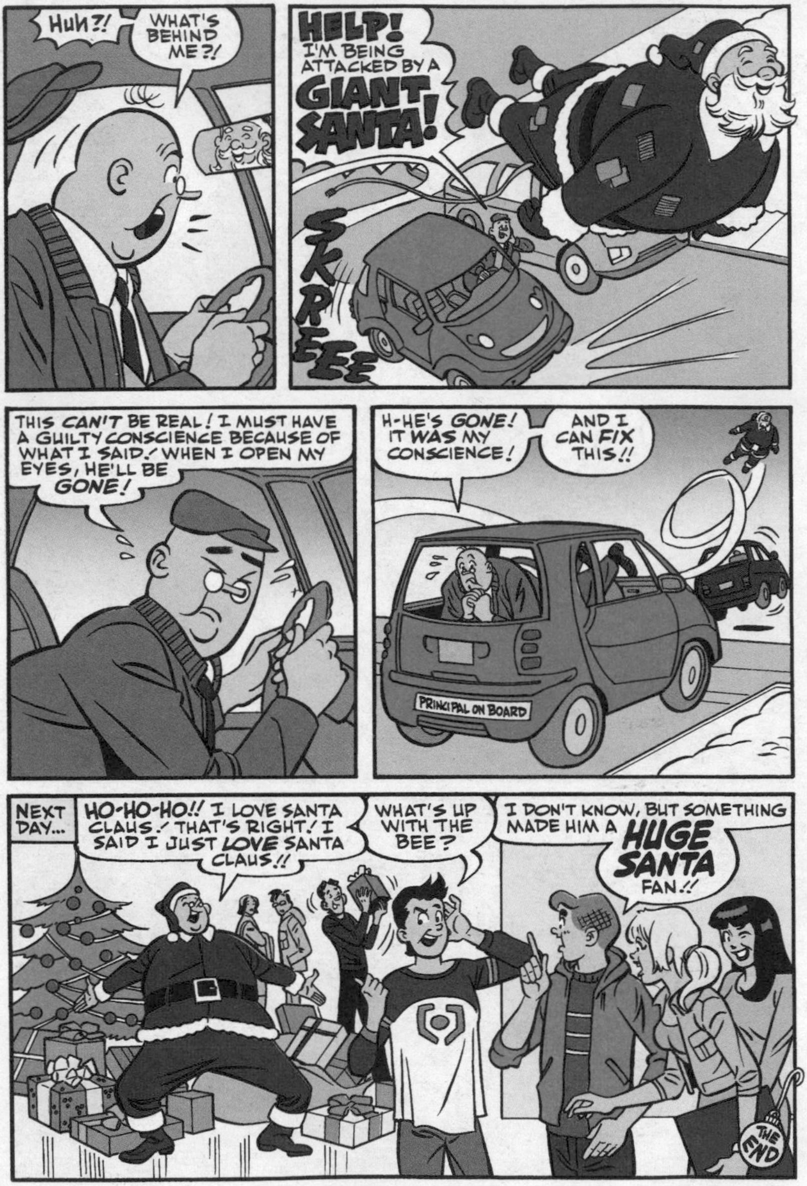
HUH?!
WHAT'S BEHIND ME?!
HELP! I'M BEING ATTACKED BY A GIANT SANTA!
SKREEEE
THIS CAN'T BE REAL! I MUST HAVE A GUILTY CONSCIENCE BECAUSE OF WHAT I SAID! WHEN I OPEN MY EYES, HE'LL BE GONE!
H-HE'S GONE! IT WAS MY CONSCIENCE!
AND I CAN FIX THIS!!
PRINCIPAL ON BOARD
NEXT DAY...
HO-HO-HO!! I LOVE SANTA CLAUS! THAT'S RIGHT! I SAID I JUST LOVE SANTA CLAUS!!
WHAT'S UP WITH THE BEE?
I DON'T KNOW, BUT SOMETHING MADE HIM A HUGE SANTA FAN!!
THE END